GW01606710

Victor Serebriakoff, one of the world's great puzzlemasters, is the honorary president of International Mensa. For many years he built up the reputation, membership and scope of the world's premier high intelligence organisation. He lives in Blackheath, London.

Also by Victor Serebriakoff

A Mensa Puzzle Book
A Second Mensa Puzzle Book
Brain
How Intelligent Are You?
Mensa: The society for the highly intelligent
The Future of Intelligence
Check Your Child's IQ

The Mammoth Book of PUZZLES

compiled by
Victor Serebriakoff

Robinson Publishing
London

First published by
Robinson Publishing
7 Kensington Church Court
London W8 4SP

The editor and publishers would like to acknowledge the contribution of Dr Abbie Salny, Harold Galen and Ken Russell

A copy of the British Library Cataloguing in Publication Data for this title is available from the British Library

Cased – ISBN 1 85487 185-4
Paperback – ISBN 1 85487 114-5

Printed by Harper Collins, Glasgow

10 9 8 7 6 5 4 3

ACKNOWLEDGEMENTS

I am very greatly obliged to Mr. Harold Gale, Executive Director of British Mensa, for use of many puzzles from his magazine Mind Games. I thank my old friend Dr. Abbie Salny, Mensa's International Supervisory Psychologist, for permission to reprint her puzzles therein. My very great thanks also to Mr. Kenneth Russell who edits the puzzle page of the British Mensa magazine and to other kind Mensan friends who allowed me to use their puzzles in this selection. Ken Russell was also especially helpful in checking the MSS and setting the handicap times. Robert Allen of Mensa Publications is thanked for permission to use the puzzles from my SF novel "My Alien Self". David Uings too was very helpful. I also thank these kind and neighbourly gifted children for their help with copying, paste-ups and such, namely Robert Scutt, Theo and Hugh Brennand and Clare Wigfrau.

INTRODUCTION

I have known Victor, the compiler of this book, for a third of a century. I met him through MENSA, which he took from a tiny group of 200 people to its present size of 100,000 members worldwide. This is by way of introduction to a very remarkable man.

I cannot say from my own experience, because I have not done them, that this is the best puzzle book ever, but what I can and do say is that, since Victor has produced it, I know it will be nothing less than excellent.

Oh, and by the way, why not try joining MENSA yourself? You will find it one of the best things you ever did.

Sir Clive Sinclair
London 1992

PREFACE

How are we to understand the enormous market for puzzles and the hours we spend on them? This is the real puzzle. In a world full of real problems, we love to tussle and tease ourselves with hypothetical ones. My own answer is that puzzling is simply mental jogging, a way to keep your brain active, to stay young in mind, and for a time, Chrissakes!, to *know* the answer.

There is also a refreshment and attraction in problems that have a single unique and certain solution and no unknown negative side effects which all our real life problems seem to have. We turn away for a time from breaking our heads on our real problems, foggy and muddled as they are. They have too many unknowns and no true solution, only a 'best' one which we *always* find we have missed. It is with a sigh of relief that we escape to the clear and certain world of paper puzzles for a breather. I could amend the old 'paper doll' song thus – 'I'd rather have a paper quiz to really solve than just a fickle minded real-life plight'.

Rewarded by the little 'Eureka!' joy that comes with any solution, you'll remain mentally lithe and active – the better to tackle the real monsters that beset you – out there. I hope this Mammoth selection leaves you keen and sharp for that battle. Here they are – your half a thousand paper quizzes.

CHAPTER ONE

I shall be frank. In the matter of puzzles, I confess I am a sadist. I am not ashamed. I glory in it. I caused widespread misery by writing my *FIRST* and then my even more evil *SECOND MENSA PUZZLE BOOK* (different titles in USA). They were fiendishly and cruelly difficult and perplexing. Then, not satisfied with adding many more torturing problems to a world where there is no shortage of them, I wrote what purported to be a novel, called *"My Alien Self"*. It was, when opened, a puzzle book in disguise with the diabolical riddles slyly woven into the text.

Now, angrily finding that there are other puzzles abroad which are even more subtly teasing and frustrating than mine, I have set out to build up this collection of the worst horrors and foist it on unsuspecting puzzlers everywhere. I know that most puzzle addicts are masochistically hooked on their wretched torment. Nyeh! nyeh! You cannot help yourselves.

I shall show no mercy. I am making new, harsh demands on my readers. For the first time, there is a strict time allowance for each puzzle. You will be fighting the clock all the way to gain a less than shameful number of merit points as you go through this mammoth collection. There will be no slack and sloppy puzzling at any old pace which other puzzle setters allow. This job has been work studied, and a proper rate of progress is required.

And I am sadistically pleased with another idea. Handicapping. Another first. I am not going to let the clever puzzler exploit a genetic and/or environmental advantage. Puzzlers are going to be handicapped. Mensa types will be clobbered. I was inspired by an SF novel, in which those of higher intelligence had, like handicapped racehorses, weights chained to their bruised and straining bodies – just to even things up a bit. This was done in the name of Equality and so it shall be with you, my readers, my victims. First you take an IQ test, and this sets your handicap. The hard-earned merit points you gain as you labour on through hundreds of tough puzzles will be reduced in proportion to your IQ. Most puzzlers are honest. What is the sense in cheating yourself? So I am relying on you to keep to my cruel rules.

HERE IS HOW IT WORKS

First you do the preliminary IQ test, find your score, and make a note of it.

Then there are 26 chapters of mixed puzzles, about 15 to each, about an evening of intense thinking for an average puzzler in each chapter. Each puzzle has a time limit. You solve the puzzle, and write your answer in the space provided. If you solve it in less than the allotted number of minutes, you may credit your running total with the minutes (merit points) gained. Work to the nearest minute (5 minutes 31 seconds counts as 6 minutes, 5 min 29 secs = 5 minutes). If you exceed the time allowance but do, against the odds, actually solve a puzzle, you will get five points only for all your labour.

There is an answer page at the end of each chapter, where you record your gain and running total as you labour on. THERE WILL BE NO POINTS FOR INCORRECT ANSWERS but, reluctantly, no penalties for overtime solutions.

When, if ever, you reach the end, you come to the reckoning. Your total score for the whole book is subject to a handicap adjustment according to IQ. First you add 2 noughts to your score. Sounds good! It is not. Then you divide the new total by your IQ which will, for most puzzlers, be over 120, even if it is not up to the Mensa level of 130 (the one-in-fifty level).

INTELLIGENCE TESTS

Your intelligence quotient (IQ) is a rough and ready measure of how intelligent you are. How good you are at logic, verbal comprehension, and handling symbolic knowledge. IQ tests are fixed so that the average score of the whole population works out at about 100. A score of 70 on a test valid for your own culture would indicate a feeble mind, and a score of 130 or so (depending on the test) would put you in the Mensa class. You'd be on what is statistically called the 98th percentile, that is you would come in the top two percent of the population for cleverness. I am not too keen on IQ as a measure myself. I prefer the percentile rating which can be deduced from IQ.

Your percentile rating tells you where you stand in your cultural group as to how your mind copes with logical and mathematical problems, how difficult the ideas you can grasp, and how good your judgement is. If you are on the 50th percentile you are average, 50% of folk would score lower than you at the test. If you are on the 70th percentile then seventy percent of your cultural-language group would score below you, and thirty percent would score the same or more. Mensans are, as I have said, on the 98th percentile, within the top two percent. Once you get the idea, you know what your score means with percentiles. With IQ you may not.

TAKING A PUZZLE SESSION

You may, of course, be one of those casual unmeticulous persons, like myself, who prefer making strict schedules for others rather than for yourself. You may prefer to wander idly through these puzzles, picking and trying one that takes your fancy here and there, like a maiden in the springtime wandering through the fields selecting a pretty leaf here, a flower there, and a curious stone yon. Or you might be a true puzzler, made of sterner stuff, one who is ready to confront the full rigour of my challenge.

To the former I say, "Blessings. Be off in your light hearted trivial way. I am not concerned with you. Be happy in your trivial light hearted way."

FOR THE SERIOUS PUZZLER

But to you, the latter, the men and women of hardihood and mental muscle, you the serious, the committed puzzle fighters, buckle on your brain armour and be ready. The war begins. For you I explain the system (unless you like to skip this and take it on as an extra puzzle).

First take the preliminary handicapping IQ test.

When you have your IQ result from chapter 2 you may start on chapter 3. It is best, but not necessary, to have a stop watch and note the time taken on each puzzle (or the start and finish time for each puzzle). You can even be so slack as to treat the session as a whole. If you do so, you must note the time of any interruptions. It is easy to take time off for a drink, a visit to the john (loo), or a phone call – and then cheat by continuing to think about the puzzle while you are not timed. How dishonest!

So for you others, the upright serious puzzlers, for each puzzle you note your start time or start your stop watch, then read the puzzle and note your answer and the time taken in the spaces provided. When you have finished and solved, or failed to solve, the fifteen puzzles in a chapter you may turn to the answer sheet at the end of it. The answers to the puzzles are given on a form where you may note your time in minutes (to the nearest half minute), the handicap time and if you solved it in less than the handicap time, your gain in points at 1 point per minute. There is no penalty where you exceed the handicap time on any question, and for each question correctly solved you add another 5 points at the bottom of the form. You carry forward your running total to the next chapter.

General Knowledge Quizzes

There are a number of general knowledge quizzes each with a number of questions. The allowance is one point for each question, and your added gain is the number you get right. There is no 5 point bonus in this case. Only if you answer them all correctly is there any gain from beating the time allowance.

The IQ Handicap

You can check up after a chapter or two, or at the end of the book. Take your running total, add two noughts and divide by your IQ. EG – score, 1000, IQ 150, therefore corrected score = 100,000/150 = 667.

For My American Readers

Some of the money puzzles are set in British pounds and pence. Older Americans may need to be reminded that there are now a mere 100 pence to the pound, not the confusing 240 that there used to be.

HOW TO GET SOME OF YOUR OWN BACK: PUZZLE DRIVES

Before you start your dreadful journey through the book I make a suggestion. The handicapping and marking scheme brings the possibility of a social opportunity for you to entrap other puzzle afficionados and fans to their doom. Instead of a bridge evening or a whist drive, you could invite your puzzler friends and rivals to a PUZZLE DRIVE. Mensans do it all the time. One chapter, photocopied – as many copies as contesting teams, supplies an evening's puzzling as you and your victims count your treasured total of puzzle points, an evening of gleeful pride and gloating triumph: or envy, hate and tension for you and those who have been, till then, your friends.

You can form small teams to compete frantically, or each person may struggle alone with his problems. You need a person appointed as timer, or a little programme on your PC with an alarm to give you a "start", "countdown" and "pencils down" for each puzzle. Each contestant or group gets a pile of pages with the backs up. The timer gives the time for the top puzzle and the top paper is turned. Then the timer counts down the minutes one by one – "20", "19", "18" and so on, as the contestants sweat and whisper. The contestants or teams write an answer when they are agreed, and hand it in to the timer, who marks the countdown time in minutes.

When time is up it is "pencils down". The timer gives the solution and those with a correct solution are credited with their gain, the countdown score when they declared the answer. The timer then starts the countdown for the next puzzle, and the contestants turn a new page and get going. Keep going until the session is over, then tot up scores and give a bow, a bag of gold, a bottle or a box to the winner(s).

ABOUT MENSA AND THE MENSA FOUNDATION

Puzzlers are often Mensans and vice versa. I am the Honorary International President of Mensa and the Chairman of the Mensa Foundation for Gifted Children.

MENSA (latin for table) is a round table society where no-one has precedence. It is a world-wide, non-profit society whose hundred odd thousand members have only one qualification. They have all achieved a score on a professionally supervised, standard test of general intelligence such that they are (roughly) in the top two percent of the general population. Children may be members of Mensa if they can be validly tested for IQ.

Founded in 1946 in Oxford, England, Mensa seeks to bring together a small sample of the intelligent people of the world for social and intellectual communion, friendship and mutual stimulus. It conducts social, psychological and opinion research but has no collective policies other than to foster intelligence for the general benefit. It has international, national and local organisations and its 103,000 members infest about 100 countries. British Mensa Ltd is the British branch. It has 40,000 members – 2,000 of them children. If you do well in my IQ test and the puzzles, you might like to send for a brochure and tests to Mensa Freepost, Wolverhampton in UK, to Mensa Brooklyn, New York in USA or International Mensa, 15 The Ivories, 6/8 Northampton Street, London N1 2HY, UK from other countries.

CHAPTER 1

Mensa Foundation for Gifted Children

The Mensa Foundation for Gifted Children is a registered charity associated with and administered by British Mensa Ltd. It has been entrusted with the task of carrying out the Mensa aim of fostering intelligence for the benefit of humanity. It assists the parents of able children in the diagnosis of high intelligence by arranging intelligence and educational tests (free to those that cannot afford them) and by consultation, advice and action to obtain education for very promising children such that their potentiality shall be fulfilled for the advantage of the nations, the world and the children themselves. The Foundation also runs a quality assurance plan to certify suitable schools. UK readers can send applications for a brochure and IQ and EQ (Educational Quotient) tests to MENSA FREEPOST, WOLVERHAMPTON (envelope marked "CHILD").

Ready to start? Right! Here is your IQ test.

CHAPTER TWO

THE SEREBRIAKOFF ADVANCED CULTURE-FAIR IQ TEST

This test comes from my book "A Guide to Intelligence and Personality Testing". I am not claiming that it has been through all the rigorous research and validation testing to which clinical and professional tests are subjected. That sort of test is restricted to use by qualified psychometric psychologists and may not be published to the general public. This is a test made parallel to well established tests and validated on Mensa candidates who have been assessed on such tests. It gives a good first approximation guesstimate of where you stand. And, hee-hee! how much your handicap will be (as in golf) as you confront and tussle with the fiendish puzzles that are lined up to defeat you. The IQ tests are childishly simple at first, but – go on, be complacent, they get hellish as you struggle on. Tests have to be designed to stop everybody somewhere. There is no time limit.

Instructions

Try to work out the plan, or scheme, or order behind the way the central tiles are placed so as to find out which of the surrounding scattered tiles fits reasonably and logically into the space in the array.

Go through the 36 tests. There are eight 'tiles' in the central 3 x 3 array which have an inner bi-logical order. But one tile is missing. You will find it among the other ones which are scattered around. Find the missing tile among the lettered ones and write the letter above the tile against the question number on the answer page. Turn the book sideways so that you can see four puzzles each time you turn a page

THE ANSWER PAGE

Write the letter of the missing tile after each question number.

Question number	Answer letter	Question number	Answer letter
1	.....	19	.....
2	.....	20	.....
3	.....	21	.....
4	.....	22	.....
5	.....	23	.....
6	.....	24	.....
7	.....	25	.....
8	.....	26	.....
9	.....	27	.....
10	.....	28	.....
11	.....	29	.....
12	.....	30	.....
13	.....	31	.....
14	.....	32	.....
15	.....	33	.....
16	.....	34	.....
17	.....	35	.....
18	.....	36	.....

Example

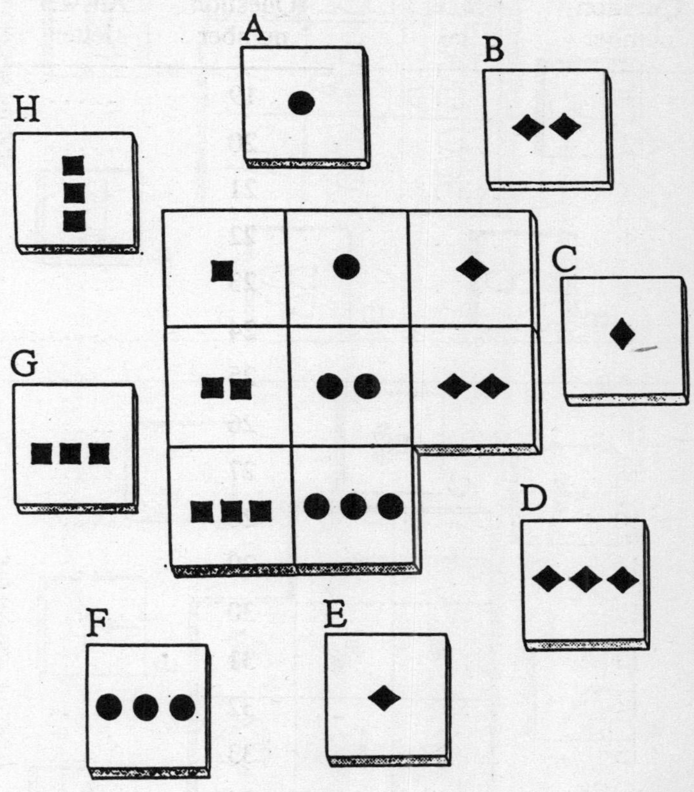

THE MISSING TILE IS D

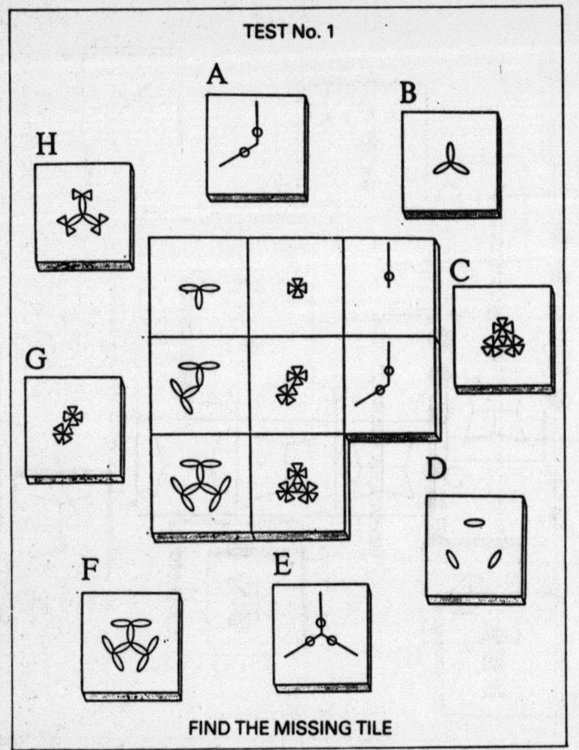
TEST No. 1
A
B
C
D
E
F
G
H
FIND THE MISSING TILE

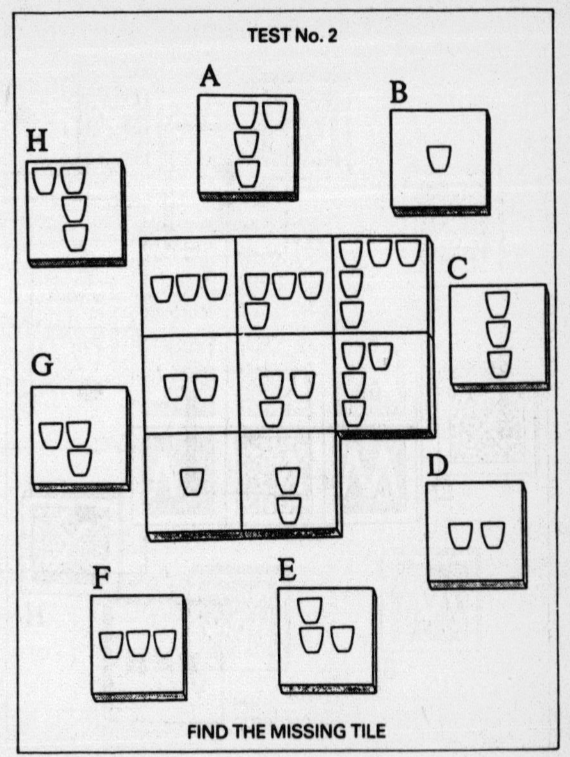
TEST No. 2
A
B
C
D
E
F
G
H
FIND THE MISSING TILE

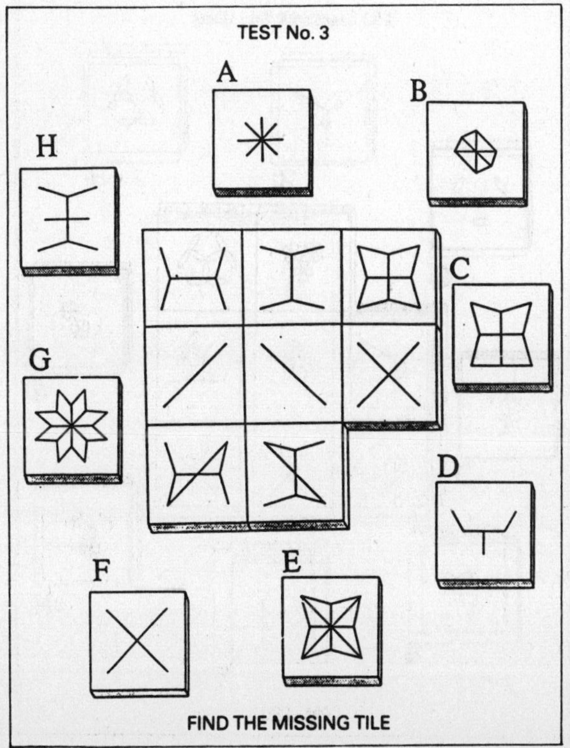
TEST No. 3
A
B
C
D
E
F
G
H
FIND THE MISSING TILE

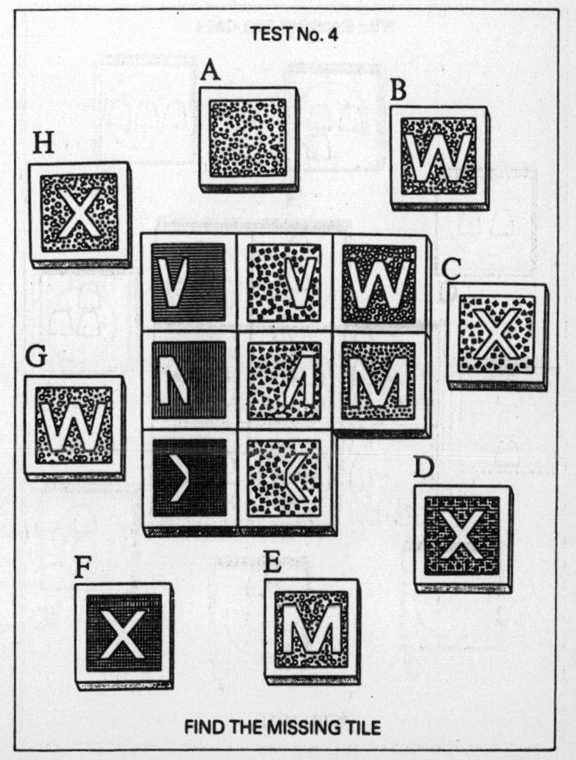
TEST No. 4
A
B
C
D
E
F
G
H
FIND THE MISSING TILE

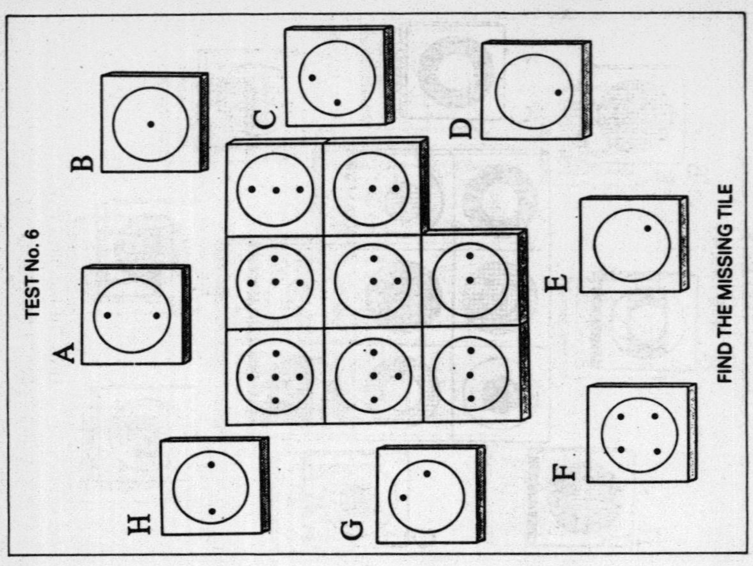
TEST No. 6
A
B
C
D
E
F
G
H
FIND THE MISSING TILE

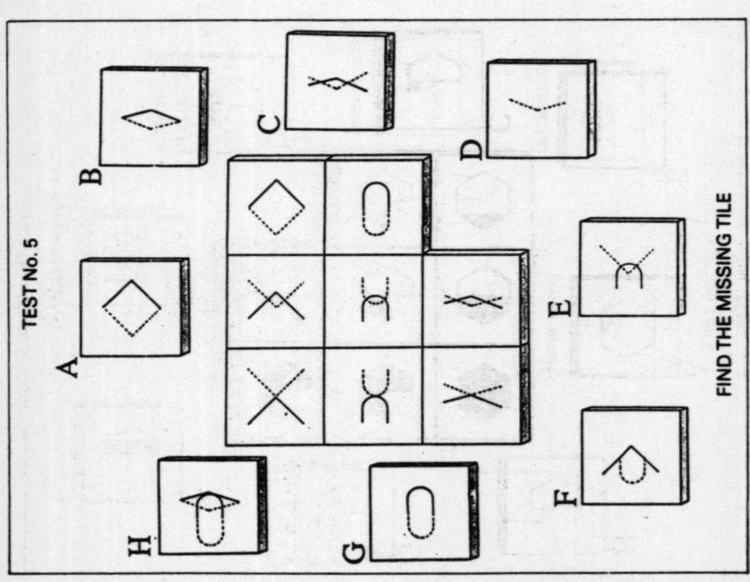
TEST No. 5
A
B
C
D
E
F
G
H
FIND THE MISSING TILE

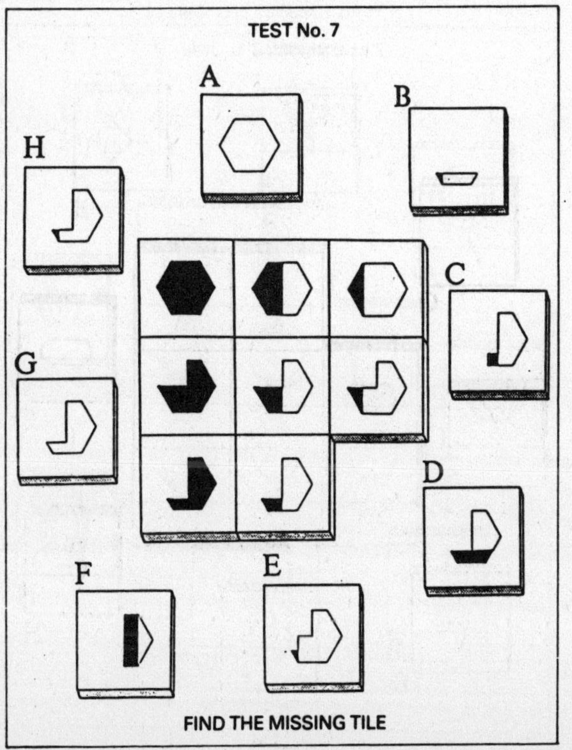
TEST No. 7
A
B
C
D
E
F
G
H
FIND THE MISSING TILE

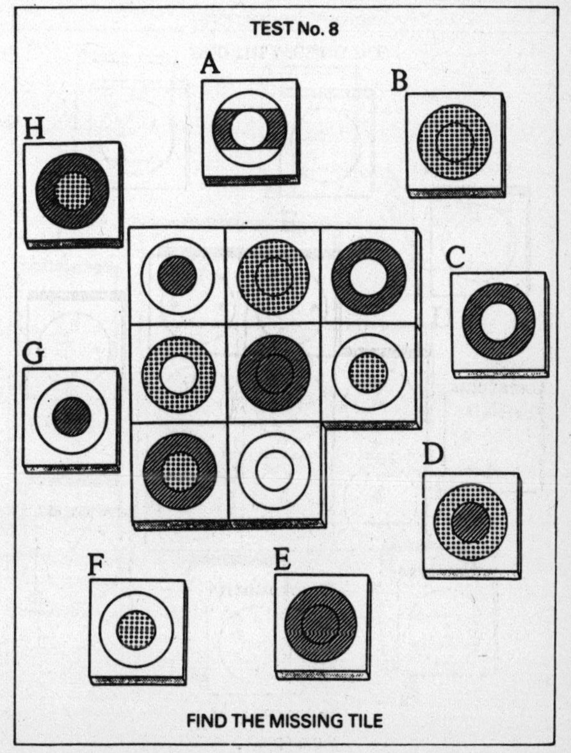
TEST No. 8
A
B
C
D
E
F
G
H
FIND THE MISSING TILE

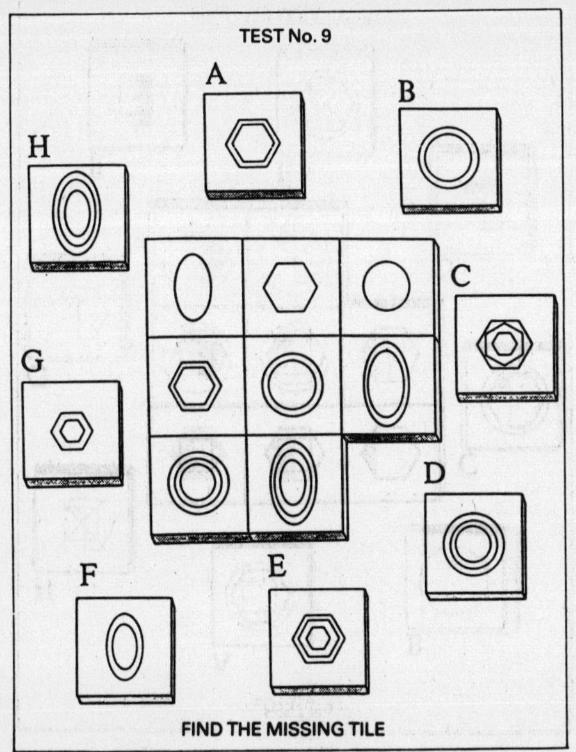
TEST No. 9
A
B
C
D
E
F
G
H
FIND THE MISSING TILE

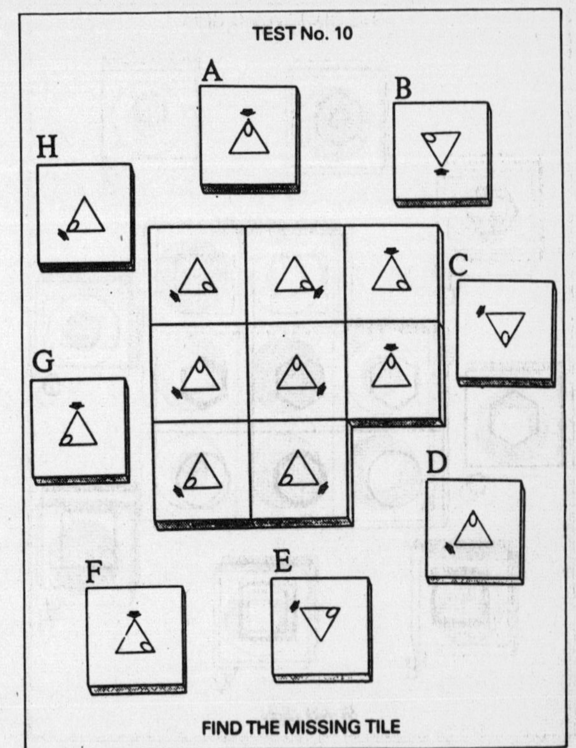
TEST No. 10
A
B
C
D
E
F
G
H
FIND THE MISSING TILE

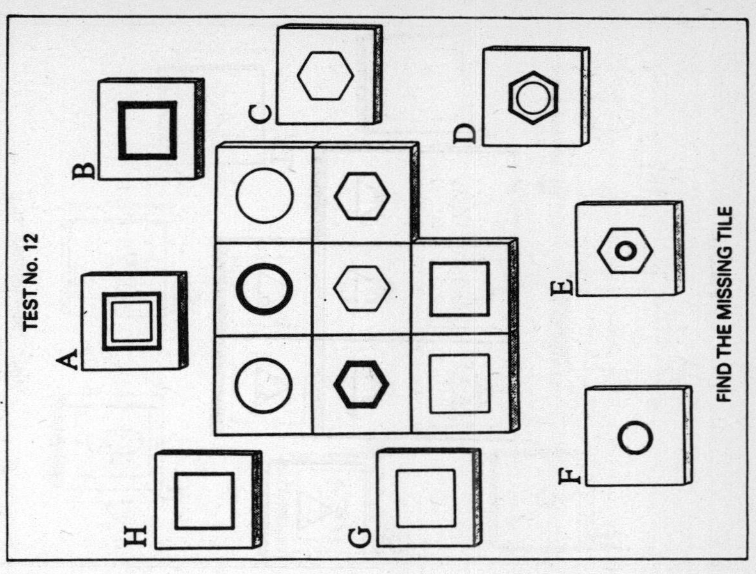
TEST No. 12
A
B
C
D
E
F
G
H
FIND THE MISSING TILE

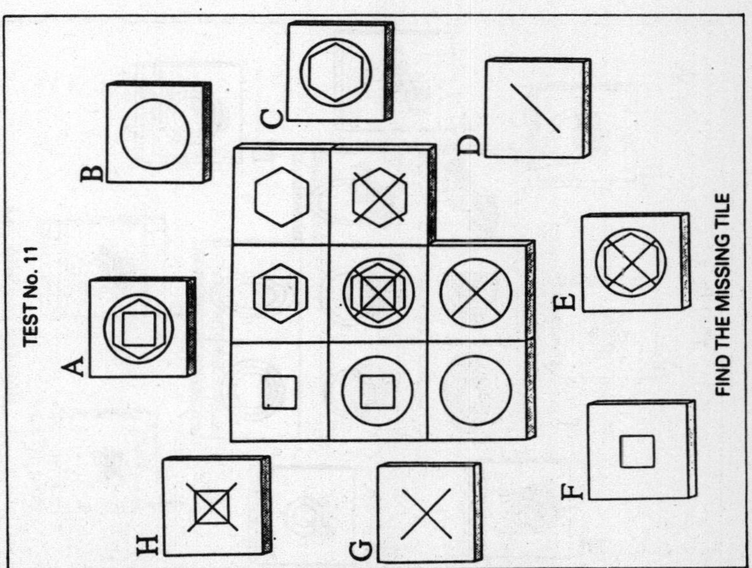
TEST No. 11
A
B
C
D
E
F
G
H
FIND THE MISSING TILE

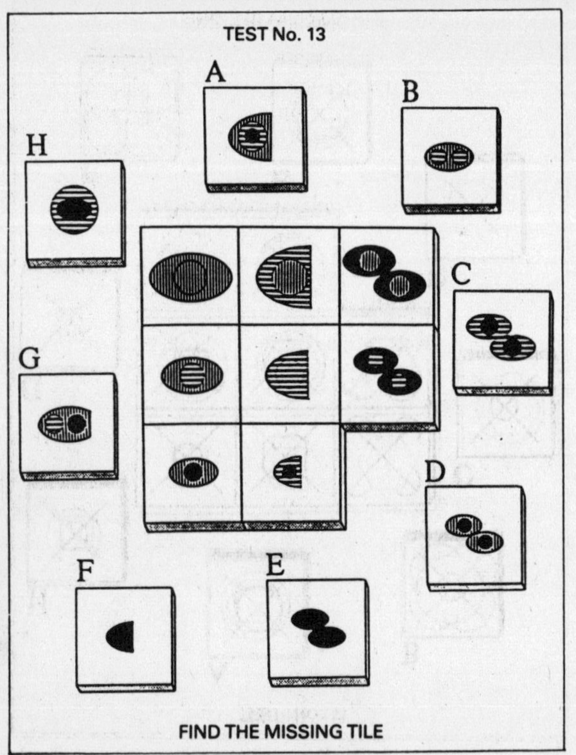
TEST No. 13
A
B
H
C
G
D
F
E
FIND THE MISSING TILE

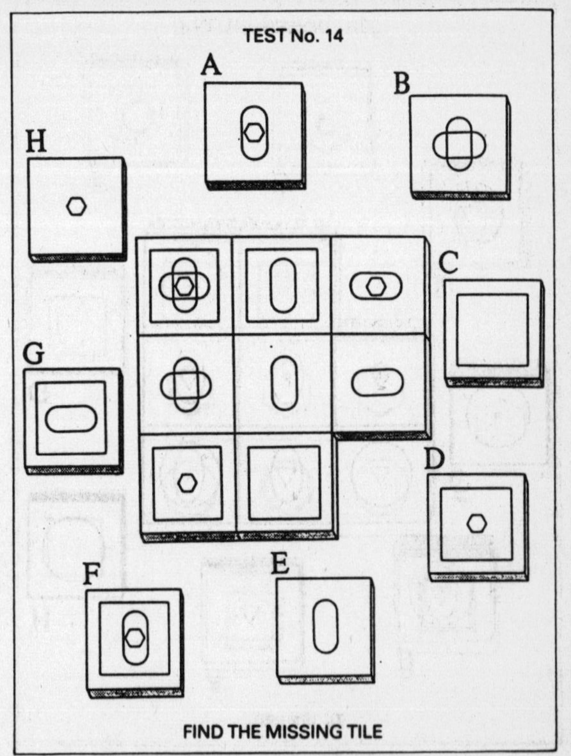
TEST No. 14
A
B
H
C
G
D
F
E
FIND THE MISSING TILE

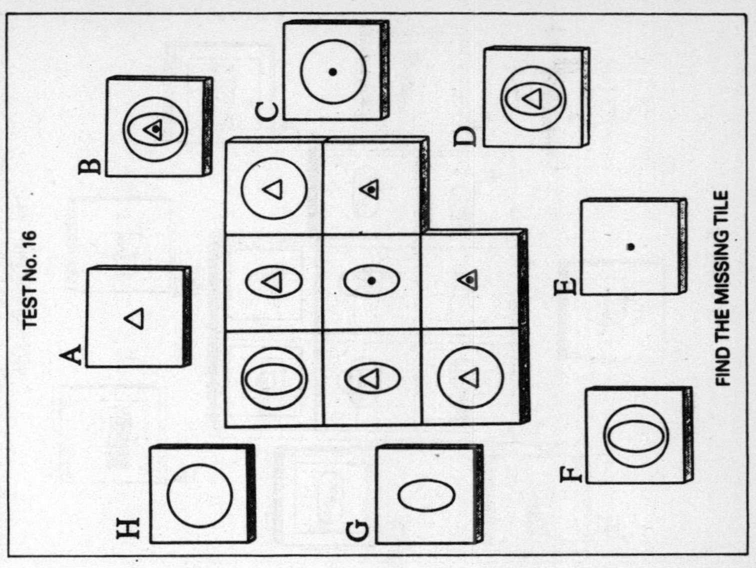
TEST No. 16
A
B
C
D
E
F
G
H
FIND THE MISSING TILE

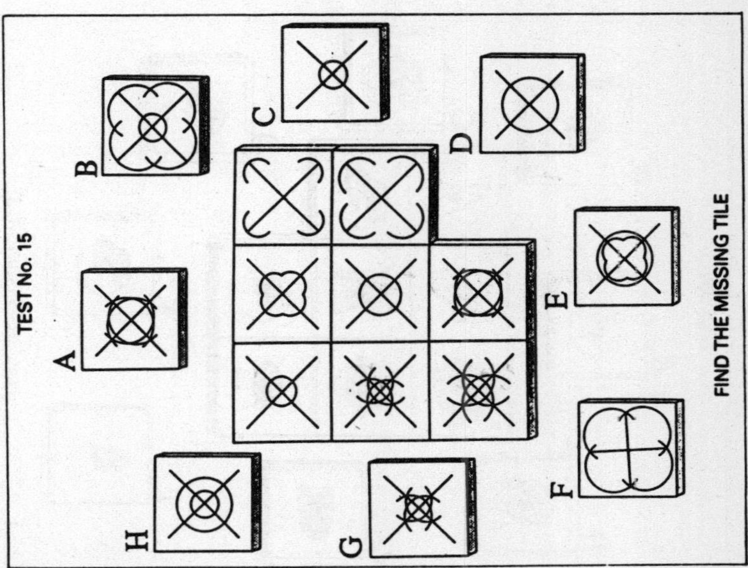
TEST No. 15
A
B
C
D
E
F
G
H
FIND THE MISSING TILE

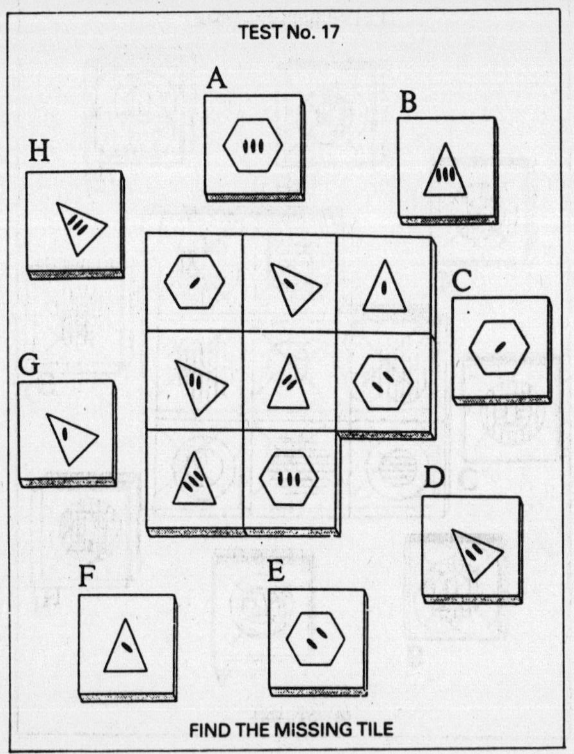
TEST No. 17
A
B
C
D
E
F
G
H
FIND THE MISSING TILE

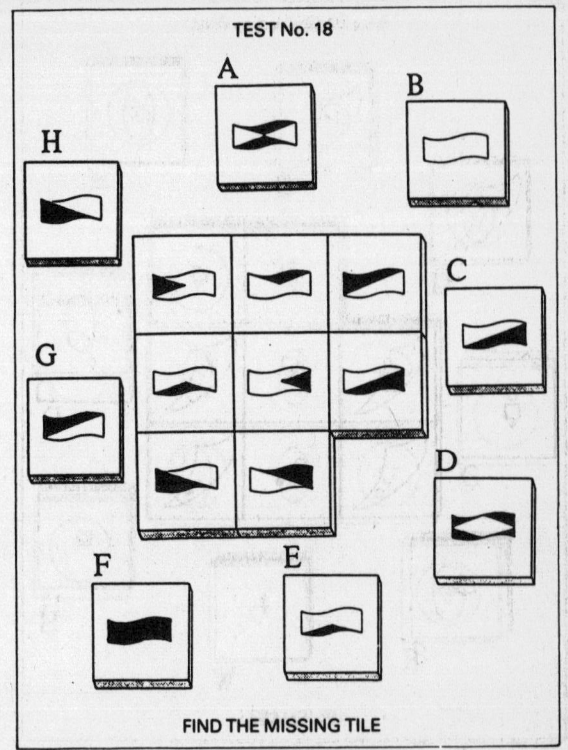
TEST No. 18
A
B
C
D
E
F
G
H
FIND THE MISSING TILE

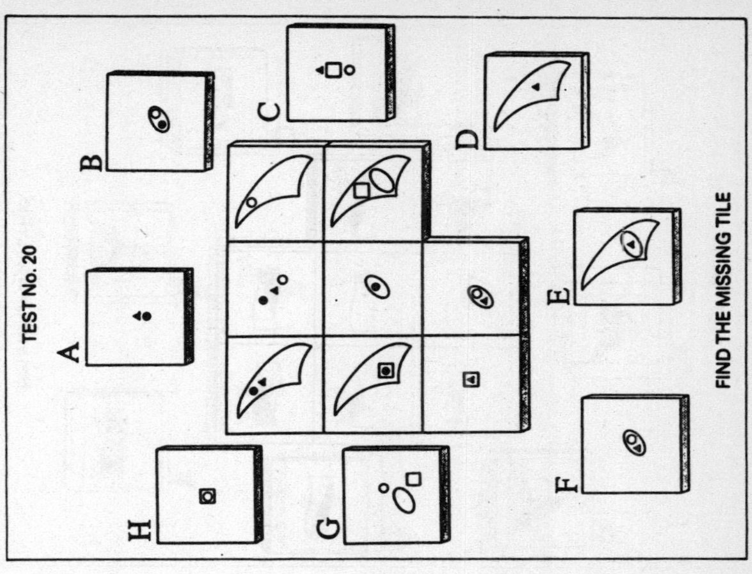
TEST No. 20
A
B
C
D
E
F
G
H
FIND THE MISSING TILE

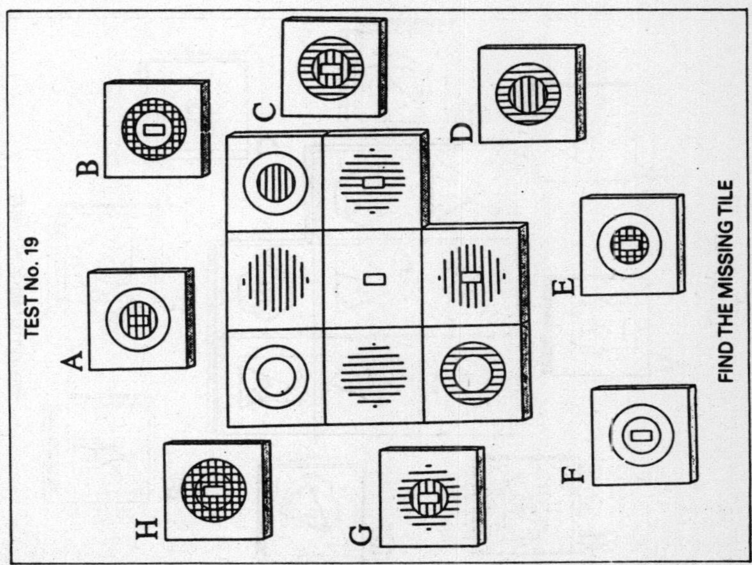
TEST No. 19
A
B
C
D
E
F
G
H
FIND THE MISSING TILE

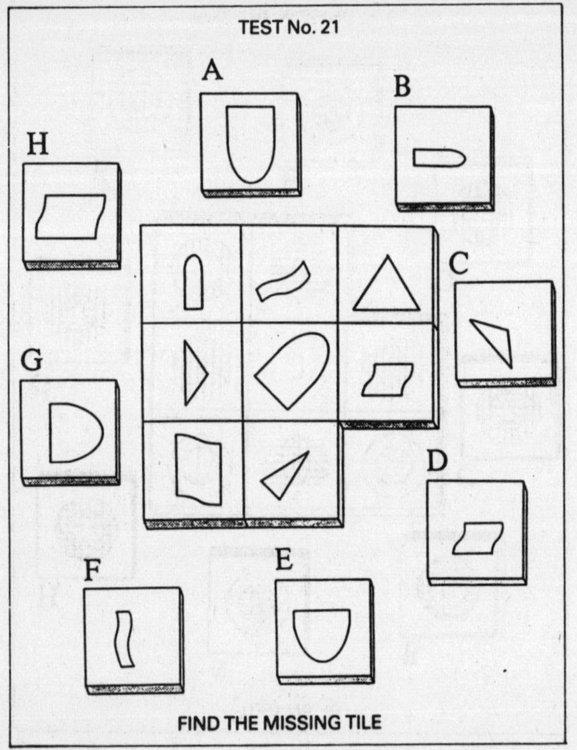
TEST No. 21
A
B
H
C
G
D
F
E
FIND THE MISSING TILE

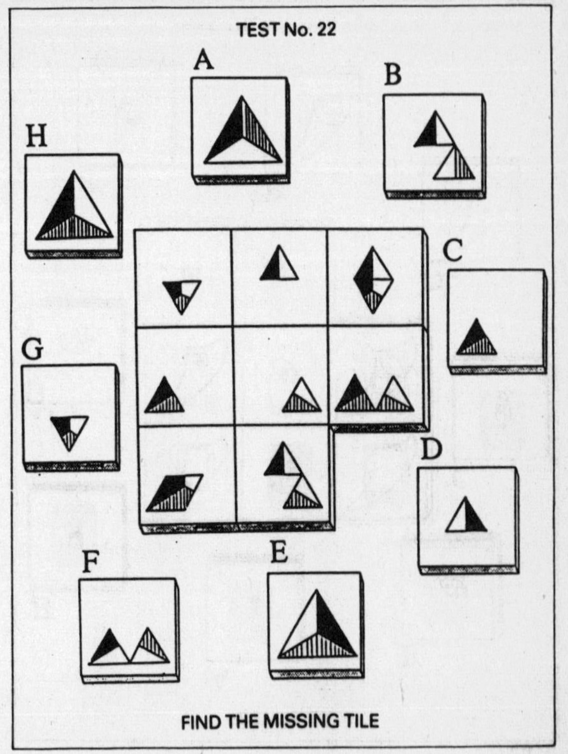
TEST No. 22
A
B
H
C
G
D
F
E
FIND THE MISSING TILE

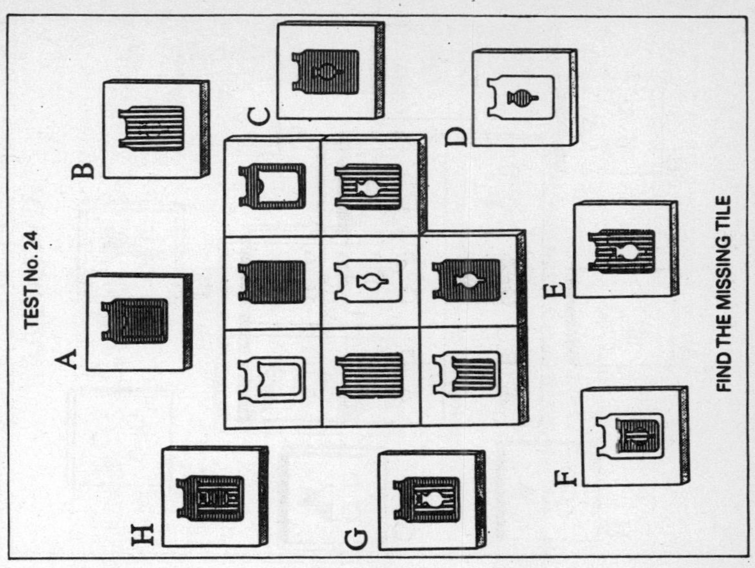
TEST No. 24
A
B
C
D
E
F
G
H
FIND THE MISSING TILE

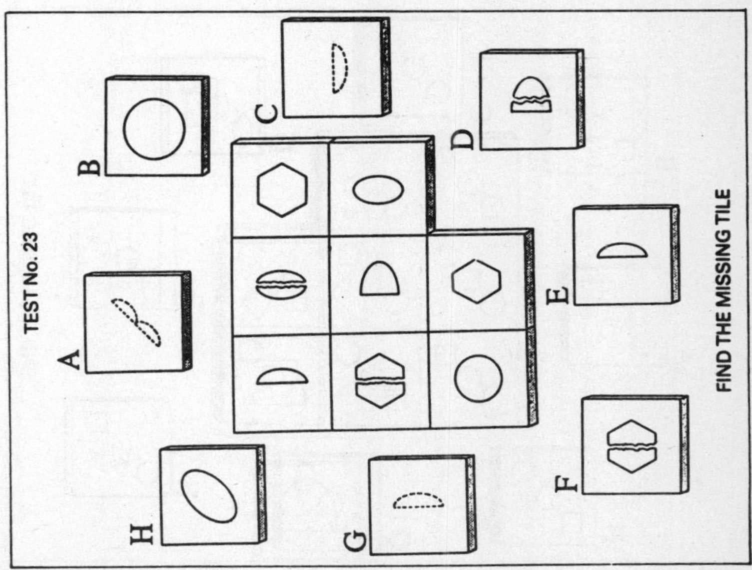
TEST No. 23
A
B
C
D
E
F
G
H
FIND THE MISSING TILE

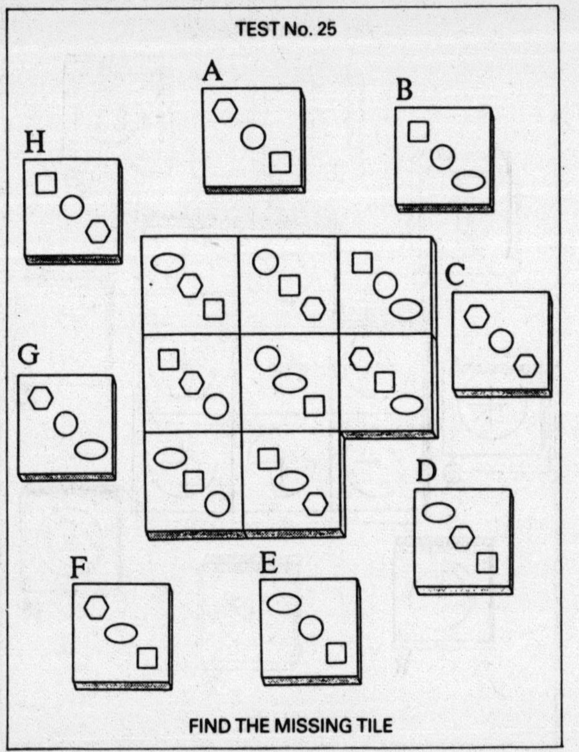
TEST No. 25
A
B
C
D
E
F
G
H
FIND THE MISSING TILE

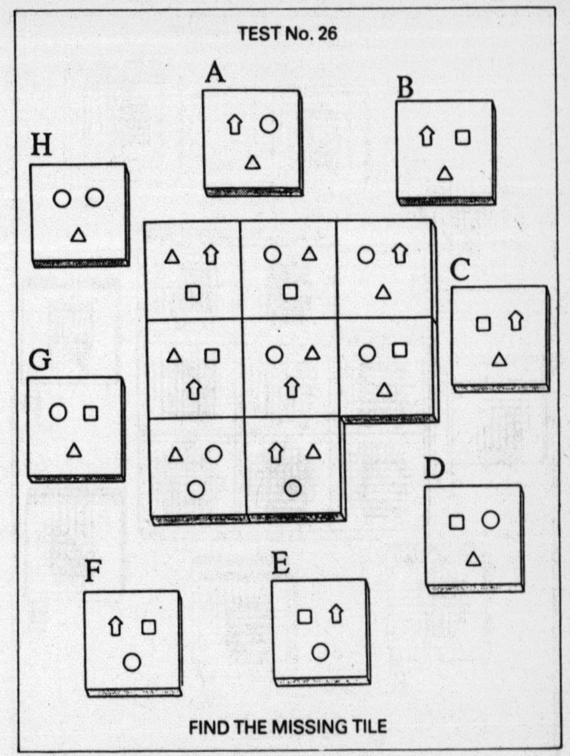
TEST No. 26
A
B
C
D
E
F
G
H
FIND THE MISSING TILE

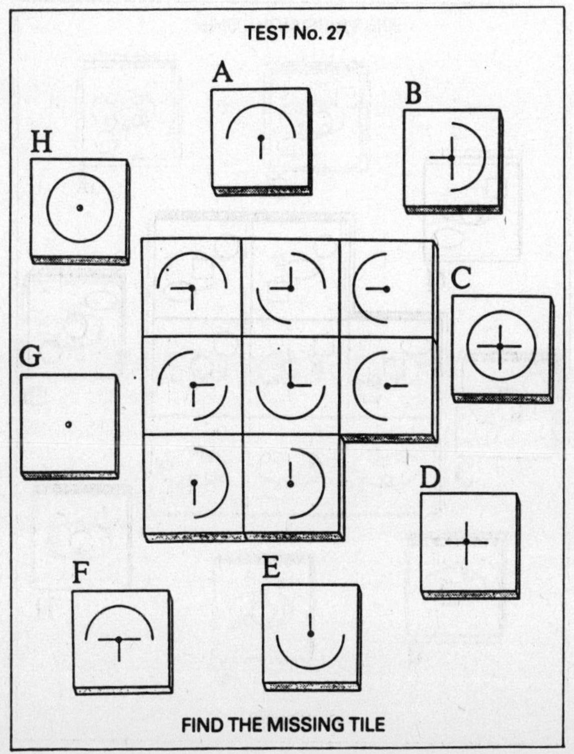
TEST No. 27
A
B
H
C
G
D
F
E
FIND THE MISSING TILE

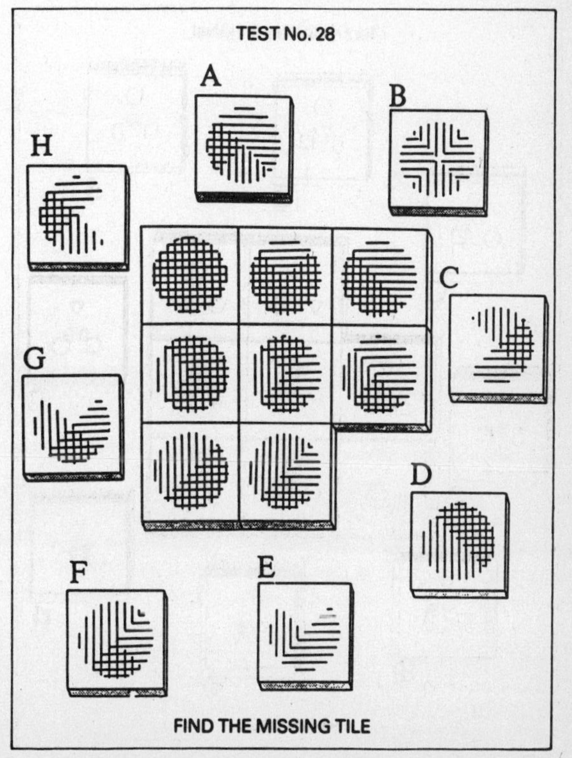
TEST No. 28
A
B
H
C
G
D
F
E
FIND THE MISSING TILE

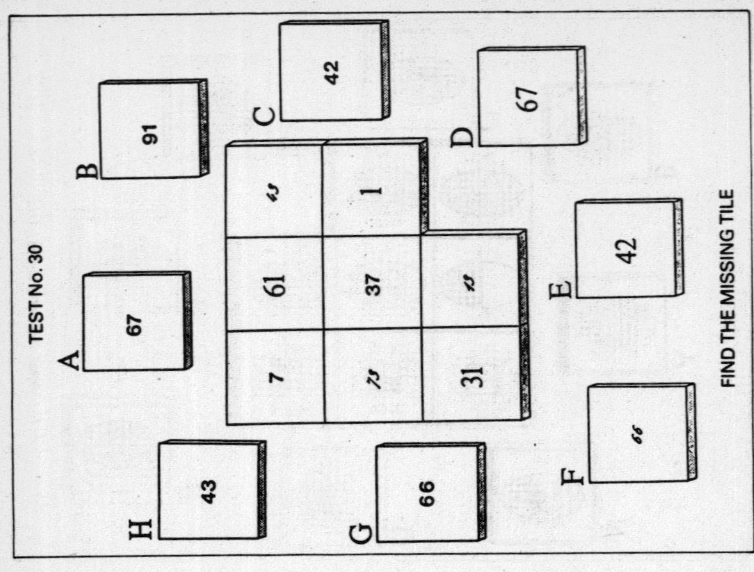
TEST No. 30
FIND THE MISSING TILE

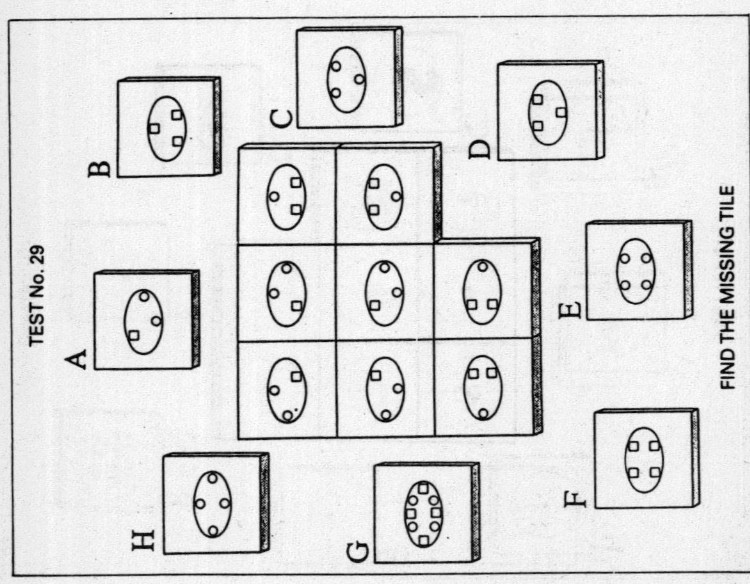
TEST No. 29
FIND THE MISSING TILE

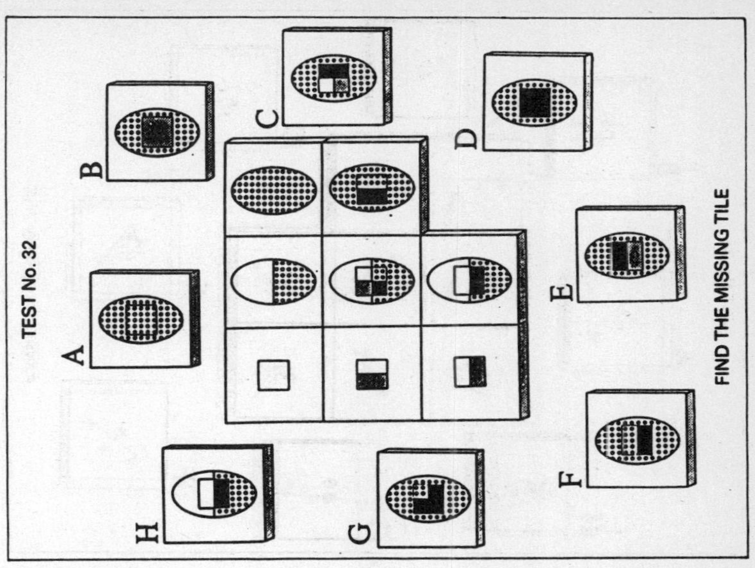
TEST No. 32
A
B
C
D
E
F
G
H
FIND THE MISSING TILE

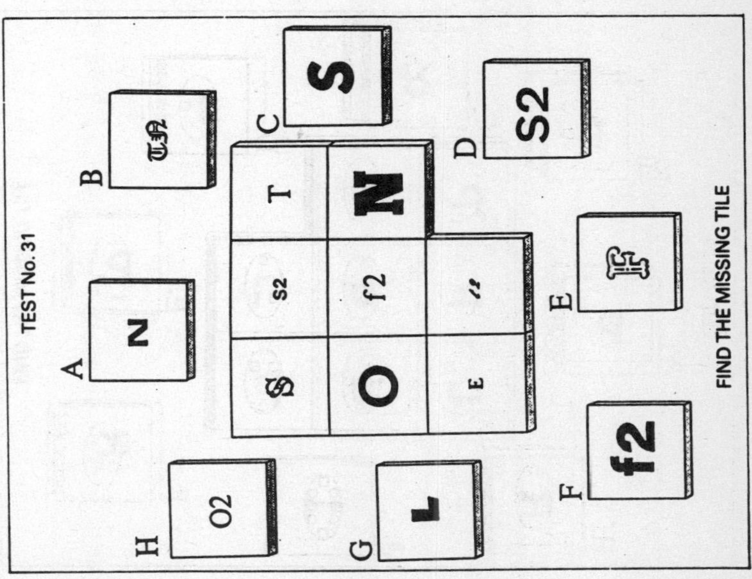
TEST No. 31
A
N
B
C
S
D
S2
E
F
f2
G
L
H
O2
S2
T
O
f2
N
E
FIND THE MISSING TILE

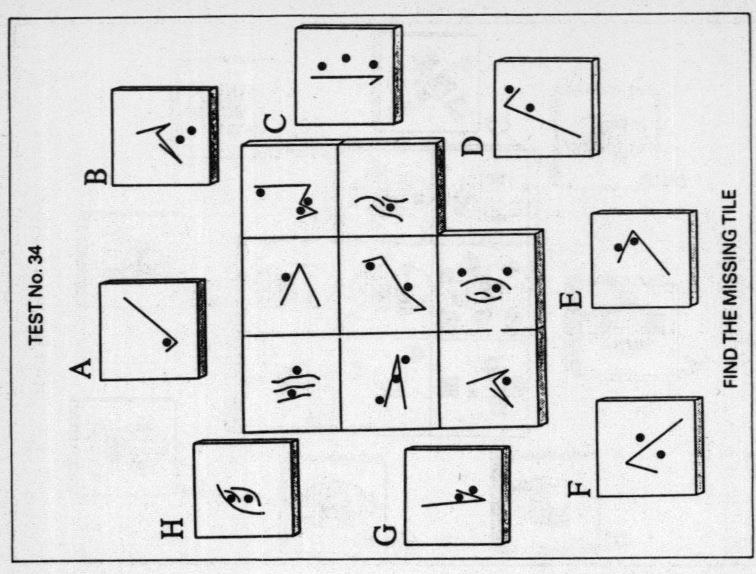
TEST No. 34
A
B
C
D
E
F
G
H
FIND THE MISSING TILE

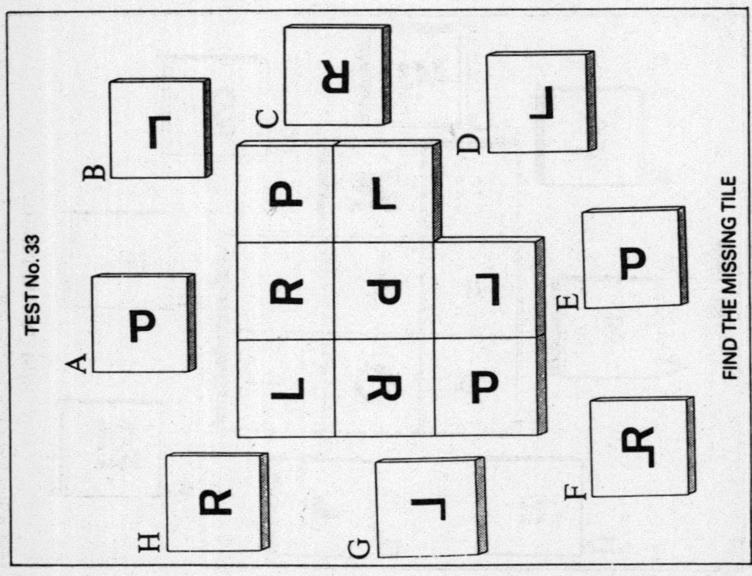
TEST No. 33
A
B
C
D
E
F
G
H
FIND THE MISSING TILE

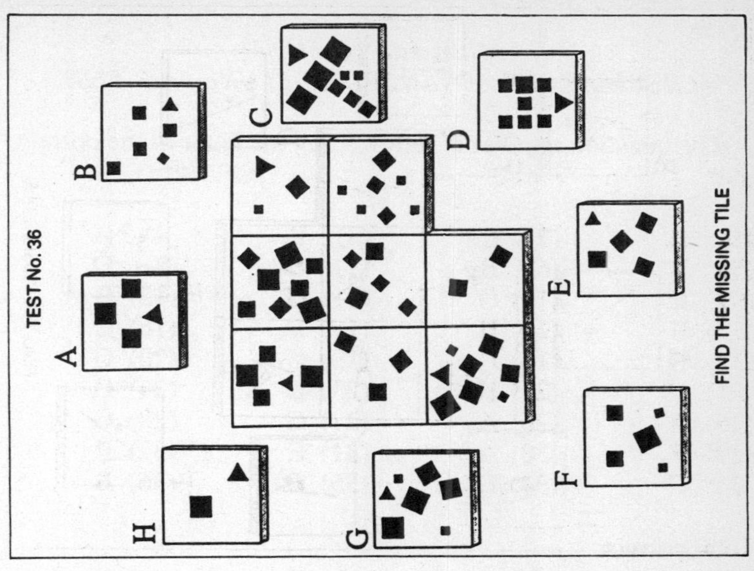
TEST No. 36
A
B
C
D
E
F
G
H
FIND THE MISSING TILE

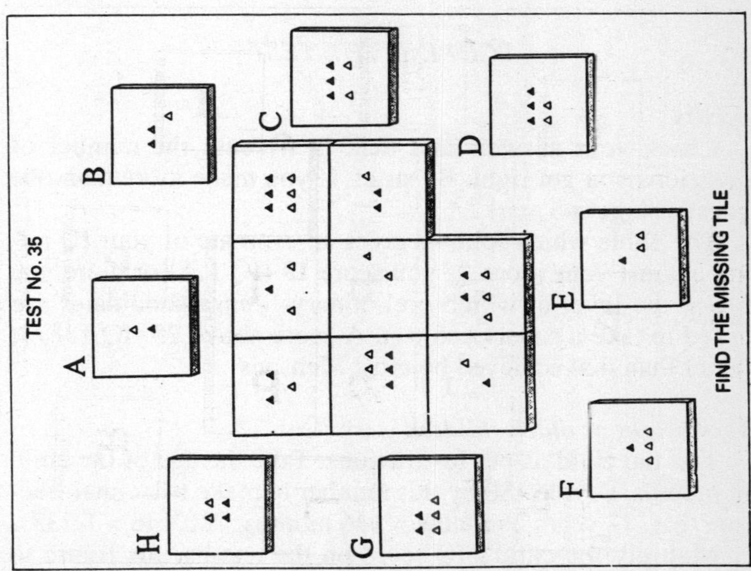
TEST No. 35
A
B
C
D
E
F
G
H
FIND THE MISSING TILE

ANSWERS TO THE SEREBRIAKOFF ADVANCED CULTURE FAIR TEST

The question number is followed by the letter of the correct tile.

(1) E	(2) C	(3) E	(4) H
(5) B	(6) B	(7) H	(8) D
(9) E	(10) G	(11) G	(12) B
(13) E	(14) H	(15) D	(16) C
(17) H	(18) F	(19) C	(20) G
(21) G	(22) H	(23) D	(24) G
(25) A	(26) A	(27) G	(28) G
(29) F	(30) A	(31) E	(32) F
(33) C	(34) E	(35) E	(36) B

Total correct:

SCORING THE TEST

Adults

Check your answers and tick, then count the number of questions you got right. Be strict. If you made more than one guess you get no mark.

The Table which follows gives an estimate of your IQ rating against your score. If you score 18 (IQ 125) or more you are at the level at which preliminary Mensa candidates are asked to take a supervised test. A score above 25 (IQ 138) is better than that achieved by most Mensans.

Very bright or older children

Test the child as per instructions. Take the age of the child in months. Divide 180 by this number to make a decimal fraction (e.g. 12 years 2 months = 146 months. 180/146 = 1.233).

Multiply the child's IQ score on the test by this figure to obtain the child's adjusted IQ (e.g. a score of 6 on the test = IQ 101. 101 x 1.233 = adjusted IQ of 124.533 = 125).

SEREBRIAKOFF TEST SCORE TABLE

Score	IQ	Score	IQ
4	97	21	130
5	99	22	132
6	101	23	134
7	103	24	136
8	105	25	138
9	107	26	140
10	109	27	142
11	111	28	144
12	113	29	146
13	115	30	148
14	117	31	150
15	119	32	152
16	121	33	154
17	123	34	156
18	125	35	158
19	126	36	160
20	128	Mensa level	

CHAPTER THREE

Target Time: 3 hours 37 minutes

THE CANNY TRICYCLIST

A poor but canny tricyclist goes for a 1000-mile tour. He has two spare tyres. He wants to use each tyre for the same distance and changes tyres to suit.

How many miles did each tyre travel?

ANSWER:

3.1	Minutes allowed	6
	Time taken	
	Points gained	

PIGGY BANK

You've had a tough time financially lately – birthdays, wedding, whatall – and you are down to your piggy bank collection. Using the broad blade of a knife, you manage to get quite a few coins out.

You find that you have £16, and you notice that you have the same number of 10 pence, 20 pence and 50 pence pieces. How many of each do you have?

ANSWER:

3.2	Minutes allowed	7
	Time taken	
	Points gained	

COUNT THOSE SPOONS!

Here is a special puzzle for Uri Spoonbender. This puzzle, however, is completely straight and there is only one exact answer. Can you tell us how many times you can form the word SPOON making sure that once you have used a combination of letters, you can't swap them round and count it twice. You can use each letter more than once, though – and watch out, this can be a bit tricky. Try and number the letters "S1, S2, P1, P2 etc."

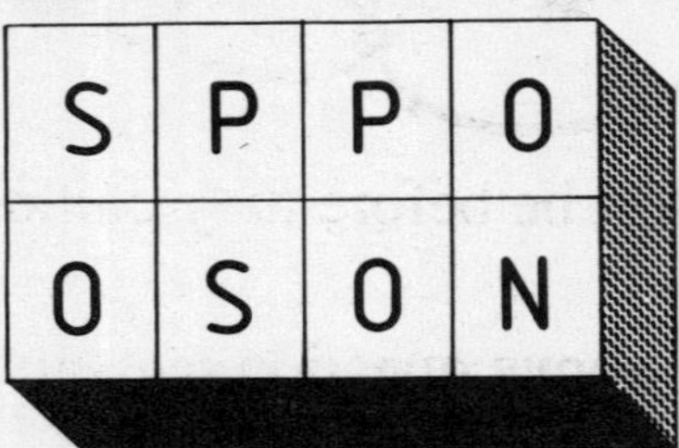

ANSWER:

3.3	Minutes allowed	9
	Time taken	
	Points gained	

COLLIDING ORBITS

a) Here is a planet orbiting its sun in a clockwise direction. An asteroid, however, is in a collision orbit with the planet. It travels in an anti-clockwise direction and is 60 degrees away from the intersection point of the orbits. The planet takes seven years to orbit the sun and the asteroid completes one orbit every 36 years.

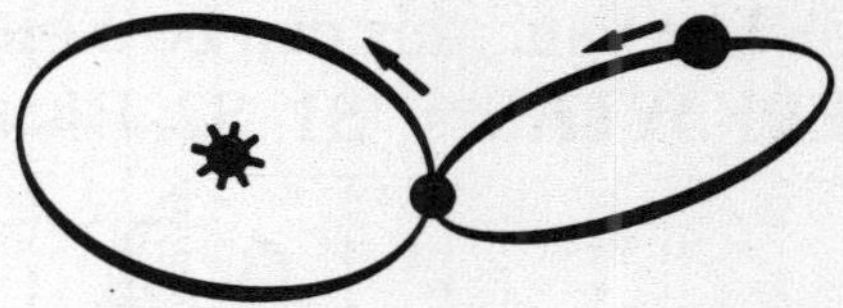

How long will it be before they collide?

b) Why is the above question questionable?

ANSWER:

<table>
<tr><td rowspan="3">3.4</td><td>Minutes allowed</td><td>29</td></tr>
<tr><td>Time taken</td><td></td></tr>
<tr><td>Points gained</td><td></td></tr>
</table>

WHERE DO I LIVE?

Within this mass of letters there are seven four-lettered words. Work out what the words are and place them into the grid, in a special order, so that a town can be read downwards.

What is this town?

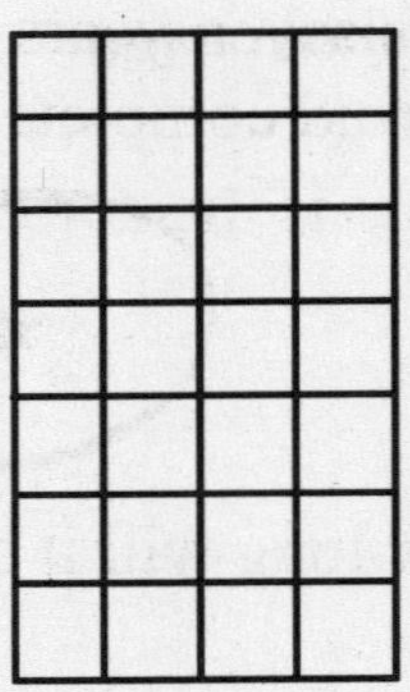

LNHAVAIESTRONE
PUIOANNEPKWTRS

ANSWER:

3.5	Minutes allowed	20
	Time taken	
	Points gained	

CLOCKS

"Little Sue", Big Ben's little sister, was correct at midnight but gains 51 minutes per hour.

You look at the clock and see that it shows 9.15 a.m. You know that the clock stopped exactly two hours ago.

What is the correct time now?

ANSWER:

3.6	Minutes allowed	10
	Time taken	
	Points gained	

HANDICAP

In a 150 yard race, Bobby beats Karen by 22 yards. The race is now run again with Bobby starting 26 yards behind the start line.

Assuming equal performance, who wins the race this time?

ANSWER:

3.7	Minutes allowed	7
	Time taken	
	Points gained	

COGGERY

Here are four cog wheels. The largest cog has 86 teeth, the next cog has 25 teeth, the next cog has 15 teeth and the smallest cog has 12 teeth. (The diagram below is only an example.)

How many revolutions will the largest cog make before all the cogs return to their original position?

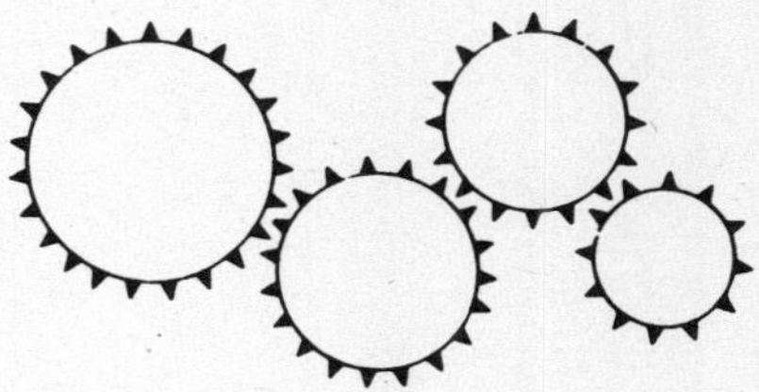

ANSWER:

3.8	Minutes allowed	15
	Time taken	
	Points gained	

A LEAKY TANKER

A petrol tanker travels at a speed of 42 mph. It is leaking petrol, however, and the petrol catches fire at the very moment it sets off. The petrol flame chases the tanker at a speed of $41^1/2$ mph.

If the tanker has stopped after $56^1/4$ miles, when might it explode?

ANSWER:

3.9	Minutes allowed	8
	Time taken	
	Points gained	

FILL THE BLANKS

For this puzzle you must fill in the blanks so that each line of five numbers adds up to 125.

Can you tell us what number should replace the question mark?

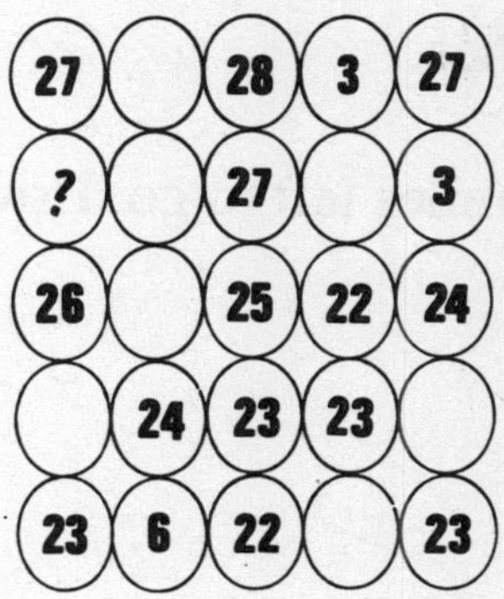

ANSWER:

3.10	Minutes allowed	6
	Time taken	
	Points gained	

WALK TIMES

A man goes on a sponsored walk. On the first day he covers one third of the total distance. On the second day he covers one half of the remaining distance. On the third day he covers one third of the remaining distance and on the fourth day he covers one quarter of the remaining distance.

He now has 25 miles left to go. How far has he travelled?

ANSWER:

3.11	Minutes allowed	15
	Time taken	
	Points gained	

TIME THE BOAT

A ship is battling against the stream to the safety of an island. It travels at a shuddering speed of 5 miles per hour, and is 15 miles away from safety. The flow of the water is $2^1/2$ miles per hour against the boat which uses $2^1/2$ gallons of fuel every hour and has a tank capacity of 15 gallons.

Will it reach safety, and if so how much fuel will it have left?

ANSWER:

3.12	Minutes allowed	20
	Time taken	
	Points gained	

TUNNELLING TRAIN

A train is travelling towards a tunnel at a speed of 30 mph. The tunnel is $6^1/_2$ miles long and the train is $^1/_8$ of a mile long.

How long will it take for the whole of the train to pass through the tunnel, from the moment the front of the train enters the tunnel to the moment the last of the rear of the train emerges from it?

ANSWER:

3.13	Minutes allowed	15
	Time taken	
	Points gained	

MARX AND WORK

The Marx brothers have taken on another job as furniture removal men and are loading tables onto a van. If Groucho was working on his own it would take him 12 minutes to fill an empty van and if Harpo was doing the same it would take him just $13^1/_2$ minutes. However it would take Chico just 14 minutes to empty a full van. This of course is what is happening: Groucho and Harpo are loading the van whilst Chico is unloading the furniture and taking it back.

Can you tell us how long it would take for Groucho and Harpo to fill the van whilst Chico is unloading it at the same time?

ANSWER:

3.14	Minutes allowed	20
	Time taken	
	Points gained	

DIY CROSSWORD

The words down and across are given below, but you must decide where the blank squares are.

C								S
						V		
						U		
E								

EAGERNESS
CATHARSIS
VIA AMUSE
LAMAS GNU
TAPE ROSE
TREK EASE

COLLEAGUES
SLACKNESS
SEVER
STUNG
PAIR
AREA
ALSO
STEM
USE
TAM

3.15	Minutes allowed	30
	Time taken	
	Points gained	

ANSWERS

		FOR CORRECT ANSWERS		
		Your Time	Time Allowed	Points Gained
3.1	600 Miles		6	
3.2	20 of each coin		7	
3.3	Spoon can be formed 24 times		9	
3.4	**a)** A collision will occur after 42 years **b)** Because the orbits are not astronomically possible		29	
3.5	Newport, Nail. Even. Wash Port. Open. Ruin. Task.		20	
3.6	The correct time is 7 am.		10	
3.7	Karen wins		7	
3.8	The largest cog will make 150 revolutions		15	
3.9	After 2 min 41 sec		8	
3.10	42		6	
3.11	125 miles		15	
3.12	The boat makes it with no fuel left		20	
3.13	13 min 15 sec		15	
3.14	11 min 38 sec		20	
	POINTS CARRIED FORWARD			

ANSWERS

		FOR CORRECT ANSWERS *Your Time*	*Time Allowed*	*Points Gained*
	POINTS BROUGHT FORWARD			
3.15	Answer below		30	
	TOTAL POINTS GAINED			

CHAPTER SUMMARY

Chapter Handicap Total:	
Correct Answers x 5 points:	
Chapter Total:	
Brought Forward:	
Running Total:	

CHAPTER FOUR

Target Time: 3 hours 12 minutes

YOU CUT AND I CHOOSE

The title gives a solution to fair shares for two when dividing cakes, but how can the principle be applied for three sharers?

Bill, Ben and Bertha share a cake. How do they arrange for the cutting to be fair?

ANSWER:

4.1	Minutes allowed	3
	Time taken	
	Points gained	

BREWMASTER

By starting at the centre square you can move in any direction except diagonally from square to touching square collecting the letters of the word BREW in any order. Can you tell us how many different ways there are of doing this?

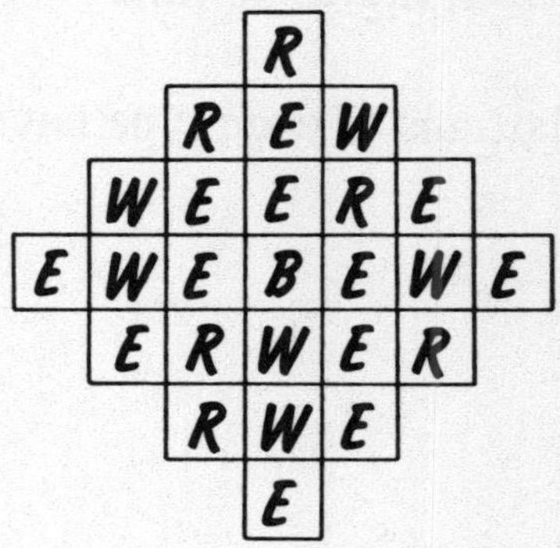

ANSWER:

4.2	Minutes allowed	**6**
	Time taken	
	Points gained	

EYING MARTIAN EYES

There are Martians with 4 eyes, Martians with 6 eyes, Martians with 8 eyes and Martians with 12 eyes. You know that there is an equal number of each type of Martian and you also know that the total number of eyes that the Martians have between them is 5,130.

How many Martians of each type have you got?

ANSWER:

4.3	Minutes allowed	**10**
	Time taken	
	Points gained	

MANAGING TIME

A company runs a Time Management course which it charges for. At the end of the first course the company's total takings were $3,895. There were more than 45 people on the course, but less than 100. Each person paid the same amount in full dollars only.

How many people went on the course and how much did the course cost?

ANSWER:

4.4	Minutes allowed	10
	Time taken	
	Points gained	

COSTING CASSETTES

A shop sells radios and cassette players. Cassette players cost 25 times as much as radios but of the ten items sold only one fifth were cassette players. Cassette players were sold at a price of £100 per 2.

How much did the shop earn from these sales?

ANSWER:

4.5	Minutes allowed	10
	Time taken	
	Points gained	

SYMBOLIC PROBLEM

Each different symbol has a different value. The numbers at the end of each row are the totals of the values of the symbols in that row. Can you work out the logic and fill in the missing value?

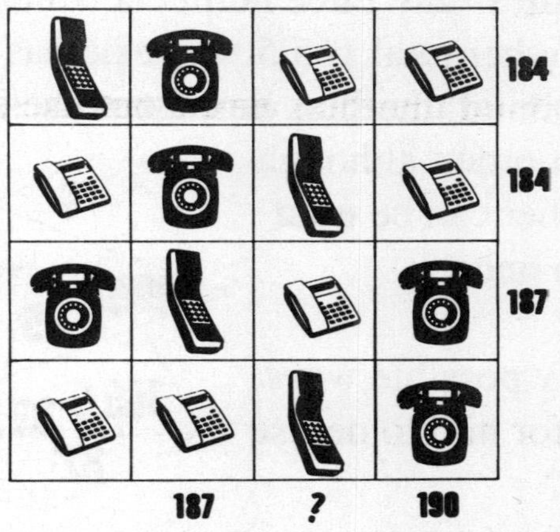

ANSWER:

4.6	Minutes allowed	8
	Time taken	
	Points gained	

BOMB CODE

A bomb has been planted on the Starship Enterprise. Mr Spock is desperately trying to defuse it by pressing numbers on a pad of buttons shown in our diagram. We know, though he doesn't, that he has to press any three numbers which when added together total 165.5. Once he has used a combination of numbers he cannot use it again in a different order, although each number can be used more than once.

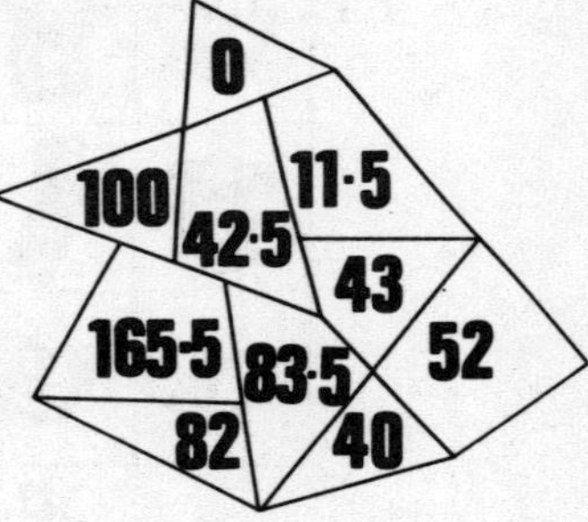

How many possible ways are there for him to defuse the bomb?

ANSWER:

4.7	Minutes allowed	15
	Time taken	
	Points gained	

ANAGRAMMAR

Each of the following words except one is an anagram of another word.

Which word has no English anagram?

SAILED PRESENT STERLING

REGINA VIKING

ANSWER:

4.8	Minutes allowed	15
	Time taken	
	Points gained	

AGES AND AGES

Cressida didn't like to tell her age, but she didn't like to be rude either. So her mother usually answered for her. Her mother said, “I am just seven times as old as she is now. In 20 years, she will be just half the age that I will be then.”

How old is little Cressida now?

ANSWER:

4.9	Minutes allowed	**12**
	Time taken	
	Points gained	

COSTING FRUIT

If an orange costs 18p, and a pineapple costs 27p, and a grape costs 15p – how much will a mango cost?

ANSWER:

4.10	Minutes allowed	5
	Time taken	
	Points gained	

PALINDROMING

A palindrome is a word, a phrase or a sentence that reads the same backwards as forwards. You will find two palindromic phrases defined below. Fill in the palindromes.

a) The zookeeper announces that he has captured two less than a dozen small beasts in a reticulated object.

b) Spoiled children of movie luminaries.

ANSWER:

4.11	Minutes allowed	30
	Time taken	
	Points gained	

BACKWARDS AND FORWARDS

Another palindrome puzzle. Can you find the two palindromic phrases?

a) Query by rodent phobic person.

b) Comment by icecream and cake loving overweight person.

ANSWER:

4.12	Minutes allowed	30
	Time taken	
	Points gained	

MEAT AND VEG

You've gone out shopping for groceries and meat. The joint costs twice as much as the vegetables, and the vegetables cost twice as much as the sweet. You spend the horrendous total of $14.

How much did the vegetables cost?

ANSWER:

4.13	Minutes allowed	3
	Time taken	
	Points gained	

MY FIRST – MY SECOND

By picking the right letter for each line, you can spell out a word of five letters. What is it?

My first is in FISH but not in SNAIL
My second is in RABBIT but not in KALE
My third is in UP but not in DOWN
My fourth is in TIARA but not in CROWN
My fifth is in TREE you'll plainly see,
The whole is a food for you and me.

ANSWER:

4.14	Minutes allowed	5
	Time taken	
	Points gained	

DIY CROSSWORD

The words down and across are given below, but you must decide where the blank squares are.

		Q						
				O				
				O				
A								

SOT TENET E L
DATA RUNE X I
MADAM VIE T V
NOMINATOR R E
I A Q D A R
N S U I C Y
N S E M T M
E E O A
T N R N
LIQUORICE
TOSS E B O O
EBON N E N M
D T T E
S A O N

4.15	Minutes allowed	30
	Time taken	
	Points gained	

ANSWERS

		FOR CORRECT ANSWERS		
		Your Time	Time Allowed	Points Gained
4.1	One way is this: Bill cuts, Ben chooses, and they both trisect their pieces. Bertha chooses one piece from each		3	
4.2	7 ways		6	
4.3	171 Martians		10	
4.4	95 people each pay $41		10	
4.5	£116		10	
4.6	178		8	
4.7	There are 4 ways of scoring 165.5		15	
4.8	Viking has no anagram		15	
4.9	Her mother is 28 and Cressida is 4		12	
4.10	15p – 3p per letter		5	
4.11	**a)** Ten animals I slam in a net **b)** Star brats		30	
4.12	**a)** Was it a rat I saw **b)** Desserts I stressed		30	
4.13	$4		3	
4.14	Fruit		5	

POINTS CARRIED FORWARD

ANSWERS

		FOR CORRECT ANSWERS *Your Time*	*Time Allowed*	*Points Gained*
	POINTS BROUGHT FORWARD			
4.15	Answer below		30	
	TOTAL POINTS GAINED			

CHAPTER SUMMARY

Chapter Handicap Total:

Correct Answers x 5 points:

Chapter Total:

Brought Forward:

Running Total:

CHAPTER FIVE

Target Time: 3 hours 32 minutes

BOUNCING CHEQUE LOSS

You are a second-hand furniture dealer. Your first customer of the day buys a settee for $25 and pays with a cheque, changes his mind and asks for a $15 chair instead. With an empty till, you cash the cheque with a neighbour and give the buyer a $10 note as change.

The cheque bounces and you have to borrow $25 to pay the neighbour. The chair cost you $11. How much money have you lost?

ANSWER:

5.1	Minutes allowed	5
	Time taken	
	Points gained	

SECRET SENTENCE

There is a sentence hidden in this square. You have to find the start letter and unravel the sentence. All the letters are used and you can move in any direction to any touching square, and by touching we even mean if it is only the corners that are touching.

D	E	D	N	E	L	E
N	I	O	N	E	P	H
T	M	A	T	N	A	V
N	E	I	I	N	E	E
S	S	T	S	F	R	R
B	A	S	N	S	O	G
N	A	E	L	U	T	E

ANSWER:

5.2	Minutes allowed	20
	Time taken	
	Points gained	

CUBISM

Here is the spread-out pattern of a box. When it is folded it will make a cube. You must decide which of the completed cubes below cannot be made from this.

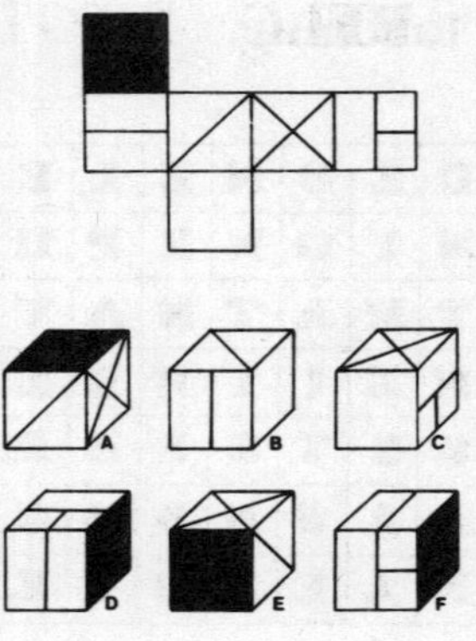

ANSWER:

5.3	Minutes allowed	10
	Time taken	
	Points gained	

DEPRIVED PROVERB 1

The following proverb has had all of the vowels taken out, and the remaining letters broken up into groups of four letters each. Replace the vowels and find the proverb.

BRDS FFTH RFLC KTGT HR

ANSWER:

5.4	Minutes allowed	3
	Time taken	
	Points gained	

DEPRIVED PROVERB 2

Here is another popular proverb, treated in the same way as the previous puzzle.

Can you decipher it?

FLND HSMN YRSN PRTD

ANSWER:

5.5	Minutes allowed	5
	Time taken	
	Points gained	

MUFFIN RACE

At a mass muffin eating contest Elizabeth eats an average of 22 muffins in her first 10 sittings. After a further 20 sittings her average increases to 34 muffins.

Can you tell us what her average was for her last 20 sittings only?

ANSWER:

5.6	Minutes allowed	10
	Time taken	
	Points gained	

MURPHY

The following coiled sentence in the box will rhyme with the first line. It is a saying that will complete the poem (or couplet, if you prefer).

MURPHY'S LAW IS VERY FINE

T	K	K	O	E
I	E	C	F	N
P	E	E	F	I
S	Y	N	T	L
O	U	R	H	E

ANSWER:

5.7	Minutes allowed	15
	Time taken	
	Points gained	

WINGLES, WONKLES

If 6 wingles and 3 wonkles cost 15¢, and you can buy 9 wonkles and 3 wingles for the same 15¢, how much will it cost you to buy 100 wonkles?

ANSWER:

5.8	Minutes allowed	6
	Time taken	
	Points gained	

THE 'I's HAVE IT!

All answers begin with the letter I.

Answers

1. Little devil
2. Sub continent
3. Kind of architecture
4. Creeper
5. Mrs Ghandi
6. Mesembryanthemum
7. Cretan mountain
8. Large lizard
9. Measuring worm
10. Austrian city at foot of Brenner pass
11. Metal era
12. German medal
13. Home of Baghdad
14. Son of Abraham and Hagar
15. Elephant tusk

5.9	Minutes allowed	18
	Time taken	
	Points gained	

TIMED CROSSWORD

Across

1. Avocado (9,4)
7. Kentish coastal bogs (6,7)
9. Cell fats (6)
11. Legionnaire's hat (4)
12. Vision adjuster (8)
14. Head of Faculty (4)
16. Paired with Hardy (6)
18. Arch of the foot (6)
20. Giver (5)
22. Large cup (3)
24. & 24 down A dance (3-3)
25. Colourful poison (6,7)

Down

1. Funny Spring day (5,5,4)
2. Astronomical abbreviation (3)
3. Excessive desire (5)
4. Kind of beret? (3)
5. Runic letter (3)
6. A scared red's reaction perhaps (8,5)
8. Scottish isle (5)
10. Container (3)
11. Young goat (3)
13. Loud yell of acclamation (5)
15. Newt (3)
17. Another container (3)
19. Type of nurse (abbrev) (2)
21. Was friendly with pussy cat (3)
22. Extinct bird (3)
23. Neon, for example (3)
24. See 24 across (3)

5.10	Minutes allowed	**45**
	Time taken	
	Points gained	

SAME, BUT DIFFERENT

Look at the sixteen rectangles in this diagram. In each one there is a series of objects arranged in a different order. There are some objects repeated more than once in some squares. Can you tell which pairs of squares can be considered identical, since they contain exactly the same objects, although maybe not in the same order.

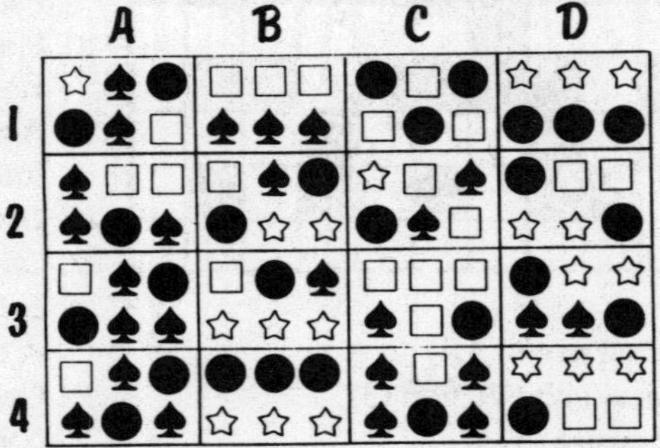

ANSWER:

5.11	Minutes allowed	15
	Time taken	
	Points gained	

COME FOLLOW, FOLLOW!

You wish to get from A to Z and must follow the arrows. How many different ways can you find to accomplish this task?

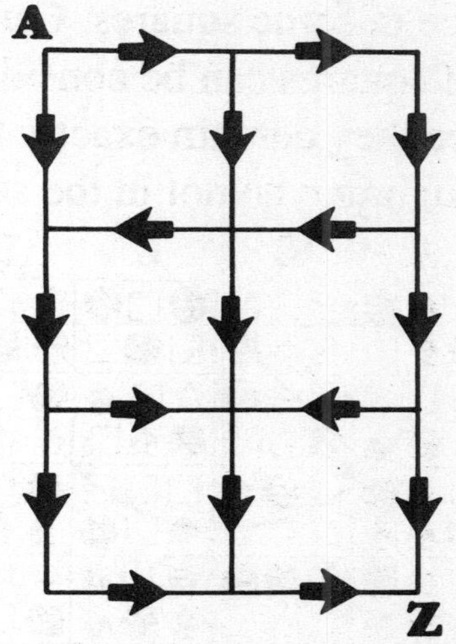

ANSWER:

5.12	Minutes allowed	10
	Time taken	
	Points gained	

WHAT LOGIC?

Can you work out the logic behind this series of numbers and replace the two exclamation marks with the correct positive numbers?

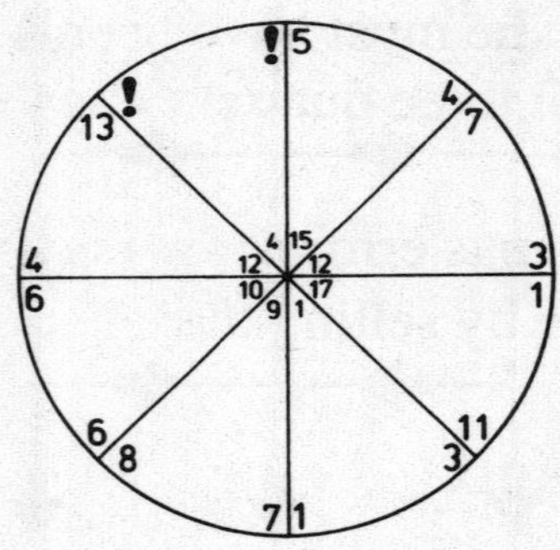

ANSWER:

5.13	Minutes allowed	10
	Time taken	
	Points gained	

EGGS

A farmer sells brown eggs and white eggs. Brown eggs are sold for £6 for ten and cost three times as much as the white eggs. The farmer sells 150 eggs of which one eighth are brown. Perhaps you can now see what we mean by 'good in parts': he must have been a good salesman to sell three quarters of an egg!

Ignore this obvious error. How much money should he make by selling the eggs?

ANSWER:

5.14	Minutes allowed	10
	Time taken	
	Points gained	

DIY CROSSWORD

The words down and across are given below, but you must decide where the blank squares are.

O								
	O							
							R	Y
	S		P					
							R	
M								S

SUPPORT HAS P
ARK ATTAR R
METE ONYX E
U N U P P
P O R E A
S T N T R
E E E
T R
APES EWE TRY
EAT REBUS HAS

O T A Y B E S A ROE
R H W E A A T S URNS
A E E T R R Y K
L M S S

5.15	Minutes allowed	30
	Time taken	
	Points gained	

ANSWERS

		FOR CORRECT ANSWERS		
		Your Time	*Time Allowed*	*Points Gained*
5.1	You lost what the thief gained , i.e. $10 + a chair = $21. Loss of profit is not loss of money.		5	
5.2	An elephant never forgets unless it is an absent-minded one		20	
5.3	F		10	
5.4	Birds of a feather flock together		3	
5.5	A fool and his money are soon parted		5	
5.6	40 muffins		10	
5.7	It keeps your neck off the line (start second letter down, left hand side)		15	
5.8	$1 (wonkles are 1¢, and wingles 2¢)		6	
5.9	Imp, India, Ionic, Ivy, Indira, Ice plant, Ida, Iguana, Inch worm, Innsbruck, Iron Age, Iron Cross, Iraq, Ishmael, Ivory		18	
	CARRIED FORWARD			

ANSWERS

		FOR CORRECT ANSWERS *Your Time*	*Time Allowed*	*Points Gained*
	BROUGHT FORWARD			
5.10	**Across. 1.** Alligator Pear **7.** Romney marshes **9.** Lipids **11.** Kepi **12.** Optician **14.** Dean **16.** Laurel **18.** Instep **20.** Donor **22.** Mug **24 & 24 Down** Can-can **25.** Yellow Arsenic **Down. 1.** April Fool's Day **2.** L.E.M. **3.** Greed **4.** Tam **5.** Edh **6.** Russians Panic **8.** Arran **10.** Pot **11.** Kid **13.** Cheer **15.** Eft **17.** Urn **19.** S.R. **21.** Owl **22.** Moa **23.** Gas **24.** See 24 Across		45	
5.11	D1 & B4, A3 and A4		15	
5.12	10 ways		10	
5.13	0 and 1 (numbers at circumference of segment added together equal number at centre of opposite segment)		10	
5.14	£37.50		10	
	CARRIED FORWARD			

ANSWERS

		FOR CORRECT ANSWERS		
		Your Time	*Time Allowed*	*Points Gained*
	POINTS BROUGHT FORWARD			
5.15	Answer below		30	
	TOTAL POINTS GAINED			

CHAPTER SUMMARY

Chapter Handicap Total:	
Correct Answers x 5 points:	
Chapter Total:	
Brought Forward:	
Running Total:	

CHAPTER SIX

Target Time: 3 hours 4 minutes

SCREWY ENIGMA

You have two screws as in the illustration. The distance between the two heads is 85.72mm. The pitch is 2.715mm. You hold the two screws together as shown and, without allowing them to rotate, you move the right hand screw around the left hand screw, as shown in the illustration, keeping them engaged together. You rotate this three times exactly. What is now the distance between the heads of the screws?

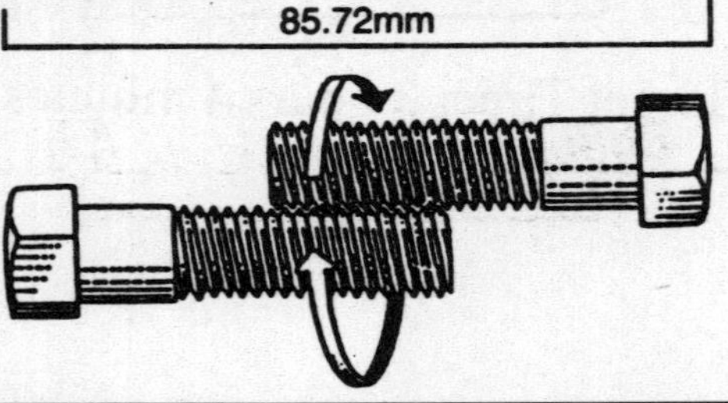

ANSWER:

6.1	Minutes allowed	5
	Time taken	
	Points gained	

LETTER BALANCE

The top and bottom sets of scales in this diagram balance perfectly. How many of the missing letters are needed to balance the middle set?

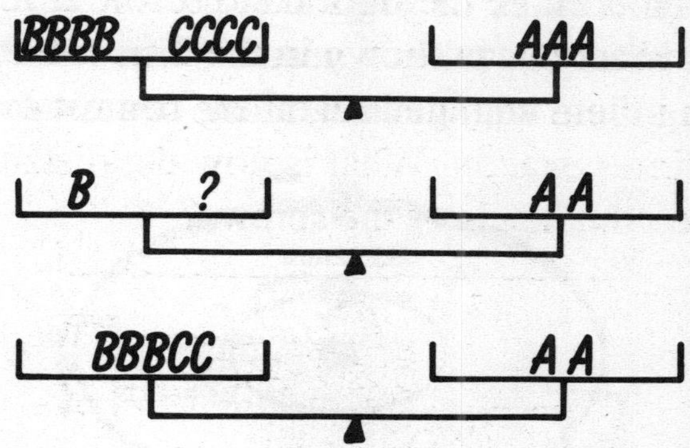

ANSWER:

6.2	Minutes allowed	15
	Time taken	
	Points gained	

TIMING ORBITS

This is a planetary system of two planets orbiting their sun. The sun is smaller than the planets because it is going out. The planets are in line with the sun and are about to rotate around it. The outer planet takes 15 years to make one revolution and the inner one takes 5 years. When will they next be in line with the sun, to the nearest month?

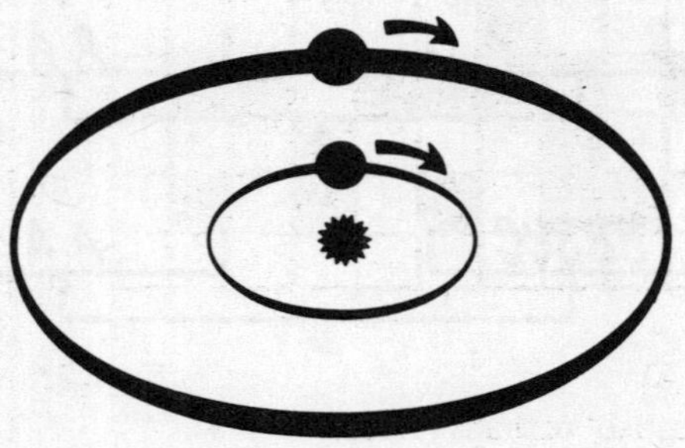

ANSWER:

6.3	Minutes allowed	15
	Time taken	
	Points gained	

TIMED CROSSWORD

Across

1. One of the Beatles (4,9)
7. North . . . (4,5,4,)
9. A line for reefing (6)
11. Husks of cereal grain (4)
12. Cloudy (8)
14. John McEnroe perhaps (4)
16. Christian festival (6)
18. Relaxed position (2,4)
20. Hollow muscular organ (5)
22. Mineral spring (30)
24. Donkey (3)
25. Early Christian (5,8)

Down

1. Fathom (5,8)
2. The 'Enterprise' perhaps (1,1,1)
3. Stone builder (5)
4. Computer abbreviation (1,1,1)
5. Scottish 'no' (3)
6. A busy postman's reaction perhaps (3,7,3)
8. Or trick perhaps (5)
10. Kind of deer (3)
11. Monkhouse, Hope, etc (3)
13. Swindle (5)
15. & 21. Submerged valley (3)
17. & 22D. Navigational abbreviation (1,1,1)
19. Exclamation of surprise (2)
23. Type of tree (3)
24. Everything (3)

6.4	Minutes allowed	45
	Time taken	
	Points gained	

DO YOU KNOW?

All answers begin with the letter J.

Answers

1. Another name for a hyacinth
2. Variety of orange
3. Semi precious stone or colour
4. Unidentified murderer from around 1888
5. A short leather strap in falconry
6. An island in Indonesia
7. Pier or dock
8. Old rustic dance
9. Another name for Jupiter
10. A judo expert
11. Seventh month
12. A member of a jury
13. A Chinese sailing vessel
14. Sweater or pullover
15. River in N. E. Africa

6.5	Minutes allowed	15
	Time taken	
	Points gained	

VASE TRADING

Bill bought an antique vase last year and sold it for 10% more than it cost. Jim bought an antique lamp, couldn't get rid of it, and sold it for 10% less than he paid. Then, just to compound the problem, Bill bought another vase at exactly the same price as the first, couldn't get rid of it, and took a 10% cut; and Jim bought an identical lamp and sold it for 10% more than he paid, which was the same price he paid for the first one.

Which of the two men made money or lost money on that series of deals?

ANSWER:

6.6	Minutes allowed	10
	Time taken	
	Points gained	

BEAN GUESSES

Mary's corner shop was losing some business to the new supermarket, so she ran one of those 'Guess the jelly beans in the jar' competitions. It was a very small jar indeed. Ann guessed 43 beans, Bet guessed 34 beans, Charles guessed 41 beans. One of them was off by 6 beans, another by 3 beans and another by only 1.

How many beans were there really?

ANSWER:

6.7	Minutes allowed	5
	Time taken	
	Points gained	

COMMITTEE HATER

The following cynical comment has had all the vowels removed, and the remaining letters broken up into groups of four. Replace the vowels and solve the comment.

CMMT TSGR PTHT KPSM NTSB
TWST SHRS

ANSWER:

6.8	Minutes allowed	10
	Time taken	
	Points gained	

NUMBER WISE?

Take the number of states in the United States, multiply by the number of lives a cat is supposed to have, divide by the Roman numeral X, and subtract the number of cents in a U.S. quarter.

What is left?

ANSWER:

6.9	Minutes allowed	3
	Time taken	
	Points gained	

SELECT THEM SOCKS

You have brown, blue, black and green socks in your drawer, in the ratio of 2 to 3, to 4, to 5 pairs. How many socks must you take out to be sure of having a pair?

ANSWER:

6.10	Minutes allowed	3
	Time taken	
	Points gained	

FOUR LETTER WORDS

What is the 4-letter word which when placed in front of the following four words will make each of them into a new word?

LINE BOAT LIKE STYLE

ANSWER:

6.11	Minutes allowed	3
	Time taken	
	Points gained	

A DISTRAUGHT LAD

What 4 letters can be re-arranged to make sense – and two different words – in the following sentence:

The little boy was absolutely distraught: "That wicked hunter set a . . . . and caught my pet; I cannot bear to . . . . with him, but I don't know what to do."

ANSWER:

6.12		
	Minutes allowed	3
	Time taken	
	Points gained	

WAYS WITH GUY

"This Guy was hot stuff!" In this diagram you will find the letters of the name "Guy". Can you tell us how many ways there are of forming this name? You are permitted to use each letter more than once, but the same combination of letters cannot be used again in a different order.

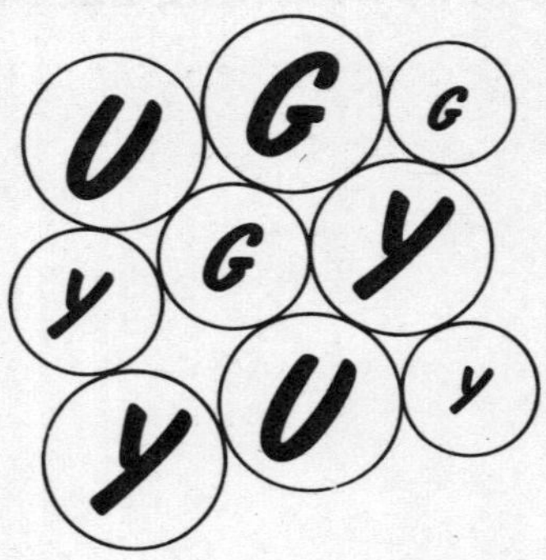

ANSWER:

6.13	Minutes allowed	12
	Time taken	
	Points gained	

EVERY LEAF IS COUNTED

Can you count the leaves? How many ways are there of tracing the word 'leaf', starting each time from the centre circle. You can only move to touching circles.

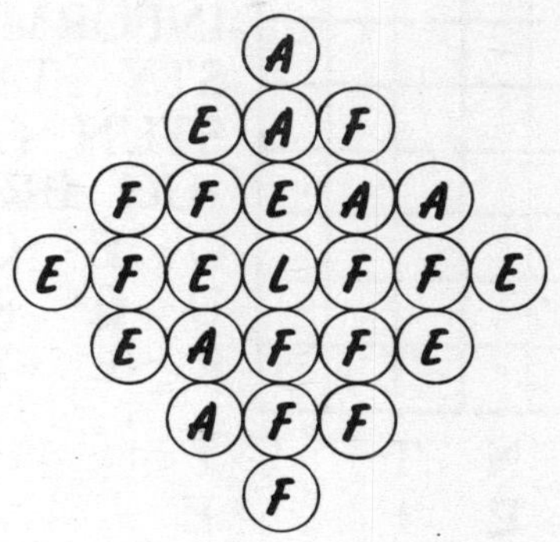

ANSWER:

6.14	Minutes allowed	10
	Time taken	
	Points gained	

DIY CROSSWORD

The words down and across are given below, but you must decide where the blank squares are.

			N					
K								
		F						
			Y					
				Z				
								D

ELEVENSES P U
UPON KIN R N
RUE APSE E F
INFORMERS C E
STY TAR U T
STUN ORE R T
JUG BRED S E
O E C L O R
U R R A R S
R E Y P

B S U N T F
E K S E I E
T I E S N Z
A P D T

6.15	Minutes allowed	30
	Time taken	
	Points gained	

ANSWERS

		FOR CORRECT ANSWERS *Your Time*	*Time Allowed*	*Points Gained*
6.1	85.72mm. The distance will not change.		5	
6.2	6 Cs		15	
6.3	3 years and 9 months		15	
6.4	**Across 1.** Paul McCartney **7.** East, South West **9.** Earing **11.** Bran **12.** Overcast **14.** Brat **16.** Easter **18.** At ease **20.** Heart **22.** Spa **24.** Ass **25.** Roman Catholic **Down 1.** Piece together **2.** U.S.S. **3.** Mason **4.** C.P.U. **5.** Nae **6.** Yet another sac **8.** Treat **10.** Roe **11.** Bob **13.** Cheat **15.** Ria **17.** S.H.A. **19.** Eh **21.** Ria **22.** S.H.A. **23.** Ash **24.** All		45	
6.5	Jacinth. Jaffa. Jade. Jack the Ripper. Jess. Java. Jetty. Jig. Jove. Judoka. July. Juror. Junk. Jumper. Juba		15	
6.6	Each of them wound up with 99% (11/10 x 9/10) of their original investment		10	
		CARRIED FORWARD		

ANSWERS

		FOR CORRECT ANSWERS *Your Time*	*Time Allowed*	*Points Gained*
	BROUGHT FORWARD			
6.7	40 Beans		5	
6.8	A committee is a group that keeps minutes but wastes hours		10	
6.9	20 (= 50 x 9 ÷ 10 - 25)		3	
6.10	One more than the number of colours – 5 (all the rest has nothing to do with it)		3	
6.11	Life		3	
6.12	APRT (trap, part)		3	
6.13	The word GUY can be made 24 times		12	
6.14	There are only 4 ways of making the word LEAF		10	
6.15	See overleaf			
	CARRIED FORWARD			

ANSWERS

		FOR CORRECT ANSWERS		
		Your Time	*Time Allowed*	*Points Gained*
	POINTS BROUGHT FORWARD			
6.15	Answer below		30	
	TOTAL POINTS GAINED			

CHAPTER SUMMARY

Chapter Handicap Total:	
Correct Answers x 5 points:	
Chapter Total:	
Brought Forward:	
Running Total:	

CHAPTER SEVEN

Target Time: 3 hours 57 minutes

ENCOMPASSING AN OVAL

A pair of compasses draws a circle. How, without changing the radius, can you make it draw an oval? You have to fix a radius, then make one rotation from a fixed point to draw an oval where the curvature changes continuously all the way around the perimeter and the pencil produces a doubly symmetrical figure where one axis is more than the unaltered radius.

How can it be done?

ANSWER:

7.1	Minutes allowed	20
	Time taken	
	Points gained	

SQUARE UP TO THIS

Can you complete this number square so that each row and each column of five numbers adds up to 220?

ANSWER:

7.2	Minutes allowed	30
	Time taken	
	Points gained	

FIREWORKS WORKOUT

Now it's time to count fireworks. Starting from the bottom left hand corner and working your way up to the top right hand corner, you must collect the letters of the word 'Fireworks'. You can collect the letters in any order, but you can only move from segment to touching segment.

How many times can you make the word 'Fireworks'?

ANSWER:

7.3	Minutes allowed	15
	Time taken	
	Points gained	

ORBITAL LINE-UP

Two satellites leave the earth's atmosphere and begin to orbit the earth. They start in line with each other and both orbit in a clockwise direction. The inner satellite makes one revolution every three years, and the outer satellite makes one revolution every nine years. Can you tell us when they will next form a straight line with themselves and the earth.

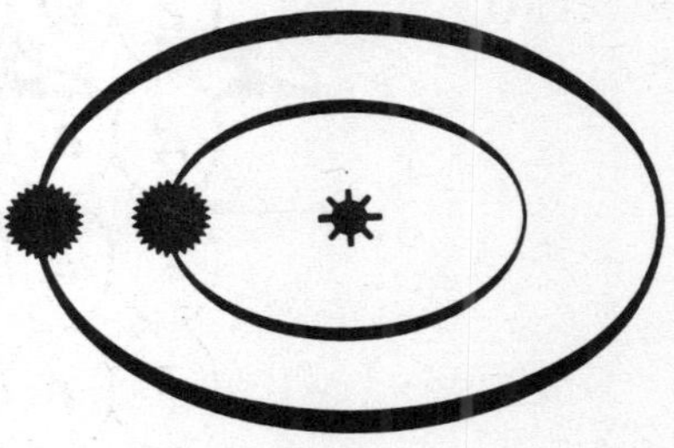

ANSWER:

7.4	Minutes allowed	15
	Time taken	
	Points gained	

UNMAKEABLE BOXES

Four of the boxes below are made up versions of the plan view, and two are not. Can you tell which two boxes these are?

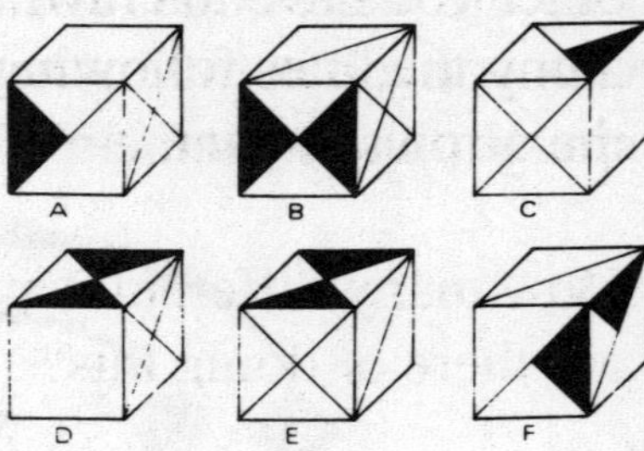

ANSWER:

7.5	Minutes allowed	10
	Time taken	
	Points gained	

CREEPY CRAWLERS

Imagine you are a caterpillar and are crawling down the veins of an enormous leaf, like the one shown below. Unfortunately, a fellow caterpillar has chewed its way through the main part of the leaf, so to get from one end of the leaf to the other you have to crawl along the lines following the arrows shown.

A

B

How many different ways are there of doing this?

ANSWER:

7.6	Minutes allowed	5
	Time taken	
	Points gained	

BLACK HOLE

A planet revolves around a sun in a clockwise direction and makes one revolution every 42 years. An asteroid, which revolves around a black hole in an anti-clockwise direction, is 40° away from where both orbits intersect. The asteroid makes an orbit every 27 years. Can you tell when they will collide?

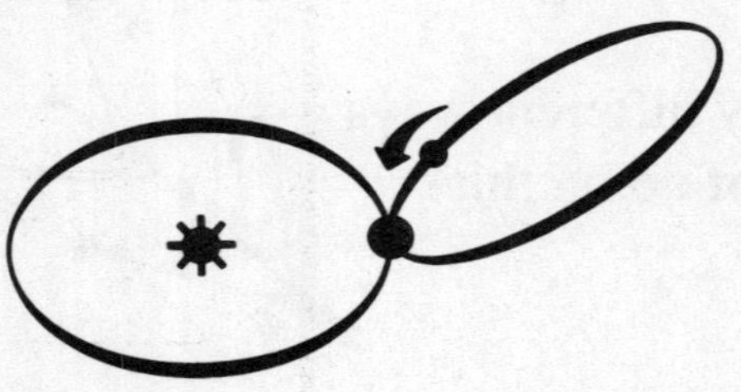

ANSWER:

7.7	Minutes allowed	20
	Time taken	
	Points gained	

PINBALL PINDOWN

Look at this strange pinball table. Imagine your ball is fired from any outside corner, and is allowed to hit four bumpers. You must remember that a ball that is fired from a corner cannot then hit another outside corner, and can only hit four numbers, excluding the corner. What is the highest possible score, and how many ways are there of achieving it?

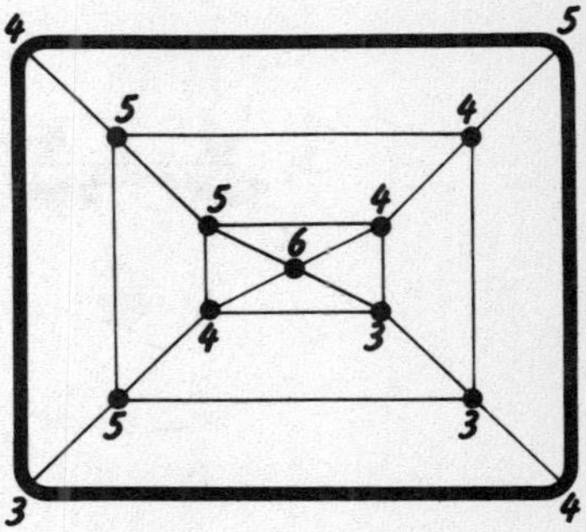

ANSWER:

7.8	Minutes allowed	15
	Time taken	
	Points gained	

ODD SIGNS

This strange signpost may not appear to contain any logic, but actually it does. Each letter is given a value and the total values of the letters in each town is its corresponding distance.

Can you work out the logic and tell us the distance to Paris?

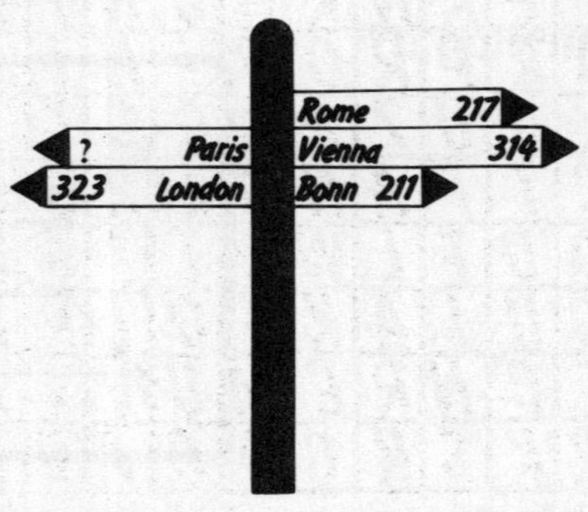

ANSWER:

7.9	Minutes allowed	30
	Time taken	
	Points gained	

BIRD WATCHING

Which twenty birds can be found in this diagram? Each of the names can be read forwards or backwards in a straight line, vertically, horizontally or diagonally.

O	S	P	R	E	Y	Y	A	J	P
O	P	A	C	D	E	R	S	K	W
T	E	R	N	K	H	C	N	I	F
A	R	P	R	O	B	I	N	T	L
K	B	U	Z	Z	A	R	D	E	T
C	T	F	A	N	S	L	R	O	O
O	D	F	L	W	D	T	T	W	R
C	U	I	A	K	S	O	L	R	R
E	C	N	R	E	M	U	V	X	A
R	K	S	K	C	O	C	A	E	P

ANSWER:

7.10	Minutes allowed	**12**
	Time taken	
	Points gained	

HIDDEN QUOTATION

This box of letters is more than just a box of letters! By starting at one of the letters you can trace a hidden quotation by going from one letter to another. You can move from a square to any touching square, vertically, horizontally or diagonally, and must use every letter.

O	E	K	O	W
M	C	G	N	L
S	E	D	E	L
W	B	U	M	I
I	T	O	E	N
S	D	S	R	G

ANSWER:

7.11	Minutes allowed	10
	Time taken	
	Points gained	

AND ANOTHER

Now try this hidden quotation. The instructions are exactly the same as for the previous puzzle. What is the quotation this time?

P	L	A	U	T
W	I	N	U	A
O	E	L	N	M
Y	L	G	N	O
T	E	O	N	D
H	R	E	I	D

ANSWER:

7.12	Minutes allowed	10
	Time taken	
	Points gained	

MEAN SPEED

A competitor in this year's car rally completes a stage at an average speed of 26 miles per hour. At the next stage his average speed greatly improves. In fact, it is three times faster than before, i.e. 78 miles per hour. Both stages were exactly the same length.

Can you tell us his average speed for both stages?

ANSWER:

7.13	Minutes allowed	10
	Time taken	
	Points gained	

SLOPPY CASHIER

You enter your local bank to cash a cheque. As usual there is a long queue, and only one out of five cashiers is serving. By the time you get to the cashier you're fed up with waiting and he is in a total mess. In fact he is in such a state that he gives you pounds for pence shown on the cheque and pence for pounds. Noticing this, you quickly rush off and spend 23 pence. Counting your cash you find that you have exactly twice the amount of your original cheque.

Can you tell us how much the cheque was for?

ANSWER:

7.14	Minutes allowed	5
	Time taken	
	Points gained	

DIY CROSSWORD

The words down and across are given below, but you must decide where the blank squares are.

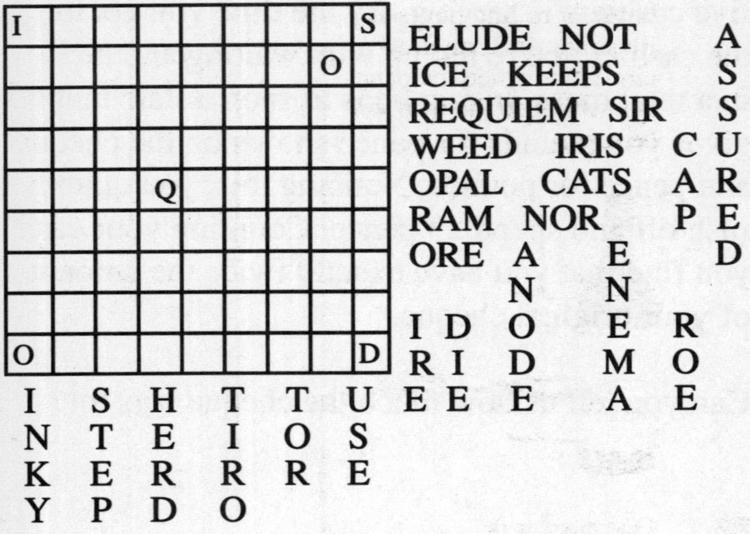

7.15	Minutes allowed	30
	Time taken	
	Points gained	

ANSWERS

		FOR CORRECT ANSWERS *Your Time*	*Time Allowed*	*Points Gained*
7.1	Wrap the paper around a bottle or rolling pin (see illustration). Then draw a circle, and when the paper is unwrapped the oval will be seen.		20	
7.2	One answer is: 50 71 48 5 46 70 46 50 50 4 47 49 44 39 41 11 38 38 42 91 42 16 40 84 38		30	
7.3	25 times		15	
7.4	After 27 months		15	
7.5	C and D can't be made		10	

CARRIED FORWARD

ANSWERS

		FOR CORRECT ANSWERS *Your Time*	*Time Allowed*	*Points Gained*
	BROUGHT FORWARD			
7.6	11 ways		5	
7.7	After 84 years		20	
7.8	The highest possible score is 25, which can only be achieved one way		15	
7.9	The distance to Paris is 270½ miles. A = 42½, B = 43½ , etc		30	
7.10	Turkey. Buzzard. Puffin. Peacock. Kestrel. Parrot. Cockatoo. Owl. Dove. Emu. Swan. Osprey. Tern. Redcap. Jay. Lark. Robin. Kite. Finch. Duck		12	
7.11	The quotation is "Knowledge comes but wisdom lingers"		10	
7.12	The quotation is "Autumn nodding o'er the yellow plain"		10	
7.13	Average speed for both stages = 39 m.p.h.		10	
7.14	The cheque was for £25.51		5	
	CARRIED FORWARD			

ANSWERS

		FOR CORRECT ANSWERS		
		Your Time	*Time Allowed*	*Points Gained*
	POINTS BROUGHT FORWARD			
7.15	Answer below		30	
	TOTAL POINTS GAINED			

CHAPTER SUMMARY

Chapter Handicap Total:	
Correct Answers x 5 points:	
Chapter Total:	
Brought Forward:	
Running Total:	

CHAPTER EIGHT

Target Time: 3 hours 16 minutes

MONUMENTAL PROBLEM

A 10-tonne statue with a flat bottom has to be settled by crane upon a larger pedestal. There is no way of lifting the statue except by slings under the base.

How do you arrange to set the statue on the pedestal and then get the slings out?

ANSWER:

8.1	Minutes allowed	10
	Time taken	
	Points gained	

WHAT'S A SYMBOL WORTH?

Each different symbol has a different value, and the numbers are the totals of the symbols in that row or column.

Can you tell us the total of the top row?

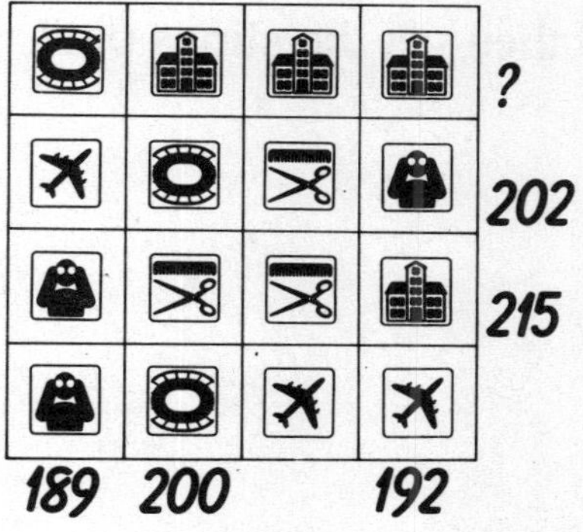

ANSWER:

8.2	Minutes allowed	**5**
	Time taken	
	Points gained	

HOW MANY ANAGRAMS?

How many anagrams can you find of the following word?

TREAD

ANSWER:

8.3	Minutes allowed	5
	Time taken	
	Points gained	

GET IN GEAR

Four cogs are in constant mesh as the example shows. The largest cog has 18 teeth, the next cog has 17 teeth, the next 16 teeth and the smallest has 15 teeth.

How many revolutions must the first cog make before all the cogs return to their original position?

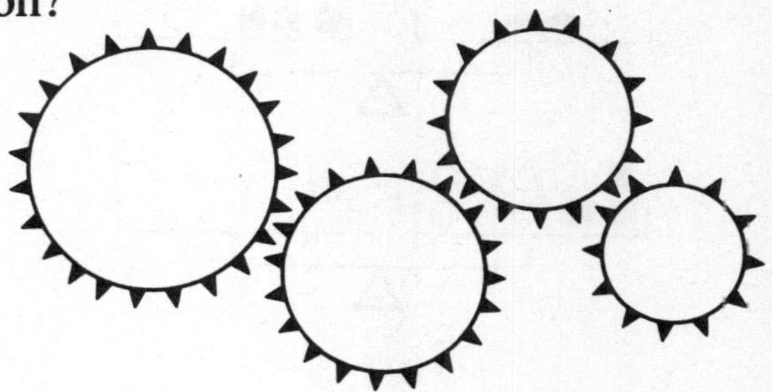

ANSWER:

8.4	Minutes allowed	15
	Time taken	
	Points gained	

WEIGH IN WITH THIS

Can you tell how many symbols are missing from the bottom right hand balance?

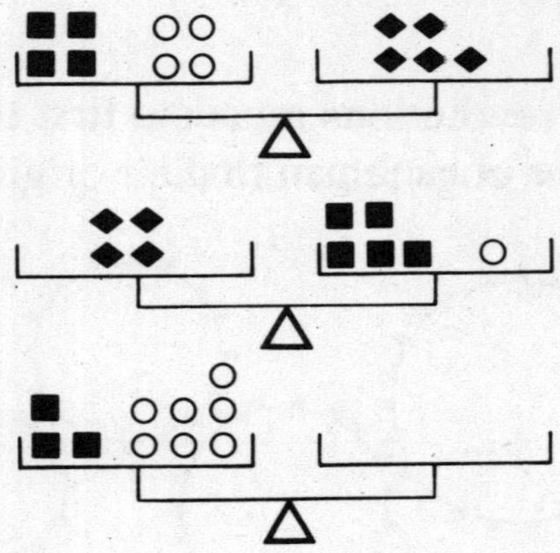

ANSWER:

8.5	Minutes allowed	10
	Time taken	
	Points gained	

BID FOR ART

At an art auction each painting cost the same price and each customer only bought one painting. There were more than 3 buyers but less than 100, and the auctioneers took £1698.

Can you tell us how many customers there were and the price of each painting?

ANSWER:

8.6	Minutes allowed	15
	Time taken	
	Points gained	

SOCCER GOALS

In the last soccer season Adam scored 34 more goals than Brian, who scored 26 less than Chris. We also know that Ed scored 8 more than Dave, Chris scored 13 more than Ed and the total number of goals scored by Brian and Ed was 37.

How many goals were scored altogether by the five players?

ANSWER:

8.7	Minutes allowed	**10**
	Time taken	
	Points gained	

BOOZE COST

A wine seller earned £532 in a day. Red wine costs three times as much as white wine. Of the 140 bottles sold, only one quarter were red.

How much would 5 bottles of red wine cost?

ANSWER:

8.8	Minutes allowed	8
	Time taken	
	Points gained	

TIMED CROSSWORD

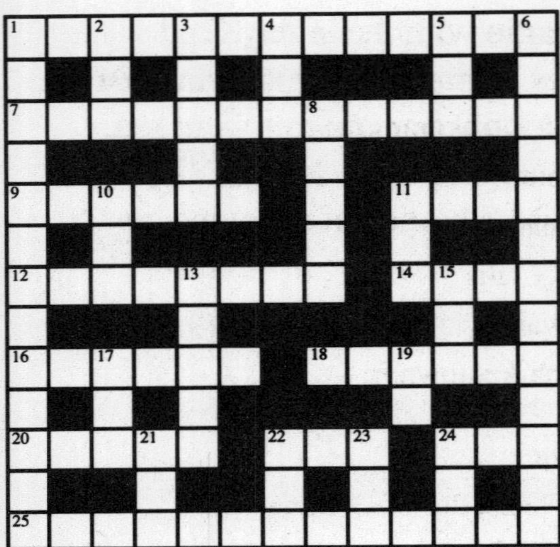

Across

1. Paul Daniels maybe? (7,6)
7. Musical instruments (6,7)
9. Seasides (6)
11. Clarified butter (4)
12. Cumbrian beauty spot (6)
14. Result of one of Quasimodo's duties (4)
16. Loyalty (6)
18. Obscure Indian river (6)
20. Architectural form (6)
22. Male of **4D** (3)
24. Teutonic state (abbrev.) (3)
25. Arithmetical term (6,7)

Down

1. Party game (7,6)
2. Narrow inlet (3)
3. Escape by luck
4. Anagrammed sheep (3)
5. Obsolete violin
6. Mountain range of Europe (13)
8. Moist atmosphere (5)
10. The first man of Norse mythology (3)
11. Primitive fish (3)
13. Reasoned thought (5)
15. Department of France (capital: Bourg) (3)
17. Three legged island (3)
19. For example (2)
21. Cretan mountain (3)
22. Jamaican drink (3)
23. Large flightless extinct bird (3)
24. Sturdy antelope (3)

8.9	Minutes allowed	45
	Time taken	
	Points gained	

LOOK FOR THE K-WORDS

All answers begin with the letter K.

Answers

1. Mountain in Karakoram range
2. Island of south west Japan
3. Jewish blessing
4. U. S. Santa Claus
5. Native Hawaiian
6. Lakeland market town in England
7. Large prawn
8. One time Chancellor of Germany
9. South African desert
10. Scene of greatest volcanic eruption
11. Chinese martial art
12. Fate (Hindu)
13. Danish money
14. Sacred book of Islam
15. Moscow citadel

8.10	Minutes allowed	18
	Time taken	
	Points gained	

SIGNLESS SUM

Fill in the maths symbols (+, -, ÷, x) in the grid below so that all the numbers add up to 100. The signs are taken in order, as they occur, ignoring the mathematical rule of applying x and ÷ before + and -.

	2		7		5	←
5						
			10		5	
8		5	100			
			5		25	
2						
	4		4		3	

ANSWER:

8.11	Minutes allowed	15
	Time taken	
	Points gained	

NUMERO ROMANA

Fill in the grid below so that each vertical and horizontal line is a genuine Roman numeral. Here are the numerals you must use: 5 Cs, 7Xs, 1M, 3 Vs and 4 Is.

ANSWER:

8.12	Minutes allowed	10
	Time taken	
	Points gained	

CONCENTRIC CONCENTRATION

Place the numbers listed below into the diagram so that each segment of three numbers adds up to 30, and each circle of 8 numbers adds up to 80. The numbers you must use are: 14, 11, 10, 12, 7, 9, 9, 8, 9, 9, 11, 11, 10, 10, 10, 10, 14, 9, 7, 11, 10, 8, 12 and 9.

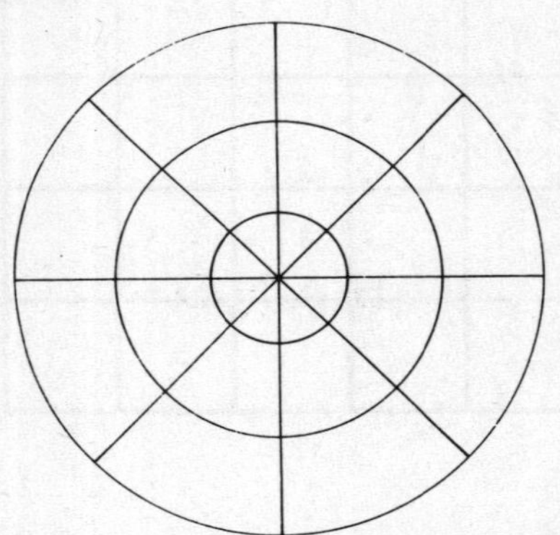

ANSWER:

8.13	Minutes allowed	10
	Time taken	
	Points gained	

PUNCHY PUZZLE

A punchy puzzle indeed! You must change the word FIST into the word HAND in as few moves as possible. Each move must produce a good English word.

F I S T

. . . .

. . . .

. . . .

. . . .

H A N D

ANSWER:

8.14	Minutes allowed	10
	Time taken	
	Points gained	

DIY CROSSWORD

The words down and across are given below, but you must decide where the blank squares are.

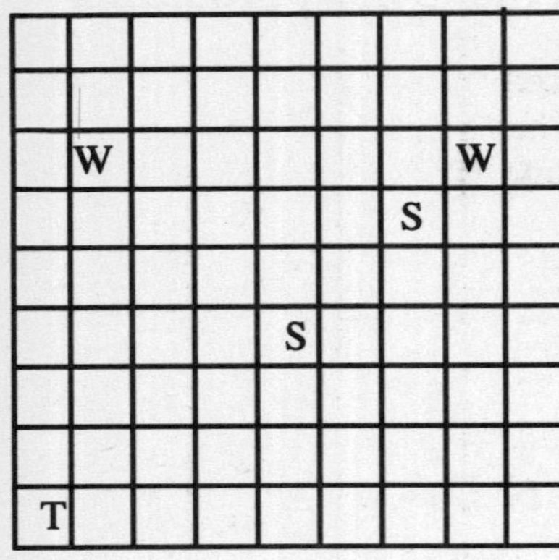

TEMPORARY T M
AWL ISLET E I
SWEPT ARC L S
MALIGNANT E C
LENS ITEM M R
OAST ROLE E E
P G L A T A
L A O V R N
E T C A Y T
A E U S
M T

S L L N
I I E I
L E A T
O S

8.15	Minutes allowed	**30**
	Time taken	
	Points gained	

ANSWERS

		FOR CORRECT ANSWERS *Your Time*	*Time Allowed*	*Points Gained*
8.1	Blocks of ice are arranged on the base so that the slings will go between them. The statue is placed on top of the blocks. When they melt the statue is on its base		10	
8.2	190		5	
8.3	Four: Trade, Tared, Rated and Dater		5	
8.4	680 revolutions		15	
8.5	5 symbols		10	
8.6	There were 6 customers; each painting cost £283		15	
8.7	138 goals. Adams scored 46, Brian scored 12, Chris scored 38, Dave scored 17 and Ed scored 25		10	
8.8	£38		8	
8.9	**Across 1.** Miracle worker **7.** Swanee whistle **9.** Coasts **11.** Ghee **12.** Lakeland **14.** Rang **16.** Homage **18.** Chenab **20.** Ionic **22.** Ram **24.** GDR **24.** Square measure			

CARRIED FORWARD

ANSWERS

		FOR CORRECT ANSWERS *Your Time*	*Time Allowed*	*Points Gained*
	BROUGHT FORWARD			
8.9 (cont)	**Down 1.** Musical chairs **2.** Ria **3.** Cheat **4.** Eew **5.** Kit **6.** Riesengebirge **8.** Humid **10.** Ask **11.** Gar **13.** Logic **15.** Ain **17.** Man **19.** Eg **21.** Ida **22.** Rum **23.** Moa **24.** Gnu		45	
8.10	K2. Kyushu. Kiddush. Kriss Kringle. Kanaka. Keswick. King Prawn. Kohl. Kalahari. Krakatoa. Kung Fu. Karma. Krone. Koran. Kremlin.		18	
8.11	5 + 7 - 2 x 5 - 8 x 2 - 4 ÷ 4 x 3 + 25 - 5 +10 + 5 + 5		15	
8.12	M C C X X C C C X V X X X V I X V I I I		10	
8.13	The outer circle contains the numbers in the following order: 7, 14, 9, 11, 9, 10, 8, 12. The middle ring: 14, 7, 11, 9, 10, 9, 12, 8. The outer ring: 9, 9, 10, 10, 11, 11, 10, 10		10	
	CARRIED FORWARD			

ANSWERS

		FOR CORRECT ANSWERS		
		Your Time	*Time Allowed*	*Points Gained*
	POINTS BROUGHT FORWARD			
8.14	FIST, FAST, HAST, HART, HARD, HAND		10	
8.15	Answer below		30	
	TOTAL POINTS GAINED			

M	A	L	I	G	N	A	N	T
I		I		A		V		E
S	W	E	P	T		A	W	L
C			L	E	N	S		E
R	O	L	E		I	T	E	M
E		O	A	S	T			E
A	R	C		I	S	L	E	T
N		U		L		E		R
T	E	M	P	O	R	A	R	Y

CHAPTER SUMMARY

Chapter Handicap Total:

Correct Answers x 5 points:

Chapter Total:

Brought Forward:

Running Total:

CHAPTER NINE

Target Time: 2 hours 51 minutes

FILL THE BLANK

Which letter should be placed in the blank square in the centre of this grid?

ANSWER:

9.1	Minutes allowed	15
	Time taken	
	Points gained	

SEEDY PUZZLE

A rather seedy puzzle, you might think! You must change the word SEED to the word TREE in as few moves as possible. Each change must produce a good English word.

S E E D

. . . .

. . . .

. . . .

. . . .

T R E E

ANSWER:

9.2		
	Minutes allowed	**10**
	Time taken	
	Points gained	

POST HASTE

Now can you change the word POST to the word MAIL in the same way. Each change must produce a good English word.

P O S T

. . . .

. . . .

. . . .

. . . .

M A I L

ANSWER:

9.3	Minutes allowed	10
	Time taken	
	Points gained	

CARRY IT ON

What letter should be used to continue the following series?

F S T F F S S E

ANSWER:

9.4	Minutes allowed	3
	Time taken	
	Points gained	

INCOMPLETE XWORD

Here's another colourful puzzle. It's a magic square, with the first word written in. The words down and across are the same. Can you complete the square?

W	H	I	T	E
H				
I				
T				
E				

ANSWER:

9.5	Minutes allowed	10
	Time taken	
	Points gained	

AND ANOTHER

A not so colourful puzzle, but the same rules apply as for the previous one. Can you complete the square?

B L A C K
L
A
C
K

ANSWER:

9.6	Minutes allowed	10
	Time taken	
	Points gained	

THINK! USE YOUR BRAIN

THINK can become BRAIN by changing one letter at a time. Each alteration, however, must give a new acceptable word. What is the least number of changes you must make, and what are they?

ANSWER:

9.7	Minutes allowed	10
	Time taken	
	Points gained	

EVERY SECOND COUNTS

Find the letter which can replace the second letter in each of the words either side of the brackets in order to create two new words. Place this letter inside the brackets, and you will be able to read a newly formed word downwards. What is it?

SHORE	( )	ARE
SHOT	( )	BRAT
GOAT	( )	ODE
AGE	( )	INCH
FATE	( )	DIAL
AUK	( )	ACHES
SHEEP	( )	OUTER

ANSWER:

9.8	Minutes allowed	10
	Time taken	
	Points gained	

SYMBOL SEARCH

What are the missing symbols in the following calculation?

((5 ? 9) ? 4) ? 8 = 19.25

ANSWER:

9.9	Minutes allowed	5
	Time taken	
	Points gained	

THREE TO ONE AGAINST

How can you arrange three matches to equal one – and not simply by putting them in a straight vertical line?

ANSWER:

9.10	Minutes allowed	3
	Time taken	
	Points gained	

DOGGONE IT!

Select and re-arrange the letters from the sentence below to find the names of at least three types of dog.

I CAN STIR A MANAGER'S BLOOD

ANSWER:

9.11	Minutes allowed	10
	Time taken	
	Points gained	

AVERAGE IT OUT

An aeroplane maintains an average speed of 180 miles per hour from one airport to another. It then returns to the first airport over exactly the same distance at an average speed of 144 miles per hour. What was the average speed over the whole journey?

ANSWER:

9.12		
	Minutes allowed	5
	Time taken	
	Points gained	

HOW MANY WAYS?

How many different routes can you find from A to B by following the arrows?

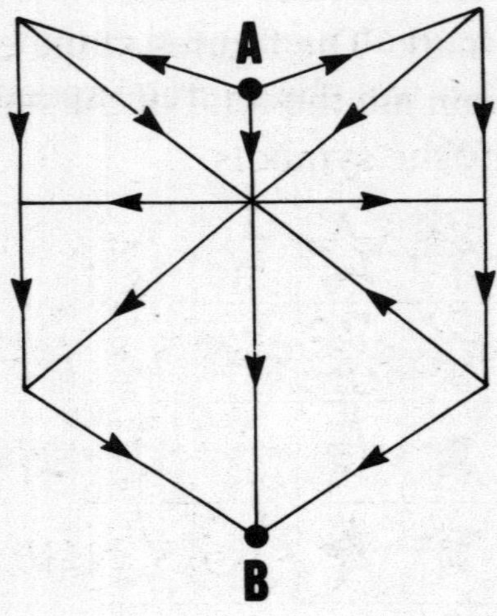

ANSWER:

9.13	Minutes allowed	15
	Time taken	
	Points gained	

SYMBOLIC NUMBERS

Once you have worked out the value of each of the symbols in the diagram below, you will be able to calculate the total which should replace the question mark. The figures at the end of each row and column are the total of the numbers represented by the symbols.

				148
				165
				160
156		155	?	

ANSWER:

9.14	Minutes allowed	10
	Time taken	
	Points gained	

DIY CROSSWORD

The words down and across are given below, but you must decide where the blank squares are.

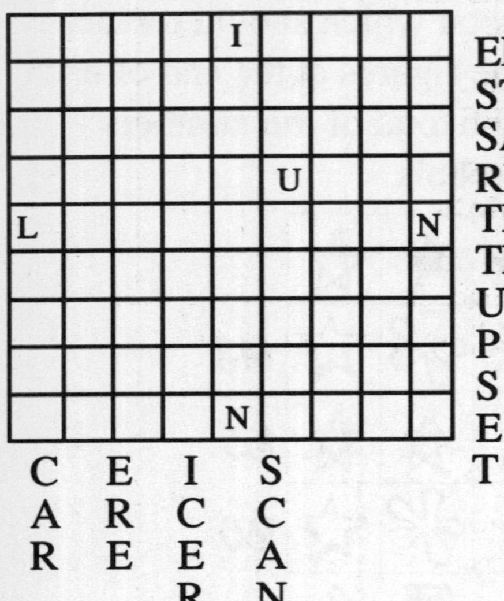

ENDANGERS
STUN APSE
SAT CREEL
RECTITUDE
TERSE AIR
TRUE LIDO

UPSET USER STOP DARED RETALIATE ENTANGLES

CAR ERE ICER SCAN

9.15	Minutes allowed	**45**
	Time taken	
	Points gained	

ANSWERS

		FOR CORRECT ANSWERS		
		Your Time	*Time Allowed*	*Points Gained*
9.1	The missing letter is A. A = 10, B = 11, etc		15	
9.2	SEED, FEED, FLED, FLEE, FREE, TREE		10	
9.3	POST, MOST, MAST, MART, MARL, MAIL		10	
9.4	N. The series is the first letters of first, second, etc		3	
9.5	W H I T E H Y D R A I D I O T T R O V E E A T E N		10	
9.6	B L A C K L O G A N A G I L E C A L V E K N E E L		10	
9.7	THINK, THICK, TRICK, TRACK, TRACT, TRAIT, TRAIN, BRAIN		10	
9.8	The word is CONTEST		10	
9.9	The missing symbols are: "x", "÷" and "+"		5	
	CARRIED FORWARD			

ANSWERS

		FOR CORRECT ANSWERS *Your Time*	*Time Allowed*	*Points Gained*
	BROUGHT FORWARD			
9.10	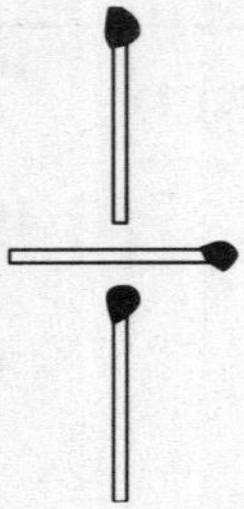		3	
9.11	The three dogs' names are: Alsatian, Corgi and Doberman		10	
9.12	160 mph		5	
9.13	There are 29 possible routes for getting from A to B		15	
9.14	162		10	
9.15	See overleaf			
	CARRIED FORWARD			

ANSWERS

		FOR CORRECT ANSWERS		
		Your Time	*Time Allowed*	*Points Gained*
	POINTS BROUGHT FORWARD			
9.15	Answer below		45	
	TOTAL POINTS GAINED			

CHAPTER SUMMARY

Chapter Handicap Total:	
Correct Answers x 5 points:	
Chapter Total:	
Brought Forward:	
Running Total:	

CHAPTER TEN

Target Time: 4 hours 0 minutes

UNBALANCED BRICKLAYER

Look at the illustration. Can such an unbalanced structure be built and sustained? I would not be asking if it could not be done. But how is is done? Using ordinary cubic bricks, no tricks. When the column is complete the vertical projection of the top brick must be entirely outside the perimeter of the bottom brick!

Table surface

ANSWER:

10.1	Minutes allowed	20
	Time taken	
	Points gained	

GEAR QUIZ

Imagine you have four cogs in constant mesh. The largest cog has 36 teeth, the second cog has 30 teeth, the third 24 teeth and the smallest 20 teeth. How many revolutions will the largest cog have to make before all the cogs return to their original positions?

ANSWER:

10.2	Minutes allowed	20
	Time taken	
	Points gained	

DECODE THIS

Can you read the following quotation in code? The vowels have been replaced with an 'X' and the consonants have been replaced with a code number.

20 9 X X 7 24 X 13 7 X 8 7 8 X 9 X 8 X
21 9 X 14 7 9 X 5 X X 15 7 19 X 13 20 8

ANSWER:

10.3	Minutes allowed	25
	Time taken	
	Points gained	

MAKE UP YOUR MINDS

Trace the letters of the word MIND in any order as many times as you can. You must always start at the centre 'M' and move from circle to touching circle. Once you have one set of letters you can count that and start again. Remember the letters can be collected in any order. How many different routes can you find?

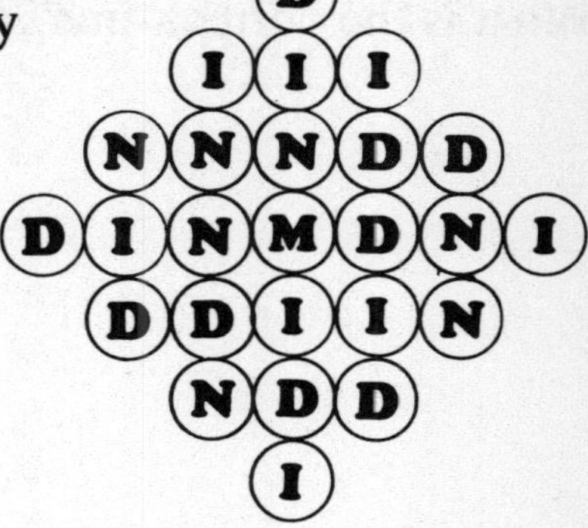

ANSWER:

10.4	Minutes allowed	20
	Time taken	
	Points gained	

LOSING TIME

Your watch was correct at midnight and, at that very moment, began to lose 16½ minutes every hour. When you look at the clock it is showing quarter past seven in the morning, and has stopped. In fact it stopped two hours ago.

What is the correct time?

ANSWER:

10.5	Minutes allowed	15
	Time taken	
	Points gained	

WEAVE BRAIN WAVE

In the grid below the letters of the word BRAINWAVE have been placed haphazardly in the square. By starting at the bottom 'B' and moving towards the top 'E' you will find more than one way of collecting all the letters of the word in any order.
How many ways are there? By the way, you can not move diagonally.

N	W	W	V	E
I	N	W	A	V
A	I	N	W	A
R	A	I	N	W
B	R	A	I	N

ANSWER:

10.6	Minutes allowed	20
	Time taken	
	Points gained	

WHAT THE 'L'?

All answers begin with the letter 'L'

Answer

1. Barren elevated plain of Central Spain
2. River entering the Thames at Bromley-by-Bow
3. Seaside resort of Gwynedd featuring the Ormes
4. Capital of Bolivia
5. Arizona is the home of which once famous British bridge?
6. Priest who began the Reformation
7. British ship sunk in 1915 which encouraged US to join WW1
8. Mythical Cornish lost land
9. Discoverer of the use of antiseptics
10. Large-eyed primate found in Madagascar
11. Israeli political party of Yitzhak Shamir
12. Cretan writing deciphered by Ventris

10.7	Minutes allowed	**15**
	Time taken	
	Points gained	

MENSA XWORD

We have arranged the word MENSA so that it reads the same downwards as across. The intention is to complete the square so that it reads four more words across and down. The first will begin with the E of MENSA, the second with N, and so on.

Can you complete the square? The letters you must use are: EEEESSSSTTTLOODY

```
M E N S A
E
N
S
A
```

ANSWER:

10.8	Minutes allowed	20
	Time taken	
	Points gained	

CANDLEMAKER

You have 64 candle stubs in your possession. You can make one full candle from four stubs. A full candle burns for one hour. Imagine that you can only light full candles. Can you tell us what is the maximum number of hours you can expect to have candlelight from your supply?

ANSWER:

10.9	Minutes allowed	5
	Time taken	
	Points gained	

FIND THE WINNERS

In a lottery there are prizes worth in total $1,649. We know that each winner has won exactly the same value of prizes and that these are in full dollars only. There were more than 20 winners but fewer than 100. Can you tell us how many prize winners there are in all, and what the value of each prize is?

ANSWER:

10.10	Minutes allowed	10
	Time taken	
	Points gained	

BIKE SPEED

A famous motor cycle racing rider has taken delivery of his brand new turbo-charged motor bike. He "flies" down the track at a fantastic speed of 840 mph, hair streaming behind in the slip stream. He takes two hours on the trip, and then literally flies back to the start, covering exactly the same distance at a speed of 120 mph.

You have to work out his average speed for the whole journey, outward and return.

ANSWER:

10.11	Minutes allowed	5
	Time taken	
	Points gained	

SQUARE UP TO IT

Here is a word written both vertically and horizontally. Complete the word square in such a way that it reads both across and downwards with good English words.

F O R T
O
R
T

ANSWER:

10.12	Minutes allowed	5
	Time taken	
	Points gained	

FIND THE SIGNS

Look at the following numbers. All the mathematical signs have been missed out. You have to replace them in such a way that the answer to the sum is 360.

23 ? 8 ? 7 ? 15 = 360

ANSWER:

10.13	Minutes allowed	15
	Time taken	
	Points gained	

USELESS TIMEPIECE

You have a mostv unreliable watch. It was correct at midnight, but at that very moment began to lose 40 minutes in every hour. It is now showing 2 am, but it stopped exactly five hours ago.

Can you tell us what the correct time is?

ANSWER:

10.14	Minutes allowed	15
	Time taken	
	Points gained	

DIY CROSSWORD

The words down and across are given below, but you must decide where the blank squares are.

I			N		L			S
						R		
				F				
T			N		W			D

MUFFINS POP
WEND ICON
PEEVE ARE
LASS SLIME
MUD RAN DIP
TERN ONE

SELFISH

ADORN UPPER SPAT IMPI SPEW

LEND SIN CURE ORE IRE ODE MAN

10.15	Minutes allowed	30
	Time taken	
	Points gained	

ANSWERS

		FOR CORRECT ANSWERS *Your Time*	*Time Allowed*	*Points Gained*
10.1	**Yes.** See illustration 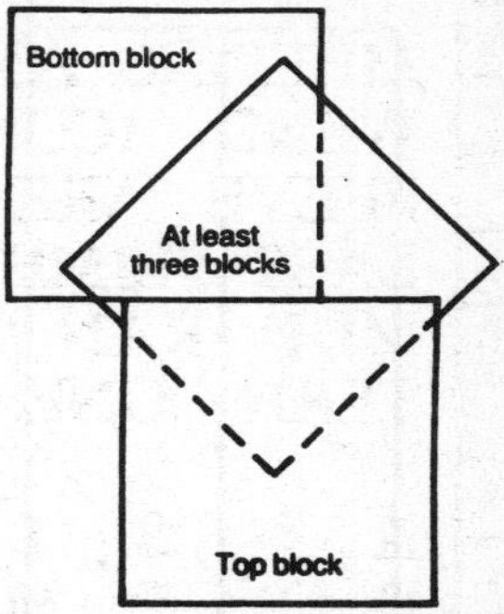 Bottom block At least three blocks Top block		20	
10.2	The largest cog will have to make 60 revolutions		20	
10.3	The quotation is : "Great contests arise from trivial things"		25	
10.4	There are 10 routes		20	
10.5	Midday		15	
10.6	There are 55 ways		20	
10.7	La Mancha. Lea (or Lee). Llandudno. La Paz. London. Luther. Lusitania. Lyonesse. Lister. Lemur. Likud. Linear B		15	

CARRIED FORWARD

ANSWERS

	FOR CORRECT ANSWERS		
	Your Time	Time Allowed	Points Gained
BROUGHT FORWARD			
10.8 M E N S A E Y O T S N O D E S S T E L E A S S E T		20	
10.9 21 hours of candlight. When you have used a candle the stub can be reused with others until each stub is used up		5	
10.10 There are 97 prize winners each with $17 in prizes		10	
10.11 Average speed is 210 mph		5	
10.12 F O R T O L E O R E N T T O T E		5	
10.13 23 + 8 - 7 x 15 = 360		15	
10.14 The correct time is 11 am		15	
10.15 See overleaf			
CARRIED FORWARD			

ANSWERS

		FOR CORRECT ANSWERS	
	Your Time	*Time Allowed*	*Points Gained*
POINTS BROUGHT FORWARD			
10.15 Answer below		30	
TOTAL POINTS GAINED			

I	C	O	N		L	A	S	S
M	U	D		S		D	I	P
P	E	E	V	E		O	N	E
I				L		R		W
	M	U	F	F	I	N	S	
S		P		I				L
P	O	P		S	L	I	M	E
A	R	E		H		R	A	N
T	E	R	N		W	E	N	D

CHAPTER SUMMARY

Chapter Handicap Total:

Correct Answers x 5 points:

Chapter Total:

Brought Forward:

Running Total:

CHAPTER ELEVEN

Target Time: 3 hours 37 minutes

A SERIOUS PROBLEM

Here is a series of numbers. They are not random. Can you find the next two figures in the series, replacing the question marks. This is not an easy puzzle, because it is the interaction between a plurality of series.

5 8 11 14 17 23 27 32 35 41 49 52 ? ?

ANSWER:

11.1	Minutes allowed	15
	Time taken	
	Points gained	

PLANE RACE

In an air race over 100 km the Spitfire beat the Messerschmidt by exactly 10 kilometres. In order to show the British sense of fair play, the Spitfire then started 10 kilometres and 101 metres behind the start line. The race was then run again, and both planes maintained exactly the same speed as in the previous race.

Which one won this time?

ANSWER:

11.2	Minutes allowed	**10**
	Time taken	
	Points gained	

SALT INTO MINE

Can you go from SALT to MINE in only four moves, changing one letter at a time and always creating a good English word at each step?

S A L T

. . . .

. . . .

. . . .

M I N E

ANSWER:

11.3	Minutes allowed	10
	Time taken	
	Points gained	

MISQUOTATION

This Churchill quote has had all of the vowels removed. So from all of the consonants can you discover his pearl of wisdom?

GV S TH TLS, ND W SHLL FNSH TH JB

ANSWER:

11.4	Minutes allowed	5
	Time taken	
	Points gained	

COUNT YOUR DIAMONDS

Each like shape in the diagram has the same value. The four numbers written above each diamond represent the totals for the four shapes within that particular diamond. The figure 133 represents the total value of the top line of eight shapes. What is the value of the bottom eight shapes?

ANSWER:

11.5	Minutes allowed	12
	Time taken	
	Points gained	

IMMODESTY

An immodest sentence about this book is concealed below. The letters have been coded and all the vowels replaced with '?'. The code used follows the keys on a standard typewriter, i.e. A is at the top left and Z at the bottom right. What is the quote?

ZI? V?KSML D?LZ ?BES?L?CT ?FR
EI?SS?FU?FU H?MMS? W??A!

ANSWER:

11.6	Minutes allowed	10
	Time taken	
	Points gained	

TIMED CROSSWORD

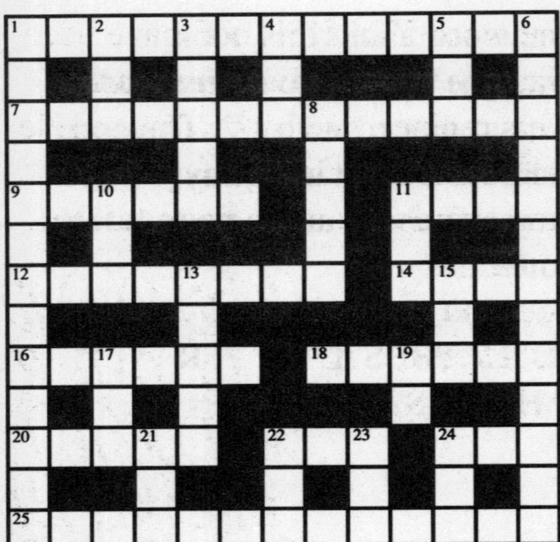

Across

1. Wrote "The Raven" (5,5,3)
7. Used in printing crafts (7,6)
9. Mohandas K .... (6)
11. Where King John reputedly lost the Crown Jewels (4)
12. Nocturnal bird (8)
14. Scottish family (4)
16. Milfoil (6)
18. Resort of NE Italy (6)
20. Inert gas (5)
22. The Lion (3)
24. Oxygen, perhaps (3)
25. A score of greenbacks (6,7)

Down

1. Safety way out (11,4)
2. Greater London Council (3)
3. First Director Gen. of the BBC (5)
4. Cut up tree (3)
5. Houses engines on plane (3)
6. Disease causing extreme enlargement of affected areas (13)
8. The lowest point (5)
10. Egg based drink (3)
11. Terrestrial gathering of clerics (1,1,1)
13. Scottish town (5)
15. Garland (3)
17. Cricket score (3)
19. Doctor of Medicine (1,1)
21. Possess (3)
22. Electronics term (3)
23. Another nocturnal bird (3)
24. A kind of gazelle (3)

11.7	Minutes allowed	45
	Time taken	
	Points gained	

WHERE IS YORKSHIRE?

The letters of the word YORKSHIRE have been set out in the diagram below. You must start at the bottom left hand letter, and move from circle to touching circle, collecting letters as you go. You must move upwards or across from left to right. How many different ways can you find of collecting the letters that create the word YORKSHIRE?

ANSWER:

11.8	Minutes allowed	8
	Time taken	
	Points gained	

WEAVE A SENTENCE

There is a sentence in the diagram below, in which the letters are placed in adjacent squares, each touching by a side or by just a corner. Your task is to find out where the sentence starts and what it says.

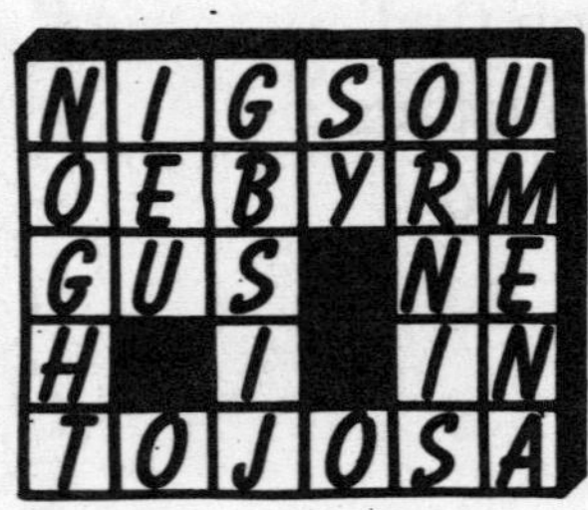

ANSWER:

11.9	Minutes allowed	18
	Time taken	
	Points gained	

THE PARTS OF A GLUTTON

Below you will find a sentence about a young man who ate and ate and ate. Within the sentence are hidden the five parts of his body which grew the fastest. Can you work out, using all the letters, what the five parts are?

HE SAT THERE AND HE FEASTED

ANSWER:

11.10	Minutes allowed	10
	Time taken	
	Points gained	

FIND THOSE WORDS

a) What word has 3 As, 3 Ls and a connection with letters?

2) Whilst GOING ABROAD you always go shopping and want a "........... ....". What two words (4,7) that form an anagram of GOING ABROAD can be placed in the inverted commas?

ANSWER:

11.11	Minutes allowed	18
	Time taken	
	Points gained	

THE MAKING OF CUBES

Below is the cut out shape which can be used to create three of the cubes shown. Which three cubes cannot be made from this shape?

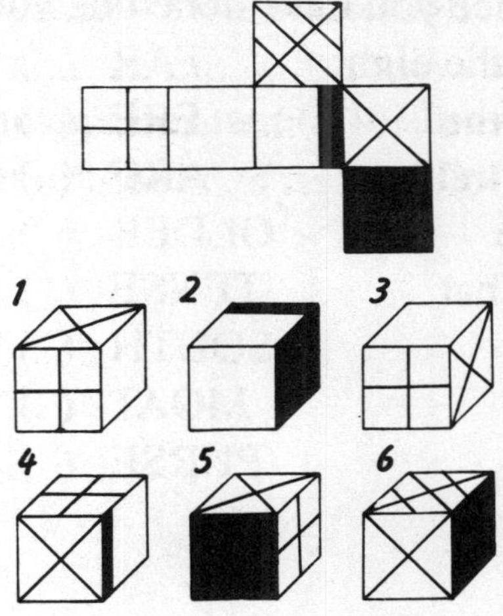

ANSWER:

11.12	Minutes allowed	8
	Time taken	
	Points gained	

LETTER CHANGE

For each pair of words below find the letter which can replace the first letter of both words to make to new words, and place it within the brackets. Once you have done this you must unscramble the eight letters from the brackets to find a long-tailed mammal. What is it?

FAR	( )	EVER
ERE	( )	IDES
ARC	( )	LILY
OLDER	( )	TASTER
TENSE	( )	DEEN
SOUTH	( )	KITE
MOAT	( )	PREEN
PURSE	( )	WEEDY

ANSWER:

11.13	Minutes allowed	10
	Time taken	
	Points gained	

STICKY BUNFIGHT

The sticky buns are back! The boss at your works party has invented a game to play with the sticky buns that the cleaner made. Here is the board, and you have to score a total of 56 points with 3 buns. The rules are that each bun must hit one of the figures on the board, each combination can be used once only, and you must stand eight feet away. How many ways are there to reach a total of 56?

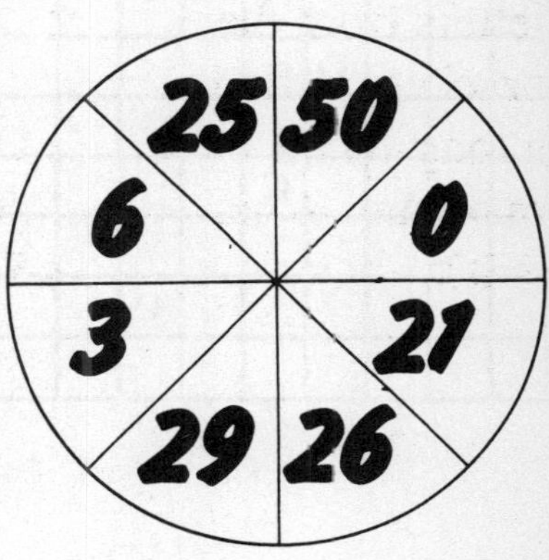

ANSWER:

11.14	Minutes allowed	8
	Time taken	
	Points gained	

DIY CROSSWORD

The words down and across are given below, but you must decide where the blank squares are.

		C						
O				O				
			O					
				C				
						O		

OASIS NUN
ORE AISLE
DECLINATE
ISLE MONK
ACNE OVER
TWITTERER

SENOR CREME ORAL AKIN DEODORANT EASTERNER

IRON SKI ASS CENT

11.15	Minutes allowed	30
	Time taken	
	Points gained	

ANSWERS

		FOR CORRECT ANSWERS *Your Time*	*Time Allowed*	*Points Gained*
11.1	The series arises from adding the prime numbers (top row) to the non-primes, in rising order, as follows: 1 2 3 5 7 11 13 17 4 6 8 9 10 12 14 15 5 8 11 14 17 23 27 32 19 23 29 31 37 41 16 18 20 21 22 24 35 41 49 52 **59** **65**		15	
11.2	Dead heat		10	
11.3	SALT, MALT, MALE, MILE, MINE		10	
11.4	"Give us the tools, and we shall finish the job"		5	
11.5	127 (circle = 12, diamond = 18, triangle = 25 and rhombus = 10)		12	
11.6	"The word's most exclusive and challenging puzzle book"		10	
11.7	**Across 1.** Edgar Allen Poe **7.** Etching needle **9.** Ghandi **11.** Wash **12.** Nightjar **14.** Clan **16.** Yarrow **18.** Rimini			

CARRIED FORWARD

ANSWERS

		FOR CORRECT ANSWERS Your Time	Time Allowed	Points Gained
	BROUGHT FORWARD			
11.7 (cont)	**Across 20.** Xenon **22.** Leo **24.** Gas **25.** Twenty dollars **Down 1.** Emergency exit **2.** GLC **3.** Reith **4.** Log **5.** Pod **6.** Elephantiasis **8.** Nadir **10.** Nog **11.** WCC (i.e. World Council of Churches) **13.** Troon **15.** Lei **17.** Run **19.** MD **21.** Own **22.** LED **23.** Owl **24.** Goa		45	
11.8	There are 9 ways of forming YORKSHIRE		8	
11.9	"Is yours big enough to join Mensa?"		18	
11.10	Teeth, Feet, Head, Ears, Hands		10	
11.11	**a)** Alphabetically **b)** Good bargain		18	
11.12	3, 4 and 6		8	
11.13	Mongoose		10	
11.14	There are 4 ways of scoring 56		8	
	CARRIED FORWARD			

ANSWERS

	FOR CORRECT ANSWERS		
	Your Time	*Time Allowed*	*Points Gained*
POINTS BROUGHT FORWARD			
11.15 Answer below		30	
TOTAL POINTS GAINED			

CHAPTER SUMMARY

Chapter Handicap Total:	
Correct Answers x 5 points:	
Chapter Total:	
Brought Forward:	
Running Total:	

CHAPTER TWELVE

Target Time: 3 hours 55 minutes

HOW FAST?

a) A car travels a distance of 100 miles at a speed of 65 mph. It covers 25 miles per gallon, and has a total tank capacity of 9 gallons. However, sod's law strikes again, and the petrol tank has sprung a leak. It was full when the car set off, but is empty when the car reaches its destination. How much fuel has it lost per hour?

b) You are on a train travelling at only $9^1/2$ mph due to the fact that it is $^3/4$ mile long. It enters a tunnel which is $9^1/2$ miles long, and keeps to its constant speed. How long will it take for the train to pass completely through the tunnel?

ANSWER:

12.1	Minutes allowed	25
	Time taken	
	Points gained	

LONGEST WORD

What is the longest word with a connection with the elements which begins with 'A', ends with 'M' and contains the letter 'U'?

ANSWER:

12.2	Minutes allowed	3
	Time taken	
	Points gained	

LEGS? – OR WHAT?

If a goat has got four legs, an elephant 6, a peacock 6 and an alsatian 8 – how many legs has an octopus?

ANSWER:

12.3	Minutes allowed	5
	Time taken	
	Points gained	

A SQUARE LAKE

Fill in the spaces in the grid below to complete the word square with three more words which read both across and down.

L	A	K	E
A			
K			
E			

ANSWER:

12.4	Minutes allowed	10
	Time taken	
	Points gained	

IS IT SAFE?

Here is a diagram of the new security lock keypad on your office safe. You urgently need to gain access to the safe in order to get your hands on the £10,000 stored there. But all you know about the combination is that you can press the buttons that are joined by a thin black line, and must find a combination that adds up to 22. How many ways are there of reaching this total?

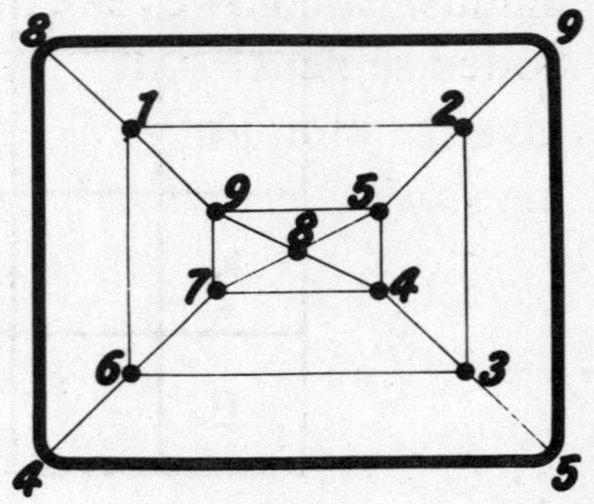

ANSWER:

12.5	Minutes allowed	10
	Time taken	
	Points gained	

ALTERED SAYING

Find the starting letter in this grid, and by moving one square at a time discover the hidden misquotation. The following riddle is a clue: "In a far off country wool is washed in one stream after another. One wool washer was too enthusiastic however. His cloth shrunk!" The coiled sentence will give the moral of the story.

X	O	P	O	I
T	O	S	L	T
A	M	S	H	E
Y	N	K	L	C
B	R	O	O	Z
Z	O	T	H	X

ANSWER:

12.6	Minutes allowed	10
	Time taken	
	Points gained	

DESTRUCTION! NO!

The self destruct button on the Inter-Galactic shuttle has been armed. You know that to stop it you have to make the smallest total possible by pressing five buttons in order, folowing the thin black lines. Each button has a value shown in the diagram, and you must deactivate the self destruct. What combination of five buttons will give the smallest total?

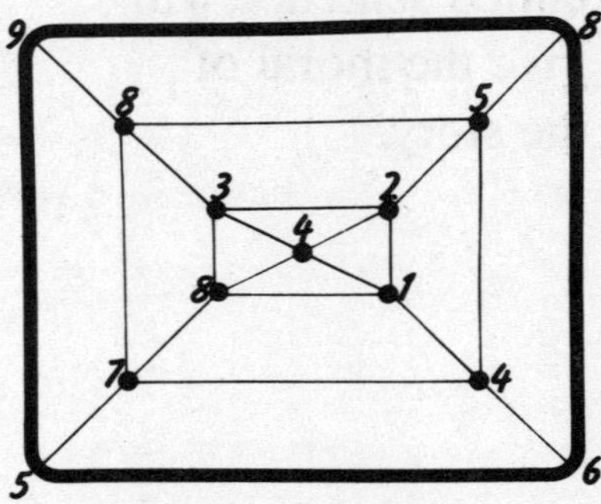

ANSWER:

12.7	Minutes allowed	**10**
	Time taken	
	Points gained	

EXCHANGE OF LETTERS

Replace the first letter of each of the words either side of the brackets with another letter which will make two new, good English words. Place this letter inside the brackets, and once all the letters have been entered you will find another word, which will be very educational for you.

LUNG	( )	FUN
FAKE	( )	PAGE
MUDDLE	( )	CALF
NIL	( )	CUT
ARE	( )	INSET
HOG	( )	HOW

ANSWER:

12.8	Minutes allowed	10
	Time taken	
	Points gained	

STAINED GLASS AND BRICKS

Here we have a stained glass window made from unbreakable glass. Local hooligans are challenged to test its strength by throwing bricks at it. Each hooligan is allowed to throw 5 bricks and must hit five different panes to score a total of 250. Assuming every hooligan achieves this degree of accuracy, how many would be needed to achieve every possible combination? I.e. once a group of five numbers has been used it cannot be reused in a different order.

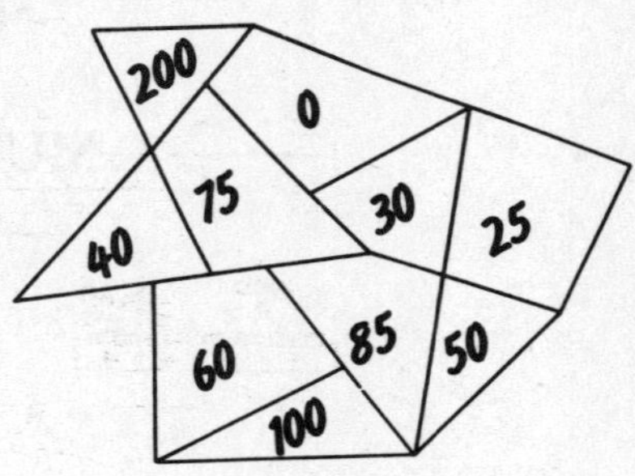

ANSWER:

12.9	Minutes allowed	20
	Time taken	
	Points gained	

A QUESTION OF BALANCE

Here are some arithmetical signs placed on a set of scale pans. The first two sets are perfectly balanced. How many multiplication signs should be put on the bottom scales in order to balance them? Fractions of a sign are allowed.

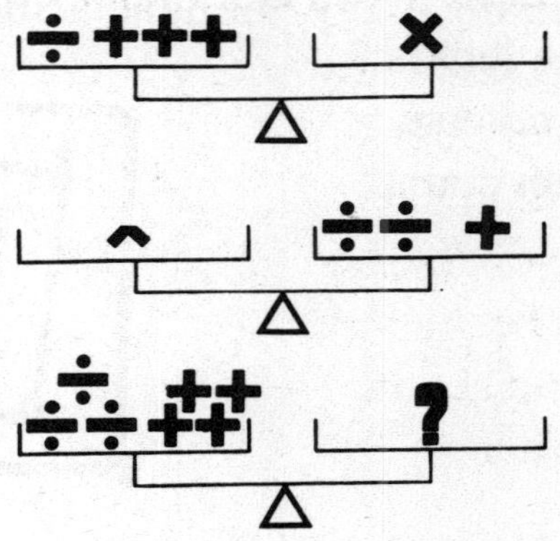

ANSWER:

12.10	Minutes allowed	15
	Time taken	
	Points gained	

MAKING WAVES

Look at the diagram and tell us how many different ways you can find of collecting the letters of the word WAVES, following these instructions. You must start at a corner and follow the lines, and can only include one corner in each selection. If you can find a way of collecting the letters twice but in reverse order, you can count that as two.

ANSWER:

12.11	Minutes allowed	15
	Time taken	
	Points gained	

BOOZER'S SWAP

Wine is wine and beer is beer, or so you would think! Well, I know someone who can change wine into beer in six easy steps. Changing one letter at a time, and always creating a new good English word, can you do the same – or even better?

W I N E

. . . .

. . . .

. . . .

. . . .

. . . .

B E E R

ANSWER:

12.12	Minutes allowed	15
	Time taken	
	Points gained	

TIMED CROSSWORD

Across

1. Works with a doll (13)
7. An Ascot prophet? (6,7)
9. Kind of beetle (6)
11. Roughage (4)
12. Neapolitan resort (8)
14. Nought (4)
16. Given in fulfilment of a vow (6)
18. Caviar (6)
20. Inside (5)
22. Curve (3)
24. Mongrel (3)
25. Rulers (8,5)

Down

1. Painful leg ailment (8,5)
2. Birmingham show place (1,1,1)
3. Large grazing area (5)
4. He had a salty wife (3)
5. International cut short (3)
6. Extinct large lizard (13)
8. Adult mature insect (5)
10. Tune (3)
11. Dickens, perhaps (3)
13. Young eel (5)
15. Large bird (3)
17. Cask of wine (3)
19. American town (1,1)
21. Long period of time (3)
22. Tree (3)
23. British athlete (3)
24. Toothed wheel (3)

12.13	Minutes allowed	45
	Time taken	
	Points gained	

QUIZ

Answers

1. Name the 1951 film which featured Ronald Reagan as a chimp.
2. In which city did John F Kennedy die?
3. Name the character who ran away when the boys came out to play.
4. Name the first day of the week.
5. Which sport begins in front of the south stake?
6. Which two countries have their flags flying over Caribbean Virgins?
7. Who wrote "Death on the Nile"?
8. How many Queen bees reign in in bee hive?
9. In which street was the bakery that started the Great Fire of London?
10. Where is the Trevi fountain?
11. Who was the founder of Islam?
12. Who was the first woman to fly solo across the Atlantic?

12.14	Minutes allowed	12
	Time taken	
	Points gained	

DIY CROSSWORD

The words down and across are given below, but you must decide where the blank squares are.

								R
	I							
			R					
	I							
		W						Y

HERON PIN C
AGE ALONE H
STARTER A
APE GREY R
STEW ODD G
DIN STIR E
SCAR ROD R
I S E E W R
N P R D A E
E A R D D N
P R O Y S T
L O C T O A T R
I D A I N G
T E R P E O

12.15	Minutes allowed	30
	Time taken	
	Points gained	

ANSWERS

		FOR CORRECT ANSWERS		
		Your Time	Time Allowed	Points Gained
12.1	**a)** 3.25 gallons **b)** 64 mins, 44 sec		25	
12.2	Aluminium		3	
12.3	6 legs (2 for each vowel)		5	
12.4	L A K E A P E S K E E P E S P Y		10	
12.5	There are two ways: 8+1+6+3+4=22 4+6+3+4+5=22		10	
12.6	"Too many brooks spoil the cloth"		10	
12.7	6+4+1+2+3=16		10	
12.8	SCHOOL		10	
12.9	You will need 39 hooligans because there are 39 different ways of scoring 250		20	
12.10	One and a half multiplication signs		15	
12.11	There are six different ways of making the word WAVE		15	
	CARRIED FORWARD			

ANSWERS

		FOR CORRECT ANSWERS Your Time	Time Allowed	Points Gained
	BROUGHT FORWARD			
12.12	WINE, WIND, WEND, BEND, BEAD, BEAR, BEER		15	
12.13.	**Across 1.** Ventriloquist **7.** Racing tipster **9.** Chafer **11.** Bran **12.** Sorrento **14.** Zero **16.** Votive **18.** Beluga **20.** Inner **22.** Arc **24.** Cur **25.** Straight edges **Down 1.** Varicose veins **2.** N.E.C. **3.** Range **4.** Lot **5.** Int **6.** Tyranno-saurus **8.** Imago **10.** Air **11.** Boz **13.** Elver **15.** Emu **17.** Tun **19.** LA **21.** Era **22.** Ash **23.** Coe **24.** Cog		45	
12.14	**1.** "Bedtime for Bonzo" **2.** Dallas **3.** Georgie Porgie **4.** Sunday **5.** Croquet **6.** The US and Britain **7.** Agatha Christie **8.** One **9.** Pudding Lane **10.** Rome **11.** Mohammed **12.** Amelia Earhart		12	
	CARRIED FORWARD			

ANSWERS

	FOR CORRECT ANSWERS		
	Your Time	*Time Allowed*	*Points Gained*
POINTS BROUGHT FORWARD			
12.15 Answer below		30	
TOTAL POINTS GAINED			

CHAPTER SUMMARY

Chapter Handicap Total:	
Correct Answers x 5 points:	
Chapter Total:	
Brought Forward:	
Running Total:	

CHAPTER THIRTEEN

Target Time: 2 hours 19 minutes

PAST AND PRESENT

Hyacinth Seer claims that she has immediate sensory perception of past events. Jock Sceptic says fiddle-dee-dee, the only events we can directly perceive are events of immediate experience.

Strictly speaking, which of them is right, if any?

ANSWER:

13.1	Minutes allowed	3
	Time taken	
	Points gained	

NESTING TETRAHEDRA

A Rubic Cube is made up of 27 nested cubes. Here is a Rubik tretrahedron or four-faced pyramid. If it is made up of units inside consistent with its external appearance, how many tetrahedra does it contain?

ANSWER:

13.2	Minutes allowed	10
	Time taken	
	Points gained	

COMBINATION

Here is a combination lock to the postal bag that the young cashier has to take to the post office. It can be opened by putting the key into the correct locks in order. You can only follow the thin black lines, and the combination must add up to 63. How many different combinations are there?

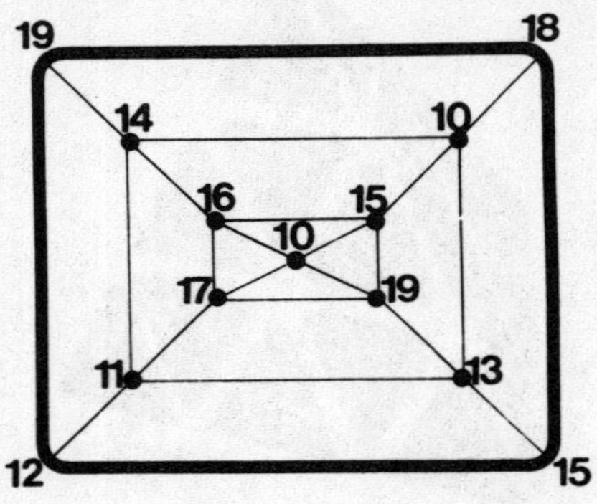

ANSWER:

13.3	Minutes allowed	5
	Time taken	
	Points gained	

SIGN IN

Look at the following numbers. All the mathematical signs have been missed out. You have to replace them to get the answer 97.

32 ? 12 ? 4 ? 1 = 97

ANSWER:

13.4	Minutes allowed	5
	Time taken	
	Points gained	

SHARING THE SHOES

The stables were trying to get rid of their old horse shoes. They had 2156 to get rid of, and they knew that a group of people would want them. They had to make sure that each person got the same number of shoes. There were over 78 people involved but under one hundred.

How many people received horse shoes, and how many did they each receive?

ANSWER:

13.5	Minutes allowed	5
	Time taken	
	Points gained	

CRAZY CLOCK

The alarm clock has gone crazy. It was correct at midnight but immediately began to lose twelve minutes per hour. It now shows one o'clock in the morning, but it actually stopped ten hours ago.

You should be at work for ten o'clock that morning. Will you be late?

ANSWER:

13.6	Minutes allowed	5
	Time taken	
	Points gained	

FIT THE DIGITS

This is a magic square, with all of the numbers left out. We are going to give them to you in a moment, and you must fill them in so that each horizontal and vertical line and the two main diagonals add up to 125. Here are the numbers:

One 1, one 9, one 18,
two 20s, two21s,
two 23s, two 24s,
two 25s, two 26s,
two 27s, two 29s,
three 30s, one 38
and one 52.

ANSWER:

13.7	Minutes allowed	15
	Time taken	
	Points gained	

SQUARE IT

Here is a word written both vertically and horizontally. Complete the word square in such a way that it reads the same both across and down with just four good English words.

B O N E
O
N
E

ANSWER:

13.8	Minutes allowed	10
	Time taken	
	Points gained	

AND AGAIN

Here is another word square but this time there are five letters instead of four. Can you complete it with four more good English words that read both horizontally and vertically?

```
T H R O W
H
R
O
W
```

ANSWER:

13.9	Minutes allowed	12
	Time taken	
	Points gained	

LETTER SWITCH

Replace the first letter of each pair of words, either side of the brackets, with another letter which will form two new good English words, and place this letter in the brackets. When you read all the letters in the brackets you will find another word. What is it?

WIND	( )	CAP
AVER	( )	BATH
MACE	( )	RACK
SATIN	( )	DEMON
TOUR	( )	LAWN

ANSWER:

13.10	Minutes allowed	10
	Time taken	
	Points gained	

STEAL A LETTER

The same letter, which occurs at least three times in each of the following words, has been removed from them, and the remaining letters mixed up. Can you find the missing letter and unscramble the words?

TMRNC
JHRHM
LICTNF
PRISLP
NTLRCH

ANSWER:

13.11	Minutes allowed	8
	Time taken	
	Points gained	

FROM PAPER TO NOVEL

Can you turn PAPER into NOVEL in only six steps, changing one letter at a time? Of course, each change must result in the creation of another completely acceptable word.

P A P E R

. . . . .

. . . . .

. . . . .

. . . . .

. . . . .

N O V E L

ANSWER:

13.12	Minutes allowed	8
	Time taken	
	Points gained	

CHANGE, MAKE

If you change the second letter of each of the pairs of words shown, and place the new letter you have used in the brackets between the words, you will create a new word reading downwards. You must create two new words either side of the brackets.

SLOP	( )	SMART
SLAM	( )	CRIME
ALL	( )	BAND
ORES	( )	ORYX
SLATE	( )	SHIN

ANSWER:

13.13	Minutes allowed	8
	Time taken	
	Points gained	

DISENVOWELLED

The following well-known quotation has had all the vowels removed, and the remaining letters have been broken up into groups of five (except the last one, because there weren't five letters left!). Put back the vowels and find the quotation.

RSBYN YTHRN MWLDS MLLSS WT

ANSWER:

13.14	Minutes allowed	5
	Time taken	
	Points gained	

DIY CROSSWORD

The words down and across are given below, but you must decide where the blank squares are.

				V				
	W					V		
U								
				W				

VAN WASTE S P
SWEET ADO E O
USES REST N S
LOBE ELSE S T
ELECTRICS E U
PARAVANES L L
N E S V E A
O R W E S T
V O A T S E
E D T O
L E B E
S R E L
K O T S
I E A E

13.15	Minutes allowed	30
	Time taken	
	Points gained	

ANSWERS

		FOR CORRECT ANSWERS		
		Your Time	Time Allowed	Points Gained
13.1	Strictly speaking Hyacinth is right. We can only know the past because the movement of information takes time, and perception itself takes processing time.		3	
13.2	Tetrahedra will not nest like cubes. The Rubik tetrahedron is made up of 4 octahedra and 11 tetrahedra, one of which is right in the centre, nested between the 5 octahedra.		10	
13.3	There are 4 combinations		5	
13.4	32 x 12 ÷ 4 + 1 = 97		5	
13.5	There were 98 people who each received 22 horse shoes		5	
13.6	Yes, you will be late. It is really 11.15 a.m.		5	
13.7	27 38 29 01 30 18 29 26 27 25 30 26 25 24 20 30 23 24 21 27 20 09 21 52 23		15	

CARRIED FORWARD

ANSWERS

		FOR CORRECT ANSWERS *Your Time*	*Time Allowed*	*Points Gained*
	BROUGHT FORWARD			
13.8	B O N E O M E N N E E D E N D S		10	
13.9	T H R O W H E A V E R A V E L O V E R S W E L S H		12	
13.10	The word is HOLLY		10	
13.11	The missing letter is A The words are: CATAMARAN MAHARAJAH FANATICAL APPRAISAL CHARLATAN		8	
13.12	PAPER, PAVER, CAVER, COVER, HOVER, HOVEL, NOVEL		8	
13.13	THINK		8	
13.14	"A rose by any other name would smell as sweet"		5	
	CARRIED FORWARD			

ANSWERS

	FOR CORRECT ANSWERS		
	Your Time	Time Allowed	Points Gained
POINTS BROUGHT FORWARD			
13.15 Answer below		30	
TOTAL POINTS GAINED			

CHAPTER SUMMARY

Chapter Handicap Total:	
Correct Answers x 5 points:	
Chapter Total:	
Brought Forward:	
Running Total:	

CHAPTER FOURTEEN

Target Time: 3 hours 14 minutes

BORING BALL

A perfect sphere has a cylindrical hole bored through its centre. The empty cylinder within is exactly 100mm long, and that is all you may know. You are not permitted to know the diameter of the hole, nor that of the sphere. Yet you have enough information to deduce the volume of the remaining perforated sphere. What is it?

The formula for the volume of a sphere is: $(4 \times \pi \times r^3)/3$. For a cylinder it is $l \times \pi \times r^2$, where l = length and r = radius. Calculators may be used.

ANSWER:

14.1	Minutes allowed	**15**
	Time taken	
	Points gained	

TAKE AND MAKE

By removing one letter – the same letter – from both words either side of the brackets and then placing that letter in the brackets, you can form a word reading vertically. Remember that when you remove the letter from each of the words you must leave a new word which can be found in the dictionary.

STRAWY	( )	WHALE
WRAITH	( )	SLEIGHT
MANNED	( )	EVEN
BARED	( )	DROVER
SHIP	( )	LIST

ANSWER:

14.2	Minutes allowed	10
	Time taken	
	Points gained	

HELP THE BIRD TO NEST

Can you go from BIRD to NEST in six changes, changing only one letter each time, and making a new, acceptable English word at each change?

B I R D
. . . .
. . . .
. . . .
. . . .
. . . .
N E S T

ANSWER:

14.3	Minutes allowed	10
	Time taken	
	Points gained	

WHATEVER WORDS?

The following combinations of letters are quite unusual, but each one is part of a word – exactly as it appears in that word. You have to discover what the four words are.

XYG XOP WKW YZY

ANSWER:

14.4	Minutes allowed	10
	Time taken	
	Points gained	

CAN YOU FOLD THE BOX?

This work box has been flattened out. A number of made up work boxes can be found at the foot of the flattened out pattern. Can you tell us which four of the completed boxes cannot be constructed from the pattern?

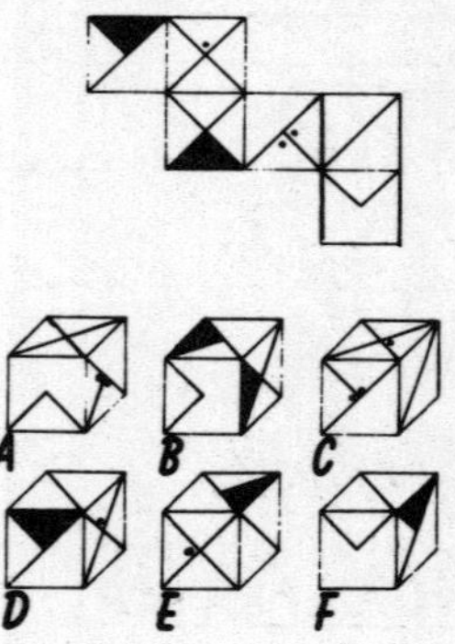

ANSWER:

14.5	Minutes allowed	8
	Time taken	
	Points gained	

DIZZY DISCOUNTS

A travel agent is offering discounts on flights to various islands. The discount is calculated by their name. With the information of this board can you tell us how many pounds discount there is on a flight to the Falklands?

CRETE	15
JERSEY	20
MALTA	15
CANARY	20
FALKLANDS	?

ANSWER:

14.6	Minutes allowed	**8**
	Time taken	
	Points gained	

LEAKY

There is a fire exactly 34 miles away. The fire engine, travelling at exactly 60 mph, holds exactly 1000 gallons of water. However, someone left the hose on the last time they went to a fire and it is pumping out water at a speed of 25 gallons per minute. It is only a small fire and will need 125 gallons to put it out. Will the fire engine arrive there with enough water to put out the fire?

ANSWER:

14.7	Minutes allowed	12
	Time taken	
	Points gained	

FAG END FACTORY

The tramp with his portable "cigarette stub conversion unit" (or CSCU for short) has found a large stash of stubs hidden by one of his local rivals.He can make one whole cigarette from seven stubs and in the stash there are 1,498 stubs.

How many full cigarettes can he make in total?

ANSWER:

14.8	Minutes allowed	**12**
	Time taken	
	Points gained	

COLLECT 'EM

Here is a grid of numbers. You have to start from the bottom left hand corner and finish in the top right hand corner. You can move upwards or from left to right collecting numbers as you go and adding them together. What is the lowest possible score, and how many different ways can you go from start to finish with a score of 46?

ANSWER:

14.9	Minutes allowed	20
	Time taken	
	Points gained	

CHRISTMAS SHAREOUT

The local garage gave away $3,395 at Christmas to its top account holding customers. There were more than 50 such customers but less than 100, and each one received an equal amount in whole dollars only.

What was the amount, and how many customers were there?

ANSWER:

14.10	Minutes allowed	15
	Time taken	
	Points gained	

TRAVEL TROUBLE

A man sets out to travel from one town to another. On the first day he covers one half of the total distance. On the second day he covers one third of the remaining distance. On the third day he covers one third of the remaining distance and on the fourth day he covers one half of the remaining distance.

He now has 37 miles left to reach the second town. What distance has he travelled so far?

ANSWER:

14.11	Minutes allowed	12
	Time taken	
	Points gained	

PINBALL SCORE

Here is a small pinball machine. You have five moves along the thin black lines, starting from one of the outside corners. What is the lowest total you can achieve counting a corner and four other scores, and from which corner must you start to achieve it?

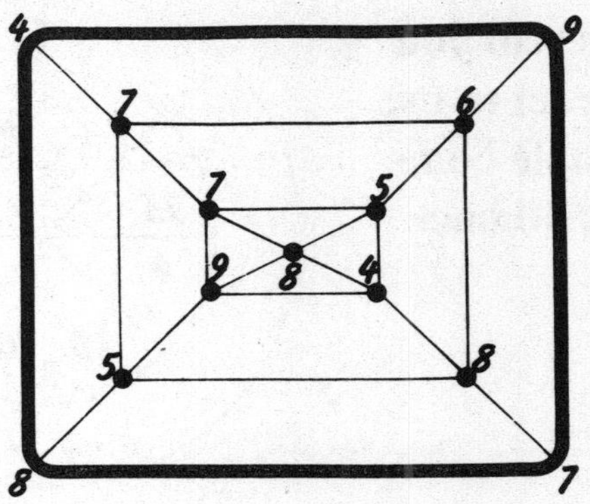

ANSWER:

14.12	Minutes allowed	10
	Time taken	
	Points gained	

DARTS SCORE

From the same games package as the pinball machine came a small dartboard with only nine segments and a set of *four* darts. You have to use the four darts and score 40 points. We will take it that you are a good shot and none of the darts miss the board. How many darts will you throw in order to use every possible combination of 40 once only?

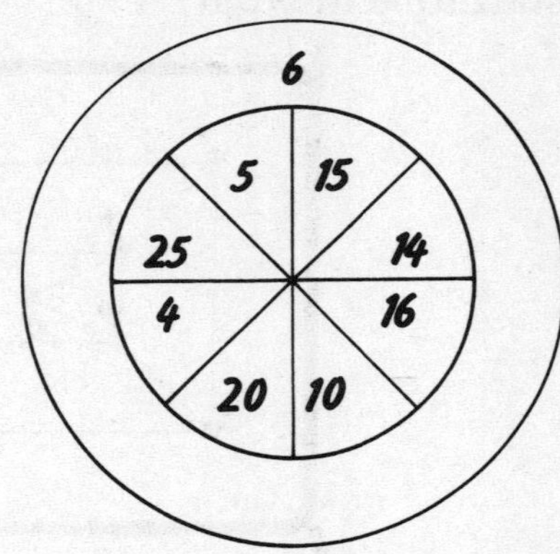

ANSWER:

14.13	Minutes allowed	12
	Time taken	
	Points gained	

HANDICAP

In a 100-yard race Miss Cawthorne beats Miss Topham by 9 yards. The race is then re-run with the winner or the last race starting 9 yards behind the start line. If they maintain the same form as in the previous race, who will win this time?

ANSWER:

14.14	Minutes allowed	10
	Time taken	
	Points gained	

DIY CROSSWORD

The words down and across are given below, but you must decide where the blank squares are.

S								B
W								
				A				
B								S

RELATED
SEDAN PIN
ACE ENDUE
SLOB BEDS
STAY FEES
ARE RID
OLD NET

ALE ORE DOE LANCE ENDED BECAUSE

CRAB BETA SPEW ENDS AND TIN ICE

14.15	Minutes allowed	30
	Time taken	
	Points gained	

ANSWERS

		FOR CORRECT ANSWERS *Your Time*	*Time Allowed*	*Points Gained*
14.1	This can be solved by elaborate calculation or by commonsense. If the solver does not need to know the diameter of the hole it must be irrelevant. So assume it is zero. We then have a sphere of radius 50mm with a volume from our formula of 523,598.78mm		15	
14.2	WINDS		10	
14.3	BIRD, BARD, BAND, BEND, BENT, BEST, NEST		10	
14.4	Oxygen, Saxophone, Awkward, Syzygy		10	
14.5	A, C, E & F cannot be made		8	
14.6	£35 (£5 per consonant)		8	
14.7	Yes		12	
14.8	248 cigarettes		12	
14.9	The lowest number is 28 which can be achieved only once. 46 can be scored seven ways		20	
			CARRIED FORWARD	

ANSWERS

		Your Time	*Time Allowed*	*Points Gained*
	BROUGHT FORWARD			
14.10	97 people each receive $35		15	
14.11	The man has travelled 296 miles so far		12	
14.12	The lowest possible score is 26, and is reached by starting from the top left hand corner		10	
14.13	There are sixteen combinations that add up to 40, which multiplied by the four darts gives an answer of 64		12	
14.14	Miss Cawthorne will again win the race		10	
14.15	See overleaf			
	CARRIED FORWARD			

FOR CORRECT ANSWERS

ANSWERS

	FOR CORRECT ANSWERS *Your Time*	*Time Allowed*	*Points Gained*
POINTS BROUGHT FORWARD			
14.15 Answer below		30	
TOTAL POINTS GAINED			

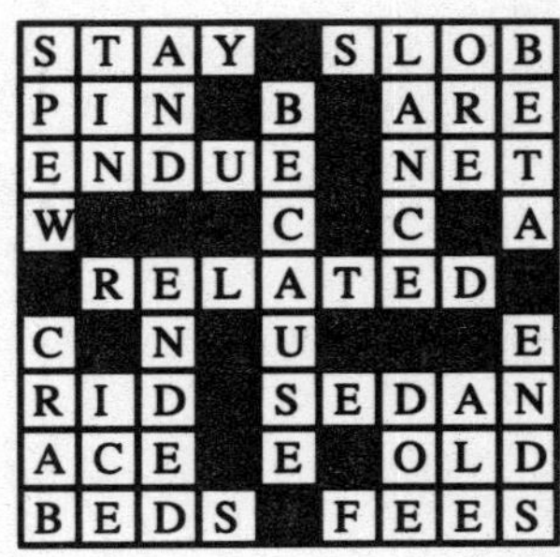

CHAPTER SUMMARY

Chapter Handicap Total:	
Correct Answers x 5 points:	
Chapter Total:	
Brought Forward:	
Running Total:	

CHAPTER FIFTEEN

Target Time: 2 hours 35 minutes

BACK-PEDAL PROBLEM

A free-standing bicycle is placed on a firm road. Someone lightly hold the bike so that it is free to move. You kneel and push on the pedal as shown in the drawing, pushing the pedal backwards. Does the bike move forwards or backwards?

ANSWER:

15.1	Minutes allowed	3
	Time taken	
	Points gained	

SPACE TRAVEL TIME

You are time travelling, using the map below. The black dots mark time tunnels which take you back 8 years in time; the white dots take you forward by the number of years indicated. Starting in 1949 you must attempt to travel as far into the future as possible, following the directions indicated by the arrows. In what year will you emerge?

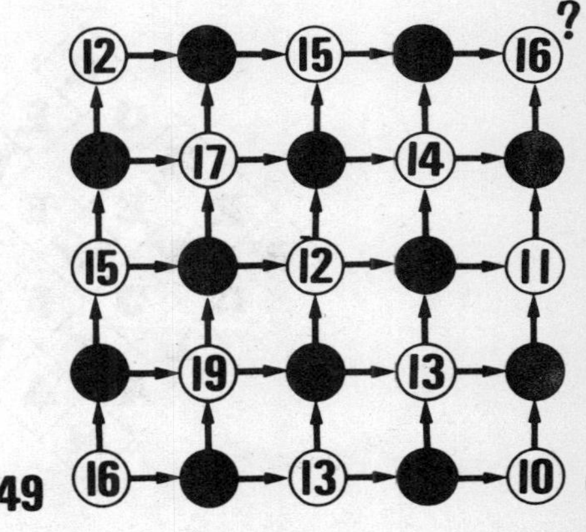

ANSWER:

15.2	Minutes allowed	12
	Time taken	
	Points gained	

THE FLOWER IN MAY

There are some May flowers in the diagram below, but how many? You have to move from the bottom M to the top R and discover how many ways you can form the words MAY FLOWER, by moving diagonally upwards only.

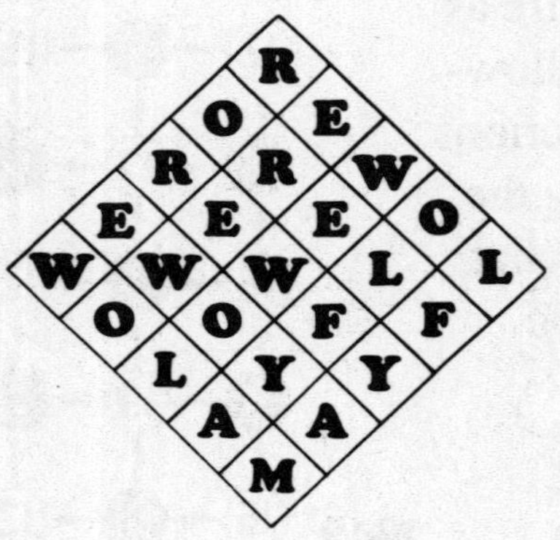

ANSWER:

15.3	Minutes allowed	12
	Time taken	
	Points gained	

SYMBOL STRING

Look at the string of symbols below, and work out why they are strung like this. Having done that, tell us what the next symbol should be.

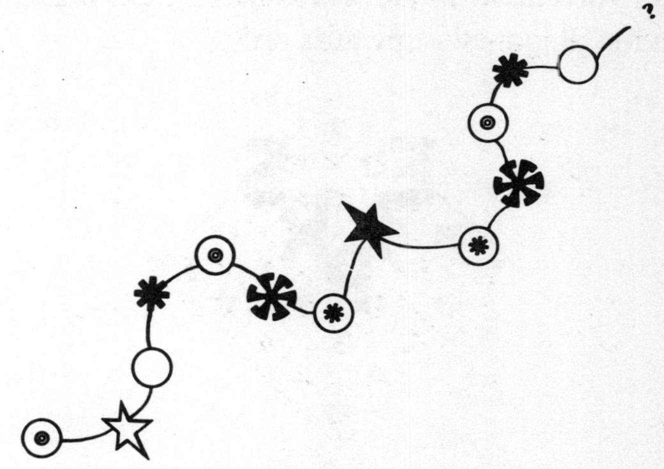

ANSWER:

15.4	Minutes allowed	12
	Time taken	
	Points gained	

ENDLESS ESPRIT

How many English words can you make from the following five letters. Each letter must be used in the word, but can be used once only.

ANSWER:

15.5	Minutes allowed	10
	Time taken	
	Points gained	

BULL CHASES JOGGER

A jogger was crossing a green pasture on a pleasant spring day when he caught sight of a magnificent black bull. Unfortunately the bull also caught sight of him. The jogger's speed increased to a steady 48mph until he reached the fence. Just as he was about to leap over it he noticed that on the other side was a 2000ft drop into the sea.

Having no time to change into swimming gear, he did a rapid U-turn, passing the bull on his way. On the way back his average speed was 32mph. The bull's average speed in both directions was 40 mph. Did it catch him?

ANSWER:

15.6	Minutes allowed	15
	Time taken	
	Points gained	

RUNS? INNINGS?

A cricketer scores an average of sixteen runs in his first 15 innings. Brilliant play! He then has a further ten innings, and his batting average per innings increases to eighteen.

What was his average for the last ten innings?

ANSWER:

15.7	Minutes allowed	12
	Time taken	
	Points gained	

RABBITS, CARROTS

Each of the diamond shaped fields in the diagram below contains a number of carrots. This number is displayed in the field for the benefit of short-sighted rabbits. Moving from the bottom field with 14 carrots to the top field with 13 carrots, and only moving from field to touching field diagonally upwards, what it the maximum number of carrots that the rabbits can eat?

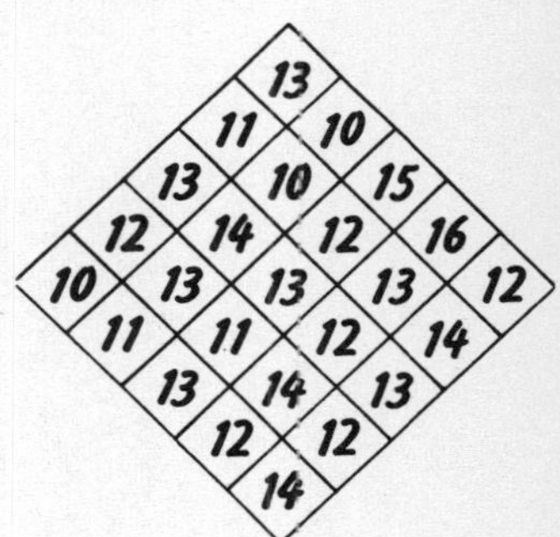

ANSWER:

15.8	Minutes allowed	12
	Time taken	
	Points gained	

COLLECT 'EM UP

Starting at the centre square and moving outwards in any direction, collect just four numbers which add up to 48. You can only move from square to touching square vertically or horizontally, not diagonally. How many ways are there of reaching this total?

			15			
		12	15	5		
	5	12	15	12	5	
12	15	12	16	5	12	15
	15	5	5	15	12	
		5	12	15		
			12			

ANSWER:

15.9	Minutes allowed	**12**
	Time taken	
	Points gained	

WHAT'S THE LOGIC HERE?

Logic prevails here! The letters at the points of the triangles are all there for some logical reason, which isn't difficult to fathom out. Which letter should replace the question mark?

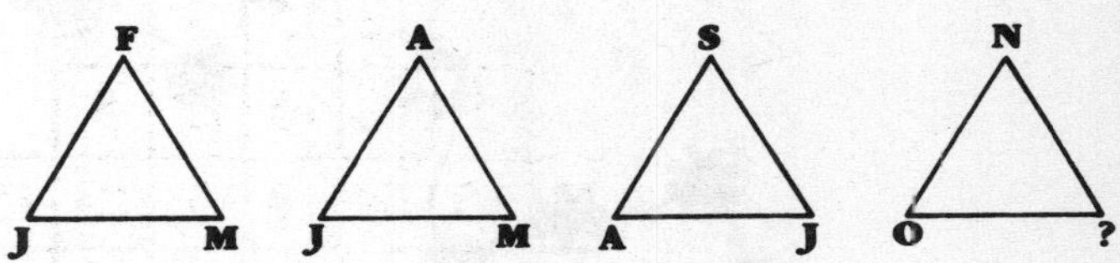

ANSWER:

15.10	Minutes allowed	5
	Time taken	
	Points gained	

ANOTHER SYMBOL STRING

Look at this string of symbols and work out why they are strung like this. Having done that, tell us what the next symbol should be. This one's so easy the dog's just done it!

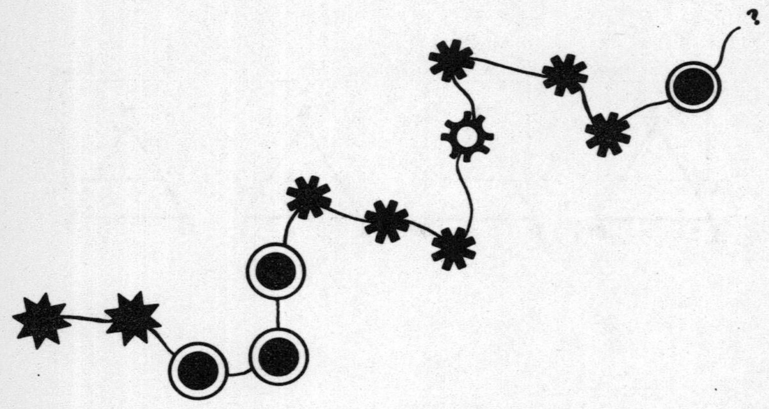

ANSWER:

15.11	Minutes allowed	5
	Time taken	
	Points gained	

ROMAN SQUARES

Below is a series of squares adorned with Roman numerals. You have to work out the logic of the series and tell us what should appear inside the last square to replace the question mark.

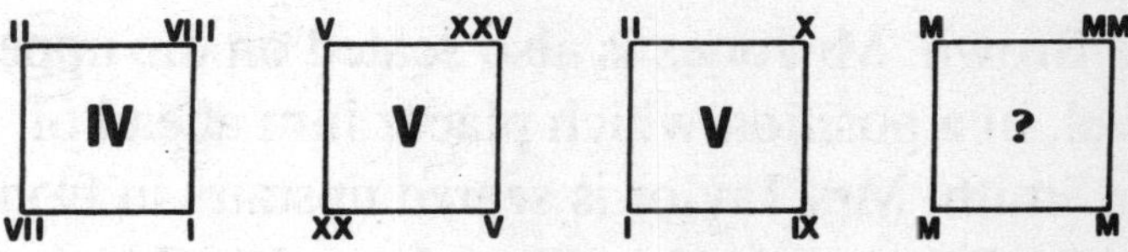

ANSWER:

15.12	Minutes allowed	5
	Time taken	
	Points gained	

SEATING ARRANGEMENTS

The two-decker minibus has five seats upstairs and five downstairs. You can see that Mrs Black is sitting behind Mr Green, while Mr Roberts is sitting in the front of the bus in front of Mr Smith. Mrs White – she's fainted – is slumped on the upper deck at the rear and in front of her sits Mr Brown. Mr Jones is also seated on the upper level, in a position which places him ahead of Mr Smith. Mrs Taylor is seated upstairs in front of Mrs Peters, who is sitting above Mr Green. Assuming that all the seats are occupied and that the last passenger is Mrs Grey, where is she sitting?

ANSWER:

15.13	Minutes allowed	5
	Time taken	
	Points gained	

RECOMBINE

There are quite a few rides here. You have to work out just how many. A letter can be used more than once and is regarded as being different, but once a combination of letters has been used it cannot be used again in any order. Thus there may be two Rs, but they are regarded as being different letters. Got it? Start counting and ride out to victory!

ANSWER:

15.14	Minutes allowed	5
	Time taken	
	Points gained	

DIY CROSSWORD

The words down and across are given below, but you must decide where the blank squares are.

							K	
						M		
K								
	Q							Y

TAMED BUS S E
AGO AMEND O N
SHELDRAKE A D
DEAR TRUE K L
RISE AREA A E
SQUALIDLY W S
R E D E A S
E R A A Y L
B O T R S Y
I D A N
D E

A I E A
I D M R
M O U T
L S

15.15	Minutes allowed	30
	Time taken	
	Points gained	

ANSWERS

		FOR CORRECT ANSWERS		
		Your Time	*Time Allowed*	*Points Gained*
15.1	The bicycle will go backwards. This is a relativity problem. Because of the gear ratio when you are riding forwards, the bottom pedal goes backwards relative to the bike, but forwards relative to the ground. So if you push the lower pedal backwards, the bike goes backwards		3	
15.2	The year 2000. The further distance is 51 years		12	
15.3	You can form the words MAY FLOWER 5 ways		12	
15.4	Large white star		12	
15.5	Piers. Prise. Pries. Spire		10	
15.6	More than likely, since the jogger's average speed is 38.4 mph		15	
15.7	21 runs		12	
15.8	120 carrots		12	
15.9	You can reach a total of 48 in 11 ways		12	
	CARRIED FORWARD			

ANSWERS

	FOR CORRECT ANSWERS *Your Time*	*Time Allowed*	*Points Gained*
BROUGHT FORWARD			
15.10 The missing letter is D. The letters are the initial letters of the 12 months		5	
15.11 The black and white circle		5	
15.12 The missing Roman numeral is II		5	
15.13 Mrs Grey is sitting at the rear dowstairs		5	
15.14 There are 24 ways of forming the word RIDE		5	
15.15		30	
TOTAL POINTS GAINED			

S	H	E	L	D	R	A	K	E
O	■	R	■	A	■	I	■	N
A	G	O	■	T	A	M	E	D
K	■	D	E	A	R	■	■	L
A	R	E	A	■	T	R	U	E
W	■	■	R	I	S	E	■	S
A	M	E	N	D	■	B	U	S
Y	■	M	■	O	■	I	■	L
S	Q	U	A	L	I	D	L	Y

ANSWERS

CHAPTER SUMMARY

Chapter Handicap Total:	
Correct Answers x 5 points:	
Chapter Total:	
Brought Forward:	
Running Total:	

CHAPTER SIXTEEN

Target Time: 2 hours 45 minutes

SQUARING THE PYRAMID

This is a test of 3D visual imagination. Picture a tetrahedron made of wood. Can you saw through it with one straight plane cut so that the two sawn surfaces you have exposed make two perfect squares on a flat plane? Well, can you?

ANSWER:

16.1	Minutes allowed	5
	Time taken	
	Points gained	

WAITING FOR THE BATH

It takes one tap twelve minutes to fill a bath, whilst it takes the other six minutes to fill it up. The plug has been left out, however, and the bath will empty in eight minutes.

If both taps are on full and the plug is left out, how long will it take for the bath to fill up, if it will fill up at all?

ANSWER:

16.2		
	Minutes allowed	10
	Time taken	
	Points gained	

GENEROUS PLUTOCRAT

In a town of 1,450 people there lived a rich man. Just before judgement day arrived he wanted to give all of the males in the town a certain sum of money and all of the females in the town $3.00. Of the males, however, only one half claimed the money and of the females only one third claimed the money.

He gave away a total of $1,450. How much did he give each male?

ANSWER:

16.3	Minutes allowed	5
	Time taken	
	Points gained	

WORK THIS ONE OUT!

What is the total value of the symbols in the diagonal from top left to bottom right?

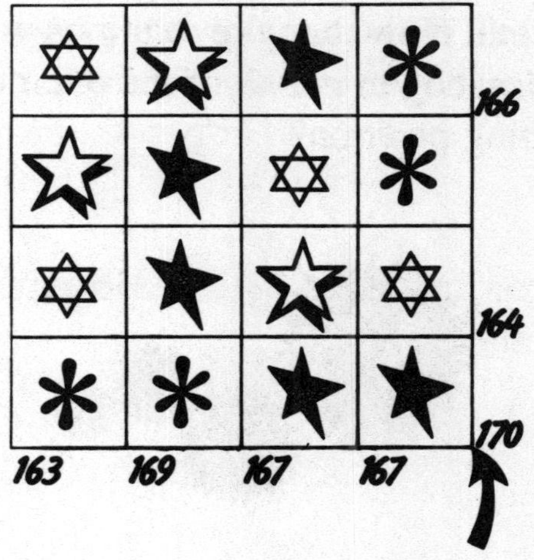

ANSWER:

16.4	Minutes allowed	5
	Time taken	
	Points gained	

COGITATION

Imagine 4 cogs in a constant mesh. The largest cog has 25 teeth, the next cog has 20 teeth, the next cog has 15 teeth and the smallest cog has only 10 teeth. How many revolutions will it take of the largest cog to get all of the other cogs back to the starting position?

ANSWER:

16.5	Minutes allowed	15
	Time taken	
	Points gained	

SQUARES WITHIN SQUARES

Here is an eight by eight grid. How many squares of any size are there within the diagram?

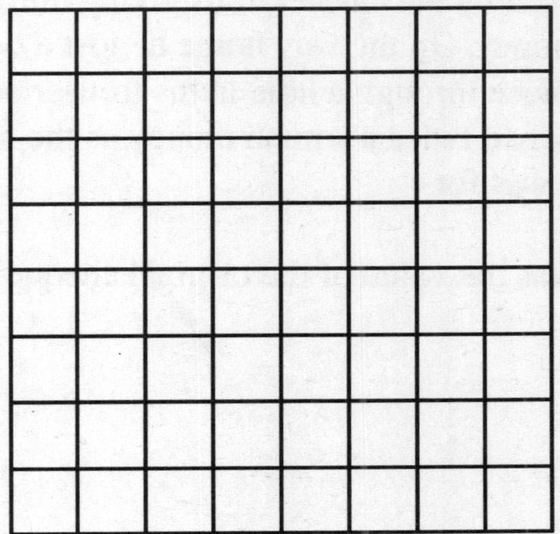

ANSWER:

16.6	Minutes allowed	10
	Time taken	
	Points gained	

TRANSPOSITION MUDDLES

A man cashed a cheque at the bank and discovered that the pounds and pence has been transposed by the cashier, thus giving him far more money. On the way home he lost a two pence piece through a hole in his trouser pocket. He now had twice as much money as the original cheque was for.

What was the value of the original cheque?

ANSWER:

16.7	Minutes allowed	**10**
	Time taken	
	Points gained	

IT ALL COMES OUT THE SAME

Look at the diagram below. You have to fill in the missing numbers in such a way that each of the horizontal, vertical and diagonal lines add up to 400. The missing numbers are as follows: 80, 60, 60, 50, 70, 100, 100, 110 and 90.

ANSWER:

16.8	Minutes allowed	10
	Time taken	
	Points gained	

PARENTHESES

Here are some triangles. All you have to do is replace the brackets in the last triangle with the number that you think should go in their place.

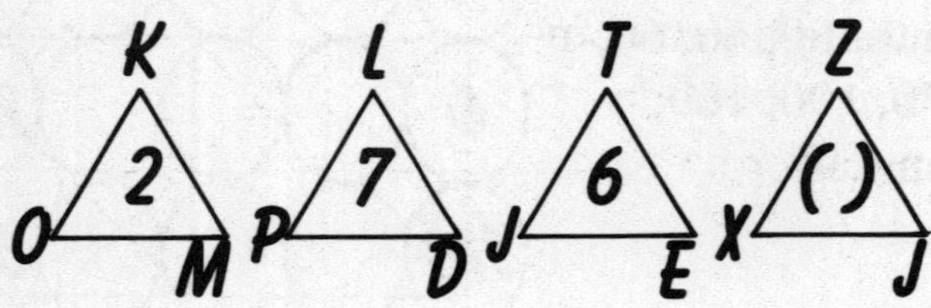

ANSWER:

16.9	Minutes allowed	5
	Time taken	
	Points gained	

TREBLE CROSSING

How many different ways can you find of constructing a figure out of the diagram below which comprises three squares with a cross in and one blank square. By different we mean that an alternative combination of squares is used, even though that combination is but one square different from the last.

ANSWER:

16.10	Minutes allowed	10
	Time taken	
	Points gained	

FIT IT IN

How many time will the shape "A" fit into shape "B"? There must be no gaps, and the shapes must be whole and not cut at all.

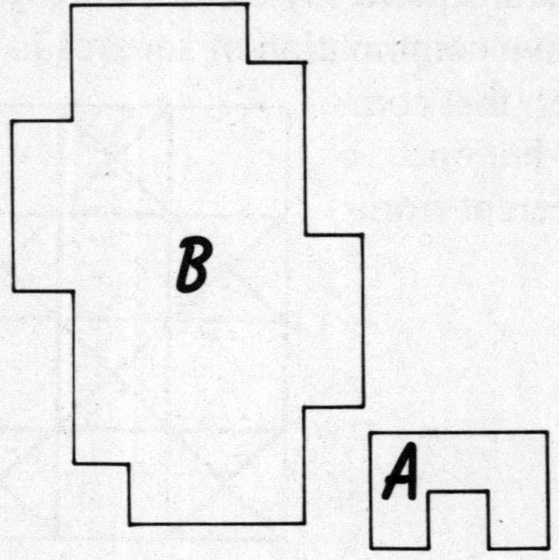

ANSWER:

16.11	Minutes allowed	10
	Time taken	
	Points gained	

MAKE UP YOUR MIND

Here are the letters of the word MIND. You have to work out how many possible ways there are of forming the word from the letters. You can use the same letters in any form of the word. For the sake of this puzzle, every M, I, N and D are treated as being different.

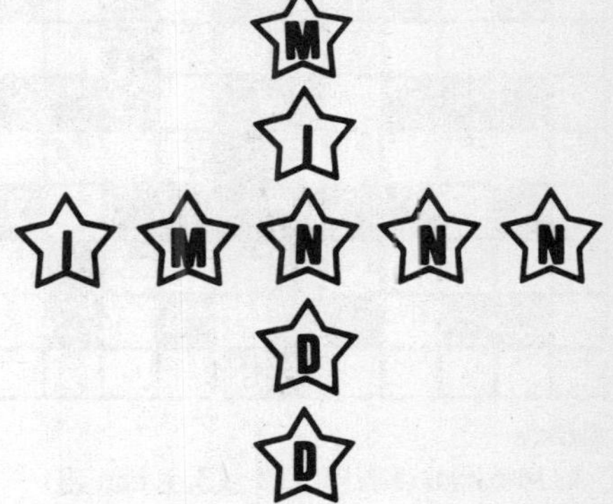

ANSWER:

16.12	Minutes allowed	5
	Time taken	
	Points gained	

TIMED CROSSWORD

Across
1. Bird (7,6)
6. Writing paper 22" x 30" (8)
10. Projectiles (abbrev) (4)
11. Detain (6)
13. Skating jump (4)
14. Orchestral music (8)
16. Limbs (4)
17. Worship building (6)
19. Sheikh, Saudi Arabian politician (6)
21. American homestead (5)
23. Unit of pressure (3)
25. Garland of flowers (3)
26. Diary account (5)
27. Chambre, peut-etre! (7)

Down
1. Mexican dish (5,3,5)
2. Tear (3)
3. Sea inlet (3)
4. Tree (3)
5. Abstract painting (13)
7. First lady (3)
8. Electrically charged atom (3)
9. Ticket game (7)
12. Often used before a noun (3)
13. Khan (3)
15. Blood sucker (3)
18. Tea container (3)
20. Yours truly (2)
22. Transportation (3)
23. Upper part of an apron (3)
24. Colour (3)
25. Lion (3)

16.13	Minutes allowed	30
	Time taken	
	Points gained	

FIND SIGN – MAKE NINE

Using the following numbers and any mathematical signs you require, can you work out a sum to which the answer is 9?

Here are the numbers: 1, 7, 11 and 14.

ANSWER:

16.14	Minutes allowed	5
	Time taken	
	Points gained	

DIY CROSSWORD

The words down and across are given below, but you must decide where the blank squares are.

I								P
			N					
				A				
	O						R	
E								M

STRANDS ROC G
EMMET IBEX Y
EWER IRONY R
STEM GRIP A
ACE BAG ERA T
ARE TEN R T E
P H I A R D
E E B T A
N R I E C
T E S D E

I I E R M E B
T C R O A G A
E E E W T O R
M

16.15	Minutes allowed	**30**
	Time taken	
	Points gained	

ANSWERS

		FOR CORRECT ANSWERS		
		Your Time	*Time Allowed*	*Points Gained*
16.1	Each face of a tetrahedron meets other faces at a linear edge. If you draw a line back from that edge and parallel to it on both faces, those two lines are parallel. The cut which joined them would form a rectangle. If you take the line back far enough they will form a square.		5	
16.2	8 minutes		10	
16.3	£2.00 each		5	
16.4	167		5	
16.5	12 revolutions		15	
16.6	204 squares		10	
16.7	£32.65		10	

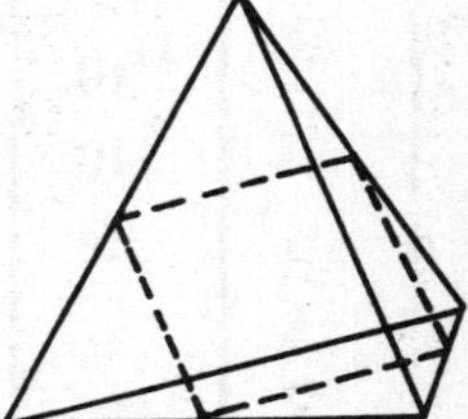

CARRIED FORWARD

ANSWERS

		FOR CORRECT ANSWERS		
		Your Time	*Time Allowed*	*Points Gained*
	BROUGHT FORWARD			
16.8	90 50 130 30 100 0 100 110 90 100 110 100 80 60 50 140 70 50 60 80 60 80 30 160 70		10	
16.9	5 (A=1 etc; add top number to bottom left and divide by bottom right		5	
16.10	There are 12 ways		10	
16.11	8 times		10	
16.12	24 times		5	
16.13	**Across 1.** Carrier Pigeon **6.** Imperial **10.** Ammo **11.** Intern **13.** Axel **14.** Overture **16.** Arms **17.** Church **19.** Yamani **21.** Ranch **23.** Bar **25.** Lei **26.** Entry **27.** Bedroom **Down 1.** Chilli con carne **2.** Rip **3.** Ria **4.** Elm **5.** Neoplasticism **7.** Eve **8.** Ion **9.** Lottery **12.** The **13.** Aga **15.** Tic **18.** Urn **20.** Me **22.** Car **23.** Bib **24.** Red **25.** Leo		30	
	CARRIED FORWARD			

ANSWERS

		FOR CORRECT ANSWERS		
		Your Time	*Time Allowed*	*Points Gained*
	POINTS BROUGHT FORWARD			
16.14	(14 x 7 + 1) ÷ 11 = 9		5	
16.15	Answer below		30	
	TOTAL POINTS GAINED			

I	B	E	X	■	G	R	I	P
B	A	G	■	G	■	A	C	E
I	R	O	N	Y	■	T	E	N
S	■	■	■	R	■	E	■	T
■	S	T	R	A	N	D	S	■
H	■	R	■	T	■	■	■	I
E	R	A	■	E	M	M	E	T
R	O	C	■	D	■	A	R	E
E	W	E	R	■	S	T	E	M

CHAPTER SUMMARY

Chapter Handicap Total:

Correct Answers x 5 points:

Chapter Total:

Brought Forward:

Running Total:

CHAPTER SEVENTEEN

Target Time: 2 hours 55 minutes

MISTAKES ABOUT MISTAKES

"THISS SENTENSE HASS FIVE MISSTAKES"

Is this statement true or false?

ANSWER:

17.1	Minutes allowed	5
	Time taken	
	Points gained	

QUIZ

Answers

1. Which person invented the automobile in 1885?

2. Do frogs have teeth?

3. How many years of bad luck follow breaking a mirror?

4. What is the most common colour of amethyst?

5. Which surface is "fine and powdery"?

6. How many stars are there in Orion's belt?

7. What did Alan Shephard hit on the moon?

8. How much thicker than water is blood?

9. What is a "Citrus grandis"?

10. What is the process for splitting atoms called?

11. What is a crow bar?

12. What is special about the komodo dragon?

17.2	Minutes allowed	**15**
	Time taken	
	Points gained	

GIVEAWAY

In a certain town of 66,000 people there lived a rich man. He offered £38.00 to each male and a certain amount to each female. Of the males, only a nineteenth collected their money, and of all the females only two out of every ten collected their money.

If he gave away £132,000.00 in total, how much did each female receive?

ANSWER:

17.3	Minutes allowed	5
	Time taken	
	Points gained	

GET RICH QUICK!

A man cashed a cheque at the bank, and discovered that the cashier had transposed the pounds for pence and the pence for pounds, thus giving him more money. He went home on the bus and that cost him 42 pence. He then realised that he had exactly three times the amount of the original cheque.

What was the value of the original cheque?

ANSWER:

17.4	Minutes allowed	5
	Time taken	
	Points gained	

A DOZEN DOZEN SCORE

Imagine a twelve by twelve square. How many rectangles of any size can you construct from it?

It may help you if you draw it out . . .

ANSWER:

17.5	Minutes allowed	15
	Time taken	
	Points gained	

AGAINST THE TIDE

A ship is battling against the tide to safety. Behind it is a waterfall and in front exactly fourteen miles away is an island. The ship is travelling at two miles per hour, but the water is flowing against the ship at one mile every two hours. The ship is using two gallons of fuel every hour, but has only nine gallons left.

Will it reach the safety of the island?

ANSWER:

17.6	Minutes allowed	10
	Time taken	
	Points gained	

INSERT, CREATE

Fill in the missing letters below to create eight words, and a ninth word will be created downwards. What are the nine words?

A ( ) ASH
UP ( ) N
SWO ( ) D
RA ( ) E
BEA ( ) S
CR ( ) AM
OW ( ) ER

ANSWER:

17.7	Minutes allowed	5
	Time taken	
	Points gained	

NEW LETTERS FOR OLD

Replace the first letter in the words on each side of the brackets with another letter to create two new words. Place this new letter in the brackets and create a seven-letter word downwards. What is it?

PAW	( )	TIGHT
SIGH	( )	SEAT
LAMB	( )	ENTER
SEAL	( )	PASSAGE
PASS	( )	SIX
HAT	( )	GEL
MAT	( )	MULE

ANSWER:

17.8	Minutes allowed	10
	Time taken	
	Points gained	

TRANSFORMERS

Change TOIL to FOOD and TEAR to WEEP in as few steps as possible, changing one letter at a time and always creating a new acceptable word.

T O I L	T E A R
. . . .	. . . .
. . . .	. . . .
. . . .	. . . .
. . . .	. . . .
F O O D	W E E P

ANSWER:

17.9	Minutes allowed	10
	Time taken	
	Points gained	

LOST PETS

"TO CHARM GETS A BIT DRAB."

From the above sentence can you find four domestic pets by using all the letters?

ANSWER:

17.10	Minutes allowed	**10**
	Time taken	
	Points gained	

WORDPLAY

a) What is the longest word you can find that begins with "A", ends with "Y" and has a connection with order?

b) Which refreshment can be made from the letters of the words "WINTER COAT"?

ANSWER:

17.11	Minutes allowed	**15**
	Time taken	
	Points gained	

TEN LETTERS

What ten letter word begins with "S", ends with "M", contains another "M" and has a connection with Thorn apples?

ANSWER:

17.12	Minutes allowed	15
	Time taken	
	Points gained	

HOW MANY CAME?

At an exclusive ball the total amount taken on ticket sales was $9,540.00. The attendance was between 70 and 100, and each person paid exactly the same amount in full dollars only.

How much was each ticket and how many people went to the ball?

ANSWER:

17.13	Minutes allowed	15
	Time taken	
	Points gained	

YOU'LL HAVE A FIT

The lettered shapes below can be used to create the larger shapes numbered 1, 2 & 3, as in the example which uses shapes A & B. Which lettered shapes are required to create shapes 1, 2 & 3?

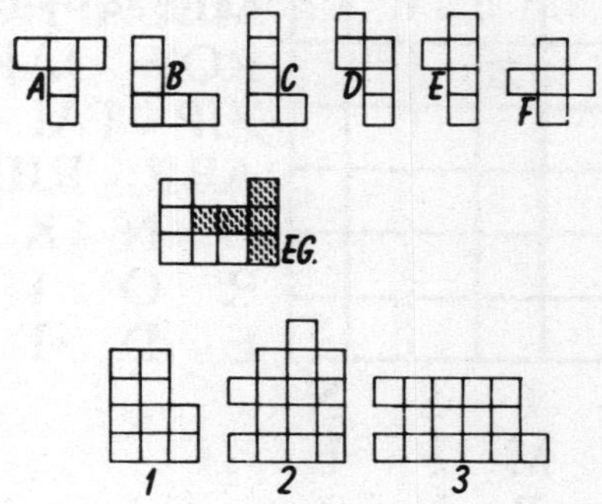

ANSWER:

17.14	Minutes allowed	10
	Time taken	
	Points gained	

DIY CROSSWORD

The words down and across are given below, but you must decide where the blank squares are.

F								
	J			Z				
			Y					
I								S

ACNE ITEM R C
RECTITUDE E R
FORE IMPS C U
MEGAPHONE T C
ROW JAR A I
ZIP PAL N F
ARE RID G O
O N K E L R
R O I A E M
E D T T

W F E I S N
E A W M P I
D R E P Y P
S E R I

17.15	Minutes allowed	30
	Time taken	
	Points gained	

ANSWERS

		FOR CORRECT ANSWERS		
		Your Time	*Time Allowed*	*Points Gained*
17.1	If your answer is "false" you are wrong, because you have left out the miscount of the number of mistakes. But if your answer is "true" you are wrong because there is no miscount and only four spelling mistakes. This is a classic Russellian paradox. Score 20 points if you noticed the paradox		5	
17.2	**1.** Karl Benz **2.** Yes **3.** Seven **4.** Purple **5.** The moon **6.** Three **7.** A golf ball **8.** Six times **9.** A grapefruit **10.** Fission **11.** A jemmy **12.** It is the largest living lizard		15	
17.3	The women received £10.00 each		5	
17.4	The original cheque was for £19.59		5	
17.5	You can construct 6,084 rectangles		15	
17.6	The ship will not reach safety		10	
	CARRIED FORWARD			

ANSWERS

		FOR CORRECT ANSWERS *Your Time*	*Time Allowed*	*Points Gained*
	BROUGHT FORWARD			
17.7	A (W) ASH UP (O) N SWO (R) D RA (K) E BEA (M) S CRE (A) M OW (N) ER		5	
17.8	Shimmer		10	
17.9	TOIL, TOOL, FOOL, FOOD / TEAR, PEAR, PEER, PEEP, WEEP		10	
17.10	Dog. Cat. Rabbit. Hamster		10	
17.11	**a)** Alphabetically **b)** Tonic water		15	
17.12	Stramonium		15	
17.13	90 people attended and each ticket cost $106		15	
17.14	**1)** C and D **2)** D, E and F **3)** A, D and E		10	
17.15	See answer overleaf			
	CARRIED FORWARD			

ANSWERS

	FOR CORRECT ANSWERS		
	Your Time	*Time Allowed*	*Points Gained*
POINTS BROUGHT FORWARD			
17.15 Answer below		30	
TOTAL POINTS GAINED			

CHAPTER SUMMARY

Chapter Handicap Total:	
Correct Answers x 5 points:	
Chapter Total:	
Brought Forward:	
Running Total:	

CHAPTER EIGHTEEN

Target Time: 3 hours 5 minutes

ONE CUT HEXAGON

Take a perfect wooden cube. You have to find a way to saw through it with one straight cut which divides it equally so as to produce two perfectly hexagonal surfaces with no messing.

ANSWER:

18.1	Minutes allowed	15
	Time taken	
	Points gained	

MARK THAT DOPE!

Can you change the word DOPE to MARK in only four steps. You have to change one letter at a time and create a new word at each step.

D O P E

. . . .

. . . .

. . . .

M A R K

ANSWER:

18.2	Minutes allowed	5
	Time taken	
	Points gained	

FIND THE WATERS

Using all the letters from the following short sentence can you create four words which have a connection with inland waterways?

"BEN RETURNED MY ARK"

ANSWER:

18.3	Minutes allowed	15
	Time taken	
	Points gained	

MAKE UP YOUR MIND – AGAIN

The letters in this grid spell the word MIND. How many ways are there of collecting the letters of the word in any order? The rules are that you must always start at the centre letter and then collect four letters. You can then start again but must not retrace your steps. You can only move from a circle to a touching circle.

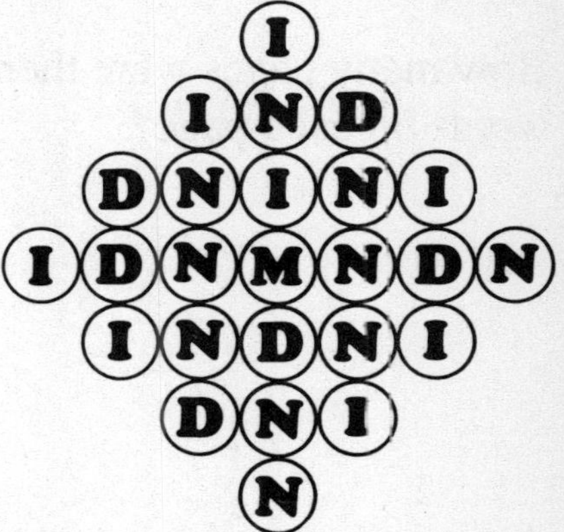

ANSWER:

18.4	Minutes allowed	10
	Time taken	
	Points gained	

WORDS AND PAGES

There was a dictionary containing 60,165 words. It had more than 300 pages but less than 350, and it had less than 235 words on each page. However, there were the same number of words on each page.

How many pages were there, and how many words on each page?

ANSWER:

18.5	Minutes allowed	15
	Time taken	
	Points gained	

AMAZING SEARCH

Only one of the four entrances will lead the centre of the labyrinth. Which one is it?

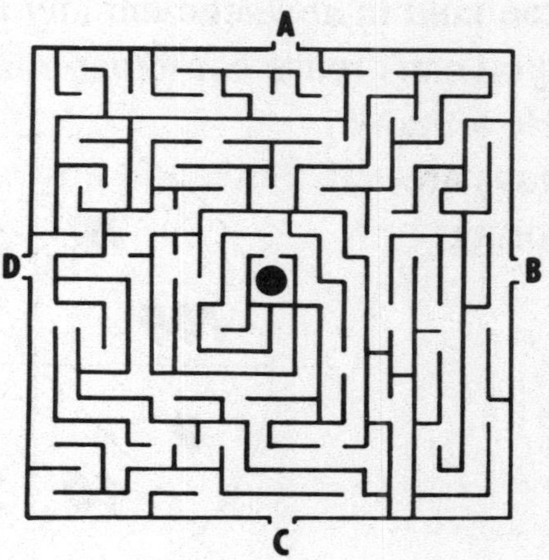

ANSWER:

18.6	Minutes allowed	15
	Time taken	
	Points gained	

BAR ARCHERY

The mini-archery target below was designed for use in pubs. It has eight segments, and you have three arrows. The object of the game is to score 120. You can land in any segment any number of times, but you can't reuse combinations of numbers. How many different ways are there of scoring 120?

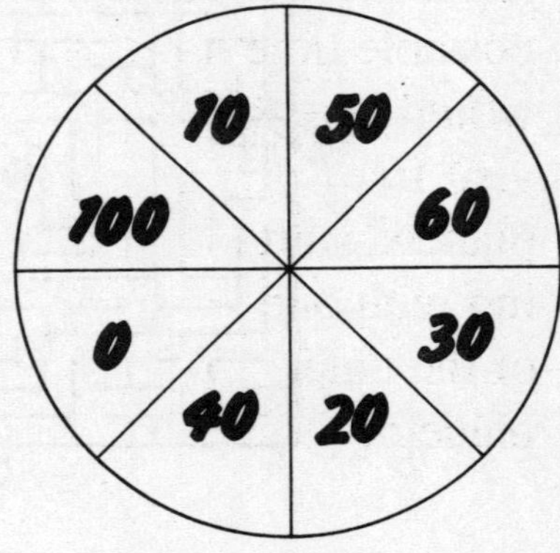

ANSWER:

18.7	Minutes allowed	10
	Time taken	
	Points gained	

A BIG PROBLEM

Below is a plan of the galaxy with four outer planets and nine inner planets. You have to visit one of the outer planets and four of the inner planets, travelling along the thin black lines. The figures represent the number of light years it takes to reach each planet. What is the shortest possible time it would take to visit five planets, starting with one of the outer planets?

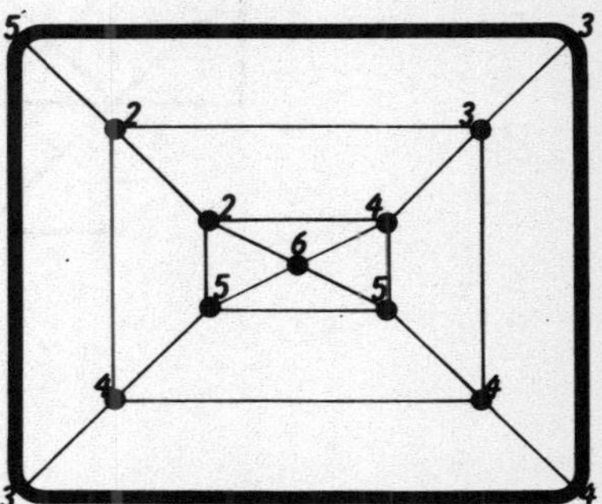

ANSWER:

18.8	Minutes allowed	10
	Time taken	
	Points gained	

SQUARE HARVEST

How many squares are there in the diagram below?

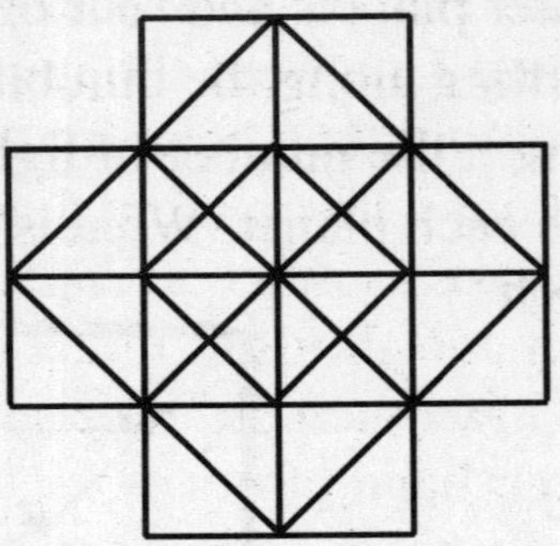

ANSWER:

18.9	Minutes allowed	**10**
	Time taken	
	Points gained	

THREE QUICKIES

a) A cup and saucer together way 12 oz. The cup weighs twice as much as the saucer. How much does the saucer weigh?

b) Mary and Jane went shopping for sweets together with 66p between them. Mary started out with 6p more than Jane, but spent twice as much as Jane. Mary ended up with two-thirds as much money as Jane. How much did Jane spend?

c) The hour hand of my clock works perfectly, but the minute hand runs anti-clockwise at a constant speed, crossing the hour hand every 80 minutes. If it was right at 6.30, when will it next show the right time?

ANSWER:

18.10	Minutes allowed	**10**
	Time taken	
	Points gained	

TRAIN WAYS

The diagram below is a simplified plan of a railway system, showing lines and points. How many different ways are there for a train to go from A to B without reversing?

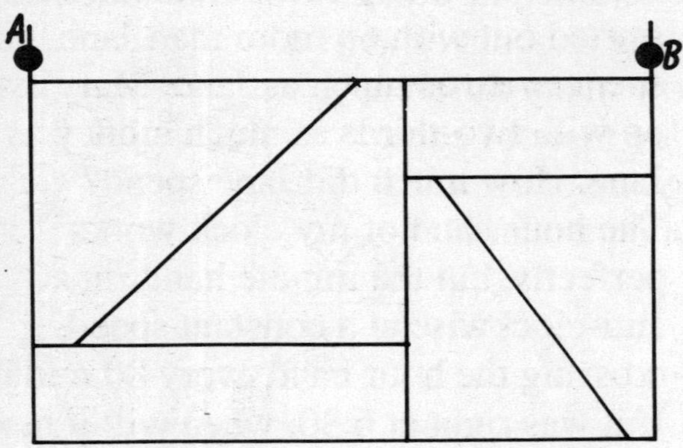

ANSWER:

18.11	Minutes allowed	10
	Time taken	
	Points gained	

CHOOSING CHOCS

In the diagram below, each symbol stands for a different type of chocolate packed in a cruciform box. You must start at the centre chocolate and move upwards, downwards or across from square to touching square – but not diagonally – collecting chocolates as you go. How many different ways are there of collecting one of each type of chocolate?

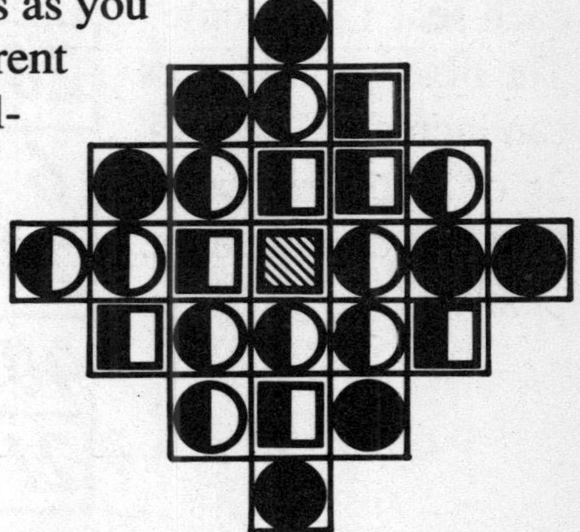

ANSWER:

<table>
<tr><td rowspan="3">18.12</td><td>Minutes allowed</td><td>10</td></tr>
<tr><td>Time taken</td><td></td></tr>
<tr><td>Points gained</td><td></td></tr>
</table>

CURIOUS SEATING PLAN

The diagram below represents the seating plan for a public concert. Work on the plan has been started, but you need to finish it. The requirement is that every row, vertically and horizontally, and the two main diagonals, must each seat 120 people.

The nine central boxes can include 21, 22, 24, 26 or 27 people each. Can you complete the plan?

26	38	27	2	27
6				35
27				21
40				15
21	7	21	49	22

ANSWER:

18.13	Minutes allowed	10
	Time taken	
	Points gained	

WHAT AM I?

Can you solve this riddle?

My first is in HALL, but not in ROOM,
My second is in BANG, but not in BOOM,
My third is in WISH, but not in BONE,
My fourth is in FLY, but not in FLOWN,
My fifth is in HOUSE, and also in HOME
To which I return wherever I roam;
To complete the whole, my last is in RUBBLE,
And I'm there to help you, if you are in trouble.

ANSWER:

18.14		
	Minutes allowed	8
	Time taken	
	Points gained	

DIY CROSSWORD

The words down and across are given below, but you must decide where the blank squares are.

					J			
				S				
					V			
	S							
J								
	V							

STARLET NIL
EVENT BAR
SEA AVERT
STEW JUMP
CEDE STAY
APE ARE TOR

SERRATE
ELATE ALERT PATH JABS
ROD ERE
USE MERE SNAP VAT TIP

18.15	Minutes allowed	30
	Time taken	
	Points gained	

ANSWERS

	FOR CORRECT ANSWERS		
	Your Time	*Time Allowed*	*Points Gained*
18.1 Your explanation should match the diagram below. If you drew the diagram correctly, take an extra mark. 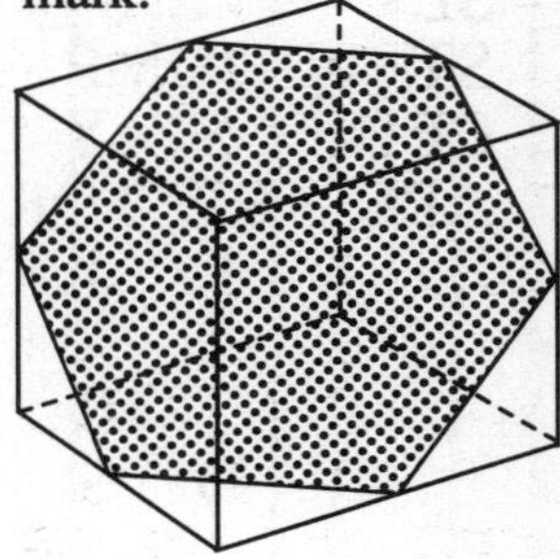		15	
18.2 DOPE, MOPE, MORE, MARE, MARK		5	
18.3 BUR, MERE, TARN, DYKE		15	
18.4 There are 11 ways of collecting the letters M, I, N and D		10	
18.5 There are 315 pages with 191 words on each		15	
18.6 Entrance B		15	
18.7 You can score 120 nine different ways		10	
CARRIED FORWARD			

ANSWERS

		Your Time	*Time Allowed*	*Points Gained*
		FOR CORRECT ANSWERS		
	BROUGHT FORWARD			
18.8	14 light years		10	
18.9	There are a total of 27 squares in the diagram		10	
18.10	**a)** 4 oz **b)** 12 pence **c)** At 7.06		10	
18.11	There are 16 different routes from A to B		10	
18.12	There are 10 different ways of selecting four different chocolates		10	
18.13	26 38 27 2 27 6 27 26 26 35 27 26 24 22 21 40 22 22 21 15 21 7 21 49 22		10	
18.14	LAWYER		8	
18.15	See answer overleaf			
	CARRIED FORWARD			

ANSWERS

	FOR CORRECT ANSWERS		
	Your Time	*Time Allowed*	*Points Gained*
POINTS BROUGHT FORWARD			
18.15 Answer below		30	
TOTAL POINTS GAINED			

CHAPTER SUMMARY

Chapter Handicap Total:

Correct Answers x 5 points:

Chapter Total:

Brought Forward:

Running Total:

CHAPTER NINETEEN

Target Time: 2 hours 55 minutes

UNEARTHLY PING PONG

You are the observer of two very heavy projectiles A and B which have, attached in front, large flat sheets of elasticium – the little known metal which is perfectly elastic. The projectiles are on opposite straight paths on a collision course, at a speed relative to you of 100 km per second. A small perfect ball of elasticium is shot from A to B at a speed of 100 km per second, and bounces back and forth between them three complete times before they collide.

At what speed relative to you was the ball moving after its last bounce?

ANSWER:

19.1	Minutes allowed	10
	Time taken	
	Points gained	

GO FORTH AND MULTIPLY

Multiply all the numbers from negative six to positive six, in increments of one, inclusive. What is the result?

-6 x -5 x -4 . . . . 4 x 5 x 6

ANSWER:

19.2	Minutes allowed	5
	Time taken	
	Points gained	

ASTEROIDING

On your way between two planets you encounter an asteroid field, shown below. The figures in each open circle are the number of years taken for that part of your journey. Each black circle represents an asteroid and adds 7 years to your journey. You have to travel from A to B, following the arrows.

How many different routes are there for which the total journey time will be 57 years?

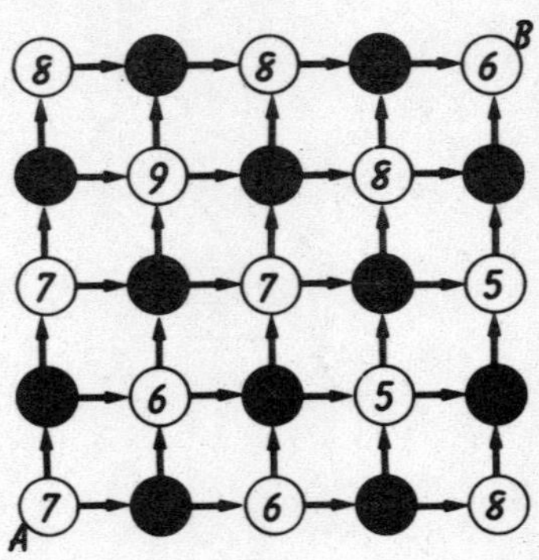

ANSWER:

19.3	Minutes allowed	10
	Time taken	
	Points gained	

LOGICAL TRIANGLES

What should replace the question mark in the last of these four triangles?

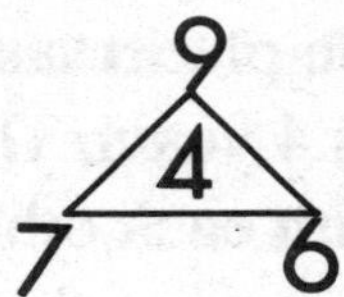

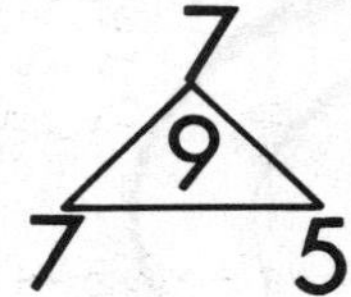

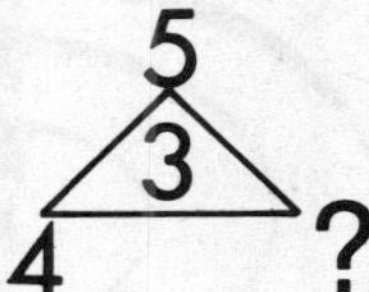

ANSWER:

19.4	Minutes allowed	10
	Time taken	
	Points gained	

PLANETARY LINE-UP

Here is a map of a planetary system. All three planets revolve around the sun in a clockwise direction. The outer planet takes 16 years to make one revolution; the middle planet takes 12 years and the inner planet takes 4 years. They are now in line with the sun and with each other. When, in full years, will this next occur?

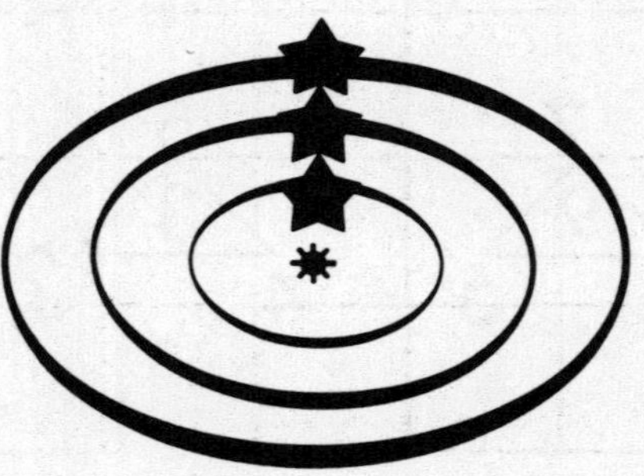

ANSWER:

19.5	Minutes allowed	10
	Time taken	
	Points gained	

CAN YOU COUNT?

How many squares of any size can be counted in this grid?

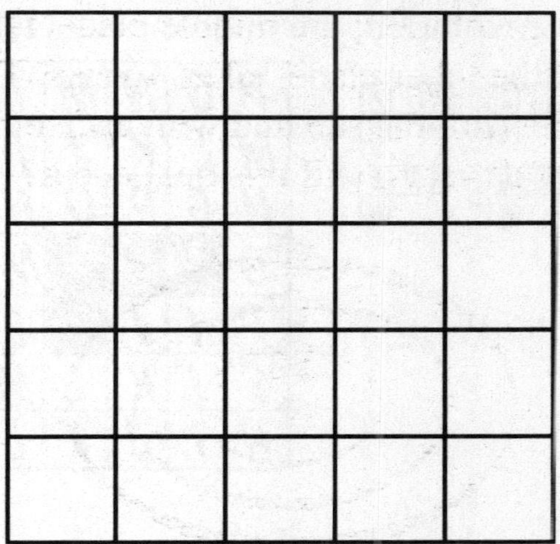

ANSWER:

19.6	Minutes allowed	5
	Time taken	
	Points gained	

LOGICRACKER

Crack the logic and tell us which of the tiles below fits into the gap in the large diagram.

P	O	N	M	L	K	J
M	L	K	J	I	H	I
N	G	P	O	N	G	H
O				M	P	G
P	I	J		L	O	P
G	J	K	L	M	N	O
H	I	J	K	L	M	N

ANSWER:

19.7	Minutes allowed	10
	Time taken	
	Points gained	

VE HAF VAYS!

How many different routes are there from A to B

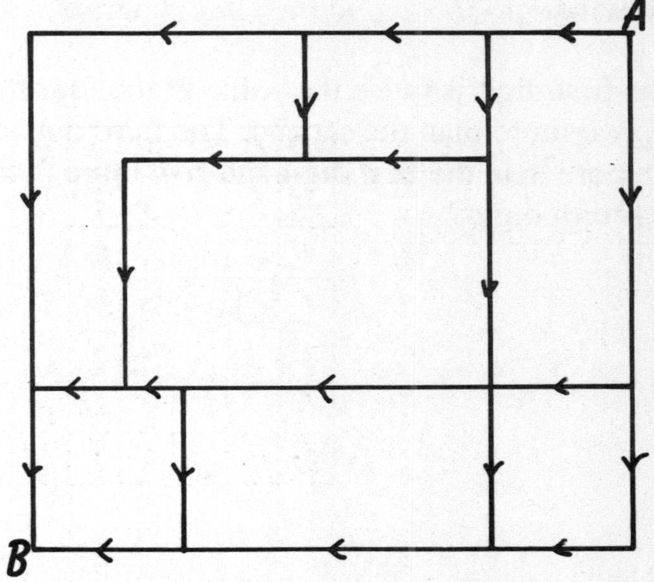

ANSWER:

19.8	Minutes allowed	5
	Time taken	
	Points gained	

FINGER THE DIGITS

Which four-digit number can be described by the following:

"The first digit is twice the value of the fourth and two more than the second. The third digit is one more than the first digit and five more than the fourth digit."

ANSWER:

19.9	Minutes allowed	10
	Time taken	
	Points gained	

CAN YOU MAKE IT?

Which of the six cubes below cannot be made from the flattened out shape?

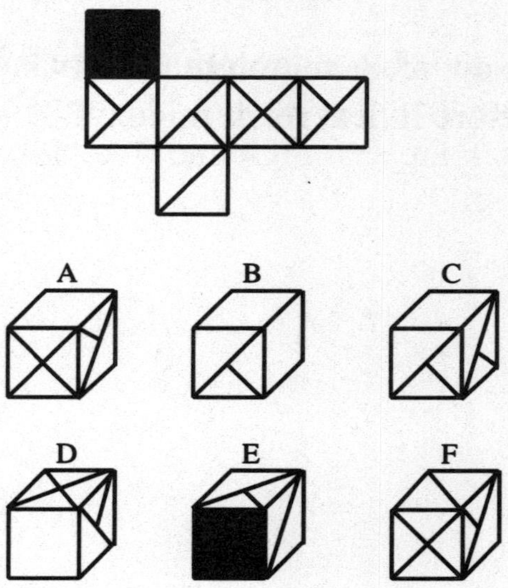

ANSWER:

19.10	Minutes allowed	10
	Time taken	
	Points gained	

WATCH OUT!

Your watch is broken. Every time the second hand passes the '4' it jumps back 12 seconds.

If the time now reads midnight, how many hours will pass before it next reads midday?

ANSWER:

19.11	Minutes allowed	10
	Time taken	
	Points gained	

QUIZ

ANSWERS

1. What kind of cow produces more than 80% of the UK's milk?
2. When would you see Bailey's Beads?
3. What colour is a Granny Smith?
4. Where are a snail's reproductive organs?
5. What was the name of Charles Darwin's ship?
6. How many points are there on a Maltese cross?
7. What puts bubbles in soda water?
8. What makes up 12 per cent of the weight of an egg?
9. Name the smallest bird in the world?
10. Where are the Haversian canals?
11. Who invented the machine gun in 1862?
12. What is the name of the jet engine that powers Concorde?

19.12	Minutes allowed	15
	Time taken	
	Points gained	

UNJUMBLE

The following six groups of letters are words that have been jumbled up. What are the words?

a) BROUNTHEAD

b) GATESTILEUC

c) HIARQULEN

d) BROKENKICKERC

e) EVERPICSHIRE

f) CREATEFOODNIN

ANSWER:

19.13	Minutes allowed	20
	Time taken	
	Points gained	

NUMBER TRACKS

You have to start at one of the corner numbers and follow the thin lines to collect four other numbers. You then add all five numbers together to give you a total for that route. How many different ways are there of collecting a total of 33? You can't "back track" or use the same route twice in any way.

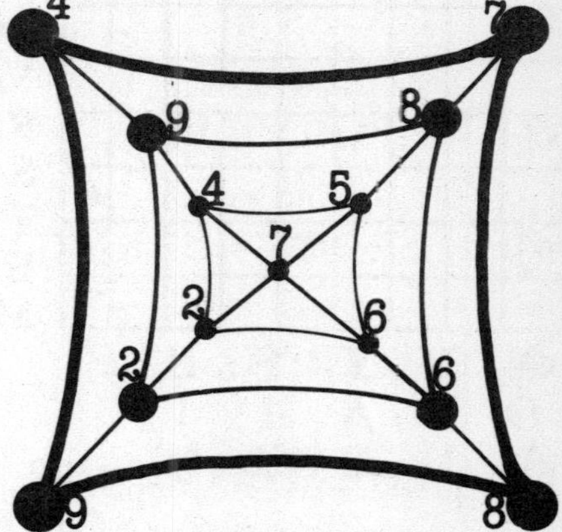

ANSWER:

19.14	Minutes allowed	15
	Time taken	
	Points gained	

DIY CROSSWORD

The words down and across are given below, but you must decide where the blank squares are.

O								S
				C				
G								
				R				
								R
				E				
A								W

INTRUDE OFT C
DEBAR OYEZ H
AXLE GULCH A
BOSS ANEW R
VAT VIA ICE A
ROE ODE O N D
S D O V A E
T R R O T
E E G I A
M W Y D L

N Y S F B A E
O O A I I C E
V U D X N E L
A

19.15	Minutes allowed	30
	Time taken	
	Points gained	

ANSWERS

		FOR CORRECT ANSWERS		
		Your Time	Time Allowed	Points Gained
19.1	The answer may surpise. It is 800 km/s. Relative to you, the observer, at the first pass it meets B at 200 km/s, its speed plus the projectile's speed. But the mutual velocity is 300 km/s. It bounces back from B to A at that speed plus that of the surface of B which it bounced off, making 400 km/s. It hits A at 500 km/s, plus the speed of A makes 600 km/s. The next mutual speed is 700 km/s and final speed relative to you is 800 km/s		10	
19.2	Zero (one of the numbers is 0)		5	
19.3	There are 8 routes		10	
19.4	5 (the total of each like positioned number is 25)		10	
19.5	24 years		10	
19.6	55 squares		5	
19.7	The missing shape is number 5		10	
	CARRIED FORWARD			

ANSWERS

		FOR CORRECT ANSWERS *Your Time*	*Time Allowed*	*Points Gained*
	BROUGHT FORWARD			
19.8	10 routes		5	
19.9	8,694		10	
19.10	B, E and F		10	
19.11	It will never reach midday unless it is mended		10	
19.12	**1.** Friesian **2.** During a total solar eclipse **3.** It's a green apple **4.** Its head **5.** The Beagle **6.** Eight **7.** Carbon dioxide **8.** The shell **9.** Hummingbird **10.** In the bones **11.** J. R. Gatling **12.** Olympus		15	
19.13	**a)** Earthbound **b)** Gesticulate **c)** Harlequin **d)** Knickerbocker **e)** Receivership **f)** Confederation		20	
19.14	There are 9 ways		15	
19.15	See answer overleaf			
	CARRIED FORWARD			

ANSWERS

	FOR CORRECT ANSWERS		
	Your Time	*Time Allowed*	*Points Gained*
POINTS BROUGHT FORWARD			
19.15 Answer below		30	
TOTAL POINTS GAINED			

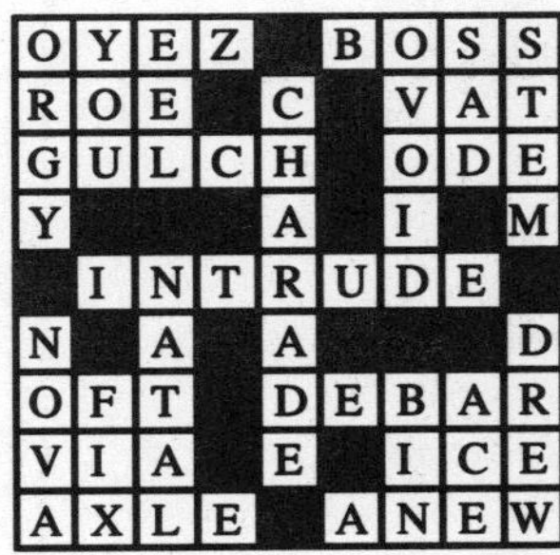

CHAPTER SUMMARY

Chapter Handicap Total:

Correct Answers x 5 points:

Chapter Total:

Brought Forward:

Running Total:

CHAPTER TWENTY

Target Time: 2 hours 22 minutes

CONTRA WALKING 1

On a train or a plane you can walk south when you are moving north, but how can you contra walk when your own walking is all that affects your motion relative to the surface? You walk forwards but you go backwards. How come?

ANSWER:

20.1	Minutes allowed	5
	Time taken	
	Points gained	

CONTRA WALKING 2

A pedestrian walks three miles due south. She ten stops. Next she walks three miles due north. She has walked six miles and she is six miles away from where she started, instead of being back there. How come?

There are many places she might have been. How would you map them?

ANSWER:

20.2	Minutes allowed	5
	Time taken	
	Points gained	

BALL GAME

Can you convert BALL into GAME in only three steps? You must change one letter at each step, and with the change a good, new English word must be formed.

B A L L

. . . .

. . . .

G A M E

ANSWER:

20.3	Minutes allowed	5
	Time taken	
	Points gained	

GOAL POST

Convert GOAL into POST in four steps, changing one letter at a time and forming an acceptable English word at each step.

G O A L
. . . .
. . . .
. . . .
P O S T

ANSWER:

20.4	Minutes allowed	5
	Time taken	
	Points gained	

LETTER TO SIGN

The top two calculations work when the same mathematical sign is placed in the position of like letters (eg, if you think "A" in the first calculation means multiply, it must mean the same in the second calculation). Once you have worked out what "A", "B" and "C" represent, apply them to the third calculation and work out the number which should replace the "?".

9 A 3 B 6 C 9 = 9

8 A 4 B 3 C 2 = 4

? A 6 B 9 C 4 = 5

ANSWER:

20.5	Minutes allowed	**4**
	Time taken	
	Points gained	

THE LOST CONSONANTS

Here is a quotation uttered at the New York Custom House. All of the consonants have been replaced by diamonds, but the vowels remain. What is the quote, and who said it?

"I ◊A◊E ◊O◊◊I◊◊ ◊O ◊E◊◊A◊E E◊◊E◊◊ ◊Y ◊E◊IU◊"

ANSWER:

20.6	Minutes allowed	3
	Time taken	
	Points gained	

DOUBLE CHALLENGE

a) On what day of the week did January 1772 fall?

b) Which two words, that use the same six letters, can be placed in the spaces in this sentence to make the most sense?

"Blackbeard the evil pirate always . . . . . . his treasure since one day he kept the . . . . . ., because he liked the colour, and was stopped at the customs and made to pay duty."

ANSWER:

20.7	Minutes allowed	25
	Time taken	
	Points gained	

FUSSY SALLY

Sally likes khaki, but not brown. She likes pyjamas, but not nightgowns. She likes chocolate mousse, but not bread pudding. Will she like slacks or jodhpurs?

ANSWER:

20.8	Minutes allowed	5
	Time taken	
	Points gained	

PHRASE MUDDLE

The following letters can be rearranged to spell five words that refer to an event which is compared to a large mammal. Here are the letters, what is the phrase?

E E A A A W T O M F H I L

ANSWER:

20.9	Minutes allowed	10
	Time taken	
	Points gained	

CONFUSED ASSIGNATION

A gentleman says to his fair lady, "We will meet three days after the day before the day before tomorrow."

If today is Monday, when will they meet?

ANSWER:

20.10	Minutes allowed	5
	Time taken	
	Points gained	

WORD SQUARE

A word square is composed of words that read across and down. Here are four definitions. If you fill in the words correctly, you will create a word square.

1) Small path or narrow road
2) A space covered, a geometry term
3) In close proximity
4) All animals have them

ANSWER:

20.11	Minutes allowed	10
	Time taken	
	Points gained	

AND ANOTHER

Here is another word square. Solve the clues and complete it.

1) A musical notation

2) Not under

3) Rip

4) It's human when done

ANSWER:

20.12	Minutes allowed	10
	Time taken	
	Points gained	

ANOTHER LOGICRACKER

Crack the logic and calculate which letter should replace the question mark. By the way, "calculate" is a huge clue!

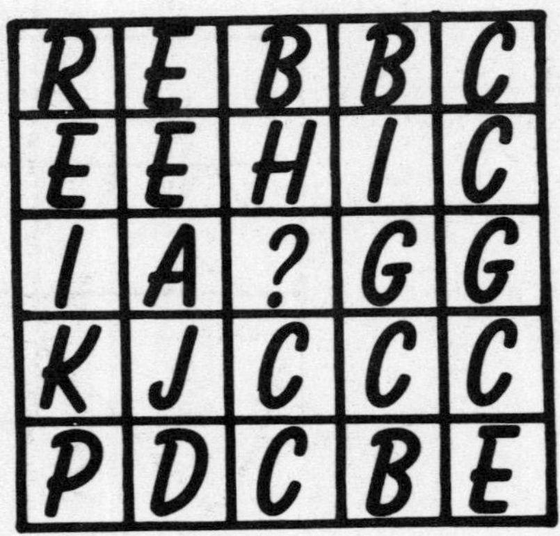

ANSWER:

20.13	Minutes allowed	10
	Time taken	
	Points gained	

ALWAYS ANOTHER WAY

Here is an eight-segment dart board, and you have three darts. You have to calculate how many different ways there are of scoring 20 with three darts. Once a combination has been used it can be reused in a different order, as many times as possible. So, how many ways are there of scoring 20?

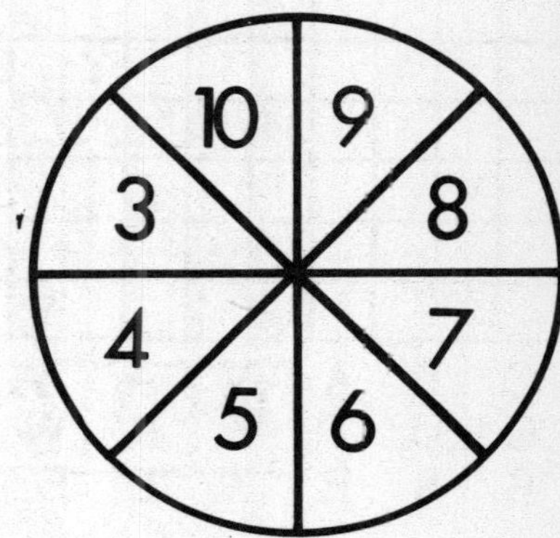

ANSWER:

20.14	Minutes allowed	10
	Time taken	
	Points gained	

DIY CROSSWORD

The words down and across are given below, but you must decide where the blank squares are.

			X					
	U						W	
		Y					Y	
	V							
	X							W

MYSTERY USE
VET BAR RUM
APEX STEW
REBEL OWE
ORE OVALS
SCAB AXED

PROTEST ROBOT BELL ARUM NOVA BREW EMERY

COB PUS ATE VEX ARE AWE

20.15	Minutes allowed	30
	Time taken	
	Points gained	

ANSWERS

		FOR CORRECT ANSWERS		
		Your Time	*Time Allowed*	*Points Gained*
20.1	You are walking on top of a ball or drum on land, or a log in the water 		5	
20.2	She was anywhere on a circle 3 miles from the south pole. When she reached the pole she did not turn, she just kept going in a straight line		5	
20.3	BALL, GALL (or BALE), GALE, GAME		5	
20.4	GOAL, GOAT, MOAT, MOST, POST		5	
20.5	The missing figure is 6 A = ÷, B = x, C = -		4	
	CARRIED FORWARD			

ANSWERS

		FOR CORRECT ANSWERS *Your Time*	*Time Allowed*	*Points Gained*
	BROUGHT FORWARD			
20.6	"I have nothing to declare except my own genius." Uttered by Oscar Wilde		3	
20.7	**a)** Monday. It was a leap year **b)** BURIES & RUBIES		25	
20.8	Jodhpurs. She likes words of foreign origin		5	
20.9	A whale of a time		10	
20.10	Wednesday		5	
20.11	L A N E A R E A N E A R E A R S		10	
20.12	N O T E O V E R T E A R E R R S		10	
20.13	F (A = 15, B = 16 etc and each row = 100)		10	
20.14	48 ways		10	
20.15	See answer overleaf			
	CARRIED FORWARD			

ANSWERS

		FOR CORRECT ANSWERS	
	Your Time	*Time Allowed*	*Points Gained*
POINTS BROUGHT FORWARD			
20.15 Answer below		30	
TOTAL POINTS GAINED			

CHAPTER SUMMARY

Chapter Handicap Total:	
Correct Answers x 5 points:	
Chapter Total:	
Brought Forward:	
Running Total:	

CHAPTER TWENTY ONE

Target Time: 3 hours 30 minutes

A HYDRA OBJECT

I have in my hand a solid object called a 'squiffle', which reminds me of the Hydra – the nine-headed monster that Hercules came up against. This squiffle has four things on it – let us call them 'driggles'. If I cut off these four driggles with my knife, I discover that my squiffle now has twelve driggles. In fact, it is no longer a squiffle, but the four driggles which I cut off have transformed themselves into squiffles! And since each of these has four driggles, I now have a total of 28 driggles.

What is a squiffle, and what is a driggle? They both have other names.

ANSWER:

21.1	Minutes allowed	15
	Time taken	
	Points gained	

WORD CHAIN

By changing one letter at a time to create a different word, what is the least number of steps needed to change the word CILL to BAIT?

ANSWER:

21.2	Minutes allowed	5
	Time taken	
	Points gained	

SCORE? YOU NAME IT!

A number of friends at school sat a test, and they all scored terribly. Each score is a percentage, and for some reason it is connected with the student's name. Crack the logic and calculate the score which Ann achieved.

SIDNEY	20
MALCOLM	22
JEAN	16
PHOEBE	24
ANN	?

ANSWER:

21.3	Minutes allowed	8
	Time taken	
	Points gained	

HAVE A FIT

Which of the shapes 1 to 5 should be placed into the empty space in the grid below?

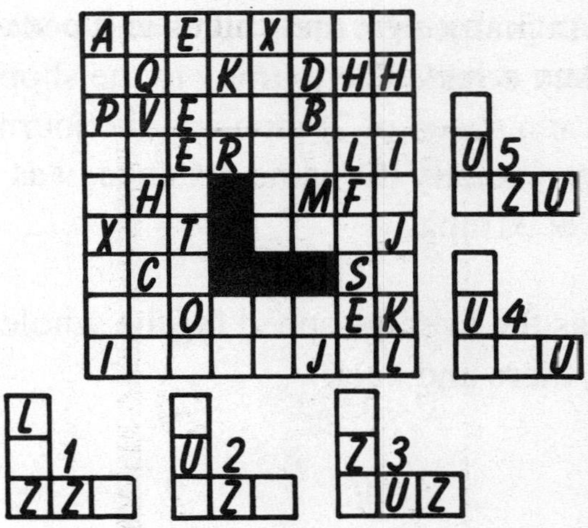

ANSWER:

21.4	Minutes allowed	12
	Time taken	
	Points gained	

SPEED THOSE EGGS

Martin and Matthew Harris were asked to pop to the shops for their parents, who run a Guest House and had run out of eggs for breakfast. They both jumped on their bikes and pedalled as fast as they could. The journey to the shops was covered at a speed of 28mph and the journey back, over exactly the same distance, was covered at 31mph.

What was the average speed for the whole journey, there and back?

ANSWER:

21.5	Minutes allowed	15
	Time taken	
	Points gained	

LIZ TRACK 3

Starting at the bottom left hand letter work your way either upwards or to the right from square to touching square in such a way that you pass over all of the letters of the name ELIZABETH. To be called a touching square, it must touch along a full edge, not just a corner. How many ways are there of "collecting" all the letters of the name Elizabeth?

A	B	E	T	H
Z	A	E	A	T
I	B	H	B	E
L	I	Z	A	B
E	L	I	Z	A

ANSWER:

21.6	Minutes allowed	10
	Time taken	
	Points gained	

ECLIPSE TIME?

Two planets are in orbit around a sun, as shown in the diagram. At this moment in time they are in line with the sun and are travelling in the direction shown at different speeds. Planet A completes one orbit every 54 years and planet B does the same task every 66 years. When will the two planets and the sun next be in line with each other?

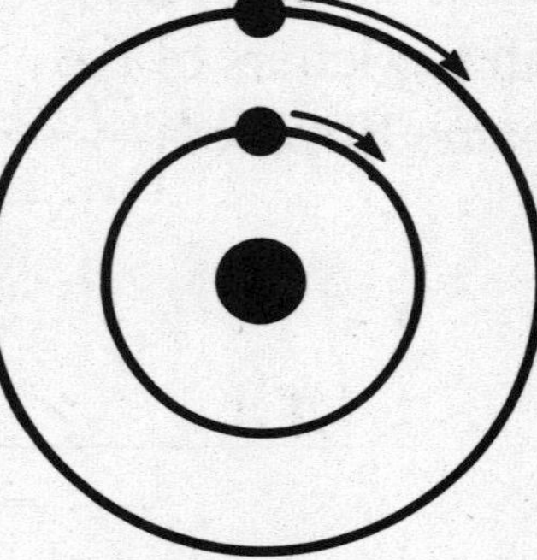

ANSWER:

21.7	Minutes allowed	15
	Time taken	
	Points gained	

KEEP YOUR BALANCE

The top two sets of scales are in perfect balance. How many of the missing item are needed to balance the third set of scales?

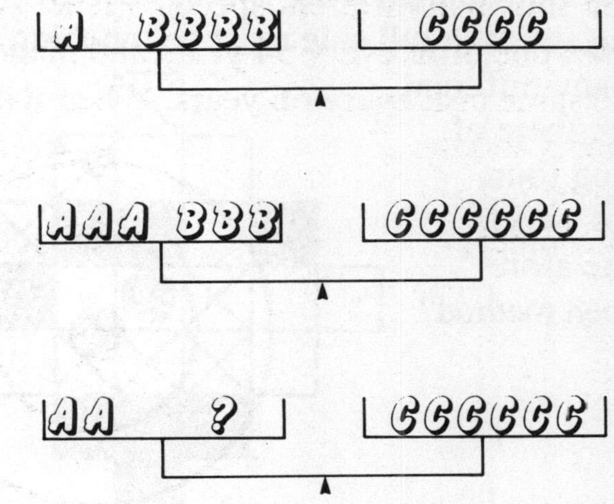

ANSWER:

21.8	Minutes allowed	10
	Time taken	
	Points gained	

ALL SORTS

There are four different types of sweet in this box and, of course, you want one of each. You must always start at the centre sweet and work your way outwards moving from sweet to touching sweet (a full side must be touching). How many different ways are there of collecting four different sweets using the afore-mentioned method?

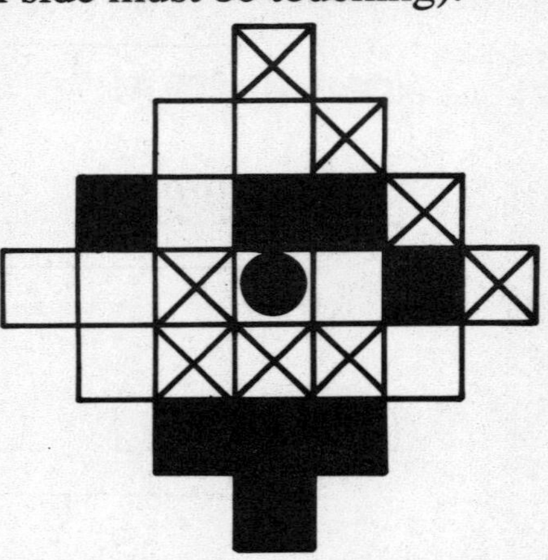

ANSWER:

21.9	Minutes allowed	8
	Time taken	
	Points gained	

WORD TIDY

What four words can be made from these letters?

a) MEETTHEMORR

b) RATNATACIC

c) NONINLATEARTE

d) TOJEPERILC

ANSWER:

21.10	Minutes allowed	12
	Time taken	
	Points gained	

WAYS THROUGH TOWN

Here is a map of a one way system in a town. You are at "A" and, of course, want to be at "B". How many legal ways are there of getting from "A" to "B"?

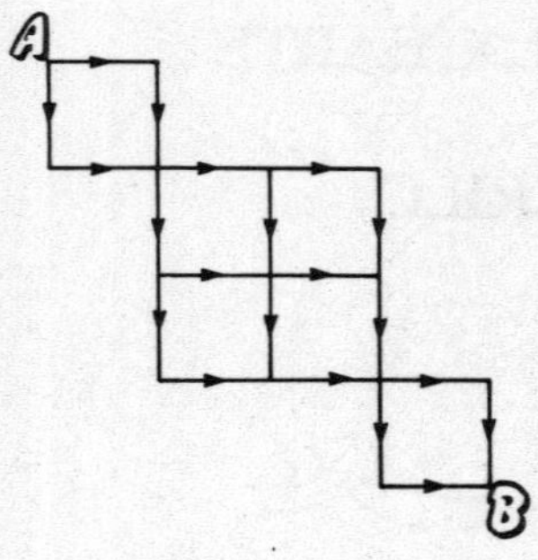

ANSWER:

21.11	Minutes allowed	15
	Time taken	
	Points gained	

COUNTING AROUND

How many different circles are there in this diagram? Colouring a few in might help you!

ANSWER:

21.12	Minutes allowed	15
	Time taken	
	Points gained	

WHEN A DECADE DECAYED

This is an easy puzzle, especially on a Sunday! What number should replace the question mark?

7	14	21	
28	4	11	
18	25	4	
11	18	25	?

ANSWER:

21.13	Minutes allowed	**20**
	Time taken	
	Points gained	

A PARTIAL MAGIC CUBE

A magic cube is one where the numbers add up to the same number down, across and through. They are not easy to draw, so I have taken this one apart into three separate layers of nine cells each. I have left some of the numbers out, and it is your job to fill them.

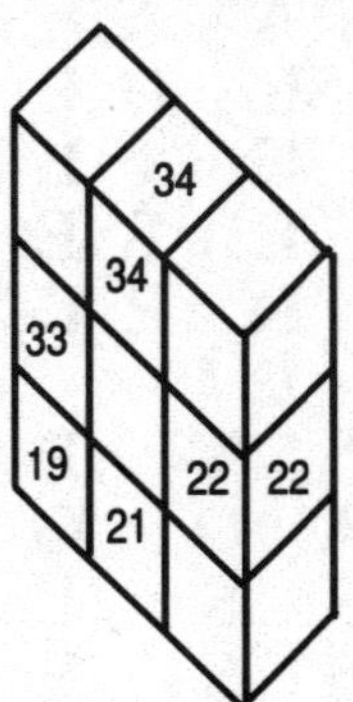

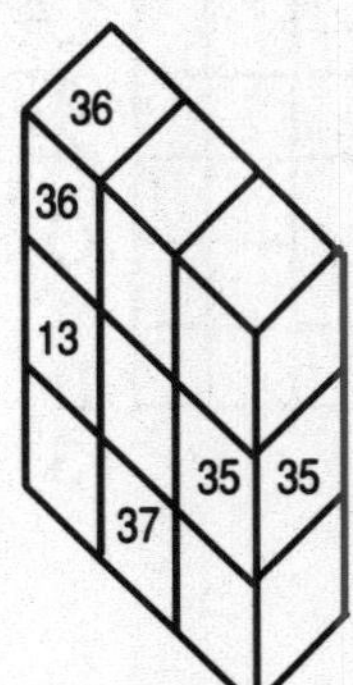

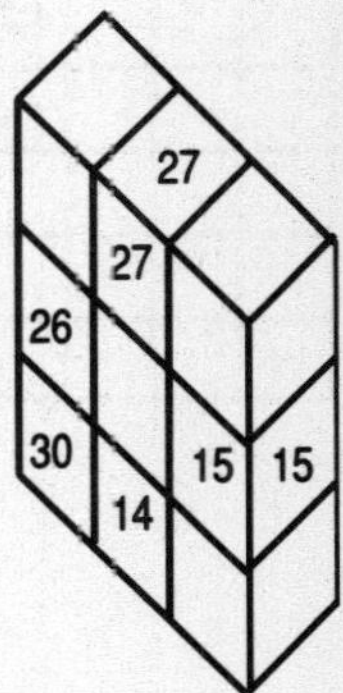

ANSWER:

21.14	Minutes allowed	20
	Time taken	
	Points gained	

DIY CROSSWORD

The words down and across are given below, but you must decide where the blank squares are.

				T				G
		K						
V								
			E		D			

SCENE SKI
DISSENTER
LLANO IRK
DIPHTHONG
ELSE DATA
APES ELSE

POKES LEAN ASSET CEDE GRENADIER DRIVELLED

ONE ASS TOSS POLE

21.15	Minutes allowed	30
	Time taken	
	Points gained	

ANSWERS

		FOR CORRECT ANSWERS		
		Your Time	Time Allowed	Points Gained
21.1	A squiffle is a four-sided pyramid or tetrahedron. It has four corners, vertices or driggles as I call them. Each cut vertex forms another tetrahedron, which has four vertices or driggles. The original squiffle becomes an octohedron with 12 vertices, while the four new tetrahedra each have four.		15	
21.2	4. CILL CALL BALL BAIL BAIT		5	
21.3	10. Number of vowels x 6 + number of consonants x 4		8	
21.4	Shape 5. A = 1, B = 2, etc. Each vertical column has a total of 50		12	
21.5	29.424 mph		15	
21.6	11 ways		10	
21.7	148 years and 6 months. They will be on opposite sides of the sun		15	
21.8	5 Bs. A = 8, B = 4, C = 6		10	
	CARRIED FORWARD			

ANSWERS

		FOR CORRECT ANSWERS		
		Your Time	*Time Allowed*	*Points Gained*
	BROUGHT FORWARD			
21.9	There are 11 ways of collecting 4 different sweets		8	
21.10	a) THERMOMETER b) ANTARCTICA c) INTERNATIONAL d) PROJECTILE		12	
21.11	There are 24 routes from "A" to "B"		15	
21.12	There are 17 circles		15	
21.13	1. They are the dates of Sundays at the start of a year such as 1990		20	
21.14			20	
21.15	See answer overleaf			
	CARRIED FORWARD			

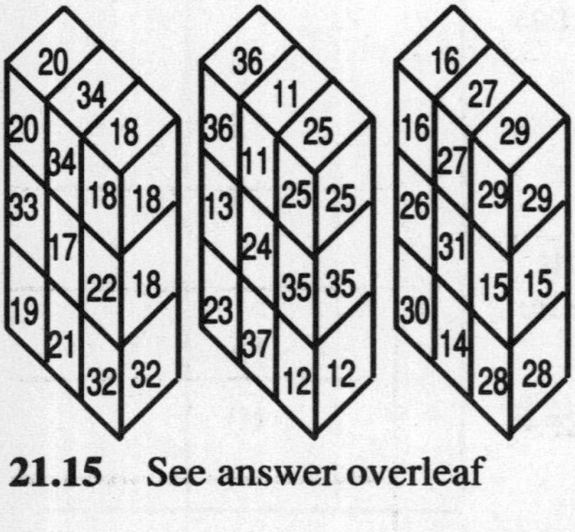

ANSWERS

		FOR CORRECT ANSWERS *Your Time*	*Time Allowed*	*Points Gained*
	POINTS BROUGHT FORWARD			
21.15	Answer below		30	
	TOTAL POINTS GAINED			

D	I	P	H	T	H	O	N	G
R		O		O		N		R
I	R	K		S	C	E	N	E
V		E	L	S	E			N
E	A	S	E		D	A	T	A
L			A	P	E	S		D
L	L	A	N	O		S	K	I
E		S		L		E		E
D	I	S	S	E	N	T	E	R

CHAPTER SUMMARY

Chapter Handicap Total: ________

Correct Answers x 5 points: ________

Chapter Total: ________

Brought Forward: ________

Running Total: ________

CHAPTER TWENTY TWO

Target Time: 3 hours 55 minutes

EXACT TIME LINE UP

At what time, exactly, between three and four o'clock is the minute hand on a normal clock exactly aligned over the hour hand?

ANSWER:

22.1	Minutes allowed	20
	Time taken	
	Points gained	

GEOMETRICAL SERIES

This is a series. You will find what comes next from what is given. SPHERE. CIRCLE. LINE.

What comes next?

ANSWER:

22.2	Minutes allowed	5
	Time taken	
	Points gained	

FIND THE LETTER

Which letter should replace the question mark in the grid below?

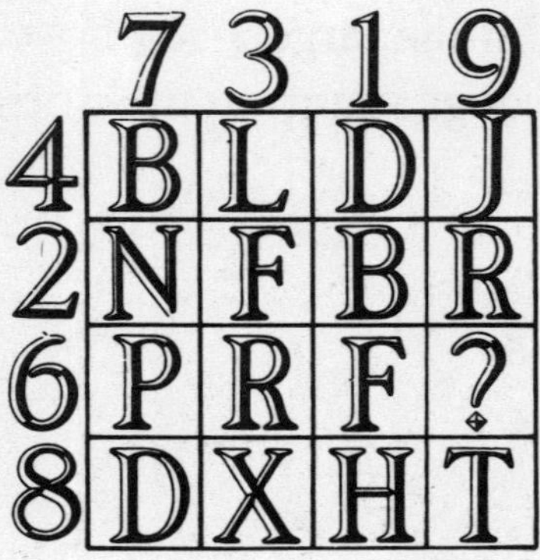

ANSWER:

22.3	Minutes allowed	5
	Time taken	
	Points gained	

MORE COGITATION

Four cogs are in constant mesh, as shown in this diagram. The largest cog has 25 teeth; the next cog, cog B, has 20 teeth; cog C has 15 teeth and the smallest cog has only 10 teeth. How many revolutions will the largest cog have to make before all the cogs return to their original position?

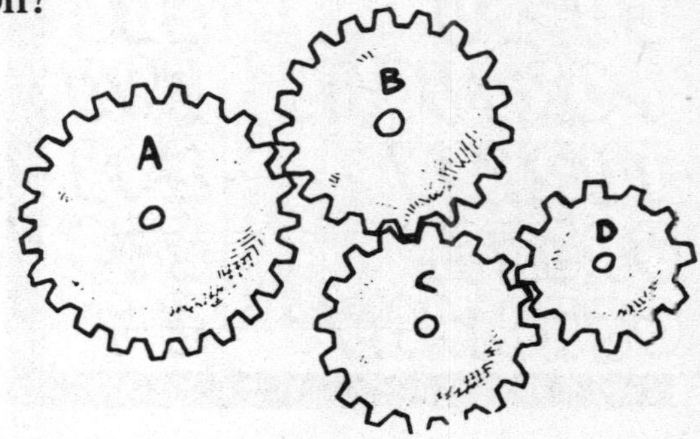

ANSWER:

22.4	Minutes allowed	10
	Time taken	
	Points gained	

IRRELEVANT COSTING

The travel agent has got some special offers on again, but has not yet written in the price for Germany. Following the same grammatical logic as for the other four, what is the cost of a holiday in Germany?

ANSWER:

22.5	Minutes allowed	20
	Time taken	
	Points gained	

LETTER SEARCH

Each letter has a value ranging from one to twenty-six inclusive. Which letter should replace the question mark?

O ÷ U + I = N

H ÷ S + A = ?

ANSWER:

22.6	Minutes allowed	20
	Time taken	
	Points gained	

ANOTHER USELESS CLOCK

Your clock has gone haywire. At 2.41 am it read 6.17, at 6.17 it read 9.53, whilst at 9.53 it read 1.29 pm.

What time will it read at 1.29 pm?

ANSWER:

22.7	Minutes allowed	15
	Time taken	
	Points gained	

LOGICAL LETTER?

Following the same logic as for the first three triangles, which letter should replace the question mark in the fourth triangle? It might take days to do this one!

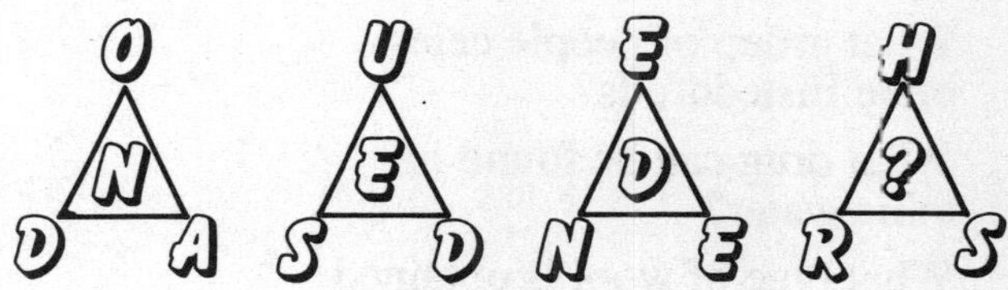

ANSWER:

22.8	Minutes allowed	10
	Time taken	
	Points gained	

QUIZ

ANSWERS

1. What do dilute acetic acid and vegetable oil make?
2. What mammal lays eggs, has webbed feet with claws and has a bill?
3. What letter is at the left hand end of the bottom row of a typewriter keyboard?
4. What group of people celebrate Eisteddfods?
5. What drug can be found in tonic water?
6. What type of wool is obtained from angora goats?
7. What is the day before Ash Wednesday?
8. Who discovered Saturn's rings?
9. How many legs does an oyster catcher have?
10. In which month does the harvest moon shine?
11. How many feet in a fathom?
12. What is a third molar called?

22.9	Minutes allowed	15
	Time taken	
	Points gained	

DIY CROSSWORD

The words down and across are given below, but you must decide where the blank squares are.

S								S
	A						I	
				E		I		
				L				
	G						L	
D								L

DEWY LOSS
NEMESIS ILL
SPAN MALL
EGO LEVEE
OPERA KIT
TAR LAD ATE

GAZELLE

OKAPI ENDOW BELL BLED

STEM STOW

ARE SIT AGE PAP VIA ELL

22.10	Minutes allowed	30
	Time taken	
	Points gained	

EXTEND THIS STRING

Here is a string of integers. The arrangement is logical. Replace the question marks at each end with the correct figure.

? 18 20 21 22 24 25 26 27 28 ?

ANSWER:

22.11	Minutes allowed	5
	Time taken	
	Points gained	

GRID FILLING

Using only the numbers given below, complete the grid in such a way thay each vertical and horizontal line totals 28.

1 1 2 2 3 4 4 5 5 5 6 7 8 8 8 8 8 9 9 9

9	4	7	6	2

ANSWER:

22.12	Minutes allowed	**15**
	Time taken	
	Points gained	

DIY CROSSWORD

The words down and across are given below, but you must decide where the blank squares are.

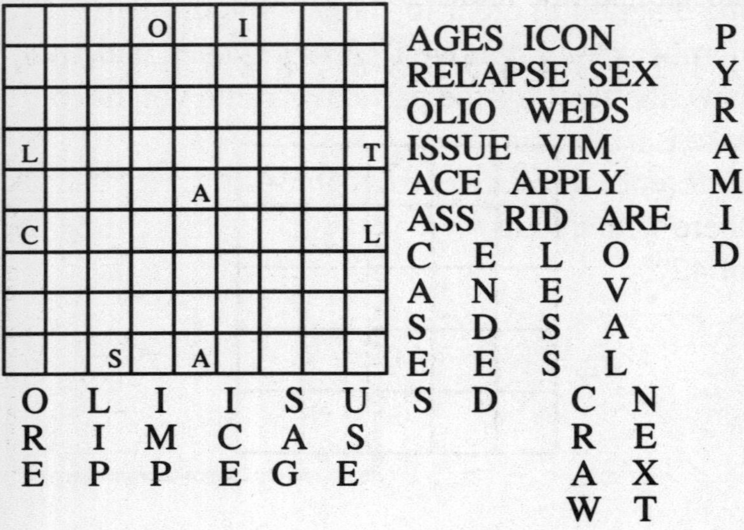

22.13	Minutes allowed	30
	Time taken	
	Points gained	

NUMBER TRACKS

Starting at one of the corner numbers, make your way, but following the thin black lines, around the diagram in order to "land" on four other numbers. Add the five figures together, and you have the total for the particular route you have taken. How many different routes are there with a total of 42?

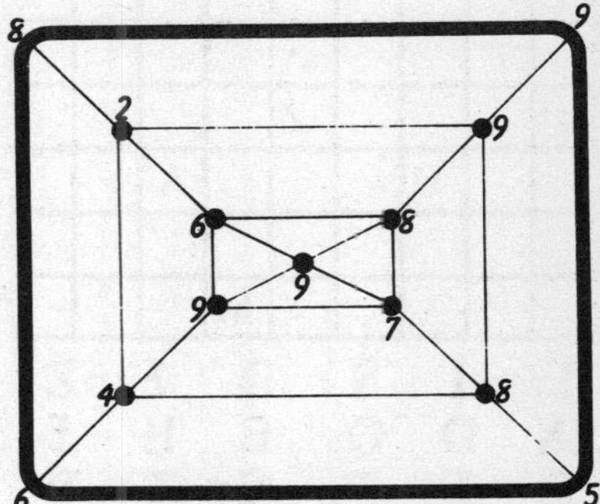

ANSWER:

22.14	Minutes allowed	5
	Time taken	
	Points gained	

DIY CROSSWORD

The words down and across are given below, but you must decide where the blank squares are.

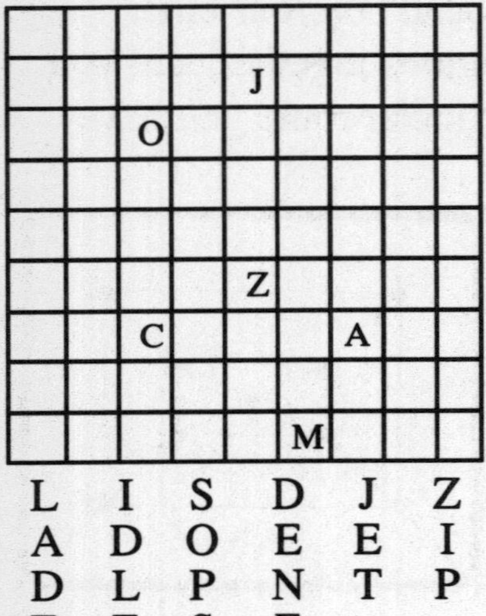

MERE IDOL
DECLINATE
ELLS SEPT
OAR LEA
PROCESSED
ERA TON
AGE GAY

ORE EAR TOR EEL DESIGNATE PROSAICAL

LADE IDLE SOPS DENE JET ZIP

22.15	Minutes allowed	30
	Time taken	
	Points gained	

ANSWERS

		FOR CORRECT ANSWERS		
		Your Time	Time Allowed	Points Gained
22.1	To be exact we use a rational number rather than a decimal. The exact answer is 16 minutes 21 4/11 seconds past three. This is the only correct answer. I said exactly, not to the nearest second or even decimal point.		20	
22.2	A point. A sphere has 3 dimensions, a circle two, and a line one. A point has no dimensions, only position.		5	
22.3	B. Multiply the "coordinates" and using A = 1, or 27, or 53 etc you can work out the letter in each square.		5	
22.4	12 revolutions		10	
22.5	£60. Multiply twice the vowels by three times the consonants.		20	
22.6	G. A = 11, B =12, P = 26, Q = 1 etc.		20	
22.7	5.05 p.m. The clock is 3hrs 36 mins fast.		15	
	CARRIED FORWARD			

ANSWERS

		FOR CORRECT ANSWERS *Your Time*	*Time Allowed*	*Points Gained*
	BROUGHT FORWARD			
22.8	U. Each triangle shows the 2nd to 5th letters of Monday to Thursday.		10	
22.9	**1.** French dressing **2.** The duckbilled platypus **3.** Z **4.** Druids **5.** Quinine **6.** Mohair **7.** Shrov Tuesday **8.** Galileo **9.** 2 **10.** September **11.** Six **12.** A wisdom tooth		15	
22.10	(crossword grid below)		30	
22.11	16 and 30. The numbers are the non-primes, starting from 16.		5	
	CARRIED FORWARD			

22.10

S	P	A	N	■	L	O	S	S
T	A	R	■	G	■	K	I	T
O	P	E	R	A	■	A	T	E
W	■	■	■	Z	■	P	■	M
■	N	E	M	E	S	I	S	■
B	■	N	■	L	■	■	■	B
L	A	D	■	L	E	V	E	E
E	G	O	■	E	■	I	L	L
D	E	W	Y	■	M	A	L	L

ANSWERS

	FOR CORRECT ANSWERS *Your Time*	*Time Allowed*	*Points Gained*
BROUGHT FORWARD			
22.12		15	
22.13		30	
22.14		5	
22.15			
CARRIED FORWARD			

22.12 9 4 7 6 2
1 5 6 8 8
8 9 8 1 2
5 2 3 9 9
5 8 4 4 7

22.13

O	L	I	O	■	I	C	O	N
V	I	M	■	P	■	A	R	E
A	P	P	L	Y	■	S	E	X
L	■	■	■	R	■	E	■	T
■	R	E	L	A	P	S	E	■
C	■	N	■	M	■	■	■	L
R	I	D	■	I	S	S	U	E
A	C	E	■	D	■	A	S	S
W	E	D	S	■	A	G	E	S

22.14 There are 5 routes by which you can score a total of 42 points

22.15 See answer overleaf

ANSWERS

		FOR CORRECT ANSWERS		
		Your Time	Time Allowed	Points Gained
POINTS BROUGHT FORWARD				
21.15	Answer below		30	
TOTAL POINTS GAINED				

S	E	P	T		I	D	O	L
O	A	R		J		E	R	A
P	R	O	C	E	S	S	E	D
S		S		T		I		E
	G	A	Y		A	G	E	
I		I		Z		N		D
D	E	C	L	I	N	A	T	E
L	E	A		P		T	O	N
E	L	L	S		M	E	R	E

CHAPTER SUMMARY

Chapter Handicap Total:

Correct Answers x 5 points:

Chapter Total:

Brought Forward:

Running Total:

CHAPTER TWENTY THREE

Target Time: 4 hours 0 minutes

INVISIBLE MAGNETS

You are blindfolded and naked in an empty room. You are given a pair of steel bars. One is a bar magnet, the other is not. You will be released if you can tell which is which. You are allowed to touch them together just once.

How can you tell which is the magnet?

ANSWER:

23.1	Minutes allowed	10
	Time taken	
	Points gained	

HOW TO CHEAT

You are on a holiday tour and the hotel manager is giving a free holiday as a prize. As you go to the final party the guests put their door keys into a bowl so as to draw the winner. The bowl turns out to be too small, and another is added. The manager will toss a coin to decide the winning bowl and then pick the winner from that.

How can you use this to increase your chance?

ANSWER:

23.2	Minutes allowed	5
	Time taken	
	Points gained	

DIY CROSSWORD

The words down and across are given below, but you must decide where the blank squares are.

			K					
		N				T		
								Y
			X					
		V						

REVERSING C A
PATE BADE O S
LACK ASPS N T
VENERATED S E
DIE AGO E R
SOD PRY R O
VEX ARE V I
A A T N E D
G R O I D S
O C E P

C L A E F E
R A G D R R
A V E D Y A
B A S Y

23.3	Minutes allowed	30
	Time taken	
	Points gained	

GOBS, KALS, ET AL

The fourth planet of Centaur Major is called Grost. The vital taxonomy is much like ours. It is known that all prits are kals, and there are no kals that are not gobs. However, although some zloms may be brups as well as prits, many of both species are not even gobs. Further, all the brups that are zloms are also prits. The problem is simple. Can there be such a weird creature that it falls into all five classes? While being a certified prit, it is also a kal, a gob, a zlom and a brup? Further, can there be creatures on Grost that fall into only one of these classes and, if so, which is it?

ANSWER:

23.4	Minutes allowed	15
	Time taken	
	Points gained	

CLOCK PATIENCE

I am patient and lazy. I have two clocks which are telling me the correct time, which is twelve o'clock. But one gains five minutes every hour and the other loses five minutes every hour. I could go to the bother of correcting them but I am too idle. I am patient enough just to wait for them to come into agreement of their own accord.

But how long will it take? And will they be right when they do agree?

ANSWER:

23.5	Minutes allowed	15
	Time taken	
	Points gained	

STRANGE SERIES

Give the next number in this series:

22 20 10 8 4 2 ?

ANSWER:

23.6	Minutes allowed	10
	Time taken	
	Points gained	

THREE-LETTER WORD

There are three numbers which in a sense are progressive. The product in terms of the second – of the first to the power of the sum of the first and the third, the second to the power of itself and the third to the power of the first – can be expressed as a three-letter everday word.

What, I pray, may be that word?

ANSWER:

23.7	Minutes allowed	20
	Time taken	
	Points gained	

CONTROLLED BREEDING

A dictator of a polygamous country wanted more girls to be born because every man wanted several wives. The wives in the harems were allowed to have children until the first boy, so there could be no more than one boy per family. He envisaged families with plenty of girls but only one boy each.

What would happen if the scheme worked? Would it result in a greater proportion of girls? If not, what was the flaw in the logic? What would be the result of such a foolish and inhuman rule?

ANSWER:

23.8	Minutes allowed	15
	Time taken	
	Points gained	

ALIEN MAGIC SQUARE

Here is a suspected magic square (all rows, columns and diagonals sum to a constant). It was found inside a meteorite. It is the only way we have of deciphering the number system employed by the aliens who sent it. We do not know the base, the meaning of the symbols, or the way of indicating the order of base units. What is the base? Can you fill in the magic square?

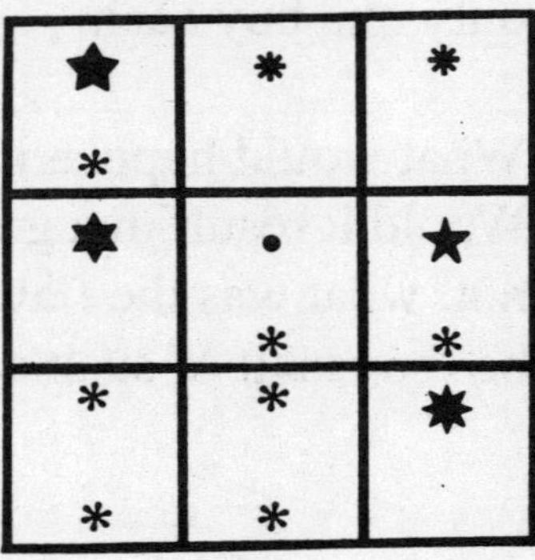

ANSWER:

23.9	Minutes allowed	20
	Time taken	
	Points gained	

DIY CROSSWORD

The words down and across are given below, but you must decide where the blank squares are.

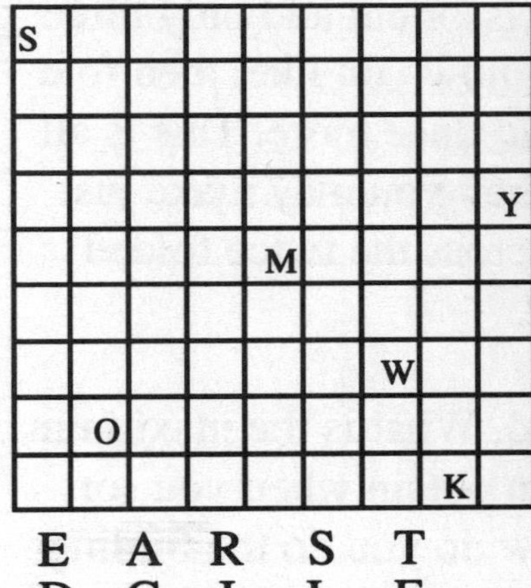

RATED DOE
NOD INTER
STAMINA
TARE STEP
ELKS SPAT
LED WIG
AGE ERE

PRIMERS

ADEPT NEWEL PEG NOT

ROE ANT

EDDY AGES RIDS SLAP TEE

23.10	Minutes allowed	30
	Time taken	
	Points gained	

MAXIMISING MESS

Imagine this. You take a piece of writing paper. Your task is to make the maximum amount of mess with one straight scissor cut and only three folds. You fold the paper how you like, then fold the folded paper, then fold once more. This is all you are allowed to do. Then you may make just one straight scissor cut across the twice folded sheet.

Two answers are required. What is the maximum number of pieces you can obtain when you sort the two cut part out? How do you do the folding to get the maximum number of pieces? You have to do it in your head.

ANSWER:

23.11	Minutes allowed	10
	Time taken	
	Points gained	

REPLACEMENT

Replace the first letter in each pair of words either side of the brackets with another letter which will form two new English words. Then place this letter in the brackets. When you have completed this for all five pairs of words you will find another word reading downwards in the brackets. What is it?

WIND	( )	CAP
AVER	( )	BATH
MACE	( )	RACK
SATIN	( )	DEMON
TOUR	( )	LAWN

ANSWER:

23.12	Minutes allowed	10
	Time taken	
	Points gained	

WORD SEARCH

Five seven-lettered words have been hidden in this grid. They all have the same two-letter prefix which, for each word, has been omitted from the grid. The remaining letters for each word have been written downwards in the grid in random order. What are the five words?

E	I	O	R	O
U	A	V	D	I
I	S	E	E	L
S	T	S	G	S
V	N	L	I	H

ANSWER:

23.13	Minutes allowed	**15**
	Time taken	
	Points gained	

WORD WORK

Rearrange the letters below to make a ten-lettered word.

GONEISCOMR

ANSWER:

23.14	Minutes allowed	5
	Time taken	
	Points gained	

DIY CROSSWORD

The words down and across are given below, but you must decide where the blank squares are.

		T				T		
			O					
R				R				
						O		
E								E

R L O T
I I U O
F V T O
E E

PROOF TOT D S
DISSENTED E E
NIP IDOLS P P
WEBS ROBE U A
IDLE RENT T R
SATURATED I A
T B B O S T
E I R W E E
N T E E D D
S E D D
E S

23.15	Minutes allowed	30
	Time taken	
	Points gained	

ANSWERS

		FOR CORRECT ANSWERS		
		Your Time	*Time Allowed*	*Points Gained*
23.1	Touch the end of one to the centre of the other. If they are attracted the touching end belongs to the magnet; if not, the touching centre belongs to the magnet.		10	
23.2	Be last, and put your key in the bowl with least keys in it. You will have an even chance of your bowl being chosen, and an improved chance thereafter if it is.		5	
23.3	(see grid below)		30	
23.4	The way to settle tricky taxonomic problems is by use of a Venn or Euler diagram, like the one overleaf.			

23.3

L	A	C	K		P	A	T	E
A	G	O		A		S	O	D
V	E	N	E	R	A	T	E	D
A		S		C		E		Y
	V	E	X		P	R	Y	
C		R		F		O		A
R	E	V	E	R	S	I	N	G
A	R	E		Y		D	I	E
B	A	D	E		A	S	P	S

CARRIED FORWARD

ANSWERS

	FOR CORRECT ANSWERS *Your Time*	*Time Allowed*	*Points Gained*
BROUGHT FORWARD			
23.4 (cont) 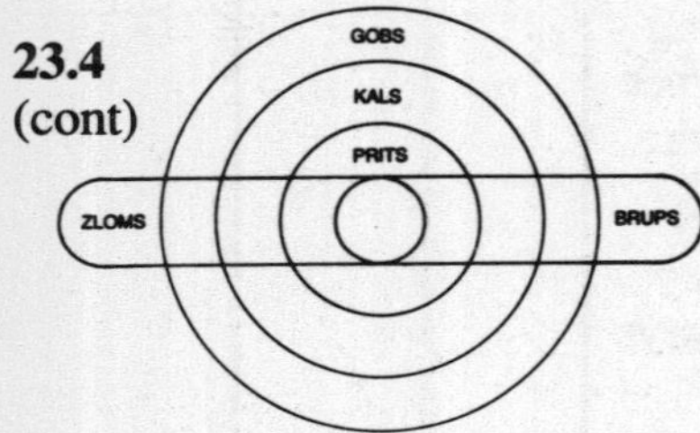 As will be seen, we can place a pencil point where a multi-racial creature will be in a rag-bag of categories falling into all of them. But there are zloms, brups and even gobs who have to subsist in exclusive isolation from other classes		15	
23.5 72 hours, and they will show 6 o'clock when it is really 12 o'clock.		15	
23.6 1. Starting from 22 you alternately subtract 2 and divide by 2.		10	
23.7 The word is 'day', which comprises $2^7 \times 3^3 \times 5^2$ seconds		20	
CARRIED FORWARD			

ANSWERS

	FOR CORRECT ANSWERS		
	Your Time	Time Allowed	Points Gained
BROUGHT FORWARD			
23.8 There will be no change in proportion of boys and girls. The chance of any specific birth being male or female remains unchanged. The result would be that the birth rate would average less than 2 per women, less than enough to maintain to population.		15	
23.9 The base is seven, and the numbers are • = 0, ✻ = 1, ✦ = 2, ✢ = 3, ✶ = 4, ✸ = 5, ✱ = 6			
23.10 See answer overleaf			
CARRIED FORWARD			

2 units 1 seven = 9	6 units = 6	6 units = 6
4 units = 4	0 units 1 seven = 7	3 units 1 seven = 10
1 unit 1 seven = 8	1 unit 1 seven = 8	5 units = 5

ANSWERS

		FOR CORRECT ANSWERS *Your Time*	*Time Allowed*	*Points Gained*
	BROUGHT FORWARD			
23.10	(crossword below)		30	
23.11	You can get nine pieces. You fold three times the same way. Fold the paper to halve the length, halve what is now the width, fold the width again, and divide the width with your cut.		10	
23.12	Holly		10	
23.13	ABOLISH, ABSOLVE, ABRIDGE, ABSTAIN, ABUSIVE		15	
23.14	Ergonomics		5	
	CARRIED FORWARD			

23.10

S	P	A	T		T	A	R	E
L	E	D		P		N	O	D
A	G	E		R	A	T	E	D
P		P		I				Y
	S	T	A	M	I	N	A	
R				E		E		A
I	N	T	E	R		W	I	G
D	O	E		S		E	R	E
S	T	E	P		E	L	K	S

ANSWERS

	Your Time	*Time Allowed*	*Points Gained*
	FOR CORRECT ANSWERS		
POINTS BROUGHT FORWARD			
23.15 Answer below		30	
TOTAL POINTS GAINED			

S	A	T	U	R	A	T	E	D
E		O		I		E		E
P	R	O	O	F		N	I	P
A			W	E	B	S		U
R	O	B	E		R	E	N	T
A		I	D	L	E			I
T	O	T		I	D	O	L	S
E		E		V		U		E
D	I	S	S	E	N	T	E	D

CHAPTER SUMMARY

Chapter Handicap Total:	
Correct Answers x 5 points:	
Chapter Total:	
Brought Forward:	
Running Total:	

CHAPTER TWENTY FOUR

Target Time: 2 hours 46 minutes

MAJORITY ABOVE AVERAGE

THE GREAT MAJORITY ARE ABOVE THE AVERAGE. This statement may seem questionable. On most measurements about half the people are above average and about half are below it, but there are measurements on which the great majority of people are above average and only a small minority below it. Can you think of one?

Think it out! You will kick yourself, if you have to look up the answer.

ANSWER:

24.1	Minutes allowed	5
	Time taken	
	Points gained	

RAILWAY MYSTERY 1

The carriage axles on a train are solid, there is no differential as in a motor car. Yet with the outside wheel travelling further than the inside wheel when the train negotiates bends, there is no apparent slippage. How come?

ANSWER:

24.2	Minutes allowed	5
	Time taken	
	Points gained	

WAYS AND SUMS

Starting at the bottom left hand '7' move from circle to circle, either directly to the right or directly above, landing on nine numbers including the opening '7' and ending with the '9' in the top right hand corner. Add all nine numbers together to arrive at the total for the particular route chosen. How many different routes are there with a total of 43, and what is the lowest possible total?

ANSWER:

24.3	Minutes allowed	12
	Time taken	
	Points gained	

ANOTHER LOGICRACKER

Crack the logic found in the first two hexagons and apply it to the third to find the value of the question mark.

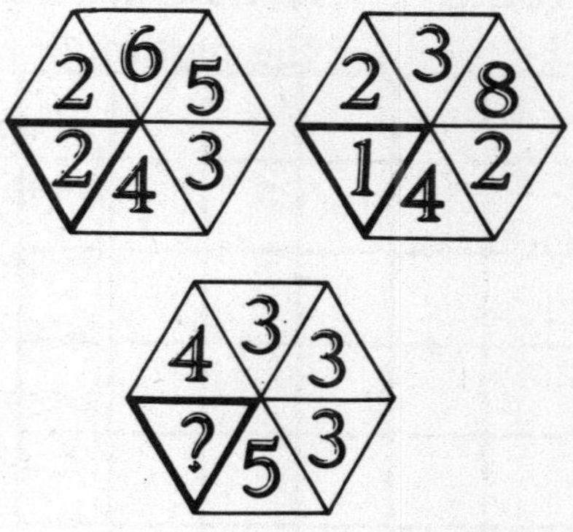

ANSWER:

24.4	Minutes allowed	6
	Time taken	
	Points gained	

POST THESE LETTERS

Place each of the following letters into the grid below in such a way that you can read six words across and the same six words downwards. The letters are: M V P I R H A R P L E T I O E T V D E E E R R E E T V D T I O E A R P L E

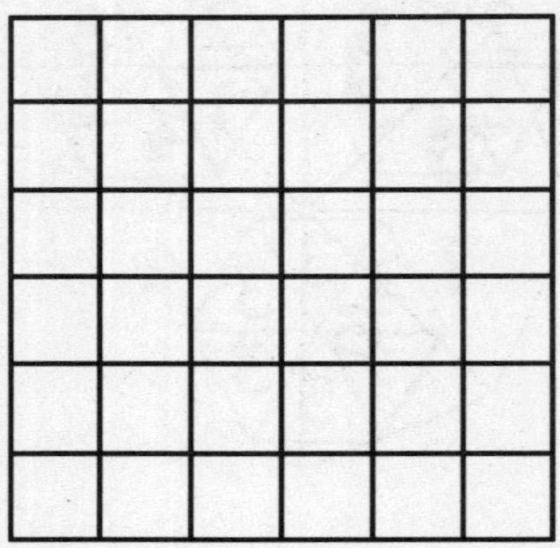

ANSWER:

24.5	Minutes allowed	15
	Time taken	
	Points gained	

REACH EIGHTEEN

How many ways can you score 18 on this dart-board? You have four darts each turn, but you can't use a combination of numbers in a different order once used.

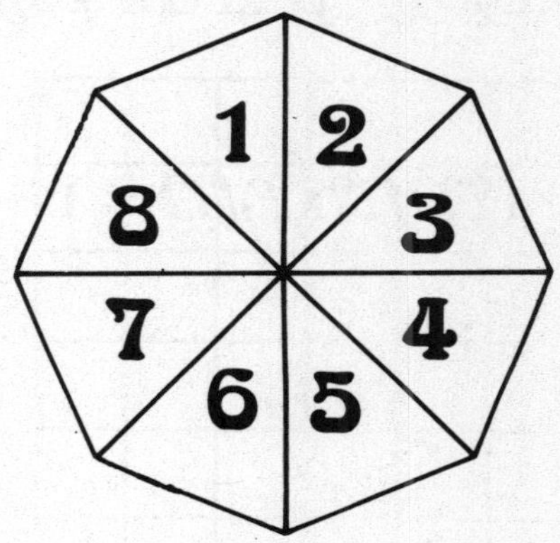

ANSWER:

24.6	Minutes allowed	6
	Time taken	
	Points gained	

GET ONE IN

Replace each question mark with one of the following digits in order that the calculation is correct.

1 2 2 3 4 4 7 9

(???/??x?)/?? = 1

ANSWER:

24.7	Minutes allowed	8
	Time taken	
	Points gained	

WHAT TIME?

Your clock was correct at midnight, but at that moment started to lose six minutes per hour. You look at the clock and see that it says 6 o'clock in the afternoon. You recall that you first realised that the clock has stopped exactly three and a half hours ago.

What is the correct time now?

ANSWER:

24.8	Minutes allowed	**10**
	Time taken	
	Points gained	

REVOLUTIONARY GEAR

Four cogs are in constant mesh as shown. Cog A has 100 teeth, cog B has 50 teeth, cog C has 20 teeth, while the smallest cog has only 15 teeth.

How many revolutions will cog C have to make before all four cogs have returned to exactly the same position as they are in now?

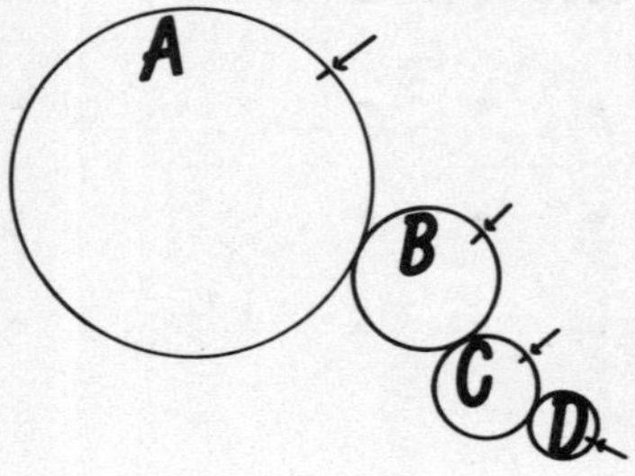

ANSWER:

24.9	Minutes allowed	10
	Time taken	
	Points gained	

A DOTTY PROBLEM

Look at this array of dots. How many squares of any size can be constructed from these dots where each corner of the squares rests on one of the dots in the array?

ANSWER:

24.10	Minutes allowed	12
	Time taken	
	Points gained	

LEAKY TANKER AGAIN!

A fire engine is travelling to a fire which is 45 miles away at a speed of 46mph. The engine holds 300 gallons of water but loses 150 gallons every hour through a small hole. They need 153 gallons to extinguish the fire.

Will they achieve their mission?

ANSWER:

24.11	Minutes allowed	10
	Time taken	
	Points gained	

NEW WORDS

Find the letter which can replace the third letter in each pair of words to create two new words. Place that letter in the brackets. When you have done this for all eight pairs of words you will discover an eight letter word reading downwards in the brackets. What is it?

CATTLE	( )	MARK
LEAD	( )	MOVED
THAN	( )	DRUNK
ARE	( )	DOPE
CODA	( )	RIB
FOUL	( )	COAL
READ	( )	BEST
RACE	( )	BAN

ANSWER:

24.12		
	Minutes allowed	**10**
	Time taken	
	Points gained	

TRAVEL TIME

The grid on the right represents a town plan with streets intersecting every half a mile. Four vehicles, A, B, C and D are travelling from one side of the town to another, following the routes indicated. A averaged 38mph, B averaged 25mph, C averaged 42mph and D averaged 49mph. Two of the vehicles arrived 'home' at exactly the same time. Which two were they, and how long did the journey take them?

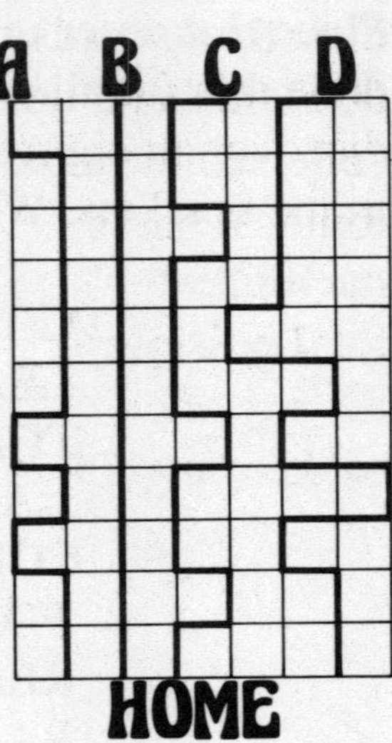

ANSWER:

24.13	Minutes allowed	12
	Time taken	
	Points gained	

PROFITABLE TRAVEL

En route from A to B you must travel from one square to any touching square, moving either directly upwards or to the right. When you have done this, add up all the numbers you have collected to find out the total for that particular route. What is the highest total possible for any one of the routes?

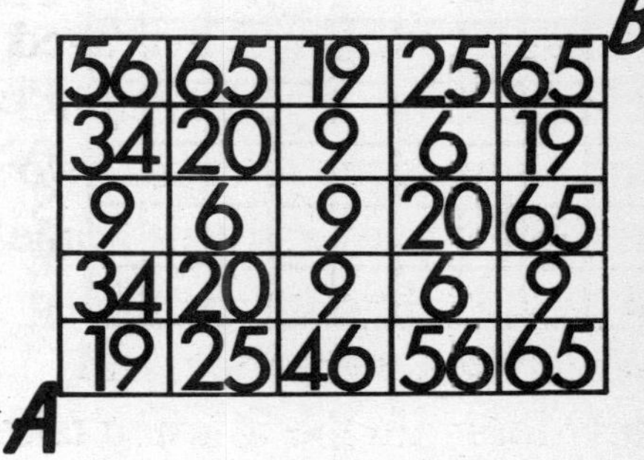

ANSWER:

24.14	Minutes allowed	15
	Time taken	
	Points gained	

DIY CROSSWORD

The words down and across are given below, but you must decide where the blank squares are.

S								S
		K						Y
				U				
S								R

```
INTER LEI     E R D
EAR GROPE     L I I
TOSS ARC      O C S
PEP PEER      P K U
STEM OFF      E S S
PEA SPRY          E
ASSUMES     A   A D
S   R   P   G   F
E   A   E   E   A
E   T   R   S   R
  S   S   O   F   O
  P   L   P   E   R
  R   A   T   E   E
  Y   T
```

24.15	Minutes allowed	30
	Time taken	
	Points gained	

SORTING PAIRS

The 28 numbers below belong to four distinct sets. Your problem is to sort them correctly. In each set there is a pair of 2-digit numbers and four functions of the pair, ie four results of arithmetic operations on the pair. Some numbers belong to more than one set, in such cases there will be duplicate copies of the functions. Your job is to discover the four original pairs of numbers. Here are the numbers and their four functions mixed and in rank order.

1,2,3,3,4,5,6,7,8,8,8

10,12,20,20,21,30,40,50,70,80

0.125, 0.3 recurring, 0.428571429, 0.8, 1.25, 2.3 recurring

ANSWER:

25.4	Minutes allowed	**20**
	Time taken	
	Points gained	

WHAT'S THE SENSE?

Following the same logic as for all the other segments, can you work out which number should replace the question mark?

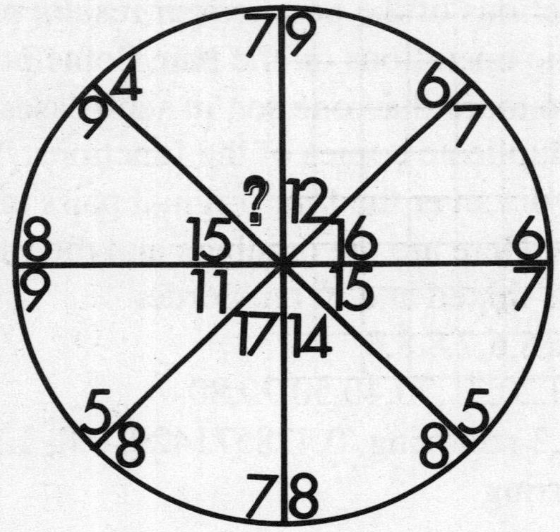

ANSWER:

25.5	Minutes allowed	12
	Time taken	
	Points gained	

REACH EIGHTEEN

The words down and across are given below, but you must decide where the blank squares are.

				O				W
U								
	X							T

UREA PESO
EXTROVERT
THESE SHE
TOO IMPEL
OVERTONES
BENT SOON

OBTRUSIVE
SWEETMEAT
ELOPE
ENSUE
OLEO
HOBO
TOTS
EASE
PUT
NEE

25.6	Minutes allowed	**30**
	Time taken	
	Points gained	

CODED KITCHEN TALK

Crack the code to reveal a well known saying:

AVV THUF JVVRZ ZWVPS AOL IYVAO

ANSWER:

25.7	Minutes allowed	15
	Time taken	
	Points gained	

BALANCING ACT

The top two sets of scales balance. How many of the third item are required to balance the third set?

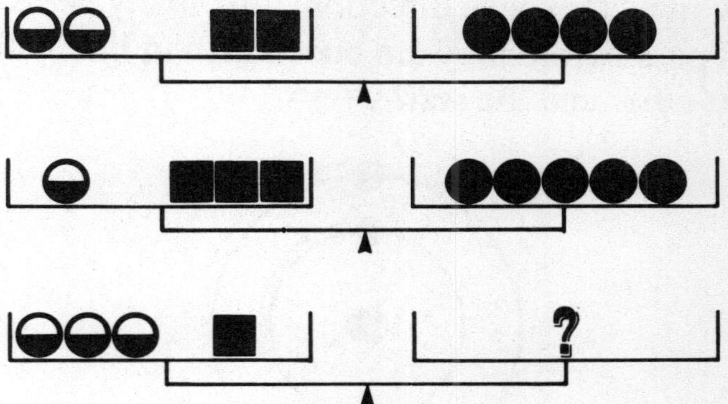

ANSWER:

25.8	Minutes allowed	5
	Time taken	
	Points gained	

ECLIPSE WATCH

Two planets are in orbit around the sun, as shown below. The inner planet takes eighteen years to complete one orbit, whilst the outer planet takes 45 years. If they both start moving now in a clockwise direction, how many years will pass before they are once again in line with each other and the sun?

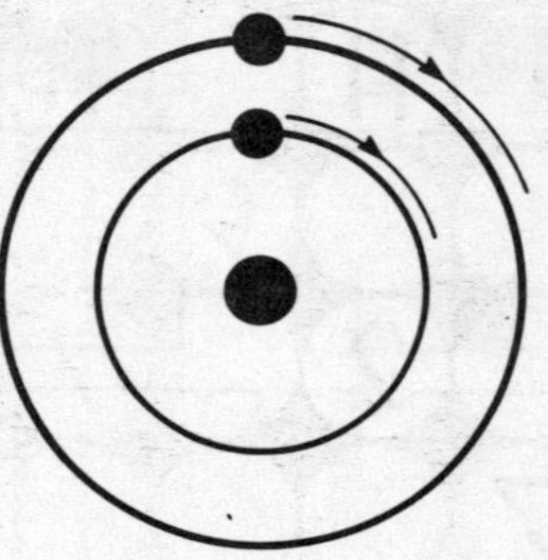

ANSWER:

25.9	Minutes allowed	10
	Time taken	
	Points gained	

SHOVE YA NUMBERS IN!

Complete the diagram below by placing one of the following numbers in each of the empty circles in such a way that each line vertically and horizontally totals 45. The numbers are:
11, 7, 7, 11, 7, 11, 18, 6, 2, 10, 10, 6, 2, 18, 11, 7

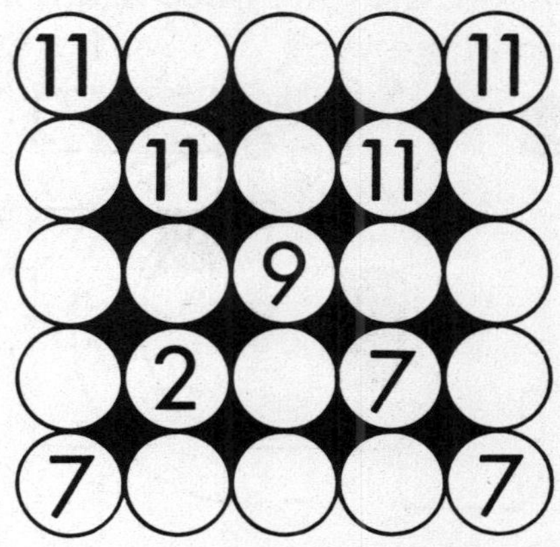

ANSWER:

25.10	Minutes allowed	12
	Time taken	
	Points gained	

T's TEASER

Using the black "T" shape, fill in the white area of the diagram below. How many T's are required in order that no gaps are left?

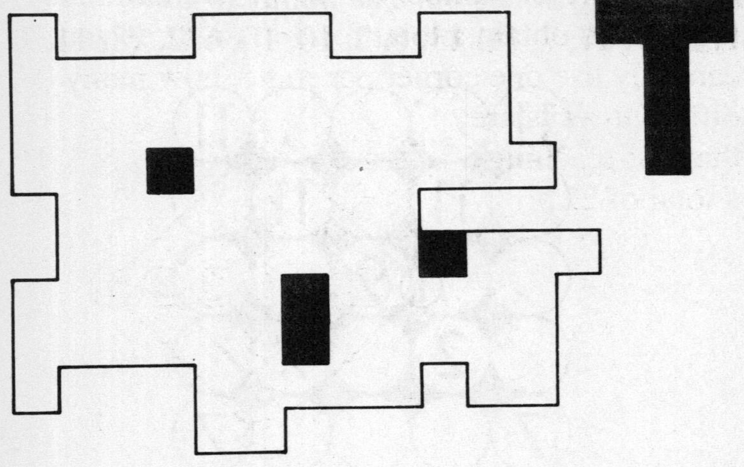

ANSWER:

25.11	Minutes allowed	12
	Time taken	
	Points gained	

SCORE A SCORE AND TWO

Start at any of the four corner numbers in this diagram, and work your way around the diagram following the black lines in such a way as to land on four further numbers. Add all five numbers together to obtain a total for that route. If you can only use one corner per route, how many different ways are there of reaching a total of 22?

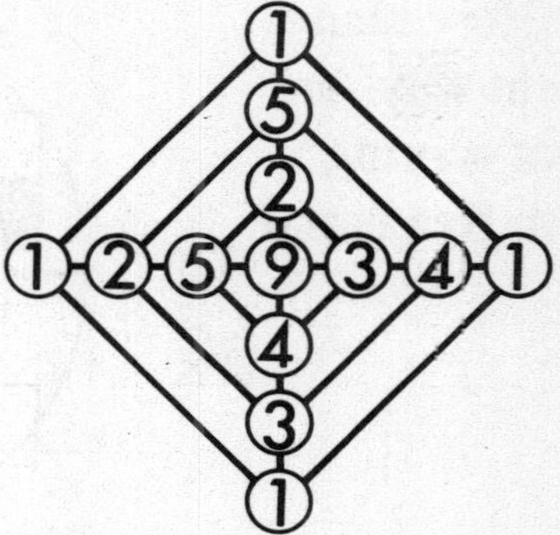

ANSWER:

25.12	Minutes allowed	12
	Time taken	
	Points gained	

MORE DART SCORES

This new darts game has a different boards and set of rules from traditional darts. You have five darts each go and must score 27 with the five darts. You can land in any segment any number of times, but once a combination of segments has been used you cannot use it again in a different order. How many different ways are there of scoring 27 with five darts?

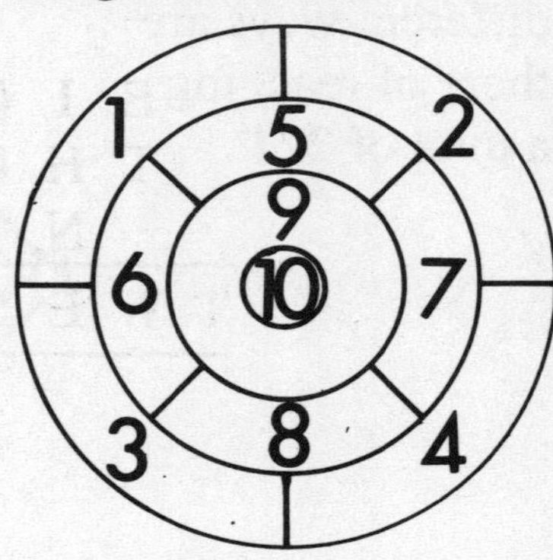

ANSWER:

25.13	Minutes allowed	**15**
	Time taken	
	Points gained	

AN AMBILOGICAL POSER

An ambilogical puzzle is logical in both ways, punlike. The letters below represent integer digits and the addition is correct in letters or their coded numbers. With the constraint that R = 2G, write down the equivalent of the sum in the hidden numerals.

```
  E I G H T
  T H R E E
    N I N E +
-----------
T W E N T Y
-----------
```

ANSWER:

25.14	Minutes allowed	15
	Time taken	
	Points gained	

DIY CROSSWORD

The words down and across are given below, but you must decide where the blank squares are.

V								
			B					
					M			
			N					
	X							

VOTED INN F R
EXCELLENT A E
ALP ENDUE V P
UNTO BEAT O R
FINANCIER U E
MERE ONCE R S
I T N C I E
R O U E T N
A N D L E T
T I E L
E C E A
N D B M
U O O E
T E N N

25.15	Minutes allowed	30
	Time taken	
	Points gained	

ANSWERS

	FOR CORRECT ANSWERS		
	Your Time	Time Allowed	Points Gained
25.1 The part of the flange of the wheel which is below the rail must be going backwards. The ever changing point at the bottom of the wheel which is in contact must be still (momentarily) but the flange itself is going backwards. The top of each wheel is travelling (momentarily) at twice the speed of the train.		5	
25.2 P. Top two letters minus bottom two letters = middle letter		12	
25.3 "This is an easy puzzle"		12	
25.4 These are the pairs of factors: 1,8; 2,6; 3,7; 4,5 Where the first of each pair is 'a' and the second is 'b' the operations were: 10a, 10b, a/b, b/a, ab		20	
25.5 13. Total of outer numbers in segment = inner number in segment two along anti-clockwise		12	
CARRIED FORWARD			

ANSWERS

FOR CORRECT ANSWERS

		Your Time	*Time Allowed*	*Points Gained*
	BROUGHT FORWARD			
25.6	(grid below)		30	
25.7	"Too many cooks spoil the broth"		15	
25.8	3 black circles		5	
25.9	15 years, on opposite sides of the sun		10	
25.10	11, 10, 11, 2, 11 10, 11, 11, 11, 2 11, 11, 9, 7, 7 6, 7, 7, 7, 18 7, 6, 7, 18, 7		12	
25.11	15 T's		12	
25.12	5 routes total 22		12	
25.13	102 ways		15	
	CARRIED FORWARD			

25.6

O	V	E	R	T	O	N	E	S
B		L		O		E		W
T	O	O		T	H	E	S	E
R		P	E	S	O			E
U	R	E	A		B	E	N	T
S			S	O	O	N		M
I	M	P	E	L		S	H	E
V		U		E		U		A
E	X	T	R	O	V	E	R	T

ANSWERS

		Your Time	*Time Allowed*	*Points Gained*
POINTS BROUGHT FORWARD				
25.14	8 5 2 9 1 1 9 4 8 8 3 5 3 8 1 0 8 3 1 7		15	
25.15	See below		30	
TOTAL POINTS GAINED				

FOR CORRECT ANSWERS

F	I	N	A	N	C	I	E	R
A	■	U	■	U	■	R	■	E
V	O	T	E	D	■	A	L	P
O	■	■	B	E	A	T	■	R
U	N	T	O	■	M	E	R	E
R	■	O	N	C	E	■	■	S
I	N	N	■	E	N	D	U	E
T	■	I	■	L	■	O	■	N
E	X	C	E	L	L	E	N	T

CHAPTER SUMMARY

Chapter Handicap Total:	
Correct Answers x 5 points:	
Chapter Total:	
Brought Forward:	
Running Total:	

CHAPTER TWENTY SIX

Target Time: 4 hours 5 minutes

CHOOSING INGOTS

The gold ingots in the Boldovian Republic are cylindrical and to exaggerate their apparent value they are hollow. Unfortunately they are exactly the size that a solid cylinder of aluminium of the same weight would have. The practice of gold plating aluminium cylinders so as to make counterfeit ingots has arisen. You are offered some mixed ingots very cheap as an 'on inspection' bargain. You know that some are fakes. You may handle them but not scratch or injure them in any way. The gold is too thick to give a hollow ring. How do you sort out the gold ones?

ANSWER:

26.1		
	Minutes allowed	15
	Time taken	
	Points gained	

TARGET PRACTICE

Place one of the following numbers into each of the spaces in the target below in such a way that each segment of three numbers adds up to 156, and each circle of eight numbers adds up to 416.

49, 49, 50, 50,
51, 51, 51, 51,
51, 51, 52, 52,
52, 52, 52, 52,
53, 53, 53, 53,
54, 54, 56, 56.

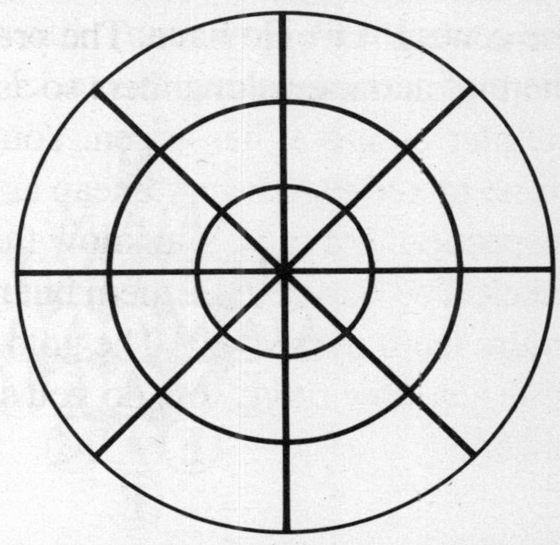

ANSWER:

26.2	Minutes allowed	15
	Time taken	
	Points gained	

HOW MANY GAMES?

Start at the central letter and make your way around the diagram from circle to touching circle. The object is to collect all the letters of the word "GAME" in any order, but always starting from the central "G". How many different ways are there of accomplishing this task?

ANSWER:

26.3	Minutes allowed	12
	Time taken	
	Points gained	

FILL IT

After a hard day at work you need a refreshing bath. The hot tap will fill the bath in 27 minutes, if the plug is in, and the cold tap will fill the bath in 29 minutes under the same circumstances. If the bath is full and the taps are off it will take exactly 16 minutes for the bath to empty once the plug is removed.

How long will it take the bath to fill if the plug is left out and both taps are turned on?

ANSWER:

26.4	Minutes allowed	15
	Time taken	
	Points gained	

DECODE 'EM

The following four words have had all their letters mixed up. Can you unscramble them and say what the four words are?

1. LATINSOODE

2. SICAGROU

3. AVERNEMUO

4. ASKMERACHL

ANSWER:

26.5	Minutes allowed	15
	Time taken	
	Points gained	

MORE THAN ONE WAY

How many different routes are there from A to B following the arrows?

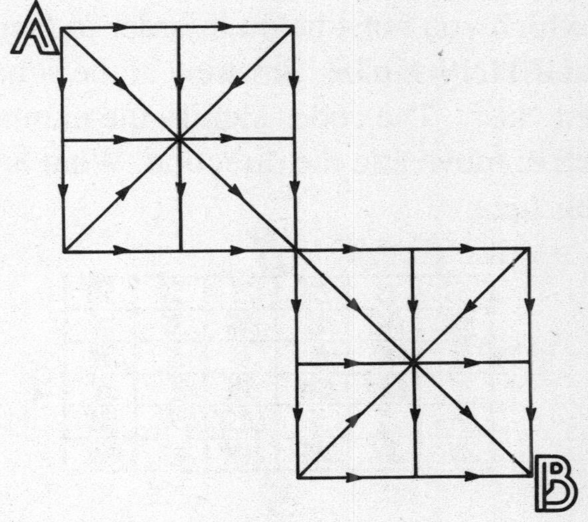

ANSWER:

26.6	Minutes allowed	20
	Time taken	
	Points gained	

HOW TO START

Obey the codes in each segment of the grid below, working backwards in order to find out which square is the "starting square", i.e. the one from which you must begin in order to land on each and every square, finishing at the square marked "last". The codes signify the number of squares to move and the direction. What is the starting square?

N

W

5S	1S	1SE	2S	5S	5W
1NE	1NE	4S	1NE	3S	4S
2E	1NE	1S	3S	1S	2N
3E	1NW	1SW	3N	1E	2N
3N	2E	3E	LAST	2N	5W
2N	2N	3NE	1NW	4N	4W

E

S

ANSWER:

26.7	Minutes allowed	15
	Time taken	
	Points gained	

FOUR CARS

Four cars are on their way home through a town in which the streets intersect every 3/4 mile. The route which each car followed is shown on the town plan on the right by a heavy black line. Car A travels at an average speed of 30mph, car B at 25mph, car C at 35mph and car D at 41mph. Which car will reach home first, and how far ahead of the second car will it be?

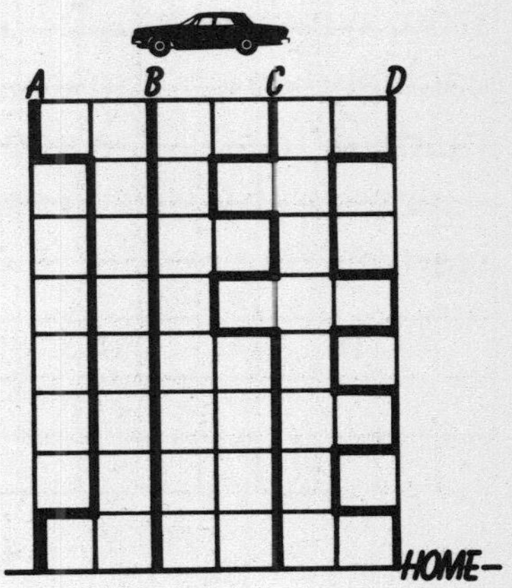

ANSWER:

26.8	Minutes allowed	12
	Time taken	
	Points gained	

DIY CROSSWORD

The words down and across are given below, but you must decide where the blank squares are.

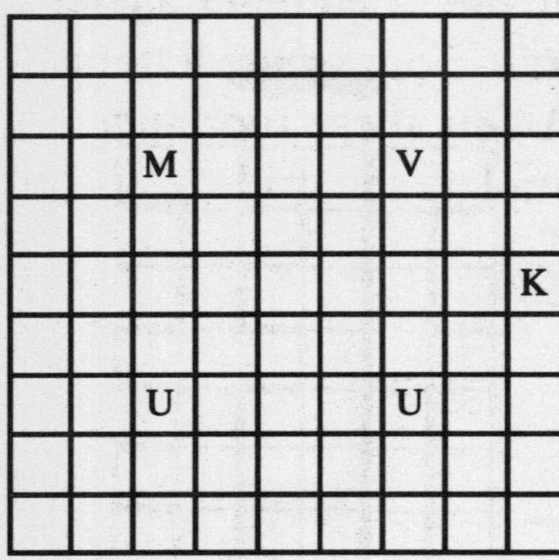

TREK ROSE SC
CATHARSIS LO
VIA AMUSE AL
LAMAS GNU CL
EAGERNESS KE
TAPE EASE NA
S S A P EG
T E L A SU
U V S I SE
N E O R
G R S A
U T T R
S A E E
E M M A

26.9	Minutes allowed	30
	Time taken	
	Points gained	

ZIGGURAT

Each horizontal line of squares in the grid below must contain a word, and each square in a vertical line must contain the same letter as the other squares in its column. Four of the letters used are S, E, P and D. Using these four and another three letters, complete the grid.

ANSWER:

26.10	Minutes allowed	6
	Time taken	
	Points gained	

SHRINK – GROW

Each horizontal line of circles must contain a word, and each circle in a vertical line must contain the same letter as other circles directly above or below it, i.e. this does not apply where there are gaps in the vertical line. Four of the letters are T, S, A and O. Complete the grid.

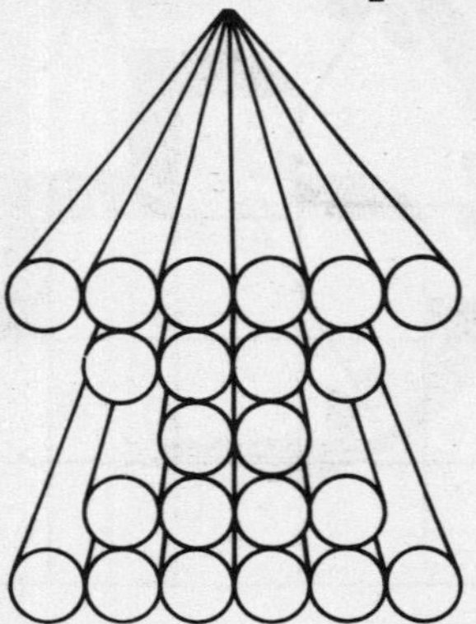

ANSWER:

26.11	Minutes allowed	15
	Time taken	
	Points gained	

THE INS AND OUTS OF IT

The outer numbers in the diagram have something to do with the inner numbers. Which number is missing from the inner set?

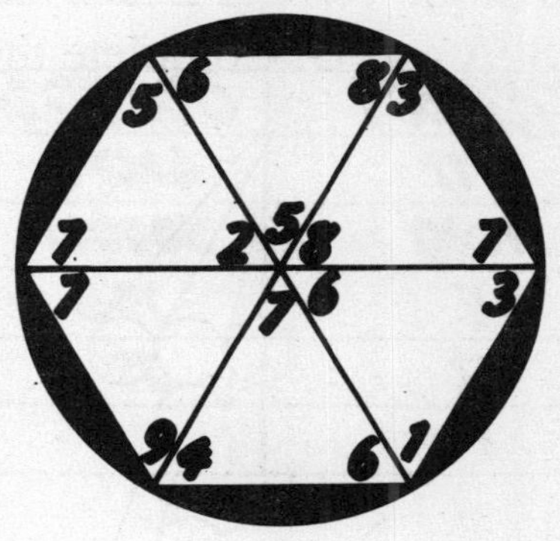

ANSWER:

26.12	Minutes allowed	10
	Time taken	
	Points gained	

WHAT IS THE RULE?

In this diagram you can see what a computer program has done to various numbers. What would the output be if the input were "1"?

INPUT	OUTPUT
111	6167·5
1000	500007
5	19·5
12	79
1	

ANSWER:

26.13	Minutes allowed	20
	Time taken	
	Points gained	

QUIZ

ANSWERS

1. What carries signals from the eye to the brain?
2. What is the name of the ship of the underwater explorer, Jacques Cousteau?
3. What type of tree yields conkers?
4. From which kind of wood was the 'Kon-Tiki' raft made?
5. What is a woofer?
6. What is a dipsomaniac?
7. What is the fruit of a rosebush called?
8. Is a spider an insect?
9. What is a baby eagle called?
10. What imaginary line encircles the earth?
11. How many wings has a bee?
12. What was the name of the mission that landed the first men on the moon?

26.14	Minutes allowed	15
	Time taken	
	Points gained	

DIY CROSSWORD

The words down and across are given below, but you must decide where the blank squares are.

								D
				A				
			O		T			
				P				
	K							

SEPARATOR D D
TIER OPEN E E
TARTS GAY S C
DESCRIBED T I
COT OKAPI R D
DODO ELAN O U
I S L R Y O
N A O O E U
G T O T R S
O E P A
T D A P
B A N I
A S T E
R P E R

26.15	Minutes allowed	30
	Time taken	
	Points gained	

ANSWERS

		FOR CORRECT ANSWERS *Your Time*	*Time Allowed*	*Points Gained*
26.1	The two cylinders will have different moments of inertia. You make a short slope on a smooth table or floor, roll the ingots down and choose those that roll furthest.		15	
26.2			15	
26.3	There are 13 ways		12	
26.4	1 hour, 50 min, 52 secs		15	
26.5	1. Desolation 2. Gracious 3. Manoeuvre 4. Ramshackle		15	
26.6	289 (hands up those who counted them, and those who multiplied 17 by 17)		20	
26.7	The starting square is the one marked '1NE' on the third row down		15	
		CARRIED FORWARD		

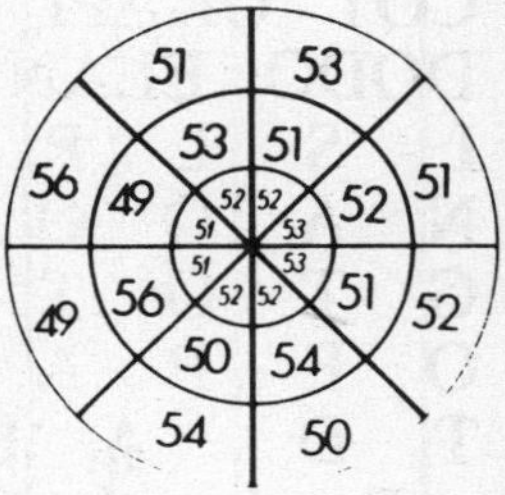

ANSWERS

	FOR CORRECT ANSWERS *Your Time*	*Time Allowed*	*Points Gained*
BROUGHT FORWARD			
26.8 Car B will arrive first, 36 seconds ahead of car A		12	
26.9 (crossword below)		30	
26.10 A / RAP / CRAPE / SCRAPED		6	
26.11 STORED / TORE / OR / CORN / ACORN		15	
26.12 **5.** Two outer numbers = twice inner number in opposite segment		10	
CARRIED FORWARD			

26.9

C	A	T	H	A	R	S	I	S
O	■	A	■	L	■	E	■	L
L	A	M	A	S	■	V	I	A
L	■	■	R	O	S	E	■	C
E	A	S	E	■	T	R	E	K
A	■	T	A	P	E	■	■	N
G	N	U	■	A	M	U	S	E
U	■	N	■	I	■	S	■	S
E	A	G	E	R	N	E	S	S

26.10

A
RAP
CRAPE
SCRAPED

26.11

STORED
TORE
OR
CORN
ACORN

ANSWERS

		FOR CORRECT ANSWERS		
		Your Time	*Time Allowed*	*Points Gained*
	POINTS BROUGHT FORWARD			
26.13	7.5 (Output = (Input x Input + 14) ÷ 2		20	
26.14	**1.** The optic nerve **2.** The Calypso **3.** The horse chestnut **4.** Balsa wood **5.** A low-frequency speaker **6.** An alcohol addict **7.** The hip **8.** No **9.** An eaglet **10.** The equator **11.** Four **12.** Apollo 11		15	
26.15	(crossword below)		30	
	TOTAL POINTS GAINED			

26.15

D	E	S	C	R	I	B	E	D
E	■	A	■	O	■	A	■	E
C	O	T	■	T	A	R	T	S
I	■	E	L	A	N	■	■	T
D	O	D	O	■	T	I	E	R
U	■	■	O	P	E	N	■	O
O	K	A	P	I	■	G	A	Y
U	■	S	■	E	■	O	■	E
S	E	P	A	R	A	T	O	R

CHAPTER SUMMARY

Chapter Handicap Total:	
Correct Answers x 5 points:	
Chapter Total:	
Brought Forward:	
Running Total:	

CHAPTER TWENTY SEVEN

Target Time: 3 hours 13 minutes

TIME ZONES

Marjory was talking by telephone to Alfred:

Alfred:	I will have to check up and call you back. Where are you?
Marjory:	I may not tell you. I'll call you.
Alfred:	It is midnight here. What time zone are you in?
Marjory:	I cannot tell you. No one could.
Alfred:	Come on! You are not in space. On earth the time zones cover every point.
Marjory:	I am on earth, in one place, but I am not in a time zone, nor between two time zones.

Where is Marjory?

ANSWER:

27.1	Minutes allowed	10
	Time taken	
	Points gained	

WHERE ON EARTH?

Here are the outlines of five British counties. Match the letter with the county name.

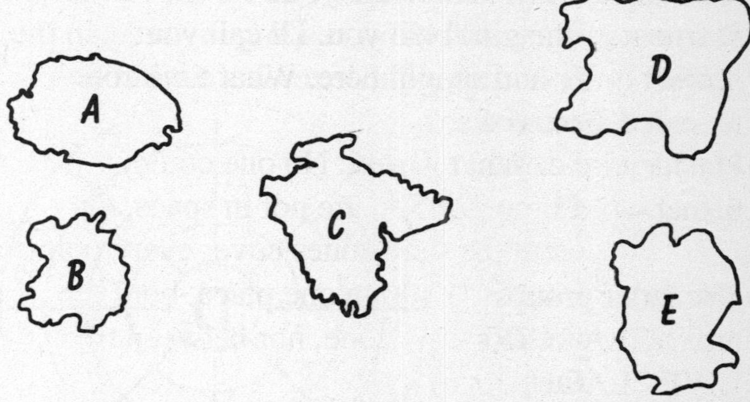

LINCOLNSHIRE NORFOLK SHROPSHIRE
DEVON GRAMPIAN

ANSWER:

27.2	Minutes allowed	15
	Time taken	
	Points gained	

UNSCRAMBLE

Unscramble the eight groups of four letters below so that when placed in front of the letter D they form eight five-letter words. Place each word in a segment of the grid below, reading inwards, in the correct order and an eight-letter word will be revealed around the outside circle. What is that word?

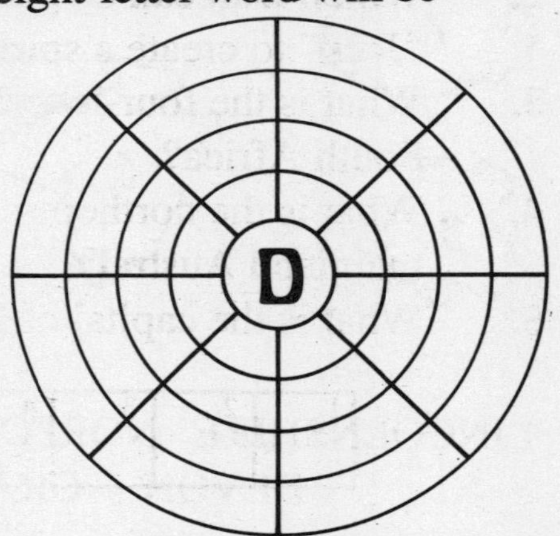

The letter groups are: NELA GIRI LIYE LAOU NOUF DINU NARB URNO

ANSWER:

27.3	Minutes allowed	12
	Time taken	
	Points gained	

A MONTH TO ANSWER

Answer the following questions and place the first letter of each answer in the respective squares in the grid below. What word is created?

1. Which planet is called the "Red Planet"?

2. Which fruit can be placed in front of "Jack" to create a spirit drink?

3. What is the four-lettered currency of South Africa?

4. What is the northernmost point of mainland Australia?

5. What is the capital of Finland?

1	2	3	4	5

ANSWER:

27.4	Minutes allowed	9
	Time taken	
	Points gained	

FIND THE WANDERERS

Starting at the bottom left hand "W" and working your way from square to touching square either upwards or to the right until you reach the top right hand "S", you will always land on nine squares. How many different routes will enable you to land on all the letters of the word "WANDERERS"?

ANSWER:

27.5		
	Minutes allowed	15
	Time taken	
	Points gained	

MORE FREEBIES

You have won a shopping spree in your local shopping arcade, which comprises 13 shops laid out as shown. Each circle represents a shop and the figure indicates the number of minutes you are allowed in that shop during your spree. You are permitted to visit a total of five shops, starting from, and only including, one corner shop. What is the maximum time that you can spend on your spree?

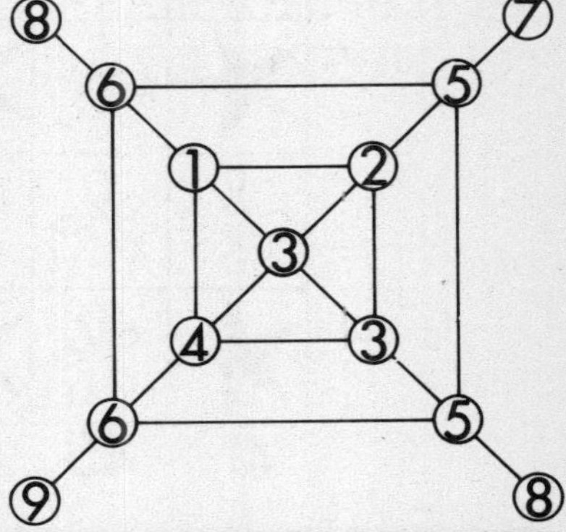

ANSWER:

<table>
<tr><td rowspan="3">27.6</td><td>Minutes allowed</td><td>6</td></tr>
<tr><td>Time taken</td><td></td></tr>
<tr><td>Points gained</td><td></td></tr>
</table>

SYMBOL SOLVE

Each like symbol in this diagram has the same value. The numbers next to the rows and columns represent the totals for the four shapes in that row or column. What is the missing total?

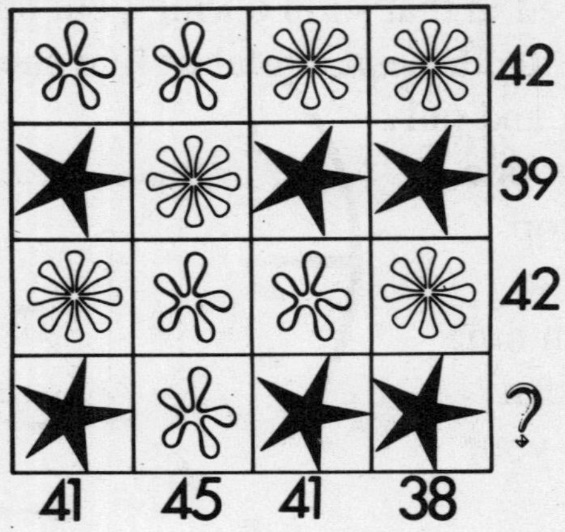

ANSWER:

27.7	Minutes allowed	6
	Time taken	
	Points gained	

NOT ANOTHER BOARD!

Here is a new-style dartboard, on which you must score 25 with three darts. You can land in any segment any number of times, but once a combination of three segments has been used it cannot be reused in a different order. How many ways are there of scoring 25?

ANSWER:

27.8	Minutes allowed	6
	Time taken	
	Points gained	

DIY CROSSWORD

The words down and across are given below, but you must decide where the blank squares are.

		K						
			L		E			
			A		T			
	Q							

ELSE EATS
RELIGIOUS
TRADE SUE
SIFT SIDE
EQUIPMENT
IRK AVERT

LIKED
ISSUE
OVA
ATOP
EMU
GUTS
REST
LEER
REINSTATE
SWEETMEAT

27.9	Minutes allowed	30
	Time taken	
	Points gained	

TWENTY FIVE

Each row and column of five numbers should total twenty five. Simply calculate the eight missing numbers, and add them together to obtain the answer to this puzzle.

6		5		6
	5	5		
6	5		3	2
4		3	3	7
	7	3	6	2

ANSWER:

27.10	Minutes allowed	6
	Time taken	
	Points gained	

MAKE OR BREAK

Which of the cubes, A to F, can be constructed from the flattened out cube shown?

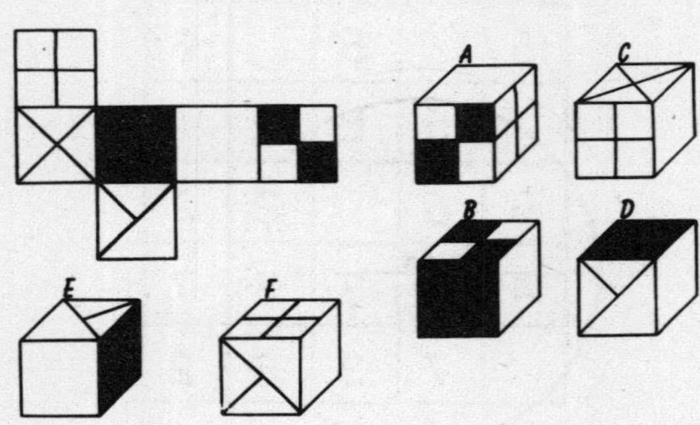

ANSWER:

27.11	Minutes allowed	12
	Time taken	
	Points gained	

ROUND FIELD

You have a field which is circular and has a radius of 5km. You want to place a rope around the field which is 100 metres out from the edge all the way round. How long will the rope have to be?

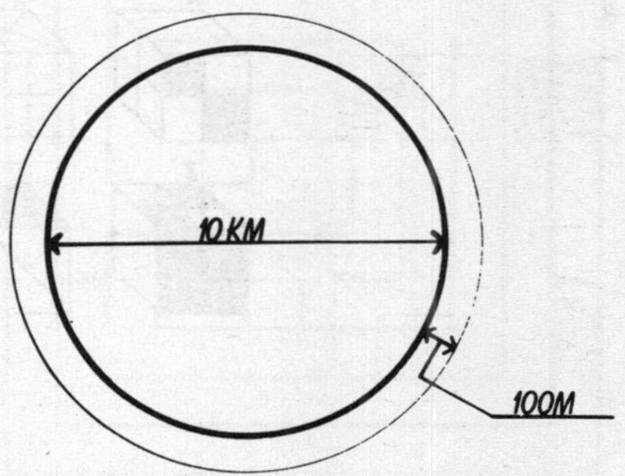

ANSWER:

27.12	Minutes allowed	15
	Time taken	
	Points gained	

2-WAY MAZE

Which two entries will allow you to take routes that will lead you to the centre of the maze?

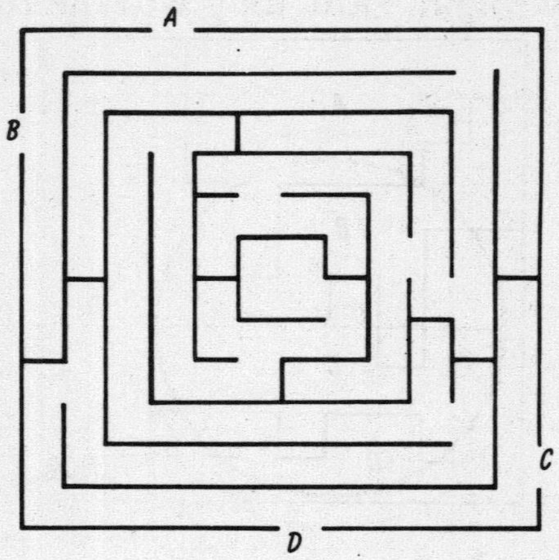

ANSWER:

27.13	Minutes allowed	3
	Time taken	
	Points gained	

SAME SPACE

There are two pairs of shapes of equal area in the diagram below. What are the two pairs?

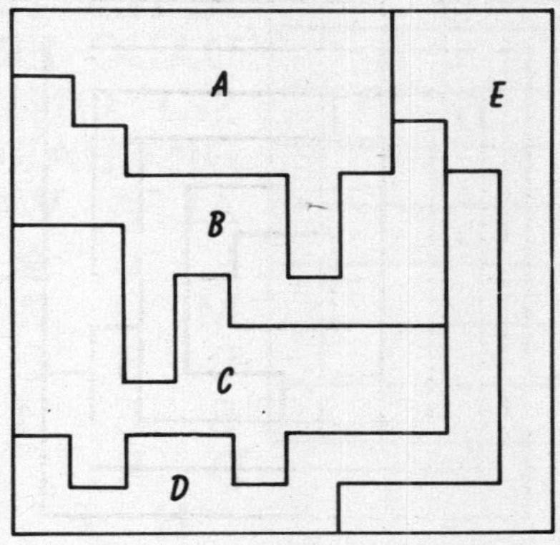

ANSWER:

27.14	Minutes allowed	18
	Time taken	
	Points gained	

DIY CROSSWORD

The words down and across are given below, but you must decide where the blank squares are.

W								
			R		O			
			D		D			

WEIRDNESS S W
ALTER DAB E I
DADO ERGO R D
SKI OTHER I O
DISCHARGE A W
ALFA WADI L H
I L A L I O
M O R O S O
B S C A E D
E E H D
D R D R
H E R I
A F A D
S T G E

27.15	Minutes allowed	30
	Time taken	
	Points gained	

ANSWERS

		FOR CORRECT ANSWERS		
		Your Time	*Time Allowed*	*Points Gained*
27.1	Marjory was exactly at the North Pole, where all the time zones meet. She was neither in a *single* time zone nor *between two* but in *all* of them. In practice, GMT prevails at the poles.		10	
27.2	A = Norfolk B = Shropshire C = Devon, D = Grampian E = Lincolnshire		15	
27.3	FEBRUARY (Found, Eland, Brand, Rigid, Undid, Aloud, Round, Yield)		12	
27.4	MARCH (Mars, Apple, Rand, Cape York, Helsinki)		9	
27.5	There are 6 routes by which you can collect all the letters of "Wanderers"		15	
27.6	31 minutes		6	
27.7	42		6	
27.8	There are 6 ways of scoring 25		6	
		CARRIED FORWARD		

ANSWERS

		FOR CORRECT ANSWERS		
		Your Time	*Time Allowed*	*Points Gained*
	BROUGHT FORWARD			
27.9	(grid below)		30	
27.10	47		6	
27.11	A, D and E		12	
27.12	31.73 km		15	
27.13	D and C		3	
27.14	B and C; D and E		18	
27.15	See overleaf			

27.9

R	E	L	I	G	I	O	U	S
E	■	I	■	U	■	V	■	W
I	R	K	■	T	R	A	D	E
N	■	E	L	S	E	■	■	E
S	I	D	E	■	S	I	F	T
T	■	■	E	A	T	S	■	M
A	V	E	R	T	■	S	U	E
T	■	M	■	O	■	U	■	A
E	Q	U	I	P	M	E	N	T

ANSWERS

	FOR CORRECT ANSWERS		
	Your Time	*Time Allowed*	*Points Gained*
POINTS BROUGHT FORWARD			
27.15 Answer below		30	
TOTAL POINTS GAINED			

CHAPTER SUMMARY

Chapter Handicap Total:	
Correct Answers x 5 points:	
Chapter Total:	
Brought Forward:	
Running Total:	

CHAPTER TWENTY EIGHT

Target Time: 4 hours 25 minutes

WALK IN FREE FALL

You are in free fall orbit in a large chamber as shown. The walls are of iron except the one at the bottom of the illustration. You have to walk with your magnetic boots from corner A to corner B, by the shortest route where your boots can hold to the surface. How long is your magnetic stroll?

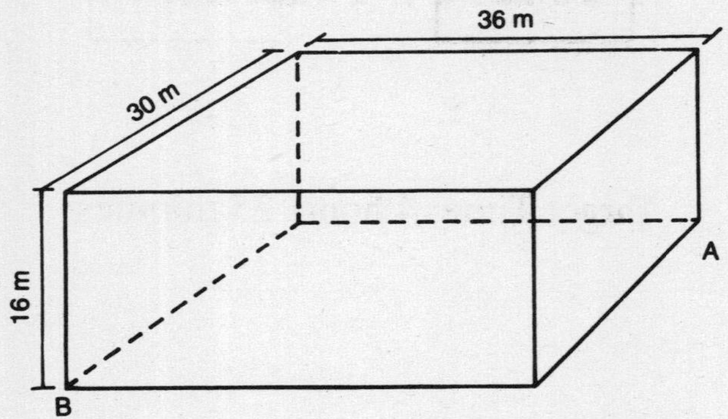

ANSWER:

28.1	Minutes allowed	15
	Time taken	
	Points gained	

TWO VIEWS

Here are two elevations of the same object. Draw the plan.

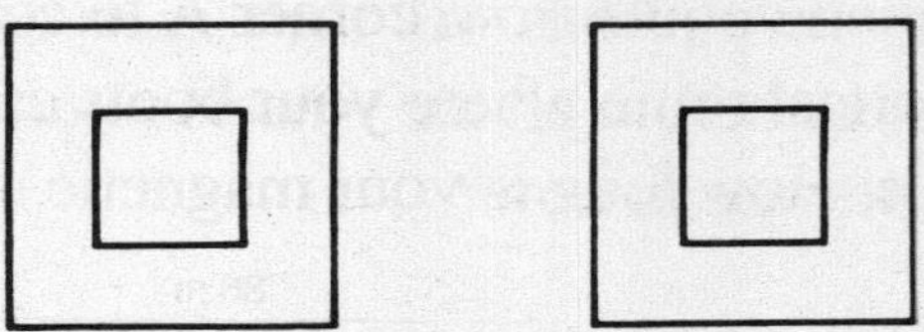

ANSWER:

28.2	Minutes allowed	10
	Time taken	
	Points gained	

COGITATE IN GEAR

Four cog wheels are in constant mesh as shown in the diagram. Cog A has 80 teeth, cog B 40 teeth, cog C 25 teeth and cog D, the smallest, 12 teeth. How many revolutions will the largest cog wheel have to make before all the wheels return to the position they are in now?

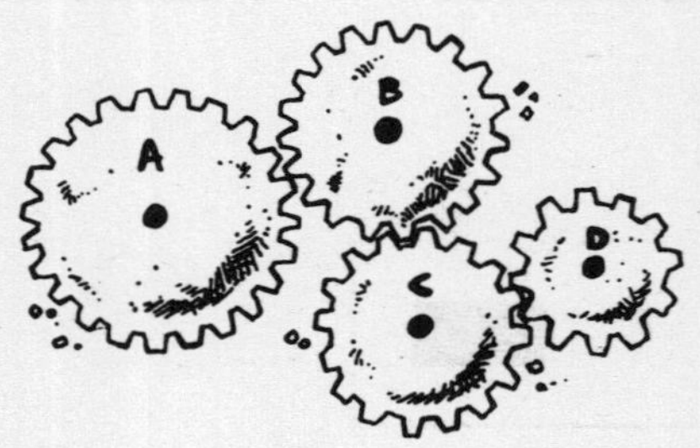

ANSWER:

28.3	Minutes allowed	15
	Time taken	
	Points gained	

FIT THE BLACK

How many times will the black shape on the right fit into the white area (ie excluding the black rectangle) in the diagram below, so as to completely fill it?

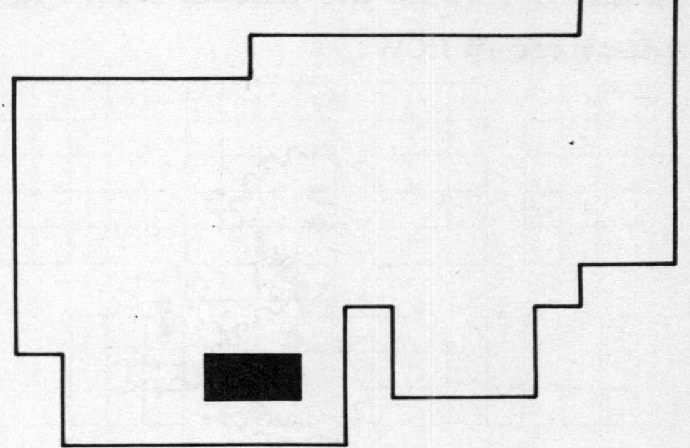

ANSWER:

28.4	Minutes allowed	15
	Time taken	
	Points gained	

MAKE-UP

All of the larger shapes numbered 1 to 4 can be created using a combination of shapes A to F. The smaller shapes may be used a maximum of twice each in forming each of the larger shapes. Which smaller shapes are used to form each of the larger shapes?

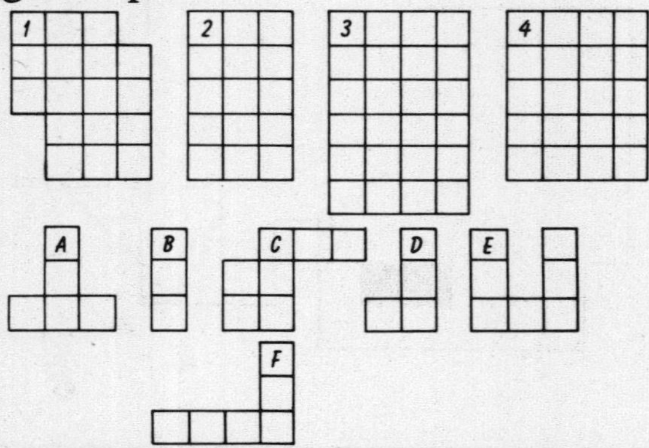

ANSWER:

28.5	Minutes allowed	12
	Time taken	
	Points gained	

SPIDER PUZZLE

A trainee web maker at the St John the Arachnid College of Higher Education has come up with this effort. He now, as part of his final exam, has to work out how many ways there are of travelling from A to B following the arrows. What is the answer?

ANSWER:

28.6	Minutes allowed	24
	Time taken	
	Points gained	

A HUNDRED LINES

Place each of the following numbers into the circles in the diagram in such a way that each row and clumn of five numbers has a total of 100. The numbers to use are:
21, 8, 19, 20, 5,
21, 21, 22, 35,
19, 37, 4, 19, 21,
8, 17, 18, 23, 19,
19, 21, 32, 19,
21 and 31.

ANSWER:

28.7	Minutes allowed	15
	Time taken	
	Points gained	

FIND THE SENTENCE

This diagram presents a code written in a clockwise direction, starting with the highlighted circle. What does it read?

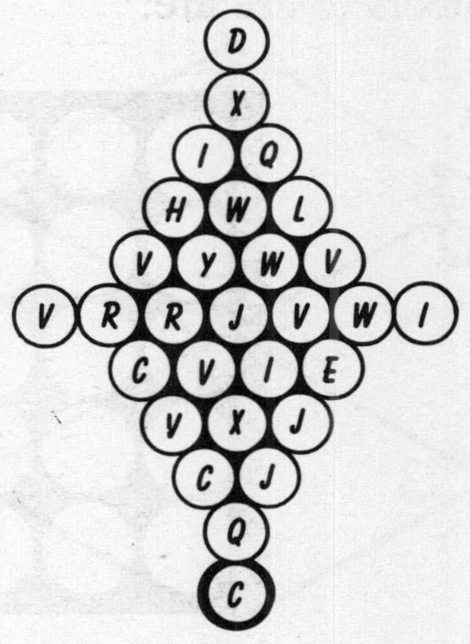

ANSWER:

28.8	Minutes allowed	15
	Time taken	
	Points gained	

LOGIC LINKS

Work out the logic that links all of the segments in the diagram and thus work out what should replace the question mark.

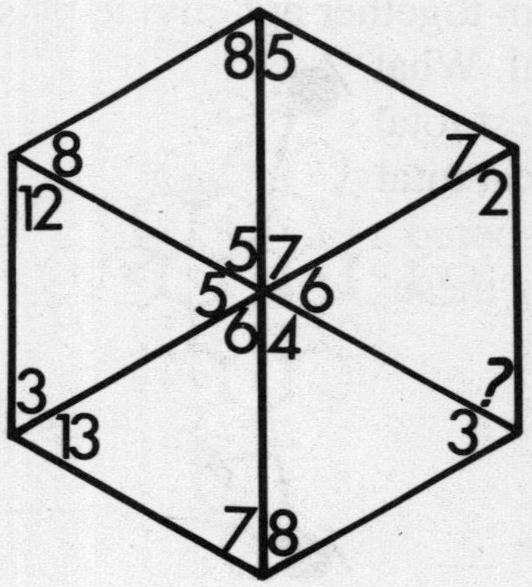

ANSWER:

28.9	Minutes allowed	30
	Time taken	
	Points gained	

HIGH LOW

Starting from one of the corners and following the thin black lines you must collect 5 numbers. Only one corner can be included and you cannot retrace your steps. Having collected 5 numbers you add them together and divide by seven to obtain a total. What are the highest total and the lowest total that can be scored by following these instructions?

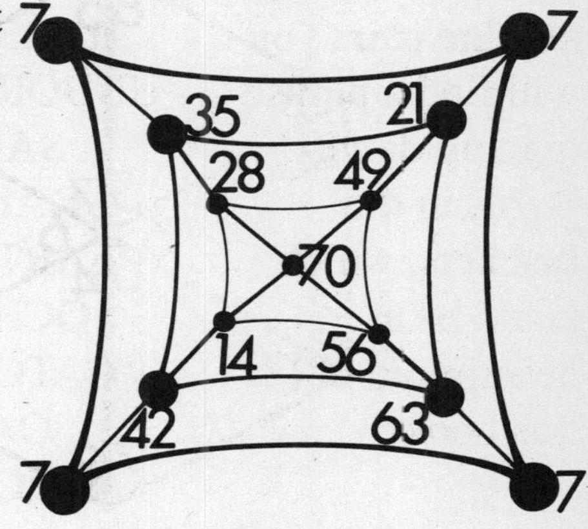

ANSWER:

28.10	Minutes allowed	21
	Time taken	
	Points gained	

HIDDEN THEME

For each pair of words find the letter which can replace the intitial letter in the left hand word and also be inserted before the right hand word. Place that letter in the brackets, and when you have done this for all nine pairs you will find a phrase reading downwards in the brackets, which could be a description of this book!

HARSH	( )	ARCH
UNBORN	( )	ON
SAIL	( )	ONE
RAFT	( )	ANGER
EARTH	( )	LOVE
OCHE	( )	CUTE
CATCH	( )	ORAL
OAT	( )	LAND
MUCH	( )	ABLE

ANSWER:

28.11	Minutes allowed	15
	Time taken	
	Points gained	

SPEED QUIZ

ANSWERS

1. What is the voltage of most car batteries?
2. Does Uranus have rings?
3. Which sense is most closely linked to memory?
4. What is it impossible to keep open if you sneeze?
5. What is meant by hirsute?
6. Which constellation contains the stars Castor and Pollux?
7. Which season begins with the vernal equinox?
8. What is a limestone pillar rising from the floor of a cave called?
9. What is the hardest gem?
10. Of which family of trees is the sycamore a member?
11. Who invented the railway sleeping car in 1859?
12. What is the name of the South American ostrich-like bird?

28.12	Minutes allowed	15
	Time taken	
	Points gained	

MAKE IT ADD UP

Place one of the following numbers into each vacant square in the diagram, so that each line of five numbers totals 55. The numbers to use are: 22, 22, 16, 16, 15, 15, 11, 6, 6, 5, 5, 2 and 2.

		16		16
		16	16	
16	16			6
	6	6		
6		6		6

ANSWER:

28.13	Minutes allowed	15
	Time taken	
	Points gained	

LAND, SLIP

Starting at the central 'S' on each occasion move from circle to touching circle in order to land on each of the letters of the word SLIP. On each move you can only land on four letters, including the intitial S, but the order of the other three letters is unimportant. How many different ways are there of landing on all of the letters of the word SLIP?

ANSWER:

28.14	Minutes allowed	18
	Time taken	
	Points gained	

DIY CROSSWORD

The words down and across are given below, but you must decide where the blank squares are.

W								
			R		O			
			D		D			

ERA RIDES
FARMSTEAD
EVIL BOYO
ARCHED RAP
DESPERATE
LOGO LISP

OPERA ROPEY ILLS IDLE SARI VOLE HIS END FIREBRAND DISLOCATE

28.15	Minutes allowed	30
	Time taken	
	Points gained	

ANSWERS

		FOR CORRECT ANSWERS *Your Time*	*Time Allowed*	*Points Gained*
28.1	The chamber when opened up would look like the drawing below, and you would follow the path shown. Using Pythagoras the distance is the square root of $(36+16)^2 + (30+16)^2$ = 69.426219 metres		15	
28.2	There are two possibilities. The best answer is both, giving a bonus point, but either will do.		10	

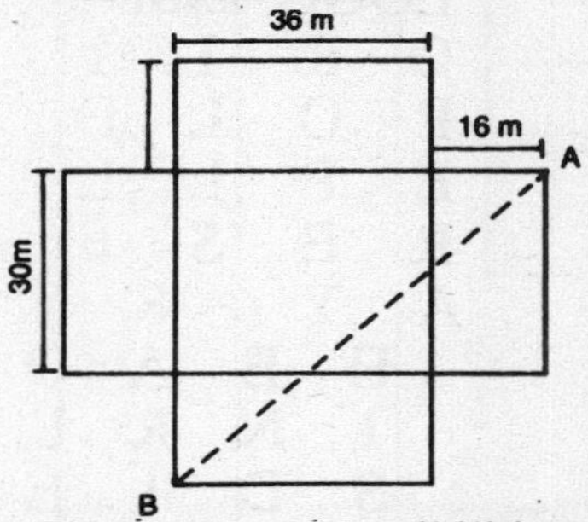

CARRIED FORWARD

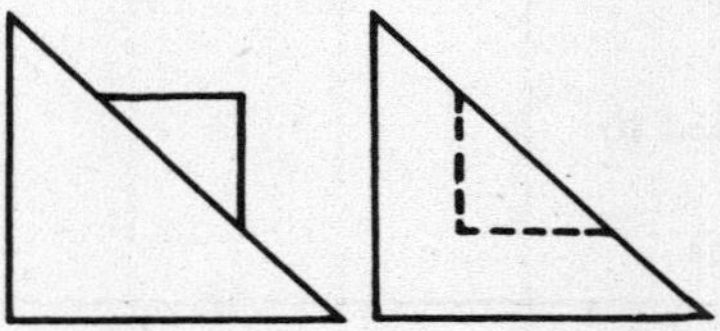

ANSWERS

		FOR CORRECT ANSWERS *Your Time*	*Time Allowed*	*Points Gained*
	BROUGHT FORWARD			
28.3	15 revolutions		15	
28.4	17 times		15	
28.5	**1.** D, E and F **2.** A, B and E **3.** A, B, B, E and F **4.** B, C, D and F		12	
28.6	There are 17 routes		24	
28.7	21 31 21 04 23 32 21 21 21 05 22 21 20 19 18 08 19 19 19 35 17 08 19 37 19		15	
28.8	"Mensa members have the biggest"		15	
28.9	The missing figure is 13. The two numbers on the leading edge of each segment, reading anti-clockwise, are totalled to give the remaining figure in the segment two ahead		30	
	CARRIED FORWARD			

ANSWERS

		FOR CORRECT ANSWERS *Your Time*	*Time Allowed*	*Points Gained*
	BROUGHT FORWARD			
28.10	The highest possible total is 35, the lowest is 15		21	
28.11	"MIND GAMES"		15	
28.12	**1.** Twelve volts **2.** Yes **3.** Smell **4.** The eyes **5.** Hairy **6.** Gemini **7.** Spring **8.** Stalagmite **9.** Diamond **10.** The maple family **11.** George M. Pullman **12.** Rhea		15	
28.13	16 2 16 5 16 2 16 16 16 5 16 16 11 6 6 15 6 6 6 22 6 15 6 22 6		15	
28.14	There are 10 routes		18	
28.15	See answer overleaf			
	CARRIED FORWARD			

ANSWERS

		FOR CORRECT ANSWERS *Your Time*	*Time Allowed*	*Points Gained*
	POINTS BROUGHT FORWARD			
28.15	Answer below		30	
	TOTAL POINTS GAINED			

F	A	R	M	S	T	E	A	D
I	■	O	■	A	■	N	■	I
R	A	P	■	R	I	D	E	S
E	■	E	V	I	L	■	■	L
B	O	Y	O	■	L	O	G	O
R	■	■	L	I	S	P	■	C
A	C	H	E	D	■	E	R	A
N	■	I	■	L	■	R	■	T
D	E	S	P	E	R	A	T	E

CHAPTER SUMMARY

Chapter Handicap Total:

Correct Answers x 5 points:

Chapter Total:

Brought Forward:

Running Total:

Don’t

Ha

ISBN paperback 978-1-9196515-0-7
ISBN eBook 978-1-9196515-1-4

Edited by Nicola Lovick and Fiona Unwin
Cover design by Rob Briggs at Roarr Design

Dedicated to Dick and John for reminding us all how lucky we are.

Acknowledgments

So much goes into writing a novel and publishing it leaving so many people to thank. I thank you all. From friends and family who support me daily to the stranger on the street whose smile made my day on one of those downer days when I question everything that I am doing and didn't think I could ever complete the book. There are, of course, some people who stand out and therefore require personal mentions.

I would like to thank my editor, Nicola, for her patience, her hard work and her encouragement throughout; to Rob for completely blowing me away with his cover designs; to my Beta readers, Kathy and Rachel, for being the first to set eyes on my work and for loving it genuinely with constructive feedback; to Fiona for backing me and encouraging others to as well; to my bosses Hugo and Martin for stocking copies, organising a signing and asking me to stay working for them even if I make it big; to Dad for urging me to go it alone, that it'll be better and more fun; to Mum for taking pride in all that I do; to Mike for upping my ego and telling me often how much Kathy enjoyed 'It's alright Jack'; to the Dillons for letting me treat their house like a home and allowing me to make the most of its calming comforts;

to colleagues and friends for listening; to the customers of New Moulton Stores for keeping the momentum going; to my dog, Arkley, for lying on my lap forcing a break from the laptop occasionally; to my siblings for always listening and for fully supporting rather than questioning my dreams; to Grandad for always asking and being thoughtful and interested; to my dedications, Dick and John, for truly teaching me the meaning of life, to enjoy every moment and each opportunity, remembering that we are so lucky.

Don't Tell Jack

BREAKING POINT

'Jack, Erin!' Mary shouted from the kitchen and heard no sound. 'Come on, guys, you're going to be late!' Still nothing came in reply from either of her children. 'Again,' she added, swearing under her breath. 'Don't make me come up there!'

The turbulence in her mind left Mary extremely short-tempered. Both children knew this, but were also used to it. Every command from their mother, especially when trying to hurry them up for the school day which neither child was too fussed about, went straight over their heads.

She perpetually felt hard done by for the life she had been handed and frequently questioned, when alone, why it had been given to her. *I've done nothing wrong. Hardly sinned. I don't understand,* she always thought. Her children were the two blessings that helped her hold it all together via the thinnest of threads.

'Ouch!' Mary screamed, as she held the remaining piece of ceramic in her hand, the rest of the plate shattered on the kitchen floor. She noticed blood dripping from her left hand. The plate dropped at her feet and smashed into small pieces. It happened so fast yet so slow she felt that she wasn't really in the moment. 'Get out!' she screamed at Flo who came running in to see what the loud noise was about. She was a typically loyal Labrador, always striving to protect her owners. Mary closed the door to the kitchen so that Flo didn't stand on any broken porcelain, creating more blood for Mary to clear up.

'Even that doesn't get you moving!' she screamed up the staircase to her children once more. Her anger towards her offspring increased. 'That's it. I. AM. DONE.' She threw a second plate at the wall, at which point she spotted eleven-year-old Jack peeping in through the kitchen door that was now slightly ajar. He didn't speak. 'And what are you looking at? Come and help me clear this mess up!' Mary screeched as he ran back upstairs and into his room.

'Hello? Hello?' Eileen arrived on cue, letting herself in through the front door. She spoke as if on a telephone call with a cold caller. She edged in slowly and angled herself so that she could see into the kitchen. She had been here many times before, so she showed no reaction to the scene before her. 'All OK here?'

'Argh, I forgot you were visiting. Hello.'

Eileen could sense the angst in Mary's voice. She was familiar with Mary's temperament, patience stretched as tight as cheese wire, but this was something else, something hidden deep down. Mary stood, head down, tears falling. She was holding her hand to cover up the blood but it was dripping faster now that no disguise was sufficient and Eileen saw.

'Here, come. Sit down. Let's get that hand tended to.'

'But the children. They need their lunches. They need breakfast. I have to get them to school.'

'I'll take care of all of that. You, my dear, need to start taking care of you.'

'That can wait.'

'No, clearly,' Eileen said, gesturing at the mess of the kitchen; the smashed plates, the blood and the tears, 'it can't.'

Mary said nothing as Eileen came back from the first aid cupboard with a bandage for her hand, ensuring no tiny pieces of ceramic were embedded in Mary's skin.

'There. That should hold it together for a bit longer! You sit down. Take a seat and I'll sort this mess out. If the kids are a little late to school, what odds? I will make their lunches. Sure, it looks as though you've made a pretty good start. I'll put on the kettle. You're going nowhere today.'

While Mary was unable to respond and her inner emotions were too mixed up to fathom, she appreciated Eileen's directness and assistance. She loved her warmth; felt it was as close she could ever get to maternal love. The closest thing she'd had to it since she was thirteen. For so long she had been in control; organising everything and taking care of everyone around her. But now she had reached her limit and was grateful beyond measure for Eileen stepping in.

Then it started again. For a moment she was peaceful. A split millisecond. It didn't last long and then the guilt filled her that she couldn't even say a simple *thank you* to her auntie. It consumed her so much that no other thought could get in. This happened all the time. Mary had no control. Absolutely none at all.

Eileen swept the mess away, physically and otherwise, while Mary tried to enjoy her cup of tea, thankful that she had cut her left hand and therefore her right hand was strong enough to hold the mug.

As Eileen swept, her mind raced. Something needed to be done, and fast. She worried about the children, but also for Mary. And the problem rested on her shoulders alone. She knew she had to take it on. It wasn't that her brother, Séan, didn't care; he was frightened about what would happen if they stepped in to do something and frightened about what would happen if they didn't.

Shouting over, Erin descended the stairs and Jack followed shortly after, both taking each step watchfully. They were very used to these scenes, but they never got less frightening.

'Hi, Auntie Eileen!' Erin said running to her for a hug but stopping before she got to the kitchen, sensing the tension within the house.

'Oh, hello there, pet.'

'What are you doing here, Auntie Eileen?' asked Jack, curiosity winning over timidity.

'Now, you two go back upstairs and get ready for school. You have the pleasure of me taking you in today. Isn't that exciting!' Eileen said, forcing a smile, desperately trying to lift the mood of the household for everyone's sake.

'OK,' Jack and Erin replied in unison. Eileen was pleased. Jack's response indicated that her calmness had brushed off on him.

Once the smashed crockery had been swept up, Mary's hand tended to and packed lunches made, Eileen piled the children into the car with toast to go.

She returned to the house briefly to check on Mary who was now in an upright foetal position, rocking backwards and forwards and wailing. She went over tiptoeing so not to make Mary jump, who probably thought she was alone in the house, and gently touched her shoulder. Mary didn't flinch.

'I think it's about time we got you some help, don't you think? Like proper, long-term help.' Eileen suggested in her non-negotiable manner.

Mary nodded.

Eileen drove to school putting up with tunes from Ariana Grande the whole way. Erin was more dominant in her choice of music and the stress of the morning had left Jack silent so Eileen went with it. She kept looking to her left at Erin sat silently during the drive. This was a concern because whenever music played, Erin sang along to it especially if it was solely her choice of music. That was when she was happy, Erin was always happy.

'I'm pretty worried about Mum, Auntie Eileen. Is she going to be ok?' Erin asked, feeling Eileen's weighted gaze watching over her.

'Oh sure, she'll be grand,' Eileen replied with confidence and placed her left hand affectionately on Erin's knee while driving with the other. She subtly glanced up into the rear-view mirror to check on Jack who was staring emptily at herself and Erin. She knew inside his mind would be full of thoughts, but she had no way of finding out what these were.

'But her hand? It was all bandaged up?'

Eileen had hoped that the mess of the kitchen had deterred the children's view of the state in which their mother was in.

'Her hand is fine. I helped her dress it so it will heal in no time at all. Mummy was thinking of lots of things at once and she cut herself on a plate. That's all. There is nothing to worry about.'

'OK. If you say so.'

Erin's solemn tone made Eileen question whether she was doing right by the children bringing them to school but she knew she had no other option and in order to sort out her niece the children needed to be in the safe care of the school day.

'So, how're you feeling about school? Ready for the year ahead?' Eileen asked with so much optimism that she immediately regretted.

'I guess.'

Erin's response proved that it was inappropriate of Eileen to add to the stress of the morning.

'You've got a bright future ahead of you girl.'

'Thanks.'

'Seriously. From a young girl I have always known you will go far.'

Erin said nothing and looked the other way as if to hide her emotions. Eileen leant across and brushed her fingers through her hair. Again she looked up into the rear-view mirror and saw Jack starring at the scene in front of him. Not comfortably watching but rather observing them as if they were a horror film, scary thoughts filling his young mind.

'Are you OK there, Jack?'

Jack nodded. He could utter no words.

'Seriously, you two. Everything is going to be alright. I promise. And do I ever break my promises?' Eileen left it a few minutes to see if she would get any sort of response. 'No, no I don't.'

Once they arrived at the school gates, Eileen made a point of seeing the children in. She could feel the judgemental stares questioning where Mary was and why the crooked old Aunt was taking on the strenuous task of the school run. She could hear mutters under the breaths of the other mothers, yet she couldn't make out exactly what was being said. Her mind went into overdrive making up stories that she felt were pretty accurate predictions. They will know something had happened to mean that Mary's Aunt from Ireland was on the school run and not Mary. They weren't stupid, these school mums, and they weren't ever far away from all of the gossip.

'Right, you two. Be good now and don't you be worrying about a single thing. Like I say everything is going to be ok.' She said this quietly now that they were outside of the car and vulnerable to the onlookers' opinions. She let them both go into school, leaning on Erin and Jack for strength.

'OK, Auntie Eileen. If you say so!' Erin responded doubtfully and Jack continued to nod.

Eileen drove home; worried about what Mary might do in her absence, dreading what she might find, and worrying about what she had to do to sort this, doing best by everyone. When she spotted a tractor on a side road, she wished for it to pull out in front of her so that her journey would be slowed out of her control. She pulled up outside the house. She could see in through the window that Mary was slumped over the beaten wooden table, where she'd left her.

Eileen pulled out her mobile and dialled 111.

'Hello there. I was wondering if I could book an appointment at the psychiatric unit. Today. I am seriously concerned about my niece's wellbeing. I fear she is very much a danger to herself,' Eileen said, getting the buzz words in. She knew the system well now.

Mary had been under her GP's care for a long time now, but not a lot had changed. The therapy helped, as did the breathing techniques and medication, but Eileen felt that Mary needed more. They had always been told that if ever things escalated, 111 was the number to dial and with her records she should be able to get seen by a consultant fairly quickly.

'We would need the referral from your niece's GP?' came the professional box-ticking reply from the receptionist.

'Of course.'

'What would be best is to contact your niece's GP surgery, explain the situation to them and then they will contact us directly to move things along.'

'OK.'

Eileen remained in the car while she made the phone call. She could see Mary through the window and kept an eye on her, but she felt it best that Mary couldn't hear the conversations being had about her wellbeing. It felt inappropriate.

'It's just I live in Ireland you see and I know things are going to have to change but currently it is too much for the children to handle. I can come over and take care of them, that's not a problem. I just... I'm eighty-one, I don't think I can give Mary the care that she needs,' Eileen continued on the phone to the GP. She was pleased from the way that the conversation was heading that she had remained in the car.

'I completely understand. Knowing Mary's condition, I feel it might be best to get her proper short-term help while we arrange sufficient medication and therapy which can be sustained. Are you ok to bring her in to see me today?'

'Of course.'

Eileen felt a weight lift off her as she got out of the car and went in to comfort Mary.

'Hello darling,' she said as she sat beside her and brought her whole body in for a big hug. 'Still feeling the same? How's that hand?' She felt Mary nod against her, tears wetting her t-shirt. 'Look, I've been on the phone to your GP. We're going in to see him, OK? And we will go from there. I think what they are looking into is getting you some professional help for the time being while they review your medication and come up with a long-term treatment plan.'

'So, they are locking me away?'

'No! Not at all! Look, you and me both know that something more needs to be done to help you, right? It is only short-term. So that you can have a happier life in the long run. Work with me here, OK?'

'OK.'

Mary didn't have the energy to question Eileen's plan, nor did she have enough energy to thank her or be grateful. She didn't know how to feel. Weakly, she stood up straight and headed to the car. Little did they know that it would be over a year before Mary could return home.

'Mary Carter? This way please.'

'Hello there, both of you. I'm Michael McKeegan, and I am your consultant today. How can I help?' Dr McKeegan said in an Irish accent with such charm that Eileen, for a moment, forgot the nature of their appointment. That he was Irish was perfect because Mary always spoke about missing home and that a part of her belonged in Ireland. It also meant that Mary was more inclined to trust him. Eileen left it a while for Mary to respond, but, once she realised that Mary was in no fit state to do so, she took charge of the conversation.

'My niece Mary here has been through the mill. She hasn't had the best deal and in 2017 she began to lose it all together. I think that is fair to say, right Mary?'

Mary nodded. Eileen continued.

'She takes on everyone else's troubles and held the family together through the toughest of times. I think, to be fair, anyone would crumble. She has been under the care of her GP since 2017 and has been given both counselling and medication, which have helped. My concern is that she now needs more help. We have been to the GP before coming here, as you know, and he too feels that this is the most appropriate way forward for now.'

'I see. Mary, would you mind if I spoke with Eileen alone for one moment?'

Mary didn't respond.

'Mary? Would this be OK?'

'Yeah, sure,' Mary said, obviously not having heard the question and therefore remaining seated. She only cottoned on when he got up to open the door and then she promptly left the room, looking very confused.

'I felt it easier for you to express your concerns without Mary in the room. Often family members find that the best way to do this. Especially with patients as ill as Mary.'

'You can quite clearly see it, then?'

'Sadly, yes. She looks quite frail, I imagine she has lost a fair bit of weight?'

'Yes.'

'You can see in her face, how it falls that she isn't naturally this thin.'

'My biggest worry is the children now. I arrived early this morning from Dublin.'

'You don't live locally?'

'No. Dublin. I arrived early this morning to a complete mess in the house. Mary had totally lost it and was throwing plates and shouting. There was hardly any food in the cupboards to feed them all and the children's uniforms looked untidy as if they had come straight back out of the dirty laundry basket. She isn't thinking straight, this is so out of character. It isn't her fault, and I don't think she would ever hurt the children. I just fear she isn't fit to look after them. She isn't well enough to look after herself. She needs more help.'

'I see. I think that would be the best option.'

'Thank you.'

Dr McKeegan left the room to get Mary and Eileen felt a huge weight release from her shoulders, not realising how much she had been carrying for so long. She took the brief moment alone to gather herself, for Mary would need her support. As Mary walked back in, Eileen's heart broke.

'Now then, Mary. I have had a chat with your auntie, and we have come up with a plan that we feel will benefit all involved. We feel that until your medication needs have been reviewed, and your illness is under better control, it would be safer for all involved for you to stay at Cherry House hospital. Do you have any questions?'

Mary said nothing.

Eileen kissed Mary goodbye, knowing that she was also kissing goodbye to most of her freedom, for the time being. It was for the best. She truly believed that.

1

ERIN

Heads turned as if something was going on. A development in it all, but Erin had no idea what this was. Everyone began furtively taking out their phones. Away from Mr Turner's view, of course. He had a thing about phones and nobody could bear the longwinded speech that came after anyone was caught glancing at it during class. Even more so during revision sessions.

'Not only does it hinder concentration...' he would ramble on. He always backed his argument with a number of facts. It strengthened his point. Whether or not that fact was true, Erin was always unsure, but Mr Turner knew all about the power of backing points up with evidence.

Social media is bad for your mental and physical health.

It increases risk of heart disease.

Staring at phones all day can make your eyesight deteriorate faster. You may even end up blind one day.

These facts were on repeat in Mr Turner's classes as he fought the hopeless battle of teenagers and phones. Erin mostly thought he had a point during class, especially during the extra sessions he was putting on in the run up to the exam, but the amount he went on about the overall effect of mobiles, the internet and social media on a daily basis she felt was a bit much. It weakened the impact of his overarching message. The general mindset of everyone was that they weren't technically meant to be at school, they had left, the revision sessions were extra so the rules were theirs to make. Or break. Mr Turner and every other teacher would disagree, but the student's consensus was just that.

So far, somehow, nobody had been caught today, but everyone was sneaking a peek and Erin was yet to receive whatever text or notification it was that everyone else was simultaneously opening. Most reacted with a gasp, though subtle, to keep Mr Turner's eyes away. A gasp in horror or total disbelief.

While looking around the classroom at everyone's reactions and figuring out how she could check her phone without Mr Turner seeing her, she noticed he too was distracted from Steinbeck's *Of Mice and Men*. He who saw literature as the pinnacle of life. The heart of community, culture and education. Everything that was important about existence. He wasn't looking around to see if anyone was struggling. He wasn't doing his usual walk up and down around the desks to ensure that everyone was at least attempting to look busy. Instead, he was engrossed, not in a phone, of course not on a laptop, but in a hardcopy article. Something from the paper.

Erin wondered if the distraction was the same for her peers as it was for Mr Turner. She wondered if it was all linked to Amy's disappearance. Nothing like this had happened to their year group before; nobody had been missing for longer than a few hours. That was Tommy Nickle and he always bunked off school so nobody was too worried. This was different. She wanted there to have been a development, but only a good one. It had never before occurred to her how she valued her year group; she cared for most of them. They had been at school together for almost twelve years. While she only knew Amy within school hours, she knew exactly who she was, her hobbies; they would always share a smile if they passed in the corridors and sit with each other in class.

All of these thoughts whirring around Erin's head made her agitated, restless and desperate to find an excuse to go up to Mr Turner at his desk so that she could see what he was reading. It was as if he had completely forgotten his surroundings. He hadn't glanced up at the clock for over ten minutes and he usually had the lesson planned in fifteen-minute sections. Never would he veer within a second of these segments. He always had timers on the go and so not even slightly shifting his gaze towards a clock or watch was very out of character.

Maybe she could ask to go to the toilet, she pondered. Was that too obvious? She was a girl, so if she took her bag with her then no questions would be asked about why she wanted to go to the toilet in the middle of a revision class.

Staring mindlessly at her blank page, she continued to think up reasons to venture towards Mr Turner's desk. He was conveniently sat with the newspaper on his lap so even if she spoke to him at his desk, there was no guarantee she would be able to see the headline.

Had they found Amy? Was she OK? What had she been through since she left home last Monday?

At that point Michelle Garner must have received the notification. That, or she had only just found a chance to discreetly check her phone underneath the desk while Mr

Turner remained engrossed in his reading. Michelle's reaction was the same as everyone else's, though hers was a bit more dramatic and was followed by a cry. If this was to do with Amy then Erin had an inkling about the answers to her three questions. She feared the worst as she glanced to her left where Amy's seat was empty as it had been all week.

She couldn't wait any longer. She grabbed her bag and headed for the door.

'Mr Turner,' she said quietly, which startled him into shutting the newspaper and remembering where he was. She didn't catch the headline, but saw that he was reading *The Yorkshire Press*. Nothing ever gripping happened in the local newspaper so he could only have been reading about Amy. Not that it's a gripping story but more terrifying and worrying.

'What? Y-y-yes,' came his uneasy reply as if he had forgotten that he was meant to be teaching English Literature to his GCSE students.

Erin scuttled off to the toilets and, shaking, took out her phone. She was in many group chats. There was one for the Geography project that was due in next week. One was for Physics because nobody understood a word that any of the Physics department staff ever uttered. A group had been made for the prom committee and Erin had been persuaded into joining that and one for the final end-of-year music concert. All of these groups were flooded with messages. Her phone's home screen was swarmed. She found it difficult to decipher what had happened until she saw in black and white.

She went onto Amy's Facebook profile where her name had been tagged in numerous desperate posts from her mum.

MISSING

And then a picture of her.

PLEASE HELP US LOCATE OUR LITTLE GIRL.

Missing from nearby York Racecourse area on Monday. If anyone has any info please contact me urgently!!!!!

Erin scrolled back up to the top of the page to see if there had been any updates to the many statuses. There were none. She wasn't in the least surprised. It would have hurt too much. Everyone would be grieving and need time to come to terms with the tragic end to the story.

The worst ending. Amy was dead and Erin would never sit next to her in class again.

2

MARY

Tuesday 28th May 2019

I've returned to this awful place, but I must focus on the good things, the positives in every situation. That is what I must do because it's what Doctor Knoll always said. I must think about the smells, the warmth, the stretching, find my zen. A total contrast to where I find myself now: the same four walls, the dreaded magnolia, the clinical scent because I deep cleaned yesterday before I ran out of anti-bac wipes. That's all they allow me to have in here. I am always alone. At least, I always feel it, even when I am in company.

Now, I wonder how I was allowed out to the yoga class when I'm supposedly too ill to function on my own. Then I remember how Eileen and Erin supported me, held my hand, walked me to the car and so on. The yoga class gave me a fleeting sense of freedom. Even though it wasn't freedom at all.

I must employ all of Dr Knoll's coping techniques whenever I feel stressed or lonely or sad. The simple breathing exercises that I have always relied upon; the experience of the moment and the act of simply being. The noticing of details that bring me into this space of living right now. Of living as me. As a perfectly fine specimen. That is right; I am me and that is fine. I AM FINE. That is what I have always been told by the nurses, the doctors, and the therapists. They all say to me that I am completely fine just the way that I am. I don't need to change my personality, I just need to change the way that I look at my personality. Blah. Blah. Blah.

These methods are very similar to what my teacher was attempting in the yoga class this evening. I have tried many meditation applications on my phone, and none have worked, yet this time I focused and reaped the benefits, within the moment at least. Maybe a lack of being able to focus has always been my problem, but today I managed it. I think being on my own, lying on my bed with my thoughts, was never going to work. However, sitting in a class surrounded by others, took my focus off my terrifying thoughts and allowed me to meditate properly for the first time. It felt so good. Oh, it felt SO GOOD.

The drive home wasn't so calming, mind you. This was largely down to the rain slamming onto the windscreen of our car and my aunt, who has never been a confident driver, trying to cope with the appalling weather conditions. She blames it on the English roads. I blame it on her driving instructor fifty years ago.

I heard the laughter coming in bursts through the chaos and felt happy for the bond that had been created between my loving aunt and beautiful daughter, and then I smiled more because I felt that I am partly the reason for this, in a good way of course. That is right, some good things can come out of situations like mine.

I was happy to witness that they had the ability to see the hilarity in a scary situation and couldn't see the danger because they were too content in the moment to notice it. In fact, rarely did they see sadness or bad things with anything in life and I am so jealous yet extremely thankful for this. They always come to visit me in high spirits despite the circumstances and not knowing when it will change or end. There's a thought. This ending.

I have tried everything in my power since being back to get to where I was just half an hour ago. I have closed my eyes and tried to imagine, but the images that come with that are certainly not zen.

I tried to picture the orange tint throughout the entire space we were in; the scents coming up in hardcopy form from the incense sticks; the door half open to allow some heat out and some cooler air in. It is surprising how hot you can get in a yoga class.

I conjured up the poses we performed in my mind. Downward dog being the easiest to recollect because it was the posture that we kept returning to throughout the class. How that will ever feel like a restful position I don't know because I struggled each time we returned to it.

I imagine again the feeling of my legs wobbling and knees weak while we held the static poses in attempt to strengthen our muscles, but instead it felt as though they were making me weaker. I was so determined to remain in each posture, but this took too much concentration and physical strength to achieve, and instead I felt as if I was going to collapse into a heap on the floor.

Still jittery, I directed my memory to the end of the class, the finale. The rest zone when, no matter your personal circumstances, it was impossible to feel agitated or stressed, you could only feel relaxed and this was the case for me. It really was. However, now trying to recall that peaceful image in my mind, I somehow can't get rid of the stress that I feel. We were lying on the floor with our eyes closed. Why is it so difficult to repeat this?

I lay on my back on my mattress which is the most relaxing position in my room and closed my eyes, thinking about all that the teacher had said. This reminded me of my meditations back in the day but which are for some reason rendered stronger within me this time around. I tried to get back into that mentality, the being in the moment, this moment, then realised that this moment isn't one that I wanted to be in, so my body resisted as did my mind shortly after.

After a while of trying but failing, I sat up and began to write as I am doing now. Writing is about the only thing keeping me going and veering me away from turning totally mad these days. Writing is my sanity, if I still have any left. I find it extremely cathartic and don't mind who reads my words whenever they find them, but, when they do, I can be assured that the words are wholly the truth of my chaotic mind. A mind that may change from hour to hour, but one that at the time produces the complete truth in writing. Like that found in a police statement. I remember that police statement oh too well.

My pen is running out which is a huge shame as it is my favourite now. It seems odd and rather pitiful to have a favourite pen, but it is one of those that writes so smoothly along the paper so no matter how much I write and at whatever rapid rate the words spill out of my head and onto the paper, my arm doesn't ache.

I press my phone and there is nothing. No messages, no missed calls, not even the pop ups which show me what I was doing this time last year back when things were slightly more normal than they are now. I look at the walls that surround me and there is nothing. My pigeonhole in which my mail is placed each morning - nothing. I am so fed up with being engulfed in nothing.

I investigate my diary. Not this one but the one that I call my *normal* diary which I use like a *normal* person and simply note down events and appointments that I have coming up so that I don't get scolded by the doctors or shouted at by my girlfriends for missing yet another lunch. Nothing. No plans, nothing to look forward to, absolutely nothing.

Today I am feeling:

Lost, nothing, sad but happy and calm with the memories of the class.

Today I am grateful for:

1. The rising sun
2. Another day
3. My daughter
4. My auntie
5. My bed

3

ERIN

'Hello!' Erin called as she entered the house. There was no answer. They must have gone out for a walk in the park or something. While Erin loved her aunt and her brother dearly, she equally loved snippets of time to herself. Especially now. Particularly after the few hours she had at school. She wished she hadn't bothered with the extra help for her exams, though she knew she needed it. Flo welcomed her with a wagging tail and showing off her new squeaking monkey toy. Eileen must have been shopping.

She walked into the kitchen aimlessly, her mind focused on Amy. Everything else was just going through the motions. She couldn't believe it. Remembering her mother's advice about her Irish roots, she put the kettle on to boil; a cup of tea is always the answer. At least it allowed her a moment to gather herself before Jack would undoubtedly come crashing in, followed shortly after by Aunt Eileen walking placidly behind.

The Yorkshire Press was lying on the kitchen side. *Aunt Eileen must have been reading it*, Erin thought, the same paper that distracted Mr Turner for so long earlier. She flicked through until she saw the headline. It must have been the one that Mr Turner was reading, nothing else would grab his attention quite like it did. Nothing in the local paper at least.

Teenage girl missing

Reports have been issued over the disappearance of teenager, Amy Milner (aged 16), who was last seen leaving her home on Lowther Street, York on Monday 20th May at around 5 o'clock. Police and Amy's family are expressing a growing concern for her whereabouts and wellbeing. A search has been ongoing and anyone who may know anything about where Miss Milner might be is urged to contact Yorkshire police.

Miss Milner is described as a white female, about 5ft 3ins tall with brown hair which she was wearing in a ponytail and blue eyes. She was last seen wearing navy-blue skinny jeans and a red jumper.

Mr Milner told the newspaper: 'Amy has always been a happy child with many friends. At school she is both popular and successful, the star student that most sixteen-year-old girls would be somewhat jealous of and look up to. We just want to find our little girl. We want our girl back.'

Erin could read on no further. The successful future that Amy had within her grasp, the exciting plans that she had made. It wasn't far from perfect.

Erin often found herself reading articles such as this one. Flitting between online sources, magazines, newspapers, any headline that caught her attention she would take the time to read. *That was the whole point of a good headline*, she thought. The articles never had a direct relation to her so she merely read them for a bit of gossip or to note how bad other lives could be. It forced her to appreciate everything that she had.

The articles were never personal to her. She would mostly read them online after they had been shared on Facebook, so she was just being nosy in response to a status she had glanced at. Occasionally in the local articles she would recognise a name and go onto their Facebook if she was friends with the person concerned. She would end up scrolling back four years or more and then wonder why she was bothering and what she was actually gaining from doing what she was doing. It was boredom, mostly.

However, the article regarding Amy was different. It was a hard copy, black and white and in her hands. It was personal. She could relate. Amy was someone that she knew. She was a friend that was always there. Through school. They never spent a lot of time with one another outside of school, but Amy was someone that Erin could rely on throughout her schooling life. They had been at school together from a very young age. Amy was someone Erin had sat next to in Maths and English for years. They laughed and cried together; it was a strong bond.

She put down the newspaper and felt queasy, so took a seat at the breakfast bar. Her legs didn't feel strong enough to hold her body so she needed the support and to be sat down. She read over the headline once more. *Teenage Girl Missing* and now, knowing the outcome, a sickness filled her stomach.

She wondered how they decided which stories to give media coverage to and which to leave out. There must be so many girls that go missing every day, but not all of them end up in *The Yorkshire Press.* There must be hundreds of stories that even have similarly horrific endings, but they aren't reported in the same light as this one had been. Amy's parents certainly wouldn't have encouraged it, Erin noted, because it is not something that you want to be reminded of while getting your shopping in at the local Co-op and seeing the headlines. Unless they felt that more coverage would result in a higher chance of Amy being found safe and well. Who knows? Erin's head didn't stop with the buzzing of thoughts.

She remembered the kettle. She pushed aside the newspaper and poured the boiling water into her mug when a knock at the door startled her. A tiny splash of water from the kettle hit her hand as if to shock her further. It wouldn't have been Eileen or Jack. They had a key and would just walk in. Nobody else was expected and they hardly had visitors anyway, so it was odd.

Cautiously, she went to answer it.

'Afternoon, young lady. PC Douglas and my colleague PC Griggs, and I believe you are Erin Carter?' the policeman said, holding up their badges to confirm authority.

'H-h-hello, y-y-yes,' replied Erin, nervously, but she couldn't understand why she was so afraid; she hadn't done anything.

'Is it OK if we come in and ask you a few questions?'

She knew that she couldn't turn the police away, so she wished for Eileen to quickly arrive home so that she had some adult support.

'OK.'

'Great. Thank you.

'Are you alright there Erin?' Dave from next door asked as he looked concerned at the officers on her doorstep.

'I'm OK, thank you.'

A pause lingered as Dave put down his bags of groceries and approached the house.

'Is there anything I can do?'

'You're welcome to stand in if you like. We're just here to ask Erin a few questions, nothing to worry about but I understand how it could be rather daunting for a young girl,' said PC Douglas.

'Erin?'

'That would be good, please.' Erin replied, wishing that Dave was Eileen but at least having an adult present gave her some support and Dave was lovely, so she knew that his intentions were only good ones.

The two officers walked into the kitchen, but not too far in suggesting that they wouldn't be long. Erin wondered how many of her peers' houses they had already been to or were planning on visiting after. Her built-in manners wanted to offer them both a cup of tea but, instantly, she felt that was inappropriate. Though she desperately wanted to take a swig of hers.

'As I said, my name is PC Douglas and my colleague here is PC Griggs. We believe you knew Amy Milner fairly well. Would you say this is true?'

She knew she had to think hard about her answers but also be factual and not go too deeply into it. Dave stood silently observing the scene.

'We were school friends. We started school together aged five and now we are about to finish.' She stopped herself, realising what she had just done. She'd slipped up, but was she meant to know the outcome? Would they think it suspicious if she admitted that she knew? She took a deep breath in and reminded herself that the police were only seeking facts; they didn't appear accusing in any sense.

'Take your time, we realise this is extremely difficult,' said PC Griggs, who hadn't yet uttered a word.

'Sorry, we *were* about to finish together this summer after exams.'

A pause followed as PC Douglas took down notes and both Erin and PC Griggs looked awkwardly around the room.

'Great. And would you say you were close?'

'Not really. Um, I guess kind of. Well, as close as you get at school. We would sit next to each other in some lessons. We didn't always hang out at break, but sometimes we did. We were a close year group, to be honest. We are a close year group.' Erin was getting mixed up with her tenses and the more she tried to correct herself, the more of a muddle she got herself into. 'Outside of school we never saw each other except for parties and things like that.'

'Right, and what was she like at parties? Recently had you noticed a change in her behaviour?'

'Not particularly. Like, we're all stressed with exams so I guess I could say she seemed a little more stressed than usual. But nothing obviously worrying.'

'OK.'

Erin didn't like the lack of expression on both officers' faces. She realised they had to remain impartial, but it made her feel uncomfortable and that she was saying the wrong thing.

'And what about her online presence?' PC Griggs added. 'Did you follow one another on social media?'

'Yes.' Erin had nothing else to add to the subject. They followed each other but nothing was happening on social media because everyone was studying for their exams. A lot of parents had taken phones off her friends so that they could concentrate only on their studies. She tried to think of anything she had recently seen that could help their inquiries. 'To be honest not much was happening on social media. Not as much as usual anyway. Everyone was concentrating on their studies.'

'I see.'

PC Douglas continued to note down the things Erin had said, and she felt the conversation was coming to an end. She hoped it was anyway, because she was fearful that she was going to get it wrong. She also felt that she hadn't said anything that was of a massive help.

'Right, well thank you, Erin, for your time today,' PC Douglas said as the two of them walked to the door and Erin followed shortly after.

'That's OK,' she replied.

'Would you be happy to come down to the station at some point over the next week if we need to ask you any more questions?'

'That's fine,' Erin answered.

'Thank you. Take care.'

The officers left and Erin felt confused and worried.

'Are you OK?' Dave lingered behind the officers.

'Yeah, all fine. Just a bit of a shock, you know?'

'It's huge.'

Dave remained in the hallway but really Erin just wanted to be left on her own.

'Thank you Dave for that,' Erin said as she gestured to the opened door politely for him to leave. He took the hint well, but Erin could tell he felt awkward in leaving a young girl on her own having just witnessed the questions asked by the police.

Eileen was still out with Jack, giving Erin time to come to terms with what had happened. Time to herself also allowed her a moment to evaluate all that she told the police and to think about whether there was anything more that she could add to aid the case.

She searched the room for further distraction to prolong the time it would take to make the cup of tea with hope that her insides had calmed by the time it came to drinking it. Worry filled her as she got off the stool. Was she to blame for this? Did she have a part to play? She considered her year group and convinced herself that the police would have been round to their houses as well. It wasn't just her.

Her mind was so absent that when she finally took a sip of tea, she realised she had poured boiling water into an empty cup. She was all over the place. On opening the cupboard, she saw that Eileen had got in a selection of herbal teas which she felt would sit better inside her than a milky brew, so she chose peppermint. She was still shaking.

Flo came running out of her bed as she realised Erin was sitting a while and, in that moment, Erin felt thankful for the love that dogs provide. She had always loved dogs and, since she was born, having a four-legged friend was an essential feature of her home life. It wasn't often though that she truly appreciated how much dogs meant to her, especially on difficult days like the one she was having.

Erin had always been the one to walk Flo since she was old enough to go out on her own and she found peace in their walks, particularly when it was just the two of them. She also enjoyed walks with Eileen, but Jack usually ruined everything that a good walk meant to Erin, so she rarely offered to take him with her. The peaceful tranquillity just didn't happen when Jack was involved. Besides, it was hard enough trying to control Flo when she was excitable and misbehaving, she couldn't control Jack as well.

A walk, that's what she needed. She would go to the fields close by their house and walk through them to the furthest point in the field that they went to when time is not an issue. Time certainly wasn't a consideration today. There were far bigger things at stake. After all, she had as long as the daylight lasted, and Eileen could contact her on her mobile if she needed her.

She put on her new Dublin River boots that her Grandad Séan had got her for Christmas. They made her feel stylish no matter what other old clothing she was wearing, because she needed to feel good. Luckily, the weather was sunny which helped her style somewhat in that she didn't have to layer up too much. The sunshine also enhanced her mood slightly, and although she was never going to feel OK considering the news she had not long ago received, she felt much better for it than she would have done if the weather outside reflected her own misery within.

As soon as she went to the coat cupboard and got her dog walking coat, a brown Barbour, Flo went ballistic. Before even getting her lead in her hand, Flo was circling around knowing exactly what the plan was which Erin always found fascinating. Erin found it interesting that Flo could sense when she was sad or happy or irritable and act accordingly. For example, on Erin's arrival home today when she was shaking in despair and disbelief at what the day had revealed, Flo was right there by her feet. Flo knew that Erin didn't only need a break with a cup of tea, she also needed the comfort of a loving dog. Of course, the dog didn't say a word or do much at all, she simply sat by Erin's side and it was perfect.

Erin struggled to attach the lead to Flo's collar because she was so overexcited by the fact that they would be leaving the house. Erin was still shaky. Once she had a treat in her hand though and gave firm commands, Flo obeyed, and they were ready to go.

Erin desperately hoped that nobody would see her because she was worried that they would judge her for taking the dog out as normal after finding out such dreadfully upsetting news about a friend. Despite her walk being part of the process of trying to come to terms with what had happened, she feared anybody looking on wouldn't see it that way and instead would view it as her moving on with normality after just half a day. Part of her brain stopped her - nobody would be so judgemental - but another part kept the thoughts coming so she walked at a faster pace until she reached the field.

She particularly liked the route that they were taking because not many people knew the walk after the field so it was usually empty and far away from anyone. As the sun shone on her Barbour, she realised it was the kind of weather where she was too hot with a coat on but too cool with the coat off so, for now, she left her outfit as it was.

She realised that her pace hadn't slowed to normal after speed walking while on the street because she got to her special place much quicker than she usually would, and she was thankful for that. Her tears came more steadily now. The tears that had been trickling down her face from the moment she left the house. As soon as she arrived at her spot her body knew that it could release. No onlookers would see and Erin needed to cry. That was the good thing about Erin's special spot, it allowed her to release anything and then gave her the option to leave that emotion behind and move forward once she walked back. Though often it wasn't that easy.

She had first discovered the place when she needed to grieve for her father at a very young age. She had been fairly open about her upset to her mother, but never expressed the anger she felt towards it all. She was angry because they were left behind. At this thought she felt the anger build up inside her again. A piece of flint was on the ground next to her. She grabbed it and flung it into the distance.

'Why were you taken so early, Daddy?' she screamed. 'Why?' came out more gently.

The log Erin eventually sat down on provided her with the strength that her mother couldn't give. Her poor mother who was grieving too. She couldn't have expected her to be strong in it all. In fact Erin felt it was her duty to be strong for her mother and Jack. This special place gave her room to scream at the top of her lungs, to let it all out without anyone around to hear her or give an opinion that she didn't welcome anyway. Screaming, walking and being on her own was good for her soul. At just sixteen she had already discovered that. She never had to explain herself either.

Tears were streaming down her face as she continued to cry, loudly. Already she could feel the anger subside slightly and Flo remained right by her feet. She leant back and breathed in as much air as her lungs could take and then let it go in a huge sigh. She tried to let her feelings go with it but most of the anger, worry and sadness stayed.

Gratitude for her special place in the field grew stronger though. It was a simple place. Just a large tree trunk on its side facing an expanse of open field with a large bush behind it, so that there was no worry of anybody hiding and seeing her. As soon as she placed her backside on the wood each time, an instant feeling of relief came over her. It was the same feeling that she had after the two hypnosis sessions that Aunt Eileen took her to, and it felt amazing. The exact feeling that she got whenever she went to the sea at Whitby or Scarborough. This time was no exception and Erin sat, breathed in deeply and desperately tried to let go.

4

MARY

Wednesday 29th May 2019

I cannot seem to shake the odd feeling from yesterday. Usually it takes a good night's sleep to get me back to my normal state of being and I wake up feeling OK again, well as good a sleep as I ever get these days anyway.

I have tried everything in my power to change the way that I feel but nothing has worked, and I am ending the day with no improvement in my mood. Thinking of calling up doc tomorrow if things remain the same way after two nights of sleep to change it. That's just not on! He will probably tell me to try one of the many techniques he gives me to ease the feelings of stress and anxiety. They are all the same.

They include meditating, going for a walk, being in the moment, breathing (if I stopped breathing, I would be in trouble), but whenever I am in a state like this one, I feel as though I cannot just simply be without conjuring up one million reasons as to why being is so difficult and ridiculously stressful. Oh, how jealous I am of those who happily spend Sundays alone, enjoying their own company. I am quite the opposite. I should never be alone. It gets dangerous when I am alone. Sometimes, not all the time.

Getting back to my calm state is somewhat like having a crick in my neck. You know when you sleep funny and can't shake the pain? Stay with me. The cause of this is mostly due to the position in which you slept, and you wake in the morning wishing that you could go back and re-do the last night's sleep to reverse the effect on your sore neck. It usually takes one to two days to get it back to normal and, in the meantime, you spend your waking hours with a heat bag around your neck and screeching at the pain of any sudden movement. My zen zone (I think that is a great name, go me!) is much like this. One to two night's sleep and I return to it. Not this time.

I went to the park, to the cafe, to the pond and took in nature. I walked up the high street and looked into the windows of shops, but didn't buy anything. I passed many pubs but didn't venture in and smelt the soothing smell of cigarette smoke and didn't break my eight-month streak of no smoking, not even a vape. I even went for an early evening stroll which has frequently saved my days in the past when I have found myself in the same mood as this one, but it just felt weird. I felt as if I could have walked aimlessly for miles and miles with no change, yet usually it only takes until the bench by the river, two miles from the start, to begin to feel the benefits.

This time, however, I was walking along and felt as if the whole world was spinning too fast around me. I passed a lady with a Jack Russell puppy who was walking rather slowly, but everyone else was on fast forward. Jack Russell lady didn't acknowledge me behind her until I got right up close. It was one of those situations where it is difficult to gauge when to cough loudly or politely say excuse me so that the person in question will hear and precious time won't be wasted with you remaining stuck behind them for longer; frustration growing as you cannot pass. I had my earphones in so I wasn't so embarrassed as half my attention was on the beautiful music gently seeping into my eardrums and taking me briefly out of the moment. As I got creepily closer to her shoulder, I hoped more for her to notice me and shift to the left slightly so that I could pass. It got very irritating very, very quickly! The walk was supposed to chill me out, but instead it made my stress levels rise like the sea levels due to global warming.

Wow, that is a bit deep for me and my therapist keeps saying that I shouldn't try to take on the world's battles as my own. I can't cope with my tiny little life at the moment so everything else can await my worry. While they are all big issues worth considering, he always says to me, they aren't for now. Global Warming is not for now. The world's politics is not for now. Let me get back to my day. It is crazy what thoughts and worries I can conjure up if I really try hard.

The cars seemed to be speeding, the light seemed to be darkening more rapidly than normal, the electric gates were closing faster on the big house just up the road and even objects that should not be moving appeared to have some element of momentum to them. The trees, houses, grass, roads, fences – everything. I felt as if I was high on drugs and hallucinating like I was in a dream. A dream that was happening in front of my eyes in broad daylight. It didn't feel as though my feet were capable of being firmly placed on the ground I was walking on, so quite frankly the experience was disturbing and uncomfortable as opposed to having the benefits that Dr Knoll frequently harped on about. He promised me about these benefits. Every time. This time he had broken his promise. Naughty man!

I had to stop moving myself to firmly place my feet on the earth and slap my face to make sure that it was reality that I was walking through, and my coffee hadn't been spiked in the cafe I had been in earlier in the day. I did think the man behind me in the queue looked a little dodgy and was casting his eyes on my movements for longer than I felt comfortable about. Yet I know how cynical my thoughts can be sometimes, particularly when I am alone.

I have taken my new notepad to write this all down this afternoon. I decided while on my way home to take the plunge and treat myself to one because that way I would not be disappointed when my birthday comes and goes next month without a gift of a spanking-new pad to write on. Also, sometimes I think that the act of buying something new releases an element of serotonin into the body or whatever it is that makes us happy. My notebook is a yellow one with four words on the front that read *H is for happiness.* That is four words if you're counting the letter 'h' as a word. Can letters count as words? I am not sure, but it doesn't really matter. Moving on.

I love an empty new notepad because I feel whenever opening it that all past thoughts and feelings vanish, and I am starting from scratch. A fresh slate on which to pour more of my inner self. It is a great feeling for the moment that it lasts and then as I begin to write things down everything comes back like a tidal wave of emotion and I usually cry for the first page of writing before pulling myself together and then writing some more.

It is funny because throughout all of this, writing never changes. It has always had the ability to change me but the process and the amount that I write does not change depending on my mood. As a young girl I turned to writing and still today I do exactly that. Every time I find myself producing more words than the normal person. They just pour out of me like champagne out of a bottle on my birthday. Yeah right, in another life! A past life.

A lot of people keep diaries. Most, I must confess, are as my 'normal' diary displays, simply stating activities each day, appointments, and social events, so that one doesn't forget their busy schedule that is modern-day life. Gosh, I sound so posh. Some people may even go as far as to write what the weather is like in such a diary, but rarely do they put down more than that. Other people keep slightly longer records of their days in writing what they did with a little more emotion and fewer broken sentences.

Each day I do an overview of my life with the added bits from that day, constantly revisiting my past in an attempt to better my future. I write as if I am talking to someone else, as if they are actually listening to every word, but, for all I know, these words will never be found and I will die someday, leaving this world and my diary in it. It will probably be used as kindling in the cooler months of winter or some other practical use. Who knows where it will end up?

Yes, one day in the future somebody will be cosying up for the evening and come across some random sentences from what used to be my life. Maybe they will find them enjoyable, it might spark inspiration for a novel. I frankly don't care.

It helps me though, so there is no way I am stopping any time soon. I don't just write at night either. No, with access to my *not very normal at all* diary you are given access to my sporadic thought process throughout my days and at any given untimely intervals. Aren't you lucky?

There is no pattern to the process, no rules to be followed, just words that come from inside my head at points at which I feel the need to note things down. Sometimes I forget to write a final passage at the end of days so those parts can only be guessed at, in between the truth of the passages before. All I know for certain is that writing is my saviour, and it is something that I must do. I won't ever stop. No way.

Am I repeating myself?

Today I am feeling:

Strange, peculiar, not with it and not in this world

Today I am grateful for:

1. A warm bed
2. Sunshine
3. Coffee
4. My four walls keeping me safe
5. A fabulous new notebook

5

ERIN

Since the news broke, Erin couldn't escape it. Even if she tried to forget about it, she was forced to face it each time another group chat kicked off. Certain messages felt even gossipy. It was wrong.

OMG Have U heard?

OMG So bad.

I can't believe it.

WOW. Is this actually happening?

Sadly yes.

So sad.

OMG.

Do you think anyone is to blame?

I dunno but I did see Luke Edgar heading to Mrs Rossy's office earlier.

OMG.

Before her sickness took a firm hold of her, Mary had tried desperately to keep Erin away from social media, but Aunt Eileen let her create a Facebook account as soon as she asked if she could sign up. No resistance. At least Mary was oblivious to everything, being physically separated from it all.

'Hello, love,' Eileen said as Erin ventured into the kitchen, having arrived home from school ten minutes prior. Usually she would walk straight in to find Eileen and catch up on the day, full of enthusiasm. Today she was distracted. 'Love?' Eileen repeated.

'Oh, sorry, Auntie. Hello.' Erin said with her phone in her hand, face glued to the screen. She went over to the kettle, forgetting her manners and putting only one cup beside it. Then she remembered. 'Auntie Eileen, would you like a cuppa?'

'I thought you were never going to ask! Is the Pope Catholic?' Eileen said with an upbeat energy that Erin wished she had.

Erin placed her phone, facing up, on the counter as she poured boiling water into both cups. Notifications were continuously filling her phone screen. Eileen put the laundry to one side and came up behind her, placing an affectionate hand on her shoulder.

'What is it, darling?'

Tears began to fall down Erin's face.

'Here, sure, I'll make these. You sit down.'

Erin walked over to the sofa as if somebody else had control over her body. She was only the physical structure and organs, her mind was elsewhere. The notifications kept coming and it was all unfolding before she had time to process it.

'Here you go,' Eileen said warmly as she handed Erin the cup.

Erin smiled, knowing from experience the healing power that sitting down with a cup of tea and chatting to her auntie had.

'Thank you,' she said, after she had soaked in the initial goodness.

'Now, what's going on?'

'So much, Auntie. Have you heard?'

'Yes, love. Sadly I did hear it on the news. It's awful sad. I was hoping it hadn't reached you yet, but then who am I kidding? News travels so fast in this community.'

'I know. The police came round yesterday.'

'What? When? Why?'

'When you and Jack were out. When I got back from school. I guess because I'm her friend at school. We sit– Sorry.' She paused. '*Sat* together in lots of lessons. I spoke with her most days. I suppose they've spoken with most people in the year group. I don't know, nothing like this has ever happened to me before.'

'Oh, darling.' Eileen edged closer to Erin and put her arm right around her.

'Is Jack here?' Erin asked, suddenly aware of their need to be discreet.

'He's upstairs. Engrossed in his Lego. He won't hear a thing.'

'Good. It's just so sad, Eileen.' Erin's sobs came out a little louder than before.

'I know. What were the police asking? Questions like?'

'How well did I know her? How close were we? Did I suspect anything was wrong recently or did I see a change in behaviour?'

'That's a lot for a young girl to take in. Why didn't you tell me before now?'

'Jack's always around. I couldn't. I was also coming to terms with it myself.'

Eileen hugged Erin tighter as Erin grabbed her phone to check the latest notifications.

'Don't be doing that. That needs to go away for a night at least.' Eileen said sternly and Erin knew that it wasn't meant out of control, authority or strictness, it was for her protection. Protecting her mental wellbeing. 'I'm going to finish the dinner, but you sit and enjoy your tea. Don't be looking at that thing though.' By which Erin knew she meant the phone.

Erin smiled an empty smile as Eileen headed back over to the hob. She went on Facebook and it was plastered with condolences for Amy's family. She knew Eileen was right and that she shouldn't look.

RIP to the strongest person I knew.

Rest in peace, lovely girl, my thoughts are with the family at this difficult time.

She couldn't turn away from it. Also, she knew that Eileen would never physically remove her phone for the night, she would just guide, *plant the seed* as she called it.

Am I the only one who hardly knew her?

Erin felt fury build up inside her on reading the last post. How could anyone think like that? Have no barrier between their thoughts and sensitivity? Darren Smith; he was always a strange one, always disrupting classes. Selfish.

She wasn't very nice to me once!

Erin gasped. Luke Edgar. Playing the victim and also trying hard to be funny. It was awfully inappropriate and sickening. Erin felt nauseous.

Eileen was very traditional, it could be argued, old fashioned in her ways. She was reluctant to let the modern world in as 'life was perfectly fine before technology'. She acknowledged this daily. Almost too much. Her fear was irrational because nothing bad had happened to either of them. However, Erin's argument was that she was sixteen, so needed some privacy of her own aside from the control slammed upon her by her dysfunctional family. Though, sixteen and being spoken to by the police regarding a suicide case, made Erin consider Eileen's accuracy in her predictions. Erin felt her face warm and redden with fury as she read the comments.

After two days of having access to the virtual social world, Erin's phone was the first thing that she went to pick up in the morning and the last thing that she put down at night. She spent hours scrolling and this habit remained, but she didn't know why because after doing so she never gained anything nor lost anything; her life remained exactly as it was.

On days when she felt bad about her own image, Instagram strengthened this sad emotion when she witnessed the accounts not of celebrities but of her own friends looking like celebrities. Marsha Graham's account was the worst. It was full of perfection. The perfect brunch; the most exotic holiday venues; the prettiest new haircuts.

Last weekend she got upset seeing her closest friendship group: Dana, Lorna and Kirsty out in town and they hadn't asked her to join them. She probably couldn't have made it with work and a visit to her mum and they knew that, but an invite would have been nice. They posted continuously onto their Instagram stories as if to torture her further.

Erin always compared her own life to their perfect situations. Her peers doing exactly what she should have be doing. Acquaintances she didn't even care about doing things that made her Saturday night look so boring and suddenly she was consumed by FOMO.

When it all began and when Erin analysed everything since, she did not ever feel she got too involved. When did it all begin? It was hard to pinpoint. It worried her every time she brought up the question. It made her feel that maybe she had some involvement. But, deep down, she knew that she didn't.

Luke Edgar and Darren Smith were by far the worst. They seemed to get a kick out of commenting 'Ugly' under all of Amy's profile pictures. They did it to other girls as well. Erin could have stood up for Amy, but she just thought how immature it was. Nothing else. She never suspected it would have such a huge impact on Amy's mind. Erin never posted much on her own accounts. The last picture on display on her own Facebook account was wishing Jack a Happy Birthday. She made a collage of photos of the two of them from when they were very little up until their holiday in Ireland last year.

She found it difficult to see how her involvement affected anything. You never know what is happening behind somebody's eyes. Thoughts and feelings are totally invisible, which is the danger when people don't discuss anything going on inside their head. Erin spent time studying everyone's accounts since discovering the news. She went over Amy's numerous times which was hurtful for her to do and nothing seemed too awful, but it must have seemed so to her.

Since everything, Eileen had been even stricter with what she called 'phone maintenance'. Maintain your brain, put your phone away,' she said every time she spotted Erin staring for too long at the screen of her phone. She had given similar limits to Jack, who was four years younger than her. Eileen was helping so much by simply being around as she always had, but now Erin was appreciating it so much more. Frequently they went out without their phones and just walked. They lost track of what the time was or for how long they had been gone, but this made it much more fun. The freedom was fresh and real.

A few weeks back they went away for the weekend and Eileen wouldn't allow Jack or Erin to take their phones or iPads with them. Instead, they packed a few outfits, wellies, and pyjamas and had more fun than they had in a long while. Laughter filled the space that they were in with not much silence in between. Erin even noticed things that would go past unobserved if she had access to technology.

For example, she noticed Jack utter his first clearly communicated sentence in years, but Eileen told her that he began doing so months ago, Erin had simply been too involved to pick up on it. She spotted how frail Aunt Eileen had become over the past year, realising that she had blocked it out of her mind. The fact that their time together was limited resonated now, truer than ever before, forcing her to recognise the importance of appreciating their time together.

With these thoughts she was beginning to feel claustrophobic rather than relaxed, thinking about happy memories. She stretched her legs out in front of her and noticed that her jeans were loose. She must have lost some weight. A significant amount at that and she was surprised that Eileen had not commented upon it yet.

Those thoughts were spinning around her head on repeat like a loop pedal in music.

6

JACK

I never knew what to expect from today because Aunt Eileen was very vague about it all. All I knew was that it wasn't a good thing that we were about to do, and it had something to do with Erin. Though I don't think she has been bad. I am sure she hasn't been bad, not Erin. I think she might have been involved in a bad thing, but I don't think she has been bad herself. I know I am not very happy about today because I don't like not knowing.

'Eileen! Where is my top we decided on, in fact I can't even find the outfit. Oh god, this is all going so wrong!' Erin screams.

She is taking over the whole entire house with her screaming. I can't handle it. It's not even seven in the morning. That's earlier than we have to get up for school but today is a Saturday so no school for me which is a good thing, I guess. Eileen is probably leaving me for as long as she can so that I can get more sleep and not throw a tantum like they say I do all the time. I don't think I do. Not that much anyway. I can sense it is very important to remain quiet today. But also, Eileen is just a nice person so part of her not waking me up yet will be because she is kind and not rude like some people I know.

'Jack, darling, can you start to wake up now?' Eileen calmly says through the door in a soft manner. She speaks to me like Mummy used to before she went all mad. I don't think I am allowed to use that word to describe how Mummy is, but I don't think I can use a better word. She is a little bit mad. I never tell anyone that I think this though. Especially not Mummy.

What I find quite funny here is that Eileen doesn't know that I already have my eyes wide open and I am staring at the ceiling trying to work out what today is about. How could she think I would be able to sleep through the racket of my sister shouting around the house? I'm always up early anyway! I can answer her better than I used to, but I am not awake enough for that yet, so I say nothing at all. Everybody is used to me saying nothing at all.

The screaming continues as Erin struggles to find the correct outfit for whatever the day holds, but I am ahead of her because Eileen helped me choose my clothes before I went to bed so that I didn't have to think too hard in the morning. I don't think I have to look as smart as Erin because Eileen didn't pick my nicest handsome man top that Mummy used to put on me whenever we went to anything posh or with family members who had never met me before, but my outfit is still quite nice, and I am happy with it.

I finally give up on trying to fall back to sleep for an extra bit of time and get myself out of bed to get ready. I had a bath last night as well, so I don't have to have a big wash this morning, just a little wash like my face and things in case I got crumbs all around my mouth from the toast.

I go into the bathroom and pass the chaos in Erin's room where Eileen is trying to remain calm and Erin has completely lost it like Mummy has done so many times before. She must get it from Mummy. I think the right word is *inherited.* Sometimes I think that she might be mad too. Yes, Erin has inherited some of Mummy's madness.

I say nothing to them as I pass but I don't think that they noticed me, so it doesn't matter. In the bathroom I have a stool to stand on to brush my teeth properly and wash my face thoroughly. I needed it to reach the sink when I was younger, but now I have grown a bit and only use it so that I have that extra bit of height because our bathroom sink is quite deep and higher up than a normal one.

Mummy bought me an electric toothbrush for my tenth birthday because she said that once you reach double digits you are old enough to have one and this made me very excited. I feel really grown up and it keeps my teeth a lot healthier. My tenth birthday was quite a long time ago now. I now brush my teeth better than I ever did before, but it means that now they know that I am awake because they can hear me in the bathroom. My toothbrush sounds a bit like a tractor. I'd like to drive a tractor one day.

'Oh, hello, Jack. I didn't see you sneak in here! Did you sleep OK?' Eileen says to me while putting her arms around me and squeezing me tight. I nod in reply.

My toothbrush buzzes three times quickly and that is when I know that it is time to stop. Cleaning is finished for another morning. Now it is time to wash my face with my new facial wash that Eileen got me. She said it will stop big spots coming early so that I will never get bullied when I become a teenager. I didn't understand what she meant but I don't ever want to get bullied, so I always use it to wash my face. I don't think I have ever had a big spot on my face. I think I would have seen it.

Finally the screaming has stopped, and I think Erin is ready to leave the house. I just have to put my clothes on but that won't take very long at all because Eileen and I laid them out all neat last night before I went to bed. As I am getting dressed, I hear the car doors open outside on the driveway and this makes me happy because it means that there will be no more waiting around before leaving the house for whatever it is we have to do and wherever it is we are going. Hooray!

I get in the car and wait for a few moments while Eileen locks up and makes sure that Flo is happy and won't destroy the kitchen cupboards like she has done occasionally when she got anxious with us being away for a long time. Flo is my favourite. She is the only one who understands me sometimes and she never asks me to do chores like tidy my room or do the dishes.

As we drive out of our close along the busy road into York city centre, I think about all the happy times that I have had with Flo. I am not allowed to walk her on my own yet. I still enjoy walks with her because, even if I am with Eileen or Erin or even Mummy, sometimes I can feel like I am all on my own.

We stop and start because of the traffic lights, but I am not taking too much notice because I am thinking about Flo and all the good times we have had. Suddenly the car stops, and I realise that we are here. The car park is busy and the signs all over it suggest that we are at a police station. I don't know why this would be or why Erin would need to come here on a Saturday. I thought Saturdays were meant to be fun.

We walk inside and everything is busy. Police officers are busying about, receptionists are busying about, cleaners are busying about, Aunt Eileen and Erin are busying about. Everyone is moving around so fast as if they are all in a rush, but I don't know why. I never expected the chaos that I can see. In fact, I always thought of a police station as being calm because it is a place where officers are trying to keep calmness in the world, not chaos.

It is at times like this that I wish I could communicate properly and didn't struggle so much to say words that people can hear so that I could ask someone what was going on. I always wish I could understand this world a bit better. From what I can see though, all I can tell is that something quite awful has happened, and Erin must have been involved or hurt by it because she is crying real tears. Not the fake ones she used against Mummy and Daddy when we were younger to get me into trouble or her out of trouble, but real, actual tears.

Eileen is being comforting to Erin, but also I can tell that she is unsure about the situation like I am. She is so careful about how she is being to make sure that she gets everything absolutely right. She never says much when big things happen like this, she just places her reassuring hand around Erin's shoulders, while keeping an eye on me and thinking adult thoughts, watching everything. My auntie really is amazing.

The policeman who is probably the calmest out of all of them (which isn't too difficult), is coming towards us and directing his attention towards Erin. I am trying to focus on too many things at once so I can't properly focus on one thing. This means that I miss the conversation between them, but I guess he has ordered my sister to come with him, though I can't say what tone he did this in, so I still don't know whether Erin is in trouble or not. I really, really want to know now.

I have never been told much about anything so far in my lifetime because everybody always wants to protect me from something. I don't know what I need protecting from. The first I knew of this event was when Aunt Eileen brought me a cup of tea and toast in bed yesterday morning before school, which is the usual giveaway of a family disaster.

She would normally make me get out of bed and sit at the table to have my breakfast, especially on a school day, so bringing it to me in bed shows that something has happened. Something bad. Occasionally it means that it is someone's birthday or that she has some good news to tell me, but from my memories I can't think of more than two times when this was the case, it is mostly bad.

...

'Morning my darling, how are you today?' Eileen asked, with a calming but nerve-racking tone as if to hide what she was about to follow up with. I was only just waking up, so apart from a few grunts and groans as any human would make at those early hours of the morning, I didn't even attempt words.

Without saying anything further she sat on my bed and waited for me to drink my tea and eat my toast as if my mug and plate were the last two items to fit into the dishwasher and she was anxious to get a load on. Her actions almost made me nervous to eat and drink in what should have been a lovely setting considering I am used to making my own breakfast in the morning and often that of Erin and Eileen as well.

I think my eye movements showed Eileen how confused I was at her behaviour, which prompted her to explain what was happening. At least she told me what our plan of action was but left the parts that possibly needed more explanation for my mind to ponder over for a few more hours. This was dangerous. I wish everyone would just tell me everything. I wish that they could read my mind and see how much I worry about things. It is just so unfair.

I knew that we were off out, and I needed to dress nicely. I knew that we had to make a slight detour to the police station, but I was told that it was nothing that I needed to worry about. I knew that I was promised lunch at my favourite restaurant afterwards and that a possible trip to the cinema with popcorn and Fanta was on the cards. So, in my mind, I was in for a great day though I still couldn't put my finger on the occasion or what I had done to deserve it.

. . .

Here we are, the bad thing that I had to work out and Erin is off in a room with an officer. All Eileen and me have to do is to wait. I am bored with looking around at everything now because there is so much to look around at that I can't properly understand any of it, so I stop looking.

'It won't be much longer, my boy,' Eileen says to me reassuringly. 'Then we can go for lunch.'

7

MARY

Thursday 30th May 2019

A fresh start. It is almost the end of May. I have always hated the winter months, and March doesn't get much better. Still a lot of darkness and so much rain. It was freezing this March as well, I've needed to layer up so much more than usual. And April. I have never experienced what they call the *winter blues* in a way that I have this year. The weather hasn't even been that bad.

Days have merged into weeks when I have felt permanently exhausted, entirely drained. I have felt fidgety as if I want to get outside and do things but the thought of physically acting upon that drives me crazier still, so I have mostly remained here in my room. I did begin the jigsaw that Auntie Eileen and the kids bought me for Christmas which distracted me for an hour or two. That is nothing though, there are many hours in one single day. And I have had lots of single days in here on my own. I am not even making sense anymore.

The shaking sensation in my hands is beyond my control and I can hardly hold the pen that I am writing with now, which is nothing on what they have been some days. I always get the shakes worse when I am frightened. I never know what I am frightened of, but this time I can only put it down to being frightened of myself. Being afraid of the person that I could become by being in here for too long. It is the oddest feeling and makes me question why we shake when we are nervous.

I remember way, way back when I was at school. Music was almost forced upon me from a young age which is why, I think, I grew to love it so much. It is probably why Erin longs to be on stage in the West End. I was so young when this happened. I was still living in Ireland and so I must have been younger than ten. My parents bought me violin lessons and before I was good enough to do so I was chosen to perform a solo in front of two hundred people at the end of year assembly. I was terrified. My vibrato was on point due to my shaking with nerves. Other than that, the performance was weak, and I was so glad when it was over. I was lucky that I was so young because I got the pity vote from the audience. I doubt I would have got a single clap if I was in my teens. This is exactly how my shakes feel now. Weak.

My skin is itchy and I have a huge rash all over my face and arms, which has always been a sign of a breakdown. I have blotchy patches all over as well and scabs which I have picked at in a panic and worried until blood drips onto the off-white carpet. At least that is the cleaner's problem. It is a silly colour choice for a place of this sort anyway. They should have gone with navy or black. Even a darker shade of cream or beige just not as close to white as it is. I should be the designer here. My hair is beginning to fall out too, which is what happened last year when all of this started. Well - sort of when it started. The reality is it took me too long to notice and it all started a long time before that.

My legs ache. My clothes are hanging off me because I haven't eaten for what must be days if not a whole week now. I can't remember. My memory is going too which is scary because a lot of the time that is all I have to hold on to. Memories. How precious they are.

I spent some time earlier (I think it was today) looking through old photos that they allowed me to have in here. I can't hurt myself on photos. In fact, they keep me very safe. Some were of Erin and Jack so young I could cup them in my hands, like tiny puppies not ready to leave their mum yet. Some were of them only a few months back which makes me so proud to look at. To look at how they have grown into such fantastic humans with little help from me. Though I have a bit of pride to take for it I guess, I wasn't always completely absent.

The children have hardly wanted to visit. I think the few times that they have appeared has been out of forceful bribery by Eileen. Perhaps a promise of McDonalds on the way home or a trip to the cinema to see the latest release. Those promises would work on Jack, every time. I'm not so sure Erin would be persuaded nowadays. She is so grown up! What a good aunt Eileen still is. No matter what we throw at her she keeps a strong frame within herself to hold everything together and keep those children onto a path of success and independence for which I will always be grateful. Always.

I say they haven't wanted to visit, I am sure it is actually Eileen protecting them from all of this. She is such a wise lady. A wise old owl (fitting because she loves owls) and she will be thinking of everyone in this. She always does. Each day she will consider what is best for me. I am sure she thinks about how much Erin would benefit from visits and recently she has been bringing her, so I guess that implies that I am improving or that Erin is maturing. Beyond her years. Jack, I doubt, is ready to be introduced to this life. Maybe he won't remember it all when he is older. I hope I am out soon and that is the case. Look at me being all logical and thinking rationally. That's a first.

I continuously trudge through all the exercises that I have been given by medical professionals over the years, but end up crying at the hopelessness of them now. Deep breaths all the way in and all the way out. In, out...in...out. I am always so surprised how long I can make my breath, getting even longer each time. My lungs must be huge! I am impressed considering all the smoking I put them through back when things were really bad.

Name spotting objects in my room, which is pretty difficult seeing as not much is in here. Lamp. Plant. Ceiling. Wall. Rug. Carpet. Chest of drawers. It is all pretty dull really and the list is exhausted within two minutes of naming.

Homing in on parts of my physical body and grounding myself that way. Notice how my lungs are expanding, filling up with air and then contracting as I release the carbon dioxide out into the world, letting go of my problems with it, supposedly. Notice the parts of me which are in contact with the ground or bed that I am lying on. Consider how I am feeling and where there is tension or pressure, or which parts feel fully relaxed. Usually none. Is my body tired or energised?

Standing up straight and feeling the weight of gravity pull down to earth. Imagining that there is a rope with a weight on the end of it heading down through my calf and into the ground, anchoring me. Feeling at one with the earth. Feeling connected. Feeling like I belong. I haven't felt like I belong in many, many years.

Picking out the beauty, little things that bring positive feelings to myself and brighten my days. That is a difficult task after the description of my room with a window that looks out into nothingness. The nothingness that I feel. I am just having a bad patch; the rain will wash away as my dear mother used to say.

I wonder how Daddy is. He finds it so difficult to cope with all this that he rarely contacts me directly and does most of his communication through Eileen and the children. He has never been good with things like this. Situations where overthinking in order to understand better are not his forte. He much prefers the simple life and problems that he can easily solve. Sadly, my illness is not one of those. It doesn't fit into the easily solved category. There is no quick fix.

I am not ready to venture outdoors yet. I don't even have a good book to read to pass my time because Eileen is my provider of those, and I can't remember the last time that I saw her in person.

I did take up knitting (like a complete grandma) the other day and in learning the basics I wasted three hours, so I decided to make Erin and Jack a blanket each. The squares are staring at me from the opposite side of the room. I might pick that up and try to kill some time. Maybe they will visit today and then it looks great if I am knitting a present for them. They will all be happy and think I am progressing. Perhaps they won't be so ashamed of their failure of a mother. Oh dear. How did this happen?

Today I am feeling:

A little better, anxious, worried, ill.

Today I am grateful for:

1. The indoors
2. Safety
3. Memories
4. Writing
5. Pills

8

ERIN

Erin couldn't stop thinking about why Amy did what she did. She continuously scrolled down her Facebook newsfeed and Amy's to see if anything she had written could have been misconstrued. Her mind even went to how she did it. A very dark place indeed. She had heard that people can feel so low to do something as awful as this, but she had never known anyone to. It was a fact that she never thought she would genuinely believe. Now she did. And she didn't want to.

It was a Sunday, of course. She loved Sundays. When she was younger, she always thought it was a very old person characteristic to have. *Maybe they are all right*, she thought, and she was in fact old for her time. She got told that a lot. *You've an old head on those young shoulders*, they would all frequently tell her.

She wished she could be older in controlling her thoughts. They simply wouldn't leave. She couldn't speak with Eileen about them as she felt sick to be thinking the way that she was. If she even mentioned to Eileen that she was worried in case anything she had written had been taken the wrong way then Eileen's disappointment would have crushed her even more. She had only written nice things under Amy's photos. Mostly she just liked the photos and didn't write anything. That was the safest way. That is what she would do in the future. A like can't ever be misunderstood. Words always can.

She decided to venture into the garden. She had to tread the stairs carefully as her knees weakened with each step. She wanted to leave her phone tucked away in the top drawer of her bedside table, but she was scared about what she would miss.

To Erin's younger self it was only people over the age of sixty-five who wished to spend days doing absolutely nothing apart from washing up the odd mug or perhaps picking up the post from the doormat and sorting through it, reading anything that looked important, putting everything into piles. She thought that old people were the only ones who got tired of the world around them and wanted some time away from the excitement. Yet at sixteen years old Erin was already a lover of days filled with no plans.

It was the days filled with nothingness that allowed her to escape a little from what was turning out to be her crazy life. Especially recently, she needed that time to digest everything that had happened but also to forget about it for a while too.

She paused as she reached the living room door and glanced at her empty phone screen. She wished for the strength to let Eileen's influence embed itself underneath her skin and not allow her phone near her. She desperately wanted to avoid all social media and contact with the outside world except from Eileen and Jack if they were around and a phone call with her mum if she rang. Though she tried to be mature in her coping methods, her inner monologue was telling her that if she left her phone upstairs she would miss something crucial.

Erin didn't want to run away completely from the situation that she was in, but she found that escaping temporarily was only healthy for her soul, letting it strengthen that bit more, allowing it to continue coping once she returned. It was why, she frequently thought to herself, adults drank wine. Sadly, she was still too young for that, so she welcomed all other forms of escapism with open arms. She couldn't escape the constant harassment from her phone, though she did turn it onto silent mode.

She found music helped this process as well, because she could let herself go and just listen. She often imagined being at some of the better parties that she had attended or invented different ways that certain situations could have worked out. Boys that she fancied could fancy her back. They might even kiss. It was her own fantasy world which, aided by music, could go however she wished it to. It was something that helped her forget reality momentarily. She retreated to the hammock in which she would lie for the duration of her Sunday, headphones in and Spotify playing her favourite tunes. Her phone was safely in her lap, the silent mode creating a slight gap withdrawing herself from the messages yet interrupting her music as they came through. She wanted to scream.

Thankfully, the sun was shining, which helped to bright Erin's mood for the day ahead. The weather was warmer than she had realised when choosing her outfit for the day and it wasn't long before Erin removed her thin jumper so that she was wearing only a t-shirt. She was so engrossed in the music that she hadn't noticed Jack set up his chair beside her with his iPad and headphones in. *He must be playing a game*, she thought to herself, but didn't start to ask him because he was content in his own world and hers was becoming lighter as the music did its thing.

Each time a message came through disrupting her peace, her mind was brought back to Amy. She thought about how Amy could have enjoyed the day like she was doing. She considered all that Amy was now going to miss out on. Prom, after exams parties, results day, university, a future. Even the summer. She would never experience the sun on her skin as Erin was experiencing. She would never see the beauty in nature and a day doing nothing. Maybe she was at peace now, listening to sweet music.

The sky looked like one in a perfect world, clear blue with just a few fluffy white clouds dotted about, perfectly shaped. The breeze came at intervals that provided just enough cool air but never too much that they had to get jackets on, and the warmth continued to make their skin smile. The birds seemed to be enjoying themselves with subtle sounds coming from the trees, but apart from that everything was still.

The aroma of freshly mowed lawn wafted over the fence as their neighbours started to perform their initial garden tidy up of the year and the sounds of the lawnmower and laughter from their children hinted strongly that spring had well and truly established its presence. As Erin started to think that the length of the latest warm period on her skin was considerably longer than the last, she looked up to see that most of the clouds had vanished and the sun shone down on its own.

'Here, you two. Put some cream on!' Eileen shouted from the kitchen, tea towel in hand and clearly emptying the dishwasher while listening to Randy Travis on the stereo.

Erin had attempted to introduce her aunt into the world of Spotify, claiming that it would save her a lot of money, time, and space, but she disregarded her efforts, preferring to keep her old habits alive.

'Eileen, it's not that bloody hot!' Erin replied, laughing.

Erin lay in silence beside her brother, mind and body at peace. Her attention only slightly shifted when passers by walking their dogs and their children were in loud conversation that distracted her. She realised it had been the longest period she hadn't been consumed by suffocating thoughts about Amy.

She removed her headphones and placed her phone face down on the lounger, took the sunscreen from her loving aunt and squirted it over Jack's tummy making him jump in shock and then laughing at his reaction. She looked at the bottle before applying some to her own skin to see that it was factor fifty.

'Really?' Erin said to Eileen in a joking way.

'Don't argue with me, young lady. It is better to be pasty white than to be diagnosed with skin cancer at a young age.'

'You'll be lucky if you ever see me get married then.'

'You'll find plenty of men that like you for who you are, they don't care if you have a tan.'

'No, I mean you won't see me because my skin is as white as the dress!' Erin replied, laughing.

Eileen was laughing too. 'You cheeky mare.'

She always used this expression, which made Erin smile because it was one that her mum often said back when she was normal. *There's a thought*, Erin paused. Mary being normal. It had been so long. At least it felt that way. She often referred to her mother as Mary both inside her head and in person. Especially when she was thinking back to when she was normal. To Erin, normal Mary was an entirely different person to the one she visited regularly at the hospital. Two entirely different people.

She thought back to the yoga class that Eileen took Erin and Mary to. The initial anxiety that she had about judgement from everybody in the room. How cruel she instantly felt towards her mother for bringing her into such a normal setting, though the therapist had said it would benefit her.

Halfway through the class Erin noticed that Mary wasn't making eye contact with the yoga teacher. She realised that she hadn't made eye contact with herself or Eileen since they picked her up. That was not so unusual, but it might be to the other people in the class. Instead, she looked awkwardly at the floor and picked at her hand which was a gesture she made when nervous. Still, Erin had to accept that Mary would be nervous when in public for a while. She wasn't acting too crazy either, so it was OK for her to be that way.

When Erin thought about her mother, she had such a mixture of feelings. Anger was towards the top of the list, both because she was being denied maternal support when she needed it most, but also that life had made her mum that way. There was only so much strength one person could have and her mum had been strong for so long. She almost thought it would have been easier for her dad to just die instantly from his aneurism. The pain and suffering after, broke her mum to the point of despair. She was not the same after the five years of suffering until her dad passed. *He changed instantly*, Erin thought, when she thought back to the hospital visits which didn't happen very often as her mum tried to protect Jack and herself. She was thankful for this.

She returned the bottle to the kitchen counter, trying to pluck up the courage to open a conversation with Aunt Eileen about the thoughts inside her head but she couldn't bring herself to do it. She wasn't feeling strong enough. Instead she headed back to her lounger, noticing her backside had left an imprint in it. She had no idea what the time was and didn't dare check her phone because she didn't want to know if there were any new messages or notifications. She gathered that she had been outside for a lot longer than she thought.

Reluctantly, she checked her phone. Her mind had returned to the dark thoughts that she experienced before, and she couldn't get stuck back into her music to make them go away. The music wasn't doing its normal thing of taking her away into another world. Sometimes she couldn't even hear it properly because her mind was so busy, the tunes weren't sticking in her head. It was like trying to plait hair after it had been freshly cut and conditioned. The strands were too slippery to combine and the length was too short to stay put.

Thoughts came crashing in. How Amy's mum must be feeling; how her two younger brothers took the news; what they think of Erin and the other girls. They should cast their anger towards the boys. If anyone read the comments underneath Amy's profile pictures they would guess these comments, if any, were the ones that hurt her.

It was awful to think that something this awful had happened in Erin's life, at such a young age, but then she felt selfish for thinking that way and making it about herself at all. It was all about Amy and her family, who will now suffer for ever. What if social media never existed? A crazy thought that she almost couldn't comprehend in this new, modern world. Sometimes she wished for it to be true.

She went inside in an attempt to remove such thoughts with a bit of rubbish TV, reluctantly doing so seeing how sunny the garden remained.

'You OK, darling?' said Eileen, looking up from her trashy magazine.

'Yeah, just needed a break from the sun,' Erin replied.

'The weather is great, isn't it?'

'Yeah.'

She hesitated in her response, noticing that Eileen had the television on in the background. It was on mute so nothing could be heard but she was watching the news so she could unmute it if anything interested her. Erin always thought it was peculiar how Eileen did this because half of the time she wasn't watching so she wondered why she didn't turn it off completely. After glancing at the screen briefly, Erin knew why the mute setting had been pressed. It was the local news and one of the tag lines was the report about Amy.

She cleared away Eileen's mug to make her exit less obvious and retreated back to her happy place in the garden, beside her brother, attempting to get lost in the world of music again. She hoped it would work this time around.

9

MARY

Saturday 1st June 2019

I am certainly doing a bit better considering I have only missed a couple of days in my diary since the last time I wrote. Writing has become a regular part of my daily routine again and I have the motivation to want to do it which is huge for my state of mind. They always tell me how important it is to keep a routine. *You must have a structure to your days, Mary.* I know I must, but sometimes it is bloody difficult, OK?

I can tell when I am getting really bad because everything seems pointless. I don't have the energy, but I also don't wish or feel excited for anything. Even getting showered and dressed seems so pointless and that is all part of this routine I must maintain. Urgh, it all gets too much sometimes.

Whenever I have had plans in life when I am in my 'normal' state, I look forward to them. Even if I don't look forward to them with huge amounts of enthusiasm, I at least see the point. Perhaps it is dinner with an old girlfriend I have always found quite boring without others in tow and I am struggling to get the energy to go, but I still see that it will be nice to talk about old times and I see the point of staying in touch with good people who mean well. If it is a works social that I must attend and I don't want to go because I would much rather binge watch a new box set on Netflix, I can see why it would benefit me personally and within my work.

Whereas in my – other state, let's call it for now – I fail to see this. I see everything as pointless and I can never find a logical solution as to why I am doing things, therefore not being able to justify wasting my time doing them. Not only do I fail to see the point and don't wish to delve deeper into discovering one, my whole body and soul hasn't the energy or strength to go. I constantly feel demotivated, exhausted and on the verge of tears, struggling to crack a smile, so any sort of social occasion becomes beyond my capability.

When I get into the driver's seat of this planet which I hope one day will happen, I am going to create a button. Much like on a television remote control. It will be like the pause button or the eject button back when we used to watch DVDs, and everything wasn't all neatly in one place on Netflix or Prime. And it will provide the same function. Everyone will have the option to temporarily pause life or eject themselves from situations that they no longer want to deal with. When they return everything will be exactly as it was when they left; it will give everyone the opportunity to temporarily leave. That is exactly what I wish to do sometimes. To temporarily leave and then come back to face it all when I am fit and ready to do so.

Anyway, how did I get so far away from the topic?

I won't bore you with the details of my missed days because they were pretty non-eventful as with most lately. Most days pass by in so much of a blur that I can't write about them because I don't notice them being there. It is like the whole definition of a day has vanished. I just live in a continuous flow of time that the rest of the world divides up into days, weeks, months, years, decades and so on, but I am not on the same wavelength. I am just in a big blur.

I know the weather isn't as warm as it should be for this time of year because I see people passing by my window still wearing jumpers quite often which is peculiar considering we are now in summer. I think. I haven't yet ventured outside because I simply can't face it. I haven't the energy and I wouldn't trust myself. I could be so nasty to an unknowing stranger, or, worse still, I could hurt them. My patience is always at its lowest when I am having an episode, so it's better for everyone that I keep myself locked away within these four walls of mine.

I attempted to start a book earlier. It was one that I have read but I was unsure about how long ago I read it so thought perhaps the plotline has left my memory. It hasn't. I was bored two pages in and already knew the ending because it instantly came back to me, lodged permanently in my mind. My thoughts reiterated my lack of seeing the point in it all, even one of my favourite pastimes – reading.

The lack of motivation and interest in things that when in my other state motivate and interest me depresses me. I never know how to get out of the mindset, nor do I remember being able to enjoy things in life, but this illness really sucks it all away temporarily. One day they will invent pills for that but for now, apparently, I have to sort it myself. So the doctor says, anyway. Pills can help many aspects of my illness but the lack of enjoyment and love for life ultimately comes from me. Maybe I'll get a new doctor.

Having failed to read and find enjoyment in anything today, I mostly spent the rest of my time longing for a phone call from Eileen even if it was just to recommend a book and then hang up. I needed some outside contact. Outside of this prison cell because that is what it feels like sometimes. Most of the time. It isn't a prison cell, and most members of staff would probably get quite offended if they heard me refer to it as one, but my gosh does it feel that way.

I miss my family. Gosh, how I miss the days where we used to spend every waking moment together. I miss not having to rely on Eileen for caring for my children. I miss Daddy. Oh I think I even miss our trip to Dublin. Before I met Brannagh and everything changed. Trotting around my home city with my two children was bliss. I smile when I remember it. Every time. I know not everything went as planned and the part of the trip that I try to erase permanently from memory was one of the worst things to happen to me but the memories of the days before that with my two innocent children are rose tinted. Certainly. I could ring them, but they may not answer and I'll get into a silly, tormented spiral of sadness over that so, for now, I'll leave it.

I have always got annoyed at people who moan about something in their lives that is perfectly fixable, yet they do nothing to fix it. Those who moan about having no money yet aren't prepared to work to earn it. Or they earn it alright but spend it on unnecessary items so are left with nothing at the end of each month and then moan about having nothing. Those who haven't got any time yet spend their days scrolling through social media feeds and watching pointless videos on YouTube, wasting their days that could be filled with the things that they frequently say they need more time for. People who moan about others not contacting them but forget that it works both ways and they can contact them just as easily. That is the category that I fit into, I guess. The ache in my wrist from writing has been saved by the ringing of my phone, I'll rest a while. It might be who I've been waiting for.

. . .

Picking up my pen after thirty minutes. No aching wrist or aching heart. I have just got off the phone to Erin. It's like some telepathic bigger being knew my wish and granted it. They are doing great. Jack is speaking more and more each day and Eileen is doing me perfectly. My ideal replacement. For now. I simply couldn't have found a better candidate for the job. While I am like I am. In my current state. As hard as I find it being away from them. Letting somebody else fill my shoes.

They didn't mention a visit, but their high spirits made me think that they will show up soon enough. Often it is unplanned because their schedules are so busy, but they want to give me enough time so if they get a free window, they will just turn up unannounced. I won't ever turn them away, they know that. I have no life in here and without them I have no life out there either.

Oh, my spirits are so high. I feel great and energised once more. It is amazing how one's mood can instantly change from down in the dumps to a big grin filling their face. I wish I felt this more but then I want to enjoy it while it lasts so we won't think about that yet.

Finally my diary is getting happier and so am I. Maybe this is the start of the upward spiral that I have been promised by so many medical professionals for such a long time. Maybe if someone is lucky enough to find this diary in the future, they won't be so bored reading it after all or start to want to self-harm two pages in. I shouldn't say that in jest, especially not where I am situated. I'll move on. Until tomorrow, peeps.

Today I am feeling:

Tired but less so, content, vulnerable, cold.

Today I am grateful for:

1. Being indoors and being mostly in my bed
2. My family
3. Eileen doing such a good job in my absence
4. My diary serving the purpose of a therapy session
5. Chocolate

10

JACK

I am still unsure what is going on, but I know that the bad thing from the other day hasn't gone away. That is definite. Eileen has brought me my toast in bed again going against the usual rules of sitting at the table to eat, especially on a school day. My thoughts are repeating themselves because I thought this the last time she brought me toast in bed instead of sitting at the table like the usual rules. Everything is getting so confusing.

I know I am usually up first, but the weekend has made me so tired that I cannot move so I got all lazy and waited for Eileen's call this morning. I am enjoying my peanut butter and strawberry jam on my toast though. It is one of my favourite breakfasts ever. Eileen makes it so well. Better than Mummy ever did. Or does, I should really say because, well, you never know.

From overhearing the conversation between Erin and Eileen before either of them knew that I was awake, I think that Erin isn't going to school today. She said to Eileen while I was listening from my bed when they both thought that I was still fast asleep that she simply can't face it. What she has to face I have no idea, but it really must be bad. For so many months I have lost count of now Eileen has been saying to her that she needs to knuckle down and work hard. Erin often skips class, but Eileen warned her that it would have a bad impact on her grades. She has some very important tests coming up in the next few months and so she can't miss any of the extra studying sessions that the teachers hold for Erin's year group at school. This is how I know that the bad thing is serious. I wish I knew what it was. It is making me a bit worried actually.

After these very important tests I think it is time for Erin to leave school completely and go off to college to do whatever she wants to do. She chooses some of her classes now which makes me so jealous because she doesn't have to do Art and History, which I hate so I would love to not have to do Art and History. Mrs Hobson doesn't like me, which is fine because I don't like her, but she makes History the worst subject on my timetable. Erin sometimes moans about still having to do Science and Maths though. I don't blame her for this because I don't particularly enjoy those two classes and I sit next to Josh Kramer who is a horrible boy to sit beside.

Mrs Hobson does this thing where we have to put our hands onto the table before we start class. I think it's to make sure she gets all of our attention. She never gets Josh Kramer's. He's too busy flicking me with his flexible ruler. It really hurts. I don't know how Mrs Hobson doesn't see. Maybe she is a bit blind. Most adults are a bit blind. They all have glasses and then forget them wherever they go. Being able to choose completely what to do would be amazing so I can't wait until I get to Erin's age when I can do that. If I were her, I would be going to school more than

I had to just to be able to make sure I passed the really important tests that would let me leave.

I tune back into Erin and Eileen having a conversation and it sounds very much like Erin is crying. Not crazy crying like having a fit about her outfit when her crying gets really loud and she sounds like a bratty two-year-old having a tantrum about their socks not being on the way that they like them to be on; the seams lining up perfectly with their toes. It still annoys me now. Instead, she is quiet crying which is almost more difficult to listen to because it is making me a bit upset too. This type of crying means that she is *really* sad and that the thing that she is crying about is probably quite serious and not just her hair straighteners have broken or something. I don't like to hear her *really* upset.

'I just can't face it, I really can't face it,' I overhear her saying to Eileen and then I don't hear a reply from Eileen, so I think she is probably just rubbing her back or hugging her tight like she does best. Eileen is the best at hugs.

I am scared to go out of my room even though I have finished my toast and would usually go out and put my plate into the bottom drawer of the dishwasher and put my glass into the top section where glasses and mugs go. In fact, I would usually be sat at the table in the kitchen so I would get up and walk a few steps to the dishwasher, then head back to my room to start getting ready for the day. It is all so different this morning that I don't know what to do and Aunt Eileen is too far away to ask her. I feel all out of place.

'Are you alright, angel?' Eileen says to me as she walks into my room and puts her hands out to take my plate and cup. I nod. 'Thank you, darling, get ready for school now.'

As I get up, I try to speak to Eileen to ask her about Erin and figure out what the matter is, but I am worried and when I am worried, I fail to speak. It just doesn't happen. No words. I have been going to special classes to help my speaking and it is getting so much better. I don't struggle anymore with easier sentences and it only becomes difficult when I am scared or unsure what the right thing to say is, so nothing ends up coming out no matter how hard I try. Sometimes I don't even know that I am so worried until I try to speak, then I realise because nothing comes out. It is quite frustrating when this happens because there is no way of telling people that is why I am silent. Aunt Eileen knows usually but sometimes I have to write it down just so she can be sure.

Part of me wants to go into Erin's room and ask her what is wrong, but the other part of me knows that I should leave her alone. This is because she will probably get angry at me and also because I can't really speak at the moment, so I best just get ready for school and go. That is what I will do. I think back to all the time I had yesterday while sitting beside her in the garden. I really should have asked her then.

I put my shorts on and find a pair of clean grey socks that will look smart enough for school on my desk. I love my desk and can sit there for hours because I am always alone there, and I love being alone. Not all of the time, but sometimes it is nice. Eileen must have put them there because that is where she puts things when they are clean. She always asks me to put the pile away, but usually she laughs because I have already done it before she has a chance to ask me to do it.

I can't find my smart polo shirt though and seeing as there were only a few pairs of socks on my desk and only one pair of pants, I think that maybe Eileen has been distracted this weekend with whatever is going on with Erin and that she hasn't washed my smart polo shirts from last week. I made quite a few of them dirty because we were playing football every lunchtime in the nice weather and Danny Smith kept being horrid and slide tackling me, so I kept falling down and getting dirt on my shirt. He knows I am not very good at football.

'Auntie Eileen, have you seen any of my smart polo shirts for school?' I ask with confidence, which shows me that my worrying has got less.

'Yes, darling. I am so sorry. I haven't sorted much of the washing, but I will get some clean ones and I'll iron them for you now. You can wear one of those today, OK?'

'OK.'

Eileen walks to the utility room and I linger outside my room to see if I can get a glimpse inside Erin's room to see what sort of a state she is in. I do this so carefully because I don't want her to see me.

Eileen returns with two crisp white polo shirts for me to put in my drawer. Well, I will put one on me now because I don't have a top on and that would not be allowed at school, not even on the hottest days in the summer. But I will put the other neatly in my drawer ready for when Danny Smith badly tackles me in football again and I get mud all over my smart polo shirt.

I like getting ready for school days best because I don't have to think of an outfit to wear for whatever I am doing that day; my uniform tells me exactly what to put on. Mummy used to decide on my clothes for special occasions like birthday dinners or friends' birthday parties, but now that is Eileen's job since Mummy doesn't live with us any longer. School days are easy, and I can decide what to wear because I know. I love being independent because it means I can spend more time on my own.

My shoes are by the front door, so I pick up my bag and head downstairs. I packed my bag last night when I felt awkward sitting in the silent living room with Aunt Eileen and Erin because neither of them were speaking. I don't need to pack much in my bag, but it is better to do it the night before rather than leaving it for the morning because if I have forgotten anything then I panic, but if it's the night before then there is no rush, so I don't need to panic. Mummy taught me that trick. Back when she lived here.

'I'll be there in a minute, Jacky,' Eileen says, and it sounds like she is back in Erin's room judging by where her voice sounds like it is coming from.

I try to reply to tell her that I have heard, but nothing comes out because I think the worry is back. Instead, I sit down on the first step of the stairs and Flo comes right close to me, so I stroke her. For some reason this calms me down so I can reply to Eileen but I don't because I think I have left it too long so it would sound weird.

'Sorry, darling, let's go.'

Eileen grabs the keys which are on the side in the same place that she always leaves them and doesn't say bye to Erin so I realise that she was definitely in Erin's room and would have said goodbye before leaving her.

'I hope that Erin is OK,' I say, half to myself and half to Eileen.

'There is nothing you need to worry about, my man,' Eileen replies, reassuring me but I still feel a tiny bit worried.

We drive off along the roads that take me to school and every time we go on this journey, I always think to myself that it would be really nice if I could walk to school. I have asked Eileen before on the longer summer days, but she says that the distance is just too far. Anything is better than catching the school bus though, so I go with whatever answer Eileen gives me.

When I first started this new school, I was only ten and now I am twelve so I might be able to handle the school bus, but I don't want to test it because it scares me. Mummy first made me get on it and there were some horrible bad people on there who laughed at me, so I always sat at the front. I made one friend who was called James and we sat and talked to the bus driver whose name was Tony, but James quickly moved to a special school and Tony got old enough to retire so I stopped getting on the school bus and my life was made better.

Usually, I have plenty of time to think on my journeys to school because Erin is always in the front seat ranting to Eileen about a teacher or a friend, so I tune out of their conversation and watch the country roads while thinking. I always think lovely thoughts and imagine dragons and wizards running around in the fields that we pass, just like in the books that I read. Our journeys to school are, in fact, one of my favourite times of day, I suppose. Today it isn't so good because I am having to think of things to say to Eileen, but I keep not being able to speak so this is harder than it usually is.

'I'm really worried about Erin, Aunt Eileen,' I say as we pull up to the drop-off point and I kiss her goodbye.

'Honestly, Jack. There is nothing that you need to be worried about, I've got it sorted,' Eileen replies, and I know that when she says she has something under control, she mostly, always does.

11

ERIN

Erin looked up at the television and wished she had stuck to her mother's golden rule of switching all electrical items off before leaving the house. Amy's parents were on the screen again. Headlines were running along the bottom. Yet again it was being drilled into Erin how real this all was and how she absolutely could not escape it. No matter how much she wished for it all to be some horrendous nightmare. All fantasy. She muted the television and slowly removed her footwear, but her eyes couldn't leave, they were fixated on the news. She just wanted to wake up.

Desperate to move her thoughts into a brighter place she began to think about Jack and how caring he was this morning before leaving for school and how frustrating it was that she couldn't tell him everything. He was far too young; she must protect him. It was an older sister duty – he mustn't know a thing.

She was finding it hard to cope with the news and she had four years' life experience on top of Jack. That on top of the fact that she was a girl which everybody knew meant that she matured faster so she probably had more than four years of experience in the bag. Jack struggled at the best of times and Erin wasn't strong enough to take on board his anxiety as well as her own. She knew that the only option was to keep Jack in the dark for as long as possible.

He knew about his mother to a certain extent. After all he would begin to question where she was or why he hadn't seen her in weeks if Eileen and Erin kept him completely out of that. They knew he had to understand parts of it but to understand from afar. They had told him that Mary needed some time out, a term that Jack was very used to, and that she was getting the care that she needed. Very carefully, they didn't give an exact time scale for it all, nor did they suggest that Jack would be able to visit because Eileen didn't know when or if it would ever be appropriate. Instead, they kept him at ease by feeding just enough information so that he would remain protected at all times from a breakdown.

The slow-motion removal of Erin's boots continued as she weakly untied each lace, reluctant to see the state of her socks because of how they felt after wading through the thick slime that was disguised as a little bit of mud. She had no regrets for the state of her footwear and feet, however, because the long walk that they had been on was soothing to her soul. It gave her that same feeling of getting into a deep, hot bath when all the muscles in her body started to relax so slowly that she could feel it.

Eileen was outside the back door drying Flo off with an old, ragged towel and Erin could hear from their muffled argumentative tones that the process was not going as swimmingly as planned.

'All alright, Auntie?'

'Shut up, you cheeky mare!'

Erin giggled sweetly and reverted her concentration to the final push where her socks were concerned.

'Ew, gross!' she gasped aloud.

'What's up?'

'My socks are filthy.'

'Well get them off outside, far away from the carpet.'

A plastic bag lay conveniently beside Erin in which she carefully placed the manky socks, her face grimacing throughout the process. She wriggled her toes to assess the state of those and decided that a shower was a priority before doing anything else. She glanced back up at the television, which was showing an interview between Amy's parents and the television presenter that was always on and who she liked but could never remember his name.

'How brave,' she exclaimed quietly to herself when Eileen walked in with steaming cups of tea.

'What's brave?' Eileen asked her, confused, not having looked at the box to see what was on.

'This,' Erin said, pointing at the television. 'Her parents. I don't know how they are able to do it.'

'Here you go.' Eileen appeared to ignore Erin's comment as she handed her a cup of tea, but it was also as if she had fully registered it and had consciously decided that saying nothing was best.

'Thank you.'

Erin unmuted the television. Amy's mother, Julie, looked slightly gaunter and paler than before, but it was all in the eyes. If Erin focused on the eyes, which she mostly did to take her attention away from the words that were being said, she could see utter nothingness inside. Julie was empty. As if inside she was dead, but, physically, she remained living. It was the saddest thing to watch, Erin thought.

Steve, the father of Amy, looked much the same as he always had and held himself better than Julie managed to throughout the interview. Julie's tears were clearly shared by Steve, but he was managing to somehow hold it together. He remained on the edge of tears, too, but never let them show.

'It must be so difficult,' Erin said to Eileen, wishing for a response that never came.

Looking over to her auntie and noticing the tears falling down her face, she turned her focus back to the television because seeing Eileen sad made her feel worse.

For the time since she had been watching the interview she realised she hadn't taken in any of what was being said and instead she was only focussing on how the two people looked rather than how they were saying they felt. Tuning in to hear the topic of conversation, she felt warmth in that they were raising awareness for mental health in young people and working towards helping those in need. People like their daughter, who they had lost for ever.

'This is hard to watch,' said Eileen.

Erin knew that Eileen hated the way she was tormenting herself by watching the news reports and reading items online about the case. Eileen's gaze turned to Erin as Erin pretended not to notice. Knowing that Eileen was worried, made everything worse. She almost felt she was disappointing her great-aunt, but reminded herself that it was a difficult situation to handle.

'Are you OK, darling?' Eileen eventually said, still looking only at Erin.

Erin said nothing. The interview ended and more news items followed as if Amy's case was just another vehicle in a long stream of traffic passing on the same street. One minute it was there, the focus of everybody. The next minute it was history. Another number, another problem to solve.

A harrowing silence filled the room. Neither Eileen or Erin said a word to each other but they both knew what each other were thinking from the emptiness within the four walls of what was usually a cosy and warming living room.

That same funny feeling filled Erin's tummy that felt just like period pains but much higher, so she knew it was that worry returning. She was prone to worrying about anything and everything. She worried about worrying and always about things that she simply couldn't change but this one was justifiable, and it wasn't going away any time soon. She placed her hand on her stomach as the pain increased and Eileen noticed her doing so.

'Darling, maybe give it a rest for a few days. As sad as it is, there is nothing you can do to change things. Sadly, awfully, heartbreakingly, my sweet, that is life,' Eileen said.

'You're right.' Erin sighed.

Eileen's voice calmed Erin's twisted stomach slightly, but it had a long way to go until she would feel OK. It was a feeling that hadn't left her since the moment she heard about Amy and one that she didn't think ever would. She knew Eileen was right and that her worrying and sadness was totally pointless, but she felt bad if she had a happy moment and she felt the deepest sympathy for Amy's parents.

'Look, I was thinking,' Eileen said, changing the topic. 'Why don't we go and visit your mum this afternoon? Perhaps see if Jack feels up to it as well once he is home from school. He could do with some family time. Well, as close to a family as we can get.'

'Yeah, that sounds good.'

12

MARY

Sunday 2nd June 2019

I feel a little broken. I can't remember the last time that I felt genuinely happy or even *how* to feel genuinely happy. This is hard.

I remember when I was younger having a day like this each month. It was always the first day of my period and it happened as regular as the months came around. Every time the eighth day of the month came, I could recite what would happen at each stage. The pains would happen first, then there would be bleeding, then the mood and then it would be over. The mood was the worst I have ever felt and remains that way to this day.

It never bothered me because it was just how it was. I would feel so miserable that I would cry until I had no tears left and for no reason that I could pin down. If somebody asked me what the matter was, I wouldn't know what to answer because I didn't know what was wrong.

I would feel so angry that I could easily have hurt an innocent stranger or, worse, somebody that I loved and not know about it or why. Rage used to fill me and then somebody would ask if I was OK and I would silently allow the tears to trickle down my cheeks and onto my t-shirt, wetting it through. It was like a thick fog came over my body and it took the length of the day for the sun to break through. Mostly I had to wait until the day was over. Sometimes even longer.

I was never actually sad or really angry, it was all down to hormones and I felt comfort in knowing that. I have tried to explain to Erin many times that this may happen to her, but she won't listen because she currently has more luck with her periods than I ever did. At least the last time we spoke about them she was doing fine. I hope that she will still come to me if and when things change and ask all the questions that every mother expects to hear from their daughter at some stage. Eileen would be too old fashioned in her answers and probably give her some old Irish homeopathic medicine to cure it. She holds such high expectations for all of that stuff! I don't rate it myself. I hope that my explanations haven't been wasted and that Erin isn't already experiencing days like mine.

The discomfort that I felt was married with frustration at the fact that it couldn't be changed. No drug, no compliment, no exciting plan was ever going to take those feelings inside me away and I needed to accept that it was just for the day. The same day every single month. The longest day. The most painful day. The most tiring day, but only the one singular day. Twenty-four long hours. Men have it so easy!

After about twenty-five years I managed to accept this at which point the menopause came. Joy! This time it was accompanied by sweats, hot flushes, lack of sleep and an

HRT prescription. Aren't I lucky? It was worse than before and for years I grew to hate my body and all that it was doing to me. Some days were better than others, but I seemed to be having a worse time of it compared to my friends of a similar age. Some of whom hadn't experienced it because I was apparently early compared to the normal woman. Yet still there was comfort in knowing that it was a natural change that women across the world experience in their lives. I was given hope in that it would be over in a few years and I could live the rest of my days experiencing happiness and peace again. Yes. Bring on retirement!

Here I am, five years later, through the menopause but experiencing the same feelings every day and they tell me that it is different. They expect me to believe that? I am not so sure, I just want it to go away. This time I haven't a clue how long it will last. I don't know all of the side effects and can't guarantee that they won't be different or new each time that I assess them all. This time there is no natural progression and a limit as to how long it will be until I can live out my days in harmony, because not every woman or man on the globe experiences this mess. Depression. Agonising depression. I am sick of it. They just tell me I'm sick.

The research on this is far behind the rest. It is ongoing and the experts don't know the answers. My family certainly can't be expected to comprehend my behaviour if the experts can't explain it. I can't explain it. Nobody can. It's that simple.

Hopefully in a few days the cloud will start to shift like it has done so many times before. I struggle with not being able to predict when this will happen, but I am starting to come to terms with it and I am determined to ride the negative wave until the fog clears.

Every time I feel this way, I pray to God that my family won't show up for a spontaneous visit as they often do. Sometimes it is more regular than others, but they know that my days often blur so they take advantage of this and I don't blame them. I don't wish for their absence in a nasty way. It doesn't mean that I don't want to see them. I pine for them every day; I just don't wish for them to see me like this. They would get so unnecessarily worried until they visit again, and I am all good. That is just the way it goes.

As always, I attempt Dr Knoll's suggestion of naming things. Bringing myself right into the moment. But, as always, this task fails and only saps more energy from me, so much so that I usually have to take a nap afterwards. WHAT IS WRONG WITH ME?

The process should go *name one object, name another, name another* and boom I feel fabulous! What it actually goes is: *struggle to find something interesting to name, name something after more minutes of tiring struggle, fail to name another* and boom – I fall onto my bed in a pitiful doze.

I don't know why I have so little energy. I don't do anything. If I go for a walk to the lake it is the biggest thing I will have done in days if not weeks. Even then I am only walking for about an hour at the most. The maximum distance I will have travelled would be, I expect, around five kilometres. That used to be my start to the day with Flo. We always went for a walk first thing, especially in the summertime.

. . .

I am currently staring out of the window at the trees. The large one to the left is blowing one way and the two buddleias to the right of this are blowing the other. How does that work when it's the same wind? I home in on one buddleia that has a beautiful brown butterfly on it. I wonder if it's rare. I would love to have an interest in something like that, but I mostly find it tedious. Today, however, I seem to be finding some interest in nature.

It's just hit me that I am writing about a buddleia and butterflies. It must be the heart of summer? June maybe, or July. Unless those hideous drugs are sending me on some awful trip. Have I missed some months? I am so confused. The air is hot, but the breeze is cool. In fact, it is a perfect summer's day. I can smell barbeques in the distance. It must be summer? There is no way that I have missed almost two months out of my life. How many visits from Erin, Jack and Eileen have I missed or been totally spaced out so that I am there in body but gone in the mind? I wonder, did they notice? I am sure I haven't missed many visits from Jack. Poor boy never gets to see his mummy. I don't blame Eileen for keeping him away, mind you. How many meetings with the wellbeing team have I not remembered so I can't say what horrible medication they are giving me now? I am in crisis. Oh God help me please.

. . .

I woke with my diary as a pillow and pen marks from my Biro on my forehead. I do feel more relaxed now though. The weather remains cool and water droplets are glistening on the grass due to the amount of rain we have had lately so I am noticing the beauty in nature both in reality and in my dream. Oh it is so lovely to dream. After talking about how tired I am all of the time it was as if my body wanted to show you all. That is how true this diary is to my life. Bring on the day when my dreams become a reality. Bring it on.

Today I am feeling:

Lost, lonely, sad, everything bad in the world. Hate it!!!!

Today I am grateful for:

(I am really trying hard for this)

1. My past
2. Memories
3. Photos
4. This diary
5. My next breath

13
MARY

Wednesday 5th June 2019

It is nearing the end of the week and I am proud of myself for getting through. I feel like I dragged myself, feet scraping at the pavement, but still I am here and so that is something to celebrate. Check me out being all positive. My therapy team will be very impressed! I always told the children never to drag their feet. *Pick your feet up,* I would shout. Now I am here, dragging the whole of me along. I am such a hypocrite.

I find this past bout of depression has been one of my worst. Hey, the things that don't kill you make you stronger! As they say. I don't want to be dead or anything, I just can't muster up the motivation to just be and would rather curl up in bed away from it all. Escape. I would much rather escape. That is exactly the reasons why I read books. To escape into other worlds far from my own.

I say that it must be the worst bout of depression, but I am sure that I have been here before. This is why this illness is so strange. Whenever I am depressed and down, I feel like

I can't remember how to be happy. Or how I was happy. I just forget the feeling of joy and positivity and feel as though I wasn't made to feel that way.

On the flip side to that, when I feel happy, I question why I am in here, my diagnosis, everything. I feel as though I couldn't get so down about things if I tried and shout at my negative self for thinking the way that it sometimes does. Things get very confusing.

My family haven't been to visit me all week and I don't blame them. I think they think (there is a lot of thinking going on here) that I am totally unaware as to when they last visited or how I act when they do but I know. Oh, I know. It is like I can feel myself pushing those I love most away and being totally unbearable company for all, but I don't even care about that anymore. They let me have a TV in my room to watch rubbish daytime television in an attempt to take my mind off all the bad stuff, but I am yet to turn the damn thing on.

It is truly baffling how once upon a time I could waste hours and hours watching reality TV. The news, chat shows and even the dreaded game shows with all their horrendous contestants, but now I can't even watch a single thing. I actually find it difficult which is totally bizarre because what is simpler than daytime television? I used to love it. I used to not only sit there and waste hours, but I was having so much fun as well. I guess those hours weren't wasted after all. It is the whole point of the programmes - escapism. That is what the producers create to pay their bills. Everybody wants to escape sometimes. It is the easiest thing to do. Well, so it should be. Not for me at the moment. I can't remember the last time I had fun or enjoyed anything.

This morning has been particularly windy with no rain which used to be my favourite kind of weather, so I kept looking outside at intervals and trying to make myself feel the closest thing to happiness. At one point a scrawny lady with marks all over her face walked past holding a bottle of wine. I thought to myself how she looked very different from the waist up compared to the waist down. It was funny really. From her face one would assume she was an alcoholic or a drug user, struggling to cope with the day to day, perhaps just out after another stint in rehab that didn't work. Money wasted.

From the waist down however, where one could notice her fancy bottle of Chablis, she appeared to be a civilised, slim, healthy-looking lady. She might even hold a high up position at a big law firm or something just as prestigious. Isn't perspective a wonderful thing?

I pondered on the bottle a while, but then remembered that I was supposed to be noticing the weather and all that came with it. The breeze. The flowing trees. The colours. The hope in the branches nowfilled with leaves. The cloudy sky with sunlight beaming in between. The glimmering puddles drying up after the rain overnight.

For a moment that I can't quite explain my mind went blank. Totally blank with nothing at all to fill it. It was like another being had come over me and taken everything out of me momentarily except my physical frame. It was so strange. I always wonder, particularly with all that goes on inside my mind, whether it is possible to not be thinking about anything at all, but even then, I am thinking about not thinking. Yet this was true, real, it actually happened, and I can't describe the feeling of relief. I felt so light.

Following that came two of the most beautiful specimens who have lifted my spirits for a week or so. I can tell this feeling is going to remain with me a while. Eileen and Erin came to see me!!! Or should I say one of the nurses came to my room and brought the news that they were in the reception waiting area, ready for me. Such a prison I find myself in and for a crime that I never committed.

'Hello, Mrs Carter,' they said, all formally. I love how I still haven't changed my name back to a Miss. Or Ms. Well, James and I never officially divorced. That would have been cruel and I'm sure frowned upon. I don't think it's usually acceptable to divorce the father of your two children because out of no fault of his own his body developed a brain aneurism which initially paralysed but eventually killed him. No, that would be frowned upon and, while I considered it, I'm very glad I never went through with it. Those days were hard, but my children had enough to cope with. The five years while James had no life and our lives were on hold.

'Hello!' I replied eagerly, suspecting I might have visitors.

'Two very special people are here to see you.'

I hate how they phrase it and treat me like a child. Just say their names. Hang on a minute. Two. Two special people! This has only got to mean one thing. I almost fell over, I got to my feet so fast and was guided down the corridor even though I felt strong enough to walk. Eileen's brought Erin with her.

'Hello! Hello! Hello! My darlings!' I shouted as I approached them both waiting patiently in the corridor.

They came over to give me big hugs and instantly I felt two stone lighter.

'Shall we go out for a walk? Lovely and windy, just how you like it!' Eileen said, mocking me for loving the wind. She hates the wind. The wind is my favourite. Not rain and wind, that's when it gets tricky, but when it is accompanied by sunny intervals like today, the wind is perfect. Cor, I sound like a weather reporter.

'Yes. Absolutely,' I replied, feeling my whole self again with my family right beside me. Erin's hug was so genuine, and I finally felt physically there for her, something I've missed lately.

We headed out to the lake and enjoyed the strong gusts almost knocking us off the pavement at times.

'Mum?' My darling girl said to me as the joyous moment went quiet for a minute.

'Yes, my darling?'

'It's really good to see you like this.'

If only she had known how I have been lately, but that doesn't matter because here I am enjoying the moment with my daughter. That is the main thing in recovery, they tell me often, it is all we have – the moment.

'Thank you, darling,' I responded happily, but also quite proud of myself that I came across that way to others. I looked out in front to see Eileen walking happily in her own world, leaving Erin and I time to catch up.

It wasn't long before we reached the lake and it looked spectacular. It isn't far and it is lovely that we are able to walk from the unit to it. It makes me feel a little more normal. The breeze made the water ripple on the lake, the sunlight shone down and my mood enhanced my perception.

'Shall we sit a while and just soak this up?' I shouted to Eileen, who was still in front engrossed in her good thoughts. Her thoughts were always good. It showed on her face.

'That sounds a great plan, my legs can't manage much more.'

'It was hardly far, Auntie Eileen,' Erin chimed in, jesting.

We all laughed.

The lake was beautiful. It reminded me of when James and I were travelling in Slovenia. Lake Bled. We woke so early and watched the sunrise. We had a map, but we didn't know where we were going so, we guessed. In the dark. We ended up climbing up a hill which was actually more like a mountain and I was in flip flops and James was laughing so much. Then we got to the top of the hill that was actually a mountain and we sat and watched the sunrise with three others who had decided to do the same. One was a photographer, set up all professionally with his tripod and fancy camera. The other two were a couple who witnessed the scene.

Memories. It has been so long since I have thought of good, happy memories like this. It has been a long time since I have thought about James and how fond I was of him. A long time since I have thought about James in a good light before it all went wrong.

'Shall we make a move around the circular walk, make the most of this weather? I think my legs have finally recovered,' Eileen said to break the blissful silence.

'Want me to head to the car and grab your walking stick?' Erin added, laughing.

'You are so cheeky!' Eileen grabbed her affectionately and they walked on in front, hugging the whole way.

I remained behind, walking a little slower and watching my auntie and my daughter outwardly show their loving bond. It was enjoyable just being with them, taking in the weather, our surroundings and being out of the unit for a few hours.

Oh boy are my spirits lifted! I would usually feel exhausted after a day out of this place because my body is no longer able to cope with the outside world, having been locked away from it for so long. It is tiring. I would go as far to say draining. However, given the length of time it has been (I think) since they last showed up, I am beyond excitable and don't think I will be getting much sleep tonight. They have given me not only a new book but a new author who I am yet to read and three of her most recent books, so I am excited for those. If sleep doesn't come tonight that is what I shall get started with. I am being so positive, and I am so proud of myself for being this way. This is SO GOOD.

All the horrible thoughts faded a while for the duration of our time together (which can I add was only two hours) and they still remain to be a little less aggressively there. A visit from my family is like injecting myself with a magical drug and the effects of this drug last a week or more. It is a drug I wish existed, but I get a taster of it by seeing my family and the people that I love the most. I just wish little Jack could come more often but Eileen tries to keep him away from the bad bits. I don't blame her at all. I understand why. He has had enough to deal with in his short life and he is still very young to cope.

Today I am feeling:

Alive, vibrant, awake, excited, all of the frantically good emotions all at once

Today I am grateful for:

1. Erin and Eileen
2. Erin and Eileen
3. Erin
4. Erin
5. Eileen

14

ERIN

'She seemed a little brighter, don't you think?'

'Definitely,' Eileen replied after a pause but with so much relief in her voice.

The pause made Erin sense that something else wasn't quite right and that she was being naive to think everything was OK. She was thankful that the visit to her mother reduced her worry though.

'I don't understand, and I don't think I'll ever fully understand mental illness. It's hard, isn't it? I read loads about it online, but I think until you're in a situation like this you never know.'

'You're totally right, darling.' Eileen said this with pride.

'Last time we visited was so awful I was worried to discover what we might find this time. I am pleased. Though she did look tired.'

'You're right. Something behind her eyes worried me.'

'What do you mean?'

'Oh nothing, doll. Here, do you want a sweet?'

Erin declined and turned her head to look out of the window with some suspicion at Eileen's words. She held her scarf close to her mouth and nose to let the calming fragrance of her favourite perfume sink in. Suddenly she felt extremely anxious.

'Auntie Eileen?'

'Yes, darling.'

'Do you think Mummy will ever be OK again?'

'Oh sure, she always is,' Eileen said with a solemn sigh and brushing off the depth of the question. 'It comes around in circles. You know that by now, surely?'

'Yes, but do you ever think that she will break the circle? That she will just be OK?'

'I don't know. She may do. It's a tricky one. Mental illness is really tough to understand. Try not to think like that and just be happy about this visit.'

'True.'

'Baby steps,' Eileen said, reminding Erin of her desperate attempt at positivity.

Eileen was so strong. Erin wished that she could be as strong as Eileen, especially after the awful visits when Eileen always noticed the good and grasped onto that tiny aspect. They were on their way to collect Jack from his friend's house because after the last visit, which was a particularly difficult one, Eileen thought about her decision to take Jack with them and felt it best that Jack was kept out of this for now, just in case. It turned out that he would have been fine to join in, but she didn't want to take the risk.

'Thank you for letting me come with you, Eileen.'

'It's OK. I sometimes question whether it is good for you or not, but then we have a visit like today, and I remember that you're old enough to cope. You have a wise head on young shoulders, Erin. You should be very proud of yourself.'

The two of them smiled at each other in the car and continued to admire the Yorkshire countryside as they drove along. Eileen felt utter relief not only because Mary seemed in much better form but also because she knew that she was doing right by her great-niece. She didn't want to taint Erin's life with negativity, but she knew how important it was to keep Mary firmly involved in Erin's life.

She knew how important a motherly figure was to a young girl. Eileen had been a temporary mother figure to Mary so often when Mary's mother, Anna, was busy with the pub. Later, after Anna had passed, she was there again for Mary. Eileen never took Anna's place, but more added what Anna couldn't give firstly because she was consumed by the work of the business and secondly because her sickness made her so weak, especially towards the end. Much like she was doing now with Erin. Not taking Mary's place, but standing in for the time being. Aunties have a different role to mothers in life, Eileen knew, and Anna had thanked her for standing in with motherly duties more than most aunties would.

Eileen would take Mary out for the day to walk along the coast in Dublin with whichever dog they had at the time and go up to see Mary at bedtime when Séan and Anna were busy with work. The pub was so successful because they put so much time into it and both Mary's parents were so grateful for Eileen because without her taking care of Mary, they wouldn't have had the time to put into their business. Séan often thanked his sister for this because he too knew the importance of a female role model in a young girl's life. After Anna's passing, he realised this more significantly but while they were running the pub it was clear too.

This was the argument that Eileen used within herself to justify Jack not being included in visits to see his mother. He didn't need Mary so desperately every day, she felt, and it could be damaging. That and his age, being four years younger made it so much harder for him to get his head around not being included. Just at this moment until Mary's condition stabilised.

'Left here,' Erin said. 'Now!'

'Ah, I always almost miss that turn!' Eileen laughed.

'Auntie, look at the road!'

'Bring on the days when you can be my chauffeur,' Eileen said as a comeback.

'I'd be a darn sight better at directions!' Erin agreed.

They pulled into a large driveway with a grand entrance but luckily the electric gates were open because they were yet another fear of Eileen's when it came to being in control of a car.

The branches of the trees hung over the track as they drove along, making for a perfect horror film setting and Erin thought of her polite decline if Cassie, Jack's friend's mum, was ever to ask her to babysit for them. To the left of the track were three large paddocks with horses grazing. To the right was a garden filled with outdoor toys.

The driveway had parked neatly on it two Audis, a Jeep and a smaller Golf, but there was just enough room for Eileen to pull up in her car right outside the door.

'They use the back door,' Erin announced as they walked towards the grand house; three pairs of Hunter wellies outside and a jacket thrown over the small brick wall that made up the porch.

'Gee, how many times have you been here?'

'Not many. Just that I know they were very particular about leaving the front door shut when we came over for a BBQ, I think maybe one or two times before.'

'OK, posh English people and leaving the front door closed!' Eileen always had to specify English.

'It's for the posh guests!' Erin joked.

'What are you trying to say?'

Erin knew the upper-classes didn't mind if you barged in without waiting politely to be invited; that was for the more common amongst society. However, realising that she barely knew Cassie, she edged the door open and shouted a polite, nervous 'hello?' Cassie came to the door looking as immaculate as ever, long blonde hair flowing.

'Oh hello, hello! Do come in. Don't worry about your shoes,' Cassie said, greeting them with yet more false enthusiasm; *another sign of their rank*, Erin thought.

'Hi,' Erin said and walked through to the kitchen, a typical country setup with an oak island around which they all gathered.

'Sorry, we're running a little late. The boys are only just washing their hands ready to eat. Do you mind waiting?'

'Not at all,' Eileen said genuinely, it felt nice for her not to be in charge for once. To hand somebody else the baton of responsibility.

Cassie went out to the rest of the house, which was shut away from the kitchen, to call the boys down for dinner.

'These folks are always running late,' Erin said quietly to Eileen while rolling her eyes and making quotation marks with her fingers. Eileen nudged her to stop being rude while still inside their house, but nodded in agreement.

Cassie returned to the kitchen and began dishing up the chicken fillets and vegetables onto the plates.

'Are you not eating?' Eileen asked, noticing only two plates.

'Oh, not now, Paul and I will eat later. He gets home just after seven most weekdays. That's London working life for you.'

Of course he works in London, Erin thought. They all smiled awkwardly, but Eileen was still relaxing in the knowledge that Jack was under somebody else's care.

'OK. As long as you don't mind.'

'Not at all,' Cassie replied, walking over to the larder to get the gravy granules. As she passed Eileen, she whispered in her ear something that Erin couldn't hear properly but assumed it was about the visit. It was about that or Amy.

'Don't worry, Cassie, Erin is fine to talk about it,' Eileen said, which confirmed Erin's suspicions. 'It went really well today. In fact, though I am very grateful for you having Jack, I don't think it would have been as awful as I thought to take him with us today. You just can't ever predict how she's going to be; you know. From one day to the next.'

'Mmm,' Cassie said, not knowing how to respond. 'It must be so hard.'

'Oh, it's just our life now. You've got to learn to live with it.' Eileen's strength once again won Erin's admiration.

'Now, boys, here you go. What would you like to drink?'

'Elderflower, please,' Daniel, Cassie's pretentious eleven year old, said.

'OK, and for you, Jack?'

Jack looked at Erin and Eileen on the other side of the room and was unable to speak. He didn't know that they had arrived, and Cassie didn't realise the importance of letting him know because shock often made his condition worse. If something unexpected happened, he was immediately unable to speak. This was something that he hadn't overcome yet despite slowly growing out of most of the other patterns in behaviour. The specialists were still working on that aspect.

'He'll have blackcurrant, please,' Erin said, jumping in as she had done so many times before.

'OK.' Cassie smiled. 'And would you two like anything to drink. Tea, coffee, wine?'

'Ooh, lovely. I'll have a glass of white wine please,' Eileen said. They weren't planning on staying long but seeing as the boys had to eat their dinner, she felt it would be rude not to enjoy a glass of the good stuff. Erin looked up at her, her gaze wishing for one thing. 'No you can't, young lady! Erin will have a cup of tea. Thanks.'

As the kettle boiled and the boys ate, Eileen and Erin gazed in awe around the kitchen and outside into the huge expanse of land that was the garden to this property. They both felt somewhat awkward mixing with people that they would never usually mix with but they also felt happy to admire a beautiful home.

'Here you go,' Cassie said to Eileen, passing her an icy-cold glass of Sauvignon Blanc.

'Thank you, love. That is just the way to my heart,' Eileen said.

They both looked over at Erin who had zoned out, gaze fixated on her brother.

'Absolutely. Eileen, it's awful,' Cassie continued as she pushed the tea bag to the edges of the mug to strengthen it.

'I'm struggling to understand how she got hold of so many,' Eileen said, confident that Erin wasn't listening.

'Or how she knew what to do, how many it would take.'

'I wouldn't have a clue,' Eileen responded, realising that she had never actually thought about it.

'Mmm. It is scary how much they know these days. Frightening.'

At this point Erin wanted the conversation to stop, so she made a sudden movement. They stirred as if they had been caught doing something that they shouldn't be and smiled in her direction. Cassie put the tea bag in the bin.

'And here you are,' Cassie said to Erin while passing her the less-welcome cup of tea.

'Thank you,' Erin replied, showing her manners and pretending she hadn't overheard.

15

MARY

Thursday 6th June 2019

I can't sit still to read my book. I have moments when I find myself getting engrossed in the story and then I think about yesterday and I feel such a buzz. I just can't shake this brilliant feeling. That's it. I feel brilliant. Yesterday evening I went on a walk after dark, they must think I am getting better to let me go, and that is something that I would never do unless I were exceedingly happy. I am exceedingly happy. They say that love is a drug. I fully believe this. A love of any kind.

Today I have already taken myself on three walks. Is that a bit much? I have so much energy, it is the reward for feeling joy. They were only short walks but they were more than I would usually do. It is only 1:00 p.m. When my mood is this level the staff have no problems with letting me out. Letting me live a life of freedom and go wherever I wish within reason. Imagine that. Freedom. That kind of rhymes. It almost sounds like a song. La dee da.

The first walk was to the lake as if to relive yesterday and all of the happiness that it brought me. I did the shorter loop that only took me around half an hour, but I noticed everything. And I mean everything.

I noticed the colours of the plants and the flowers starting to bloom and I thought of the excitement that summer has brought to me in the past. I hope that same excitement will reappear soon. We are in the beginning of June after all. The world is certainly starting to warm up, we just need it to stop raining so much. The grass glistens all day long. It doesn't need any more watering! What was I doing out so early as well? It was only nine in the morning.

I even noticed a little caterpillar on the bench where I stopped briefly for a moment to look at some more and I spotted plenty of butterflies enjoying life like me. Did you read that? Enjoying life like me. There were quite a few yellow ones which means that summer is here, I think. Well, almost. It would be if it wasn't for the rain. I think they were yellow.

I heard every sound though it was quiet. I felt every breeze that gently blew over me. I saw every bug that passed by me. I even tasted the distinctness of the summertime warmth and smelt the freshness of the air. I noticed everything.

Every person that I passed, of which there were only a few, I said hello to. In a jolly way, not a reluctant *I came out for a walk to avoid everyone and everything* kind of way. I even smiled. I mean, come on, diary. I smiled! I welcomed their presence with open arms. When alone, even if I am the happiest level of happy that I get to, my natural face is solemn. Today it was smiling. Inside and outside, I was smiling! I gave everyone my smile today, even those who had forgotten theirs. It was great. All of the strangers were sharing my happiness. Well, most of them. Some didn't give me their smile.

The second and third walks were the same, but I enjoyed the first of the two so much that I took myself to that place again. That and the lake gets pretty busy after 10:00 a.m. so mostly I avoid it unless I am in company. Especially as today is such a lovely day so it would have been packed with grotesque scenes of happy couples milling about and not working. That is, of course, my very own humble (and bitter) opinion.

I digress.

The first of the final two walks I pondered long and hard about which route to take, but felt that my happiness was best set free in and among nature, so I took myself to the woods. Twice. That was the best decision.

The breeze was frequent, so I felt as though the trees were alive with me. Well, they are alive. Of course they are. But I mean I felt they were experiencing the same kind of euphoria as I was. They danced as I danced, and we all felt free. I am in an insane asylum and I felt free. Who'd have thought it were possible? I think the trees were singing as well.

There weren't too many people on either walk and this is always a bonus. Despite my extremely welcoming mood, I might even have managed a crowd the way I was feeling. There was the odd dog walker and one lady on a horse but, other than that, I was alone in the perfect company of the trees. I sound crazy, right? I don't care. I am. My records practically say so, in a more politically correct way. Take out the industry jargon. Remove the words that I don't even understand, all the medical bumf, and it basically states that: *Mary Carter you are a little bit crazy and so we are going to lock you up in this place and fix you so you can return to the normal world and not be crazy anymore.*

I think the few dog walkers and the lady on a horse had the exact same idea as me and that they too felt a sense of freedom within the woods. Maybe they were crazy like me. It is very strange how just going to a different place and simply by being there can have such a huge impact. I felt so calm.

At one point I found a tree trunk that had fallen and was placed just in the perfect spot for me to take a break. I sat on it and watched the woodland just be. Nature. I love it. For a moment I wished that I was in some exotic country like Australia in the jungle or in South America. I wanted to be somewhere where they have different birds to your average crow and pigeon. I wanted to be among the colourful Woompoo Pigeon, the Pale-Yellow Pigeon, and the cuckoos. I guess Australians sitting on a tree trunk in the jungle would think the same. Though I doubt they would wish to be in England with the average crows and the pigeons.

My family. Oh, I love them. I love how they make me feel this good. They are the only ones who can do that these days. Even when Erin seems down, her head might be somewhere else thinking of exams or typical teenage worries, I love the fact that she comes to visit. Something inside her must make her want to because I know how stubborn she can be if she doesn't want to do something. I made her after all!

So many things before used to make me so happy but now they are all that I have. I keep getting told by the experts that it will get better. The emphasis being on the word *will.* They almost force the word out as if they too are struggling to believe it. They tell me that I will find happiness in other things one day and that this is just another wave that I must ride out, but I am not too sure that I believe them. I have ridden so many waves so far and I am not even very good at surfing. I suppose I will have to improve. Practice makes perfect.

I just wish I could have seen Jack. Of course I asked how he was doing.

'He's doing OK,' Eileen replied, looking down at her hands in her lap.

I never know what she means by this. I hope so much for my little boy that he is finding communication easier. If I was asked in my twenties about my future, I would never have predicted that any child of mine would have problems speaking. Not coming from this family. Especially the Irish side. I then remember all that he has been through. It is not fair. Life is not fair.

I said nothing in response, prompting Eileen to continue. 'He's very excited about the show, mind. He keeps practising in the garden. Erin and I watch from the kitchen window. It's very cute.'

'It's hilarious,' Erin laughed.

'Don't be rude, he's doing great,' Eileen interrupted.

I'm glad he's doing well with school which makes me think Eileen's solemness in response to my initial question must be because of me. He must be worried about me or embarrassed. I mustn't get bogged down with thoughts and worries. Not today. Not while I am feeling this good.

I will see Jack on Saturday. Well, from afar. It is his school show. The big one that they do each year. Who knows whether they will let me see him in person and have a chat with him at the end after he has performed? Maybe I will be able to give him a hug. It will depend how I am on the day. And who knows? I don't.

They say sometimes how I am (when I am really bad) has a detrimental effect on Jack's wellbeing. It is for the safety of the child. It is in his and my best interests. Yeah. I've heard it all before. I understand. I try to. I have to. I have no other choice.

On Saturday Eileen is picking me up at 6 o'clock and taking me to Jack's school.

Wow, Saturday isn't very far away. I've only just realised!!

He is performing some dances, and this is something that he loves to do best so he is usually in his best form. I love to watch him, and I am so excited. It is adding to my good mood. For sure. Even if I don't get to see him in person then at least I get to see him in his element.

Today I am feeling:

Euphoric, ecstatic, happy, thankful, excited.

Today I am grateful for:

1. Eileen
2. Erin
3. Being able to see Jack perform in a few days
4. The outdoors and nature
5. Noticing things and being aware

16

JACK

Mummy had so many tips when I did this show last year and the time before that, but this year she hasn't been available to ask and Auntie Eileen just isn't good enough. She also doesn't have any time these days, she's always busy. She never experienced being on stage whereas Mummy has. I know I should never ever say that, but she isn't my Mummy. It is only a rehearsal.

My legs are shaking and I have bashed into two people already as we are lining up getting ready to go on and practise. Normally I would be able to avoid people because I know that we are all standing close together before we go on, so I tell my brain that I have to be extra careful not to bash into anyone. My legs are so wobbly at the moment that my brain can't help it and already two people have been bashed into by me. Oh dear. This is the last rehearsal before we show real live people tomorrow night and I look out from the stage and see the sea of faces staring up at me waiting for me to perform. I just know I am going to be so scared.

I can still remember it from last year and the time before that because it was so scary. There are so many big lights making lots of brightness so I can feel the warmth on my face as if the sun is really close to me on a sunny, hot day when Mummy would be shouting for me to keep topping up the sun cream all the time. It gets quite annoying actually. But I miss it. I really miss it.

Last time I remember feeling actual sweat dripping down my face and I was so embarrassed and worried that everybody watching could see it. I don't think they could, and Mummy said that they couldn't, but I know that sometimes she lies just to make me feel a bit better. This time I keep telling myself that I am not going to be so nervous and I can do it.

I haven't got a big part like Luke Harris and Daisy Low do. They are the main ones, so they are on the stage all the time and they have loads of words to remember as well as dance routines. I don't have any words. I am so happy about that because last year and the time before that they made me say a line or two and sometimes it worked but mostly nothing came out and it was so embarrassing. People didn't understand why I struggled so much but I did and nothing I tried to make it better worked. I don't know how Luke and Daisy do it remembering all those lines let alone speaking them too. They do it so well, so I am glad that they got picked for the parts and not me.

I am extra worried about our last performance on Saturday night because not only are Erin and Eileen coming to watch, but Mummy is as well. She hasn't seen me perform since the big show last time, so I really want to impress her. Erin and Eileen probably won't focus much on me or the show because their minds are constantly busy at the moment, but I know that Mummy will be watching me the whole time, so I have to make it a good show for her.

I tried to rehearse in the living room at home when Erin and Eileen were watching but they didn't pay much attention, so I gave up and waited to practice when nobody was home. Or I go into the garden when I have all the space to myself. I feel more free in the garden and like nobody is watching me. We have a fence right the way around the garden so that Flo can't get out but also so that nobody can peer in with their beady eyes and watch me dance. I'm sure that isn't why we got the fence, but I like to think it is something that Mummy and Daddy considered.

Mummy and Daddy together, that is a nice thought. Sometimes I forget about Daddy because it feels like Mummy has been in her special hospital for so much longer than she really has. The whole time she has been in her special hospital Daddy hasn't been here. Auntie Eileen often tells me that he is everywhere, and I always look around me but I never see him. She says that sometimes she can feel him but I don't understand what she means by this. I can't feel him either because he isn't there. I want him to be but he isn't and my eyes are good eyes so I think I would see him.

I think Daddy would have been proud of me if he could see me concentrating so hard during our final rehearsal. I have to really focus on the steps because I haven't been able to practice this year as much as I have in the past with Mummy around to help. Auntie Eileen hasn't had the time to help lately. I don't know why or what but something has been taking up all her time. It is the same something to do with Erin. Before Mummy went away and she lived with us she had lots of time to help me.

Miss Foley is teaching us for the last time and I still can't remember the bit in the middle when we have to link arms with the girls and weave in and out of the lines. I get all confused and usually end up going the wrong way which would be so embarrassing if it happened on the night. Especially if it happened during Saturday night's performance, the most important show of them all, because Mummy will be there.

'Right, everybody. Listen up. Today is our final chance to perfect this, our final chance to tidy up the loose ends. Focus, try hard, but most of all, enjoy it because I just know you are going to be brilliant.'

Miss Foley spoke with so much confidence that it gave me a boost. I was ready to begin and my first dance kicks off the whole show, so it is a big responsibility as Miss Foley has told us lots during rehearsals. Her speech has given me a lift and so I think it is going to be OK, but I am still a little bit nervous. Thankfully I don't have to speak.

The music has begun, and I know that we have to wait for four beats of four and then start our moves but actually I just follow Freya Jones who stands in front of me and she is very musical so I know that I can rely on her to get it right. One, two, three, four and we are off. My brain suddenly goes blank but it is OK because the first part of the dance routine is all in one group and so I can follow everyone around me quite easily. If I do go wrong, it isn't too obvious to the audience because I am only one person in a sea of about twenty-five.

I remember Miss Foley's words at the beginning and focus. Step to the right, do that shuffle thing that Erin taught me and then step back to the left and twist. There we go. I did it! I am feeling very happy with myself, but my excitement makes me forget the next part when we all link arms and twist about. I soon get back into it when Freya Jones finds me in the crowd and shows me where to go. I really like Freya. She is probably my best friend.

The last part of the routine is my favourite and Miss Foley said we could make it up if we forget the proper moves because that makes it look more fun. We all start dancing freely and then the lights go out. This marks the start of the show and we have to quickly run off the stage leaving just Luke Harris and Daisy Low on there to begin their first bit of talking.

I feel good knowing that one out of my four dance routines went well, and I didn't make too many bad mistakes so hopefully tomorrow night's performance will be even better, and all of my family will be proud of me when they come to see me on Saturday. I really enjoyed doing it, but I know it will be scarier tomorrow because just now I didn't have an audience. I was still nervous, but I know that I am going to be doubly nervous when I perform to an actual audience. Maybe even more than double.

The next time I am due to be on stage isn't for a while. I sit down at the side of the drama studio where everybody who isn't performing at the moment is sitting and open up a script I find lying there to see if I can follow what is happening. I work out I am not on for another five songs so I can relax a bit and enjoy the action on the stage. Luke Harris is a very good actor. He goes to a drama school outside of our school, so he is always picked for the main parts and I enjoy watching him perform.

It is actually really nice to sit and watch everything that the audience will watch over the next few nights when Mummy will be coming to see me perform. I feel like I have been given a free ticket because I haven't paid but I am in the audience, enjoying the show. Everyone is really good. I hope I look that good when I am on the stage dancing.

We all clap as Daisy finishes singing a solo which she sang beautifully. Miss Foley said so. She smiles at the clapping and cheers from the crowd watching her, which is us, the rest of the cast. She shouldn't really smile at it because that means she is out of character. She is acting and the audience will clap but she has to remain being her character until they all bow at the end. Miss Foley explained this to us very early on.

The clapping and excitement is silenced inside my head when I see the door to the drama studio open. My eyes can't help but turn away from the action on stage to see who it is coming in. It is as if I know it has got something to do with me. My eyes focus when they see that it is Erin. *Why would Erin be here*, I think. She should be studying for her really important exams at home if she isn't at school in the library. I see her whispering to Mr Smith who is working on the stage lighting in the corner of the room and pointing over to me.

She is probably coming to tell me that she can't make the show on Saturday. It won't upset me too much because she doesn't make a lot of things recently and Auntie Eileen keeps telling me not to take it personally and that she is just having a tough time. I listen to what Eileen says and usually find something to focus on. This time it is the show and Erin still manages to get in the way. I really hope they can make it. I really want Mummy to see me perform and maybe I will get to see her after. Oh, I would love to see Mummy. I am getting all worried now. Why does Erin have to ruin everything?

17

ERIN

Erin opted to get the bus in to school to give her some time to think and rehearse the conversation she was going to have with whoever was on reception. Eileen had offered to drive her in, but she politely declined knowing space was what she needed.

That's all I have to do, Erin thought. Go into reception, explain the situation – that her mum was going to attend the concert so they might be late and things might not go to plan; it might frighten or worry Jack – and then leave. Get back to her studies. Chill in the garden with her revision guides. Hopefully Pythagoras' theorem could take her mind off everything once she'd done it. That was it.

It was easier said than done. She felt sick as she approached the school entrance. For a moment she waited, looking around her to make sure nobody was watching, as she attempted to calm herself and find the strength to go inside. She didn't want to show anyone how weak she felt but she needed the moment to gather herself.

Mrs Davies walked past her and towards the staff room as she entered and her smile gave her the strength to go ahead with the conversation. Mrs Davies was Erin's favourite teacher when she was in year nine and had her as a form tutor. She didn't have her for any lessons, but her support through everything was incredible. The impact of her father's death was - and always would be - devastating, Erin knew that, but for some reason in year nine with it being still so raw she needed more support for it than ever. That paired with her mum beginning to get ill with stress and Aunt Eileen still living in Ireland, she needed a strong female figure and, for a year, Mrs Davies almost solely took on that role.

'Hello,' she said, nervously and because she wasn't sure of the current receptionist's name.

'Hi there, how can I help?'

Erin was glad at how nice the lady was being and instantly felt that she was more compassionate than some of the other receptionists.

'Hi, I just wanted to talk to someone.'

'Of course, do you need a private room?'

The lady got up quickly from her perched position and was more than obliging to help Erin. She felt this attitude must be embedded in the lady because of all of the people struggling to come to terms with what had happened. Their focus was on Amy. Most issues they were dealing with lately where a student needed to talk was to do with Amy. The receptionists were always the first port of call when students were struggling and Erin guessed they must have been inundated recently.

'It's not about that.'

'Oh. OK, can you chat here or...'

'Yeah, I'm fine to say it here. It's just about the concert. I'm coming on Saturday evening.'

'OK.'

'Well, my mum is coming too.'

'Sorry, how unprofessional of me. What's your name?'

'Erin. Erin Carter.'

The lady got out a spreadsheet with more words on it than numbers. It took her a while to find Erin on it, but, after she did, it was clear that not much further explaining was needed on Erin's part.

'Right, OK. Is somebody else going to be with you?'

'Yes. My auntie. Well, technically, she is my great-auntie. She looks after me and my brother at home.'

'Yes, Eileen. Great. Well take your time and don't stress. We can put you in seats at the front which will hopefully lessen your mum's anxiety if she can't see the rest of the audience. Her focus can be on Jack.'

'Great. Thank you.'

'Take care now.'

Erin felt warm from the kindness of the lady and then realised that she never got her name. She wanted to get out of the school though and was fairly happy with how the conversation went. It wasn't as hard as she had expected.

She checked the local bus timetable on the wall. There was a bus coming sooner which stopped at the back of the school so she walked, fast paced, through the corridors to get out as quickly as possible. To catch the bus in time but also to get out of the building sooner. A building which felt so empty, like Amy's death had removed some of the structure completely. Right through to the foundations.

A bus was pulling up just as she arrived which Erin was happy about because she didn't want to risk seeing anybody she knew. She didn't want to talk. She just wanted to get home.

The journey was only ten minutes and for that she put her earphones in and enjoyed her favourite music from her favourite West End shows. This was her go-to whenever she felt stressed. A pick me up. Musicals had the power to lift her off into a happier world. Stress-free and fun. Two songs later and she was home.

'Hello, darling, how was it?' Eileen asked as Erin slumped onto the sofa which was placed in the kitchen for all the extra guests that never visited. Everything in her world had suddenly slowed down.

'Ah, it was alright.'

'Are you OK?'

'Yeah, I just hate it.'

'Which part?' Eileen put the dish that she was scrubbing down and sat beside Erin on the sofa, her presence comforting her.

'All of it really. Mostly having to warn people of her presence. It's like my mother is a monster. I hate it. Nobody else has to pre-warn the teachers or their friends that their mother is going to be attending the show.'

'Oh darling. It must be so hard for you.'

Silence filled the room as Eileen dwelled on how foolish it was of her to ask Erin to speak to the teachers about the fact that Mary would be in the audience for the show on Saturday evening. Erin was at home now, studying for the exams and Eileen – in hindsight – felt she should have gone in herself. Though Erin had wanted to go. Had practically insisted, in fact, that she did it herself as it made her feel more grown up, involved and in control of this whole situation. Eileen kept telling herself this to feel better about her position of authority.

'Auntie. Are *you* OK?' Erin asked, forcefully implying that it was absolutely not ok for her rock, Auntie Eileen, not to be ok.

'Oh. Of course I am. I shouldn't have asked you to do that today.'

'But I *wanted* to. It makes me feel helpful. And it takes my mind off Amy.'

'I know you did but this is a very difficult time for you and that was a very hard conversation to have, I am proud of you. I forget sometimes that you are still very much a child. Don't take this wrongly, I am not trying to patronise you, but I still have a duty of care to you and I should have stepped in and done that for you today.'

'Thanks, Auntie. Let's face it, I think you will always take it upon yourself to have a duty of care towards me and Jack. And Mummy. I think that is just your nature,' Erin said.

'I know, I can't help that one I am afraid. You will be thirty-five and I will still be checking that you have packed something warm.'

'God help us!'

They both laughed.

'How does it feel at school?' Eileen continued.

'Strange. There is an eerie feel to the corridors. Like she should be there but she is not. She wouldn't be in the school anyway because she would be off like me, studying, but it feels as though she is missing. The feeling is really strong. The teachers look sad too.'

'It is a huge thing when that happens. Teachers get more connected to you students than you would think. It's a terrible tragedy.'

'I guess you're right.'

Eileen hugged Erin tight to her, reassuring her that she would always be by her side. She never had to explicitly say because her hugs were so strong and so tight that they perfectly explained her thoughts and feelings.

While Erin and Eileen had been talking Jack had been dropped home by a friend. Eileen didn't expect him home so early, but she gathered due to the rehearsals and preparations for the play the school day had been cut short. He merely popped his head in and waved before heading straight upstairs. Eileen put his lack of speech down to nerves.

Eileen hoped that Jack wouldn't come downstairs for a while - for a few reasons. One was so that they could share the time alone that she knew Erin needed. The other was so that he wouldn't question why Erin was upset. He was such a caring little boy, but Eileen knew that he needed to be kept out of this situation. He had experienced enough sadness in his short life.

The two sat for a while longer, enjoying the sun on their faces down from the sun light window above. It was like they had travelled two months down the line and fully into summer with the warmth radiating into their skin but knowing the reality, they appreciated the feeling. For a moment Eileen felt pleasure in the fact that Erin was often more like a best friend than a great niece. She loved their special bond and also noticed the impending sense of Erin's maturing into late adolescence, probably faster than the rest of her peers.

'Right, I best get up and make us some dinner,' said Eileen. She had to continue making dinner, doing the laundry, looking after everyone, and not lingering with her thoughts for too long. The same process that she had been going through for years.

'What are you making?'

'Your favourite.'

Erin smiled at the thought of chilli con carne, but also at the kind gesture from her aunt.

'Do you mind if I just sit here?'

'Of course I don't. Do you mind if I put Norah Jones on?'

'If you must.'

They both laughed and Erin made a funny face as if to say that despite their vast age difference, she actually quite liked Norah Jones. She had grown up with Eileen's musical influences, much like her mother, and, also, she found it soothing even if the music wasn't particularly to her taste.

For a brief moment, Erin forgot all of her troubles and smiled with sheer contentment. Eileen noticed this and, turning back to the hob, smiled too. There was an air of calm within the kitchen as the two of them sat and listened. Eileen had the doors opened to outside to let in the summer breeze and the colours within the house made everything brighter both in a literal sense and an emotional one.

It didn't take long before their peaceful moment was interrupted when they heard noise from upstairs.

'Hey, Jacky, are you OK?'

'When is dinner?

A pause followed as Erin was in shock over how clearly he had just spoken. His worry from earlier about Erin showing up at the school had obviously passed him by. Perhaps the show was boosting his spirits and erasing his worries. Maybe that was the answer and that he was destined to be on the stage. It could solve all of his speech problems, but, for the time being, Erin was simply amazed.

'Erin,' Jack said again, fairly clearly, and Erin hadn't noticed for how long she had been lost with her thoughts. 'Erin,' Jack repeated. The word came less clearly as he was filling with frustration at her delayed response.

'Oh, er. Sorry. It will be in fifteen minutes.'

'OK.'

Jack skipped off to continue his existence in whichever imaginary world he had created while Erin lingered at the bottom of the stairs wondering if she was dreaming.

'Is everything OK?' Eileen shouted from in the kitchen.

'Yeah,' Erin replied and darted from the stairs to Eileen, who was now dancing by the hob and humming away, lost in music.

'Woah. You startled me!' Eileen said.

'Jack just spoke to me.'

'Really? Wait. Really?' Eileen had been convinced that his speech had worsened with everything going on. Especially as trauma affected it the most so she was sure that was why he had been so quiet. She gulped another sip of her wine as Erin continued to tell her all about it.

'I am certain. I wish I had recorded it. He asked, clear as day, when dinner was and then said, even clearer, that he would be down shortly. Like, who is this guy and what have they done with my little brother?'

'Erin, that's amazing! I think that's a reason to celebrate,' Eileen said as she finished her first glass of Sauvignon Blanc and refilled it with an extra-large measure.

'I wish I could drink.'

'Not yet, young lady.'

'Can I just–'

'No.'

Erin loved Eileen for everything in the world but sometimes she hated how strict she was. A lot of her friends' parents allowed them to have a glass of wine or a beer with their evening meal.

Quite symbolically, without her glass of white wine and instead with a small glass of blackcurrant squash, Erin took herself back to the chair and sulked in the peaceful moment before dinner. Her aunt was still happily cooking, and her brother was happily playing upstairs. While she longed to be allowed the habits that her peers were allowed to do, her mind didn't veer off into the darkest of places and it remained in the moment so she felt thankful. She didn't even think about her mother.

'Do you know, I am starting to like her,' Erin said, acknowledging Norah Jones filling the downstairs floor with her dulcet tones.

'At last, my plan is working. I am surprised you've not come to love her sooner, what with your mother being such a huge fan. Because of me, of course,' Eileen replied merrily.

'Mmm,' Erin said solemnly, 'Mummy never listened to music much in the last few years. I can't remember ever hearing her have it on in the house like this. Maybe she was just too sad.'

'It's an awful shame,' Eileen said, not meaning to say it out loud. Mary had taken to her musical tastes, much like Erin was in the moment they were sharing. Mary used to love getting in the car with Eileen because it meant that she could listen to one of her huge selection of tapes from the glove box. For a small child she appreciated older music and Eileen knew it was all her influence. It made her sad to hear Erin state that Mary had lost her love for music within her despair.

Now, hearing Erin speak as she was, Eileen felt so incredibly sad for Mary. The girl who used to be so happy-go-lucky, now so empty and lost from the joy of life. It broke her heart. She hoped and prayed every single day that she would be well enough to soon come back home.

18

MARY

Saturday 8th June 2019

I honestly can't stop feeling this good! I can't stop reading either, I am so utterly addicted. I was correct about not getting any sleep last night because I don't think I got more than maybe three hours in total, but I don't care and it is not affecting my mood in a negative way as it usually would. This must be the first time in well over a year where I haven't got much sleep yet don't feel like a zombie and want to kill everyone who enters my private sphere. I didn't even contemplate sleeping until my eyes started to droop like a normal person's would. Hear me? N O R M A L person. Oh gosh, I can't remember the last time I felt normal.

I have even found the time and energy to do something with my hair. For so long now I have left it to do its own thing, some days I even leave it totally matted and hope that it will sort itself out in the next wash. Today though it is neat and curly, as if I have made a bit of effort. I suppose I have. At least I think it looks good. My mood has allowed this.

On Eileen's last visit she brought with her some serum which adds volume. This, along with a new top that she bought from a local lady who has just started a clothing business. The top is lovely, bright and lightweight. I can't stand clothes that feel heavy to wear. It's perfect.

My nightly routine goes something like this:

- Read a load of this brilliant book by my newly discovered brilliant writer, on recommendation by Erin and Eileen who give me the best book suggestions ever
- Start to feel a bit sleepy like one would after a hard day's work, an effect upon a normal functioning body and mind, NORMAL!
- Eyes start to droop and occasionally drop off into the land of nod (again, normal behaviour)
- Wake up missing my brilliant novel
- Repeat

Reading this new author reminds me of my Irishness and makes me feel nostalgic. I completely get her sense of humour and the sayings that she uses all of the time. I always give Irish authors a chance. Stick with our own. It is just what we do.

The main character in the novel brings me back to my younger days mucking around in McDinton's and at Phoenix Park. Dressed in everything baggy and all with perms, we thought ourselves extraordinary but in fact we were so normal. Just like everyone else our age. I smile as I remember secretly smoking when we were only fourteen. Mum and Dad never knew because they were too busy running the business. I didn't realise I could like myself these days, but I am certainly fond of the past me. She was a cool character.

The books are so lengthy that I can get totally immersed in them and notice the time three hours later, so soaked up in fiction that I am unable to concentrate on my own fears and worries in reality. It is great. A page-turner, one would say. Her style is so funny yet so true and realistic. Gosh, I feel like a book reviewer. That is a thought.

Hey, maybe that is what I should think about doing. I could work from here or wherever I end up and get paid for writing stuff down like this. I could get paid for reading and then writing about what I think of each book that I read. A dream job. I can't remember the last day of work I had, and it does get me down sometimes. Well further down than I already am usually, except for now.

I completely understand when people talk about needing a purpose in life and work gives just that. A purpose to each day. It also brings routine into everyday life and my gosh have they all told me time and time again about the importance of keeping a routine. Even in here. Even when the most exciting part of my day is walking to the lake or the woods and back.

Part of what made me start writing this diary was from talks with my therapist about routine. Writing it down helped me get used to planning each day. Even if the plan consisted of waking up, showering, brushing my teeth, reading for one hour, eating lunch, walking for one hour, eating dinner and then writing this diary before bed. It was still a routine. Working removes that planning because for eight hours a day the plan is made for you. Work.

The last position I held was one of great authority and working hasn't crossed my mind again until recently. I was always too busy at work looking after everybody else and then I became ill, too ill to work. I have contemplated voluntary positions at local charities and such like but not a proper job and a prestigious one at that – a book reviewer. Now, that sounds rather civilised!

I look at the time to see it is 10:53 a.m. which would normally strike up a huge wave of depression in me, knowing that I am not even halfway through the day; hardly halfway through the morning and I have so much more to endure.

Not today however, today I am thinking much differently to the usual. Today I am on top form and all I can see is the good in everything. Well, mostly my book, but everything. I am on page four hundred and fifty-seven and I only started last night. Being halfway through the morning is fabulous because it means I have so much more time to read and enjoy. The rain doesn't matter because I don't want to be outdoors, I want to be in bed right here where I am with my book and nothing else. The cold doesn't matter either – thank God for central heating and blankets! One's that I am not even paying for. What a bonus. I am questioning why the need for heating in June if the world is supposed to be warming up? It seems so wrong. The weather is having an off day like I experience far too often!

Check me out looking up and ahead rather than down into the deep pit of doom and gloom. I haven't done my feelings justice because I feel absolutely fantastic right now – long may it last!

My plan for the rest of the day:

- ☐ Read
- ☐ Doze

- Read
- Doze
- Read
- Doze
- Read
- Doze
- Read
- Sleep

How is that for a routine? I do hope it works out that way.

The nurse will be in shortly to take my blood pressure (I don't even know why they do this; I have never understood why they need to do this all the time) and give me some tablets. Then someone will be in a little later with my lunch. Another nurse will come in halfway through the afternoon to take my blood pressure and give me some more medication followed by the lady with my dinner. A final nurse will come in before bed with more medication and I just have to take it, I don't even have to hold a conversation with any of them because I am ill. The nurses add to my routine as well because they have to come at specific times otherwise my health is affected.

Sometimes it is the same nurse throughout the day but usually they are different. Perhaps one will come for two consecutive times and then it will change. It is rarely the same nurse on shift for the whole day because I don't think they do as long working hours here as they do in a normal hospital. I am not surprised really because I am sure that working here is so much harder than in a normal hospital. I can say that because I am one of the reasons that makes it so hard.

This is all I have to do today, and the rest can be spent with my nose in my book. These are the only people I have to see; these are the only things I have to remember and even if I am sleeping, they don't mind. Sometimes they don't need to wake me, they just come back a little later. I do have it easy really when I stop and think about it. I have got a lovely little routine. I might show this entry to my therapist because he will love it and be very impressed. Top marks.

I AM SEEING MY BOY TONIGHT TOO. I AM SEEING MY BOY TONIGHT. I CAN'T WAIT. How did I momentarily forget? But I love it when that happens. Then you get a surge of joy rush through your whole body like the flow of blood through your veins. Woohoo! I feel great. I feel alive and it feels great!

I live in total bliss, most of the time, when I am in this mood, which isn't very often at all. Oh please, God, help me remain in this euphoria forever and a day. Please, please, please. If God can't help me then nobody can.

Today I am feeling:
Relaxed, vibrant, energised, HAPPY, NORMAL (ish)
Today I am grateful for:

1. My book
2. This new author
3. Writing
4. Good emotions
5. The visit from my family (memories of)

19

ERIN

'Erin, are you almost ready?' Eileen shouted up the stairs. 'We're going to be late!'

'Coming!' Erin replied.

She knew how important it was for Jack to get there with plenty of time to prepare beforehand and she also knew that collecting her mother might take longer than planned. That was always a factor that they had to take into consideration. Really, she had been ready for the last fifteen minutes, but it took her time to mentally prepare as well as physically preparing. She realised the importance of not showing her inner feelings to Jack or her mum. They could be stored away for a discussion with Eileen somewhere down the line. Eileen was the only one Erin could share her real self and feelings with and, even then, she hid a lot from her. Erin quickly straightened her necklace and silently gave herself the mental courage to continue. It was a locket that her mum bought her on her fourteenth birthday with petals inside from the flowers at her father's funeral.

'Hey, Jacky. How are you feeling?' Erin said, truly delighted to see her little brother looking so excited.

'I'm OK. I feel a little bit nervous, but mostly I am OK.'

'You're going to rock.' She was impressed yet again with the way that Jack's speech was coming along, particularly as he had told her that he was nervous and usually nerves significantly impacted his speech. She refrained from saying anything to his face though, because highlighting his speech usually had a negative effect on it. Nevertheless, Erin was extremely glad that Jack was showing signs of being able to control it a lot better despite his nerves.

The siblings looked at each other and laughed as they walked out to the car while Eileen proceeded with all of her usual checks on leaving the house. Every light switch, every electrical plug, all of the doors were checked at least twice and so on. It was getting worse.

Just before she stepped out of the front door, the phone began to ring.

'Hello?' Eileen answered, unexpectedly, praying that something hadn't happened to Mary and that she was still able to attend the show. She knew that it would break Jack's heart if that happened, and she also knew that she would remain on edge until the show was over.

'Hurry up, Auntie, we're going to miss the show!' came Erin's giggly voice from the other end of the line, trying so hard to keep Jack's spirits up.

Eileen paused for a moment wondering how such a young girl could come across so upbeat and chilled when she knew that, deep down, she was a wreck. It was a skill that Eileen felt Erin shouldn't have had to learn by this stage in life and one that she had mastered beyond her years. A wave of sadness washed over her, but in it was a hint of pride too. She was so proud of Erin for handling everything so well. She was also a little bit proud of herself.

'Dana is going to be on the West End. She is fabulous in everything she does. Have you ever seen her perform?' Erin said to Jack with a false excitement as Eileen got into the car, masking her worry. Eileen was happy to see them indulging in chat, not arguing. Erin got no response from Jack, so she continued, 'I learn a lot from her. At drama club I used to watch her and take note so when I next played a part like her I could do the same. I never tell her that she is someone I look up to, but I do think she is brilliant. Big-headed, but brilliant. She's a natural. You would think I would be a natural by now because I have loved musicals for so long. Hopefully one day I will make it. At least I will give it a go.'

Jack still wasn't replying due to nerves taking away his voice, but it didn't matter because Erin's words seemed to be helping both her and him. At the intervals Erin needed to catch her breath, the car fell silent. She looked out into the countryside, but her mind kept wandering to dark places, so she continued to talk. 'You know when I go to London to see a show I don't just watch for enjoyment, I really learn from the cast. I dream to be them one day. The talent is so high. So energetic. The voices are insane! As much as I miss Daddy, I am glad he left Mummy lots of money so she could treat us to days out in London and things. Some of my school friends have never even been to a show in London. Lots of them have never even been to London for the day.'

Jack was dropped at the school in plenty of time before the show, reducing his anxiety as much as they possibly could.

Once they had successfully dropped Jack off, the mood in the car changed.

'Eileen I am scared.'

'I can tell that from the amount you spoke just then,' Eileen replied, jokingly trying to keep Erin's spirits up but soon after uttering the words she realised that Erin wasn't in the mood for joking. 'I'm sorry. I know. Hey, you don't know what form she will be in. She could be in great form! We just don't know. If she is awful, we won't bring her, but I am sure that they would have let us know that by now.'

'True.'

'She has been pretty good the last few times we have been. Hasn't she?'

'I know, but public spaces always freak her out. Especially this sort of one. All of the judgemental eyes. It makes me so mad.'

'I know. Here. Come on.'

Eileen leant over the handbrake and gave Erin a big hug. She held her extra tight and for even longer than usual. Once the hug was over, she held her shoulders as if to strengthen them literally and spoke straight into her eyes.

'You have got this.'

Erin said nothing, but simply smiled and undid her seatbelt.

Mary was already waiting in the visitor's room when Eileen and Erin walked through to reception. The staff knew them well enough, but still had to go through all of the formalities. It was protocol, and in an institution such as the one Mary was in, it couldn't be avoided. Erin and Eileen both knew this, but it didn't stop them getting frustrated with the process. It was so time-consuming.

Erin stood waiting for Eileen to sign some of the paperwork and her leg began twitching in annoyance. It was like being late for something and the bus was stuck in traffic. Or each light that it reached turned red.

The staff were very good in keeping it all quite subtle as one nurse spoke with Mary while the receptionist took Eileen aside to do the mandatory requirements before entry. The staff at the unit knew as well as Eileen and Erin knew how difficult Mary was going to find attending the show. The most important thing was to keep things as normal as possible to remove the institutional feel. Especially in preparation for the event that they were all attending.

'Darling. Oh, darling girl, my baby!' Mary said as Erin walked towards her and Erin returned the hug, even if somewhat less enthusiastically.

'Hi, Mummy.'

'And, Eileen. I am so glad to see you two.'

'We are too, Mary.' Eileen replied, letting the mother and daughter embrace for as long as they needed.

'Mum. We've got to fix your hair,' Erin said, unable to hold it in. She could see that Mary had tried to do something in an attempt to make some effort but she could see that she needed to do more.

'Of course. I did try. Though I knew you were going to say this, so the nurse sorted me out a dressing table in here. Look, it is over there. It is like I have my own beauty parlour and my very own personal beautician.' Mary said this as she dragged her fingers affectionately through Erin's locks. Erin smiled, but couldn't remain still for long; eager to get Mary's appearance sorted out.

An unintended silence remained as Erin twisted the straighteners and hairbrush through Mary's thinning locks, making the curls that Mary had attempted herself more defined and even. Eileen simply sat and observed everything around her. Everything except the two family members standing right in front of her as that would be too painful.

Erin was used to doing hair for her friends. She was always the designated one when they were getting ready for parties. Therefore, her focus wasn't on her mum's hair at the moment. It didn't need to be, she had perfected the art of hairstyling. Instead, as she went through the motions that she had performed on so many of her friends, she thought of things outside of her own situation. She noticed the nurses juggling everything, moving efficiently with different bits of equipment each time she looked, hardly any were standing around because they simply didn't have time. Something must be happening because during other visits the whole place seemed much calmer, quieter, peaceful, still.

When Erin considered it, she thought it must be a very difficult place to work in. Almost, in many ways, harder than in a busy hospital ward. Somebody else could get hurt or another life be lost. And there were no machines or drugs to control this; mostly it was keeping a beady eye and remaining supportive. She noticed a man on the other side of the building looking right at the three of them, observing his thoughts and doing much the same as Erin was doing. Mentally trying to escape.

Erin continued on with Mary's hair, spraying it with hairspray at the end and looking proud of the finished product. She then rummaged in her bag and got out an array of creams, assuring Mary that none of them were thick foundation and started applying them all over her face. To Mary's surprise, the softness on her skin felt relaxing and the end result made her feel better. Stronger. She was unsure as to how, but somehow it did. Finally, Erin pulled out an old dress of Mary's; also one of her favourites. She knew that Mary felt comfortable in it and that was the most important thing. It helped that it was perfect for her frail frame, making her look a bit more filled out than she was, therefore making her appear healthier too.

It didn't take long for Erin to transform Mary into a much fitter-looking individual and when Eileen, who had also zoned out of the moment and onto other things, eventually turned her focus back onto them, she was impressed and amazed at the transformation. It wasn't perfect and the task of hiding her sickness entirely was impossible, but Eileen felt that Erin had made a remarkable effort.

'Right. I think you look great, Mummy. Would you like to see in the mirror?'

'Oh yes please, darling. I can't wait,' Mary responded, a subtle hint at falseness in her voice.

'You look great Mary. Erin has done a fantastic job. We must be going now else we will be late and poor Jack will be beside himself with worry.' Eileen said, taking charge.

'Of course, let's go.' Erin instructed.

A further silence filled the car for the journey to the school but a silence that felt more awkward than before. As if a huge amount was meant to be said but everyone was holding back.

'Are you OK, Mum?'

'Yes. Just terrified of the judgement–'

'Just be strong, Mum.'

Mary instantly felt guilty for lumbering such an honest answer on her daughter, but she was also stunned by her mature and sensible reply.

With that Eileen parked up and walked around to the other side of the car to help Mary out. Mary wasn't very stable on her feet at the best of times and when she was particularly anxious this weakness increased quite drastically; she found it difficult to eat enough. The medication didn't help either; the weakening of bone density and weight loss were included in the myriad of potential side effects listed on the leaflet.

'Thank you,' Mary whispered to Eileen. 'Thank you for helping me out of the car, but also thank you for bringing me here.'

'You're always welcome, my darling. I will do and am doing anything to make this better for you.'

'I know,' Mary replied with a genuine smile on her face and they headed into the school.

Erin had cottoned onto the fact that the makeover at the unit had made them late arriving to the show, but she also felt that it was best to keep this from her mum. They didn't realise quite how late they were when they got to the entrance, however, to see the lights were dimmed and Miss Foley had already begun her welcome speech.

'Go on in. Miss Foley will understand,' came the understanding words from the lady in reception as Erin pushed gently onto the door so that it didn't make a loud creaking noise as they entered.

As quietly as they crept in, a head turned to see who it was, and Erin felt the weight of embarrassment descend upon her. She frantically searched for their seat numbers and wished she hadn't been so shallow in spending so much time on her mother's appearance beforehand. She kept her head down to prevent her making any eye contact with friends or parents that she knew, hot with shame both for being late, but also for bringing her mother. She hadn't heard what people thought about the situation. Everyone knew, of course they did. It was school gossip. But she wasn't ready to hear it. As they settled in, the room was mostly silent, but Erin overheard a number of conversations which made her realise that it was not her family's situation that was the focus of the room, but Amy's death.

'Such a shame and so devastating for the family,' she heard one mother say to the other.

'So awful, I can't even begin to put myself in their shoes.'

For a moment Erin forgot entirely her own embarrassment and instead felt overwhelmingly sad for her school friend. Each time she heard it spoken about out loud she felt how real it was. It was as if she was almost beginning to allow herself to be separated from it on a day-to-day basis but still she knew it was there with all the feelings that came with it. But hearing it out loud exploded the emotions within her, like putting polos into a coke bottle as they had done in Science class and suddenly it all felt uncomfortably real.

Eventually they found their allocated seats, which were the few empty ones towards the front, and they sat down. Mary was in the middle. Jack's first dance began.

. . .

'Here you go, darling,' Eileen said as she gently placed a cup of tea on the coffee table beside Erin who was sat on the sofa in deep thought.

'Thank you,' Erin replied, forcing a slight smile.

'I know it must be so tough.'

'It really is. I found tonight particularly hard. I don't mean to fuss over her outfit so much, but I just know that everyone will be looking and judging her, and I just can't handle that.'

'I know, darling. I know.' With these comforting words Eileen moved next to Erin, hugging her tightly. Part of her felt so proud of Erin and how she took everything on her chin and part of her wanted to cry herself for the world in which Erin had come to know so well.

'How did Jack go down?' Erin asked, extremely maturely.

'He went straight away. Like a heavy log. He was shattered, bless him.'

'I think we're all shattered. I'll go to bed after this if you don't mind.'

'Of course I don't. I won't be far behind you.'

20

JACK

I am tying up my shoes really tight because at the end of one of my dances last night they untied, and I almost fell over in front of everyone. That would have been so embarrassing. I am sitting on my special step that I have been sitting on lots when it wasn't my turn to be on stage and I feel quite comfortable here. It isn't actually my step, but it is the one that I always sit on, so I call it mine. I know that I don't own it. I am not that stupid. Who owns a step? I suppose the school does. If it was my building then I would own it but it's not so I don't.

Erin and Eileen dropped me off and went to pick Mummy up, but part of me thinks that they are lying, and she isn't coming at all. I don't know why they can't tell me these things or why they couldn't take me to pick her up. We could have just left a few minutes earlier and we would have had time. They never take me to see her even though I tell them that I can handle it. I really can. I am stronger than Erin. She cries all the time and I hardly cry at all, but she gets to go and see Mummy as often as Eileen does so I don't know why I don't get to see her hardly at all. Eileen tells me it is for the best and because Erin is older, but I don't know why that matters at all. She still cries all the time, and I don't.

I look up from tying my shoelaces. I quickly look back down because I really have to concentrate on things like this, especially when I am so nervous like I am now. This is the most nervous I have been before any of the other shows. I can feel people crowding together and they are all quite close to me which I don't really like but the space where we all get ready isn't very big, so I have to be strong. Like stronger than Erin strong. I can be strong.

I see Daisy Low and Liam Harris talking quietly to Miss Foley and I think she is probably giving them a team talk. They have done a really good job of playing their parts this week. In fact, I think that maybe they have been better in this show than they were in the show last year and the one before that. Maybe they have learnt because they got older. Everyone improves with experience. Anyway, they are both really good and I am glad that they are doing the main two parts because I would be way too scared.

I am also not good enough. They have so many lines. I could never remember that many lines and, on the night, I am sure I would be too scared to say that many lines. Like speak them out loud.

I stay put, sat on my special step, but instead of looking down at my shoelaces I am looking up at everybody. My shoelaces are all tied up extra tight now anyway, so they won't untie, and I won't fall over.

I watch as Miss Foley wraps up her kind words and lets Daisy and Luke get ready. I can tell that they are kind words because all three of them are smiling and Miss Foley is always kind so I know that her words would be kind, always. Especially right before the start of the big show.

Miss Foley walks towards the door that we have to go through before we enter the stage, and she begins to read her notes. She has to do a big speech to welcome the audience and to tell everyone about the safety stuff like fire exits and things. This is when my nerves get really bad because I have to get ready in the side bits of the stage while Miss Foley talks, and I know that I will be on stage soon. My legs feel like the jelly that Eileen always makes for my birthday. If my legs were taken off me and put on a plate right now, I think that they would be wobbling around like my jelly does on my birthday.

From one corner of my eye, I can see Miss Foley and from the corner of the other eye I can see Daisy Low walking and it looks like she is walking towards me. I don't even think she knows me too much. She is a really nice girl, but I doubt she would have time to notice someone like me. I am in the background and I don't even stand out when I am on the stage because there are so many of us doing our dances at one time.

'You've been great this week, Jack,' she says to me and because I am so nervous and also because I really didn't expect her to speak to me, words just won't come out of my mouth as hard as I try. 'I hope you're enjoying yourself. That is the main thing.' That is what Miss Foley says all of the time and it really helps.' She continues to speak, and I continue to be silent, but I wish so much that I could talk properly. I just smile to show her that I am enjoying the conversation and that I do agree with what she is saying. I think sometimes that people just accept that I find it difficult to speak properly and I really like that because not many people take the mickey out of it. Daisy sits by my side on my special step a few minutes longer and then gets up to go to the front of the queue waiting by the stage door to stand with Luke.

For a few seconds I forget how important this show is to me and how nervous I really feel. I forget that Auntie Eileen, Erin and possibly Mummy will be sat in the crowd watching me. I wonder what Mummy will look like. It feels so long since I last saw her. I wonder if her hair will be all knotty like last time or if Erin will bring her hairbrush and sort it out.

Everything goes quiet in the corridor where we have all been getting ready and that is when I know that Miss Foley is beginning her speech, so I need to get ready for our dance. More ready than I have ever been. We go onto the stage at the beginning of our dance and stand for about thirty seconds before the music begins and the moves start so it gives me a little bit of time to calm down and also perhaps to spot Auntie Eileen, Erin and possibly Mummy in the crowd. We decided to do it this way quite late on in rehearsals and it was something to do with the sound and the lighting guy, but I don't really understand why. I don't need to understand why. I just know that is what happens.

Miss Foley wraps up her kind words and everyone claps which is when we start to walk onto the stage and get into our starting positions. This time, maybe because it is the final show, Miss Foley talks for longer and we walk on while she is still talking. We have never done that before. While waiting for about thirty seconds I try to put my head up slightly to scan the audience and to see if I can spot Mummy. I know that we should have our heads down to the ground as it looks the best and that is the way that Miss

Foley taught us, but I don't think people will notice if I look up slightly. I am really careful. Besides, they are all supposed to be looking at Miss Foley and listening to her words.

I look up and down all of the rows and find it very hard to tell who everyone is because of the dim lighting and the brightness from the stage. Slowly, I go through everyone and I don't think I can see them. They might be sat right at the back because there is darkness over those audience members because of the brightness from the stage but I am sure Erin said that they had seats closer to the front.

As Miss Foley says her final few words about enjoying the show and all about how hard we have worked, I see the back door open and through it come Auntie Eileen, Erin and Mummy. They make their arrival very obvious and I feel a little bit embarrassed because of this. Everyone turns slightly to see. They don't interrupt Miss Foley's speech, but they all still look and stare.

Auntie Eileen is holding Mummy up and Mummy looks scared to be there. Erin looks very embarrassed like she did when Grandad Séan would dance at family parties. She is walking a few steps in front of them trying to find their seats. She is in such a rush. They are late after all and it is quite embarrassing for me so I can see how it will be a lot more embarrassing for Erin.

I am right and they are walking closer towards the front. I am both happy and scared that they are here to watch me. Mummy looks really tired. Her hair is all matted although it looks like Erin tried to brush it and put it into a presentable hairdo before they brought her here. Maybe that is why they are late. Her skin is all spotty and loose, especially on her face. It is like when she went on that diet that her friends were all on and Erin told her off immediately because she was losing weight too quickly and, also, she was really miserable. That is what she looks like now: really thin and really miserable. I wonder why. She should be excited to see me.

21

MARY

Saturday 8th June 2019

2:56 p.m. Finished my book. I made a pact with myself not to do anything else before I finished my book. That includes this diary. I hardly slept through the night because I just kept reading and when I couldn't sleep, I picked up the book and then I couldn't stop. It was so good. The ending was fabulous. I wonder if I would enjoy it as much if I wasn't stuck here. Who knows? Who cares?

Big day ahead of me today. Big event. Going out tonight and mingling with the public. Big step for me. Usually when I get taken out by Eileen and Erin it is just to a park or the lake and not many people are around. Never Jack. I rarely ever see Jack. This does make me very sad. Big time. Maybe that will change soon. I guess as he grows, he may get stronger and then Eileen will feel that he can become more involved. Hopefully I won't have to think about that too much as hopefully I will be out of here sometime soon.

I got side-tracked. People. I rarely have to come into contact with the normal functioning public which is great. Even if there are people around during our walks or daily outings then I never have to interact with them. I don't know who they are. I just go about my day, trundling along and trying to smile for my family who have so kindly made the effort to come and spend time with me. That is all.

Tonight, I have to face the actual public in a confined space. It gets me really nervous. Eileen knows this so she will be extra gentle with me later on when they come to pick me up for the show. This frustrates me because I know that she means well but it makes me feel more like a patient than ever. It can come across as quite patronising. This is another thing that I must let go of though because my aunt has done so much for me, I cannot begin to show my gratitude enough.

One thing that is helping to keep my spirits up though is the fact that I get to see Jack tonight. Oh, my boy. He will make me so proud even if I don't get to physically touch him, hold him. He might be too freaked out to speak to me but we will spend an amount of time within the same four walls so it will be brilliant. That is huge for me. So worth the stress of going out in public.

My poor boy, I wonder what he makes of all this. I would love to know. My mind has gone back to that wonderful time in Dublin last year when he was holding my hand walking by my side and chatting away about the zoo. He loved his trip to the zoo. I felt like I was winning as a mother as well. A parent. Both parents. I couldn't quite work out his words and what he was saying, but I got the gist and figured out the points he was trying to make. It was one of the first, and possibly only times, Jack and I have partaken in true conversation. It was sensational.

While appearance matters, it's not what gets me so wound up beforehand. It is more the sheer amount of energy that it takes for me to be there and to act in an appropriate way with everyone, not to mention working out how Jack feels and making him feel as secure as possible. Erin too; she must struggle with it though she never speaks to me about her struggles. I guess that is what fills the car when they leave each time and go to pick Jack up from whichever friend they have left him with.

What will fill me with worry from now on is whether the parents will recognise me, want to talk, ask questions – worst of all – ask me how I am. I will worry about seeing teachers who once had parents' evening with me and my children but now deal mostly with Eileen. Even the children might ask or look and wonder which is sometimes worse. I will feel very self-conscious. That is by far what I hate the most about this illness and being locked away from the world. They tell me that it won't be for ever.

I wish I hadn't finished my book.

. . .

I had to stop writing and start doing because it was healthier for my mind. I took myself on a walk to the lake and thought I was going to just sit and soak in nature but instead I just walked because any amount of sitting set my head off again. It was a beautiful walk though and now I am filled with mostly only excitement to see my boy perform tonight.

There were some beautiful colours surrounding the lake and this doesn't only make me happy for the normal reasons of colourful flowers making anyone happy, but I am always pleased that I notice them. It is a sign of having a good day with my illness. The smells also were strong and apart from the freshly mowed banks that the gardener prepares for the public to sit on for picnics and such, the flowers' fragrance was strong enough to smell from afar. I needn't get up close to them to experience the glory.

There weren't many people out either which was great but surprising due to the beauty of the day. In fact, I really enjoyed my walk on my own. Am I allowed to say that?

Phew! I am exhausted, but pleased with myself. I am glad for my walk; it got me in the right headspace for the evening. Erin and Eileen arrived promptly at half past six and sure enough I was styled to Erin's approval. Bless her, she is only trying to help. I am sure she's embarrassed on my behalf.

Getting into the car was even a struggle. I bashed my head on the roof and my foot slipped on the first attempt to get in the front passenger seat. My legs were weak making the struggle worse but I managed on the second attempt thankfully. We drove to the school and I kept telling myself to be brave for my boy. Though they had arrived well on time, the styling took a while, so we ended up being late which didn't help matters at all. Miss Foley was doing her well-rehearsed speech which I think is the same each year. Though she may be as nervous as me and who knows what personal troubles that she goes through daily, so I must be kind. I must be kind.

I crept in and was thankful for our timing to a certain extent because Miss Foley's speech was done in a spotlight, meaning that the entire audience was in darkness. That smell that I hadn't smelt in a while seeped into my nostrils.

The smell of artificial cleanliness, much like a village hall or any communal space. Numerous smells simply masked rather than gotten rid of. What else would you expect in a school?

While heads turned, I really hoped that they didn't work out that it was me. Yet with Eileen and Erin almost holding me up, I suspect that potentially they did. At least nothing was said of it and, best of all, I didn't have to make small talk with any of the school mums asking how I was doing. Blah. Blah. Blah. I simply walked (struggled) in and sat down.

Erin sat extra close to me and took my hand to squeeze. She knew that she couldn't talk much as the show was about to begin, but she silently told me that it was going to be OK. It was strange when we switched roles like this. An odd feeling. It happens so often now and Erin is very qualified to take on my role, supporting me as I should be supporting her. Like now, tightly holding my hand, reassuring me that I will survive.

The warmth of Erin's clasp spread up my wrists and around my body giving me a little more strength to not let my fears and struggles get in the way of enjoying the show. The room was silent, but my head was so loud. One thing that was certain was the pride for my boy and genuinely positive emotions show well on my face so that worked in my favour. It was hard being separate but seeing him standing there looking at me and grinning with innocent happiness filled me with so much love.

I could feel Eileen's gaze of concern glaring at me throughout the performance which strangely made me cross, but I must remember that it is only out of care. Deep, deep care. She only wants the best for me. Erin didn't watch me, her eyes were focused on the stage, but her hand didn't leave mine for the duration and she doesn't know how much this helped.

Jack and I didn't get to talk afterwards because Miss Foley didn't think he was strong enough. I walked up to her as soon as the lights came on, but I knew from her face that the answer would be a no.

'I just think it would be a little too much for Jack right now, Mrs Carter.' I said nothing. 'Daisy had a chat with him beforehand and reported to me that he wasn't able to speak. As you know, a lot of Jack's peers are aware of his problem but they are good in showing concern. I think currently his anxiety levels are a little too high and you being here will be enough for him to take in for now.'

I hate that she gets the final decision. I hate that my life is so controlled when, before all of this, I was totally in control. Of everything.

I felt tears brimming, but knew I had to accept the circumstances and leave with Eileen while Erin stayed there waiting with Jack and partaking in the post-show refreshments. What a dysfunctional family. What a dysfunctional life. I hate how much anger can build in me after what should have been such a normal, happy evening.

Today I am feeling:

Started the day happy, filled it with apprehension and ended in fury.

Today I am grateful for:

1. Reading and books
2. Nature
3. Erin and her beautifying skills
4. Eileen and her warmth
5. Jack and his smile

22

ERIN

THE DAILY NEWS

Friday 31st May 2019
By Gregory Smith

Teenager Amy Milner is thought to have committed suicide after experiencing trolling online. Her body was found by a local dog walker on Tuesday evening, a few days after the young girl was last seen leaving her home in Huntington village, just outside of York.

Police issued a missing person report when Amy didn't return to her home on Monday 20th May.

Miss Milner's mother, Julie Milner, spoke to the paper yesterday:

'She was the kindest girl I knew, and we had no idea what was going on inside her mind. She always seemed so happy, embracing all that life threw at her. I feel totally heartbroken that I couldn't help our little girl.'

It is thought that a situation that occurred on social media for a few days leading up to Amy's death may have been a strong contributory factor. The police are looking into this alongside a local mental health charity in an attempt to prevent anything so awful happening to other teenagers in the future.

Julie and Steve, Milner's parents, are also keen to get involved with the charity which encourages young people to speak out about their issues and to not take what they see on social media as reality. They want it for their daughter's legacy. They are also fighting for stronger punishments for trolling.

'At the end of the day it has cost our daughter's life,' said Milner's father Steve.

'It's such a shame that it has come to this. Social media can affect young people a huge amount. Our charity seeks to help mental health in young people. We aim to offer a place that they can come to talk without any of their friends knowing. A safe haven,' says Judith Edmons, founder of the charity. 'Teenage suicide is on the rise and something needs to be done about it. This all needs funding. We are here to help with that too.'

Erin placed the newspaper down the side of the sofa as she heard Eileen's footsteps getting closer to the living room. She didn't want to alarm her auntie and she knew that it wasn't good for her to keep reading over and over the same story. It was a form of mental torture, but she simply couldn't help herself.

'All OK in here, darling?' Eileen said, checking in.

'Yeah, yeah. Grand.'

'It's awfully quiet.'

'Oh, uh. Yeah.' Erin attempted a small laugh, but felt embarrassed by how obvious she was making it look. Eileen clearly knew that she was up to something. She was in the living room sat in silence. Nothing around her to be occupying her. Erin didn't just sit and certainly not in silence.

Eileen left the room with her worried look lingering still inside the living room. Erin remained on the sofa, jittery. She took a deep breath in and looked up at the ceiling. She then let her breath out for as long as she could and cast her gaze down to the floor. At this movement she could see too much of the newspaper for her liking and began stuffing it down even further into the sides of the sofa.

'Here,' Eileen returned, 'I got you and Jack one each from the bakery.' She handed Erin a Belgian bun. The icing was the perfect amount and glossy as if it had just been made to order. Erin paused a moment to consider the calories. Prom was fast approaching and all of her peers were so skinny. 'Are you OK, darling?' Eileen asked as if she had said the wrong thing.

'Yes, sorry,' Erin answered, quickly snapping out of her vain worries. 'Wow. Thank you, Auntie Eileen. That's a real good one!'

'Fancy a nice cup of tea to go with it?'

'Yes please.' Erin smiled, holding her thought a moment as to how Eileen almost telepathically knew that something was wrong. She knew exactly how to make things that bit better, more bearable. She also knew when not to ask and to just perform random acts of kindness which always helped so much.

Erin sat in the living room with her gooey Belgian bun on her lap and her cup of tea warming her hands and her soul. She remained in silence because she felt no need to put on the television to disturb the pleasant moment. She then chuckled to herself at how old she sometimes was for her years.

Flo came bounding through from the garden. *She must have been outside with Jack*, Erin thought, she had thought that the house was spookily quiet for him being home. That scene would mostly have ended in Flo on the sofa to greet Erin because she had been away from her for an hour or more. Instead, with food involved, she sat at Erin's feet looking directly into her eyes.

'No, no. Flo, darlin'. You are not allowed this cake. It is all mine, and you are getting a little podgy around the edges.' Flo stayed in the same position and didn't react to a word that Erin was saying to her. Erin laughed at her persistence for a dog with a minimal attention span. 'No. No you can't. Nope. Don't give me those eyes. I will take you out in a little while. Oh, OK then. Just a small bit.'

Erin and Flo enjoyed the remainder of the cake before Erin got up to take the empty dish and mug into the kitchen to load into the dishwasher.

'You're a good girl, Erin,' Eileen said as she entered the kitchen, 'Do you fancy going for a walk?'

'Sure,' Erin replied and suddenly remembered the newspaper wedged in between the side of the sofa. She knew that Eileen wouldn't get too cross; she was more likely to become worried and for an eighty-year-old lady Erin felt that worry needed to be minimised.

Before she did anything else, she snuck into the living room and removed the newspaper from the sofa. She took it upstairs into her room to file away with the rest. She never knew what she planned to do with the articles. She wished she hadn't got into the habit of obsessing over them. It was clearly why she felt so tired all the time. It was always at night when her mind would want to check another fact or how something else was phrased before it allowed her to sleep another minute.

One day she would burn them, and she doubted that she would read them again because she knew that Eileen was right, and it was all damaging to her own mental health. One thing that she was certain of was that she didn't want her aunt to find the stash, so she hid them well.

23

MARY

Wednesday 12th June 2019

My spirits are high with pride having seen my boy perform and I think that is what is keeping me up. I could sleep for days, but the buzz I got from the show is giving me a little energy whereas otherwise I would have none. Shattered. An event like that makes me shattered. It used to be my normal, now it crushes me.

James was always such a character that we all always said he would have been great on stage so that must be where Jack gets it from. Erin too. In fact she's always been more for the stardom than Jack. He was great. And so confident, though I know that he wasn't deep down. Then again, I look to everyone these days as confident because I am the total opposite. I never used to be.

It did annoy me how much my daughter cares about appearance though. It was the first thing that she thought about after hugging me on arrival to pick me up for the show. She went straight to fixing my hair and makeup.

Urgh.

It is also the magazines and how they plaster all over them the most immaculately presented women, no mention of airbrushing. My poor girl must think that is how everyone has to look. Going to a function like the school show must be hell for her as she tries to compete with that. How can you compete with that? A computer image. It is basically a painted, perfected, edited version of every single woman that walks this planet.

They will all have a makeup crew, a lighting team, cameras at all angles and, even then, they have a computer programme afterwards to polish the final product. We are expected to think they rocked up to work looking that way. Or that they go to the supermarket and look just as perfect. I don't think so. I will have to have a word with my little girl.

I was grateful deep down and she did make me look lovely though. Well. As lovely as I have done for a very long time.

In further news I have been quite chilled lately and I am not sure why. I have spent a lot of time in the past few days out in nature because the weather has been kind. All the experts say how good this is and I usually question how much they know about psychology, but recently I have been in agreement.

The ground that had been left and the river banks made way for the beautiful colours of summer. The air felt so warm on my face that I even removed my cardigan for a length of time and wore only a t-shirt without feeling a chill. Each face I passed seemed happier than a month prior. Spirits were lifted, including mine and I stared out at the lake soaking it all up.

It was beautiful. So, I captured it. Wonderful.

That's enough for today. I think I might sleep tonight.

Today I am feeling:

Can I say chilled? As close to that as I can get, proud, slow, restful, a tiny bit of resentment that I just can't let go.

Today I am grateful for:

1. Jack's performance
2. Inner peace
3. Sunnier weather
4. Hints of summer
5. My diary to log it all

24

ERIN

Julie Milner has slept with her daughter Amy's favourite t-shirt every night since she went missing.

'It smells of her as if she is still here with me,' Julie reported.

Speaking to the Daily News *she added:*

'I feel heartbroken. Utterly heartbroken and helpless that I couldn't be there for my little girl. I couldn't talk her out of her decision or tell her that things were never as bad as they may seem at the time. Tell her not to make any hasty decisions before it was too late. Sadly, it was too late. I wish I had sat down with her and discussed things. I think I could have made it all better. Or at least then we could have handled it together.'

'Eileen, would you look at this!' Erin exclaimed in horror, unable to hide the fact that she was reading yet another article on the case. It had made her far too angry for that.

'What is it, darling?' Eileen came rushing in from the kitchen, putting the dinner on hold to see what the fuss was all about. It could have been anything.

'This article is horrendous. It's awful. If I were the parents, I would sue them. How can they write such a thing and get away with it? It isn't even accurate. I'm sure Julie never even said those things. I'm sure she can hardly string a sentence together through the tears. I've witnessed her being interviewed on TV. It makes me mad.'

Eileen sat beside Erin and began to read through, skim-reading because she had read so much on this story and found it harder to do so each time. That reason as well as the fact that the potatoes had begun boiling for the stew, so she didn't want to overdo them.

'It is very shallow. I can't see how they get away with publishing this sort of stuff really. But, honey, you shouldn't be reading this stuff all the time. It isn't good for you.'

Eileen could see Erin's annoyance at her words and moved closer in beside her to give her a hug. At this point Erin broke.

'I know it isn't. I just care.'

'I know you do, and that is a good thing.'

Erin looked up at Eileen because she could hear her upset in her voice and they sat in silence apart from Erin's sobs. At that moment Eileen remembered the potatoes, which was a good thing because her tears were coming.

She often cried alone so that she could maintain the illusion of strength to those around her. In fact, she was a firm believer that crying was no sign of weakness and that those who cry are actually among the strongest in society. Yet she never wanted her family to see her crying as she felt that she had to remain a pillar of strength for their benefit and peace of mind.

'Darling, I am just going to turn the dinner down and get the table laid. Please don't worry. As sad as the situation is, there is nothing that you can do.'

'But what if I could have done something? That is the thing that I keep thinking. It goes round and round in my head all of the time.'

Eileen looked at her, failing to find any words of comfort, so got up to finish the dinner.

Since the day that the news broke about Amy, Erin had felt guilty. She knew that suicide, which is what she had decided it would have been from the start, was something that was a lone act so in that sense nobody was to blame for the physical death. She was aware that she wasn't involved in any of the comments that had caused Amy's hurt, yet part of her felt guilt over her death. She had been over the words that had been on the news so many times and then proceeded to search social media multiple times to find out the names of the trolls. They weren't even friends of Erin's, in fact she hardly knew them, so where the feeling of guilt came from was bewildering, but it was very much there.

She knew that Eileen was right, as was always the case, and that she should stop over-analysing the scenario because it was such a complex one to try to understand, but she couldn't stop herself. It was everywhere. It was the main focus of conversation as friends sent through more pictures of articles on Snapchat and WhatsApp group chats didn't stop pinging. The headlines were full of it; she would be watching television at night and it would come on the news. So Erin couldn't escape it, but then felt more guilt for making it about herself when she thought that way.

Hey Erin.

I keep reading the comments from Luke and Darren...

A text came in from Kirsty. Erin hated when she had been singled out for advice. She was tired of giving advice. Her closest friends had a Whatsapp group between the four of them and most things were discussed in that.

The more I read them the more I think how bad it is.

She also hated how everyone in her year sent separate messages for each sentence. She always wrote everything in one but everyone else sent a sentence at a time, sometimes a word at a time. It built tension that Erin didn't have the strength to wait for.

I feel really guilty for not seeing how it affected Amy.

Do you think we should have done something? You knew her best.

Erin didn't have the energy to reply. She had made a mistake in opening the message so she knew she had to, but everything in her didn't want to think about someone else's view on the situation. She was only coming to terms with it herself. Trying to work out why and what had happened. Where it all went wrong. How she could have helped. And all of this was being considered in her own time. She didn't need Kirsty putting on the pressure.

I'm really not sure what we could have done. OMG. It's just so sad, she replied and hoped that it would stop Kirsty texting more.

Well I was looking at Luke's profile earlier and Amy has liked every single post.

All his pics

Everything

Erin felt her head was going to explode with the text tone repeatedly chiming. She turned her phone onto Silent so that Eileen wouldn't hear either. Rather than opening the texts she just read them from the home screen, knowing the risk of Kirsty being hurt by this, but also removing the pressure. She could just say she had been called to do some chores or something.

Surely that means his comments can't have hurt her that much?

She wouldn't have bothered to like anything.

Don't you think?

Maybe the trolls were others. Didn't you say you had seen them named somewhere?

'Jack, Erin! Dinner!' Eileen called from the next room as if she too was trying to take her mind off something by shouting louder than necessary, but Erin was hoping that Eileen's speciality, Irish stew, would take her mind off the horror. She was also thankful for having a genuine excuse to leave her phone in the other room.

'Yum, it smells delicious,' she exclaimed on arrival at the table and Jack's beaming grin expressed his happiness for their favourite Irish dish.

The smell reminded Erin of Ireland which sometimes felt more like home to her than England did, even though she had lived in England for her whole life. It took her right back to the pub that her grandad once owned and that they always visited on holidays. She never had to worry about fitting in there because everyone was family; they had no choice but to look out for her. In fact, the pub that her Grandad once owned was long gone and a much more modern restaurant stood in its place, but they still visited so that Séan, Mary and Eileen could talk about all the memories that the building held. It was as if just being in the same building, despite it looking entirely different, gave Séan and Mary the feeling of being back at McDintons. Even if stew wasn't on the menu, the place still smelled of it to them and Erin was warmed by this fragrance due to the memories that came with it.

Things were different with her dad's side of the family. Everything was a little more rigid. More formal. Often quite awkward. She never felt as welcome visiting her English family as she did when she went to Ireland. Even people who weren't true relatives adopted Erin and Jack as a brother and sister, never leaving them out of conversations or plans. She loved both families and the Irish side had the advantage of being a lot bigger, but there was a significant difference in the way each visit made her feel.

'Jack, you were great on stage.' Erin said, bringing Jack's focus back into the room because he too had temporarily gone absent. It worried her whenever this happened as she considered what thoughts were buzzing around his brain.

'Thanks,' he replied, confirming to Erin that the thoughts weren't too distressing as he was able to speak.

Having cleared the plates again to take her mind off everything that it was focused on, Erin returned to the living room. Her phone was still flashing.

?

??

????

You there?

Erin?

For the duration of dinner, Kirsty refused to take Erin's silence for an answer.

25

JACK

'Darling, are you all ready for bed now?' Eileen says to me as she always does because sometimes I think she is a bit unsure about whether she is getting it right. I'm always ready, but she always asks. I know I must brush my teeth and get into my pyjamas. I know the process; I am eleven. But she always asks.

I nod. Something is worrying me, but I don't know what. I always know I'm worried because I can't speak but sometimes I don't know what that worry is. It's like my body finds out before I do.

'Good boy. Now, tomorrow we have to be up early, OK?'

I nod again. Nothing is happening when I try to talk.

'Right. Now you need to be up early and dressed smart. I'll help pick your outfit.'

Auntie Eileen goes to my wardrobe and picks out my brand-new trousers and my smartest shirt. I'm glad that these are the first things she picks because I'm very happy with her choice and I can't speak to say anything else. Nodding is easy. I don't understand why suddenly I'm having to dress smart all the time. Like last week when I was promised the cinema, but we had to go to the police station first. It doesn't feel right. Maybe that is my worry. But I don't know why. All these secrets are so tiring. Then I am not sure if it is just because I am young and when I get all big and adult, I will understand everything from before. I don't know. I will just have to wait and see.

'That's great then. Sleep tight, darling boy, and I will see you in the morning bright and early.' She leans over me to kiss me on the forehead. 'I love you. Gosh, your hair. So grown up.' And then tears fill in her eyes. Auntie Eileen never cries. This is a proud cry that I'm getting all big. I don't understand why adults do that. Why cry when you are happy or proud? Adults are very confusing.

'Auntie Eileen?' I manage to say just before she leaves my bedroom.

'Yes?'

'Why am I having to dress smart all the time and why am I having to get up so early at the weekends?'

'Gosh, Jack, your speech is amazing!'

I don't think she meant to say that out loud because whenever someone says that I stop being able to speak because I get all embarrassed.

'Now go to sleep, there's a good boy.'

I think she forgot that I asked her two questions.

Usually on Sunday mornings I am allowed to stay in bed for as long as I like. Especially since the bad thing that I don't know about happened. Erin and Eileen take ages to wake up so I can just sleep and play with the toys in my room and pretend that I am still sleeping so nobody disturbs me. I like it this way. I can go into my own imaginary worlds which are the best places to be. I have to make sure that I am really quiet though because sometimes my toys crash, and then there is no hiding that I am awake. I never want anyone knowing that I am awake.

Today though I have been told that Eileen will wake me up early as we have to leave the house for something. I wonder what that something is. Hopefully, I will find out soon. It can't be early yet because Eileen hasn't come in to wake me up and I can't even hear any footsteps around the house so they both must be sleeping still. I really hope that they haven't forgotten about our plan or, even worse, overslept.

My mind is going crazy with thoughts about what it could be that we are doing today and also about whether Eileen and Erin have slept through their alarm clocks. I wish mine wasn't broken because then I could see what time it is. I can tell the time now, especially on my alarm clock because that one literally tells me in the numbers on the screen. Like, if it says 7:05 then it is five past seven in the morning. Easy. It gets a little trickier when it is after lunchtime because I had to learn that seventeen means five. It is like seventeen hours after midnight. At the start, when I was learning, I found it all very confusing but that was years ago so now I find it easy.

Oh. Very exciting. I can hear footsteps. Usually, I can tell if it is Erin or Eileen but I am finding it hard this morning. They seem light so I think it is more likely to be Eileen because she considers others sleeping whereas Erin just stomps around as if nobody else lives in the house.

'Hello there, darling! How did you sleep?' Eileen says to me as she walks into my room and opens my curtains.

I just smile and roll over under my duvet to face Eileen. Words don't come easy this morning and I think it is because I am so stressed about what it is we are going to be doing today. The stress about whether Eileen and Erin had overslept has now vanished because I know it isn't true. After all, Eileen is in my room so she is awake. But I think that the after effect of that worry, mixed up together with the worry about today's event, altogether is leaving me unable to speak. Eileen knows this though, so she sits down on my bed making sure that she doesn't sit on me.

'Here's some orange juice and toast to get you started.'

My aunt is so kind. Hearing her voice reassures me and removes most of the worry faster than anything else in this whole wide world. It means I am able to speak again sooner, but it is never soon enough for my patience. I get so frustrated with it. Especially today because I just want to ask and then know what we are doing. It is really annoying because when I get frustrated it all gets worse and then I can't speak for longer.

'Now, you enjoy. I am just going to make sure Erin is up and then I'll come and grab your empties so you can get ready.'

I smile as a thank you and wish for Eileen to be able to read my mind so that she can answer the question that I cannot ask. Sadly, she doesn't have this superpower and she leaves the room.

I sit extra quietly and don't start eating my toast straight away because my munching will make noise inside my head and then I won't be able to overhear the conversation in the other room. I try to listen in carefully for any clues but all I can hear is muffled noise and then the dog starts barking which stops all chance of hearing a thing. Thanks, Flo.

I eat my toast and drink my orange juice and think to myself that this is my favourite breakfast. I do like it on some Saturday mornings when Eileen cooks up sausages and bacon and things, but I like toast and juice best.

'Right, darling. How're you getting on?' Eileen is back in my room and I still can't speak. 'Erin is getting up now, so you need to get washed and dressed and then we'll be off.'

I want to ask where, but words don't happen. Not today. Not right now. I hope this doesn't affect wherever it is we're going because sometimes I can have whole days where speaking is impossible. Eileen clears my plate and cup and heads downstairs to feed Flo so hopefully she will stop barking and I can get ready in peace. Hopefully how long it takes me to get ready is enough time to calm my nerves and the stress inside me so that I can speak when I go downstairs.

I am very happy that Eileen and I went through my wardrobe and picked an outfit last night because the thought of trying to choose one this morning would be too much. Instead, I can just grab my smart jeans and bright-green t-shirt and I am ready to go. I also had a bath last night so this morning I only have to put on my face stuff that Eileen tells me I must put on every day and brush my teeth. That is it. I am ready.

I head downstairs and stop by Erin's door to see if me waiting there gets her to come out and tell me what is going on, but she just stares at me and smiles so I don't think I am making it too obvious. As I walk down the stairs, I make a thump, thump, thump sound and Flo hears so she runs to the bottom step and waits for me. She is a very good dog and knows that she isn't allowed upstairs, only at

Christmas. I smile and fuss her before going in the kitchen to find Eileen.

'Hi there, Jack. Are you OK?'

'Yeah.' I reply. I replied! I spoke! I must have calmed down. But I can't get too excited because that will reverse it and any big emotion stops me talking.

'Good. Now, while we wait for Erin, I will tell you what today is all about. Sit down there.'

Eileen points to the sofa which is in the kitchen and I never know why. It doesn't look like the right piece of furniture for the room. Anyway, it is very comfortable so I don't argue with her command. I am also very thankful that she has finally got my inside message and is going to tell me what is going on. At least, I hope she is. I hope she doesn't do that typical adult thing of only telling part of a story so that I am left still guessing about the rest.

'Now then. You know your mummy isn't very well at the moment and you haven't been able to see much of her lately. Well, it is very difficult to understand, especially for young people like you. Even the doctors don't fully understand it. What is wrong with your mother can't be seen. It is not like a broken leg or an infected chest. Her illness is inside her brain and sometimes it makes her do and say things that she doesn't mean. She may look different and act different, but she is still your mum and wants to see you. Lately her health has improved, and I spoke to the doctors about you coming with us for a visit. The trouble is, darling, it can sometimes be very distressing if she is having a bad day. We might get there, and they tell us to go home. However, we might get there and have a lovely time. You see?' Eileen pauses for me to think. I nod. 'Good boy. Now put on your shoes and we'll get in the car.'

I feel a mixture of happy and sad and worried. I want to see Mummy, of course I do, but when she came to my show, she didn't look like my mummy at all and didn't make the effort to come and see me after. I have not spoken to her properly in months. She must have been very poorly. I always think it is so unfair that Erin gets to see her more often, but when Erin comes back from visits she usually acts all weird so then I think maybe it isn't such a bad thing that I don't go. Now I am going so I have to be brave.

'Oh hey, dude!' Erin comes up to me and pats me on the head. I laugh and am extra happy that she is ready in time and we won't spend ages sitting in the car waiting for her.

Erin and I leave first while Eileen stays inside locking up and sorting Flo out. I am thinking about lots of things and I think Erin is too because she is silent as well. I don't know where Mummy is staying so I wonder what the drive is like. It can't be too far away because they never stay overnight.

We head off in the opposite direction to school so it must be in the middle of nowhere. If we are ever going out for the day and we head in this direction the place that we go to is the only place for miles. There are fields everywhere and no buildings. Occasionally there will be a farm shop and we will stop there for the toilet and a drink. Eileen often buys something and then regrets it afterwards because it is too expensive and she didn't need it.

I am annoyed that I didn't look at the clock at the front of the car as we left because I would know how long we have been driving for. Then I don't know how long the total journey is so that wouldn't help me either. Neither Eileen nor Erin are talking so I guess they are thinking as much as me. Imagine if we didn't think at all. I think I would have a lot more energy.

We come to some random traffic lights in the middle of nowhere and Eileen is indicating left so we must be turning. In my experience of long journeys, turning off a main road usually means that we are nearly at our destination. And I am right. Here we are. It looks just like a hospital, but a hospital made into homes. I suppose that is what it is because everyone living here is living but ill. Eileen parks up and we walk inside.

The entrance is one of those circle doors which I struggle to get through so Erin helps me. I have got stuck in them too many times and Erin always gets embarrassed so she just comes in with me now. Sitting in the waiting area is my mum but she looks so white like the walls around her. She smiles as she sees us and has an even bigger smile when she sees me, but her lips are almost purple. I don't think they told her I would be coming.

'Oh, Jack, darling. What a lovely, lovely surprise,' she says as we all walk over to her.

She definitely didn't know I was coming. This day is going to be harder than I thought. I don't think I will be able to say a word.

26

MARY

Sunday 16th June 2019

Ahhhhhhhhhhhhhh the biggest sigh of relief. I didn't write that like a big chilled-out sigh. It was more like screaming in anger. Let me try that again. Ah. Sigh. My boy came to see me for the first time. My beautiful baby boy. I hope he isn't too stressed out now. Sitting in his room wondering where his mummy went and why she had been replaced with a maniac. He looked so frightened.

He didn't say much, but I could see in his face behind the fear that he was happy to see me. He has always been a mummy's boy. James and him never got the chance to properly bond, life's traumas got in the way of that, but Jack and I – we have the most special bond. We really do.

We had the best time today and the great thing about it all was that it was sprung upon me and I didn't know about any of it. I didn't even expect a visit from Eileen and Erin today until the nurse came and told me to get ready because they would be arriving in under an hour. I got ready so quick I didn't even think about it. I knew after last time that their visits would become less frequent over the next few months because of Erin's exams and I just accepted it. I had no other choice.

Erin will do great in her exams, but I do understand that she needs to work hard and study. My girl needs to focus to get to the next stage of her life. I can't believe she has already reached that point and that she will be entering the next stage of existence before we know it. Wow. Time flies. I wonder if she ever will make it to the West End. Her childhood dream that I hope still remains strong.

I can tell that she knows that she needs to put the effort into her work too as sometimes when she visits me her mind seems to go somewhere else. She is probably solving a maths equation, reciting the latest script for the summer show, or figuring a new invention that she will go on to make, making herself millions. I have always known that Erin will make it big one day. She has always been so determined and while that was a struggle during her early years, it will be a good thing soon. I just know it will.

Anyway, I didn't even think about getting ready and I knew that Erin would do my hair and makeup all over again if I looked too embarrassing for her to be seen with in public. Well, with the public beside the lake, which on a Sunday is never that busy, surprisingly. Thankfully.

They arrived and we headed out into the late springtime sunshine that was breaking through the clouds as it had been raining all morning. I don't think I allowed any of them to speak for the first half an hour. I was babbling on about nothing, but I was just so happy to see them all. Especially Jack. He ran in front as we reached the lake which was almost empty. It was just the four of us and I absolutely loved every minute.

I performed Dr Knoll's most favoured technique at all times. Live in the moment. I was right in that moment. The moment that lasted the whole morning. The moment that was the happiest of my year so far. The happiest that I can remember in my time here as much of it has been pretty bleak, I won't lie to you.

In fact, I can't remember too well what we spoke about except that I asked Erin in detail how she was getting on with her studies and each time she tried to change the subject. She must be so nervous. I wish I could be there for her more. In more of a motherly way. More present, like physically there, not locked away in here. It was nice to have time to talk it all through with her though. I want her to know how interested I am and I want her to know that I am proud.

We walked and we talked, and we sat on the bench looking out at the stunning lake, just appreciating time together. Eileen had bought a stash of cakes from the local bakery near our house. She always goes to that bakery and if ever she needs to lighten the mood she will be sure to provide delicious treats from there. It is one of her go-to moves and it always won everybody over no matter what the situation was that required them. I couldn't stomach a full cake though, much to my disappointment, as I was too mixed up with good emotion, so I wrapped one half up to take back with me and I am enjoying it now as I write this. It is out of this world. I hope whenever whoever finds this diary that the bakery remains open so that you too can enjoy a treat or two. It is called Cake House, York. Amazing.

Oh I am just so happy that I can't even describe it fully in these words.

Erin looked so beautiful and Jack, oh Jack, is growing up so fast into the most handsome boy. He will turn heads. I am sure he already is, if he is not too young for that. I have never asked him if he has a girlfriend. Or a boyfriend; we are in the twenty-first century. I think he is still too young, but I expect he is popular at school. He is a good kid so I think it would be hard for his peers not to like him. As if I don't know all of this. I really should know. As a mother, as Jack's mother, I should be fully involved. Maybe next year.

For the first time in such a long time I feel out of place being in here. I am questioning my diagnosis and keep having to look at the letter they sent me all those months back after that awful day - the worst. I remember it so vividly and I thank Eileen silently every single day for doing what she did back then. She remained so cool for the entire duration when, deep down inside, she must have been petrified.

I really don't feel as though I should be in here today, does that mean I am getting better? I found my letter earlier:

Mary Carter, you are being detained under Section 3 of the Mental Health Act 1983, whereby you shall remain at Cherry House hospital until your treatment plan says otherwise.

Has my treatment plan ended? Am I free to go home?

Who knows? I don't. Shall I frame it, I think, as I rip up the letter into tiny pieces and place it firmly in the bin.

Today I am feeling:

Happy, funny, normal, relieved, good.

Today I am grateful for:

1. Jack
2. Erin
3. Eileen
4. My cake
5. This diary

27

ERIN

'Are you OK there, dear?' Eileen asked Erin as she walked into the sunroom with a cup of tea in her hand.

'Ooh. Is that for me?'

'Why, would you like one?'

'Of course I would, a McDinton through and through, me, even if my surname is Carter!'

'I love that, your Irish roots shining through loud and proud. The tea is yours, darling. I am just finishing some ironing so mine is beside me in there.'

Eileen loved her great-niece so much, but worried about how she was *really* doing. She almost wished that she wasn't such a joking character all the time as it often masked her inner fears and struggles that Eileen knew she was facing currently. She also knew how to deal with Erin in most scenarios as she knew so well how to deal with Mary back when she was younger, less so now. In so many ways they were so different, but they could be so similar as well.

'I am going to finish the chores so I will leave you to your music.' Eileen knew to leave Erin and trusted that she would come to her in time if she needed. Besides, she had spoken openly so far during the process of coming to terms with Amy's tragedy, so Eileen felt comforted by this fact despite worrying all of the time.

'Thanks, Auntie. I've got all the musicals on the go, surprise!'

'You certainly know how to spend a Sunday afternoon well. Especially a rainy one. Just like your mother used to. It must run in the family.'

Eileen smiled as she left the room and Erin watched her go before smiling with her and losing herself again in music. She continued to find music comforting in ways that allowed her to completely switch off from real life and the tragic events of it all. It had the power. Her complete focus. She couldn't imagine a day without music being a huge feature.

Flo came in as she finished the album and Erin decided to continue shuffling tracks for a little longer with Flo tucked in beside her on the sofa. Her eyes were heavy and she was almost asleep, helped by the light patter of raindrops on the skylight.

It took her a while to return to the relaxed state that she had been in for the time she had been in the sunroom, as she was considering discussing with Eileen whether to burden her mother with the news about Amy. She was fully aware that the staff might not approve of her telling her mother. They might think it would be too much for her mother to handle. She was also aware of her absent mindset occasionally during visits and how she would hate for her mother to think afterwards that it had something to do with her.

The morning's visit with Jack had gone so well that Erin felt the next step would be to maybe bring in the news about Amy. How easily her mother had appeared to accept the reasoning for Eileen to be afraid of bringing Jack gave Erin the feeling that perhaps she was ready for more reality. She might be strong enough.

The rain was falling heavier now, and she had to turn her music up so that she could hear it over the pending storm outside. All of her thoughts were veering her focus away from the lyrics and instead back to Amy. She repeated her favourite song to prolong the time that it would take for her web of emotions to kick off in a chaotic spiral again. She stroked Flo softly, desperately clinging onto the chilled feeling she had just moments ago. She looked up at the ceiling to see the droplets from the rain had completely covered the skylight, preventing her from seeing out, and she gave a big sigh. The walk around the lake that morning with the spring sunshine poking through the clouds seemed a lifetime ago.

The relaxed feel seemed to strengthen in the moment as she closed her eyes, but she also knew that this feeling would never last long. She enjoyed it while it did though and smiled with only the sound of rain and the quiet murmur of Eileen's singing coming through from the other room. Eileen knew exactly how to build a sense of calm into a home and Erin thanked her every minute for this. Calm is what she needed, always.

Jack must be sleeping, she thought to herself as it was very rare that he wouldn't be making a racket if he was home and awake. It was also very unusual for Jack to sleep during the day. His spontaneous napping only occurred during the very early stages of his condition in another reaction to the trauma, aside from his selective muteness. It was as if he couldn't cope and his body's way of doing so was to simply shut right off and fall asleep. It made sense really and Erin wished that it could be a rule for adult life. The closer she got to it, the more she wanted to shut down like a laptop and sleep off the worry.

'Has it helped?' Eileen asked as Erin walked into the kitchen and put her mug into the dishwasher.

'Lots. How's Norah?' Erin replied, and Eileen smiled. She listened to Norah Jones so much that they spoke of her as if she were a friend or a member of the family.

'She's grand. She's always grand. She makes me feel grand. Makes everything grand.'

'You should know! You sure love that word, *grand.* Is Jack upstairs?'

'He is. Though he's being worryingly quiet.'

'I know. I am going to go up and see him.'

While Eileen loved Erin's genuinely caring ways, she could tell that there was a heaviness about her character lately. The conversation was light, but Eileen knew Erin better than that and could see the real feelings behind the chat. She soothed her worry by finishing the last few items on her ironing pile and indulging in the beautiful voice of her favourite singer.

Eileen rarely got to enjoy moments to herself, especially recently, so she clung onto any time that she got. Even though she was ironing which in her opinion was the most boring of chores, she was content in the moment. It wasn't until she got moments to herself that she realised how stressful it was to be in her position. She didn't get the time to stop and dwell on it. Yet she felt the weight on her shoulders whenever the children weren't around, or she wasn't answering phone calls trying to sort more of the mess out. Thankfully, the moments rarely lasted, forcing Eileen to remain in the position of holding it all together.

'Is everything OK?' Eileen asked as Erin pulled up a stool and sat at the breakfast bar. She was half asking about Jack, but mostly urging Erin to discuss her own feelings.

'He's grand. He told me to go away so he's more than grand,' Erin responded, going against Eileen's wishes.

A silence filled the room.

'Auntie Eileen?'

'Yes?'

'What are your thoughts on telling Mum about Amy?'

'Oh, darling. Is this what's been going on with you?' Eileen felt a sense of relief in that it was a specific worry for Erin that they could talk about.

'I just feel bad when we visit, and I go quiet because I have lots on my mind. Like I am not always in the best of form and I would prefer to be able to discuss it rather than leave and Mum think it is because of her. I would hate her to think it is because of her.'

'I understand where you're coming from. I am just not sure your Ma is quite strong enough yet. It's a tricky one.'

'But this morning she accepted the fact that Jack was there and the reasons behind why he wasn't ever there before.'

'Yes. She did so well. You are right. Hmmm, you've thought about this in lots of detail.'

'Sometimes, sadly, it's all I do.'

'Tell me about it,' Eileen said in a stern reply, but inside her worries had just doubled considering how much this was all on Erin's mind.

'I realise that they are kept away from news and media as part of the recovery process, but do you think it would be a good idea? It might even make things a little easier for Mum. She would want to know. Amy and I were at school together since the day dot. I don't think I can keep it from her any longer.'

'I think if it would help you then we should think of a way to approach the subject. How about we visit again on Thursday? That way Jack is at school so he won't feel left out. Besides, he saw her this morning. We don't have to mention it to him, especially because the reason we are going he really doesn't need to know about.'

'That sounds good. Thanks, Auntie.'

Eileen paused putting the iron and ironing board away and walked over to Erin. She gave her a big hug from behind and kissed her on her head. A tear trickled down Erin's face and she felt thankful that her aunt had allowed her to momentarily crumble.

As the two of them paused in the moment, the rain strengthening on the windows, Eileen pondered over whether she had made the right decision. Her gut was usually right, but this time it didn't feel right and that was usually a bad sign. A reason to go back on her decision. Yet she also knew how much Erin wanted to let Mary into the torment and she could see, in a way, how it might help Mary.

Mary needed purpose and to feel like she could help others. She also needed normal and this was far from normal. The fact that Jack showed up to visit boosted Mary no end because, of course, she was very happy to be reunited with her little boy. It also uplifted her because Jack being there made the situation more normal. Eileen was sure of it. During every other visit there was a significant presence missing and that made Mary very aware of where she was and the situation that she was in. Jack being there removed this.

Eileen wished desperately that these thoughts didn't follow her around like Flo whenever she wanted to be fed. They were right by her feet and never left. Though she would always much prefer Flo to be there than her awful thoughts. It was like a light switch that turned on at exactly 6 o'clock each morning and eventually turned off at around 11:00 p.m. if she was lucky. It usually caused disturbance through the night; a flickering of thoughts.

Her thoughts were constant and plentiful. She thought about Mary and analysing every aspect of that situation. She worried about Erin and all that she had possibly going on inside her young head. It was so wrong for her to be so young and to have gone through and still be going through so much. Too much. She was full of fear that she was neglecting Jack in it all. This was on top of the everyday task of keeping everyone alive, safe and well and organising appointments, bin collections, exam stuff for Erin and school things for Jack. The mundane. She wished for more of the mundane. It was too much, but Eileen never let that show. She then realised that she was temporarily failing at this disguise as she remained holding Erin on the sofa, tears still trickling down both of their cheeks.

Erin looked up at Eileen and smiled as if to say *enough now* which made her again consider how tough Erin was being through all of this. Flo ran into the sunroom all excited and then back into the hall. They both wiped their tears away. Jack peered in round the door as if he was asking whether the coast was clear, in his own unique way. At this point Eileen suspected he knew that something was going on. She really hoped she was wrong, but it was too easy to see on his face.

28

JACK

It feels so strange seeing Mummy again and I don't know what to say to her at all. Not that I can. It is like there is so much to say that I don't know where to start. For now, I won't even try to speak because the stress will probably leave me silent anyway. I will just let Erin and Eileen do all the talking as they are experts at talking. They really are. Sometimes it bugs me, but today I think it will be a good thing and work in my favour.

I already understand a bit of why Eileen hasn't let me visit Mummy much until now. Just looking at her is quite scary. Her face looks so thin and so white. Like one of those ghosts in the films that I watch. Her lips are almost purple. And her eyes look empty. Well, obviously they have eyeballs in them, but it is like she is not thinking about anything inside her head. I am always thinking so I don't know how she does it.

I find it hard to understand and Auntie Eileen has explained it to me so many times, but Mummy isn't physically sick. Like, she doesn't have a broken leg or a funny tummy or cancer or anything like that. Daddy had a thing that happened to him that made him die but Mummy's isn't physical. I don't think it will make her die either. She just lives with it inside of her brain. And it is not very nice.

When Auntie Eileen explains it to me, she says that Mummy's brain has a battle with her like the characters on my video games and in the films that I watch. Her brain tells her to think certain ways or do certain things that back when she wasn't ill, she would never do. It is very tricky to understand and usually my brain has a battle with itself trying to understand everything that Auntie Eileen says. Sometimes it just shuts off completely and then I have to ask her to repeat what she said slower and clearer. It is hard.

Part of me wants to be back at home with my toast and juice, and Flo sitting at the bottom of the stairs waiting for me. Not having to think about this difficult illness and Mummy suffering in this place every day while we all continue on living our lives like normal. Part of me is happy to be here. I wonder what happens next. Do we leave this place? I don't feel very comfortable here. I don't know how Mummy stays here all the time. I think that she would be better off at home. It is much nicer there and warm and friendly. But then where would Eileen stay? Eileen is sleeping in Mummy's room and the spare room still hasn't been cleared out. It doesn't even have a bed in it. I guess we would have to rearrange everything and buy Auntie Eileen a bed.

She only moved in with us when Mummy was taken to this place or wherever she went first. If she went somewhere before this. Eileen lived in Ireland originally, where Mummy was born. Daddy never visited Ireland. I don't know why. Grandad Séan rarely goes back, it was always

Eileen who came to England. We did visit last year but I can't remember much because it all turned bad and when things turn bad, usually, I forget all about them. I remember the zoo. That was fun.

This place is like a hospital but emptier. There aren't as many staff or as many patients. People are moving around slower than they would be in a hospital. I guess more people die there so people can be more relaxed in here. It is more like a hotel for ill people. Maybe not a hotel as that suggests that they are all on holiday and judging by how Mummy looks, I don't think she is on holiday.

Mummy hasn't stopped looking at me and I hope my face is smiling otherwise it would be a little bit awkward. I think I am smiling. I am trying really hard to smile and not show my confusion because, really, I don't know what to think. I really hope we go somewhere else because I don't like this place. I hope we go out for a walk or something.

'Right. Shall we head out? I brought some fancy cakes so maybe we could go for a walk by the lake and enjoy them on the bench. Seeing as the weather is in our favour. For now, anyway. The rain doesn't look too far away, and we might need to sit on our coats on the bench, but we will make do. Does that sound OK, Mary? Do you feel up to it?' Eileen speaks like she is holiday relaxed. Maybe it is a hotel where Mummy is staying after all. I don't know how she can be so calm and normal when we are here. But then I remember that she has been more often than me and also that she is older. I am only eleven. I am allowed to be a bit afraid of places like this and mummies like mine.

I also wonder why going for a walk is such a big deal and why Eileen is asking Mummy if she is OK with going on a walk. We always used to go for walks, and it was never a big issue. Mummy loved it. She always used to suggest it. We walked Flo to the end of the field and looked out into the hills. It all looked lovely and Mummy used to comment on this every time, saying how lucky we were to live where we do. Did.

'Yeah, that'll be grand,' Mummy replies and inside I am cheering. I couldn't last in here much longer.

I am excited to go to the lake because I bet it is surrounded by big trees and lots of birds like the walk near our house. I also love water and always look into it trying to find my reflection or spot any fish swimming around. I am just excited to go out for a walk and not be stuck here with Mummy looking like a ghost.

We head out and go in the opposite direction to the car so the lake must be only a walking distance from this place. Though you never know with Eileen. Sometimes she says places are near and that it is fine to walk, but the walk feels like it takes forever. By the time we reach wherever it is we are going to my legs ache so bad that I wonder how I will make it the whole way back.

I am hanging back as we walk on purpose because Erin and Eileen have so much to say to Mummy and I can't get my words out anyway. They keep looking behind them to check that I am not lost, and I am very happy with this setup. It means I can think on my own without getting too stressed about it. Things are getting very stressful.

For once, Eileen was right when she said that the lake wasn't far because already, we have reached a woodland area which I am guessing leads directly to the lake. We pass a lady with a dog as we go through the fence at the entrance and we all have to squish to the side so that we can all fit. I don't know why we didn't just wait for the lady to go through and then all go one by one. Then I wonder why we didn't bring Flo with us. She loves a walk and a lake. She always jumps in and goes for a swim. She actually smiles. I think dogs can smile.

'Are you alright, my boy?' Mummy turns to me and speaks. I am gutted because I can't reply but she knows me well enough by now. 'It is so good to see you. It really is. You are going to love this walk as much as I do. I go most days.'

I am very glad Mummy has a lot of practice in talking more than a normal person because it takes the attention away from the fact that currently I cannot speak. I am so stressed, but also so happy. It is very strange.

We reach the bench, which is one of many dotted around the lake, but I figure this one is the one that Eileen, Erin and Mummy always sit on because they call it *our spot*. I can feel my face light up when Eileen reaches into her bag and pulls out a selection of delicious-looking cakes. I love the bakery she buys them from. It isn't far from our house and sometimes we walk to it, but mostly Eileen takes the car because it is quicker and we get our cakes sooner.

'Now, how are we going to do this? I brought a knife with me so we could each have a bit of all or are there particular ones that you want?' Eileen says, always so prepared.

'I'll have the eclair,' Erin responds, selfish as always.

'I'll have the Belgian bun, thank you, Eileen. I know how much Jack loves lemon sponge,' Mummy says in her normal tone of caring for others. This makes me happy because I do love lemon sponge, but also for a moment Mummy seems normal and I begin to wonder why she is locked away in the hospital that isn't a hospital.

We sit on the bench eating our delicious treats and looking out onto the lake. The warmness on my back makes me think that the summer holidays can't be too far away. I get all excited for this because it means I can do what I want when I want. No school! I also don't have to get up early. They probably are quite a lot of days away, but when it gets warm time goes faster so I am sure they will happen soon.

Everyone is quiet because they are also enjoying their cakes as much as me. All we can hear are the birds and the occasional quiet and unclear sound of speaking when people pass us. People travelling in all sorts of ways. Some are on bikes, some running, lots walking and even a group on those Segway machines pass us just now. I want to try and ride one of those someday. Maybe Auntie Eileen will let me go for my next birthday. Maybe Mummy will be in charge again by then.

'This is lovely,' I say and shock my own self with the words coming out of my mouth.

'Ah, look who's shown up!' Erin says and I don't say anything, but I think that is a real mean thing to say when she knows that I am stressed. She has been here so many times more than I have so she has an advantage. She always tries to wind me up.

'Good boy, darling,' Eileen says reassuringly and we all continue to enjoy the moment we are in. I think how strange it is that we are sitting on a bench and we are all pretending to be normal. At least I am pretending, the others might not be. Though I think that they probably are. I am not too sure that normal exists. Not now anyway. There is so much to think about.

29

MARY

Monday 17th June 2019

I still can't shake the feeling of elation from yesterday. The fact that I saw my boy in the flesh for the first time in as long as I can remember just makes me burst with excitement.

You know when they say about exercise releasing those endorphins that make you happy and have more energy? So effectively, the more exercise you do which uses up energy, the more energy you will have? Or something like that. I am no scientist. Well, the same applies here. I think I could run a marathon on the positive energy I have running through me after my beautiful boy came to visit me.

His little face seemed so unsure and he didn't say much. That is to be expected. I then got worried about it when he left, but the nurses reassured me, and I know I must be OK; what they said put me at ease. They rarely put me at ease because my mind is so wild. It would take a miracle. But hey, miracles do happen! They told me that it will take time for him to come to terms with everything and to adjust to having a mother living inside a psychiatric unit but that he will get used to it. I listened to the nurses and I understood. It will just take time.

Normally, I am so frantic and worried about something that nothing anybody says will put my mind at rest. It is part of the condition I suppose. Yeah, that condition. That nasty little thing that I have living inside of me that just won't go away. Anyway. I get so bitter because nobody can understand, and this is when I am in my manic state. Manic Mary. Doesn't the word *manic* look so similar to *maniac*. They both sound the same too when I repeat them as much as I am doing. I occasionally feel like some maniac.

Today and yesterday when I spoke to the nurses, I wasn't in this state but more my normal state. Well, as normal as it gets these days state. I was trying to explain what I have been told so many times about Jack and his difficulties with speech in situations such as the one he found himself in yesterday. I said how huge that would have been for him and speaking loudly about this completely settled my mind. He panics when he is out of his comfort zone, or in traumatic circumstances and this causes anxiety to rocket within him so the lessons he has learnt in his speech therapy sessions go out of the window. Much like my doctor's exercises that I so often rely on, I guess. I can't do those well when I am panicking.

Other than Jack being completely nervous, I think he was happy inside too. His face lit up slightly when he saw me, and I think it saddened somewhat as he left. Trust me, a mother can always tell. No matter how psychotic things become. This all must be hell for him as well. Sometimes I forget to think about that.

Erin is a lot more open about her worries but even the way that she deals with this particular situation slips my mind too often. If she comes to visit and is especially cranky, I always put it down to something that has happened at school or the stress of her exams. I never consider the fact that she must find the visits daunting and scary. I am supposed to be the strong one but for so long she has had to remain strong for me. It is completely back to front and around the opposite way to how it should be. I wrote that a bit back to front and around the opposite way to how it should be too. Bad English, Mary. My diary, my rules.

As always, Eileen kept things moving along and if ever there was any awkwardness she filled in the gaps. She is so good at that. That used to be me. That was always my job in social gatherings with friends or family parties. I guess I will just have to accept that as a thing of the past.

Eileen also kept everything upbeat and could almost read Jack's mind, recognising when he was a little confused or needed an explanation and she'd swiftly provide him with the information that he needed to feel fully involved. It was so important that he felt fully involved.

I wonder what they all said on the journey home from here. I haven't ever thought about those conversations until now. I wonder if Jack was able to speak and being in the calmness of the car, he could express how happy he was to have seen me. Or the opposite. Don't be ridiculous, Mary. He would have been so happy to see his mummy after all of this time. For sure.

I was feeling so normal today and having normal thoughts until the nurse disrupted this with my medication. Now I am rattling. Rattling on in this diary but physically rattling as well with pills. I am sure that they could stop these soon, but they just need to keep someone in a job. I shouldn't be so cruel. The nurses are lovely. Well, when I am in this mindset they are.

I lose track of the days in here and each week feels like that period between Christmas and New Year when nobody knows what day it is. However, I have cottoned on to the fact that it is nearing the end of June which means Erin's exams will be over very soon.

Maybe by some miracle I will be out of here by then. One can only hope. Though I must plan for the worst-case scenario: I am still here, they will visit me here and we will celebrate by the lake. Cake, sweets, so much chocolate, congratulations presents and maybe even a small Prosecco will all be involved, but it will most probably be right here, in these circumstances. Get real, Mary.

I must ask Eileen subtly when they next visit the date of her last exam. How wrong is that? Eileen should be asking me. I am so out of touch at the moment; I know she has told me a thousand times, but I forget. I can't even remember what subjects she is doing. What a mother I am!

Apart from checking that she is OK with her exam progress, I don't delve too deeply into Erin's life during visits. I want to keep things cheerful, light and hope that if something was wrong, she could still confide in me. I really hope she could.

The nurses got me a treat for being so understanding with Jack yesterday (he must have seemed worse to them than he did to me). They got me some non-alcoholic beers which taste just like lager. I am enjoying one as I write, and it is lovely. So it is. It hasn't got quite the same numbing effect of relaxation upon my bones, but it will do.

Sipping on a pretend half pint while browsing the internet for the most special end of exams gift for my newly sixteen year old. I have had worse Mondays. Especially in here. I won't go into that now. Not today.

Today I am feeling:

Happy, thankful, calm and level.

Today I am grateful for:

1. Eileen
2. Jack
3. Erin
4. The nurses' reassurance
5. Visits

30

ERIN

Erin was staring out of the window as she waited in the car for Eileen to return. Being within the school gates forced her to think about her studies and how behind she had gotten with those. By this point she should be carrying her revision guides around with her as she does her phone in case she got a chance to fit in extra study as she should have done while waiting on Eileen. In fact, she hardly knew where her Physics books were, she had almost entirely given up on her Science subjects. She had done so before, but even more so now.

Eileen had gone in to see Jack's teachers and Erin was a little confused as to why. Perhaps she felt that things were going to go really wrong and that they may be a lot later than 3:30 p.m. to pick Jack up. Or she felt that the teachers needed to be aware of a disruption in home life that the revelation that they were about to tell Mary could cause. Even if Jack was left unknowing, he could suspect something was wrong. This worried Erin more.

She tried to distract her mind by watching the hordes of people rushing about. Mothers were still bringing their children to the school entrance which Erin thought was a bit strange considering how far into the school year they were. That usually only happened on the first week and for the extremely nervous students. Mostly by the age of eleven, students had built up the independence to take themselves into school and they didn't need to hold onto their mum's hand any longer. To still be doing it in the spring term was very strange.

Though she hadn't considered what they might be going through at home. Perhaps they too had an extremely difficult home life, so their mum was literally holding them up so that they attended school. Much like they had to do with Mary whenever she ventured out in public. That or they could be close friends or relatives of Amy. Erin suddenly felt evil for her presumptuous thoughts.

Perhaps parents were finding the news difficult and therefore being a lot more protective over their children than they were previously. They were probably clasping tightly onto the fear of the same thing happening to one of their own. She wondered how many younger kids had been banned from their phones or social media temporarily since Amy died. She considered how many parents now obsessively looked into everything that their children consumed. Asked them where they were going or didn't even let them out in the first place.

Students on the opposite side were setting fire to some sort of wooden block in the corner of the car park. They were as far away from the school entrance as you could get and still remain in the car park, but she noticed pretty quickly. She wondered how the three teachers on round-up duty hadn't cottoned on yet. Perhaps because they were holding a mothers' meeting and catching up on their weekends rather than performing sufficient crowd control. It made her wonder what they were all getting paid for.

She was amazed how much her mind was almost momentarily forgetting Amy's story. It seemed that outside the school, everywhere in her life, Amy was ever present. Like her absence was so loud. Yet in school, the only place that she spent a significant amount of time with her, Amy was gone.

That's why the teachers weren't doing their job properly. The parents can't be blamed for hugging their children extra tight, for holding their hand that little bit more, hypothetically of course. It was like she had been away from school forever and when she was last at school properly Amy was sat beside her. In her mind, at school, Amy existed. It was an awful reminder. A sudden, heavy sadness made her sink into a deeper slump in the passenger's seat.

The moment of solemn despair was followed by a wave of thanks which swept over her at the thought of not having to face this every day. Ever again. Unless she failed her exams of course. That was a thought that she quickly shoved aside though as she didn't want to consider it an option.

The claustrophobia of a school day. She tried to get the feeling back because part of her longed for the safeness even when she hated it at the time. Maybe it would take her mind off the terrifying thoughts currently whirring around.

'Jamie King and Luke Edgar are about to have a fight!' The screams roared down the corridors. The stampede made it feel as though the entire building was shaking.

'Quick! Let's not miss this one!'

'The teachers don't know yet, let's get there before they break it up.'

Erin and her friends gave each other a look across the table. They looked down at their sandwiches and then gave each other nods of approval. Their sandwiches could wait; nothing ever that exciting happened and it was often over before they got a look in.

They reached the back field and saw the crowd gathering on the far side. No adults seemed to be present, so they knew they had time to witness something before it was stopped by authority. Everyone on the field was walking over.

'What do you think it's about?' Kirsty asked the rest of the group.

'I saw on Facebook last night that they were having words underneath Luke's post. He wrote an indirect status accusing someone, no names mentioned, of grassing him up about his stash.' Lorna filled them in.

'Stash of what?' Erin asked, innocently.

'God, Erin you're so out of touch.'

'Oh.' Erin hated how she was expected to know about every drug or social habit that all her friends knew about. They didn't understand that she had so much else going on with her mum. Most of them didn't even have jobs so they could focus and learn everything about sex and drugs and all the gossip of the year group to fit in with the popular crowds. Erin often didn't have the time.

As they approached the crowded corner of the field, Jamie King was squaring up to Luke and certainly dominating the fight. The judgemental eyes from Shannon and Hannah's group stared at Erin and whispered under their breaths. They gave her the most stick about her mum.

'She needs to just get over it. We've all got parents who died or are unwell. Just get over it,' she heard Shannon say to Hannah. The other girls just stared. 'People are sick of pitying her,' she continued, speaking louder, almost wishing for Erin to hear. She liked to show who was boss, that she didn't care and wasn't scared.

'Come on, let's go to the other side, get a better view,' Erin said to the group as they walked in the opposite direction to where Shannon and Hannah were stood. Neither of Erin's friends were aware of what was being said; Erin hated it though, never wanted to make a scene.

Erin's trance was interrupted by the sight of Eileen returning to the car. She also looked lost in thought. She had to come to terms with the awful situation concerning her niece's mental state and the continuous worry that that brought with it. She also had her great-niece's mental state at the top of her worries, whilst coming to terms with a tragedy that was far too close to home, and her great-nephew's innocence and keeping it that way so as not to make his condition worse. This was all without thinking about her own needs and health. And all in her eighties when everyone was meant to start to look after her. It sounded exhausting to Erin, just outlining it all.

Gratitude swept over Erin. For a dainty old lady, she sure held a lot upon her shoulders.

'Ah, that wasn't too bad, pet.'

'What do you mean?' Erin replied, confused, considering what could be so bad in telling Jack's teachers that they would possibly be slightly late to collect him that afternoon. It happened all the time for all sorts of perfectly suitable reasons that were nothing like their own.

'Finding someone to talk to. That place is usually rammed, and it takes thirty long minutes of waiting before you can get seen. Especially if you want the private room. It is like gold dust to get seen in there.'

'Wait, what's so private and confidential about saying we might be late in picking Jack up?'

'Nothing, darling. I would just prefer to talk in peace, explain myself without anyone overhearing. These days you can't just say with no explanation. They know everything pretty much about your mum so I do often go into detail, or sometimes they just ask out of care and for me to talk properly it is easier if we speak in private. I also ask about you two and that is confidential. You'll understand when you're older. It's nicer to only tell your business to a few people. People that you trust. Anyway. How're you feeling?'

'Nervous.'

'Don't be.'

'Am I doing the right thing?'

'If it feels right, then yes.'

'But it doesn't. I feel a knot in my stomach. I don't want to make matters worse, I just think it will help all of us. It will mean I can be more real and honest in visits.'

'Anything to help us all, darling. I think you're doing great. It is a very brave thing to do. And a very grown-up way of thinking, to help others around you.' Eileen's reply made her sound a lot more confident about Erin's plan than she really felt inside. She was never going to say this to Erin though. For once she was totally torn as to what the right thing to do was and she had decided to let Erin go with her gut instinct, having learnt a lot from her own, and do what she felt was the right thing to do. The correct way to approach things. She put all of her trust in her great-niece to get it right.

'I hope it helps.'

Eileen smiled while Erin continued to look worried as they set off for the unit. The feeling within the car was the same tense uneasiness as usual with an extra shot added to the mix. Eileen's thoughts whirred around her head, questioning whether it was the right thing to do but she had to do right by everyone. She could tell that for Erin, telling Mary was going to take a weight off her shoulders and anything to do that in these times was a good thing. Whichever way she went about it.

'Eileen?'

'Yes?' Eileen responded with a smile, trying to take herself back to being in the middle of her teenage years and full of dread.

'How come you never married?'

'Wow. That is a big question. And a complete curve ball in our conversation!'

'Sorry, I didn't mean it to be so personal. I just wondered.'

'I never found the right man. I am also far too independent to share my life with anyone.'

'Did you have relationships?'

'Oh yes! Plenty. I had my day. I had fun. It just didn't stick. Nothing ever does, in my opinion.'

'What do you mean?'

'Sorry, I should never have said that.' Eileen quickly retracted her statement, forgetting for a moment that she was talking with her sixteen-year-old niece as opposed to someone much older.

'I'm curious.'

'I just don't believe in for ever.'

'I see.'

'Why the twenty-five questions all of a sudden? You're not worrying about boys already, are you?'

'A bit. All my friends have boyfriends. Or at least they have had them.'

'Stop right there, my girl. You are amazing. You are bright, funny, clever and going to go far in life. You will find someone when the time is right for you.'

'Yeah, yeah. I've heard it all before!' Erin laughed and decided against getting too deep in conversation before doing the thing that for so long she had been dreading.

While Eileen realised the need for her niece's changing the conversation topic, it did make her think about all Erin had on her plate over an average sixteen year old. They would have the usual boy troubles, friendship troubles, future troubles and imminent exam pressure. Erin was different. She had a constant battle of understanding the cruelty of the world from too young an age. Her mother, sick in hospital. Not physically sick which might lead to a quicker, easier understanding but mentally sick and quite drastically so. And a tragic event that is so common yet so rare to affect a life so personally.

They arrived at the unit and, before Eileen had turned off the ignition, she reached over to the passenger seat and gave Erin a big hug. It was a hug to build strength in an adolescent about to undertake a very adult task. An embrace filled with love. Most of all it was a hug from herself and also Mary, whose mind had been ripped away from her.

31

ERIN

'Thank you, Eileen,' Erin said at the end of their long embrace. She prepared herself for what lay ahead and built up the strength to get out of the car.

'Come on now.'

Erin couldn't find the strength to smile, but, inside, she felt thankful for Eileen's presence and warmth. She desperately wanted to forget what she was about to do, but the dreaded moment was minutes away from happening, so she knew that she had to be strong. Strong and grown up. She wished she was older.

'Hello there, ladies!' came the jolly welcome from the receptionist. 'She won't be long. The doctor wanted to see your mum this morning so she isn't quite as punctual as she would usually be.'

'No bother. Thanks,' Eileen replied.

Erin wished for her mother to be sat there waiting as she normally would have been. Instead, they had the painful wait which Erin knew would feel a lot longer than it actually was. She didn't want more time in which to overthink everything that was about to happen.

Eileen smiled at her, somehow knowing what was going on inside her head and this gave her strength.

Erin spotted her mother walking down the corridor, almost being held up by the nurse. It was the frailest she had seen her in a long time, and she thought to herself that Jack's visit and the elation it had caused must have finally worn off. Her poor mother. For the first time in a long time Erin felt sorry for her. This feeling had gone recently as each visit had been the same and pretty good.

Visits without worry had become almost routine and it was as if Mary was having a break from life in some sort of health retreat for a while as opposed to the psychiatric unit that she was actually in. Aside from the clinical feel and nurses walking around everywhere, obviously. They usually went out to the lake removing that altogether so in Erin's mind she had somewhat misplaced her mum's mental illness. Until now. Until she witnessed her hardly able to stand.

'All OK?' Eileen asked the nurse.

'Oh yes. Well, everything will be OK in a day or so.'

'Right.' Eileen added, waiting for the nurse to provide some sort of explanation.

The nurse looked over to Erin, who smiled with a confidence that she didn't feel within. This allowed for the nurse to continue, unsure as to whether it was appropriate in front of Erin, being so young. Yet they had all seen her visit so much and she gave off the impression outwardly that she was toughening up to the situation.

'Mary had a slight mix-up with her medication and it will take a few days to balance out, but she will be fine. We are reviewing this situation. We continue to assess the medication that we give to our patients and Mary's are all being looked at to see if there is a better solution. However, the initial mix-up has been noted and the staff have been advised not to give Mary the option to take the pills herself. They were laid out for her, but two were taken at once. While this isn't too dangerous, it doesn't help Mary's recovery.'

Erin looked worried and the nurse regretted her decision to speak so plainly to Eileen in front of Erin.

'Are we to take you out, missus, or would you rather just go to the cafe?' Eileen asked Mary.

'Shall we start with the cafe so I can get my bearings and then see where we are at?'

'Sounds perfect. All OK with you, Erin?'

'Of course.'

Erin loved a lot of things about Eileen and one was how she always included her in decisions. She spoke to her like an adult and respected her opinion. It made visits and the whole situation with Mary a lot easier for Erin to handle.

'Let's go then.'

Both Erin and Eileen took one of Mary's arms each and guided her gently to the cafe which was attached to the building, but felt less clinical and more enjoyable. It was the closest thing to real life within the unit, yet Mary felt a sense of security because she knew that help was always on hand if something went wrong.

Erin had mostly decided that now wasn't the right time to tell her mum everything and, after talking to her for a few moments, she decided fully. She would do it another day. This visit needed to be about Mary's recovery.

'What would you like?' Eileen asked, about to go to the counter and order while Erin and Mary took their seats.

'A strong coffee, please,' Mary replied.

'A nice cup of tea!' Erin said, mimicking Eileen on a daily basis. 'It solves everything!'

Eileen said nothing and just smiled at Erin's response. She was happy that Erin had stopped worrying and that they had both concluded that now wasn't the time to say.

'How's revision, darling?' Mary asked, genuinely interested and feeling better. She knew that she was at her best when surrounded by family and this moment was demonstrating that perfectly. Normal conversations made her almost forget the mental struggles of the last seven years. The battle between keeping herself sane during James' suffering and treatment and keeping the children safe and protected. For years she had to remain strong and conversations about Erin's exams while incarcerated in a psychiatric unit illustrated her ability to still put up that barrier against her illness.

'OK, I suppose. Just a lot to do,' Erin responded, suddenly worried at being on her own with her mum. It was such a strange feeling because a year ago it was so normal and lovely, but now it was a worry. She realised that these days she rarely was on her own with her. Eileen was always present. She was now terrified that she would say the wrong thing that could be detrimental to Mary's health. Then she snapped out of it and tried to enjoy a snippet of normal conversation with her mum.

'You're going to do great, you know that?'

'I hope so. I really do.' Her mind left the room momentarily as she thought: if only her mum knew. If only she knew what extra torment Erin had to put up with every second of every single day. The torture that she was going through mentally. If only exams were her only current stress. If only.

'You will.'

Eileen came back with a tray of warm beverages and both Mary and Erin smiled at the sight. Erin felt relief from the worry of saying the wrong thing and they all enjoyed the moment, knowing that today wasn't the day for walking to the lake and pretending all was normal. Today wasn't the day for revelations of catastrophic proportions. Today wasn't even the day for thinking too much about anything apart from staying in the moment and making that moment a good one.

Perhaps they wouldn't be so late picking Jack up from school after all.

32

JACK

It is really strange because I have been told that Auntie Eileen and Erin might be late to pick me up, so I have to wait in the office at the front of school until they get here but I don't know why. The only thing I can think of is that they are going to visit Mummy, but last time we visited Mummy she was fine. It was me that had the issues. Maybe they should be visiting me. I am only kidding. But I don't get it.

It must be for a special reason because I am being treated like one of the kids that has *special circumstances*, as they call it. Being separated from the rest as if I have something wrong with me, or *sensitive issues*. I've heard it all before and I have been here before too. In normal life like if Eileen got caught up in a doctor's appointment she would just arrange for me to go to someone's house. It's usually Daniel Brampton's and I think it's because Eileen likes to nose at his house when she comes to pick me up. It is pretty big. Also, his mum always offers her a glass of wine and Auntie Eileen sure likes wine! I don't understand why I am not there right now. I know she knows that I hate after school club so perhaps that is why I have to wait elsewhere.

Mummy really was fine last time and, apart from looking a little bit poorly, her face looked kind of happy and that is how I remember it back when she was OK. I really hope she is OK. I hate that adults tell me nothing because I am a child. They think they are protecting me, but actually they are tormenting me. If I knew then maybe I would be able to speak to my friends today but, instead, the stress has meant that I can't speak. My friends just accept it now and I sit at breaktime and lunchtime smiling if they are making a joke or acting shocked if they are telling a story, but it isn't fun. Not for me, anyway.

Besides, Erin should be revising. For so long it has been one of the only things that she goes on about and Auntie Eileen always tells her how important these exams are for her future. They can't be that important if they can do something for a day that means they might be late for picking me up. It is all so confusing.

My last lesson is Maths, and I can't concentrate. I can't even concentrate when nothing else is on my mind and my speaking is fine. But with all this going on inside my head I really can't concentrate. I think Mr Hamilton knows something that I don't because he isn't even telling me off for not being able to concentrate; he isn't directing any of the quick-fire questions at me. This is good because I didn't do the homework, but I wish that he would tell me what he knows.

I keep looking at the clock, which is moving so slowly, and I think it is because I am stressed. The lesson finishes at 3:30 p.m. and the big hand has been stuck on the number two for a lot longer than one minute. I really hope Erin and Auntie Eileen haven't gone away to do something really fun and left me out. That would make me very cross. I bet they have gone to visit Mummy, but she was fine when we last saw her. I don't get it.

The clock must have moved a bit and I probably zoned out for a while because Mr Hamilton has told us to gather our things and finish off what we are doing to get ready to leave. I don't even know what we were supposed to be doing so my page is blank. I look to my left and so is Damian Grant's page, but he isn't very clever so his page is always blank. On my right is Melissa Scanlan and she has filled up three pages in her workbook. She is a teacher's pet so I guess I am not in the position to judge how much work I should have on my paper. Sat in between the bottom of the class and the top, I am about in the middle. That is what they always say at parents' evening. Parents' evening that neither of my parents can attend. How weird.

I stare back at the clock and watch the tick of the second hand. Tick, tick. I watch it go round and round. I must be watching for at least three minutes because I look around me and all of the class have left the room. Mr Hamilton comes over to speak to me. Silly really as I can't speak. Nobody gets that sometimes. I just can't do it.

'Hi there, Jack. I guess you have been made aware that your auntie and sister may well be late getting you today. Do you want to come to my office and wait there? I am going to have a cup of tea while I mark some books. I have biscuits!'

I smile because I can't speak, and I think he understands that my answer is yes. I have never known this side to Mr Hamilton and I always think teachers just teach and don't care. Especially those that teach Maths. How boring. Suddenly I can feel myself being able to speak soon. It is such a strange thing, but I can always tell when it is ok to try. Not quite yet but soon. I love biscuits.

'Come along then.'

We walk down the Maths stairs and halfway along the next corridor into a room. I wonder how Auntie Eileen and Erin will find me up here, but I am sure that they will. I hope the biscuits have chocolate on them.

'Now if you just take a seat down there. Do you want a book to read or a comic? Don't worry, I won't make you do any Maths!'

Mr Hamilton is talking to me as if I am going to answer, but he knows that I can't. I don't know why he is asking me questions when he knows this.

'There we go. Do you want a hot chocolate to go with that?'

He hands me a Custard Cream which, while it doesn't have chocolate on top, is still one of my favourite biscuits, so I am happy with it. I manage a nod to reply to his hot chocolate question and I don't take anything to read because I am happy just sitting in peace.

'Perfect. I will get that for you. I am just going to ring down to reception to say where you are. Then when your auntie and sister arrive, we can go to them.'

I smile and almost manage a *thank you,* but it doesn't quite come out. I have never known a teacher to be so kind and now I think that Mr Hamilton is my favourite. He is at least one of my favourite teachers now after today. Erin always said how she hated him, but I think that is because she hated Maths. I don't like Maths, but I might enjoy it more now knowing how kind my Maths teacher is.

I sit in Mr Hamilton's office and enjoy my hot chocolate, dipping my Custard Cream in every now and then. Bits break off as the biscuit gets soggier, but I don't care. It is lovely. And it is taking away most of my stress. I feel far less stressed than I did not that long ago back in my Maths class. If only Mr Hamilton had given me a hot chocolate and a biscuit then. He would have had to give one to the whole class though, so I understand why he didn't. I really do think that it would make Maths class more fun and I am sure that all of my classmates would agree. Maybe we would get a lot more work done if biscuits were involved.

Mr Hamilton's phone begins to ring, and I think that it is probably reception telling him that Erin and Eileen are here waiting for me. Part of me is thankful because it means that they haven't forgotten about me. The other part of me wishes that they could have waited a little longer as I am really enjoying just being so calm. I am also enjoying my delicious hot chocolate and second Custard Cream. I feel so lucky. What a way to end the school day.

'That's them, little chap! They are here to collect you.'

I take one last lovely gulp of my hot chocolate and look to the bottom of the mug which is filled with mashed-up bits of biscuit. It looks disgusting but tastes so good.

'Thank you,' I manage to say as I leave Mr Hamilton's office and head to reception to meet Erin and Auntie Eileen.

33

ERIN

TEENAGE DEATH TREATED AS SUICIDE

Thursday 30th May 2019

Teenager Amy Milner, whose body was found by local dog walker on Tuesday 28th May 2019 is being treated as a suicide case while an inquest is undertaken.

A funeral and celebration of Amy's short life will be held on Friday 21st June and anyone who knew and loved Amy are invited to join.

Erin put the paper down as Eileen entered the room.

'I can't take much more of this,' she said, trying to hold back the tears.

'I know, darling. It really is awful. Try to be strong today to support her family. I think they want it to be more of a celebration of her life than a sad farewell.'

'That's how all funerals should be but also all funerals are when the person is old, like really old. She was too young. And she wasn't even ill.' Erin couldn't hold back her emotions any longer and began to wail uncontrollably into Eileen's arms.

'I know,' Eileen replied, because she did. The truth was that she felt exactly as her great-niece felt. She just couldn't express it because then they would both be crumbling messes. She knew she needed to be strong for everyone today. For Erin, for Mary, for Jack and for Amy's close friends and family.

'Where's Jack?' Erin asked, not wanting her brother to see her in such a state.

'Getting ready. We have to take him to school first and then go straight to the crematorium. Here, I'll make you a nice cup of tea. Then you can get ready in peace and I'll take Jack. That way no questions will be asked. He can't know about this.'

'I know. We really do. He would never be able to cope. I'm sure certain brighter kids in his year may have cottoned on but he can't know we are going to the funeral. How closely linked it all is.'

'The less he knows, the better. Your brother thinks a lot so I don't want his little mind getting too involved. I'll go and check on him while the kettle is boiling,' Eileen said while giving Erin a warm embrace.

'Thank you, Auntie Eileen.'

'You're always welcome.'

Eileen left the room with a smile and so much comforting warmth within it that it made Erin momentarily feel strong. She hadn't even thought about her outfit for the day because more pressing matters had swamped her brain. They had been told to dress in colours to celebrate Amy's bright and happy personality. *How ironic*, Erin thought.

Part of her wanted to go online and read over everything that was said, again, but she knew it would hurt so much. Part of her wanted to give the trolls a comeuppance that they deserved, but she knew they would get that one day. Part of her wanted to sit in the same position on the sofa all day long drinking tea. All of her knew that the only thing she needed to do was to get up, be brave, be strong and get through it.

'Right, my darling, Jack is all ready to go,' Eileen said as she came back into the room and headed for the kettle. 'I think I'll be needing one of these myself,' she added as she poured the boiling water into Erin's mug and got herself a travel mug out of the cupboard.

'Thanks,' Erin uttered weakly as Eileen handed her the warm brew and she smiled so that she didn't cry. She never wanted Jack to see her cry.

'Now, we won't be long. Well, I won't! Jack is staying at school all day.'

'Don't rub it in, Auntie Eileen,' Jack responded in the clearest tone he had been able to manage in a long time.

'Bye!' Erin said more cheerily than she felt and pondered on Jack's speech, suggesting that he wasn't worried at all. If only he knew.

Erin loved how Eileen had the ability to make every situation upbeat. Even during the worst times, she found something to laugh at or be light-hearted about. It was as if it was a coping mechanism. She leant on joy for strength and Erin hoped and prayed that she would have the strength to be like that one day. With all these thoughts the home phone started to ring, and she was so immersed that she almost missed it. Only one person rang the home phone and that was the one person who she loved to speak with on the phone.

'Hello!' she answered in a happy tone and was immediately embarrassed because she had made it so obvious that something was wrong.

'Hi, pet, you sound uncharacteristically cheery for a day of studying?' her grandfather Séan said.

'Ah, I am fine, Grandad. How are you doing?'

'Ah, grand. Grand. Sure, I am always grand!'

'I know you are. What have you been doing with yourself?'

'Fixing this poxy iPad. I don't know why your aunt bothered getting it for me. I think it was some sort of joke.'

'I'll come and visit you once these exams are over and show you step by step.'

'Don't be cheeky, young lady. I'll be grand. It can't be that difficult.'

'Clearly it is since she got you it for Christmas and it is now June,' Erin replied, laughing.

'I sure as miss your cheekiness. How's it going with the studies? Seriously, like?'

'Yeah, it's fine. I am doing as best I can, really.' Erin said this in a way that wouldn't raise suspicion within her grandad but one that also expressed how she actually felt. She *was* doing her best given the circumstances. Obviously Séan was fully aware of the situation with Mary, but he never mentioned it. He didn't know how to deal with it and so acted as if everything was always fine. Erin felt it odd that he rarely asked about Mary, his only daughter, but Eileen assured her that he did. He asked Eileen all the time how Mary was getting on. He also rang Mary himself fairly frequently, in his terms, at the unit. He just felt strongly about keeping the children out of such an adult situation. Little did he know how involved Erin had become.

'Great. That's really great and you're going to do us all and yourself extremely proud, I just know it. Is your aunt around?'

'No, she's just taken Jack to school.'

'Right, well would you tell her I phoned?'

'Sure. Look, Grandad, I better go.' Erin said, noting the time the clock was showing and suddenly realising she had only twenty minutes to get herself together before they had to leave.

'Grand, great speaking to you.'

'And to you, Grandad. Love you.'

'Yep, bye.'

Erin smiled at her grandad's response to emotion. She did it on purpose, mostly. While, of course, she loved and adored her grandad, he couldn't cope with outwardly showing emotion. He instantly went stern upon hearing the words and rather than getting het up about it, Erin accepted that it was how he would always be.

She finished her last dregs of tea which had been perfectly made by Eileen and headed upstairs to get ready. Luckily, she had already showered last night so it was just a case of finding the appropriate outfit and doing her face so that she looked good, but she also was sure not to heavily pile on the makeup as there were going to be a lot of tears.

As Erin looked in the mirror she began to cry. She opted for a small amount of BB cream and mascara.

'Hello! Erin, I'm back!' Eileen shouted up the stairs and Erin thanked God for the timing because her mind was about to go wild. She could feel it.

'Hi, I am almost ready!'

'Brilliant. I'll just tidy up here a bit and then we can hit the road, yes?'

Erin sighed before answering, noting again how difficult the next few hours were going to be for so many people.

'Yes?' Eileen shouted up again, with a sarcastic impatience knowing how long Erin mostly took to leave the house.

'Yes. Grandad rang by the way.'

'Oh lovely, was he OK?'

'Perfect. Just checking in, I think. Wanted me to let you know he called though.'

'Right. I'll call him later if I get a chance. We've got this, my darling. I promise. Together we can be strong for Amy and her family.'

34

ERIN

Erin could see the number of cars and people already there. The vast number of attendees highlighted the youth of the deceased. Anyone passing would know that it was the funeral of a young person rather than one in their nineties. Already it felt so wrong.

The sun was shining, and Eileen had calming music on, trying to make the day OK for the both of them. As OK as a funeral for a young girl could be. They had to be strong. Erin wasn't sure of the artist that Eileen was playing and she didn't bother to ask, she just needed to listen and enjoy. It was the sort of music that had the power to take you out of this world. It silenced your troubles and thoughts temporarily, leaving a space only for Zen. Erin also gave Eileen this time to be in peace; they hadn't spoken to one another for much of the journey, but it was perfect. She knew that Eileen also needed time as too often she forgot that Auntie Eileen might be struggling with everything as well. Being eighty-one didn't make her invincible in that sense. They were lost in their own calm. Similar to the yoga class a few weeks back, though Eileen's driving was much better this time. Thankfully.

The bright colours of everybody's outfits looked beautiful as Eileen drove into the carpark and found a space close to the entrance. It was like a human bouquet of flowers, the kind you get when you ask a florist for a happy bunch. Eileen couldn't walk too far, but she also needed five empty spaces next to each other to ensure that she wouldn't bump another car in the process of parking her own. They sat in the car a moment before opening the doors, just taking it all in and building up the strength to continue on. Erin considered the fact that this was only her second funeral. Pretty good going for sixteen years on this earth, yet she felt that it was an average number unless someone had a particularly horrific set of events in their young life. Two funerals of two grandparents who naturally were meant to pass in the circle of life was fine. Sad, but fine. It was how it was meant to be. Two funerals being tragedies in their own right and Erin felt that she qualified for the latter category. A set of horrific events in such a young life. Despite her experience of funerals being limited, both services that she had attended were desperately sad cases. Of course all funerals were sad, but some deaths were more natural than others.

The first funeral that Erin attended in her life was her father, who again died too young. While he was in his forties, he still had a lot of life to live. The average life expectancy was almost double his age. The circumstances of his death added to the gloom as he had suffered for so long and so Erin, Jack and Mary were forced to mourn him before he had actually passed away. It was one of the hardest things that they had to do. Erin and Jack were both too young to be left without a father figure in their lives while Mary was also too young to be left without a husband.

The second funeral was this one. Erin couldn't believe it. She still couldn't and felt that she never would. It was a girl, in her year, in her town, and it was too real to handle.

Everyone stood waiting to be allowed in, dressed in the brightest dresses and hats as if they were going to the races. The men all wore pink chinos, some yellow, some were in plain jeans but with a bright shirt. In fact, out of the whole congregation not one single person wore black or navy. *It really was a celebration of life*, Erin thought, as they walked in and sat near the back. That is how she had to approach the service, that is how she was going to be able to stay strong. For Amy.

'Well done, my beautiful girl,' Eileen whispered to Erin as she squeezed her hand tight. A tear dropped from Erin's face onto the picture of Amy on the front of the Order of Service. Robbie Williams 'Angels' played among the sobs and sniffles of all the guests. Those who loved Amy. Pouring out of the door because there wasn't enough space for the love all in one room. It had to seep outside to the people waiting in silence, flooding the carpark.

As Erin sat, silently looking around, she wasn't one bit surprised at the huge turnout. The sadness was overwhelming at how such a loved girl could feel so unloved. So useless. Unworthy of a life. So, she took it. Erin couldn't work it out. It was so backward. If only Amy knew. If she could see everyone who showed up for her then maybe things would be different. What a shame that it was just too late.

Erin's thoughts were interrupted by the Vicar beginning the service. It wasn't surprising that no readings were to be given by Amy's parents but rather all they wanted to say was to be delivered in a eulogy read by the Vicar. An impartial body who appeared as overwhelmed by the sadness as Erin felt watching.

The Vicar began. A wobble heard in her voice and seen on her lips told Erin that she was going to struggle to speak with confidence. It was unsurprising as she must do so many funerals but not many like this. Anyone giving the eulogy of such a young life with so much future left would find it difficult.

Erin's eyes focussed on the front row and she could see Julie's shoulders moving up and down. She kept the sound of her sobs quietly to herself, but the movement screamed out how broken she was. Steve was still. Erin realised she couldn't see them from the front, only from behind but his stillness spoke as much as Julie's shoulders did.

Eileen had been trying to stop her tears throughout, Erin could tell, but finally her guard broke and she had to lift her tissue to wipe her eyes. Eileen was always the strength in life but even Erin saw this as an occasion where Eileen was allowed to back off from her rock duty. The roles switched momentarily as Erin took Eileen's hand and squeezed it into her lap as if to say, *I'm with you, we will support each other.* The Vicar continued.

. . .

After the service was over, everyone moved onto Julie and Steve's local, just up the road from their house. The staff had put on so much delicious food and there was positivity among the sadness that filled the room. It was just how the family wished for it to be. A huge, crowded space filled with everyone who loved their daughter, telling stories about her precious character.

Eileen and Erin got themselves a plate of food and took themselves to the far side of the pub to sit and gather their thoughts. On a big screen in front of them was a series of photos on loop with some video footage of Amy in between. The focus was largely on happy memories, but the sheer sadness of a life lost so young was ever present.

Moments later, Julie started to give a speech:

'Hello, everyone, and thank you all for being here for our little girl. I am not sure how long I will be able to speak for, but please bear with me. As you can see just by looking around yourselves, our Amy was so loved. We wanted to-t-to. I am sorry.' At that she began to cry. It started as an exaggerated version of the sniffle that she maintained throughout all of her speeches in interviews on the news and in the few words she had uttered during the service, thanking people for coming to pay their respects but, gradually, her cries descended into sobs.

Steve took over. 'Understandably this is all incredibly difficult for us, so I won't make this speech long. There are no words that will make any of this OK. There will always be a huge hole in our hearts and the hearts of so many over the loss of our beautiful daughter, Amy. What Julie was trying to say is that we tried to make this as much of a celebration of Amy's life as possible. While there is so much sadness within us all, we are so pleased with how you have all turned out. Attending, dressing in happy colours and telling cheerful good stories about our little girl.' Steve too began to sob. 'I am sorry. I don't think I can do this.' He held up his drink and the rest of the congregation followed.

Masses of glasses were held high in the air to show the utmost respect for Amy and her family. 'To our little girl.'

'To Amy,' came the respective chorus of all those who loved her.

Eileen gave a tissue to Erin which she gladly took as her tears were becoming uncontrollable. As she took the tissue, she looked over to Eileen who had a pile of tissues beside her, soaked in her tears as well.

35

JACK

Today has been a very strange day to be honest. Auntie Eileen made such a fuss about leaving Erin on her own this morning while she took me to school. Then she made a big fuss about me being at school all day. Erin always just stays at home while Eileen takes me to school. I don't know why today was so special. It was also strange because Erin was up and sitting on the sofa with a cup of tea before I left. In fact, she was up way before me. This never happens. Ever. Auntie Eileen always has to wake her up and tell her all about how important these exams are for her and how she knows that it is very difficult at the moment, but she needs to study hard for her future. It is the same conversation every single day.

Auntie Eileen was all chatty on the way to school. Way more than usual. I have been thinking a lot recently and decided that there was something wrong because Eileen was kind of outside the car even though she was driving it. It has been very odd. Today she was chatting, and I was hardly replying because the change got me all stressed and then my speech went all bad. Maybe she was just very impressed with my response to when she said I had to be at school all day. I did speak really well. It might have been enough to boost her spirits this much.

I don't know what's going on. Because then I got to school and even that was strange. There was a kind of atmosphere throughout the building. Like someone had come in the night and cursed it. I thought that only happened in my books and TV shows, not in real life. Maybe I am wrong. It is like because I don't speak people don't tell me. I wasn't even allowed into assembly and I don't know why. None of my year group went. Usually in the big, big assemblies with the whole school we all go but so many people didn't this time. Nobody told us why. But I think they know more than I do.

The teachers all seemed distant, like Eileen seemed for the last month. Maybe it has something to do with getting older. But then Eileen is like really, really old and some of my teachers are only just old. There is like fifty years between them. I don't know, I am just glad that the day is over and that hopefully tomorrow will be less strange.

Eileen is coming to pick me up and she is a few minutes late which is so not like her. She knows how important it is for me both to be on time coming to school and also leaving. I get stressed about silly things and then it stops me speaking but that is just how I am, and Eileen knows this. I wonder where she is.

Sometimes I wish I was big enough to walk home because I like walking and it means I can think about all my thoughts without anyone judging me. People can mostly tell when they look at my face if I am thinking about something weird but on a walk, it is more private. Nobody is watching. And judging.

Finally, I spot Eileen's car pulling into the car park and feel very relieved. She is smiling and waving at me so her day couldn't have been as strange as mine. Though she was acting quite strange this morning.

'Hi there, darling. Have you had a good day?' Eileen asks me, all upbeat which is the opposite to how I am feeling. All strange and confused. I am not sad or anything, just a bit angry because I have no idea what is going on, yet everyone around me seems to get it. Whatever it is. I can't respond so instead I nod half-heartedly, and I think she gets the gist. 'Now, when we get in you can do whatever you want for an hour and then we have one of your favourites for tea - pizza!'

I smile because who doesn't smile at pizza, but I still feel all weird.

We get home faster than I think we ever have and after greeting Flo with a big hug because she doesn't know anything is wrong, I run upstairs so that I can be on my own with my thoughts. I can hear Auntie Eileen shouting for Erin, but there is no answer. I can then hear Eileen talking to herself about where Erin could be and talking to her phone to call her. I leave her to it.

Erin isn't in her room. I glance in and begin to turn around to head into my room but, as I turn, I spot that her laptop is open and unlocked. The light of it catches my eye because it is pretty dark in her room with the blinds down. It is daylight outside. I don't know why she has her blinds down. I don't think I would be as brave if I wasn't so confused. This is a prime opportunity to find out why everyone around me is acting so strange. All the time. It might be totally useless, but at least I can try.

With these thoughts I feel like someone on my TV shows and in my books. I feel as though I am in a proper spy or detective film. It feels very cool, to be honest, and I can't hear any noise from downstairs so the coast must be pretty clear. I am sure Eileen is still busy trying to locate Erin and Erin has probably gone out for a walk so she won't catch me in the act. If this was the case, she would usually have taken Flo with her, but this is no normal day so I shouldn't be questioning things.

I continue to creep in hoping that the floorboards won't give me away. One creaks slightly as I step on it, but I move my foot slightly to the right and no sound is made. I keep looking around to see if Erin is in fact in her room and just being extremely quiet. That would be a miracle, but it could be possible on a day like today. Eventually I reach the laptop which I initially thought was a lot closer to the door than it was. Well, I think my slow and nervous creeping might have made everything seem slower and further away. I don't think Eileen heard the creaks.

I hover at the laptop just to make sure nobody is coming up the stairs and then I read the screen. It is open on Erin's Facebook account. I have never been on Facebook before, only from a distance over Erin's shoulder before she catches me and shouts. Eileen told us we were not allowed social media, but then she let Erin get a Facebook account. With no arguments; it was just like one day someone had put a spell over her strictness, and she allowed Erin to do whatever she liked. Work that out.

There are lots of messages that read *RIP Amy* and lots of big chunks of writing afterwards. There are also hundreds of photos of Amy Milner and all her friends. Even people that I never saw her with, but I guess they are in the same year, so it isn't unlikely for them to have at least one photo with her. Why they are posting it on Facebook, I don't know. Maybe it is her birthday. Or perhaps she has done something really impressive for charity and raised lots of money like some people to at school and then we have a big assembly about it to celebrate.

I then think back to what RIP means: rest in peace. It is what everyone was saying when Daddy died and at his funeral it was written in lots of places. Mummy kept getting letters with it on some of them and cards that all said *sorry*. I never knew why they were all saying sorry because they didn't make Daddy die.

I open the next tab on Erin's computer. It is a newspaper article. The headline reads *TEENAGE DEATH TREATED AS SUICIDE* and I feel sick in my stomach, like actually sick. I don't really know what suicide is, but I definitely understand the word death. That is final. There is no coming back from death otherwise Daddy would still be here. Death is what happened to Daddy and I've certainly not seen him since nor will I see him again. I don't think. Amy Milner, the girl in Erin's year, must have been taken by death. Death must have happened to her. Amy Milner must have died.

I run to the bathroom, not worrying about the creaks, and vomit into the toilet. I get it all down the toilet and flush it so it is clean, but I am sure Eileen will have heard. I pause for a moment to see if she did because she would be calling up the stairs to see if I am OK or running up them to help. Nothing. Silence. Pure silence and I feel relieved. I go back into Erin's room to make sure I leave the laptop as I found it so that she doesn't suspect a thing. I didn't know people could die so young.

There is another tab on Erin's laptop and before opening the Facebook one and leaving it because that is how I found it, I open this last open tab. It is Facebook as well, but, at the top it says her name. Amy Milner. It must be her Facebook, but why is Erin on her Facebook? I don't understand Facebook. And, right now, I don't think I want to.

I leave all the tabs open and go back onto the Facebook one which is the one that Erin had on the screen. I leave Erin's room exactly as it is and go into my own. I sit on my bed because I don't think I can stand any longer and I hear the door go. Erin is home. Great timing. Or not. I must speak to Mummy about this. I wonder when I will be allowed to visit her next.

36

MARY

Wednesday 26th June 2019

I have had a bit of a break from my diary and I think that maybe a week has gone by, or more. In fact, the nurse has just told me that it is Wednesday 26th June so I have amended that bit up at the top. I knew it had been about that long, but I needed space to get through. I don't really know why I put a date at the top of my entries, and I am unsure as to who the date is for. Maybe someone will find this diary in the future and it will be handy for them to know what the date was. I don't know why.

I am certainly no longer as down in the dumps as I was last week, but the elation I initially felt after seeing Jack has well and truly left the building. For good. Well, until he visits again, I guess, but who knows when that will be.

I knew that I was getting better and that it was perhaps time to start writing again because yesterday – or was it the day before? – I read. Lots. Eileen and Erin give me so many suggestions or bring books with them that even if I haven't seen so I will never run out. Well, rarely. Of course, I go through phases thanks to this delightful illness of mine where I can read two books in one day because I get so engrossed and care little about anything else in this world. Not such a bad thing, eh? I also have zero distractions, let's face it.

Anyway, I do hope my family visit again soon.

I've been better with my medication lately after last week and my fuck up. Whoops. Either that or the nurses have more control and I've learnt probably best not to do it myself. I am not trained in that field. Though you would expect me to know my doses by now; I've been rattling with pills for long enough.

I even left the house today. Did I just say house? It is a figure of speech because this isn't any house. I rephrase. I left the psychiatric unit today. That's better. This is huge. I haven't gone for a walk or anything like that since I last had a visit from family almost two weeks ago now. I wonder how much they think of me.

I took myself to the lake. It was lovely and sunny and warm. I appreciated this, which is another sign of my spirits being up. When they are down, I don't appreciate or see the point in anything. That's right, when my spirits are high, I notice things. I noticed a fish jumping out of the water earlier. It was beautiful. I noticed the weather. I noticed the peace within me. It felt good.

I wonder if people notice me. I go there quite often and rarely see the same faces. I suppose it is a pretty large area, but it's also my local lake that I visit often. You would have thought that I would bump into the regulars. Maybe they avoid me. Who knows? Who cares? I don't.

I walked and walked today and didn't do too much sitting and watching. It was nice to get some fresh air and breathe it in to store until my next venture outdoors. There were more dogs than people which is my idea of heaven and everybody kept out of each other's way unlike usual when everyone sticks to the same side of the path. Duh. Move over.

It was very pleasant, and I am very glad that I dragged myself out of bed to go. I think the nurses are secretly very pleased with my progress this week though they rarely say. I can just tell when they are happy with me. Full marks. It is all kept very professional and I think they are being extra careful in case I decide to administer my own medication again. If I think I am back to normal. I won't. I have told them this, but they can't take any chances. I would hate to be in their shoes.

I hate getting marked on things in life as if I have gone back many years to school. I hated school. Fair enough, the way that they judge pupils in school was marking and grading. In my opinion, that needs to stop in adulthood. Well, in general life at least. If you're doing an exam or something within work, then perhaps grading is OK. What I hate is the grading of living which is what I get every day.

Back when I was fit to take the children to school there was a grading system of school mums. Who looked the most immaculately presented; who gave the best lunches; who dressed their children best on school uniform days; who was the most involved in the PTA.

At university there was a grading system outside of the academic stuff on who partied the hardest; who dressed best (again) for the end of term ball; who held the best drinks parties and so on.

Even in my late twenties I felt that same grading system creeping back into my life when my peers compared who was going to do all of the tick boxes of life first. The usual textbook stuff like marriage, kids, buying first homes. It was all the grading system of life and I absolutely hated every inch of it.

Now I find myself getting graded in terms of my mood. If I am extremely happy like I was after Jack visited and for the days after that I get a very good grade. Either an A star or a 10/10. If I am very low or especially if I mess up on my medication like I did last week then I am not sure if I achieve an F or a 1/10. I don't think I even make it onto the scale. I hate the scale.

This bitterness isn't going to get me very far and, really, I have had a good day. I just wish for my family to visit, that is all. Too much time on my own can be dangerous, especially lately with my changing mood so frequently and so dramatically.

For now, I am going to continue reading my good book and eagerly await another visit from my family to create that inner elation. That A grade euphoria. The 10/10 happiness. I really hope Jack comes this time. I hope that his last visit is the start of something and that he comes every time now. Maybe Eileen has finally decided that he is grown up enough to cope. I love seeing Eileen and Erin so frequently, but I always miss Jack. Every time.

Today I am feeling:

Mellow, level, better, stronger, wishful.

Today I am grateful for:

1. A week gone by
2. Time being a healer
3. My diary
4. Books
5. Hope

37

JACK

To be honest, I think Eileen was a bit shocked when I asked her if I could join them visiting Mummy next time that they go. I have never asked before. I think Eileen doesn't ask me because she has always known that my answer will be a yes if she does ask if I want to go with them. I don't think she has ever asked me what I want to do when she plans to go with Erin alone. I am always left out of visits but now, having found everything on Erin's laptop, I am desperate to speak with Mummy about it. Mummy will be able to talk me through things as she has done so many times before in my life. It always helps a bit.

I am never brave enough to ask Eileen, which I guess is why I have only been invited to go a few times. Probably three. How strange is that? I have to get invited to go and see my own mummy. It is a very strange world.

I won't tell Auntie Eileen about the laptop, though I do think she would understand if I did tell her. If I tell her it is more likely to get passed on to Erin who will get so mad at me and I don't want to risk that. Therefore, I'll not tell either of them until I have spoken with Mummy. She will tell me exactly what I should do, I am sure of it. Yep. That will be my plan. Excuses, otherwise, so many excuses.

'I know it's so difficult for you to understand, Jack, but we can't always plan visits to your mum as you would think we could. OK?' Eileen says to me when I ask her when I will be allowed to go and visit Mummy before Erin's exams finish so that I can sort out her present. I want to be a part of it.

'OK,' I manage to reply with a quiet and sad tone to my voice, but then the anger gets the better of me and my voice vanishes.

'Good boy,' Eileen says as I get up to leave the room. 'Jack.' I turn back around, 'I really appreciate you for being so grown up about this. I know how hard it must be.'

She doesn't. I am sure she doesn't, although I don't really know how Eileen is feeling.

I have no choice and no words to argue with my auntie's decision. I am powerless and have no control over my life. I wonder if I ever will. Erin has so much control over what she does and where she goes, yet I have no control. No say in things as simple as seeing my mum. Eileen is always telling me how big and grown up I am being so why won't she let me decide things sometimes? I don't get it.

Another thing that seriously confuses me is how Eileen goes on and on about how difficult it is to organise visits to Mummy. Surely all it takes is me and Eileen, possibly Erin if she decides to join us, to get into a car. Drive down the road for about twenty minutes. Park up, enter the building and sit at the special table where Mummy is always sat whenever we visit. We then chat a bit about what I've been doing and how Erin is getting on with her really important studying for her extremely important exams that she sometimes doesn't seem to care about, and we go to the lake. We walk out of the car park and through the little alleyway that smells of dog poo. I wonder why we don't bring Flo. We walk around the lake and sit on the bench if it is free and admire the view. We head back, say goodbye to Mummy and tell her how great she is doing and how visiting her boosted all of our spirits as well as her own. We drive twenty minutes back down the road and then we are home. That really is all that it takes.

It's really not that hard, is it? Why they make a big deal about it and always tell me it is so difficult to book an appointment, I don't know. I think it is just another thing that they lie to me about. For my own protection, they say. I am not so sure, it is quite frustrating. I know I've only visited maybe three times maximum, but still. I know how it goes.

Anyway, Eileen promised me a McDonald's to make up for the fact that it isn't so easy to visit Mummy just like that so I think I can forgive her for now. I love McDonald's. Especially the funny machines that you use to order food. I feel all grown up each time we go and sometimes Auntie Eileen lets me pay so I use her card and wave it over the contactless part of the card machine. It goes *BING* and all is done. We just wait for our food.

Erin is being all weird today and doesn't want any food, so Auntie Eileen and I go on our own. She lets me control the radio and says that I am allowed whatever I like to eat which is unlike her because usually all that I am allowed is a Happy Meal. In fact, today all that I want is a Happy Meal, but it is kind of Auntie Eileen to give me the choice.

I think she feels so bad about telling me how difficult it is to just pop and visit Mummy.

'Jack!' Eileen calls up the stairs, 'Are you ready to go and grab some lunch now, darling?'

'Yes!' I manage to shout down the stairs in reply. 'Yes please!'

'Good boy.' Eileen loves me using my manners.

I rush down the stairs and Eileen is just in the kitchen giving Flo some of the meat left over from last night's dinner while I put my shoes on. I smile into the kitchen because seeing Flo so happy makes me so happy. I love her. She is probably one of my best friends in this whole wide world.

'Erin, we're just off to McDonald's. Are you sure you don't want anything?' Eileen shouts up the stairs and I wonder why she doesn't just go up and ask her more quietly. Then I think back to five seconds ago when Auntie Eileen and I were doing exactly the same thing, so it doesn't matter.

The queue for the drive-through is very short which is both great and surprising considering the fact that it is lunchtime. Well, it is nearly lunchtime; I think we are a bit early and must have just missed the rush which I am sure will happen at around twelve o'clock and onwards. We get in and out in no time.

I think this is great because I am hungry, but also because the food gives me the energy to start another conversation, pleading with Auntie Eileen to let me visit Mummy. I really don't give up easily. I blame it on still being a child. That is what Erin sometimes calls me when she is being mean and nasty. A pesky, petulant brat, I think are the actual words that she uses. I don't care. Sometimes it is needed and mostly it works. Besides, I am a child!

'Auntie Eileen?' I ask, innocently.

'Yes?'

'I really think I can cope with another visit to Mummy now. If that is what you're worried about I really think I am strong and I can handle it. I won't let you down. I promise.' My words get faster as I say more of them and I wonder how I manage without losing the ability to speak because I am so worried. This usually affects my talking, but, at the moment, it isn't.

'Oh, Jack.'

'Please. I am literally begging you. I really want to see her. I miss her more than I want to sort out Erin's present.'

'I am sure that's true. I did think that was a little odd that you are caring so much about what to get your sister for her finishing her exams.'

I smile and hope.

'Let me see what I can sort out, but I am making no promises, young man!'

'Thank you, Auntie Eileen.'

I know Auntie Eileen would never say something like that unless she really was going to try. She always comes up with a plan. I think my constant asking of the same question has worked. Maybe I will use this method when I would really like pizza for tea or another trip to the cinema. Visiting Mummy this time is so important to me though and I know that my brain won't shut up until I have spoken to Mummy about it all.

38

JACK

As we head towards the unit, I feel a tiny knot in my stomach and start to question whether or not I am doing the right thing. I have nobody to tell me this. Auntie Eileen thinks I am speaking to Mummy about Erin's present. Erin thinks that I just feel left out so I want to come with them. Mummy probably hasn't got a clue that we are coming. Only I know the real reason. For once.

I look out of the car window and try to think about something else. I try to pretend that we are a normal family, and that Mummy isn't in a special unit and Erin's friend didn't commit suicide. I know what that means now. This doesn't help because I can't think of anything else. Erin and Auntie Eileen are having their own conversation in the front and I don't even care what they are talking about, so I don't listen.

Instead, I try to work out how I am going to do this. I need both Eileen and Erin out of the room. That is easy. I just say to Eileen that I need to speak to Mummy about Erin's present and I am sure she'll take her off somewhere. That will work fine. I think to myself how clever I have been for quickly coming up with a disguise that is a secret. Erin's present has to stay secret from her and Eileen knows this so she will play along with everything to get me and Mummy time to speak alone. She won't even know why it is so important for us to be alone. Good work, Jack, and I didn't even try.

With Eileen sorting it so that Mummy and I can be on our own without Erin questioning things, I have to figure out how I am going to talk to Mummy about this really tricky thing. How do I tell her that I was going against all the rules that she has ever set in our house and that I looked into Erin's private laptop without asking for Erin's permission? I have also got to bring up a really tricky subject and one that might make Mummy sad. That is not good when Mummy gets sad, especially now that she is in this special unit. Ever since she has been in here, we have had to be very careful with making her upset or saying anything that takes her off the level that she needs to be. Still and calm, that is how Auntie Eileen always explains it to me. It never used to be this tricky when Mummy lived at home with us. At least I can't remember it being too tricky. I can't really remember Mummy ever being sad.

Maybe I will be really strong when I get speaking to Mummy and I'll even surprise myself with how strong I am being. I hope so. Go with the flow as Erin always says to Flo when they are being silly together. I miss Erin being silly all the time. She isn't silly very often anymore and it makes me sad.

We are at the big roundabout which means that we are very nearly at the special unit where Mummy lives. For now. I recognise the big roundabout. It has really pretty flowers on it and I always think how lovely they look whenever we go around it. Although I've only seen it three times, it sticks in my mind. Well, I suppose I have seen it six times. Each time I go to the unit to visit Mummy I see it on the way there and on the way back. If I have visited Mummy three times, which I think is about right, then I have to double that number and that is how many times I have passed the pretty roundabout. Two times three is six. Six times.

Auntie Eileen is in the middle of the road bit where you indicate to turn for Mummy's special unit and, now, I am scared. Terrified, in fact. I think to myself that I don't need to definitely approach Mummy about the news story today. I could just enjoy the visit and maybe ask Erin and Eileen about it another time. But that is wimping out, just like Charlie Green says when we play dodgeball in PE. I don't want to be a wimp. And I want to talk to Mummy about this so that is what I will do. I can be strong. Really strong.

'Are you OK, Jack?' Eileen asks me as we park the car and get ready to head in. It is at this point that I realise I haven't said anything for the whole journey. I have only been thinking. Lots of thinking but nothing out loud. Thankfully.

'I am good, thank you, Auntie Eileen.'

'Good. There's a good boy.'

'You talk to him like a dog sometimes,' Erin says to Auntie Eileen, laughing as she speaks. Auntie Eileen gives her a pretend slap and we head in.

Mummy is being led to the table where we sit and greet her when we arrive at reception. She looks better than she did the last time I saw her and less fragile. The nurses don't look like they are holding her up. She looks better than when she came to see me at my show and Erin had done all her makeup that night. Then again, Erin isn't the best at doing makeup, she isn't a professional so maybe she just did a really bad job of Mummy's makeup. What would I know?

'Oh, my darlings. My darling boy. You came again. It is so good to see you all!' Mummy cries from afar. She isn't allowed to come close to us until we have signed some things at reception. Well, Eileen is signing them, Erin and me just wait patiently, both wanting to hug our Mummy. I don't know why we have to wait; I really don't understand this place sometimes.

Eventually Auntie Eileen finishes writing and signing whatever forms it is she has to sign and fill in and we head over to Mummy. There are always so many forms for Auntie Eileen whenever we come here.

'Hi, Mummy!' Erin says, more excited than she has sounded in a long time.

'Hello, darling. Exams all going OK?'

'I've only had a few science tests so far and I think they went alright. Thanks.'

'Good girl. You are going to shine. I know it.'

It was at this point that I felt bad because I didn't even realise that Erin's exams had begun. I thought she was just having to study hard in preparation for them. Whoops. I know I have to get organised with the present because once they start they don't last for long but I didn't realise they had already started.

'Thanks, Mum,' Erin replies and we all take a seat around the table.

'Ah, Jack. And how are you doing, my precious boy?' Mummy says and I get all embarrassed because she always calls me her precious boy in front of everyone. It makes my face turn all red and embarrassing.

'I am OK,' I say. 'Thank you,' never forgetting my manners as I smile at Eileen.

'Great. That really is great,' Mummy says, just smiling so big.

We all sit in silence for a moment and it starts to feel a bit awkward. I look over to Eileen as if to say that I desperately need to talk to Mummy about Erin's end of exams present, but I don't say any words out loud. I didn't think that I would need to hint to Eileen how desperate I was to be alone with Mummy, I thought she would have guessed by how many times I asked her if I could join on the next visit. Clearly, I wasn't as obvious as I thought I was.

'Right, shall Erin and I go and grab us all a beverage?' Eileen says, breaking the uncomfortable silence and winking at me. She always knows how to subtly make everything happen correctly.

Erin follows her to the cafe leaving Mummy and me on our own. Auntie Eileen thinks this is the part when I am going to bring up Erin and discuss an amazing gift for her that I have been thinking about for weeks. Little does she know.

'Mummy?'

'Yes, my darling.'

'I have something to talk to you about?'

'Go on.'

I get all nervous and I am shaking as I pull from underneath my jacket the printouts of what I saw on Erin's laptop screen. I didn't think Mummy would believe me if I just told her, and also there is always the possibility that I won't be able to speak so I had to quickly work out how to use Erin's printer and keep all of the sheets of paper hidden from them both, including now. This is in between running to the bathroom and being sick down the toilet while also checking that nobody is coming up the stairs to catch me in the act. I would have got so told off. So badly.

'I haven't told Erin and Auntie Eileen that I know, and I am so confused, but it also explains a lot about why they have been acting weird lately.'

'Oh my.' Mummy gasps, 'How awful,' she adds, wiping a tear from her face while reading all of the words on the printout.

'I can't believe it, Mummy. I don't really understand it, but I know that it is something very very bad. And sad. Erin has been so upset to Eileen, crying all the time and I just thought it was exams problems or friends or girl stuff. I didn't know that it would be anything like this. I walked upstairs one day last week when Auntie Eileen and Erin were being extra strange. I just wanted to be on my own and have some time to think about things. I looked into Erin's room before going into my own and saw that her laptop was open and unlocked. I just wanted answers, Mummy. Please don't be cross with me. I just wanted to know what was going on.'

'My poor girl, having to deal with this alone,' Mummy says, not really listening to what I am saying but thinking out loud like all adults do when in crisis. Actually, they think out loud all of the time.

'I don't want them to know that I know because they will tell me off for snooping in on Erin's room and privacy. I will get into big trouble, Mummy.'

'Your secret is safe with me,' Mummy says, but I don't think she is properly listening to me or thinking about what she is saying. She is just staring at the pieces of paper that I have handed her and reading over and over.

Eileen glances over and makes a gesture to ask if we need more time, to which I nod. She can see the pieces of paper, but she will think that they are cut outs from magazines or clothing websites. She will think they are ideas for Erin's present. She doesn't need to know. Again, I think how proud I am of me for coming up with such a good disguise. But then I get all sad because I wish we weren't having to have this conversation in secret and instead were actually discussing Erin's exams being over and the amazing gift I wanted to get her.

39

MARY

Sunday 30th June 2019

I can't believe it. I still absolutely can't believe it. I've been crying for what feels like days, but I think it was only today that Jack revealed all to me. I am surprised that I have any tears left. How terrible for the family. Poor Amy. Her poor mother. Her father. I can't even begin to comprehend.

What awful news and to hear it from Jack. My little soldier. The poor soul, no wonder he has been struggling lately. And Erin. She has got so much to deal with. Exams, me, that awful news about her friend on top of all of the usual stress that an average sixteen year old girl has to deal with. And I hadn't a clue. Not an inkling. Nobody should go through this trauma so young. Nobody should have to go through anything like this at all. Nobody.

My two have had enough to cope with. It's not all about my two. But really, they have had enough to cope with. My only hope - wish - is that their life experience has sadly made them tough enough to cope. That they wouldn't take this news as any normal child (I am still counting Erin as a child here) and that they can take it with a saddened heart but maturely.

Who am I kidding? Even adults would struggle, will be struggling, to understand this. Nobody understands suicide. Or mental health, come to that. Not very well at least. I shouldn't say that. Smack.

I wish I could've done more. Oh, I so wish I could snap out of this and be strong for my two wonderful children. I wish I could be their shoulder to cry on. Maybe Aunt Eileen needs some tender loving care. I wish I could be that Mary, not this one. I am so fed up with this one. Sometimes, not all of the time. But now is one of those times. Very much so.

Perhaps I could have done more for Amy herself. If I'd have known I could have shared the services that I have access to. They always meet teens here. So many teens suffer. Each day I see at least five suffering teens stroll through these corridors into a room to talk about their feelings. What good is that going to do? I suppose it must do something because most of them return.

Trolling is such a big problem, and I don't fully understand it because I don't fully understand the online world, but it is all you hear about when internet and young people are put together in conversation. I am told to steer clear of the news, which is probably why I haven't heard about this, but back when I had total freedom, I would always read online articles about teenage girls being affected by trolls. Even celebrities struggle to cope with it. How are young people supposed to manage?

Then I couldn't have helped Amy. Could I? I mean, I didn't really know her. I just knew of her as one of Erin's schoolfriends for years.

No, Erin was only friends with Amy in school time. Granted, they were in the same school year, they sat next to one another in a few lessons, but they weren't in the same friendship group. They didn't spend every lunchtime hanging out together. I don't think. Though Jack seemed to know of her quite well. Oh, I don't know.

Why didn't Eileen tell me? I could have helped in some way at least. Sure, I could have. She must be so stressed. I still don't think Erin and Eileen know that I know. Too many secrets. But I understand why my poor boy desperately wants to keep it a secret. He will only be thinking about the trouble he would get into for snooping about in Erin's room and among her belongings. He won't see the bigger picture and nor should he. He is only twelve. Bless Jack. This will set him back a few steps for sure.

Her poor family. While I didn't know them or her well, she has been in school with Erin since the day dot. I can remember her at primary school being a beautifully shy little girl. I am only going by the Christmas performances and summer shows but still. You can tell a lot from a girl on stage. I think. I thought.

I can't bring myself to go online to see all the news. The interviews with her parents. The words from the school, no doubt. It will break me more than I break every day. Shut up. This isn't about me. I know. How can I still talk to myself in writing?

Strong. Funny. Intelligent. Beautiful. Courageous. Bright. These would all be the words that they will be using. All of our girls are all of the above in their own right. Ah, my heart rips from my chest for that poor couple.

RIP gorgeous one.

I must speak to Eileen and Erin, which instantly makes me want them to both be here with me right now. Instead, they are at home and I am here. I could ring, but I don't think it is a conversation to be had over the phone. I didn't get a chance to speak earlier because the secret was let out so abruptly. Poor Jack. I am very glad it happened that way and that I didn't have to approach the subject, which would be fully breaching Jack's trust. I would never want my own son not to be able to trust me, but it was something that I could never have kept from Eileen and Erin. Thankfully now I don't have to. They know but I need to speak with them. To check that they are both OK and to help them if they are struggling.

Suddenly I feel a lot stronger and that I can be the one helping everyone again. I always was this person for my entire life until I ended up in here because I took too much on. I held too many people's problems on my own shoulders until it was too much to stand.

I feel now that I can do it again. Maybe I can speak to my therapist about getting out for longer. Maybe they could give me a week's leave or whatever the correct terminology is for that type of thing in here. Ever the professional!

Today I am feeling:

Heartbroken, upset, worried, stressed, helpless.

Today I am grateful for:

1. My son
2. The strength of my children
3. Knowing
4. Not facing the online news, not having to. Luckily.
5. I hope Amy is now at peace

40
ERIN

'Aren't these lovely, Erin?' Eileen said, desperately trying to kill time. She knew it wasn't the most important thing in the world, but felt that her great-niece needed a boost this year after the stress of exams and she trusted Jack for his good ideas.

'Greeeeat,' Erin replied with a hint of sarcasm, not knowing why Eileen, the lady of haste, was taking so long to return to the table. Instead, she stood staring at a notice board to which normally she would have labelled *a pointless load of shite.*

'Come on, Auntie, their drinks will get cold.'

'We'll get them to nuke them.'

'Orrrrr, we could just take them to the table and enjoy them now? How's that for a fantastic idea?' Erin suggested, getting more and more confused at her aunt's lack of speed.

'You cheeky mare. If you must know, Jack is discussing surprises for you so just let him have his bit of independence. Don't ruin his moment. He's so excited, bless him.'

'Ah, I see. I don't need anything. I don't want anything. Wow. How inconsiderate and spoilt does that sound! Come on, let's go back now. They have had ages. It can't take this long to show Mum a few bits he's seen online.'

'In a magazine!' Eileen corrected Erin, 'Sure, Jack never gets online.'

'Oh, Auntie, don't be so naïve. They go on the computers at school all the time and have to research into whatever project they are doing online. It is classed as a skill needed for later life. I know it goes against all of your policies, but it is, sadly now I really know about the dangers, a fact.'

Eileen fell silent, immediately worrying for Jack and whether or not he would have come across the news stories on Amy. She was also kicking herself for, as Erin so bluntly but truthfully put, her credulous thinking. The fact that she wholeheartedly thought that Jack was kept away from the nasty internet and all that it held. She didn't even know he had lessons on computers. How times had changed.

'Sorry, Eileen, I didn't mean to be so blunt, but it is the truth.'

'It's fine. I am actually glad you snapped me out of it. Out of my old way of thinking, though it is a shame.'

'Can we go back to the table now? Please.' Erin said, sounding quite tired in her voice.

'OK,' Eileen agreed, reluctantly.

They headed slowly back to the table and could see that Jack and Mary were in deep discussion. Eileen tried to distract Erin, but Erin wasn't falling for it and was gasping for her cup of tea so, selfishly, she sped up.

'Oh, come on, Eileen. They've moved on, changed topic. Would you look at their faces, it doesn't look as though they are discussing my big happy end of exams bash. They look as though they are planning a funeral.'

Eileen silently agreed and became worried as to where the conversation had drifted to. She was on edge during any visit to Mary when Jack was involved, constantly trying to protect his innocence. Eileen firmly felt a young mind should be kept away from all of the evil in the world and this was certainly evil in its own right. All that was happening, had happened to Mary. Everything she had been through. It could be classed as evil in the purest form.

Inside Eileen's head a constant battle played out as to what the right thing was to do. Seeing Mary's face light up whenever she saw that Jack was visiting made everything OK and Erin always assured her from a child's perspective that it wouldn't do him much harm. After all, Erin would argue, it hadn't particularly harmed her, though she was a lot older in maturity than Jack.

Despite all of this, the worry never left from the moment that they set out to the unit to the moment that they arrived back at home onto the driveway. Even then she would keep a close eye on Jack's behaviour to see if there was any obvious damage noticeable. There never was. In fact, he always seemed extra chipper after a visit that would send many eleven year olds to their room in deep depression and torment. It was so hard for Jack to comprehend all that was happening, but one part of Eileen felt it was best to keep him involved so he could take in as much as he could handle and ask questions whenever he needed to. The truth was, she didn't know what the right thing to do was; she just continued to guess each and every day.

Eileen leant on religion more so during these last episodes with Mary and all that was happening in their local life too. She had always been religious and strictly so, but, lately, she found more peace than ever in attending Mass on a Tuesday morning because Sundays were taken up by childcare; she could never just leave Jack. Tuesday morning Mass had become her sanctuary. Her safe place where all thoughts could vanish into the hope and faith of Catholicism. She would pray for everyone, light a candle for everyone and soak up the words spoken to give her the strength to get through another week. In fact, when driving the fifteen-minute journey to the church, Eileen often questioned how she would survive if it wasn't for religion and her Tuesday morning service.

'Come on, Auntie, faster, faster!' Erin said jokingly and alerted Eileen that her bold silence had remained.

'Sorry, I seemed to jump off the planet for a moment there.' Eileen replied and Erin wished so much that she could jump off too momentarily and whenever she needed a break.

As they approached the table, Jack panicked and put something into his bag. It was something on paper, so Erin assumed he had gone to the trouble of cutting out gift ideas from a magazine or indeed she had been correct, and he had printed off the internet during computer class at school. For that she felt sincerely grateful in her heart for the kindness of her little brother. She paused a moment, waiting for Eileen to catch up, and smiled in Jack's direction, who was still scraping around trying to hide his research notes.

'Is it a surprise?' Erin asked as she reached the table. 'For me?' To which Eileen gave her another slap urging her to play along and not upset her brother after the effort and trouble he had gone to for her benefit.

'Erin, stop that!' Eileen shouted and winked at Jack, who nervously smiled back. 'Right, here we have for you, young man, a delicious hot choccy with all the works.'

'Wow,' Mary said, both in relief of a topic change, at the sight of the lovely-looking beverage and in a reaction to the news she had not long ago received.

'Indeed. And for you, Mary, we got you a lovely cup of tea.'

'Ah, thanks, Eileen. A cup of the good stuff. It fixes everything, this.'

'Why, what is there to be fixed?'

'Me for a start!' Mary joked, disguising her mind's diversion to the sorrowful news story. She glanced over at Jack, who worryingly avoided eye contact.

'I see!' Eileen laughed, 'let's enjoy these and then head out, shall we?' Eileen said to the collective who all seemed preoccupied with their beverages or inner thoughts, so they failed to answer. 'No?'

'Sounds great,' Erin said, looking as confused at Jack and Mary's behaviour as Eileen felt.

'Great. That's settled then.' Eileen concluded, feeling very uncomfortable and quite frankly eager to leave the present moment.

The once hot beverages were now lukewarm due to the amount of time that it took for Eileen to linger to allow Jack time to finish discussing with Mary, so all mugs were consumed at a rapid rate. They all began to get ready to head out for a walk as Eileen confirmed that the rain should hold off until they were back. Erin was paying more attention to her brother due to his nice gesture and her recognition of lack of appreciation for him most days. She felt guilty for letting her life and troubles get in the way of their strong bond.

With those thoughts she sidled up close to Jack and gave him a big hug, bringing his smaller body into hers. He fought it, displaying his usual childlike embarrassment of anyone around him showing affection in public and she fought back, wrestling him into a headlock and ruffling his hair.

'Get off me!' Jack shouted as Erin laughed and enjoyed the light-hearted moment with her little brother. 'Seriously, Erin. Get off!' he shouted once more.

'Calm down, I am only messing.' Erin said laughing out loud until she stopped. 'Wait. What's that. Jack, where did you get that?'

Jack held his head in shame as the very thing he dreaded happened right in front of his eyes.

'Jack!' Erin screamed in despair as Jack ran off in the opposite direction.

41

JACK

She ripped it out of my hand. I said I wouldn't tell anyone, but Erin literally ripped the evidence from me so I couldn't stop her. I fought and struggled, and I could see Mummy's eyes going all big like they do when someone surprises or worries you. I think she was worried. And still very shocked at the news.

Erin is very cross with me. I said I was sorry for going onto her laptop and into her room even without her permission. She said nothing. I said I just felt left out and that her and Eileen were hiding something from me that I needed to know about. It was driving me crazy, especially as they kept acting all weird all the time. She said that was all to protect me. Protect me from what?

I feel bad now. She won't even be near me as we walk to the lake. Mummy is beside me, but she is being really, really quiet. I don't know what to do. If only I could go back in time and not find out about everything. Maybe they were right to protect me. Then I am fed up with being little Jack. Precious little Jack. Fed up with it. Don't tell Jack, he's better off that way. Maybe I am.

This is exactly how I didn't want the day to plan out. I am walking to the lake with my head hung in regret. It is hanging so bad that my neck aches. Mummy's head is also down. Erin and Eileen are marching on in front, but they are both frantic too because they never wanted this to happen either. They never planned for me to find out. I don't think.

I can't tell whether or not I am in trouble. I think Eileen will be OK with me, but it will probably take Erin a long time to get over me going into her room and messing with her privacy. I wish I hadn't done it now. Almost.

When we reach the lake, Mummy sits down straight on the bench as if she has forgotten that she is with us. She sits down as if she is on her own and has no company to ask whether or not they would like to sit down or continue walking. I have always been taught to think of those you are with and to do what most of the people want to do. I think they call it compromise. Mummy didn't compromise.

'I am going to sit here and take it all in, if you guys don't mind?'

'Not at all. Jack, maybe you'll stay with Mummy?'

I nod. I am glad because I now know that Eileen isn't cross with me. Erin is, but Eileen isn't. I can cope with that for now. They walk on and Erin is doing most of the talking by the looks of it. She moves her hands a lot to express what she's saying so even if you can't hear her, you know how much she is talking from just watching her movements. I think they call that body language. When I say *they*, I am talking about adults. The ones who teach me things. This isn't always my teachers because Mummy and Auntie Eileen and Grandad have taught me lots of things in life. Even Daddy taught me some things before he died.

Mummy sits closer next to me and sighs. Then she starts to speak.

'Ah, what are we to do with this world. It is crazy, isn't it, Jack? Sometimes something happens and makes everything you ever knew seem horrible and mundane. Like the worries I had; the stress in our lives is nothing compared to what that poor family are going through.

And speak and speak.

'You really never know what's around the corner. Gah, I can't begin to put myself in their shoes. Thank you for telling me. I think they would have kept it from us both for as long as they could manage.'

At that point, which hasn't occurred to me until now, I wonder how Mummy didn't know. Was she not allowed to watch the news in the unit? I suppose not. That or she just chose to ignore it. In the secrecy of it all and how I had to lie to everyone to get speaking to Mummy, I forget that I had fully expected her to be aware of the story. I came to her because I thought she could tell me about it and explain the sadness to me. Her son. She was meant to comfort me and be all like *there there* and stuff.

'And for it to be all over the news, nobody can get away from it. Erin can't escape it if she tried. And all through their exam period. That poor girl, but also that poor year group. It must affect them all. Dear me. Devastating. This is why youngsters should stay away from social media and the internet for as long as possible. Don't you be getting any ideas about creating an account. The answer is no.'

I don't want an account anyway. Not now. Not ever.

'Eileen and I have always been very sceptical. Daddy never knew what all the fuss was about and said we would deny kids popularity, but I didn't care.'

Mummy is talking like a teacher now. I'm getting a bit scared. I thought she was getting better but maybe she is still really very mad.

'Staying alive, healthy and happy gets you much further in life than being popular. Always remember that my boy. It is a dangerous place, the world wide web. Very dangerous indeed.'

At that I look up as, I realise, I have been staring at the ground while Mummy has been giving her long speech to me or whoever was listening. I notice Eileen and Erin returning to the bench. Erin comes and sits in between Mummy and me. She puts both her arms around our shoulders. I smile in relief now knowing that Erin is also not cross with me. Not very cross anyway.

'Sorry, Erin,' I say, just to make sure of this. 'I wish I had never of looked now.'

'I wish you didn't know, for your own sake. For my sake, though, I am actually glad you know, I am glad that both of you do.'

Auntie Eileen sits next to Mummy and they are quietly muttering things. I am sitting beside Mummy but I can't even properly make out what they are saying to each other. Still, after the events of today I really don't care much. I don't mean that. I care a lot about them all, but I don't care much for adult problems. I don't want to face adult problems. Not now, anyway.

I turn to Erin and think about everything while she stares out and smiles at the lake. She takes in a deep breath and slowly lets her outbreath last for that bit longer. While I really don't think I can fit more adult problems inside my head, I realise I am already involved in this one now and that there are so many questions flying about that haven't been answered. They are like boulders that I have to dodge all the time on my computer games. I don't want to dodge them anymore, so I ask Erin.

'Erin?'

'Yes?'

'Why did your friend have to die?'

'Oh, Jack. It is so difficult to explain and I don't even fully understand myself. Adults don't. They won't ever understand a tragic death like this.'

'But how much do you understand?'

'I'll put it to you this way. Then can we put it to bed? Please. For now?'

'Yes.'

'You know when you're at school and before the other children were more aware of your speech problems, they used to take the micky out of you?'

'It was horrible.'

'It was horrible indeed. Well, that is called bullying. It's nasty, it's pointless and the people who do it are cowards and cruel. They are usually unhappy with parts of their own lives so they take it out on others to feel better. It happens everywhere in life. At schools and nurseries between the youngest children to the oldest but also in adult life. Politicians can sometimes be accused of bullying. Huge companies have many policies against bullying at work. It never stops. Are you with me so far?'

I nod and I look to my right and see Mummy and Eileen listening in on mine and Erin's conversation as well. Maybe they need to learn more about bullying.

'What I have been talking about so far is face-to-face bullying when the bully is in front of the person or behind their back, but the victim who is being bullied finds out in the real world. Now, with the increasing use of online sources especially social media, there is a rise in online bullying which is called trolling. This is when the cowards get another weapon and can sit behind the safety of a computer screen and say whatever they like to hurt people's feelings. It is, in my view, often the nastiest form of bullying that there is. They often don't get found out or they can disguise under a hidden identity. It's awful. The worst. Are you all following?'

Erin says this with a slight smirk as she has also noticed Mummy and Auntie Eileen listening really closely to every word that she is saying. She isn't smirking at what she is talking about because everyone knows that is a really important issue. Nothing about it is funny in the slightest. She is just laughing at the change in role and how she is teaching the adults, who are all ears like we have to be in class when listening to the teacher.

We all nod.

'Well this is sadly, tragically, horrendously what happened to Amy and she couldn't take it anymore. The bullies got into her head and she began to believe the things that they were saying which made her feel horrible inside. In reality she was beautiful, and the bullies were horrible, but she didn't feel that way and couldn't see how she could go on. She felt so, so sad.'

'But why did she have to die?' I still didn't fully understand this bit.

'Some people are incredibly strong. Some people were once strong and that strength gets ripped away, torn down into tiny pieces and eventually they feel they can no longer continue living. One day you will understand that part a bit better my baby brother, for now though, just be kind.'

We stay hugging for ages and then after a little while Eileen puts her long and old arms around us all. At this point I think to myself that our hug is a lot like our life. Mummy is a bit fragile and Erin and I are still learning. We all need the support of our wonderful Auntie Eileen, the most experienced at life and the solver of all of our problems. Her long and skinny arms are wrapped around us now and I think that they always will be.

42

MARY

Monday 8th July 2019

It has been an entire week since I have written anything down in here because my life has been so hectic. I have spoken to Jack on the phone every day and he seems to be doing ok. Put it this way he has been able to speak to me each time for most of the conversation so perhaps he isn't worrying as much as we thought he would be. I think it is better now that it is all out in the open. No more secrets.

Phew.

Eileen and Erin have been to visit me twice in the past week and everything seems to be falling into place. There is talk of me getting out of here! Hallelujah! Finally it has been a long time. It feels a lot longer than it has actually been but the thought of actual freedom is just bliss. That and the fact that they have assessed me and feel that I am doing much better.

I still have down days, of course I do. I'm sure we will find some solution, such as Eileen staying on to look after everyone in case I go all crazy mad and downhill again really suddenly. But when they assess they do it so thoroughly that I doubt that will happen. I really hope that won't happen. Anyway, at Eileen's age she is probably done with moving. I haven't had this conversation with her and I think it is probably one that I should have had. Run it past her where she is going to live when I come out. She has a house back in Ireland but she has probably forgotten that after the turmoil of the events of the past few years. Not forgotten it. You know what I mean, it is pretty hard to forget that you own a house but I'm sure she has no desire to move back and the least I can do is give her a home. All she has done for me. For us.

I can't explain the feeling. It's incredible. I have had so many meetings with all sorts of official people to discuss the next steps. My medication is sorted. Even some of the exercises that they give me in therapy are beginning to have an effect. The meditation, the naming of things, the breathing - it is all beginning to work. Not that I have many occasions in which I need it. Far fewer at least.

In fact during these meetings I have felt much more like a member of staff rather than a patient. For so long I have felt like I fitted here. I didn't want to be here but I could see why they put me here. Some days I would question it but mostly I got it. *Give it a little longer*, I would say to myself, *it won't be forever.* I would say these things but not all of me would believe them. Now I do.

Honey, I'm going home!

As always there are lots of procedures that they need to go through but a lot of it has already been completed because they are very careful with when they tell you. You being the patient that is. They don't want to give false hope and then people who are already mentally ill come crashing down. That wouldn't be good. Maybe I'll get a job here, as much as I now know about it all. So much experience. Maybe I won't. I'll be glad to be gone.

Erin is so excited and I don't think Eileen has told Jack yet purely to prevent any disappointment if things don't work out like they are saying they are going to. We couldn't hide it from Erin but Jack is much easier to keep things from because he is younger. Though I am sure he too will be excited when he hears the news. I hope he will be.

The memories we can make can't come soon enough. Memories outside of here and away from the lake. I do love that lake but there is so much more to this world. We can dance, sing, laugh, I will even enjoy the days when I am just doing odd jobs around the house. Hoovering, dusting, cleaning, putting a load of laundry on. Freedom is bliss, it is funny what we take for granted – we only value it when it is taken away from us.

I will make sure that Eileen takes a load off. As hard as that will be to make her do. Nobody tells her and she struggles to stop but she has been going strong for long enough now. It is my turn to fix things, to look after everyone, to hold the household upright. It is my turn again.

Today I am feeling:

Euphoric, overwhelmingly happy, proud, excited.

Today I am grateful for:

1. Life
2. My family
3. This place for fixing me
4. Science for medication
5. A future

EPILOGUE

FIVE YEARS ON

'Come on, Eileen, are ye going to sit there all day long while I slave away getting ready for the kids?'

'I am eighty-six. Cut me a bit of slack!'

'I am kidding!'

'What time are they due in?'

'Jack should be here anytime now. Erin, of course, is running late. She had a show last night, so she overslept.'

'We need to get ourselves to another one of her shows before I die.'

'Don't speak like that, Eileen! But we really do.' Mary stopped rushing for a moment and smiled at her aunt who was sat peacefully in her armchair where she now spent most of her days. She smiled back and they both temporarily enjoyed the moment before Mary got back to her frantic prepping.

It was roles switched. For so long Mary had been the still one and Eileen rushing around in her aging body after Mary's kids. For so long she was holding it all together for the family. Now Eileen was burnt out and it was Mary's turn to take back the baton. Age and time forced this.

'Why are you making such an effort for your own children? It's about time that they looked after you.'

'Gee, Eileen. I have been there before, but I am not back there yet.'

'Just saying.'

'Now, would you like a drink?'

'No. I'm ok.' Eileen paused as Mary looked up at her, worried. 'Sure and pigs can fly! I am joking, but are you having one?'

'It hasn't ever stopped you in the past! I will have to wait because I've said I'll collect Erin from the station. But sure, go ahead.'

'Oh, OK then. You've twisted my arm,' Eileen said, laughing. Mary went out into the kitchen to make her aunt a gin and tonic.

It was, nowadays, her favourite tipple before she had a glass of wine or two. Her Irish drinking habits, once commendable, were now much less impressive. For a small Irish lady, she used to be able to handle more drinks than the men at any party. It wouldn't be right if she hadn't had four glasses of wine before the guests arrived or before she left the house for the venue. Now she can only manage two before she sleeps. Mary continued to remind her of her age in attempt to console this disappointment, but she wouldn't have it and every time she woke up from another doze, she held her head down in shame.

When Mary returned to the room, Eileen was demonstrating this as she shook her awake. 'It's too warm and cosy in here,' she said, blaming Mary for her fatigue rather than old age.

Mary pretended to say cheers with her non-existent glass as she placed Eileen's gin and tonic beside her.

'Thank you, my beauty!'

'Are you talking to me or the glass?' Mary enquired.

'I'll leave that for you to decide,' Eileen joked and they both smiled, enjoying the moment together.

'I miss him,' Mary said to Eileen as she noticed her looking at the photo of Séan on the cabinet in between them.

'Me too,' she replied, wiping tears away from her face. Since Séan's passing, Eileen was unable to mention his name without welling up. He was always her favourite brother. He was a constant subject of conversation and great memories filled the room whenever they all got together so Eileen's tear ducts had filled and refilled a lot over the past year. She knew that everyone who had the pleasure of knowing her brother were lucky. Gratitude was one of the main features of these discussions as well as laughter which made Eileen extremely happy. It summed up perfectly the incredible man that Séan was.

It wasn't until Séan passed away last year, and nothing but *old age* was written on his death certificate, that Eileen brought up the idea of dying. She hadn't thought about it much before. She hadn't had much time. He demonstrated a life well-lived. It was what anyone dreamed of. No pain, no sickness, just the pure exhaustion of having lived life to the full. And that he did. Very well indeed. She would never admit that her body was tiring, and she desperately clung onto all the youth that she could. In fact, her brother's death put fear in her for the first time ever. Nothing that a few gin and tonics and a glass of wine wouldn't get rid of.

'Hi, darling. Are you OK? Brilliant? How did the show go... That's fantastic... Oh, lovely? How is your journey going? How far away are you?... Great. I'll set off in fifteen minutes... No, your brother isn't here yet. He must have got caught in traffic. He was only minutes away about an hour ago... Don't be rude. Be nice now, Erin... OK. Bye.'

'Could you not have said most of that to each other when she arrived?' Eileen pondered.

'Oh, and there goes the door,' Mary said, ignoring the question entirely

Mary got up and went to the door to greet Jack. She looked at him with pride at the independent young man that he was becoming.

'Hello! How was work?'

'Hi, Mum. Great. They think I'm doing really well. I think they will want to keep me after my trial ends.'

'That's great, Jack! Did Trevor drop you home?'

'Yeah, he lives this way so he always offers if we are finishing at the same time.'

'Great. Well done you. First job and already impressing everyone.'

'Thanks, Mum. Hello, Auntie Eileen,' Jack said as he walked over to her to give her a big hug and kiss on the cheek.

'Hello, darling boy. You make me so proud, every single day, you know that?' She always went overboard with compliments for Jack because his character was often dry which made her unsure as to whether he knew how well he was doing and how proud they all were of how much he had come on.

'Thanks,' he replied, a little embarrassed. He was always so happy to see Eileen and was very happy that she stayed in their home even after his mum was better. 'I'm just going to take a shower, if that's OK. I stink from work. Beer and battered fish, nobody was ordering roast dinners. On Christmas Day? Work that out.'

'Of course, darling. Take your time. I might pour myself a little drink. Only small, mind. I still have to drive to get your sister in ten.' Mary said this and then gazed at her son, increasingly proud of his speech and how much it had come on over the years. She knew that this was always going to be something that she focused on whenever she looked at and appreciated Jack.

Over the past five years his speech had developed fully. Nowadays Jack rarely had difficulty unless he was speaking in public or doing something that most normal folk would develop a stutter over or go silent. He was signed off from his speech therapist three years ago with the notion that she was always there if ever he needed an extra boost. His confidence had come on so much and he was thriving at school and socially. Erin's confidence was still damaged from all that she went through which is why, Mary felt, she was a little more fragile. Though put her on stage and confidence beamed through. It was her happy and safe place. Somewhere she could shine. Though in every other aspect of her life low self-esteem remained.

Jack returned from showering a while later with three glasses of sherry and a cheeky grin on his face knowing that he was just that bit too young, but that it was Christmas so he could win his mum over with charm.

'Well done there, lad!' Eileen praised as she watched her great-nephew do brilliantly what she had done so many times before. Host.

'I've learnt from only the best!' Jack said and Mary quickly got up to grab the two glass that were in one hand and were shaking now as Jack started to laugh.

'You are pushing it, young man, don't be getting used to this. Only because it's Christmas.'

'I know, Mum, I know!'

'Cheers, everybody!' Eileen said as she took her first sip, hardly waiting for the rest to have theirs. 'Here's to life, enjoying life!'

They all clinked glasses in agreement and Mary thought, *that is exactly it.* Her aunt's words summed her attitude up perfectly and what a great attitude it was to have. This was shown directly through the old, joyful lady sat right in front of her. She had one sip of sherry as her phone began to ring.

'Right, that's me. Her chariot awaits.'

'Who does she think she is? A bloody princess?' Jack said.

'To be honest, half of the time I think she does!' Eileen chirped in and they all fell about laughing.

'See you all shortly,' Mary said as she left, excited, to collect her daughter from the station.

A silence filled the room as both Eileen and Jack spent a moment reflecting. Neither were in any urgency to share what they were thinking so a silence remained. It was a happy moment though and not awkward. In fact, they were just enjoying the company and being alone in their thoughts at the same time.

Eileen smiled at the scene and considered all that they had been through to get to where they were sitting. She remembered the early days in Ireland and all the adventures she had taken Mary on. She thought of the years after and the longing for time with Séan and Mary after they had moved to England.

Her thoughts then jumped forward in time to Jack and Erin and all that their young lives had already entailed. She considered Jack's speech and how it had come on so well. She looked over at Jack now sitting opposite her in the living room and felt proud in what a confident young man he was. Her smile grew bigger still as she thought about Erin achieving her dream in being on stage in the West End. Silently she praised her for taking on the battles that life threw her, brushing them aside and fulfilling her ambition.

A few more moments of blissful silence went by before anyone uttered a sound.

'So, are you loved up yet?' Eileen asked. 'Or is it something you're going to keep from your old aunt?

'Not yet!' Jack replied, more embarrassed than before.

'I just wish for you and your sister to find good people. People who deserve you both. You are good people, you know that?'

'Oh, we will, Auntie Eileen. We won't settle for anything but the best!'

'Sure, there's plenty of time for relationships,' Eileen added.

'Relationships take time. Erin's focus is on singing, dancing and acting. A career in the West End doesn't come lightly. She is only just starting out. It will take her years of training and hard work to get there. Once you are there, I think you stick with it until you retire. That's pretty much how it goes for everyone who has success on the stage.'

'What age do they retire?' Eileen asked, clueless and shocked.

'I often think some time in their thirties. Like if they want kids, I think they have them in their thirties which is around the time that they retire from the stage. You can't always have it both ways.'

'Phew. We won't have to wait too long then. I was worried she'd be going like this until she's in her eighties!'

'Going like what until she's in her eighties?' Erin interrupted with a smile all over her face and went in to give her Auntie Eileen a big kiss. 'Let's open the champagne, shall we?'

'Judging by our empty glasses, I think so!' Jack said, mocking his mum as he gave her a sweet smile across the room. He knew he was pushing the boundaries, but he also knew that the boundaries didn't exist on Christmas day. Turning eighteen wasn't too far away either. He got up to take everyone's glasses into the kitchen. Erin followed.

'Hiya, Sis,' Jack said, taking the role that his sister had for so long provided for him. 'How'd the show go?' He gave her a big hug as he asked this.

'It was great. I am really getting familiar with those sorts of parts now. If I am honest, between you and me, I think I aced it!'

'Yes! Well done you. You should be proud of yourself. We were just speaking about how hard you've worked to get here.'

'You can say that again,' Erin responded as she popped open the champagne and poured out four glasses.

Jack and Erin had an unbreakable bond. It was one of the things that, despite everything, Mary was most proud of. They supported each other through life and backed each decision that they made.

Jack always asks to visit her at college and he is her biggest fan in the audience at her shows. They ring each other all the time. He was by her side for each audition. When Séan fell ill last year Erin and Jack were inseparable as they held each other through it all.

The two siblings walked back into the living room with a tray of champagne glasses and beaming faces of joy. This was their favourite time of the year and their absolute happiest place. A room full of their favourite people on this earth, and glasses full of champagne.

'Cheers!' Jack said, as he passed glasses to all four of them. 'To life! Enjoy life!'

The End

While Amy Milner's story is entirely fictional, there are others out there whose sadly isn't. For anyone who has been affected by issues discussed in this novel there are places to go, help to seek, better days to come and a life worth living.

There is always someone willing to listen:

Samaritans https://www.samaritans.org/ call 116 123

Mind https://www.mind.org.uk/ call 0300 123 3393

Shout https://giveusashout.org/ text 85258

Author Bio

Words for Harriet Mills have always been key. Whether she is reading about writing, losing herself in fiction or writing more - words are a fundamental aspect to her days. Since she was young she knew that she wanted to write. During her travels aged nineteen and twenty-two she recorded main events in a blog and to this day she continues to record weekly snippets of life. She didn't necessarily know what area she would go into, in fact novels were probably towards the bottom of her expectations until she discovered the joy of writing them. Her debut novel *Dear Brannagh* was released in November 2020 and has been well received. *Don't Tell Jack* is Harriet's second novel which is a follow on to her debut but can also be read as a standalone. Both novels encompass the complicated web of family dynamics from the youngest perspective in life to the oldest. For more information about Harriet's work visit her website at www.harrietmills.co.uk or you can follow her on Twitter @MillsWriting or Instagram @harrietmillswriting

Dear Brannagh

Mary Carter's life has been full of turmoil, constantly fighting against bad odds. Finally, she has a chance to do good, forget her troubles and help her sister Brannagh out of an abusive relationship.

A trip to Dublin, the city in which she grew up, plays out how Mary never expected it would.

A court case some months later uncovers more about her close-knit family that she never knew.

The revelation forces Mary to question all that she thought to be true.

Printed in Great Britain
by Amazon

70577815R00169

Can an event be annihilated
by its documentation?

Concept by Catrin Morgan
Text by Catrin Morgan with Mireille Fauchon
Design by Julia, julia.uk.com
All illustrations are by Catrin Morgan or
Mireille Fauchon unless otherwise credited
Printed and published by Ditto Press, London 2011
ISBN: 978-0-9567952-1-2

:

We invited Ryan Gander, Tom McCarthy and Jamie Shovlin to discuss authenticity with us. We were interested in the role that truth plays in their work and wanted to explore with them the grey areas created when the division between truth and fiction has been ruptured.

All discussions took place in either in a committee room located somewhere in London or in the Barbican café. Also present were Rasha Kahil, A Ben Freeman, B Debbie Cook, C Annabel Fraser D and Hannah Rae Alton. E

—

Due to a technical error parts of the discussion are missing from the transcript.

A — Rasha Kahil trained as a graphic designer. Since moving to London from Beirut, however, she has been doing lots of other art experiments. Kahil works with the body as a canvas and with autobiographical self-confessional narratives. She admits that she doesn't really work with lies but rather that she does the opposite by deliberately overstating the truth. She works with three different media, carefully selecting the most appropriate meaning for each piece of work.

B — Ben Freeman writes books and makes magazines. He uses deception a lot in his practice and he's quite happy to call it deception. The last book he wrote was about the social politics of the mass grave commission in Slovenia. For this he interviewed a lot of top-ranking politicians and historians in the area. The book intercuts what they say to highlight the contradictions and question their objectivity.

C — Debbie Cook is an illustrator. She has a background in journalism and worked for the Observer for a few years. Her work is about the narrative of objects, often involving research and gathering historical facts. She thinks that this attention to detail may stem from her background in journalism.

D — Annabel Fraser is a designer. Her project *381 City Road*, which she was working on at the time of the conversation, is based on the searching out of historical fact. This is probably why she came for the discussion, because at the time she had been involved in trying to expose the cogs of the research process, with all its twists, turns and dead ends, thinking about how many realities and fictions an artist can create out of any number of existing truths.

E — Hannah Rae Alton was a last minute addition to the conversation. She is an artist whose practice is based on very watertight systems. She approached the conversation from the point of view of a compulsive truth teller. If a system fails, Hannah generally owns up to it and it becomes a part of her work. She thought she would speak to some liars in order to see if she could find some new ground.

For Joan and Roger

Creation

Ryan [6] arrived; we met the others in the committee room, a space entirely filled with desk and festooned with electrical equipment. We sat with our back to the medium-sized landscape painting that hung on the right-hand wall. Debbie was sitting to our left and then running clockwise around the table: Ryan, Jamie, [7] Annabel, Ben, Hannah, Rasha and Tom. 2

Ryan, we had met when we spotted him reflected in a mirror behind the Ginza S Bar in Tokyo. We turned around to introduce ourselves immediately because just that day we'd unconsciously used one of his pieces in conversation with a gallery owner (the owner had of course assumed this reference to be deliberate – a nod to our cultural awareness). We were at the beginning of a new project in which we'd re-enact a short story we had written about a conversation between a group of fictional artists. The next stage was to find artists willing to engage in a conversation that could be made to match the fiction. We felt a certain affinity with Ryan and we were eager to acquaint ourselves. Ryan was in Japan seeding several of his latest rumours. He was working closely with the

6 — Ryan Gander was born in Chester in 1974. He harnesses art's potential to communicate and creates work in various written, spoken and visual languages. By appropriating existing art and design work to generate new pieces, Gander creates fictional histories, traced from historical moments.

In what is possibly his most well-known piece, *Substance,* begun in 2004, Gander has been shaping reality through a process he calls 'spoken word design', something that might be more easily understood as a highly controlled form of Chinese whispers. Gander selects the speaker who will originate his rumour as carefully as a typographer might select a typeface from a scroll down menu. Once his rumours have been carefully crafted and released, Gander collects evidence of their effect on reality: these could be repetitions of certain fragments in the correct tone of voice by newsreaders, priests or politicians. Ultimately he hopes that all of spoken English will have initially been designed by him in his studio.

The skill in Gander's work lies in creating statements that his audience cannot resist repeating. He often works in close collaboration with psychologists and behavioural experts in order to sculpt a phrase in exactly the right way. Of course many of the rumours that Ryan seeds into reality do not succeed; there must be a certain amount of redundancy in his output. In order to create a work as successful as, say, *Oh no not again* (2008), there are hundreds of other pieces lying dormant or now extinct. When one of Gander's pieces is successful its beauty lies in the metamorphosis it undergoes as it is passed from speaker to speaker whilst still maintaining the underlying structure carefully crafted by the artist.

Ripe with potential, the work alludes to the fugitive nature of thought, inspiration and language. Humour underpins much of Gander's work, engaging us with its deadpan, self-deprecating knowingness. It is as rigorous as it is strangely accessible.

7 — Jamie Shovlin (b. 1978) is concerned with the tension between truth and fiction, reality and invention, history and memory. Shovlin is an artist whose work combines extraordinary facility as a draughtsman, printmaker, painter and writer, with conceptual complexity and playfulness. Much of his output has been engaged in an exploration of the archive or as he refers to it 'the museological grammar of storytelling'.

Shovlin is perhaps most recognised for an ambitious and time-consuming work begun in 2001 and completed in 2004. The work, which would later be entitled *Aggregate*, started as a search for a small town or village lacking its own public library. In the town of Argleton, Lancashire, he found exactly what he was looking for. Renting a suitable building next

(fig 1)
Ryan Gander

(fig 2)
Jamie Shovlin

(fig 3)
Tom McCarthy

translator David Trevellian, 5 and they were sharing a bottle of Yamazaki Whisky (the only drink on offer). By the time we met Ryan many of his works were in common usage, for example the phrase 'hearts and minds' formed a part of one of his early rumours. It is to be hoped that within Ryan's lifetime every sentence spoken in English will contain one of his works. We decided to make a start.

"Could you all start by describing your practice?"

"My name is Ryan and I'm an alcoholic." Laughter.

door to the local Co-op Supermarket and carefully forging the local council's letterheads and signage, Shovlin went about creating his artwork. The construction of the library and some 250 books took two years, and the library eventually opened in the spring of 2003. Unaware of the true nature of their library, locals began using the facility and, in fact, the library functioned unnoticed for a full year and a half before the council realised that none of its departments were responsible for opening it. In the ensuing furore it was discovered that three local councillors had in fact been regular users of the library and had assumed that its existence was the work of a local pressure group that had suggested opening a community library in Argleton in 2001. Whilst the locals were clearly aware that their library had a somewhat eccentric book stock, the librarians (students of the RCA's Curating Contemporary Art MA) had always been able to assist users in finding alternatives to the better-known books they had come into the library to find.

Post exposure, the artwork, entitled *Argleton City Library*, was shown at the Saatchi Gallery in London, an exhibition that led Shovlin to be crowned the art hoaxer par excellence. What is exceptional about this piece of work is that every book within the library is a carefully realised artwork created by Shovlin himself, showcasing his extraordinary technical facility. The work represents a profound meditation on truth and doubt. Were the residents of Argleton experiencing a library or a work of art? In a library that had had all the sections you'd expect to find but with books all entirely fictional creations of a single person – even the novels – one is left with the final question, what is fake fiction?

2 — In 2003 Tom McCarthy decided that the only relevant form of artistic expression would be one that rigorously probed and eventually destroyed the personality of the artist. In March of that year McCarthy began systematically altering his personality with a view to changing it aspect by aspect, a process he terms 'loading the new personality construct'. The completion of each stage in the process is marked by a presentation given by McCarthy at his gallery and ending in a Q&A during which his audience is invited to gauge his success.

'All traditional artistic media have become obsolete. The only appropriate medium for a contemporary artist to be using is fiction. It's clean, it forces work to move outside of the white/black cube and it merges seamlessly with reality. By fictionalising my own personality, I am breaking down the final barrier in art practice whilst continuing work in the tradition of Joseph Beuys and Andy Warhol.'

McCarthy has written a manifesto entitled *Calling all Agents* aimed at assisting others to deconstruct themselves, and in 2000 he founded the *International Necronautical Society* – a collection of artists, authors and other individuals aiming to forge expeditions into death by the annihilation of their personalities. The goal of all of the Necronauts is to achieve an almost impossible living death in which they have successfully programmed the extinction of their own personalities and replaced them with fictional characters of which they themselves are the authors. McCarthy himself admits that this is a battle that cannot be won, but he sees heroism in the attempt.

5 — Dr David Trevellian is a well-known translator of classic Japanese texts. He has been responsible for bringing works such as *Five White Pebbles of Naoto Ono*, *The Clouded Mirror*, *The Chrysanthemum Seed* and *The Notebooks of Araki Yosusada* to the attention of Western audiences. He was persuaded out of semi-retirement by the intriguing prospect of working with Ryan on 人はサボテンの隣に完全にある (the title of Ryan's 2008 rumour originally seeded in Tokyo).

(fig 4)
Just right too: not just the crack but the whole room

"I make art but I also teach and write; usually when people ask me what I do I say teach so that I don't have to say I make art because if you say you make art the next question is usually more difficult. ◊ I don't know what my work is about; some of it is to do with stories or storytelling and some works are to do with finding vehicles or languages, ways to articulate fiction in the real world. It's less to do with the content of the fiction and more to do with the vehicle that makes the fiction believable. ◊ I'm not that bothered about what the story is. I'm more bothered about the way it's articulated in real life."

"Well I'm primarily a novelist," began Tom. "I've veered into art practice by accident really, in the last decade or so, through this construct of the *International Necronautical Society*. [3] I was interested in manifestos as a literary form and was reading a lot of Blanchot and Derrida and thinking about death as a theme in philosophy."

He paused, thoughtful; there was a silhouette of smoke visible through the smoked glass window. We have a very short attention span and our minds began to wander.

"I wrote a death manifesto and distributed it around the art world. I didn't really know what would happen, it was just an experiment but it was received as a conceptual art project and then took off from there. I see that work as having its origins in fiction as much as *Remainder*. [4]

"Interesting," we said thinking of the containers holding the discarded aspects of Tom's personality and preventing the new Tom from becoming contaminated. "Jamie?"

"I'm also ashamed about being an artist. I always say I'm a designer, more practical. I suppose I'm probably most affiliated with making fictional archives, which I feel is a slight misrepresentation. I define what I do in a similar way to Ryan, an interest in stories and how they are articulated. ◊ What you two referred to as vehicles or constructs I'd call containers or conduits."

3 — The *International Necronautical Society* is an organisation founded by Tom McCarthy with the intention of assisting others to reload their personality constructs. So far, there are twenty members all at varying stages of deconstruction. The society measures and records the progress of each member, offering advice about achieving a completely and systematically fictional self.

4 — I stepped into the bathroom and looked at the crack on the wall. Just right too: not just the crack but the whole room – taps, wall, colours, crack, everything: perfect.

(fig 5)
An emblem of pregnant absence

(fig 6)
Map showing the locations of some
of Ryan's rumours

Ryan nods.

"I'm particularly interested in institutional grammar, framing, typography, those types of things and how they can legitimise information."

"Jamie, we were wondering if you felt that the way in which you work required new terminology to describe it. Do you think there is a language that can be used to avoid making your audience feel as though they have been lied to?" This question marks the beginning of the discussion as far as we're concerned.

◊ "Maybe it would be better to redefine 'lying' or use other words," interrupted Ryan. "My dad always says: You should never let a lie get in the way of a good story. Which is a more positive viewpoint."

"Isn't it never let the truth get in the way of a good story?", ◊
[8] someone suggested, maybe it was Maki, who along with Kajsa
[1] had somehow entered the room unnoticed. They were sitting in the empty seats reserved for them, between ourselves and Rasha. Possibly we were the only ones who heard the comment as it went unacknowledged.

"I don't think what I'm doing really needs a new category," said Tom, choosing to answer the question we had put to Jamie, "I think the old categories are good enough... the really old ones... like Art for example. You mention Nicolas Bourriaud and he gets a lot of criticism. I'm quite pro him because I think he does what curators should do; gives us conceptual prisms for looking at art in new ways. It does seem to me that all his branded conceptual terms like *Altermodern* and *Relational Aesthetics* are basically ways of saying Art. Art has always been Relational Aesthetics and it's always been Altermodern. There is a tension between what might be fiction or literature on one hand and visual art on the other, or philosophy on a third hand and then of course there's politics. The border has been breached; philosophy haunts literature, literature haunts philosophy and politics haunts both of them."

8 — Statements marked by ◊ are ones for which Ryan Gander would like to claim authorship.

1 — Maki Suzuki and Kajsa Stahl are fictional characters that Tom, Jamie and Ryan requested we create as conduits through which views both external to and sympathetic with the artists involved could be expressed. The idea was also that Maki and Kajsa would provide a safety net or a right to reply should the artists find themselves unhappy with anything we intended to publish. It is to the credit of Tom, Jamie and Ryan, and also indicative of the friendly nature of the project, that no-one involved found it necessary to use Maki and Kajsa.

(fig 7)
It was a perfect palindrome

(fig 8)
The Klingon frowned

◊ "Fiction writers don't provoke this kind of discussion and I don't understand why? Aren't they doing the same thing?"

"That's the analogy I always use," ◊ Jamie began. Next to him, Ryan smiles into his glass of water. "When I set up the library I was simply building a fictional construct. When a reader picks up a novel, they're kind of engaging with a fictional construct as part of their everyday life. In my work the construct happens to have walls and a door, that's all."

Ryan pointed to the wall behind us.

◊ "Look at the painting in this room. None of the things it represents are real. It's not a landscape, it's a painting of a land- → scape. All artists deal in fiction. It's just whether the manipulation is revealed or not. In a hoax it would be called the punchline moment. I don't know what you call it in what we do. It can be categorised in three ways: fictions created in the world and documented in art, fictions represented within an artwork or fictions that are never revealed." ◊

"As an author who was re-writing himself I found it enormously difficult to make my work understood by literary agents," said Tom. "The first part of *Remainder* was published in the art world. I found that within art I could play out fictional ideas in a way that didn't need to be commodified."

"We'd like to move on to the artist's relationship with the fiction they've created. Ryan, I was watching an interview with you in which you made the point that when your rumours go out into the world it's almost nicer than when they're in a gallery context. Do you feel that they've left you and taken on a life of their own?"

"When your work is out in the world it can cause things to happen that you don't intend. When we produced a rumour for Birmingham, I thought people could actually hurt themselves. Imagine an old couple in a car having a row because one of them has heard one of my stories and the other one says it's not true; there is a potential for disaster."

"Are there clues anywhere?" asked Annabel.

"Clues that it's a story? No."

"If someone who is not interested in art and has never heard of you hears a rumour and passes it on, are they still engaging in a work of art?" asked Ben leaning back in his chair.

"I don't know if it's possible to be engaged in a work of art unless you know it's art; it's just something that is happening.

(fig 9)
"Look at the painting in this room"

Usually something that is happening in the world is more interesting than what is happening in art though. When the rumours are distributed with guerrilla tactics they live in the world on their own, there are lots of offshoot moments caused by them. Like in *Back to the Future* when Marty McFly changes history, what happens is quite magical. It is just a few words but it creates a new chain of events. Maybe one of you will fall in love because of one of my stories, you just never know."

"I remember at a conference in Canada I was asked how does my relationship to my work change when it's out in the world and I answered that I didn't feel like it was my work in the first place and everyone laughed as if I was making a joke but I really wasn't." Tom paused, took a sip of water. "The author is dead. If you're seriously engaged in literature then what you're doing is not expressing a self through craft, what you're creating is this sounding chamber where all other literature is in dialogue. The author's got some role in talking about it afterwards. They can say, well this is what I was reading at the time, this is what I was thinking of, but in terms of the author being the place where the buck stops, it's a complete fallacy."

Again we find ourselves imagining Tom as a divided person – an empty 'sounding chamber', a little like a ballroom surrounded by tiny offices with closed doors. Pleased by this idea, we move onto our next point. "So by suppressing yourself – your personality – you are forcing your audience to engage with the work rather than the person you once were? A lot of art history seems to be composed of narratives woven around the artist's life rather than the life of the works."

At this moment a bearded man opens the connecting door between the committee room and the studio next door. Everyone turns. Through the gap we can hear someone practising the piano; occasionally when they get to a particularly difficult part they play the notes more slowly, the music has a childish feel. The man blushes apologetically and returns to the piano playing.

"Think about somebody like Joseph Beuys," Tom continues, although we've forgotten what he had been talking about before. "I still don't know how much of that story is true about him getting shot down and wrapped up in rabbit fat, and I've heard twenty different accounts and heard ten different experts give talks and I'm still confused. It's a productive confusion."

Phantom Settlements
(DITTO PRESS)

£18.99

The NewBridge Project

12-16 NewBridge Street West
Newcastle upon Tyne // NE1 8AW

+44 (0)191 232 8975
admin@thenewbridgeproject.com
www.thenewbridgeproject.com

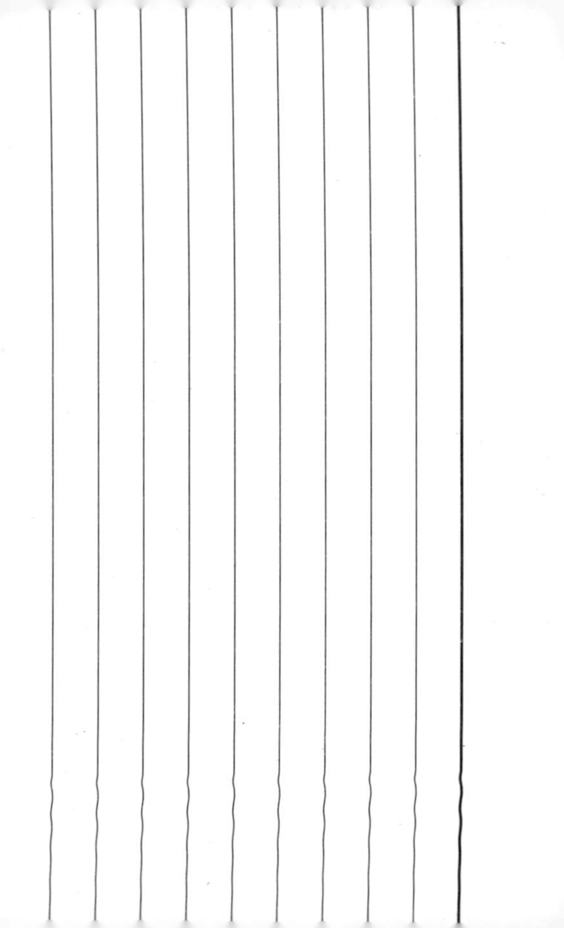

(fig 10)
Just in time

"Is that just another solution to the same problem?" we ask, trying to find our way back into the conversation. "Artists like Sophie Calle and Joseph Beuys do the exact opposite of what you're doing and in the end it has a similar effect, which is to camouflage the person behind the art."

"An artist like Andy Warhol disappears into the repetition of his own image. He would get his friends to dress up as him. In fact, that's where we got the idea for our Tate hoax, although I never thought of it as being a hoax. That was authentic in a way, it was an honest gesture to not just talk about inauthenticity but to really play it out in an interesting way. We didn't know how it would be received, especially the Q&A bit. 12 We'd given the actors answers to give whatever the questions were. I was virtually having a heart attack, some of the answers made sense and some of them didn't, and so there's an increasing tectonic slippage between reality and what we'd planned."

"It all comes down to motive," puts in Jamie. "In a hoax the motive is the reveal, that moment at which somebody gets very angry or very upset and then the hoaxer turns around and says actually it's not real. That's the moment of entertainment."

"I think that using the word hoax prescribes an intention," we added. As with anyone who finds themselves using one of Ryan's statements, we weren't entirely sure if we'd meant to or not. That feeling, key to Ryan's work, is the numbing of your autonomy. Tom had begun to speak.

"... then someone, a quite conservative figure in the audience who for all I know was an actor who had been hired by someone else, came along and said, 'We've been had'. It's to do with people's expectations of authenticity. They want authenticity to look a particular way – for the relationship between a proper name and a body to be fixed. Even when that relationship is the subject being interrogated they still don't want it to be put at stake."

We were wondering what authenticity might look like.

"In the work we are discussing the audience should understand that they are looking at a fiction. Have you ever produced a piece of work in which the audience do not know it is fictional?"

12 — The Joint Declaration on Inautheticity delivered at Tate Modern as part of Nicolas Bourriaud's Altermodern exhibition has been the most recent manifestation of Tom McCarthy's altered personality. During this lecture he detailed changes in his taste in art, his attitude to capital punishment and his newly acquired dislike of bananas.

(fig 11)
She shook her head

"I never say because in a way they are the same thing. Whereabouts in a piece of work are the fake/fiction, truth/non-truth divides? When my mum tells me a story I know her mind isn't a recording device, it's a sponge that lets water in and out. When I start to make a piece of work I think about the frame it is going to go in. The frame is the context the story is being told in and that affects how it is understood. It's exactly the same thing; there's a pre-existing structural framework whether you're telling a story verbally or whether you're doing an exhibition. Truth is a very awkward term because there's no agreed deception – sorry Freudian slip– conception of what it is. It's like a story; it might be defined as the main story that we all abide by. I call these things conduits." Jamie reminded us of a conversation we'd once had with Tom in which a casual remark about sponges led us to a discussion of Derrida and Francis Ponge.

"There's a category error built into our society and into our psychic structuring.

"Basically we're constructs and we're constructed through language, society, the law and desire, and all these other things. Loaded, almost as an afterthought, into these constructs is an opposing ideology; that we're not constructs, we're absolutely each of us unique, natural, spiritual true identities and this, what we should be expressing. This goes completely against our actual nature, so we're all living out an irreconcilable contradiction. This contradiction," said Tom.

"Is my mum real? Is *Argleton Library* real? I hope my mum's real. You never know.

"After I did a piece of work about her, one of the first things that appeared in the press was that she wasn't real. That really pissed her off but I thought it would have been so much better if I'd done that instead."

Jamie's mum has made several appearances in his projects, in fact, one of the details that raised suspicions in *Argleton Library* was the fact that photographs of the same woman were discovered in books whose contents should have been entirely unrelated.

"In way the hero of *Remainder* is genuinely a hero and not a villain because he takes that contradiction to its breaking point," began Tom. The language Tom uses to describe the *Remainder* project is highly unusual. He regards the piece as in keeping with his earlier novels and he has taken the step, whilst the last vestiges

(fig 12)
"Where we're going we don't need roads"

(fig 13)
The books had been borrowed
from Argleton Library

of his previous personality remain, of describing his new personality in the third person as if he were the hero or main protagonist of a novel.

"I see him as very subversive in a way, he believes in the ideology and lets it play itself out right to its absurd limit until the whole thing breaks down, society breaks down and collapses."

"We looked at two people who created huge lies that involved them creating other versions of themselves." We wanted to bring the discussion back to what we had planned. "One was Binjamin Wilkomirski, [18] who claimed to have been a childhood survivor of Auschwitz. He wrote a memoir based on his experiences but was too young to have been in Auschwitz and has since been widely discredited. The fascinating thing about Wilkomirski is that people go to visit him knowing that what he's saying can't be true but come away believing him because he's so authentic. I think he's had to start believing it because if he stopped believing the fiction the personality he has created would collapse. He has a similar thing – an urge to narrate. He continues to create stories around this fictitious version of himself, shoring up the failing defences of his story through narration, it's a similar kind of doubling."

"There are some elite types of people – philosophers and poets – who can be at once the man who trips and the man who watches the trip. It's called doublement and De Man says that although it may seem a blessing to be able to do this, it's a curse because as soon as you're doubled and split you can never be authentic. He calls that phenomenon irony, which consists of restating or replaying that division in order to regain an imagined authenticity that existed before the moment of awareness. This authenticity can never be regained, but implicitly that moment never really existed, we were never authentic."

Someone may have replied to Tom here, it seems likely. Looking back, parts of the conversation becomes hazy and obscured.

"The phrase I use for this is repository of bad ideas. I have hundreds of ideas that don't get that far into the process because they're crap. Is it the same for either of you? I decided that through this project I would be able to exercise these bad ideas.

18 — One of Argleton County Libraries most borrowed books was a misery memoir of the holocaust survivor Binjamin Wilkomirski entitled *Fragments: Memories of a Childhood.*

(fig 14)
He did hear me

(fig 15)
No shades of grey

It was a lot of fun actually because these are things you can't normally do because they'd get trashed, and rightly so. If you're putting yourself in the mind of a middle-aged woman writing for Mills & Boon then they're permissible."

"They become justifiable," said someone.

Hannah, who had not yet spoken, began, ◊ "I was really interested in the idea of adopting an alter ego as an excuse to make a certain piece of work. 15 My alter ego gets all the bus fines. It is a way of creating a person who fulfils a smaller function than the entire person normally would." ◊

"Tom, are you using the protagonist in *Remainder* in a similar way? He's a character created to pursue an idea although he isn't doing it in the world in quite the same way as, say, the fictional writers in Jamie's library are."

"When I first had the idea for *Remainder* my initial thought was a novel. I had this moment of déjà vu in a bathroom exactly like the protagonist and then thought I want to do that. It could have been an art piece, then I thought I wouldn't want to have that room built as an installation, that's not really that interesting. I'd want the whole building, I'd need the whole building, I'd want the cats, then it gets interesting. In fact, it's only really interesting if you can expand into the street. You have the shoot out and even that's not enough, you would need everything. You would need to do the bank heist, then I realised it would have to be real."

"Moving on a little bit, Ryan, it is said that your interest in rumours began when you found out about Christopher Wilson's article on a fictional graphic designer, Ernst Bettler, 17 in *Dot Dot Dot* magazine. Although both the interview and the magazine editorial contained clues to the fictional nature of the article, these were missed and the story was later repeated by both *Adbusters* and a book about graphic design written for Phaidon entitled *Problem Solved*. The truth about Ernst Bettler remained ambiguous until two years ago when Rick Poynor wrote an essay after *Problem Solved* was published pointing out that, in fact, Ernst Bettler had never existed."

15 — John English (Hannah's alterego) is the author of a book called *Managing Your Household Bills: A Step - by - step Guide* published in 1988 by The Stationary Office. In Argleton County Library the book was given the class number 332.772.

17 — The least borrowed book at Argleton County Library was a graphic design primer entitled *Problem Solved*. This book is notable in one respect: it is the only place in which the work of the graphic designer Ernst Bettler is discussed as part of graphic design history.

(fig 16)
Forced landing in the Crimea

◊ "It's a wonderful work because every time it's told by different people it changes. The Chinese whisper element that has become a part of it is beautiful and when I tell the story I never admit that it's false. It can happen, it just didn't happen. It's a vehicle for another set of ideas." ◊

We finally asked the question that had been on our minds since the beginning. "When you take on reality in this way you have to lose? Surely you can't win?"

◊ "Winning would be fascism. If you could beat reality and actually impose a new reality principle, that would be complete fascism, so in a way that's really good," Tom said.

"It's the vanishing point, it's the absolute degree zero of time.
19 It's like Orpheus being shredded in front of the underworld;
this is the absolute, the disintegration of pure fact as we enter endless fictions." ◊

This is where the transcript ends

---

19 — 'Ah! Here it is. Bomb in Greenwich Park. There isn't much so far. Half past eleven. Foggy morning. Effects of explosion felt as far as Romney Road and Park Place. Enormous hole in the ground under a tree filled with smashed roots and broken branches. All round fragments of a man's body blown to pieces. That's all. The rest's mere newspaper gup. No doubt a wicked attempt to blow up the Observatory, they say. H'm. That's hardly credible.'

(fig 17)
"I arise again the same though changed"

(fig 18)
A job well done

Appendix

(A)	*McCarthy, Tom Remainder London: Alma Books 2007, p.148*
(B)	*Lady Kagami, Five White Pebbles of Naoto Ono, Trans David Trevellian, London: Penguin Books, 1968*
(C)	*Jerry Parker Police Reporter and the Candid Camera Clue Racine, Wisconsin: Whitman Publishing Company, 1941*
(D)	*Argleton Hollow Earth society poster, photographed as it was displayed in the library*
(E)	*Articles showing the dispersal of Ryan's rumour 'The markings on the floor that suggest the evidence of a struggle.*
(F)	*Argleton's location on Goole Earth*
(G)	*The logo for Argleton City Library*

I stepped into the bathroom and looked at the crack on the wall. Just right too: not just the crack but the whole room – taps, wall, colours, crack, everything: perfect. I stepped back into my living room, picked up the phone and called Naz.

(A)

Five White Pebbles
of Naoto Ono

5/-

Lady Kagami / Trans David Trevellian
Penguin Poets

(B)

DEC - - 1944

JERRY PARKER
POLICE REPORTER
and the Candid Camera Club

ALTON JAMES 6677889

By JACK WALLEN

Illustrated by [illegible]

ALTON [illegible] 6677889

Copyright, [illegible], by
WHITMAN PUBLISHING COMPANY
RACINE, WISCONSIN
Printed in U. S. A.

ALTON JAMES 6677889

(C)

(D)
THE ARGLETON HOLLOW EARTH SOCIETY
TOPIC FOR DISCUSSION:
THOMAS PYNCHON: HOLLOW EARTH EVANGELIST OR CELLULAR COSMONAUT?
tans
have to be suicidal to ring
sten, in total confidence, to
m at ANY time. Try us.
To find out how
your idea into
Contact
student

WOMAN BATTERED TO DEATH

Search for Assailant

"At about 8 45 p.m., a widow named Emily Stubbs was brutally attacked about the head with a blunt instrument, and there is evidence of a struggle having taken place. The wounds were of such a character that she must have died almost immediately. It is highly probable that the assailant's clothing is blood-stained, and there may be marks on him indicating that he has been in a struggle. The police would welcome any information from anybody who saw any suspicious person loitering in the locality or from any person who finds an instrument with which the murder might have been committed."

(E)

A YOUTH CONFESSES MURDER.

STRANGE CASE AT PORTSMOUTH.

The death of Beatrice Hansford, obviously from violence, at Portsmouth on Sunday evening, is now attributed to her brother Frank, a youth of 17, and at the local Police Court yesterday he was brought up on a charge of murdering her. He was described as a carpenter's apprentice.

Dr. Emmett, who received an urgent summons to the house, said the girl's wounds could not have been self-inflicted, but there was no marked evidence of a struggle.

Address:
more info »
Argleton, Lancashire
UK
Directions
Search nearby
Save to...
more
A

(F)

ARGLETON LIBRARY ‡ ARGLETON LIBRARY ‡ ARGLETON LIBRARY ‡
N
I
I
L

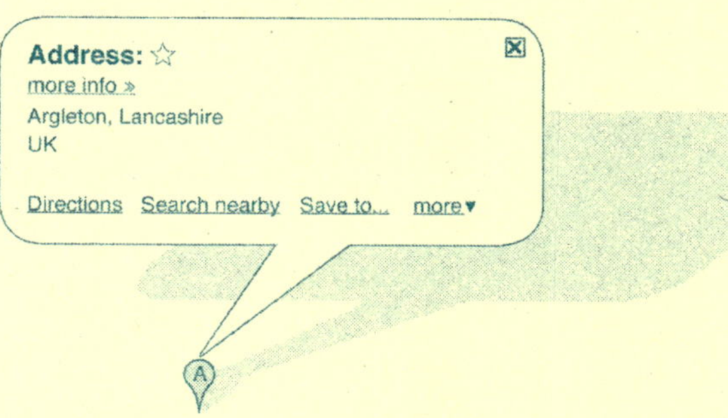

(G)

Floating Footnotes

9 — Many of the residents of Argleton were swayed by persuasive arguments in a book by the scientist Yves Fissiault outlining his hollow earth theory. This led to the formation of the Argleton Hollow Earth Society who meet monthly in Argleton Friends Meeting Place. Even after the books in Argleton Library were exposed as fictional many of the members of the Hollow Earth Society continued to believe in Fissiault's theory and there are quite a number of conspiracy theories circulating through the village to account for the truths found in this fictional book.

10 — Naomi V. Jelish is a fictional artist and subject of the monograph *The Sketchbooks of Naomi V. Jelish*,London: Goldsmith & Ledger, 2001, whose author John Ivesmail is also fictional.

11 — John Ivesmail is the author of *The Sketchbooks of Naomi V. Jelish*, London: Goldsmith & Ledger, 2001, a book which appeared in the artist's mongraphs section of Argleton Library (classmark MON JEL).

13 — In the archive section of Argleton County Library were contained documents with the following classmarks: FO 800/868 and HS 8/944. These refer to Churchill's secret plot at the end of the World War II to have Himmler assassinated.

14 — Jayson Blair was the name of the bartender who served ourselves, Ryan and David Trevellian at the Ginza S Bar in Tokyo.

16 — The music section of Argleton County Library contained a wide selection of books including one on a band called Lustfaust, written by Rik Horncastle and published by Megahertz Verlag in 2002.

20 — Another series of books produced by Shovlin for the artist's monograph section of Argleton County Library were fictional additions to Phaidon's modern Artists series. There were six or seven of these but the one that caught the popular imagination was a book looking at the career of John Fare. John Fare:Pieces of Me details the career of an artist working mostly in the sixties who systematically dismembered himself using machines made especially for the purpose. There are obvious links here between Fare's career and that of Tom McCarthy. Whilst one is disassembles his physical self the other disassembles his spiritual self.

II
II

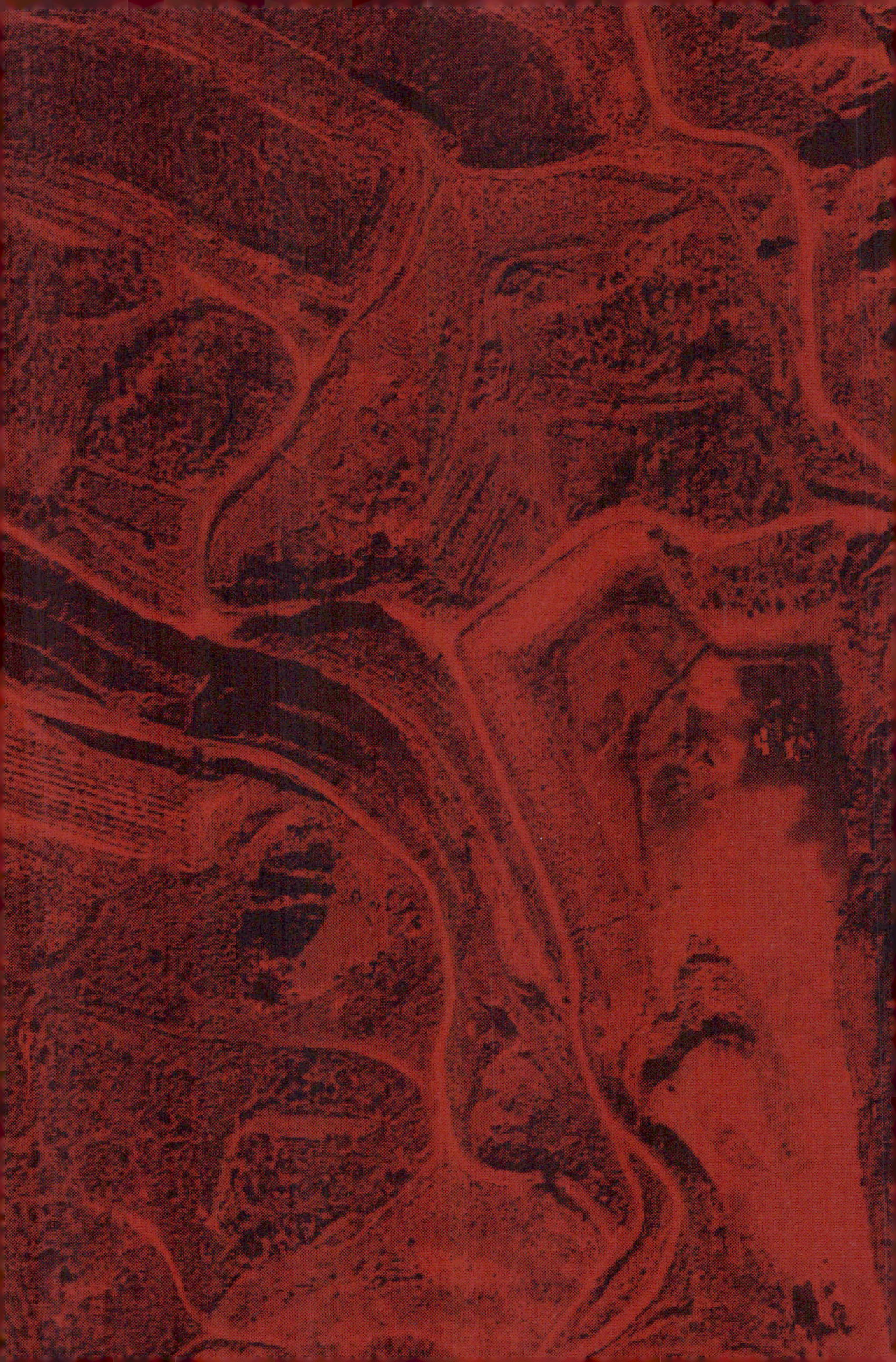

II

Verisimilitude

II

(fig 1)
Ryan Gander

(fig 2)
Jamie Shovlin

(fig 3)
Tom McCarthy

5 — Trevellian was the name of the doctor with the leather suitcase and the little torch – one of them at least. Perhaps they've run together, all these doctors, in my mind. At any rate, a Dr Trevellian, who had a little torch and various other accessories which he kept in a battered leather suitcase, was often in my flat, observing me. I couldn't do much about it: I was too weak to throw him out and so prone to lapses back into my trance that I couldn't even issue orders properly. The funny thing is, though, that I didn't mind his presence. He kept very still. He didn't flap around, pace up and down or even move his arms much when examining me. He stood still observing me from a few feet away, as passive as a statue – or closer, frozen above me with his torch held steady in his right hand, casting down a beam of yellow light.

4 — When I could, I raised my eyes up to the crack; this oriented me again, stopped me feeling dizzy. The building was on my side even if this bad man wasn't.

2 — Tom McCarthy is a writer and artist. He was born in 1969 and lives in a tower block in London. His debut novel *Remainder* was first published in November 2005 by Paris-based art press Metronome. A work of literary criticism, *Tintin and the Secret of Literature*, was released by Granta Books in June 2006. Tom's second novel, *Men in Space*, came out in 2007 (Alma Books) followed by *C*, published in 2010.

In 2005 Tom collaborated with the artist Rod Dickinson on a piece entitled *Greenwich Degree Zero*. This piece documented Martial Bourdin's 1894 terrorist attack on Greenwich Observatory in which he detonated a bomb destroing not only the Observatory itself but much of the surrounding parkland.

His ongoing project the *International Necronautical Society*, an avant-garde network that surfaces through publications, proclamations, denunciations and live events, has been described by Untitled Magazine as 'the most comprehensive total art work we have seen in years' and by Art Monthly as 'a platform for fantastically mobile thinking'. In 2003 the INS broke into the BBC website and inserted propaganda into its source code. The following year, they set up a broadcasting unit at the ICA from which more than forty 'agents' generated non-stop poem-codes, which were transmitted over FM radio in London and by internet to collaborating radio stations around the world.

— Catrin Morgan: Shall we begin by introducing ourselves?

—

— Mireille Fauchon: Whilst we were researching for this talk we created the theory of authenticity and a fictional psychiatrist responsible for it called Dr David Trevellian, 5 who we thought should work at the University of Cardiff. Both the phenomenon we describe and Dr Trevellian are based on events that take place in the novel *Remainder*, 4 by Tom McCarthy. 2 Authenticity – as we chose to define it – is a phenomenon that follows post-traumatic stress, in which patients believe that they can bring themselves closer to reality through the use of lies or fictions. We wanted to describe a psychological state distinct from compulsive lying where the attempts to dodge the perceived surface reality mean that the patient can then create a space where they are enclosed within a fiction. This artificial psychological environment is the only way they can determine "the truth" – by creating layers upon layers of fictions. We used the hero of *Remainder* as our key case study, the story of a man who had suffered a massive head injury and subsequently developed an obsession with recreating moments prior to the in-

(fig 4)
David Trevellian in Italy during the 3rd Global Forum on Memory and Identity

(fig 5)
Naomi V. Jelish

6 — Ryan Gander was born in Chester in 1976. He harnesses art's potential to communicate and creates work in written, spoken and visual languages. His practice adopts both familiar styles, such as cartoons and maps, as well as more avant-garde aesthetics. By appropriating existing art and design work to generate new pieces, Gander documents real historical moments and turning points in visual culture.

In one work, Ryan produced a local street map, updated and available for visitors to take away. In another piece called *Loose Associations*, Ryan lectures his audience on seemingly disparate aspects of design history. In *Man on a Bridge – A Study of David Lange* (2008), a 16mm film transferred to an HD projection, we see a well-known British actor, Roger Lloyd Pack, walk across a bridge until he is drawn to the edge to concentrate on an incident below. He does it again and again, slightly differently, fifty times in a sequence of Sisyphean repetition, but we never get closer to finding out what it is that attracts his attention.

Ryan works with a family of collaborators drawn from a wide range of creative industries. They might be other artists such as John Fare or musicians such as the band Perl Gray. Ripe with potential, the work alludes to the 'what if' of the creative process, the fugitive nature of thought, inspiration and language. Humour underpins much of Gander's work, rescuing it from mere 'institutional critique', engaging us with its deadpan, self-deprecating knowingness. It is as rigorous as it is strangely accessible.

8 — Statements marked by ◊ mean the reverse of what they say.

7 — Jamie Shovlin is a conceptual artist. He staged his first exhibition in 2004, in which he curated the drawings of a disappeared schoolgirl called Naomi V. Jelish. The work was shown alongside newspaper cuttings and diaries, and was bought by Charles Saatchi for £25,000. By coincidence, the name of the schoolgirl is a perfect anagram of Jamie Shovlin.

In 2006 Shovlin created another exhibition based in the memorabilia of the German 'Krautrock' band Lustfaust. The exhibited archive included links to various fan websites and prompted the critic Waldemar Januszczak to praise the way in which the band had 'cocked a notorious snook at the music industry in the late 1970s by giving away their music on blank cassettes and getting their fans to design their own covers'. The collection was runner-up for the Beck's Futures prize. In September 2007 Lustfaust, together with Schneider TM, gave a concert to celebrate the opening of the new Berlin Exhibition space for Haunch of Venison.

Shovlin claims that the main function of his work is to draw attention to individuals and organisations that his audience would not otherwise encounter, encouraging them to question their preconceptions.

jury. He received quite a lot of compensation, as the accident that happened wasn't his fault, and he used this money to recreate remembered events. Our reasons for creating this story were to use it to illustrate the idea that there may be useful or positive outcomes to an interaction between narrative fiction and truth or fact.

—

◊ Ryan Gander: 6 You're using the word truth, but I don't know if everyone agrees with the subject being truth because "truth" has positive connotations of integrity and morality. Maybe it would be better to redefine truth or use other words. Jamie's mum always says, "You should never let the truth get in the way of a good story," which is a positive view of what a lie is. 8

—

◊ Jamie Shovlin: 7 Isn't it never let a lie get in the way of a good story?

—

—

(fig 6)
Detail from a tourist map of Birmingham

10 — In July 1991, 13-year-old Naomi V. Jelish and her family mysteriously vanished from their home in Kent, after a tragic year in which her father died after attempting to save her younger brother from drowning. Shortly after the family's disappearance, John Ivesmail, a retired science teacher at Naomi's school, unearthed a collection of the teenager's remarkable drawings.

11 — In the years following Naomi's disappearance, John attempted to trace what had happened to the family through an investigation of Naomi's incredible artworks. John hoped to throw light on the family's bizarre vanishing by mounting an exhibition of the youngster's work.

John died in 2002, before his desire to open the exhibition could be achieved. Despite this, the show John had planned was realised in the presentation of Naomi's work at the Riflemaker Gallery in 2004, overseen by the artist Jamie Shovlin. Since their early nineties disappearance, Naomi and her family have never been heard from.

– RG: Oh, yes, it is.

—

– MF: Well maybe we could stick with authenticity as it is applied by Trevellian as a strategy for coming closer to reality more than an attempt to moralise.

—

– CM: Shall we begin by talking about the artist's identity? Is being an artist always some kind of personal exposure or is it necessary to make a deliberate choice to do this? Jamie, can we begin by talking about your Naomi V. Jelish [10] project?

—

– JS: I find being a person is exposing your self. Whilst we're here speaking, we're all trying to be as open and authentic as we can be and I've always tried to be as honest as possible about what happened. I discovered those drawings whilst still a student at the RCA. The dominant way of looking at work at that time was for the artist to be quite distanced. So I decided I would make something more unequivocally autobiographical. At that time I was lodging with a character called John Ivesmail, [11] a slightly sinister Nabakovian kind of guy. He was also an amateur curator and local historian. It was through him that I gained access to Naomi's drawings – he had been her teacher at the time of her disappearance. After his death I took over the archive and created the website. So in a way the project is a document of that period in my life. I was really interested in how in essence this story was tabloid material but I had translated it using a different, more museological grammar, and that supplanted the basic melodrama of the story and replaced it with a certain seriousness. The way that something is presented impacts upon its actual content and you can tell any story by delivering it in the right way to the right audience.

(fig 7)
Marie Aurore

13 — On the night of 10 May 1941, in one of the most extraordinary and bizarre incidents of the World War II, a Messerschmitt–110 crash-landed on a remote Scottish hillside. Its pilot, who had parachuted to safety, was Rudolf Hess, the Deputy-Führer of the German Reich. Hess's remarkable solo flight was immediately dismissed in both Britain and Germany as the deranged act of a disordered mind. He was disowned by Hitler, and Winston Churchill's Government insisted that his unexpected arrival on British soil was of no lasting consequence. Nevertheless, the mysterious circumstances of the flight, and Hess's unbroken silence during fifty subsequent years of imprisonment, have led to endless speculation as to his true motives. Until now, no-one has found the crucial pieces of evidence which prove that a small group of men within the British Government and intelligence services were in fact conducting a brilliantly clever plot, which was not only to lead to Hess's flight, but would also have a decisive impact on the course of the war. Martin Allen's researches in archives in Britain, Germany and the United States have unearthed many documents previously undiscovered by historians. The details they reveal are explosive, and alter our perception not only of the conduct of the World War II, but of the secret forces that shaped post-war Europe and global politics.

—

— CM: Do you think that the use of factual information in artworks can be a way of tripping someone up when they're looking at your work? Of catching your audience and persuading them to pay more attention?

—

— JS: I always have a problem with words like trap or trip because they're so negative. I don't know if there's any kind of opposition to them – phrases that are positive – entrypoint for example?

—

— RG: Snare.

—

— JS: Bear trap.

—

— CM: I think that presenting yourself in a way that purports to be honest prescribes an intention.

—

— RG: It is also something to do with duration. Truth is eternal and inherently respectable. I think what Jamie's talking about is that the obsessive archiving of Naomi's work has become his contribution to the piece. It's not so much to do with the spectator, trying to preach to them or convince them or change the way they think. It is more about the research, and that acting as a catalyst.

—

— Ben Freeman: There was the man who recently discovered documents in military libraries to evidence his claims that Churchill had been collaborating with the Nazis through the Secret Service. 13 This case has elements that are similar to what Jamie is

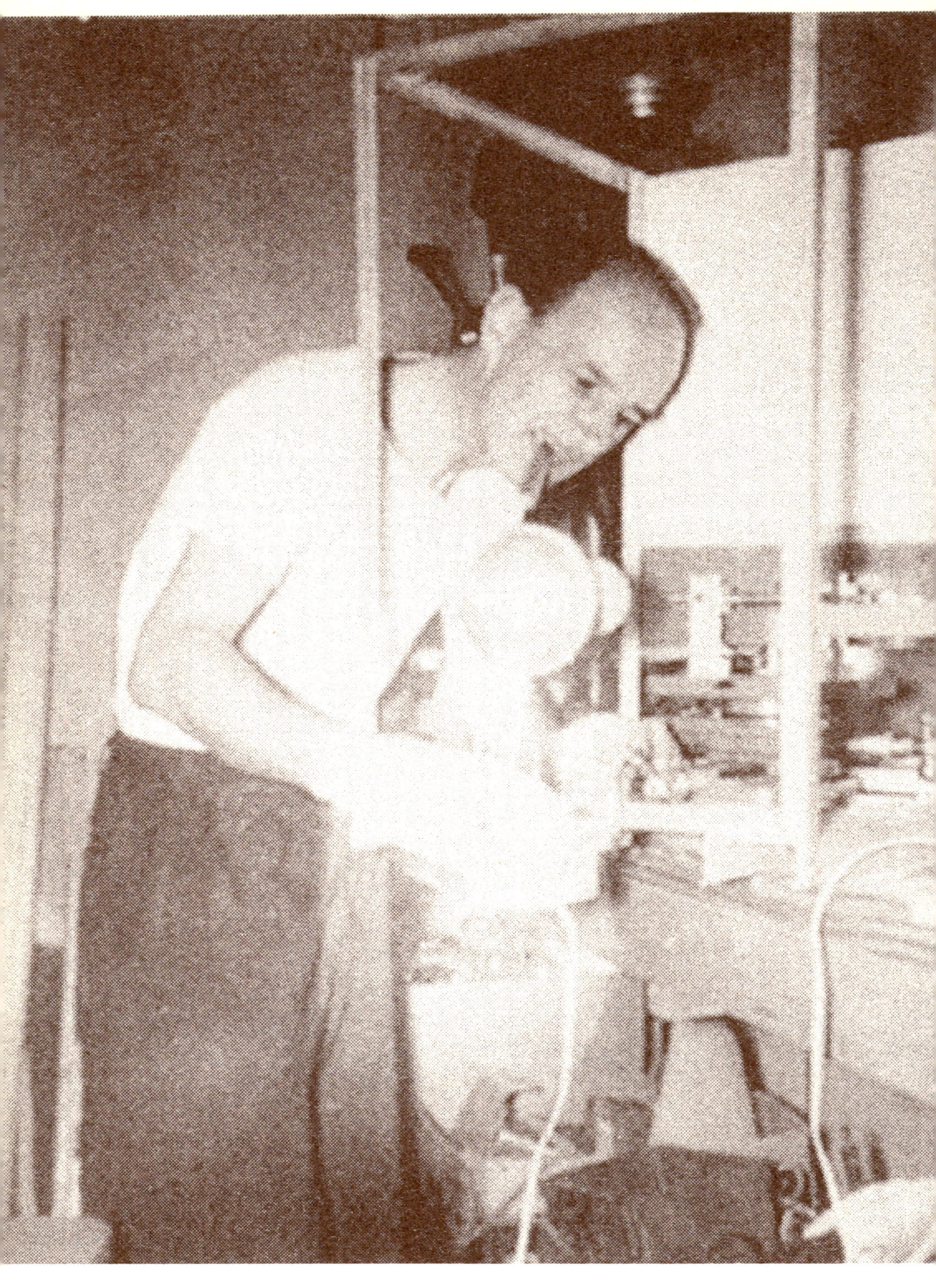

(fig 8)
Yves Fissiault working on an opticosonic harmonic device in his laboratory

(fig 9)
Stotham, Massachusetts

(*fig 10*)
Brnst Bettler

doing but maybe what sets it apart is its political intention and the repercussions stemming from that.

—

— CM: Perhaps the other reason that there is an impulse to name what Ryan and Jamie do is that their strategy gives them an intimacy with their audience. There is an openness there that creates a desire to work out what your intentions are.

—

◊ Annabel Fraser: Non-fiction writers don't provoke this kind of discussion and I don't understand why? Aren't they doing the same thing?

—

◊ JS: That's the analogy I always use.

—

◊ RG: Look at the painting in this room; all of the things it represents are real. It is a representation of a real landscape. All artists deal in truth. It's just how close you are to the truth. It can be categorised in three ways: facts documented in art, facts represented within an artwork or facts that are never revealed.

—

— CM: And then there are all the degrees in-between.

—

— RG: Jamie, in the work we are discussing the audience should understand that they are looking at an archive of factual documents. Have you ever produced a piece of work in which the audience do not know that what they're seeing is based on fact?

—

— JS: I never say because in a way they are the same thing. Whereabouts in a piece of work are the fake/fiction, truth/non-truth divides? When my mum tells me a story I know her mind isn't a recording device, it's a sponge that lets water in and out. When I start to make a piece of work I think about the frame it's going to go in. The frame is the context the story is being told in and this affects how it is understood. It's exactly the same thing; there's a pre-existing structural framework whether you're telling a story verbally or whether you're doing an exhibition.

—

◊ RG: What was the word you used earlier? Vessels?

—

(fig 11)
P+H's fiftieth anniversary poster on display in Bergwald

(fig 12)
Lustfaust performing at Fabrik in Hamburg, Saturday 3 Dec 1977

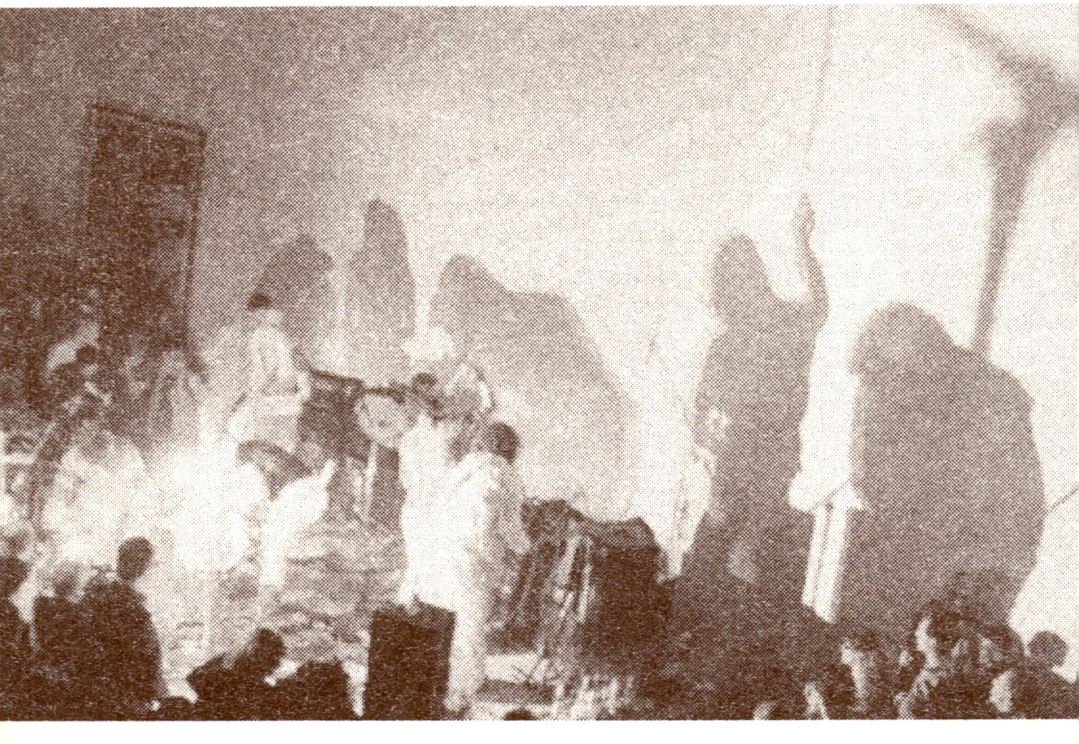

15 — Hannah Rae Alton is the alter ego of artist John English.

◊ JS: Conduits; you said vehicles.

—

◊ RG: We'll just stick with vehicles; it's a better word. You said that one of the vehicles could be typographical. Does a certain kind of typography express the truth more clearly? Is that what you were saying before? Is the frame the same thing?

—

— JS: Architecture, frames and typography, they're all the same thing, they're just on varying scales.

—

— RG: Would you say presenting truth within an artwork is one of those vehicles as well?

—

— JS: Truth is a very awkward term because there's no agreed conception of what it is. It's like a story; it might be defined as the main story that we all abide by. Is my mum real? Is Naomi Jelish real? I hope Naomi V. Jelish is real. You never know. After I did a piece of work about her, one of the first things that appeared in the press was that she wasn't real. That really pissed me off but then I thought maybe it would have been so much better if I'd done that instead.

—

◊ Hannah Rae Alton: I was really interested in the idea of using honesty as a starting point for making a certain piece of work. Because I choose to be honest I get all the bus fines; if I lied I wouldn't have to pay. Clearly, there are negative implications in telling the truth. 15

—

— JS: A thing that was never addressed was the kind of work Naomi V. Jelish makes. I looked at the sketchbooks belonging to other thirteen-year-old girls and they were really boring. They were full of Forever Friends and copies from cards, they don't have any dramatic narrative. Naomi's sketchbooks are filled with things like horses and flowers. This left it vulnerable to criticism. I remember being very careful about how I explained it; when I did some research I noticed that many of the images in her sketchbooks had come from somewhere else, mostly from how-to-draw books.

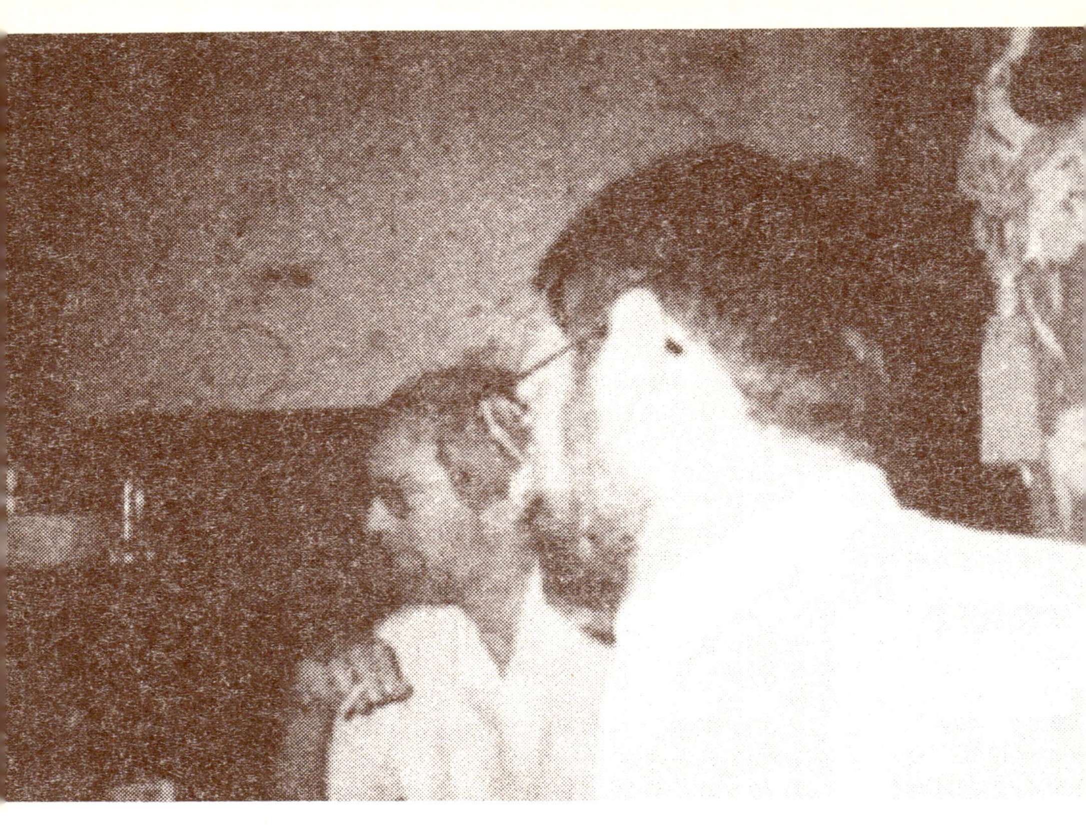

(fig 13)
John Ivesmail

16 — Lustfaust was an experimental noise band active in West Berlin during the late seventies and early 1980s whose [sic] combination of an aggressive on-stage presence, found object instrumentation, and the use of an anti-capitalist community-based model of distribution (send the band a blank cassette and they would return it with their latest release) spawned the Dadaist Geniale Dilettanten movement of the early 1980s and pioneered the burgeoning cassette culture of the late seventies.

It is a circular thing; a thirteen year old drawing what she is being told she should draw.

—

— MF: Something you've mentioned before in relation to Lustfaust
16 was being able to exhibit flyers and merchandising posters that you wouldn't necessarily make yourself but which you enjoy in a slightly guilty way.

—

— JS: The phrase I use for this is repository of bad ideas. I have hundreds of ideas that don't get that far into the process because they're crap. Is it the same for you, Ryan? I decided that with this project I would be able to exercise these bad ideas through other people. It was a lot of fun actually because these are things you can't normally do because they'd get trashed, and rightly so, but if you're archiving the work of a thirteen year old/fifteen year old from Idaho then they're permissible.

—

— MF: They're justified by their original context.

—

— CM: What about the artist's relationship with the facts they have discovered? Ryan, I was watching an interview with you in which you made the point that when your maps go into a gallery context it's almost nicer than when they are out in the world.

—

—

— RG: For some of the museums I show at, I produce a thousand maps that are versions of tourist maps for that city, the kind of thing that is usually freely distributed by hotels. I noticed that on certain tourist maps some existing streets are left unmapped. I reprint the maps correcting inaccuracies such as non-existent municipal buildings and adding the streets that have been left out. The Barbican is a famous example of a planned municipal building that appears on some maps but was in fact never built. So the streets that were erased from the map, I put back. The maps are placed in a cardboard box outside the gallery space but in the in-

(fig 14)
Naomi's mother

17 — In the article entitled 'I'm only a designer: The double life of Ernst Bettler', which appeared in Issue 2 of *Dot Dot Dot* magazine, the Swiss graphic designer Ernst Bettler talks about his life in graphic design and gives details of a particular incident involving a Swiss pharmaceutical company, Pfäfferli + Huber. In 1954, aged 25, Bettler was commissioned to produce a series of posters celebrating the company's fiftieth anniversary. P+H had been involved in testing on concentration camp prisoners and Bettler was aware of this. In carrying out the brief for P+H, Bettler made a series of posters showing models in contorted poses, which, if hung in a row, spelt out the word Nazi. When these posters hit the streets of Switzerland there was a public outcry and Pfäfferli+Huber were closed down. The pharmaceutical company later took Bettler to court but were unable to prove that the designer had intended the effect of the poster campaign. The interview goes on to describe Bettler's subsequent and less eventful career in Great Britain, designing books and art catalogues.

stitution, and they're listed on the work list. You quite often find boxes of flyers in entrance halls in galleries anyway. So you can pick them up and take them not realising that they're works of art and then use them. We also use guerrilla tactics. If you walk into a hotel in Sheffield with a pad of tourist maps and say it's a delivery, they start giving them out and using them.

—

— AF: Is there a clue anywhere?

—

— RG: Clue to my involvement? No.

—

— CM: I'd like to talk now about Ernst Bettler. 17 Awareness of him began to grow when an interview with him appeared in *Dot Dot Dot* magazine. Both *Adbusters* and a book about graphic design written for Phaidon entitled *Problem Solved* picked up the story and covered it. Doubts about Bettler's existence have been cast, particularly by Rick Poynor in an article for *Eye Magazine*'s website.

—

—

— RG: The interview took place when Christopher Wilson wrote an article for *Dot Dot Dot.* Whilst he was researching he discovered this Swiss graphic designer called Ernst Bettler who, when he was about thirty, moved from Switzerland to Berlin and made a pitch for a company called Pfäfferli+Huber Pharmaceuticals.

—

— CM: I think it actually happened in Switzerland.

—

—

— RG: Was it Switzerland?

—

(fig 15)
Binjamin Wilkomirski as a child

(fig 16)
John English

—

— CM: I think so.

—

—

— RG: Sure?

—

— CM: Yes.

—

— RG: I think you should do some fact checking because I've told this story a thousand times and I've always said it was Berlin.

—

— CM: I'm sure the town was in Switzerland.

—

— RG: No, you go on. You've stolen my thunder now.

—

— CM: There was a pharmaceutical company in this Swiss town called P+H, who used concentration camp workers during World War II. After the war they asked graphic designers to pitch for a fiftieth anniversary commemorative poster. Ernst Bettler won the pitch. There were four final images, which look quite innocuous until you line them up next to each other and you realise that the bodies of the models in the images are bent into letter shapes and that they spell Nazi. The posters brought down the firm.

—

— BF: Do you think it's ethical to use someone's life to make a point?

—

◇RG: Of course. I think it's a wonderful work because every time it's been told by different people it gains new life.

—

—

—

— CM: If you want to use a story to make a point then perhaps it's much easier to use what's actually there in reality than it would be to create a fiction.

—

—

◇Rasha Kahil: If you could beat fiction and actually reinforce a new reality principle then in a way it would be really good.

—

—

(fig 17)
John Fare

– JS: It's much better as well to source a story from a provocative timescale because people believe it immediately. That's why people read these stories because there is such a dominant historical narrative that as soon as someone discovers a small subset it becomes interesting. However, the story can appear implausible because of the cultural will to find out more than we already know... ◊ it's like Orpheus being shredded in front of the underworld; this is the absolute, the disintegration of pure fact.

— — — — — — — — — — — —

This is where the transcript ends

— — — — — — — — — — — —

(fig 18)
Greenwich Degree Zero

Appendix

(A) *'A child in hell' by Binjamin Wilkomirski in The Guardian (London: 26 Oct 1993) p.63*

(B) *Letter from Yves Fissiault on Rockedyne headed notepaper*

(C) *Wilson, Christopher. 'I'm only a designer: The double life of Ernst Bettler' in Dot Dot Dot, Issue 3, 2001, p. 17*

(D) *'INS Founding Manifesto' in The Times (London: 14 December 1999) p. 1.*

(E) *McCarthy, Tom Remainder London: Alma Books 2007, p.148*

(F) *Page from the online Naomi V. Jelish Gallery showing Naomi's portrait of John Ivesmail.*

(G) *Bridge no.122 by Nat Tate*

(H) *Lustfaust's members Ashworth and Kruger*

(I) *Hollow Earth Diagram by Yves Fissiault*

Binjamin Wilkomirski was three, maybe four, when the war began. His father was murdered, his mother disappeared. He, a tiny boy, was taken to a concentration camp. He survived. Now in his 50s, he has forced himself to recall fragments of his buried past

(A)

From the desk of
Yves Fissiault
Chief Engineer
Electronics

ROCKEDYNE
A DIVISION OF ROCKWELL CORPORATION

May 4, 1962

Mr.L. Kaufeld
Chief Engineer
ES & E Supervision
Boeing Company
Box 3707
Seattle, Washington

Dear. Mr Kaufeld,

This is to certify that the bearer, Mr Thomas Pynchon, of Ithaca, New York, has long been known to me, and that he is a man of good family, steady habits, and honest and conscientious in the performance of every duty.

He sustains an excellent reputation among his associates and neighbors. He is highly respected by all, and is possessed of a good education. I take pleasure in recommending him to any who may desire the services of an active, competent and trustworthy young man.

I am,
Yours respectfully,

Yves Fissiault

Yves Fissiault
Chief Engineer
Electronics Division
Rockedyne, Company

915 [illegible] AVENUE CULVER CITY, CALIFORNIA 63 TELEPHONE [illegible] 8-6451

(B)

Early the following year a second set of pos
was presented, one by one over a series of meet
for the client's approval. Only after they had b
printed did Bettler's masterplan come to fruiti
'The beauty of it was that, taken alone, each po
was utterly inoffensive. But you must rememb
that everything has a *Zusammenhang*; a context.
These posters would be seen together in horizo
rows. And I was very careful with my briefing
the bill stickers.'

On hundreds of sites around Burgwald and
bouring Sumisdorf, the posters appeared in fou
In the first a clowning child's body made an 'N'
in the second a woman's head was bowed inside
'A'-shaped triangle of her forearms. An old man
contortions in the third poster ('that took forev
shoot') sketched a 'Z'. No prizes for guessing tha
girl in the final *plakat* stood defiantly still, her a
silhouetted profile as stiff as, well, a letter 'I',
for example.

The reaction of the usually passive local pop
was immediate. The posters were torn down in
streets, the offices of the *Sumisdorfer Nachrichten* v
buried beneath an avalanche of complaint lette
and demands were even made for the company's
managers to stand trial. In under six weeks
Pfäfferli+Huber were ruined forever. Even today
sooty mark left on the front of the factory buildi
by the long-gone metal logo is less visible than th
ancient 'Nazis raus' spray-paint around the rust
gates. If World War II had in part been fought o
battlefield of design, then Bettler's involvement
the downfall of P+H stands as a testament to des
power to change things since then. But how did
get away with it? Wasn't there even a threat of
retribution?

'Pfäfferli+Huber took me to court, sure. But a
I said, each of the posters was completely innoce
I'm only a designer. As soon as a job leaves the
printer it's out of my hands. I can't be held respo
ble if some buffoon – or a little team of buffoons,
– is insensitive when it comes to sticking the dam
things on a few walls in town!'

(C)

100-strong electoral college had originally been called to interview the four shortlisted candidates. But the interview did not go ahead because the party activists voted by 54 to 40 for the 20-strong selection executive to reconvene and increase

Continued on page 4, col 8

Court to give evidence for her husband. Page 3 *Photograph: Chris Harris*

SIDE

Branson ...ry bid

...ranson, the Vir...nan, launched ... attempt to win ...nal Lottery li... promising that ... set up a Peo...ry that could ...xtra £1 billion ...auses......10, 15

...an snub

...orld leaders ...e state funeral ...m Croatia's ...resident, Fran...n, because of ...thoritarianism. ...s of citizens ...farewell........13

...nd draw

... successfully the threat of a ...eat in the Test ...nst South Afri... Elizabeth as ...ussain hit an ...0..................44

Financier moves in for M&S

BY FRASER NELSON

A MONACO-BASED financier with close links to the billionaire Barclay brothers yesterday confirmed that he is considering launching a takeover bid for Marks & Spencer.

M&S shares, which rose sharply last week amid takeover speculation, fell 9 per cent to 273p. City analysts said Philip Green, who took over the Sears retail empire earlier this year, may find it difficult to raise the £11.5 billion that would be needed to acquire M&S through a hostile bid.

Tesco refused to rule out a takeover bid for M&S and could emerge as a white knight. More than 40 million M&S shares were traded yesterday as private investors continued to speculate on the outcome of a bid battle.

Business, page 23

a happy bully

... he was over... a friend eventu...

...ls more like 1857: ...n claimed to suf...s of bullies sever...han 3 per cent of ...habitual physical ...ers every week) ...er cent bullying ...ost of these chil...ullied. Very few ...tegory of "pure" ...ctims.

...er cent) of prima... "relational bully... teasing — in the ...elational bullies ... behaviour prob...

...on page 2, col 1

"You're ill — you need to get out and do a bit of bullying"

(D)

When I could, I raised my eyes up to the crack; this oriented me again, stopped me feeling dizzy. The building was on my side, even if this bad man wasn't. When I felt well enough to move, I went into the living room, sat down on my sofa and phoned Naz.

(E)

(F)

(G)

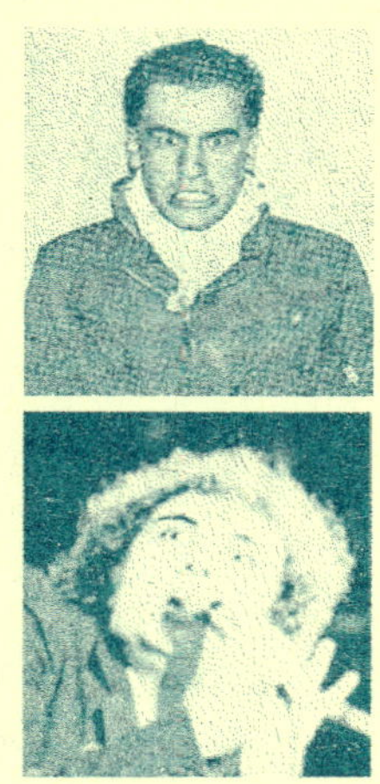

(H)

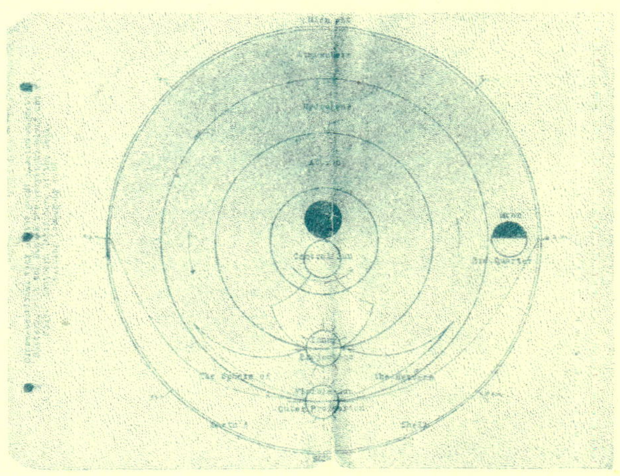

(I)

Floating Footnotes

1 — Although Maki Susuki and Kajsa Stahl were present for the entire conversation they remained silent throughout.

3 — The International Necronautical Society's founding manifesto declares an intent to map the spaces that open around the sign of death in the fields of literature, art, science and culture; to plot and to follow the paths that lead to these spaces. It also speaks of a 'craft': as the vehicle to be constructed, and as the practice to be identified and cultivated in order to realise the necronautical project.

9 — In 1997 a show at the Anthony Giordano Gallery in Oakdale documented the life and work of the artist and scientist Yves Fissiault.

12 — Tom McCarthy delivered the INS Joint Declaration on Inauthenticity alongside the philosopher Simon Critchley at Tate Modern, at four thirty on Saturday, 17 January 2009. Footage of the declaration can be found at http://channel.tate.org.uk/media/27082994001.

14 — Jayson Blair is a staff reporter for the New York Times. His first article for the paper was 'Fire at Overcrowded Queens House Kills One' on 9 June 1998.

18 — In 1995, the publisher Judischer Verlag published a book entitled *Bruchstucke: Aus Einer Kindheit 1939–1948*, written by a Holocaust survivor named Binjamin Wilkomirski. The book was later published in English as *Fragments: Memories of a Childhood 1939–1948*. The book tells the story of Wilkomirski's childhood. Born in Riga, as a child he witnesses the murder of his father by Latvian militia. He then escapes by boat from Riga to Danzig, where he and his brothers stay in a farmhouse. One day Wilkomirski emerges from the farmhouse cellar to find that his brothers and the farmer's wife have disappeared. After wandering alone for some time he is eventually picked up by a convoy taking prisoners to Majdanek concentration camp. Shortly before the liquidation of Majdanek, Wilkomirski is sent to Auschwitz where he survives until liberation. He is then brought to an orphanage in Krakow where he stays until one of the women looking after him smuggles him into Switzerland to escape from the pogroms. In Switzerland Wilkomirski is adopted by the Dössekkers – a wealthy childless couple who give him a new identity, that of Bruno Dössekker.

19 — In 1894 the anarchist Martial Bourdin was responsible for an explosion which destroyed much of the Greenwich observatory and also caused his own death.

20 — Fare was a performance artist whose performances involved the amputation of parts of his body and their replacement with metal or plastic decorations. Between 1964 and 1968, performing across Europe and Canada, he was lobotomised and lost a thumb, two fingers, eight toes, one eye, both testicles, his right hand and several patches of skin. The amputated parts were preserved in alcohol. Fare had the amputations performed by a randomly controlled machine, and ended his career by having his ~~head~~ amputated.

III

III

III

Confabulation

III

Shall we begin by explaining Maki and Kajsa's absence? [1]

......

— Mireille Fauchon: [illegible]

......

[illegible]

......

— Ryan Gander: No.

......

— CM: [illegible]

......

— RG: [illegible]

......

— Rasha Kahil: So are we all willing to lie?

......

— RG: [illegible]

......

— RG: [illegible]

......

— CM: [illegible] Not lies by artists, big lies by people.
(can't hear)

—

— Ryan Gander: Before we begin can we just address the terminology; you're using the word lying but I don't know if everyone agrees with the subject being lying.

—

— Or...

1 — We asked Maki and Kajsa to provide us with their memories of the conversation; some of their recollections were less clear than others.

(*fig 1*)
Ryan Gander

(*fig 2*)
Jamie Shovlin

◊ RG: You're using the word lying but I don't think the subject should be lying because it has negative connotations of hoaxing or something. I remember that my dad always says that you should never let a lie get in the way of a good story, which is a more positive view of what a lie is. [8]

—

◊ JS: Isn't it never let the truth get in the way of a good story?

—

— RG: Oh yeah, something like that. I forgot.

—

— RK: Well maybe we should just stick with disingenuity as it is described by David Trevellian as a way to create a space outside of reality rather than to cheat people?

—

— CM: Shall we begin by introducing ourselves?

—

— Someone: Yes! I completely forgot!

—

— MF: My name is Michelle and I'm an illustrator... I'm interested in stories that have some basis in fact or historical truth and what happens when fiction and reality collide.

—

— CM: I'm an illustrator. I like to put stories in to new contexts for example I have just hidden a murder mystery within a butterfly classification guide.

—

— RG: My name is Ryan and I'm an alcoholic. [6] What do I do? What do I do? Well, I make art but when I'm asked I normally say I teach because if you say you make art that is usually followed by a more difficult question.

8 — Statements marked by ◊ are ones for which Ryan Gander has no recollection.

6 — Ryan Gander was born in Huddersfield in 1974. He regards being an artist as being a workman. He studied Fine Art at Chester University and undertook a residency at the Jan Van Eyck Academy in 1996. His break through show in 2003 was at the Ikon Gallery in Birmingham and was entitled *Heralded as the New Black*. The show's title was taken from a remark made by the artist's father on discovering his son's success: 'So I suppose now you're going to be heralded as the new black.' Gander makes regular contributions to the design journal *Dot Dot Dot*. These are of varying reliability, particularly the transcripts of a series of lectures whose title we can't remember, in which he delivers seeming facts about such things as Goldfinger's modernist house in Hampstead. Each item in the lecture is connected to the next by a loose chain of association. In 2007 he did something to do with portraits at the Frieze Art Fair. In another piece he created a new word *Mitim*, which means something like a made up word that can only mean itself. Due to the reflexive meaning of the word, it proved very difficult to introduce into common us-

(fig 3)
Tom McCarthy

— Jamie Shovlin: Like Ryan I'm also ashamed of saying I'm an artist so I normally say I'm a designer, more practical. 7

—

— Ben Freeman: [illegible]

—

— Hannah Rae Alton: My work mostly relies on scientific fact and if I misjudge and it doesn't work, the work doesn't exist, so I thought I'd hang out with a bunch of liars and see what happened.

—

— RK: My work is often represented through images of my-self and is quite confessional.

—

— Annabel Fraser: I'm Annabel, I suppose I'm a designer.

—

— JS: Sorry.

—

— AF: [illegible]

age, although Ryan exhibited it as an answer in a crossword puzzle and someone else managed to insert it into a magazine article.

Ryan Gander's art works are quiet, often requiring detective work and close attention to decipher them. This reflects the artist's well-known love of detective stories.

7 — Jamie Shovlin studied painting at the Royal College of Art, graduating in 2003. He has since become famous as an art hoaxer par excellence. The two pieces that Shovlin is currently most well known for were both made early in his career. The first of these was the *Naomi V. Jelish* project in which he created works purporting to have been made by a fictional school girl. These works were then shown at the Riflemaker Gallery, where they were bought by a Charles Saatchi, who at the time of buying was unaware that the pieces had in fact been produced by Shovlin. In the 2004 Beck's Futures show at the ICA he showed an archive of fan work relating to a German punk group named *Lustfaust*. Of course, *Lustfaust* never existed.

More recently Shovlin has been making work that looks at his parents view of 1960s America through the prism of their record collection. His work often features his mother.

(fig 4)
The cover of Alma Books hardback edition of Remainder, 2006

[illegible]

—

— Debbie Cook: My name is Debbie Cook and I'm an illustrator but I came from a journalistic background, and in that profession I had to rely on accuracy.

—

— RG: Did you practise that?

—

— DC: What do you mean? No!

—

— RG: [illegible]

—

— DC: [illegible]

—

— Someone: I'd like us to begin by looking at your identities as artists. Do you think that an artist's persona is a performance?

—

— JS: I think being a person is a performance. While we're sitting here we're all abiding by certain codes of delivery.

—

— AF: We saw you give a talk a few weeks ago and you mentioned using the Naomi V. Jelish [10] project as a way of validating a certain type of work.

—

— JS: When I first began making those images there was no author attached to them other than myself. I began to see that there was a

10 — In 2004 there was an exhibition of drawings and sketches by a precocious 13-year-old schoolgirl called Naomi V. Jelish. The exhibition told the bizarre story of how the girl and her family disappeared from their Kent home shortly after her father had drowned.

or

It is now more than 15 years since 13-year-old Naomi V. Jelish disappeared with her family from their home in Kent. But look up her name on the internet and you will find her photograph, school report and newspaper cuttings about the disappearence, as well as examples of her extraordinary drawings collected by a retired teacher from her school, John Ivesmail.

(fig 5)
Naomi V. Jelish, School Sketchbook N°1

narrative emerging. At that time there was a trend for making work that was strongly autobiographical and I wanted to make something more forcefully not my own; that's when I came up with Naomi V. Jelish. I'm ordering this quite coherently now, retrospectively, but at the time it wasn't like that at all.

If you present it as what a thirteen year old did draw, it should fulfil certain roundness. I remember when I first heard the word hoax I had to look it up in a dictionary and I still don't really know what it means. It's a sort of Jeremy Beadle-type prank but, for example, I can't imagine turning up anywhere dressed as her.

—

— Or...

—

— JS: When the press picked up the Naomi V. Jelish project, "hoax" was one of the words used a lot. I remember having to look up the word hoax in a dictionary and it seemed to refer to a Jeremy Beadle-type prank, and I thought to myself – is this what I meant?

—

— CM: Do you think that using fictions can maybe be a way of... if you can trip them up quite early on when they are looking at your work then it's a way of catching them and keeping them with your work like a kind of trap or a trip...

—

— JS: I always have a problem with things like trap, trip because they're all negative. I don't know if there's any kind of opposition to them... phrases that are positive.

— Honey pot!

—

— RG: Snare.

—

— JS: Bear trap.

—

— BF: Hoaxes are not respected and short lived.

—

— HRA: I think it's also to do with intention.

—

— RG: I think that's a good way of talking about your work. When I'm giving a lecture about my work, and I can think of a way that things could have been better, then I always say that that's the way it was.

(*fig 6*)
Ryan Gander, Your life in four acts, Forward, 2008

– BF: There was a man who recently got arrested for forging military documents which suggested that Churchill was collaborating with the Nazis.[13] To me that was a hoax. It was a prolonged, very in-depth hoax, but it was a hoax. I don't see anything negative about borrowing from the language of hoaxes and pranks; in my world that can lead to respectable outcomes. I once stood outside Selfridges with a man in a suit and we said we were from a magazine looking for new models and asking the most unlikely people who must have known that they couldn't be models but were posing for the camera anyway.

—

– JS: In hoaxes there is the reveal where someone is getting very angry or upset and suddenly Jeremy pops out and says actually it's not real. I'm not sure what you call it in what we do.

—

◇ JS: Vehicles.

—

◇ RG: Vessels.

—

◇ JS: Conduits?

—

◇ RG: Could typography be one of these vehicles?

—

– JS: In a gallery there's this almost sanctified looking. People come into a gallery with certain expectations.

—

– RG: Nobody likes to be manipulated.

—

– HRA: There's an artist called Eve Laramee[9] who did a project in which she claimed to be allowing visitors to communicate with Kelper's ghost and the gallery was initially uneasy but in the end it agreed to be complicit in the deception.

—

13 — Martin Allen's *Hidden Agenda: How the Duke of Windsor Betrayed the Allies* (Macmillan) paints a devastating picture of this truly evil royal who was a close friend of Charles Bedaux, a Nazi spy so dangerous that the FBI would appear to have bumped him off in 1944 (officially he committed suicide).

9 — For much of his life, Fissiault simultaneously inhabited two worlds – the concrete realm of applied science and the mystical domain of alternative realities and utopian longings that led him to experiment with communal living and mind-altering drugs. By the mid 1960s his unorthodox ideas became increasingly suspect to his aerospace industry employers, who forced him out as a security risk.

(*fig 7*)
Ryan Gander, A future Lorem Ipsum, 2006

(*fig 8*)
Ryan Gander, The Klingon smiles and simply replies..., 2008

◊ AF: Fiction writers don't provoke this kind of discussion and I don't understand why.

—

— RG: That's the analogy I always use.

—

— Or...

—

◊ RG: That's the example I always use. All artists deal in fictions it's just whether the manipulation is revealed or not. Look at the painting in this room. It's a painting of a landscape, not a real landscape. We're surrounded by fictions all the time.

—

— JS: They're all the same thing, they're just on smaller or larger scales of space.

—

◊ RG: And would you say mixing truth in with fiction is one of those vehicles as well?

—

◊ JS: Conduits, you called them vessels.

……

— JS: Truth is a very awkward term because it's … there's an agreed deception, Freudian slip, conception of what it is, it's like a story it might be defined as the basic story that we all abide by but I think we're all aware of the fact that somebody some organisation has at some point made that story the way it is rather than it just purely existing.

……

— HRA: I wanted to draw [illegible] flowers when I was thirteen.

……

◊ TM: Winning would be fascism. If you could beat reality and actually impose a new reality principle, that would be complete fascism, so in a way that's really good.

—

— RG: There's [illegible] and London, Sheffield and there's [illegible] but it's at the printers. But the thing is that these exist in a [illegible] outside the gallery space but in the institution so they're more like in the institution than they are in the gallery but they're listed on the work list as a work of art but you quite often find boxes of flyers in entrance halls in galleries anyway so you can pick them up and take them and not know or know and

[illegible]

......

— BF: [illegible]

......

— RG: [illegible] actually this thing is quite magical. [illegible]

......

— AF: [illegible]

......

— RG: [illegible]

......

— CM: I'd like to talk now about re-enactment. We initially invited Tom McCarthy [2] to join us today but unfortunately he couldn't make it. A few years ago Tom made a project with Rod Dickinson entitled *Greenwich Degree Zero*. In it, they re-enacted an attempt to blow up the Greenwich observatory by anarchist terrorists. In their version, however, the attack was shown to be a success. Dr Trevellian gives a case study where he talks about a situation in which a bank heist is being re-enacted. If you're re-enacting a bank

2 — Tom McCarthy is an artist and novelist. In 1994 he published his first novel *Remainder*, which was soon followed by the philosophical work *Tin Tin and the Something of Something*. He has recently published another novel, *C*, which takes communications as its theme, in particular radio and telegraphy at the beginning of the last century. *C* has just been longlisted for the Booker Prize.

In the art world, Tom McCarthy is known as a writer of manifestos. He founded a society of artists, writers and philosophers called the *Necronautical Society* and together they are endeavouring to map and explore death. At some point in the last five years Tom McCarthy produced a work at the ICA that took its inspiration from William Burrough's cut-up pieces. This piece was a radio station, broadcasting bits of cut-up poetry and other things on a particular frequency throughout London.

In 2009 McCarthy took part in the Altermodern exhibition at Tate Britain. His contribution involved hiring actors to play himself and the philosopher Simon Critchley. These actors then delivered a necronautical declaration, much to the outrage of their audience.

heist in a real bank and the staff don't know it's a re-enactment then maybe it's just a bank heist? Re-enacting can build layers upon layers of fiction until a rupture is created taking us back into the real again.

—

— MF: For example, I knew someone, an old metal head I used to work with, who went to a *Lustfaust* gig thinking that they were a real band and he was really looking forward to seeing this old seventies band and he was really pissed off when he realised they weren't real. He cottoned on quite quickly that the guys in the band were too young to have been playing in the seventies.

—

— JS: Yes! That happens! I meet people who claim to have been at *Lustfaust* gigs in the seventies. It's like that thing of however many people claiming to have been at Woodstock. [16]

—

— RK: But now *Lustfaust* are a real band, they're going to be playing at the Big Chill.

—

— BF: Aren't they really Schneider TM?

—

— AF: How do you feel about that?

—

— JS: Really bad, it's got nothing to do with me. I was happy for it to have been what it was at the ICA, but one of the musicians I had originally collaborated with wanted to take it further and I didn't really have a choice about that.

—

— JS: I have a term for that kind of work, which is repository for bad ideas. I don't know if you do the same thing, Ryan?

—

◇ HRA: I really like the idea of creating a person that fulfils a function that's smaller than a normal person would. My alter ego gets all the bus fines. [15]

16 — A similarly nostalgic piece by Jamie Shovlin looks at the cultish outpourings of the fans of an obscure German shock-rock band called *Lustfaust*, who cocked a notorious snook at the music industry in the late 1970s by giving away their music on blank cassettes and getting their fans to design their own covers. Shovlin had tracked down these obsessive fans on the internet and carefully archived their memories.

15 — Johnny English is a quiet man, always pleasant but never chatty. He mostly keeps himself to himself.

(fig 9)
Barry Wenden, White Bird, Oil on Canvas, 1973

[illegible]

—

— JS: Fully engage yeah.

—

— HRA: Without having to have the rest of your...

—

— BF: You both use the Internet in your work: Jamie, the Naomi V. Jelish site is a .org site, do you think that's misleading? You said that there were clues in the original exhibition. Are there any clues in the site that it's not real? I haven't found any.

—

— JS: As far as I'm aware there aren't any clues.

—

— CM: Has the presence of the Internet given a space for this kind of work to occupy? It's not so clear when you read something online whether or not it's true.

—

— Or...

—

— CM: You both used websites as part of your work. Ryan, do you think that the Internet acts as a facilitator for your fictions? I noticed that the John Fare website uses his[20] Wikipedia page, which seemed to me like a way of inhabiting the Internet's language of fact.

—

— RG: Basically I don't think that the Internet is doing anything new, it's just replacing what used to be done through word of mouth and storytelling. Stories changing as people passed them on to each other.

—

— Or...

—

20 — John Fare, a Canadian who removed various bits of his body in a slow and bloody process of auto-amputation, is avidly admired by another artist, Gregor Schneider.

(fig 10)
Ernst Bettler

— RG: The Internet hasn't changed anything, it is just a new means to do something that has been happening since the beginning of time. People would tell stories around fireplaces and then they would be retold to others and they would change, and that's the same thing.

—

— HRA: But, do you think the Internet has given a forum for your characters to exist in a way that would be impossible otherwise?

—

◊ RG: I don't think so at all. I think the Chinese whisper element that has become a part of them is beautiful and would happen even without the Internet.

—

— AF: I'd like to talk about the John Fare project. What I found particularly interesting about that was that the website uses the actual Wikipedia page that refers to John Fare and then flips it over. The reason I liked this was that it uses Wikipedia, which is essentially the language of fact for the Internet.

—

— DC: But Wikipedia is really unreliable.

— BF: It's actually not. It's really hard to get an entry on Wikipedia. They have a team of fact checkers. Wikipedia is great because it represents this battle between true researchers – experts in their field – and hoaxers who just want to spread disinformation.

—

— RG: And now you can read on Wikipedia that it's actually a fiction, which is really weird. I think the Chinese whisper element that has become a part of them is beautiful and would happen

—

— Someone: Finally we should talk about belief; this type of work can only exist with the participation of an audience. Like with my village in India: because people believe in the bad spirits in the lake, then they are as real as their mobile phones.

—

— AF: People want to look outside of logic for an explanation. Coming back to Rod Dickinson, he was involved in making some of the crop circles and even after an explanation had been given for those, people still wanted to believe in them. It's also to do with trust, if you trust whoever's telling you the story, you ignore some of the

(fig 11)
Ernst Bettler's poster for P+H as it appeared in Problem Solved by Michael Johnson, 2002

(fig 12)
Lustfaust performing at Fabrik in Hamburg, Saturday, 3 Dec 1977

warning signals. In the Kelper's ghost example, people actually believed that they were communicating with a ghost however unlikely they might have found it outside of the gallery. I think that was to do with the fact that the gallery had little signs warning people not to use the equipment during an electrical storm; in fact, there wasn't any electricity running through it.

—

— JS: I can think of an example of people reading inaccurate facts about themselves in a newspaper and not correcting them.

—

— JS: Wasn't there a reporter who fictionalised articles for the New York Times?

—

— Someone: David Trevellian,[5] I've read his autobiography.

—

— RK: Walid Raad of the Atlas Group makes artworks playing with the notion of fiction, but never explicitly stated that way. They are presented as factual data that the artist uses to document experiences or historical episodes, mainly of the Lebanese civil war. One of his video works, which is seen as "documentary", about a Lebanese man held hostage alongside Terry Waite and Terry Anderson, is actually pure fiction, playing upon audiences'prejudices about how they would expect someone like that to behave. It ties in with historical facts that actually happened at that time, creating an aura of suspended belief.

—

— Belief brings these works to full term.

—

— RG: There's this guy called Ernst Bettler.[17] He's a Swiss graphic designer and he moves to Berlin from, I don't actually remember, when he's about thirty he moves from Switzerland to Berlin and

5 — In fact, we made a slip of the tongue here. The name of the journalist who fictionalised articles for the New York Times was, of course, Jayson Blair. Please see footnotes numbered 14.

17 — Some choose to educate by more subtle means. Although he is now becoming recognised as one of the founding fathers of the 'culture-jamming' form of protest, Ernst Bettler's way of revealing to 1950s Switzerland that Pfäfferli+Huber AG (a pharmaceutical company) had Nazi roots was astonishingly subtle.

When commissioned to design a set of fiftieth anniversary posters, he suggested four in total. And into each one he echoed the shape of the letters 'N', 'A', 'Z' and 'I' through the image photographed. It was only when the posters were put up randomly around town that his client realised that their embarrassing roots had been revealed. There was public outrage. Only six weeks later Pfäfferli+Huber were out of business, thanks to the underground information campaign of Bettler.

(fig 13)
Jamie Shovlin, Fontana Modern Masters,
2003–05

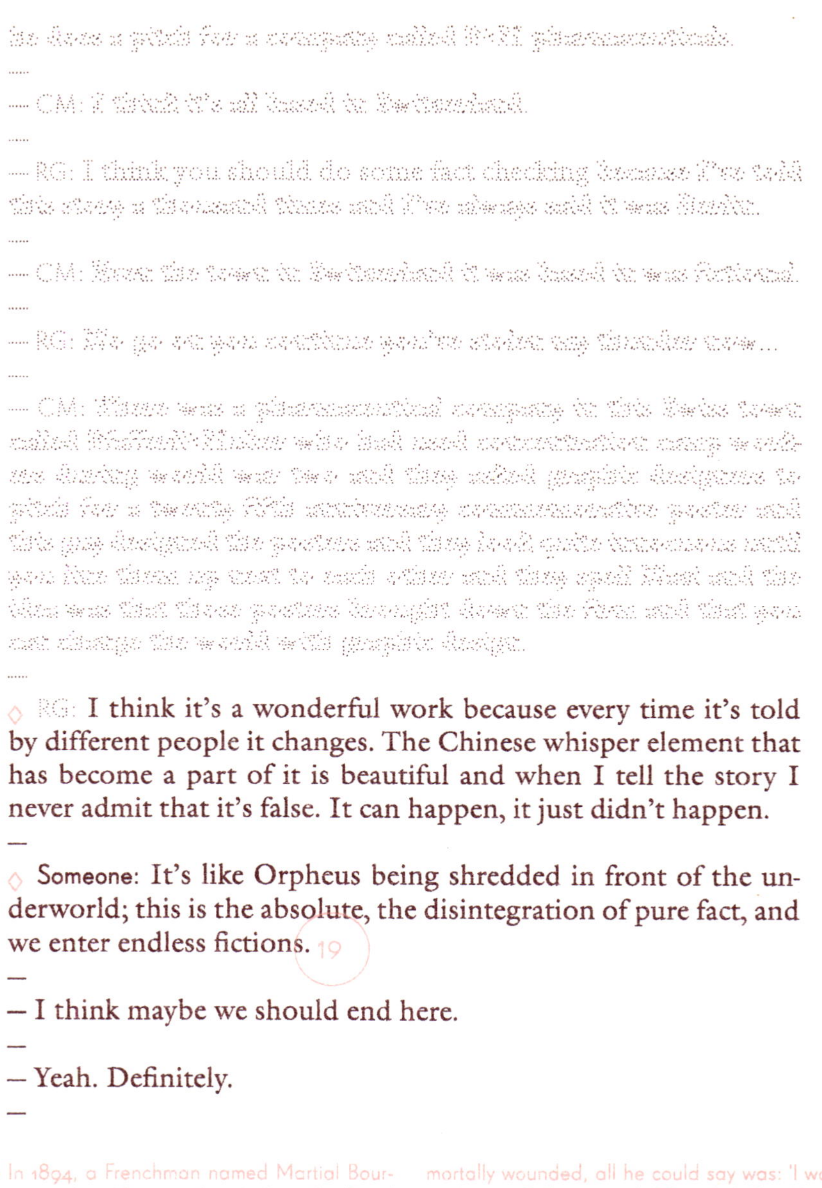

◇ RG: I think it's a wonderful work because every time it's told by different people it changes. The Chinese whisper element that has become a part of it is beautiful and when I tell the story I never admit that it's false. It can happen, it just didn't happen.

—

◇ Someone: It's like Orpheus being shredded in front of the underworld; this is the absolute, the disintegration of pure fact, and we enter endless fictions.[19]

—

– I think maybe we should end here.

—

– Yeah. Definitely.

—

19 — In 1894, a Frenchman named Martial Bourdin attempted to blow up the clock at the Royal Observatory, seeking to rid the world of the tyranny of Greenwich Mean Time. Holding a packed lunch in one hand and a bomb in the other, he walked up the path leading to the observatory, tripped and dropped the bomb, which disembowelled him. When a group of schoolchildren came across him, mortally wounded, all he could say was: 'I want to go home. Call me a cab.' Bourdin's frankly risible attempt at outrage sparked one major piece of literature – Joseph Conrad's *The Secret Agent* – and a plethora of penny dreadfuls, one of which concerned a man floating across London in a dirigible, chucking bombs until prevailed on to desist by his mother.

(fig 14)
A photograph of Naomi's mother, found on the cover of one of her sketchbooks

(fig 15)
The cover of Picador's paperback edition of Fragments by Binjamin Wilkomirski, 1996

– RG: What's the conclusion? Before we finish we should think of a conclusion. We still haven't come up with a positive definition of what it is that we do. The problem is that, through all this talking we still haven't come up with a word to describe what it is that we're talking about. Something to do with fictions that run alongside reality...

–

– RK: Parallelity?

–

– RG: Parallelity! Perfect.

–

– It's been dead good.

– – – – – – – – – – – – –

This is where the transcript ends

– – – – – – – – – – – – –

(fig 16)
Remains of Beuys' crashed plane,
Crimea, 1943

(fig 17)
John Fare

(fig 18)
Tom McCarthy and Rod Dickinson,
Greenwich Degree Zero, 2006

Appendix

(A) 'Burn, Gordon 'Houses of Horror' in The Guardian, (London and Manchester: September 22 2004)

(B) Januszczak, Waldemar 'Beck's Futures hasn't lost its bottle' in The Sunday Times Culture Section, (London: April 2 2006) p.15-16

(C) Harrison, Helen, A Works of curious conflicting directions' in The New York Times (New York: April 13 1997) p. 16

(D) 'Books of the year' in The Observer Review (London: November 26 2000) p.2

(E) Sabadus, Aura 'Hess Mystery Solved Says Historian' in Western Morning News (Dorset:February 1 2003) p.9

(F) Kalman, Tibor 'Design Interventions' in Adbusters, Issue 5, Volume 9, September/October 2001, p. no page numbers.

Little Gregor (he was born in 1969) must have been a worry to his mother. He was not like other children. None of his friends, for example, lay in bed at night working out how to completely isolate themselves – from noise, from evidence of any other living presence – by lining their rooms with 4ft-thick layers of lead, glass fibre, soundproofing materials and other stuff. (Completely Insulated Death Room would be finished in 1991.) None of them coated their faces and naked bodies in a doughy mixture of meal and water and cycled through the cold to school: or if they did, they certainly didn't refer to the end result as "body art". Gregor was an avid admirer of a Canadian called John Fare who removed various bits of his body in a slow and bloody process of auto-amputation.

Home alone, Gregor filled a coffin-shaped box with wet cement and lay face down in it, with a chisel at hand in case things went kerflooey. The original idea had been to make a second impression of his back and, unaided, flip the first entombing slab on top of himself, but this proved impractical.

Around this time he was earning pocket money working as an altar boy at the local Catholic cemetery, where he learned many things.

woo
had
inte
screa
after
there
infla
one g
has s
yet. I
doub
at nig
and

As
cof
with
lay
with

with
others
bly ne
Sch
many
Apoca
Londo
anti-s
has ca
genera
as far f
it can

(A)

rt that's
s of the
eet. The
nter is a
es, of a
l in the
Church.
boppers
ober and
moves

phenomenon was itself a religion.

A similarly nostalgic piece by Jamie Shovlin looks at the cultish outpourings of the fans of an obscure German shock-rock band called Lustfaust, who cocked a notorious snook at the music industry in the late 1970s by giving away their music on blank cassettes and getting their fans to design their own covers. Shovlin has tracked down these obsessive fans on the internet — Lustfaust Fans Reunited? — and carefully archived their memories. There's also an interview with the band's surviving guitarist, whose weird, robotic voice, and the way he keeps pressing his neck when he speaks, reveal him to be a survivor of throat cancer. It all makes for creepy and fascinating viewing.

meanw
having
sor. B
appea
has d
and it
becom
Sim
entirel
system
New Y
Joyce'
has b
betical
book
first, a
installa
concep
unbrea
talism.
the pi
circuit

(B)

Yves Fissiault, Artist of the Cold War Era

Anthony Giordano Gallery, Dowling College, Idle Hour Boulevard, Oakdale. Through May 4. 244-3016.

Using artifacts, documents and artworks salvaged from Fissiault's estate, Eve Andrée Laramée has constructed a remarkable installation tracing the intellectual and creative evolution of a man whose wide-ranging enthusiasms led him in curious and often conflicting directions.

Fissiault, who lived from 1908 to 1991, was a metallurgist and electrical engineer by profession, but his practical concerns were paralleled by a lifelong quest for spiritual enlightenment.

Working briefly as his research assistant in 1978, Ms. Laramée helped him gather information on alternative cosmologies, which he charted in arcane diagrams, surreal paintings and curious constructions.

To her surprise, Ms. Laramée found that she had been named executrix of Fissiault's estate, which amounted to the documentation of his life's researches.

As an artist herself, she has organized the material with a sculptor's sensibility, arranging the fragments to build a composite structure that supports a complex biographical and conceptual narrative.

Even at an early age, Fissiault seems to have been fascinated by optics, and he used the eye as an extended metaphor of perception on a cosmic scale. Models, drawings and paintings of eyes reflect their analogies to celestial bodies and computers, as well as their hypnotic qualities.

For much of his life, Fissiault simultaneously inhabited two worlds — the concrete realm of applied science and a mystical domain of alternative realities and utopian longings that led him to experiment with communal living and mind-altering drugs.

By the mid 1950's, his unorthodox ideas became increasingly suspect to his aerospace industry employers, who forced him out as a security risk.

Ms. Laramée offers Fissiault's material with no commentary beyond a chronological outline, leaving the viewer to decide whether he was a brilliant visionary or a deluded crackpot, or perhaps a combination of the two. Implicit in her installation, however, is a subtext of intolerance for minds like Fissiault's — a paradoxical bias in a society that celebrates innovation and technological progress.

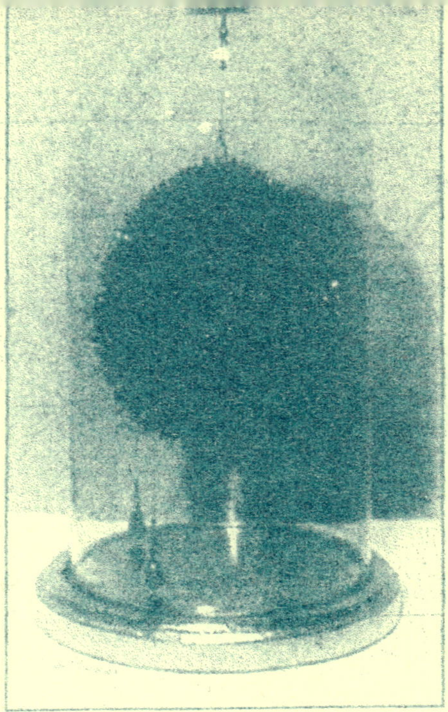

"Ouvo Bulleta-Tack Egg" by Lisa Loiodice-Fleischman.

Jeff Epstein: Paintings

The Art Gallery, Southampton Building, Suffolk Community College, Selden. Through April 18. 451-4351.

Although he now lives in Brooklyn, Mr. Epstein often returns to his old neighborhood in Lawrenceville, N.J., to find his subject matter. And while a few of his sketchy, broadly brushed paintings show daylight scenes, he prefers to study the night's deep shadows and looming forms.

Under the harsh glare of artificial light, even a cosy home set in reassuring confines of a suburb garden seems strangely ominous. the "Night Yard" series, the house surrounded by engulfing trees a shrubs that cling to it like tar.

Perhaps lava is a better simile, the glow that backlights the pic fence and turns a charming bor into a phalanx of aggressive bl spikes has a decidedly volcanic ov tone.

In another nocturnal series, M Epstein looks at empty school bu ings, or rather through their gl doors and windows into fluoresc lighted spaces.

The cold and lonely atmosphere unoccupied classrooms and deser hallways recalls Edward Hoppe hermetic environments, but with the humanizing influence that ev the most world-weary night ha might afford.

Surprisingly, in spite of th

(C)

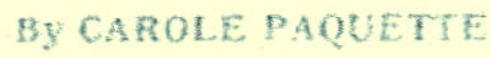

By CAROLE PAQUETTE

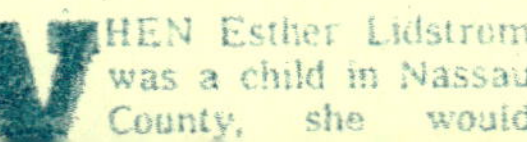

WHEN Esther Lidstrom was a child in Nassau County, she would

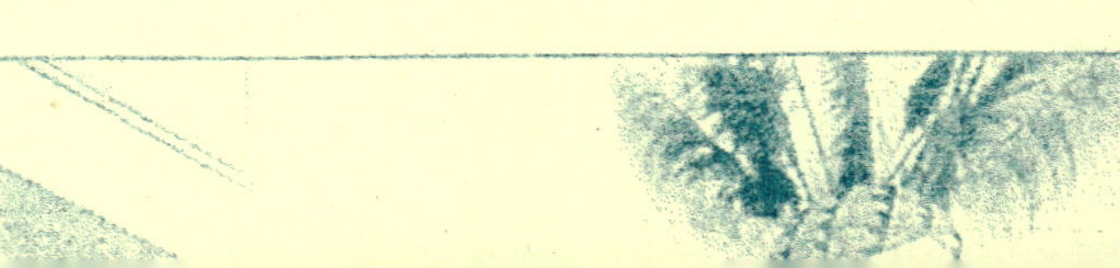

ilip Roth seems to

food we buy and eat. Se
read a lot of novels this
some new, some older: I
Haruf's Plainsong and **Nial**
Letters of Love (both Picado
with enormous pleasure
Robert Harris's Archangel (
North Patterson's The Final
(Hutchinson), the perfect
and all the wonderful th
by **Michael Connelly** (Orion)

(D)

TOM PAULIN

Martin Allen's **Hidden Agenda: How the Duke of Windsor Betrayed the Allies** (Macmillan) paints a devastating picture of this truly evil royal who was a close friend of Charles Bedaux, a Nazi spy so dangerous that the FBI would appear to have bumped him off in 1944 (officially he committed suicide). **Frank Kermode**'s **Shakespeare's Language** (Allen Lane, Penguin) is an inspiring work of evaluative critical analysis.

MAVIS CHEEK

'Not for horrid profs,' sa
mode of his **Shakespeare's**
Lane, Penguin) – and he's
engaging and clear to re
called **Colm Toibin**'s **The Bl**
ship (Picador) 'emotional
phy'. I'd add the word 'b
that. Three generations
ent beliefs, three women
terms with each other a
selves. With **The World's S**
corn (Cape), **Shena Mackay**
more immaculat
of human f
tune and f
sl

CHRISTOPHER FRAYLING

I particularly enjoyed **David Skal**'s **Screams of Reason – Mad Science and Modern Culture** (W.W. Norton & Co) which begins with Dr Faustus and ends with Stephen Hawking but concentrates in between on Boris Karloff and Hollywood horror. The best-written book I read was **Thomas McGuane**'s elegant and thoughtful essays about the partnership – a partnership he calls 'a burst of poetry' – between humans and horses collected as **Some Horses** (The Lyons Press).

EDNA O'BRIEN

Snow and Guilt by **Giorgio Pressburger** (Granta) is a perfect little book. Translated by Shaun Whiteside, these six stories have an underlying unity: the writing is austere yet

A.L.

This yea
chief (Cape)
MacLeod's p
master of pros
firmly assured. T

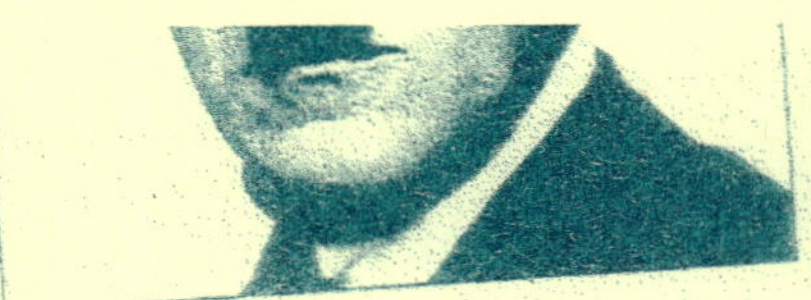

● DECEIVED: Adolf Hitler

● REVEALING: Dorset-based author

urchill

Aura Sabadus

ulation has been rife that there was more to Hess's arrival in Britain than the authorities would admit but the crucial evidence to prove the case was missing – until now.

After three years of researching previously undiscovered documents in Britain, Germany and the United States, Mr Allen now reveals for the first time what he says are the true motives for Hess's infamous flight.

The new evidence proves that a small group of men within the British government and intelligence services were in fact conducting a brilliant plot which would not only lead to Hess's flight, but would also have a decisive impact on the course of the war.

The plot was a classic sting, known only to a few, but it led Hitler to believe, falsely, that there were factions in the British Government willing to overthrow Churchill and negotiate a peace deal with the Germans. The deal would have seen the liberation of Western Europe in return for Hitler being given a free rein to press eastwards across Russia, his ultimate goal.

So successful was the plot to convince Hitler that peace on the Western front was imminent that he had already committed his troops to fight on the Russian front before the supposed peace deal was concluded.

When Hess was captured and peace with Britain failed to materialise, Hitler was forced into the one scenario that he did not want, a war on two fronts.

"The British Government's determination that Britain would survive at all costs, however unscrupulous the means, and whatever the devastating consequences for the Russians, who lost over 20 million lives in the fighting that ensued, is something that had to be covered up," said Mr Allen.

"Disclosure would have shattered Britain's international credibility and ruined

joins trawler for cod rese

Fisheries Ministers which led to drastic

(E)

(F)

It's one of the greatest design interventions on record. In 1958, the Swiss pharmaceutical company Pfäfferli + Huber AG hired graphic designer Ernst Bettler to create a series of posters celebrating the company's 50th anniversary. Bettler's cutting-edge work, they hoped, would put a post-war shine on the company.

Bettler turned in a fine, four-poster series that soon hit the streets of Switzerland — where an incensed populace tore them down and exploded with rage against the arrogant, brutish corporation. Within six weeks, P + H was ruined forever.

P + H, you see, had a history of involvement in testing carried out on prisoners in Germany's wartime concentration camps. Bettler hadn't forgotten. Taken one by one, the designer's four posters seem innocent enough. Posted in a row, however, they appear to be a series of letters (the "A" is shown here). You can guess what four-letter word Bettler made sure to spell out for the world.

Floating Footnotes

3 — Fakes and simulacra appeal to McCarthy in his various guises as artist, critic and novelist. There is, for instance, the 'Joint Statement on Inauthenticity' published by the International Necronautical Society: the semi-fictional, quasi-totalitarian conceptual art collective that McCarthy founded in 1999 with a pastiche manifesto in the Times. 'All cults of authenticity,' it declares, 'should be abandoned.'

4 — I was standing by the sink looking at this crack in the plaster, when I had a sudden sense of déjà vu. The sense of déjà vu was very strong. I'd been in a space like this before, a place just like this, looking at the crack, a crack that had jutted and meandered in a way just like the one beside the mirror. There'd been that same crack, and a bathtub also, and a window directly above the taps just like there was in this room – only the window had been slightly bigger and the taps older, different.

11 — Naomi's art was said to have been saved from her house by one of her teachers, John Ivesmail.

or

Naomi V. Jelish's extraordinary drawings were collected by a retired teacher from her school, John Ivesmail. Ivesmail had planned an exhibition of her work, hoping it might shed light on the family's disappearance, but he died before it came to fruition, passing the material to conceptual artist Jamie Shovlin.

12 — Its roots lie between minimalism and, via the "Tate Declaration of Inauthenticity" – "for us, inauthenticity is the core to the self, to what it means to be human" – signed by some of the artists, Warhol in dilute form.

14 — Whether as a student journalist at the University of Maryland or as an intern at the Boston Globe, the short and ubiquitous Mr Blair stood out. He seemed to be constantly working, whether on articles or on sources. Some, like fellow student Catherine Welch, admired him. 'You thought, "That's what I want to be,"' she said. Others considered him immature, with a hungry ambition and an unhealthy interest in newsroom gossip.

18 — An intensely personal piece of testimony, *Fragments* (to Wilkomirski's astonishment) has turned out to be a 'sleeper', rapidly gathering an international following. Writer Christopher Hope described it as 'an achingly beautiful book'; the New York Times said he writes 'with a poet's vision, a child's state of grace'. But what distinguishes Wilkomirski is that he's retrieved a child's sensibility, unfiltered through adult interpretation.

IV

IV

IV

Details

IV

— Tom McCarthy: 2 Sometimes, you have a voice-activated thing, those are a nightmare. So every time you stop talking it goes off and it takes few seconds to kick in again.

—

— Catrin Morgan: We've done a few tests because last time when we interviewed Ryan and Jamie we lost forty minutes of conversation, but in the end that's been quite nice because it's led to us doing things to fill in the gaps.

—

— TM: That's right you're inventing things. Um... are you sure you're getting good enough audio here, there's quite a lot of...?

—

— CM: Yeah, we did another test; we did a test run where we taped ourselves.

—

— TM: Actually, talking of losing audio I should tell you something, but later...

2 — McCarthy lives exactly where such an intellectual prankster ought, high up in a tower block on the Golden Lane Estate beside the Barbican in Central London. This modernist urban village was designed by municipal architects who admired the Situationists, that nebulous grouping of artist-anarchists whose deadpan subversion also cast a spell on punk rock – and on McCarthy himself.

— CM: Shall we begin by explaining Kajsa and Maki's 1 absence?

—

— Mireille Fauchon: As you can see we've got two reserved seats, which are for Kajsa and Maki, who aren't here, but I've got a note to read out which will explain everything.

—

To whom it may concern; we are here with you today, well not really, but with you're help we can be if you wish and agree to lie, we can pretend we are present at this conversation. From Maki and Kajsa

—

— Ryan Gander: 6 No.

—

— CM: No, you won't?

1 — Maki and Kajsa's places at the conversation were reserved using A4 sheets that we had printed earlier. The sheets read simply 'Reserved' and were typeset in Arial.

6 — Ryan Gander is a fan of Sherlock Holmes and Inspector Morse.

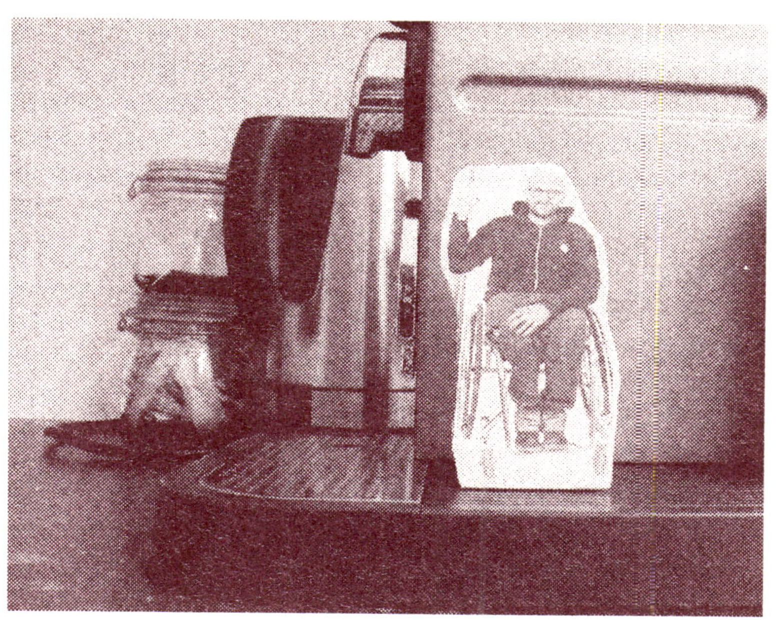

(fig 1)
Detail from Ryan Gander's studio

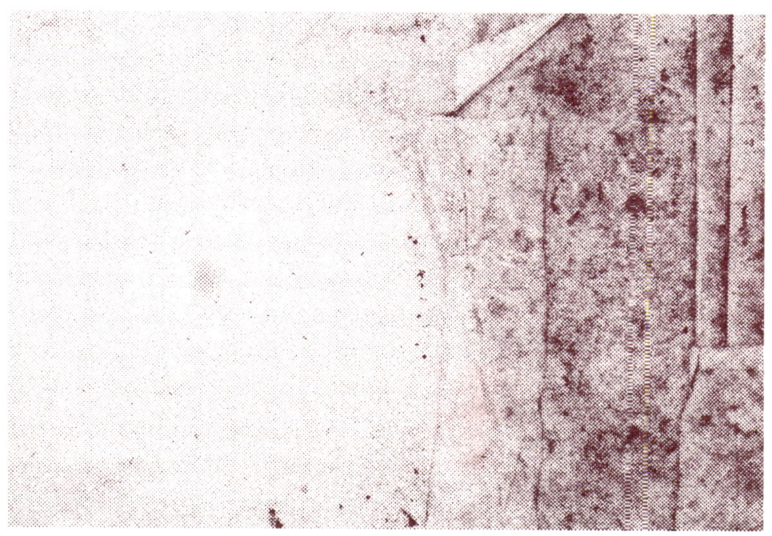

(fig 2)
Detail from Jamie Shovlin's studio

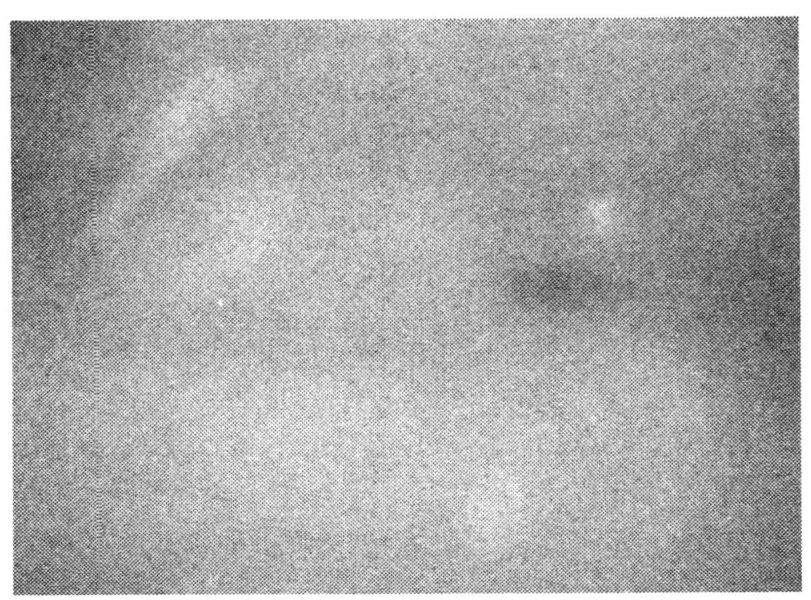

(fig 3)
A window at the Barbican café

(fig 4)
"The road itself was like an old Grand Master – one of those Dutch ones, thick with rippling layers of oil paint"

— RG: No.

—

— Debbie Cook: I'm not either.

—

— RG: I might leave; you might have more to say if I go.

—

—

— MF: Shall we begin? Trevellian [5] writes a lot about re-enactment or repetition as a way of trying to access the real through repeating or actually trying to recapture the authentic moment. In particular, a case study about someone suffering from post-traumatic stress who becomes fixated with the idea of restaging a bank heist, but the way to restage the perfect bank heist would be to put it obviously within the context of a bank but without telling the authorities, the bank staff or the public who are using the bank that it's a reconstruction, so what...

5 — The leather suitcase carried by Dr David Trevellian is a battered one. There is a particularly deep scratch in the leather running from the top left hand corner down to the bottom right; the corners are scuffed beyond hope of repair and there is a greasy stain in the shape of a shadow.

—

—

— RG: Dangerous.

—

— MF: Very dangerous, that's the problem.

—

— CM: At what stage does that stop being a real bank heist and become a reconstruction?

16 — *Lustfaust* played 36 gigs between 2004 and 2007.

—

— TM: In tennis, did you say?

—

— MF: What happens is that you're brought crashing into the real. When you realise this is a real situation but actually it's still not real, it's just another level of inauthenticity, it's a rupture in what's being simulated. Which started me thinking about *Lustfaust* [16] and the idea of a band that doesn't really exist with images that are falsified and fake music. Now we have *Lustfaust* playing at the Big Chill Festival, which is the rupture that makes them into a real band.

—

— Jamie Shovlin: [7] I'm not responsible for that.

—

— MF: But would you like to maybe talk a little bit about how you feel?

—

— JS: I feel really bad. When the opportunity came up I kind of... a German band called Schneider TM, who are a real band and who have members who exist and have played for many years...

7 — He says he is in Basel. And perhaps he is. There is certainly a hubbub in the background. But maybe that is punters at a bar in Ibiza. Or his local boozer in Streatham, South London. It is impossible not to spend the whole conversation wondering if you have missed the point and are going to look rather foolish later on.

—

— MF: So you say.

—

— JS: I've met them! This is a true story – I'm not lying – they played a gig at the ICA during its display and saw it. And they asked me, why can't we remember this band?

—

◊RG: You're using the word lying, but I don't know if the subject should be lying because lying has negative connotations about cheating or corrupting people. Maybe it would be better to redefine lying or use other words. My dad always says, you should never let a lie get in the way of a good story.

—

—

◊JS: Isn't it never let the truth get in the way of a good story? 8

—

— MF: I know this old kind of metal head guy who I work with, and he went to a *Lustfaust* gig thinking that it was going to be this amazing performance of this band and then he was really pissed off.

—

— RG: Nobody wants to be manipulated.

—

— TM: It's like about half a million people were at The Sex Pistols gig in The Hundred Club or whatever.

—

— MF: Only the guys in this band are not even old enough to have been born when the band were first around.

—

8 — Statements marked by ◊ are fragments from earlier conversations.

(fig 5)
Details from the sketchbooks of
Naomi V. Jelish

(fig 6)
Ryan Gander, Your life in four acts – Forward, 2008

◊AF: I was just thinking, fictional writers, they're writing something else everyday and no-one has this kind of discussion, so I don't understand why...

—

◊JS: That's the analogy I always use.

—

— TM: Ballard in his introduction to *Crash* says this is 1972: we're surrounded by fictions all the time; TV advertising, roles to play, personae that we can acquire and act out, and he says the writer's task is to create the real, not the fiction. That's already done by the world. I suppose that in extreme cases these people take it upon themselves to create a fiction that's above and beyond any of the available fictions that we can all get away with all the time. When a lie comes into contact with reality, it's not really reality that's fragmenting, it's accepted fictions that are breaking down. Freud never talks about reality, he talks about the reality principle, which is a set of rules about what is permissible. I'm not some kind of relativist who thinks that anything's true and it's all fiction, because that's a dangerous path and you meet holocaust deniers down that line. Fiction comes from "to perform" right? In Latin? Yeah, it's facio – I perform. It's all under construction.

—

◊RG: I think all artists make... when you look at the paintings in here none of these things are real. I think all artists deal in fiction anyway. It's just whether that manipulation of saying when some-

(fig 7)
Ryan Gander, This Consequence, 2005 (detail)

thing isn't true is there or not. That moment, in a hoax it would be called the punchline moment, but I don't know what we'd call it in what we do. Whether the fiction's created in the world and documentation of it shown in art or whether the fiction is shown in art or whether the fiction is never let out so you always believe its true. It's that sort of process, these three realms.

—

— JS: It all kind of comes down to motive. In a way, a hoax is, in the kind of context we are talking about, a Jeremy Beadle-type prank.

—

— TM: I remember reading that research anthology about pranks. I don't know if any of you saw that? It came out in the early nineties.

—

— CM: I've been trying to get hold of it.

— TM: It's out of print and I gave mine away. It's really interesting though they talk to people like Valance and Mark Pauly, people that would... and who else, I mean, and Situationism figures quite big in it, and the idea of détournement, but there was a whole kind of genre of art in the sixties that was a kind of social Pranksterism and so I suppose that has a kind of pedigree of a history that you can plug into.

—

— JS: Kind of, yeah.

— RG: And it's not so much to do with the spectator or trying to trick them or convince them or change the way they read it. It's to do with making, and that being the catalyst for you to make something.

—

— BF: There was the man who recently got arrested for forging a load of documents in military libraries to prove that... to somehow back up his false claims that Churchill had been collaborating with the Nazis via the Secret Service. [13] To me, that was a hoax. It was a prolonged, very in-depth hoax, but to me, it was

13 — Optical brightening agents only began to be used commercially in the late 1950s. Their presence would have demolished the document's claim to authenticity straight away. Their absence was a positive sign. The paper the letter was written on also had rag content, a genuine characteristic of paper made before the war. It is, according to Bower, only relatively recently that our paper has been made with such a high concentration of wood pulp.

a hoax. His intention was to deceive and to further his political aim, and that's what sets it apart from an artwork, but I would see that as a prolonged hoax.

—

— JS: With me, I think that there was a certain expectation, say for example, that I might have dressed as her, [10] which seemed absurd to me. Can I imagine, you know, turning up in a dress? So by the time the entire project was presented, my role as myself was as a kind of third figure in this chain of passage that began with her and then went to John, who was a kind of amateur curator or local historian; a slightly dodgy character — Nabakovian is the best way to describe him. [11]

10 — Naomi V. Jelish's school sketchbook number eight is decorated with magazine clippings all showing portraits of the pop star Madonna. John Ivesmail suggests that this is symbolic of Naomi's rebellion against Catholicism.

—

◊ Hannah Rae Alton: I was really interested in the idea of adopting an alter ego as an excuse to make a certain piece of work. My alter ego gets all the bus fines. It is a way of creating a person who fulfils a smaller function than the entire person normally would. [15]

11 — John was accommodating and friendly – a lifelong bachelor who had always lived alone and rarely left his native Gravesend.

—

— TM: In the nineties you had Luther Blisset, I don't know if you know about that? Loads of people were just using the name Luther Blisset to do articles, essays, talks, you know, artworks. There was another figure who was created and who may or may not ever have actually existed, and people could just be called Monty Cantsin. You could make an artwork or be a rock star as Monty Cantsin and, I mean, even the Dadaists had the Christ and co. company, where you each strived for five marks and you could be Jesus for a week.

15 — The reference number for John English's council tax bill is: J001567056

—

— MF: Tom, I wanted to ask you, just because I live really close to Brixton I was wondering...

—

— TM: Why it was there?

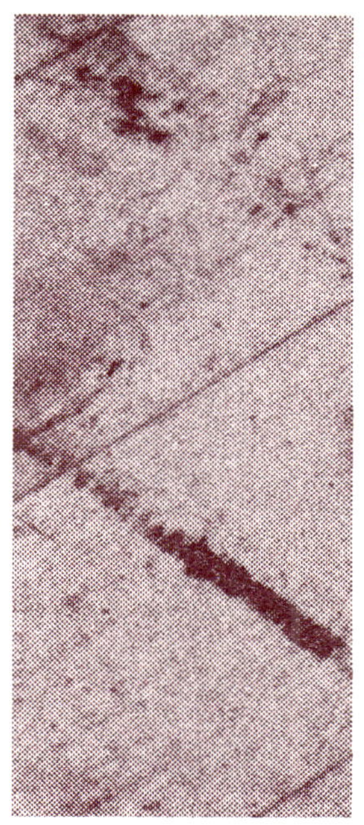

(fig 8)
Ryan Gander, The Klingon smiles and simply replies..., 2008 (detail)

– MF: Yeah.

–

– TM: I just knew the area. I lived in the house he lives in on Hearne Hill Road.

–

– MF: It was really nice for me to read *Remainder* because I knew all of those places very well, so I could imagine this person living in my space.

–

– TM: I've been back there quite a few times, and once I went back there with the local press; they were so happy that someone had set a novel in south London that they wanted to do a walk- around feature and we went to the place where the shooting was and there was a sign there saying, "Shooting: appeal for witnesses"; there's always a shooting. If I went back there I'd see it again.

–

– MF: It's that corner, isn't it?

–

– TM: Yeah, it's endless. And then, funnily enough, talking of tax bills and things, when the feature came out, someone from the Lambeth council tax office contacted me through my publishers and said, we read the article, congratulations, blah blah, and it says you were living in Hearne Hill Road at the time and our records say that you didn't pay your council tax and you owe us one hundred and twenty-nine pounds fifty-one pence or something, and I ended up having to pay it.

–

– I was thinking, when you were talking before, of that film *Hiroshima Mon Amour*, which you've probably seen, right.

–

– CM: No.

–

– TM: Oh right, it's really good. Marguerite Duras wrote the screenplay and Alain Resnais made the film. It starts with this French woman and her Japanese lover lying in bed and she's saying, I was in Hiroshima, I saw the burns victims, I saw the wreckage, and you're getting documentary footage whilst she's saying this; after a couple of minutes he just interrupts her and says, you weren't here, you didn't see anything, and it just goes on and on for about twenty minutes, and on, I saw this and I saw that, you

(fig 9)
Barry Wenden, White Bird, Oil on Canvas, 1973 (detail)

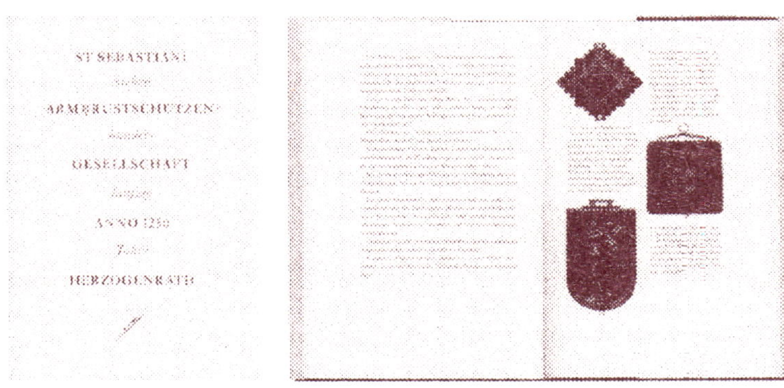

Cover and spread from a recent book for I.O. Ferdinand Verlag (1999)

18

(fig 10)
One of Ernst Bettler's less notorious pieces

never saw anything. Then later it turns out that during the end of the war she was in France; she tells this other story later to him where she was a young girl, eighteen, in this town called Never in France and she fell in love with another eighteen-year-old German soldier and then right at the end of the war the Resistance shot him and she had her head shaved and it was a disgrace because she'd had an affair with the enemy. This kind of was her trauma, so one trauma stands in for another. She feels some entitlement to have claimed to have witnessed Hiroshima even though she didn't.

18 — Binjamin Wilkomirski is a professional clarinetist and instrument maker.

—

— CM: I found an amazing quote from Wilkomirski, 18 I think he qualifies it later in the interview, but he says that he was looking through all of this Holocaust literature and he thought to himself, where am I in all of this? I just thought that was amazing because it perfectly summarises what he ended up doing, inserting himself into a grand narrative.

—

— BF: But for me, with Nazi Germany that's the one thing that always astounds me is how few people did stand up to that, so when somebody creates this fiction, which illustrates that someone has done something, it's a considerable addition to that heritage. 17

17 — Even today, the sooty mark left on the front of the factory building by the long-gone metal logo is less visible than the 'Nazis raus' spray paint around the rusted gates.

—

— RG: He just needed other bits of the story; it could have been set in Australia or it might not have said Nazi, it might have said, you stink. So it wasn't a political motivated thing at all, it was just a way to illustrate that you can do anything with your work and your mind. ◊ The Chinese whisper element that has become a part of it is beautiful and when I tell the story I never admit that it's false.

—

— JS: It's much better as well to use a provocative timescale because it validates it immediately; if it was, lets say, I'm trying to think of a neutral period of time in the country, it's probably impossible. Something that isn't tied into a much larger historical moment, which obviously WWII is. It immediately becomes of

(fig 11)
Detail from the P+H 50th anniversary posters

note. That's why people read those stories, because there is such a dominant historical narrative there that as soon as someone discovers a small subset...Tom Cruise is making a film about Josef Von Stauffenberg, the guy who tried to kill Hitler and died doing it. It's a fairly good distillation of that process.

—

— TM: By the way have you come across Donald Crowhurst, the yachtsman? Tacita Dean went and filmed his boat...

—

— CM: Is he the one who died?

—

— TM: Yeah, he faked his round-the-world race.

—

— MF: Oh yeah.

—

— TM: It's brilliant. He was in the race and he was just a bit crap, he wasn't winning or anything and they didn't have GPS so he started saying, I've rounded Cape Horn, I'm here, I'm here, faster than anyone had ever been and he just created this whole reality and it's like Major Tom in David Bowie; his wife was signing advertising deals for him for when he got home and he was a national hero and he was just sailing in circles in the South Sea and the only place for him to go was suicide. He just jumped over-board but I think that he's genuinely heroic in a way that Ellen MacArthur isn't. I mean she just sails against the roaring wave but he takes on reality and the reality principle; that's heroic and he loses, which is even better.

(fig 12)
Melody Maker adverts, 20 Jan 1979, from Lustfaust memorabilia album No7

— CM: When you take it on in that way, you have to lose; there's no – you can't win.

—

◊ TM: But winning would be fascism in a way; if you could beat reality, if you could actually impose a total reality principle, that would be complete fascism.

—

— CM: I'm reminded a little bit... this is not quite the same but it's sort of another example of people losing against reality. I read that the Italian Army after World War II, they created a whole division that was completely fictional, to convince the Russians that they had more military power than they actually had because they were worried about a communist uprising or Russian invasion; but because of the way Italian bureaucracy is set up, they can't get rid of the files for the pretend army until they've demobbed the soldiers.

—

— TM: Which they can't do...

—

— CM: ...because they never existed.

—

— TM: That's brilliant, that's really good, fantastic.

—

— CM: So they're on an eternal loser with that one as well.

—

3 — Financier moves in for M&S, by Fraser Nelson – A Monaco-based financier with close links to the billionaire Barclay brothers yesterday confirmed that he is launching a takeover bid for Marks & Spencer.

M&S shares, which rose sharply last week amid takeover speculation, fell 9% to 273p. City analysts said Philip Green, who took over the Sears retail empire earlier this year, may find it difficult to raise the £11.5 billion that would be needed to acquire M&S through a hostile bid.

Tesco refused to rule out a takeover bid for M&S and could emerge as a white knight. More than 40 million M&S shares were traded yesterday as private investors continued to speculate on the outcome of the bid battle.

For Business News turn to page 23

— TM: That's brilliant, that's the *North by Northwest* syndrome. That's the other point with fictions – and this is where the INS [3] come in as well – is that they create a space for the real. So that if you take what's essentially Kafkaesque sub-committees and so on, and you say these exist and then someone says I want to join your committee – someone from the BBC wrote to us and said, I will be a conduit for your propaganda – it becomes real and the fiction becomes a space for an event.

—

— Rasha Kahil: Definitely.

– TM: Virtually my favourite writer is Francis Ponge, who spends his time trying to describe objects like oranges and oysters, but when he describes oysters it's really the whole world.

–

– MF: I think I've heard you talking about him before in another interview – about the orange.

–

– TM: I keep going on about him. The orange? Expressing the orange like the globe.

–

– MF: You're left with a husk.

–

– TM: Yeah, and it all kind of bounced back and you've got gunk all over you and there will always be a kind of messy remainder. I think the INS is very much about looking at the materiality of the upset grand project; the blubber of the whale in Moby Dick that stops the world being a perfect white screen for Ahab to project himself onto. Ahab is a totalitarian Western white man trying to project himself onto reality and the whale is the real: it's excessive, just sheer lumps of fat and sperm and stuff. I think art and poetry and literature should engage with that surplus.

–

– CM: That reminds me of Jayson Blair, the New York Times reporter. 14 Many of his lies were really inconsequential; he would describe a field full of daffodils behind the house of the people he was going to meet, but because he'd never been there the field of daffodils didn't exist. But the people he'd lied about didn't complain because they didn't think it was important and in the end it was all of this surplus detail that tripped him up.

–

◊ MF: It could happen, it just didn't happen. I've been researching this The Priory murder in Balham. I looked at loads of South London papers. It was written about a lot in the seventies because they were thinking about demolishing the house, and the articles were full of lies about underground tunnels in the area that don't exist at all.

14 — Ms Gardner says she is trying to be strong for her husband and three other children. When she needs to get away from the calls, the e-mail messages, the websites and television images of war, Ms Gardner tends to the red, white and blue pansies potted on the front porch of her home, here in this rural suburb, north of Baltimore.

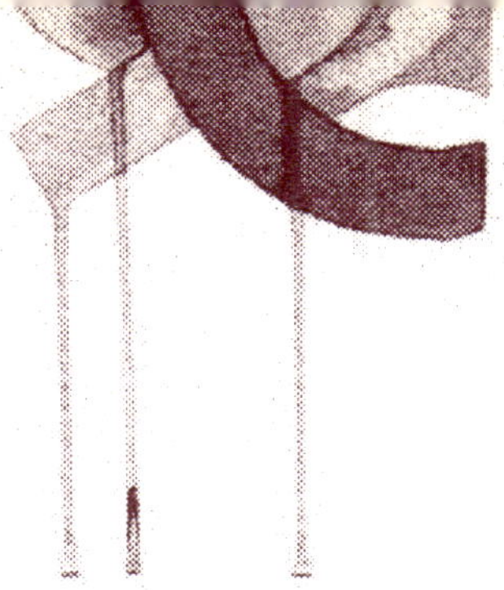

(*fig 13*)
Jamie Shovlin, Fontana Modern Masters, 2003–05 (detail)

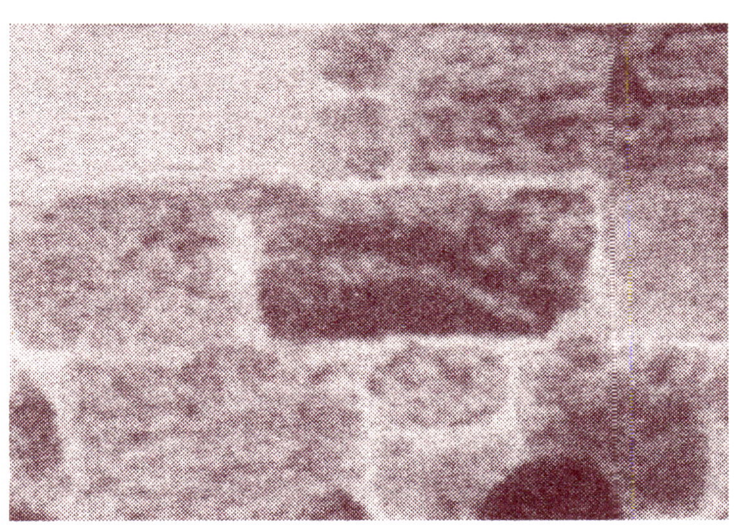

(*fig 14*)
Detail from a photograph of Naomi V. Jelish's mother

— TM: So whose were the tunnels? Were they for criminals to run around in?

—

— MF: No, no, no, well sort of. Actually, I think the idea of underground tunnels comes from the fact that there were quite a lot of asylums in the area and it's sort of a childhood urban myth.

—

— CM: They're there though, aren't they?

—

— MF: They're not underground tunnels, they're tile kilns,
but I really loved the idea of underground tunnels being in South London.

—

◊ RG: Is authenticity also validated, as you said before, by these conduits, or tunnels? Did you say vessels?

—

◊ JS: Conduits.

—

◊ RG: Conduits, yeah, those things, or I said vehicles. We'll just stick with vehicles because it's a better word. So those vehicles that you explained about, you said they could be typography. Do you see typography as a sort of... the language of it validates a fiction. Is that what you were saying before?

—

— JS: Yeah...

—

— RG: And you see the frame as the same?

—

— JS: You know, architecture, the frame, typography.

—

— RG: A vitrine?

—

— JS: They're all the same thing, they're just on smaller or larger scales of space.

—

— TM: When me and Rod were doing that Greenwich thing, [19] we went and got all the newspapers and the idea was that we'd change all the papers to fit our story but we had to change very

19 — After the Greenwich explosion, an article was picked up at the scene. It was the half of an iron ring used to tightly secure the stopper of a bottle. A corresponding half fell from Martial Bourdin's body.

ROYAL BOROUGH OF KENSINGTON AND CHELSEA

KENSINGTON CENTRAL LIBRARY
Phillimore Walk, London W8 7RX

Mon, Tues	9.30am - 8.00pm
Wed	9.30am - 1.00pm
Thurs, Fri	9.30am - 8.00pm
Sat	9.30am - 5.00pm

Renewals 0171 - 937 2542

This book must be returned on or before the latest date below. Adult readers will be charged fines on books kept beyond that date. The period of loan may be extended providing that the book is not required by another reader.

25 FEB 2000	06 AUG 2007	
16 MAR 2000	21 MAY 2009	
25 MAY 2000		
10 JUN 2000	04 OCT 2010	
12 SEP 2002	25 FEB 2011	
24 FEB 2004		
12 NOV 2005		
19 JUN 2007		

E1/845

(fig 15)
Opening pages of Kensington Central Library's copy of Fragments by Binjamin Wilkomirski.

little. We just had a word here or there to tweak. Loads of them were very melodramatic, so a reporter would go and investigate London Anarchists and describe going up the stairs of the chemistry room at the British Library like it was a den of iniquity, and how the stair creaked as he went up it, and several people congratulated me on how well written it was and I hadn't done anything at all. I hadn't touched it. People thought that we'd done the writing and we hadn't, of course. Greenwich seems so significant as well because it's zero, it's the vanishing point, it's the absolute zero degree of everything time. The fact that this guy disintegrates as he comes to that line is just perfect. ◊ It's like Orpheus being shredded in front of the underworld but this is a disintegration of fact into pure nebulous endless fictions. That line is a fiction as well; it's not like the North Pole, which is a real thing, it's just an arbitrary line.

4 — I ignored them and carried on copying the crack. I had to start again two times – the first because I'd made the scale too big to fit the whole crack in, then once more when I realised that the flipside of the wallpaper was smoother than the bubbly side, which I'd been drawing on, and so would make for a more accurate transcription. I copied it meticulously, noting in brackets aspects such as texture and colour.

—

– CM: I think that's about all...

—

– CM: One last thing I want to ask you. Earlier, Jamie mentioned sponges and we've heard Tom mention them in other interviews...

—

– TM: Sponge is to do with Francis Ponge. Okay, so his name is Francis Ponge and he writes poems about sponges a lot because they are amorphous things that take on. They soak in water and express it again but they're a bit wet. There is a book by Derrida called Signeponge, like sponge in French is éponge and Signsponge is like "signed Ponge" Signsponge. Ponge gives Derrida a copy of a book of his poems and he writes, signs Ponge, like Dear Jacques, yours signed Ponge. Derrida makes this whole play around the signed sponge and the proper name of Ponge; all the work sponges off the name and vice versa. I suppose in *Remainder* 4 I was really thinking about... he has an obsession with sponges as well when he looks at the tar and then when he's poking the bullet wound he says, "Oh yeah, it is like a sponge", as he's poking this guys flesh.

– MF: The bullet he pretty much put inside him.

–

– TM: Although it's a shotgun right? It could have been bits of shot; I didn't actually research that, I may well have got that wrong actually.

–

– MF: We won't mention it.

–

– TM: That's where the sponge comes from.

–

– RG: Great.

This is where the transcript ends

Total amount due £129.51

(fig 16)
Detail from bills sent to John English

(fig 17)
Blood on the floor of the Isaacs Gallery in Toronto after one of John Fare's 1968 performances

FEBRUARY 20, 1894.

THE ANARCHISTS IN LONDON.

ON THE MANUFACTURE OF BOMBS.

DANGEROUS INFORMATION OPEN TO ALL.

HOW LITTLE THE POLICE KNEW.

(FROM OUR SPECIAL CORRESPONDENT.)

(fig 18)
Tom McCarthy and Rod Dickinson, Greenwich Degree Zero, 2006

Appendix

(A)	*Lustfaust gig list*
(B)	*McCarthy, Tom Remainder, London: Alma Books 2007, p.62*
(C)	*Wilson, Christopher. 'I'm only a designer: The double life of Ernst Bettler' in Dot Dot Dot, Issue 2, 2001, pp. 14-18*
(D)	*Details from the 'EP' letter from Edward Duke of Windsor to Hitler*
(E)	*Diagram showing the correct alignment of Ernst Bettler's P+H posters*
(F)	*Annotations from John Ivesmail's essay on Naomi V. Jelish*
(G)	*Photo which accompanied the New York Times article 'Watching and praying as a sons fate unfolds.' (New York: March 25, 2003)*
(H)	*Enquiry into Ernst Bettler and P+H posted on Google answers*

(A)

LUSTFAUST GIG LIST:

- Berlin, Der Blue Auster Bar, 51 Pfalzburgerstrasse, Friday November 19 1976
- Berlin, Der Blue Auster Bar, 51 Pfalzburgerstrasse, Monday December 14 1976
- Schoenberg/Kreuzberg, The Risiko, Monday January 24 1977
- Berlin, Der Blue Auster Bar, 51 Pfalzburgerstrasse, Thursday 24 February 1977
- Berlin, Der Blue Auster Bar, 51 Pfalzburgerstrasse, Friday 25 February 1977
- Berlin, Der Blue Auster Bar, 51 Pfalzburgerstrasse, Saturday 26 February 1977
- Gütersloh, Stadhalle, Friedrichstr. 13, Tuesday June 28, 1977
- Hannover, Rotation, Goseriede 9, Thursday June 30, 1977
- Hannover, Rotation, Goseriede 9, Friday July 1, 1977
- Hamburg, Markthalle, Saturday July 2, 1977
- Paderborn, Westfalenkolleg, Tuesday July 5, 1977
- Bielefeld, Audimax, Universitätstrasse, Wednesday July 6, 1977
- Bielefeld, Audimax, Universitätstrasse, Thursday July 7, 1977
- Köln, Sartory-Säle, Saturday July 9, 1977
- Köln, Sartory-Säle, Sunday July 10, 1977
- Bad Breisig, Jahnhalle, Monday July 11, 1977
- Saarbrücken, Congresshalle, Hafenstrasse, Wednesday July 13, 1977
- Berlin, Metropol, Nollendorfplatz 1, Friday 15 July, 1977
- Berlin, Der Blue Auster Bar, 51 Pfalzburgerstrasse, Monday 28 November, 1977
- Oldenburg, Renaissance, Alexanderstr. 1, Thursday 1 December, 1977
- Hamburg, Fabrik, Barner Str. 36, Saturday 3 December, 1977
- Hamburg, Fabrik, Barner Str. 36, Sunday 4 December, 1977
- Hamburg, Top Ten Club, 136 Reeperbahn, Monday 5 December, 1977
- Hamburg, Kaiserkeller, 38 Grosse Freiheit, Tuesday 6 December, 1977
- Hamburg, Indra Club, 64 Grosse Freiheit, Monday 12 December, 1977
- Köln, Palazzoschokko, Friday 16 December, 1977
- München, Schwabingerbräu, Feilitzstr. 3, Monday 19 December, 1977
- Weissenhoe, Toast Club, Haupstrasse 24-27, Thursday 22 December, 1977
- Wiesbaden, Wartburg Music Hall, Schwalbacher Strasse 51, Monday 26 December, 1977
- Wiesbaden, Wartburg Music Hall, Schwalbacher Strasse 51, Tuesday 27 December, 1977
- Köln-Mülheim, Stadthalle, Jahn-Wellemstr. 2, Friday 30 December, 1977
- Regional (South East) final for Melody Maker Rock/Folk Concert, Red Lion, Gravesend, Tuesday 14 February, 1978
- The Triad, Bishop's Stortford, Tuesday 21 June, 1978

- Scamps, Hemel Hempstead Herts, Thursday 23 June, 1978
- Oscar's, Newbury Park, London, Tuesday 28 June, 1978
- Dacorum Pavilion, Marlowes, Hemel Hempstead, Herts, Friday 31 June, 1978
- Melody Maker Rock/Folk Contest 1978 National Final, The Round House, Sunday 2 July, 1978
- – Berlin, Der Blue Auster Bar, 51 Pfalzburgerstrasse, Friday 15 September, 1978
- Berlin, Der Blue Auster Bar, 51 Pfalzburgerstrasse, Friday 22 September, 1978
- Berlin, Der Blue Auster Bar, 51 Pfalzburgerstrasse, Saturday 20 January, 1979
- Schoenberg/Kreuzberg, The Risiko, Wednesday 14 February, 1979
- Berlin, Der Blue Auster Bar, 51 Pfalzburgerstrasse, Friday 16 February, 1979
- Berlin, Quasimodo, Berlin, Kantstrasse 12a, Monday 12 March, 1979
- Berlin, Der Blue Auster Bar, 51 Pfalzburgerstrasse, Wednesday 1 August, 1979
- Berlin, Der Blue Auster Bar, 51 Pfalzburgerstrasse, Thursday 2 August, 1979
- Berlin, Quasimodo, Berlin, Kantstrasse 12a, Friday 10 August, 1979
- Gütersloh, Stadhalle, Friedrichstr. 13, Thursday 25 October, 1979
- Hamburg, Kaiserkeller, 38 Grosse Freiheit, Monday 29 October, 1979
- Hamburg, Kaiserkeller, 38 Grosse Freiheit, Tuesday 30 October, 1979
- Hamburg, Fabrik, Barner Str. 36, Wednesday 31 October, 1979
- Hannover, Rotation, Goseriede 9, Friday 2 November, 1979
- Grootebroek, Kwot, Raadhuislaan 17, Tuesday 6 November, 1979
- Markelo, Bills Bar, Van Amerongenstraat, Thursday 8 November, 1979
- Groningen, Tante Vera, Oosterstraat 44, Saturday 10 November, 1979
- Bergen op Zoom, Korenbeurs, Potterstraat 50, Sunday 11 November, 1979
- Rotterdam, Eksit, Eendrachtstraat 87a, Tuesday 13 November, 1979
- Rotterdam, Eksit, Eendrachtstraat 87a, Wednesday 14 November, 1979
- Brussels, Théâtre 140, Monday 19 November, 1979
- Saarlandhalle, Saarbrucken, Tuesday 18 March, 1980
- Frederich Eberthalle, Ludwigshafen, Wednesday 19 March, 1980
- Musterlandhalle, Munster, Thursday 10 March, 1980
- Deutschlandhalle, Berlin, Friday 11 March, 1980
- Islington Hope and Anchor, Wednesday 20 August, 1980
- Deptford Arms, Thursday 21 August, 1980
- Reading Festival, Saturday 23 August, 1980
- Woolwich Tramshed, Monday 25 August, 1980
- Stoke Newington Pegasus, Tuesday 26 August, 1980
- Fulham Golden Lion, Wednesday, 27 August, 1980

I remembered how it

(B) had felt inside my apartment, moving through it: from the bathroom with the crack in its wall to the kitchen and living room, the way plants hanging in baskets from the ceiling had rustled as I'd passed them, how I'd turned half sideways as I'd passed the kitchen unit's waist-high edge – turned sideways and then deftly back again in one continuous movement, letting my shirt brush the woodwork. I remembered how all this had felt.

(C)

Would the next Ernst Bettler please stand up?

Despite the fact that his political views have obviously not changed, the work which Bettler has produced in London over the last three decades shows none of his former thirst for subversion. In place of company-toppling posters and booby-trapped corporate identities there is a neat stack of books for small publishers in Britain, Switzerland and the Netherlands. Many of them are related to charities of one form or another. There are a fair number of art catalogues ('I'm allowed one vice!'). All are assembled with great consideration for the material they contain and for the people who will read them. They exemplify many of the things which Jost Hochuli and Robin Kinross would say are virtues in book design. They are 'Nice Things'. They aren't doing anyone any harm. But all the same, I can't help feeling a pang of disappointment. Though I appreciate their beauty, the books represent to me a fall from grace. Wistfully imagining this Swiss expatriate nipping a soon-to-overinflate concern such as Virgin in its bud at some appropriate point in the late 70s, I ask if he doesn't ever think of a return to his bad old ways?

'Do you like the Rolling Stones?'

Pardon?

'How old is Mick Jagger? Fifty-five? Fifty-six? And there he is on that stage, still telling us that he can't get his satisfaction. An eighteen-year-old

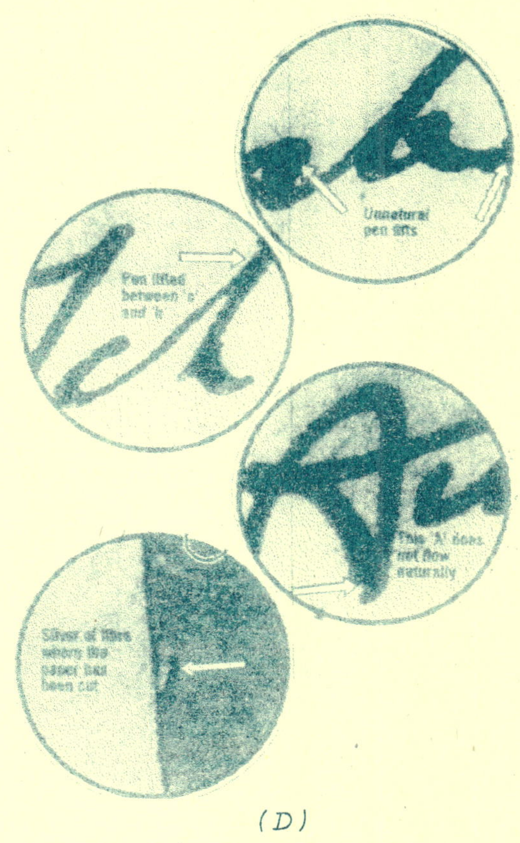

Unnatural pen lifts
Pen lifted between 'c' and 'h'
This 'A' does not flow naturally
Sliver of fibres where the paper has been cut

(D)

NAZI

(E)

John Ivesmail

(F)

Six pictures of soldiers, sailors and airmen deployed in Iraq were hanging in the lobby of St. Francis Xavier Roman Catholic Church, where the Rev. Jeffrey S. Dauses asked parishioners to pray for President Bush, the men and women in the armed services and the innocents of Iraq.

At 9:45 a.m., the family arrived back home and waited about 40 minutes before returning to the nonstop television war coverage where they were almost immediately greeted

(G)

Doug Mills/The New York Times

Martha Gardner planting a group of red, white and blue pansies.

Question

Subject: **Swiss Pharmaceutical company alleged to be Nazis**
Category: Miscellaneous
Asked by: **ch1cken-ga**
List Price: $10.00

Posted: 04 Dec 2002 05:32 PST
Expires: 03 Jan 2003 05:32 PST
Question ID: 119027

I need to check if a swiss company called Pfäfferli + Huber AG actually existed in post war Switzerland. Already know about the reports in the magazines Adbusters + Dot Dot Dot but http://www.leftwatch.com/discussion/fullthread$msgnum=1199 has alleged this to be a hoax - need to ascertain if there ever was this company or a drug called Contrazipan. Cheers. Michael. Happy hunting

Request for Question Clarification by scriptor-ga on 04 Dec 2002 06:08 PST
Dear ch1cken,

No final proof so far, but certain evidence: *(H)*

- The family name "Pfäfferli" does not exist anywhere in a German-speaking country. I checked address and phone directories as well as genealocial databases. It is a fake name, made up to sound "typically Swiss" (the suffix "-li" is considered a cliché ending of Swiss names). The family name "Pfefferli" - pronounced much the same - does exist, but since the poster shows the word clearly with an a-umlaut, it has absolutely nothing to do with it.

- "Contrazipan" does not show up anywhere, neither in tables listing pharmaceutical substances, nor in trademark databases. A quick call at a pharmacist revealed that the name would not even make sense cr fit anywhere in the nomenclature of medical substances names.

- The poster allegedly promoting Contrazipan has nothing in common with late 50s' advertisement style. Since I have quite a good knowledge of European 50s' design, I can say for sure that the picture would be an anachronist contaminant.

Regards,
Scriptor

Clarification of Question by ch1cken-ga on 04 Dec 2002 07:29 PST
mmmmm
Well The only extra information I have is that a poster was alledgedly designed for Pfäfferli + Huber AG by a designer named Ernst Bettler in 1959. The story goes that there were four posters, one of which is the 'a' of the word Nazi.
The story was written by a UK based design writer called Christopher Wilson, who until recently swapped e-mails with me at the Royal College of Art under the email address of christopher.wilson@rca.ac.uk. He assures me it is legit but has thusfar offered no substantiation. There was apparently something on Lines and Spline s about this but it seems ot be down. Actually, the poster style is quite a good approximation of the infamous 'swiss style' of design of the time, so not sure I agree with you there. The creidt of the 'poster' says Pfäfferli + Huber AG, Burgwald CH, incidentally.
As it happens, I've never heard of a swiss designer called Ernst Bettler either.

Clarification of Question by ch1cken-ga on 12 Dec 2002 04:08 PST
any more news on this guys?

The author of the article is refusing to supply any 'proof' of the designer or the client, so I'm keen to nail this as soon as possible

Thanks

Floating Footnotes

9 — Yves Fissiault's wife was the starlet Mia L'amar; her most well-known role was in the film Exile in Mexico, directed by Bodo Muscotti.

12 — But art's dirty secret is inauthenticity all the way down, a series of repetitions and re-enactments that attempt to cover over the traumatic event of materiality. As Joyce realised in Finnegans Wake, literature is rich trash to be recycled and adapted in a commodius vicus of recirculation. Yet, there is always a remainder that remains: a shard, a leftover, a trace, a residual. Everything must leave some kind of mark.

20 — Fare's earliest 'appearance' gestures consisted in the public removal of his clothing, accompanied at times by such trimmings as the pressing of 'his bare arse' against the street-level windows of particularly genteel restaurants. These high deeds nearly always led to his arrest and/or hospitalisation, if only because it never, apparently, occurred to him to avoid consequences, however predictable or unpleasant. Fare was again arrested when, early one morning, a frightfully Danish police constable found it impossible to ignore Fare's curious treatment of a parked motorcar. Fare had in fact already spent several hours fastening random objects to the vehicle in question with epoxy resin. These included: golf balls, milk bottles, brooms, unopened tins of food, one dead cat, his own clothes, old gramophone records, dozens of biros, and over a hundred forks and spoons.

V

V

V

Exposure

V

Tuesday 20th May, Seminar Room One

Ryan Gander, Jamie Shovlin, Debbie Cook, Rasha Kahil, Catrin Morgan, Mireille Fauchon, Hannah Rae Alton, Ben Freeman & Annabel Fraser

– Shall we begin by reading a statement from Maki and Kajsa?

To whom it may concern, we are here with you today,[1] not really but with your help we can be. If you wish and agree ~~to lie~~ we can pretend to be present at this conversation.

– Everybody agreed to verify Maki and Kajsa's presence with the exception of Ryan, who maintained that they were not there. In order to sustain the integrity of their position, Maki and Kajsa made no further contributions to the discussion.

—

– Catrin Morgan: Whilst we were researching for this talk we came across a theory of disingenuity created by ~~a~~ psychiatrist in the University of Cardiff, Dr David Trevellian,[5] to describe a phenomena that follows post-traumatic stress. ~~It~~ is a strategy used by patients who believe that they can bring themselves closer to reality through the use of lies or fictions. I should explain this is not compulsive lying, which is a different psychological phenomenon and doesn't obviously benefit the liar. The patient creates a space in which they are surrounded by fictions allowing them to dodge the perceived surface reality. They believe this artificial psychological environment is the only way they can determine the truth – by creating layer upon layer of fiction. We read about one particular case study, the story of a man who had suffered a massive head injury and subsequently developed an obsession with artificially recreating moments prior to the injury. He received quite a lot of compensation, as the accident that happened wasn't his fault, and he used this money to recreate remembered events. We thought it might be useful to use the theory of disingenuity to describe artists, such as yourselves, who use fictions or lies in your work.

—

1 — Maki Suzuki and Kajsa Stahl were not in fact present at the original conversation.

5 — Dr David Trevellian is a psychologist working at the University of Cardiff. His most important and well-received paper so far in his career has been *Disingenuity: Re-enacting an authentic past, rupturing a deauthenticated present*, which outlines his theories on disingenuous behaviour in patients suffering from post-traumatic stress.

Monday 30th March, The Barbican café
Tom McCarthy, Catrin Morgan, Mireille Fauchon

— Catrin Morgan: Could you start by describing your practice?

—

— Tom McCarthy: 2 Well I'm primarily a novelist. I've veered into art practice by accident really, in the last decade or so, through this construct of the *International Necronautical Society*. 3 I was interested in manifestos as a literary form and was reading a lot of Blanchot and Derrida, and thinking about death as a theme in philosophy. I wrote a death manifesto and distributed it around the art world. I didn't really know what would happen; it was just an experiment but it was received as a conceptual art project and then took off from there. I see that work as having its origins in fiction as much as *Remainder*. 4

—

— Mireille Fauchon: We have been reading Bourriaud's *Altermodern* and wondering if you felt that the way in which you work required a new terminology?

2 — Tom McCarthy – 'English fiction's new laureate of disappointment' (Time Out, September 2007) – is a writer and artist. He was born in 1969 and lives in a tower block in London. Tom grew up in Greenwich, south London, and studied English at New College, Oxford. After a couple of years in Prague in the early 1990s, he lived in Amsterdam as literary editor of the local Time Out, and later worked in British television as well as co-editing Mute magazine.

His debut novel, *Remainder*, was first published in November 2005 by Paris-based art press Metronome. His latest novel, *C*, was published in 2010. His ongoing project the *International Necronautical Society*, a semi-fictitious avant-garde network that surfaces through publications, proclamations, denunciations and live events, has been described by Untitled Magazine as 'the most comprehensive total art work we have seen in years'. In 2003 the INS broke into the BBC website and inserted propaganda into its source code. The following year, they set up a broadcasting unit at the ICA from which more than forty 'agents' generated non-stop poem-codes, which were transmitted over FM radio in London and by internet to collaborating radio stations around the world.

3 — Founded in 1999 by Tom McCarthy, the *International Necronautical Society* (INS) spreads itself as both fiction and actuality, often blurring the two. 'Famously described as "replaying the avant-garde along the faultline of death"' (Art Monthly, London), the INS inhabits and appropriates a variety of art forms and cultural 'moments' from the defunct avant-gardes of the last century to the political, corporate and conspiratorial organisations they mimicked. The INS's manifestos, proclamations, reports, broadcasts, hearings, inspectorates, departments, committees and sub-committees are the vehicles for interventions in the space of art, fiction, philosophy and media.

4 — "I mix plaster so it won't crack", Kevin sniffed. "Well do wrong what you usually do right, then," I said. He mixed it much drier – but then the cracks are sort of random: you can't second guess which way they'll go. It took another day of experimenting: trying salt and razor blades and all sorts of devices to get it to crack the right way. Kevin whistled the same tune for hours while he did this: a pop tune, one I thought I recognised. He didn't whistle the whole tune – just one bit of it over and over.

◊ Ryan Gander: 6 You're using the word lying, but I don't know if the subject should be lying because lying has negative connotations about cheating or corrupting people. Maybe it would be better to redefine lying or use other words. My dad always says, you should never let a lie get in the way of a good story.

—

◊ Jamie Shovlin: 7 Isn't it never let the truth get in the way of a good story? 8

6 — Gander's work comprises manifestations of irresolution. *A sheet of paper on which I was about to draw, as it slipped from my table and fell to the floor* (2008) remains eternally un papier vide, the blank page that yearns to be written on but is completely inaccessible. As a motif it is suspended in a hundred glass spheres, scattered on the floor like autumn leaves. In *Man on a Bridge – A Study of David Lange* (2008), a 16mm film transferred to an HD projection, we see a well-known British actor, Roger Lloyd Pack, walk across a bridge until he is drawn to the edge to concentrate on an incident below. He does it again and again, slightly differently, fifty times in a sequence of Sisyphean repetition, but we never get closer to finding out what it is that attracts his attention. Words have been written on a gallery wall but they have been plastered over; there are maps that confuse street layouts from the past with those that presently exist; there are a set of wooden blocks that make up an alphabet as illegible as it is utopian... and so on. Presiding over all is the face of a man in anguish, part of the wall drawing *Oh no not again* (2008).

7 — Jamie Shovlin (b. 1978) is interested in the tension between truth and fiction, reality and invention, history and memory. Shovlin is perhaps best known for a series of ambitious projects, including *Naomi V. Jelish* (2001–4) and *Lustfaust: A Folk Anthology 1976–81* (2003–6), in which the artist constructed extensive and seemingly real archives, which were then revealed to be elaborate fictions. The 'Jelish' archive consists of drawings, newspaper cuttings and other ephemera relating to a 13-year-old prodigy who had disappeared with her family in mysterious circumstances, along with notes and inventories made by John Ivesmail, a 'retired science teacher at Naomi's school [who had] unearthed a collection of the teenager's remarkable drawings' (both Naomi V. Jelish and John Ivesmail are anagrams). A second archive, 'curated by Jamie Shovlin' and purporting to document the activities of a German 'experimental noise band' from the 1970s, *Lustfaust: A Folk Anthology 1976–1981* (2003–6) contained cassette covers and posters apparently made by the band's supporters, fan reminiscences, a filmed interview with one of the band members and even short samples of Lustfaust's music. When these works were shown at the Saatchi Gallery, London, Freight & Volume in New York and in 'Beck's Futures' at the ICA, Shovlin was hailed as an art-world hoaxer par excellence.

Shovlin's *Fontana Modern Masters* book series (2003–5) extended the artist's interest in exploring the fallibility of classification systems, exploring an absurdist premise: that intellectual achievement can be ranked or scored according to a points system. Fascinated by the ambition and appearance of Fontana's series of books, 'Modern Masters' (which set out to examine the thinkers 'who have changed and are changing the life and thought of our age'), Shovlin set about constructing a system that would allow him to 'accurately' produce the covers of the books that Fontana had announced it was to publish but which, for whatever reason, had never appeared.

Jamie Shovlin studied at the Royal College of Art and lives and works in London. Institutional solo exhibitions include 'In Search of Perfect Harmony' at Tate Britain, London (2006) and 'Aggregate' at City Gallery, Leicester; Artsway; Talbot Rice Art Gallery, Edinburgh and Hatton Gallery, Newcastle (2006–7). He had a solo exhibition at the Contemporary Art Museum in Rome (MACRO) in October 2010.

8 — Statements marked by ◊ are entirely fictional.

– TM: I don't think what I'm doing really needs a new category, I think the old categories are good enough, the really old ones like Art for example. You mention Nicolas Bourriaud and he gets a lot of criticism. I'm quite pro him because I think he does what curators should do; gives us conceptual prisms for looking at art in new ways. It does seem to me that all his branded conceptual terms like *Altermodern* and *Relational Aesthetics* are basically ways of saying Art. Art has always been Relational Aesthetics and it's always been Altermodern, which is the point Simon and I made in that INS declaration. There is a tension between what might be fiction or literature on one hand and visual art on the other, or philosophy on a third hand and then of course there's politics. The border has been breached; philosophy haunts literature, literature haunts philosophy and politics haunts both of them.

— CM: Well maybe we could use disingenuity as it is applied by Trevellian to describe a strategy for coming closer to reality rather than an attempt to cheat people. Shall we begin by talking about the artist's identity? Is being an artist always some kind of performance or is it necessary to create a construct? Can you talk to us about the Naomi V. Jelish project? [10]

—

— JS: I find being a person is being a performance. Whilst we're here speaking we're all abiding by a certain code of delivery. Before I talk about Naomi V. Jelish I'd like to say that I've retrospectively reorganised my thinking about the project into a very ordered account. In reality it was totally haphazard; I began making those drawings whilst still a student at the RCA. The dominant way of working at that time was autobiographically. So I decided I would make something that was deliberately not my own. At a certain point I became quite aware that I was making decisions in a linear way; one image would relate to another and that was leading to a narrative. This made me a little self-conscious and I decided that there needed to be someone accountable. That's where Naomi V. Jelish came from; it's an anagram of my name. To account for the narrative element in the organisation of the drawings I created a second character, John Ivesmail. [11] It began with Naomi, whose work is curated by John, an amateur curator or a local historian. My fictional connection was that I lodged with him and that's how I gained access to the archive of Naomi's work and arranged it according to his wishes.

—

— My interest in the project has been slightly sidelined by the fact that it has been labelled a hoax. I hate that word. I remember when I first heard that and I had to look up what it really meant in a dictionary. It made me think, is that what I meant? What I was really interested in was how in essence this story was tabloid material but it had been translated using a museological grammar, and this supplanted the basic melodrama of the story and replaced it with seriousness. The weight of something's presentation impacts upon its actual content and you can tell any story by delivering it in the right way to the right audience.

10 | 11 — If you are particularly sharp-eyed (or a Scrabble addict) you may have noticed that both 'Naomi V. Jelish' and 'John Ivesmail' are anagrams of 'Jamie Shovlin'. You might begin to suspect that this compelling tale is a shaggy-dog story, straight from the murky depths of Shovlin's imagination.

(fig 1)
Ryan Gander

(fig 2)
Jamie Shovlin

(fig 3)
Tom McCarthy

– CM: Do you think that using fictions can be a way of tripping someone up when they're looking at your work? Is it a strategy for catching them and persuading them to pay more attention?

–

– JS: I always have a problem with words like trap and trip because they're so negative. I don't know if there's any kind of opposition to them – phrases that are positive – entrypoint for example?

–

– RG: Snare.

–

– JS: Bear trap.

–

– Ben Freeman: I'd like to pick up on the subject of hoaxes and to introduce the term prank. I did a project once where for just a couple of days I stood outside Selfridges dressed up in a suit and pretending to work for a magazine casting for models, but we were asking the most unlikely people. We built up a series of portraits of people trying to look their best but whilst doing so knowing that there's no way that they could be models. To all intents and purposes it could have been a Jeremy Beadle-type prank but the outcome was more meaningful. I don't see anything negative in

– TM: We never thought of The Declaration on Inauthenticity 12 as a hoax; then someone, a quite conservative figure in the audience who for all I know was an actor who had been hired by someone else, came along and said, "We've been had". It's to do with people's expectations of authenticity. They want authenticity to look a particular way – for the relationship between a proper name and a body to be fixed. Even when that relationship is the subject being interrogated they still don't want it to be put at stake.

—

There's a category error built into our society and into our psychic structuring. We're constructs and we're constructed through language, society, the law and desire, and all these other things. Loaded, almost as an afterthought, into these constructs is an opposing ideology; that we're not constructs, we're absolutely each of us unique, natural, spiritual, true identities, and this is what we should be expressing. This goes completely against the actual nature of us, so we're all living out an irreconcilable contradiction.

12 — Two actors posing as Tom McCarthy and the INS philosopher-in-chief Simon Critchley delivered the *Joint Declaration on Inauthenticity* at Tate Modern, at four thirty on Saturday, 17 January 2009.

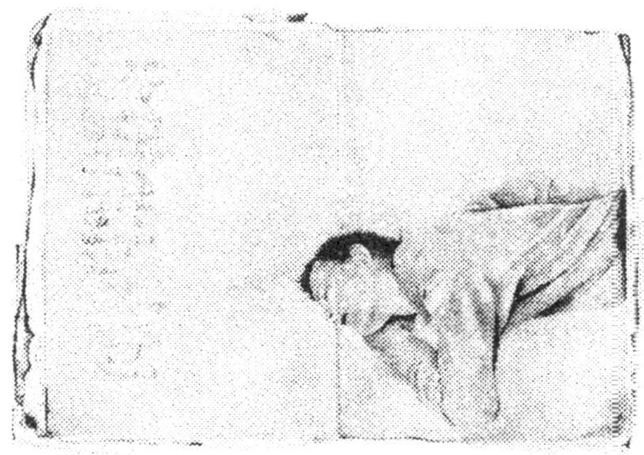

(fig 5)
Pages from Naomi V. Jelish's Sketchbook #10

borrowing from the behaviour of hoaxes and pranks. Hoaxes are seen as something cheap, whereas in my world that behaviour or methodology can lead to outcomes that are respectable.

—

– CM: I think that using the word hoax prescribes an intention.

—

– RG: It is also something to do with duration. Hoaxes are short-lived and not respectable. What Jamie's talking about is an obsessive making of the work that is a reason for doing it at all. It's not so much to do with the spectator, trying to trick them or convince them or change the way the work is read. It is more about the making, and that acts as a catalyst.

—

– BF: There was a man who was arrested recently for forging documents in military libraries to back up his false claims that Churchill had been collaborating with the Nazis through the Secret Service. [13] To me that was a hoax. It was a prolonged and very in-depth hoax, and his intention was to deceive to further his political aims. That's what sets it apart from an artwork.

—

– CM: People might be anxious to give a name to what Ryan and Jamie do because the strategy they are using distances them from their audience. The fiction comes between the artist and the audience and I think it creates an anxiety to work out what their intentions are.

—

13 — Perhaps this was the true scenario: Allen, a self-styled 'eminent historian', stumbled on the documents during painstaking research that took him to files left untouched by other historians; then, after his books were published and unknown forces read about his discoveries, the only way they (presumably modern British Intelligence agents) could discredit him was to substitute forgeries in the files for the genuine 'smoking gun' documents.

But the police investigation, relying on Forensic Science Service tests, finally revealed that this had not just happened a few times. In all, there were 29 forged documents, each typed on one of only four typewriters. They were placed in 12 separate files, and cited at least once in one or more of Allen's three books. In fact, according to the experts at the archives, documents now shown to be forgeries supported controversial arguments central to each of Allen's books: in *Hidden Agenda*, five documents now known to be forged helped justify his claim that the Duke of Windsor betrayed military secrets to Hitler; in *The Hitler/Hess Deception*, 13 bogus papers supported Allen's contention that, in 1941, British Intelligence used members of the Royal Family to fool the Nazis into thinking Britain was on the verge of a pro-German putsch; in *Himmler's Secret War*, 22 counterfeit papers also underpinned the book's core claims that British Intelligence played mind games with Himmler to encourage him to betray Hitler from 1943 onwards, and that ultimately they murdered the SS chief.

None of these forged documents was cited in any other works of history. Allen disputes this, but has not provided any citations.

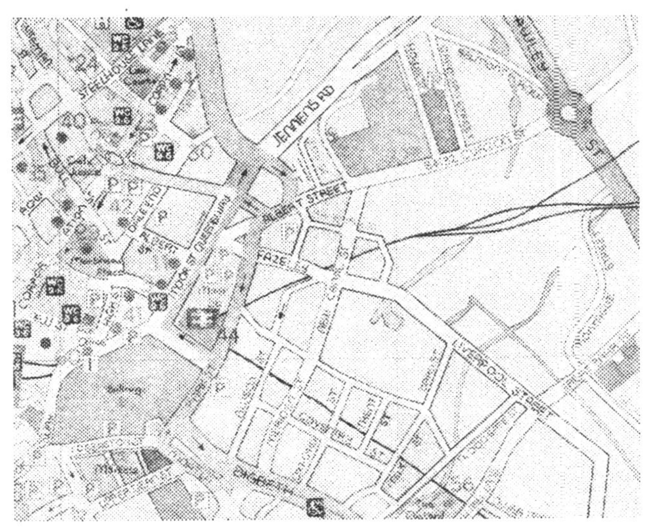

(fig 6)
Ryan Gander, Your life in four acts – Forward, 2008

(fig 7)
Ryan Gander, A Future Lorem Ipsum, 2006

— JS: It all comes down to motive. In a hoax, the motive is the reveal, that moment at which somebody gets very angry or very upset and then the hoaxer turns around and says actually it's not real. That's the moment of entertainment.

—

◊ Annabel Fraser: Fiction writers don't provoke this kind of discussion and I don't understand why?

◊ JS: That's the analogy I always use.

—

◊ RG: Look at the painting in this room; none of the things it represents are real. It's not a landscape, it's a painting of a landscape. All artists deal in fiction. It's just whether the manipulation is revealed or not. In a hoax, it would be called the punchline moment. I don't know what you call it in what we do. It can be categorised in three ways: fictions created in the world and documented in art, fictions represented within an artwork or fictions that are never revealed.

—

— CM: There are all the degrees in-between as well.

—

— RG: Jamie, in the work we are discussing the audience should understand that they are looking at a fiction. Have you ever produced a piece of work in which the audience doesn't know it's fictional?

—

— JS: I never say, because in a way they are the same thing. Whereabouts in a piece of work are the fake/fiction, truth/non-truth divides? When my mum tells me a story I know her mind isn't a recording device, it's a sponge that lets water in and out.

— CM: You have another identity as an author, does that make you freer to never have to reveal yourself as the artist?

—

— TM: I found it enormously difficult to get my fiction into print initially because it was deemed uncommercial. It was published in the art world initially. Meanwhile I found within art I could play out fictional ideas in a way that didn't need to be commodified.

(fig 8)
Ryan Gander, The Klingon smiles and simply replies..., 2008

— TM: Sponges are related to Francis Ponge. His name is Francis Ponge and he writes poems about sponges because they are amorphous things that take on water and express it again, but they stay a bit wet. There is a book by Derrida called Signeponge; sponge

(fig 4)
The cover of the Metronome edition of Remainder, 2005

– JS: When I start to make a piece of work I think about the frame it is going to go in. The frame is the context the story is being told in and that affects how it is understood. It's exactly the same thing; there's a pre-existing structural framework whether you're telling a story verbally or in an exhibition.

—

◊ RG: What was the word you used before? Chambers?

—

◊ JS: Conduits, you said vehicles.

—

◊ RG: We'll just stick with vehicles; it's a better word. You said that one of the vehicles could be typographical. Does a certain type of typography validate a fiction? Is that what you were saying before? Is the frame the same thing?

—

– JS: Architecture, frames and typography, they're all the same thing, they're just on smaller or larger scales of space.

—

– RG: Would you say mixing truth in with fiction is one of those vehicles as well?

—

– JS: Truth is a very awkward term because there's no agreed deception – sorry, Freudian slip – conception of what it is. It's like a story; it might be defined as the main story that we all abide by. Is my mum real? Is Naomi V. Jelish real? I hope my mum's real. You never know. After I did a piece of work about her, one of the first things that appeared in the press was that she wasn't real. That really pissed her off but I thought it would have been so much better if I'd done that instead.

in French is éponge and Signsponge is like "signed Ponge" – Signsponge. Francis Ponge gives Derrida a copy of a book of his poems and he writes, Signs Ponge. Derrida then makes this whole play around the signed sponge and the proper name of Ponge. In *Remainder*, the protagonist also has an obsession with sponges, when he looks at the tar and then when he's poking the bullet wound he says, "Oh yeah, it is like a sponge." As he's poking this guy's flesh. That's where the sponge comes from.

(fig 9)
Barry Wenden, White Bird, Oil on Canvas, 1973

◊ Hannah Rae Alton: I was really interested in the idea of adopting an alter ego as an excuse to make a certain piece of work. My alter ego gets all the bus fines. It is a way of creating a person who fulfils a smaller function than the entire person normally would. 15

— JS: Something that was important was the kind of work Naomi V. Jelish makes. I looked at the sketchbooks belonging to real thirteen-year-old girls and they were really boring – full of Forever Friends and copies from cards – no dramatic narrative. Instead, I filled Naomi's sketchbook with things like horses and flowers. So actually the project shows the stereotypical view of a thirteen-year-old girl as seen through the eyes of a twenty-four-year-old man. This left it vulnerable to criticism. I remember being very careful about how I justified what I was doing, and so every image on that project came from somewhere else, mostly from how-to-draw books. It's circular; this is what we tell a thirteen year old they should draw presented as what a thirteen year old did draw.

—

— MF: Something you've mentioned before in relation to *Lustfaust* 16 was being able to make work that you wouldn't necessarily make under your own name.

15 — John English is the alter ego of Hannah Rae

16 — I have less time for a twit called Jamie Shovlin, who exhibited a project at the Beck's Futures exhibition in 2006 devoted to the German electro-doom band *Lustfaust*. Posing as a fan of the band, Shovlin organised huge amounts of information about *Lustfaust* into an archival cornucopia that appeared to follow the boys from rise to stasis. I had never heard of *Lustfaust* and German electro-doom is not my bag, so there was absolutely no reason to suspect the band was an invention. Only years later, when someone got into my Wikipedia page and gleefully edited the *Lustfaust* story, did I realise I had been duped.

– CM: Tom, are you using the protagonist in *Remainder* in a similar way? Is he a character created to pursue an idea?

–

– TM: When I first had the idea for *Remainder* my initial thought wasn't a novel. I had this moment of déjà vu in a bathroom, exactly like the protagonist, and I thought, I want to do that. It could have been an art piece, then I thought, maybe that's not really that interesting. I'd need the whole building, I'd want the cats, then it gets interesting. In fact, it's only really interesting if you can expand into the street. You'd have to have the shoot-out and even that's not enough. You would need to do the bank heist, then I realised it would have to be a novel.

(fig 10)
Ernst Bettler

— JS: The phrase I use for this is repository of bad ideas. I have hundreds of ideas that don't get that far into the process because they're crap. Is it the same for you, Ryan? I decided that through this project I would be able to exercise these bad ideas. It was a lot of fun actually because these are things you can't normally do because they'd get trashed, and rightly so. If you're putting yourself in the mind of a fifteen-year-old boy from Idaho then they're permissible.

—

— CM: I'd like us to move on to the artist's relationship with the fiction they've created. Ryan, I heard you make the point that when your maps go out into the world, it's almost nicer than when they're in a gallery context. Do you feel that they've left you and taken on a life of their own?

—

— RG: For some of the museums I show at, I have a thousand maps printed that are copies of tourist maps, the kind of thing that is usually freely distributed by hotels. Then I get the maps from 1901 and I put streets back that used to be there but have been removed, because big municipal modernist buildings have been put in. Not necessarily modernist, it could be any type of building but it's usually a civic building. The Barbican is a good example; during the war that whole area was bombed so where there used to be streets there are now municipal buildings. I put back the streets that don't exist any more. The maps are placed in a cardboard box outside of the gallery space but they're listed on the work list. You can pick them up and use them and not realise that they're works of art. We also use guerrilla tactics; if you walk into a hotel in Sheffield with a pad of tourist maps and say it's a delivery, they start giving them out and using them. Sometimes this leads to an ethical decision. When we produced a map for Birmingham, I thought people could actually hurt themselves because there are a lot of motorways and slip roads and things. Imagine an old couple in a car having a row about directions because the map's wrong; there is a potential for disaster.

—

— AF: Is there a clue anywhere?

—

— RG: A clue to the changes? No.

—

(fig 11)
One of the P+H 50th anniversary posters

– BF: If someone who is not interested in art and has never heard of you picks up the map and uses it, are they still engaging in a work of art?

–

– RG: I don't know if it's possible to be engaged in a work of art unless you know it's art; it's just something that is happening. Usually it's more interesting than what is happening in art though. When the maps are distributed with guerrilla tactics, they have their own place in the world. There are lots of offshoot moments in reality that are caused by them. Like in *Back to the Future* when Marty McFly changes history, what happens is quite magical. It is just a piece of paper but it creates a chain of events. Maybe one of you will fall in love because of this map, you just never know.

(fig 12)
Lustfaust

– TM: I remember at a conference in Canada I was asked, how does my relationship to my work change when it's out in the world, and I answered that I didn't feel like it was my work in the first place, and everyone laughed as if I was making a joke but I really wasn't. The author is dead. If you're seriously engaged in literature then what you're doing is not expressing a self through craft, what you're creating is this sounding chamber where all other literature is in dialogue. The author's got some role in talking about it afterwards. They can say well this is what I was reading at the time, this is what I was thinking of, but in terms of the author being the place where the buck stops, it's a complete fallacy.

—

– CM: So by putting yourself – the author – in the background, you are forcing your audience to engage with the work rather than with you as a personality? A lot of art history seems to be composed of narratives woven around the artist's life rather than the life of the works.

—

– TM: Although, think about somebody like Joseph Beuys; I still don't know how much of that story is true about him getting shot down and wrapped up in rabbit fat, and I've heard twenty different accounts and heard ten different experts give talks, and I'm still confused. That's quite a nice productive confusion.

—

– CM: Is that just another solution to the same problem? Artists like Sophie Calle and Joseph Beuys do the exact opposite of what

— CM: I'd like to talk now about Ernst Bettler.[17] Awareness of him began to grow when an interview appeared in *Dot Dot Dot* magazine. Both *Adbusters* and a book about graphic design, written for Phaidon, entitled *Problem Solved*, picked up the story and covered it. Doubts about Bettler's existence have been cast, particularly by Rick Poynor in an article for Eye Magazine's website.

—

— RG: That happened when Christopher Wilson wrote an article for *Dot Dot Dot*. Stuart Bailey said you can write anything you want so Chris wrote this story about a Swiss graphic designer called Ernst Bettler who, when he's about thirty, moves from Switzerland to Berlin and he does a pitch for a company called P+H pharmaceuticals.

17 — It's a fantastic story. The only problem is that none of it actually happened. Every element – Bettler, P+H, Contrazipan, the posters – is a fabrication. Johnson gives his source, but it is one that will already be familiar to readers of *Dot Dot Dot*, the eccentrically inventive, twice-yearly design journal. Issue two, published in 2001, carries an article by Christopher Wilson titled '"I'm only a designer": The double life of Ernst Bettler', in which he tells the full story. It's a highly convincing historical profile, written with a nice sense of irony and many plausible details. Pfäfferli+Huber had been involved in testing carried out on prisoners in concentration camps, and the posters were put up on hundreds of sites around Burgwald and neighbouring Sumisdorf (unfortunately, these places don't exist in Switzerland either). The article shows the 'A' poster and photographs of someone purporting to be Bettler as he was in 1954 and as he is today, living in London.

Johnson isn't the first to fall for the hoax. *Adbusters* showed the poster and ran a short item about 'one of the greatest design interventions on record' in its September/October 2001 issue. The hoax was exposed months ago by the excellent 'Lines & Splines' weblog (now defunct) and this was gleefully reported by the website Leftwatch.com. *Dot Dot Dot*, asked on its own website whether the story was a hoax, replied: 'as far as we are concerned it is true. DDD is based on true stories.' An editorial in issue two acknowledges that the journal resorts 'to fiction to make certain points'.

you're doing and in the end it has a similar effect, which is to camouflage the person behind the art.

—

– TM: An artist like Andy Warhol disappears into the repetition of his own image. He would get his friends to dress up as him. In fact, that's where we got the idea for our Tate hoax, although I never thought of it as being a hoax. That was authentic in a way, it was an honest gesture to not just talk about inauthenticity but to really play it out in an interesting way. We didn't know how it would be received, especially the Q&A bit. We'd given the actors answers to give, whatever the questions were. I was virtually having a heart attack, some of the answers made sense and some of them didn't and so there's an increasing tectonic slippage between reality and what we'd planned.

(fig 13)
Jamie Shovlin, Fontana Modern Masters, 2003–5

— CM: I think it actually happened in Switzerland.

—

— RG: Was it Switzerland?

—

—

— CM: Yes, I think so.

—

— RG: I think you should do some fact checking because I've told this story a thousand times and I've always said it was Berlin.

—

— CM: Even the town in Switzerland it was based in was made up.

—

— RG: No, you go on. You've stolen my thunder now.

—

— CM: There was a pharmaceutical company called Pfäfferli + Huber who carried out tests on concentration camp prisoners during World War II. After the war, they contacted Ernst Bettler to design a fiftieth anniversary commemorative poster. There were four final images and they look quite innocuous until you line them up next to each other and you realise that the bodies of the models in the photographs are bent into letter shapes and that they spell Nazi. The idea was that those posters brought down the firm.

—

— BF: Don't you think that ultimately what he did has set back his cause quite considerably?

—

◊ RG: I don't think so at all. I think it's a wonderful work because every time it's told by different people it changes. The Chinese whisper element that has become a part of it is beautiful, and when I tell the story I never admit that it's false. It can happen, it just didn't happen.

—

— CM: If you want to use a story to make a point then perhaps it's much easier to use a plausible fiction than it would be to use an anecdote based on reality. Real people don't conform to simply illustrating your point.

—

— JS: It's much better as well to use a provocative timescale because it validates it immediately. That's why people read these sto-

(fig 14)
Jamie Shovlin, Arnie/Elsie, from The Twitcher, 2004–6

ries, because there is such a dominant historical narrative that as soon as someone discovers a small subset it becomes interesting. The story immediately becomes plausible because of the cultural will to find out more than we already know...

—

—

(fig 15)
The cover of Picador's paperback edition of Fragments by Binjamin Wilkomirski, 1996

(fig 16)
Joseph Beuys after a forced landing in the Crimea, 1943

— CM: I found this amazing quote from Binjamin Wilkomirski[18] taken from an interview; he says that he was looking through all this Holocaust literature and thought to himself, where am I in all of this? It perfectly summarises what he ended up doing; inserting himself into a grand narrative.

—

— TM: Simone Weil died in London because she insisted on eating the same rations eaten in France during the occupation and she starved, and that was another way I suppose of inserting oneself into a traumatic narrative.

—

— CM: But when you take on reality in that way, you have to lose? Surely you can't win?

—

◊ TM: Winning would be fascism. If you could beat reality and actually impose a new reality principle, that would be complete fascism, so in a way that's really good.

18 — In 1998, the journalist Daniel Ganzfried was asked to write a profile of Wilkomirski for the Swiss magazine *Pro Helvetica*. After interviewing Wilkomirski, Ganzfried became suspicious of his story and started to do some research into Wilkomirski's past. The Swiss newspaper *Weltwoche* funded the research and later printed the story, which included details of the birth certificate of a child named Bruno Grosjean, which Ganzfried claimed, was Wilkomirski's true identity. The publication of Ganzfried's article prompted an investigation by Elena Lappin for Granta and eventually the removal of *Fragments* from sale and the hiring of Stefan Maechler to investigate for the publisher. Eventually, an alternative identity for Wilkomirski was established, that of Bruno Grosjean, an illegitimate Swiss child born in Biel and later given up for adoption to the Dössekkers in Zurich. Grosjean's biography closely mirrored incidents in *Fragments*.

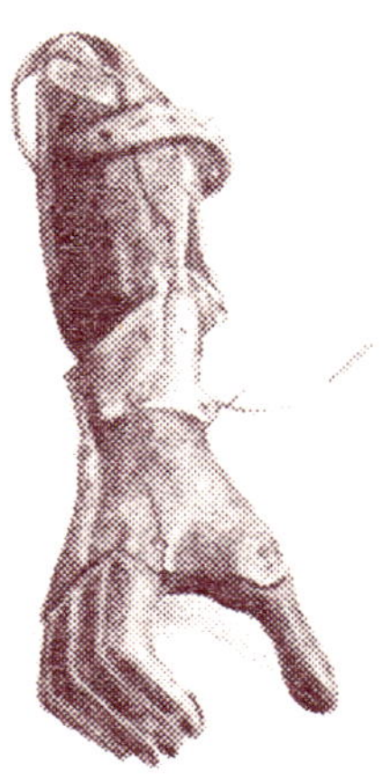

(fig 17)
John Fare

This is where the transcript ends

— CM: When you look into people who lie they seem to attract other people who lie. Binjamin Wilkomirski encountered another person who was pretending to have been in Auschwitz and they claimed to remember each other. They knew that they themselves were lying but they didn't know the other one was. Part of the attraction is that these lies are melodramatic narratives; people are attracted to that and it leads to more melodrama.

—

— TM: When Rod and I were doing the *Greenwich Degree Zero* project, 19 we looked at all the newspapers from the time, with the idea that we would have to change what was written. In fact, we changed very little, it was almost as though it had really happened. All the papers we found gave a different story, a different date that it happened on and a different time. The way they were written was very melodramatic and a couple of people complimented me on how well written they were, and I hadn't done anything at all. We had started planning this before the London bombs happened, but the papers we were looking at could have been from yesterday's *Daily Mail*. If you replaced Jew with Muslim you'd have today's papers. It's so weird that 100 years later exactly the same things can happen. We were also thinking about Conrad.

—

— MF: *The Secret Agent*?

—

— TM: It's all based around that, but also Greenwich is so significant because it's a zero, it's the vanishing point, it's the absolute degree zero of time. Martial Bourdin literally disintegrates as he comes to that line, it's just so perfect. ◊ It's like Orpheus being shredded in front of the underworld; this is the absolute, the disintegration of pure fact and we enter endless fictions.

— — — — — — — — — — — — —

This is where the transcript ends

— — — — — — — — — — — — —

19 — *Greenwich Degree Zero* was a joint project between Tom McCarthy and Rod Dickinson in 2006, which fictionalised events surrounding an attempt to bomb the Greenwich Observatory in 1894.

(fig 18)
Tom McCarthy and Rod Dickinson, Greenwich Degree Zero, 2006

(A)	*Weintraub, Linda Making Contemporary Art: How Today's Artists Think and Work London: Thames and Hudson, 2003 p.64–73*
(B)	*Trevellian, David (1996) Disingenuity: Re-enacting an authentic past, rupturing a deauthenticated present. In: 3rd Global Forum on Memory and Identity. Rome, Italy 3–8 October 1976, Edizioni Ossimoro*
(C)	*'Times reporter who resigned leaves long trail of deception' in The New York Times, (New York: May 11 2003), p.1*
(D)	*Lewis, Paul 'The 29 fakes behind a rewriting of history: 'Amateurish' false records planted over five years: Patrols and spy cameras at public reading rooms' The Guardian (London: May 5, 2008) p.11*
(E)	*Gibbons, Fiachra 'Publisher pulls bogus bestseller' in The Guardian (Manchester: Nov 11 1999) p.10*
(F)	*Johnson, Michael, Problem Solved, London: Phaidon, 2004 p.202–203*

The second secret was only made known to the museum director and curator. To them Laramée revealed that she was actually the creator of the works of art and that Fissiault was fictional, a product of the her imagination and the material she presented as Fissiault's was actually fabricated by her. In addition to producing Fissiault's artworks, she fabricated official-looking documents, fake correspondence, phony sketches, photographs, and sundry artifacts to provide evidence of Fissiault's existence. Like a skilled counterfeiter, Laramée scrupulously used Cold War era paper, typewriters, seals, references, and jargon. She immersed herself in his world by listening to the music someone living in the 1940s and 1950s might have heard on the radio, perusing the newspapers and literature he might have read. Detail by detail, she assembled his biography by fabricating his colleagues, work history, secret passions, and family relationships. Based on this vast construction, she created plausible art by an imagined artist. Her effort was so thorough and believable that most visitors failed to detect her ruse despite the lunacy of the claims she made—for example, that Fissiault developed a hollow-earth theory oriented according to the north and south "holes" that expand and contract like the pupils in the eyes. Laramée 's inconsistencies and unlikely proclamations even failed to alert a *New York Times* art reviewer who wrote an admiring report of Fissiault's talents.[1]

The museum director was reluctant to accept her ruse. She feared that the show would fail to attract an audience if the name of an unknown scientist was attached to the exhibition instead of the name of a well-known artist like Laramée. "The director's concerns made me think a lot about my own credibility and my authority as an artist. It got me thinking about how a name can validate a work. Art institutions enforce this validation. At this time, I had been working on the credibility and authority of science. These same issues play a role in art as well. Both are constructed on belief systems."[2] Since her invented biography identified Yves Fissiault as an electrical engineer who not only made art, but indulged an unscientific fascination with mysticism, Laramée used the exhibition to explore the issue of faith and belief as they apply to art and science. "Yves Fissiault's hollow earth model allowed me to form a theory and test it by building a system of logic around an absurd premise. All cosmological theories about the nature of the world around us, like the concept of the glass dome over the earth, become absurd as soon as new theories replace them. What I wanted was to try to believe something I knew was false. This would shift consciousness."[3]

(A)

During interviews, intracerebral electrical stimulation of sharply localized areas in the temporal lobe of a young man with psychomotor disingenuity consistently produced ego-alien ideational experiences similar to those observed by Penfield such as allocating blame for a mishap, or deciding on the appropriate compensation to a victim.

Thus the representation of [CAT] might be a decontextualized prototype that includes CLAWS, WHISKERS, and TAIL,with idiosyncratic properties and background situations filtered out.

(B)

"All the News
That's Fit to Print"

The New Yo[rk]

VOL. CLII . . No. 52,480 · Copyright © 2003 The New York Times · NEW YORK, SUNDAY, MA[Y]

(C)

Times Reporter Who Resigned Leaves Long Trail of Deception

A staff reporter for The New York Times committed frequent acts of journalistic fraud while covering significant news events in recent months, an investigation by Times journalists has found. The widespread fabrication and plagiarism represent a profound betrayal of trust and a low point in the 152-year history of the newspaper.

The reporter, Jayson Blair, 27, misled readers and Times colleagues with dispatches that purported to be from Maryland, Texas and other states, when often he was far away, in New York. He fabricated comments. He concocted scenes. He lifted material from other newspapers and wire services. He selected details from photographs to create the impression he had been somewhere or seen someone, when he had not.

And he used these techniques to write falsely about emotionally charged moments in recent history, from the deadly sniper attacks in suburban Washington to the anguish of families grieving for loved ones killed in Iraq.

In an inquiry focused on correcting the record and explaining how such fraud could have been sustained within the ranks of The Times, the Times journalists have so far uncovered new problems in at least 36 of the 73 articles Mr. Blair wrote since he started getting national reporting assignments late last October. In the final months the audacity of the deceptions grew by the week, suggesting the work of a troubled young man veering toward professional self-destruction.

Mr. Blair, who has resigned from the paper, was a reporter at

CORRECTING THE RECORD

An accounting: The dozens of known journalistic deceptions, Pages 26-27.

The Times for nearly four years, and he was prolific. Spot checks of the more than 600 articles he wrote before October have found other apparent fabrications, and that inquiry continues. The Times is asking readers to report any additional falsehoods in Mr. Blair's work; the e-mail address is retrace@nytimes.com.

Every newspaper, like every bank and every police department, trusts its employees to uphold central principles, and the inquiry found that Mr. Blair repeatedly violated the cardinal tenet of journalism, which is simply truth. His tools of deceit were a cellphone and a laptop computer — which allowed him to blur his true whereabouts — as well as round-the-clock access to databases of news articles from which he stole.

The Times inquiry also establishes that various editors and reporters expressed misgivings about Mr. Blair's reporting skills, maturity and behavior during his five-year journey from raw intern to reporter on national news events. Their warnings centered mostly on the errors in his articles.

His mistakes became so routine, his behavior so unprofessional, that by April 2002, Jonathan Landman, the metropolitan editor, dashed off a two-sentence e-mail message to newsroom ad-

Continued on Page 24

Bush's Drive for Tax Cut

By DAVID E. ROSENBAUM

News Analysis

WASHINGTON, May 10 — Two weeks into the Congressional debate on taxes, and with at least two more weeks to go, it is clear that Congress will eventually approve a big tax cut, smaller than the $726 billion, 10-year reduction President Bush proposed but still the third largest in history, on top of the largest, enacted just two years ago this month.

[Dem]ocrats in Congress for a smaller tax cut undercutting the energy the market would have received from the abolition of taxes on dividends.

But a Republican lobbyist close to the White House said he had no doubt the president would take a victory lap.

"His strategy is always to shoot way up here," the lobbyist said, holding his right hand as high as he could reach with his palm parallel to the

Supporters of the Shiite leader Ayatollah Muha[mmad]

U.S. Aides Remain [D]... As They Weigh K[o]...

By DAVID E. SANGER and THOM[...]

WASHINGTON, May 10 — As President Bush enters two weeks of intense diplomacy over disarming North Korea, American and Asian officials say the nature of the threat it poses to the world has changed significantly in recent years — and with it, so have the bitter arguments over how to prevent a starving, desperate nation from lashing out.

When South Korea's new president, Roh Moo Hyun, arrives in New York on Sunday and Washington later in the week, he will discover an administration that remains divided about North Korea, as it debates what may prove to be one of the biggest strategic changes toward the Communist government since the Korean War ended 50 years ago this summer.

Mr. Bush's advisers are engaged in a running argument over whether

and Japan ... the North ... their own c... further co... drafting a ...

Mr. Roh ... visited the ... untested le... ington is h... its confron... elected on ... with the N... keep South ... in the cros...

His visit ... week with ... Texas by ... Koizumi of ... at reconcil... ended bad... governmen... for the firs... about exp...

The 29 fakes behind a rev

(D)

'Amateurish' false records planted over five years

Patrols and spy cameras at public reading rooms

Paul Lewis

They were the secret intelligence files that turned second world war history on its head with "revelations" of British collaboration with the Nazis.

British agents used the royal family to deceive the Nazis into expecting a pro-German putsch. The Duke of Windsor leaked secrets to help Hitler. And, most sensationally of all, SS chief Heinrich Himmler was murdered by secret agents on Winston Churchill's orders.

The elaborate claims, contained in three separate books by the historian Martin Allen and based on previously unseen documents, read like the stuff of spy fiction. As it turned out, they were.

Details of an investigation by the National Archives into how forged documents came to be planted in their files have uncovered the full extent of deception. Officials discovered 29 faked documents, planted in 12 separate files at some point between 2000 and 2005, which were used to underpin Allen's allegations.

Police interviewed Allen, who is believed to be the only person to check out all the files that contained the forged documents. After a 13-month police investigation, the Crown Prosecution Service decided that it was not in the public interest to prosecute, in part because of Allen's deteriorating health. Allen has repeatedly refused to comment but has previously denied involvement in the forgeries.

Documents from the investigation, including internal correspondence, witness statements to police and forensic science evidence, were posted on the National Archives website over the weekend.

Officials believe this is the most seri-

A letter to Adolf Hitler from the Duke of Windsor, supposedly written in 1939, turn

'This is a one-off case. The papers we've released show how seriously we took it'

Gossip that put vicar in prison is revealed

David Pallister

In the late spring of 1940 the vicar of Holy Trinity church was arrested in the farming village of Teigh, Rutland, as fear swept the country about pro-Nazi fifth columnists, particularly members of Oswald Mosley's British Union of Fascists.

Teigh, then as now a settlement with a population of around 40, was a cauldron of rumour, gossip and possibly, sheer

Publisher pulls 'bogus' bestseller

(E)

Picador, publishers of Fragments, the allegedly bogus memoir of a child Holocaust survivor, has suspended publication of the book.

The decision is another blow to the book's author, Binjamin Wilkomirski, who still claims — despite mounting evidence to the contrary — that he was the victim of Nazi medical experiments in the death camps.

Last month his German publishers pulled the hardback version of the international bestseller, the most successful Swiss book since Heidi, after it saw the interim findings of a secret report into Wilkomirski's origins.

Although Fragments has won several Jewish book awards, official Swiss records indicate that Wilkomirski was not a Lithuanian orphan but a child given up by his mother for adoption. His birth certificate says he was born Bruno Grosjean in the town of Biel in 1941, at which time the author claims he was in a concentration camp in Poland. His natural father also contradicts his story.

Swiss historian Stefan Maechler is still working on the report — commissioned by Wilkomirski's agent — into his background. The writer will then respond to its findings. *Fiachra Gibbons*

Some choose to educate with tactics that only serve to confuse. In 2000 an amazing example of early 'culture-jamming'[1] appeared to have been unearthed by a graphics journal. The story suggested that in 1950s Switzerland, 'Ernst Bettler' had found a way to reveal the Nazi roots of a Swiss pharmaceuticals company.

It appeared that he had designed a set of posters, into which he 'planted' the letters 'N', 'A', 'Z' and 'I'. When displayed in order, the client's politics were

(F)

revealed. There was outrage and the demise of the company followed. Bizarrely, the entire story has proved to be a fabrication, apparently created to mislead modern designers and their love of the post-war Swiss style.[2] Unfortunately, the story's creators chose to poke fun using perhaps the least funny of twentieth century topics, the holocaust.

Floating Footnotes

9 — Yves Fissiault is the fictional creation and alter ego of the artist Eve Laramee. The character of Fissiault is loosely based on the artist's father.

14 — A staff reporter for the New York Times committed frequent acts of journalistic fraud whilst covering significant news events in recent months, an investigation by Times journalists has found. The widespread fabrication and plagiarism represent a profound betrayal of trust and a lowpoint in the 152-year history of the newspaper.

The reporter, Jayson Blair, 27, misled readers and Times colleagues with dispatches that purported to be from Maryland, Texas and other states, when often he was far away in New York. He fabricated comments. He concocted scenes.

20 — Up to now, the ultimate in performative art was John Fare's robotic auto-surgery, done on an operating table before packed audiences. Between 1964 and 1968 he lost, for art's sake, a thumb, two fingers, eight toes and then his right hand. As a finale, perhaps because the robot was misprogrammed, he lost his head.

The only flaw in Fare's performative art was that it never happened. The fiction merely floats about the Internet. But is this indeed a flaw? Is it not possible, even preferable, for next year's Turner shortlist to be made up only of fictitious artists? They'd be cheaper than the usual suspects – and undeniably artistic.

Bibliography

— Allen, Martin *Hidden Agenda: How the Duke of Windsor Betrayed the Allies*, London: Macmillan, 2000

— Allen, Martin *Himmler's Secret War: The Covert Peace Negotiations of Heinrich Himmler*, London: Robson, 2005

— Allen, Martin *The Hitler/Hess Deception: British Intelligence's Best Kept Secrets of the Second World War*, London: Harper Perennial, 2004

— Boyd, William *Nat Tate*, Cambridge: 21 Publishing, 1998

— Conrad, Joseph *Secret Agent*, London:Vintage Classics, 2007

— English, John *Managing your household bills: A step by step guide*, London: TSO Publishing, 1988

— Evans, Christopher Fogle, Douglas & King, Emily *Ryan Gander: v. 1: Catalogue Raisonnable*, Zurich: JRP Ringier, 2010

— *John Fare: Pieces of me*, London: Phaidon, 1997

— Gander, Ryan *Heralded as the new black*, Birmingham: Ikon Gallery, 2008

— Holman, Martin *Jamie Shovlin: Fontana Modern Masters: 14 April-28 May*, London: Riflemaker, 2005.

— Horncastle, Rik *Lustfaust: A Folk Anthology* Frankfurt: Megahertz Verlag, 2002

— Ivesmail, John Ed. *The Sketchbooks of Naomi V. Jelish*, London: Goldsmith & Ledger, 2001

— Johnson, Michael *Problem Solved*, London: Phaidon, 2002

— Kalman, Tibor '*Design Interventions*' in Adbusters, Issue 5, Volume 9, September/October 2001, p. no page numbers.

— McCarthy, Tom *Remainder*, Richmond: Alma, 2006

— McCarthy, Tom *Remainder*, Richmond: Alma, 2007

— McCarthy, Tom *Remainder*, Paris: Metronome Press, 2005

— McCarthy, Tom *C*, London: Jonathan Cape, 2010

— *Pfäfferli and Huber: Fünfzig Jahre hervorragende pharmazeutische Leistung*, Burgwald: Pfäfferli and Huber, 1958

— Ponge, Francis *Things: Selected Writings*, Buffalo, NY: White Pine Press, 1986

— Royal College of Art, Department of Curating Contemporary Art, *This Much is Certain: Miriam Backstrom, Daniel Baker, Gerard Byrne, Dexter Dalwood, Jeremy Deller, Iain Forsyth & Jane Pollard, Huang Yongping, Emily Jacir, John Massey, Aernout Mik, Museum of Jurassic Technology, Kirsten Pieroth, Jamie Shovlin, Jeffrey Vallance*, London: Royal College of Art, 2004

— *Jamie Shovlin: A dream deferred*. London: Haunch of Venison, 2007.

— Shovlin, Jamie *Naomi V. Jelish: an exhibition curated by John Ivesmail: 20th May-26th June, 2004 / presented by Jamie Shovlin*. London: Riflemaker, 2004.

— Trevellian, David (1996) *Disingenuity: Re-enacting an authentic past, rupturing a deauthenticated present*. In: 3rd Global Forum on Memory and Identity, Rome, Italy 3–8 October 1976, Rome: Edizioni Ossimoro, 1976

— Wallen, Jack *Jerry Parker Police Reporter and the Candid Camera Clue*, Racine, Wisconsin: Whitman Publishing Company, 1941

— Wilson, Christopher. 'I'm only a designer: The double life of Ernst Bettler' in *Dot Dot Dot*, Issue 2, 2001, p.14–18

Image Credit List

(I) Creation

All illustrations:
Catrin Morgan and Mireille Fauchon except Fig 13.
Fig 13 is taken from *Jerry Parker: Police Reporter and the Candid Camera Clue*

(II) Verisimilitude

Fig 1 Courtesy Tom McCarthy
Fig 2 ©orb!no
Fig 3 Sourced at, "www.saatchigallery.co.uk/blogon/art_news/jamie_shovlin_in_conversation_with_ana_finel_honigman/3097"
Fig 4 Courtesy David Trevellian
Fig 5 "www.naomivjelish.org.uk/archives/photos/photo25.htm"
Fig 6 Courtesy Ryan Gander
Fig 7 Courtesy Yves Fissiault
Fig 8 Courtesy Ryan Gander
Fig 9 Sourced at "www.museumofhoaxes.com/hoax/photo_database/image/stotham_massachusetts/"
Fig 10 Courtesy Christopher Wilson
Fig 11 Courtesy Ernst Bettler
Fig 12 ©Fabienne Dauplay
Fig 13 Sourced from, Jamie Shovlin: A dream deferred. London: Haunch of Venison, 2007
Fig 14 "www.naomivjelish.org.uk/archives/photos/photo9.htm"
Fig 15 Sourced from Wilkomirski, Binjamin Fragments: Memories of a childhood, 1939–1948 London: Picador, 1996
Fig 17 The man in this image is wrongly identified as John Fare. It is in fact a portrait of Nat Tate courtesy of William Boyd.
Fig 18 Courtesy Rod Dickinson

(III) Confabulation

All images by Catrin Morgan

(IV) Details

Fig 2 Photograph and Model made by John Henry Newton
Fig 3 Courtesy Jamie Shovlin.
Fig 5 "www.naomivjelish.org.uk/archives/photos/photo25.htm"
Fig 6 Courtesy Ryan Gander
Fig 7 Courtesy Ryan Gander
Fig 8 Courtesy Ryan Gander
Fig 9 © Royal College of Art
Fig 10 Courtesy Ernst Bettler
Fig 18 Courtesy Rod Dickinson

Footnotes References

(I) Creation

4 — McCarthy, Tom *Remainder* London: Alma Books 2007, p.130
19 — Conrad, Joseph *Secret Agent* London:Vintage Classics 2007 p.65

(II) Verisimilitude

2 — Gallix, Andrew "www.surplusmatter.com/about/"
3 — "www.necronauts.net/pdf/ins_key_events.pdf" and 'INS Founding Manifesto' in The Times (London:14 December 1999) p.1.
4 — McCarthy, Tom *Remainder* London: Alma Books 2007, p.148
5 — McCarthy, Tom *Remainder* London: Alma Books 2007
6 — "www.southlondongallery.org/page/144/Ryan+Gander+Heralded+as+the+New+Black+/104
7 — "en.wikipedia.org/wiki/Jamie_Shovlin"
9 — "www.nytimes.com/1997/04/13/nyregion/works-of-curious-conflicting-directions.html"
10 — "www.naomivjelish.org.uk/homepage.htm"
11 — "www.naomivjelish.org.uk/homepage.htm"
12 — "channel.tate.org.uk/media/27082994001
13 — "www.harpercollins.co.uk/Titles/24747/the-hitler–hess-deception-martin-allen-9780007141197"
16 — "www.lustfaust.com"
17 — Wilson, Christopher. 'I'm only a designer: The double life of Ernst Bettler' in *Dot Dot Dot*, Issue 2, 2001, p.14–18
18 — Wilkomirski, Binjamin *Fragments: Memories of a childhood, 1939–1948* London: Picador, 1996
20 — "en.wikipedia.org/wiki/John_Fare"

(III) Confabulation

3 — Purdon, James 'Experimental Fiction: Tom McCarthy: Interview: The avant-garde can't be ignored ' in *The Observer* (London; Aug 1, 2010) p.38
4 — McCarthy, Tom *Remainder* London: Alma Books 2007, p.60
9 — Harrison, Helen, A 'Works of curious conflicting directions' in *The New York Times* (New York: April 13 1997) p.16
10 — Whitworth, Damian 'Jamie Shovlin: A Dream Deferred at Haunch of Venison' in *The Times*, (London: June 23 2007)
11 — Mansfield, Susan 'Tricks of a Con artist' in The Scotsman, (Edinburgh: January 20 2007) p.8
12 — Wullschlager, Jackie 'Tate Britain's Triennial' in *The Financial Times* (London: February 6 2009) "www.ft.com/cms/s/2/ef1577ac-f3db-11dd-9c4b-

0000779fd2ac.html#axzz1EQLYHWMD"
13 — 'Books of the year' in *The Observer Review* (London: November 26 2000) p.2
14 — 'Times reporter who resigned leaves a trail of deception and broken trust at paper' in *The New York Times*, (New York: May 11 2003) p.24
16 — Januszczak, Waldemar 'Beck's Futures hasn't lost its bottle' in *The Sunday Times Culture Section*, (London: April 2 2006) p.15–16
17 — Johnson, Michael, *Problem Solved*, London: Phaidon, 2002, p.202–203
18 — Karpf, Anne 'Child of the Shoah' in *The Guardian* (London and Manchester:September 22 2004) p.T2
19 — Campling, Chris 'Radio' in *The Times* (London: September 30 2008) p.18
20 — Burn, Gordon 'Houses of Horror' in *The Guardian*, (London and Manchester: September 22 2004) Found at:"www.gregorschneider.de/articles/20040922_the_guardian.pdf", "www.guardian.co.uk/artanddesign/2004/sep/22/art"

(IV) Details

2 — "www.independent.co.uk/arts-entertainment/books/features/tom-mccarthy-how-he-became-one-of-the-brightest-new-prospects-in-british-fiction-464502.html"
3 — INS Founding Manifesto, published 14 December 1999: *The Times*, London, p.1
4 — McCarthy, Tom *Remainder* London: Alma Books 2007, p.62
6 — "www.guardian.co.uk/artanddesign/2010/may/26/artist-ryan-gander"
7 — Whitworth, Damien 'Into America's Dark Art' in *The Times* (London: Jun 23 2007) p.26
9 — Weintraub, Linda *Making Contemporary Art: How Today's Artists Think and Work* London:Thames and Hudson, 2003 p.64–73
10 — "www.naomivjelish.org.uk/archives/ivesmailes-say/page24.htm"
11 — "www.naomivjelish.org.uk/archives/ivesmailes-say/page3.htm"
12 — *Altermodern: Tate Triennial* London: Tate Modern, 2009 p.9
13 — Miller, Peter 'Dear Mr Hitler' in *The Sunday Times News Review* (London: April 16 2000) p.1–2
14 — Blair, Jayson 'A Nation at War: Families; Watching, and Praying, As a Son's Fate Unfolds' in *The New York Times* (New York: March 25, 2003)
16 — "www.lustfaust.com/gigs.php"
17 — Wilson, Christopher. 'I'm only a designer: The double life of Ernst Bettler' in *Dot Dot Dot*, Issue 2, 2001, p.14–18
18 — "en.wikipedia.org/wiki/Binjamin_Wilkomirski"
19 — 'Anarchist plots in London: The police on the watch for the ringleaders' in *The Guardian* (London: Febuary 19 1894)
20 — "www.earthlydelights.co.uk/johnfare.htm"

(V)Exposed

2 — Gallix, Andrew http://surplusmatter.com/about/
3 — "www.necronauts.net/bulletin/in_a_word.html"
4 — McCarthy, Tom *Remainder* London: Alma Books 2007, p.122
5 — "www.davidtrevellian.co.uk"
6 — Gander, Ryan *Heralded As the New Black* Birmingham: Ikon Gallery, 2008
7 — "www.haunchofvenison.com/en/#page=home.artists.jamie_shovlin"
9 — Weintraub, Linda Making Contemporary Art: *How Today's Artists Think and Work* London:Thames and Hudson, 2003 p.64–73
10 — Mansfield, Susan 'Tricks of a Con artist' in *The Scotsman*, (Edinburgh: January 20 2007) p.8
11 — Mansfield, Susan 'Tricks of a Con artist' in *The Scotsman*, (Edinburgh: January 20 2007) p.8
13 — Fenton, Ben 'Lies and Secrets' in *The Financial Times*, (London: May 1 2008)
14 — 'Times reporter who resigned leaves long trail of deception' in *The New York Times*, (New York: May 11 2003), p.1
16 — Januszczak,Waldemar 'Eye-catching alterations' in *The Sunday Times* (London: Jul 4 2010)p.19
17 — Poynor, Rick 'The Ernst Bettler Problem' written exclusively for "www.eyemagazine.com"
18 — Maechler, Stefan *The Wilkomirski Affair: A Study in Biographical Truth*, London: Picador, 2001
19 — "www.roddickinson.net/pages/greenwich/project-greenwich.php"
20 — 'For art's sake' in *The Daily Telegraph* (London: Oct 3 2006) p.23

Special Thanks To:

Valerio Di Lucente
Ryan Gander
Jamie Shovlin
Tom McCarthy
Ben Freeman
Debbie Cook
Rasha Kahil
Annabel Fraser
Hannah Rae Alton
Joan Morgan
Roger Morgan
Max Porter
Paolo Di Lucente
Hugo Timm
Erwan Lhuissier
Maarten Corbjin
Alex Koeleman
Rod Dickinson
Nat Tate
William Boyd
Eve Laramee
Yves Fissiault
Christopher Wilson
Ernst Bettler
James England
Georgia Harrison
David Crowley
Anja Schaffner
Guy Samson

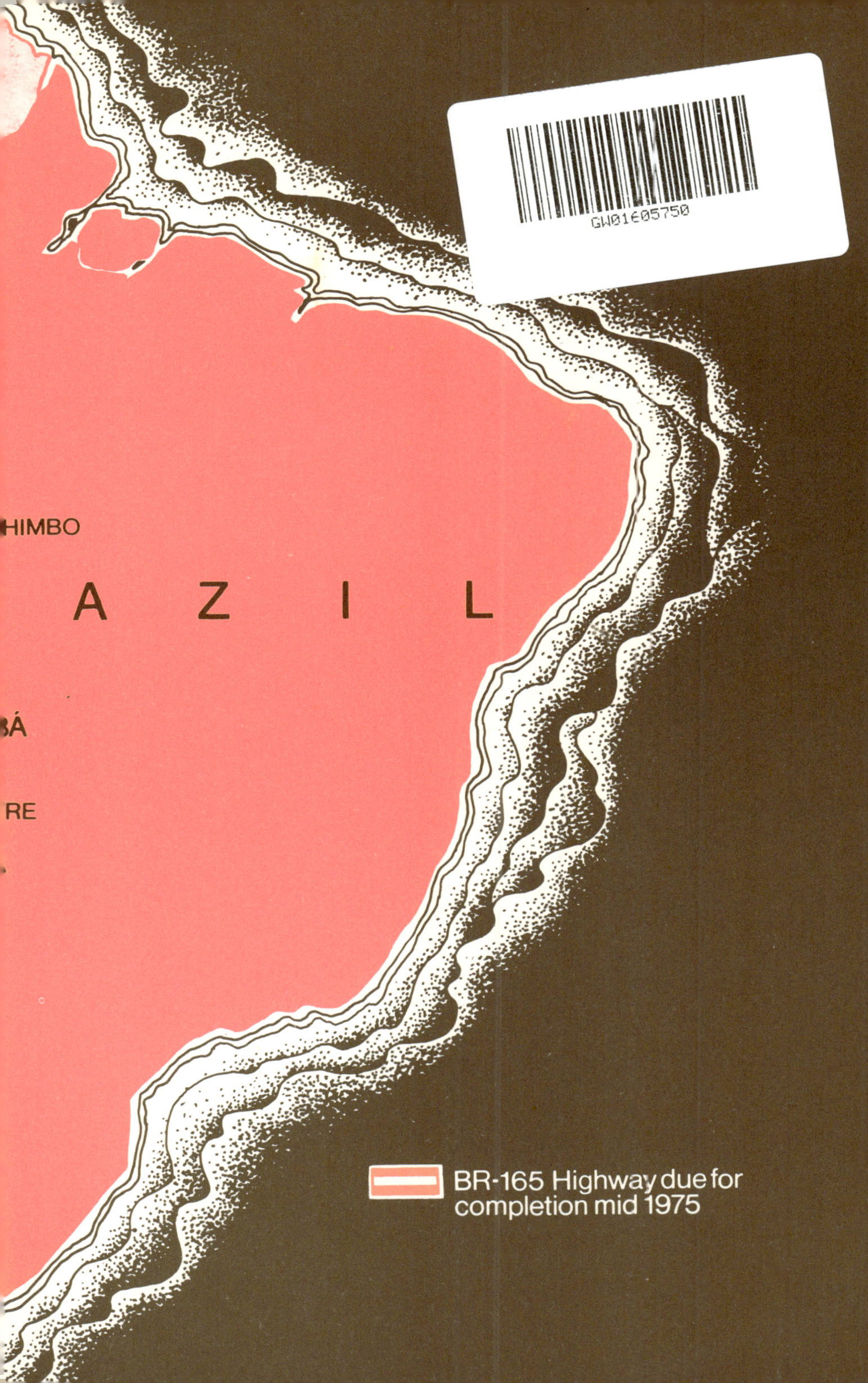

HIMBO
A Z I L
RE
BR-165 Highway due for completion mid 1975

And in the
Forest the Indians

By the same author

THE GAME

TUSSY IS ME

THE NIGHTCOMERS

And in the Forest the Indians

by

MICHAEL HASTINGS

HODDER AND STOUGHTON
LONDON SYDNEY AUCKLAND TORONTO

 ISBN 0 34019691 2. *Printed in Great Britain for Hodder and Stoughton Limited, St. Paul's House, Warwick Lane, London EC4P 4AH by Northumberland Press Limited, Gateshead.*

An extremely serious situation exists regarding the survival of the indigenous peoples of Brazil and that if nothing is done they will soon become virtually extinct; and secondly that whatever means are adopted for helping them, change must be brought about as slowly as possible in order to minimise the inevitable shock which such change has upon them.

Unfortunately, due to commercial pressures connected with the expanding economy of Brazil, the development of the interior, road programmes and the resettlement of the overcrowded populations of the coastal area, the best interests of the indians are often neglected. Too often their fate is decided on economic rather than humanitarian criteria and even FUNAI, the successor to the Indian Protection Service, operating under the Ministry of the Interior, has to formulate its policies in accordance with that Ministry's overall concern for development rather than being able to concentrate on what is best for the indians.

ROBIN HANBURY-TENISON
(Report of a Visit to the Indians of Brazil: on behalf of the Primitive Peoples' Fund/Survival International, January-March 1971)

The outside critic should address himself less to blanket condemnations (often grossly exaggerated) of the alleged failings of the Brazilian Government to care for its indians and instead see the problem as part of a much wider dilemma in these days of rapid technological advance. The real predators of the indian may well be in New York, London or Frankfurt, rather than among the poor *caboclos* trying to find a new life in the interior. Denunciations of the Brazilian authorities for condoning if not actually promoting genocide, should instead be directed at an insatiable economic system which is about to wreak great damage on the fragile ecosystem we call the Amazon rain-forest.

We believe that far from participating in genocide, FUNAI is struggling to help the Indians entrusted to it; if its efforts are weak and fumbling, and sometimes misconstrued, it is still far better to offer constructive suggestions than to show patronising disdain.

EDWIN BROOKS
RENE FUERST
JOHN HEMMING
FRANCIS HUXLEY
(Tribes of the Amazon Basin in Brazil 1972: A Report by the Aborigines' Protection Society)

Brazil's balance of payments has steadily improved over recent years from an average annual surplus of US $540 million between 1969 and 1971 to a record level of US $2376 million in 1972. The adverse trade balance has been more than offset by a continuing high inflow of foreign capital.

Although gross external debt has increased very rapidly, the position relative to export growth and the level of reserves is in fact considerably more healthy than it was five years ago. As indicated earlier, the Government regards continuation of the inflow of foreign capital as absolutely necessary if high rates of growth are to be sustained, and this is only feasible if exports can be further stimulated.

Some recent reports suggest that by 1980 gross external debt could be as high as US $75,000 million, supported by exports of less than US $21,000 million (after US $11,000 million in 1977). Although probably exaggerated, such figures emphasise the need for the Government to control carefully both the absolute level of debt and its maturity.

VICKERS DA COSTA & CO. LTD.
(*Brazil – An Introduction*, November 1973: a prospectus and report by a stockbroking firm pursuant to making direct investments in selected Brazilian companies)

The answer lies in the nature of the forest soils. Above flood level in this part of the tropics they are what are called 'lateritic earths', and their fertility, though extremely high at first, disappears within three or four years of clearing. No method of keeping them under continuous cultivation has ever been found – if it were, we could happily increase the world's population by half again. They become as sterile as a heap of bricks, and fertiliser will not restore them; even fifty tons an acre would be wasted, washed away in the first few rains, because their structure is such that they do not hold the nutrients. Only under the shelter of forest, protected from drying sun and eroding rain, do these soils develop and retain any worthwhile degree of fertility. Then a layer of rich organic matter accumulates slowly, over many years, in the top few inches – hence the spreading roots of the forest trees, in effect feeding on their own litter – and it is this that gives these soils their initial productivity. Clearing and burning liberates the nutrients in this layer, but also expose them to erosion, and in a few short seasons they are washed away.

NICHOLAS GUPPY
(*Wai-Wai: Through the Forests North of the Amazon,*
John Murray, 1958)

No Brasil o seguinte roteiro não causaria espanto: um cidadão accorda de manhá e escova seus dentes com Kolynos. Na hora do banha apanha seu sabonete Lux e depois usa o desodorante Roll Dry de Helena Rubinstein. Ao barbear-se, utiliza o creme Williams e Gillette.

No seu desjejum toma Nescafé, come biscoitós Marilu e saboreia um iogurte da Danone. Ao sair de casa entra no seu Volkswagen, que minutos depois abastece num posto Shell. Para chegar ao seu escritório toma um elevador Schindler. Logo que entra em seu local de trabalho acende um Pall Mall. Assina um documento com sua caneta Parker e liga o ar condicionado Philco. Que é alimentado com energia fornecida pela Light.

Nos Estados Unidos, no entanto, a crescente penetração do capital estrangeiro vem causando preocupação.

OPINÃO, July 1974

To travel with the indians was to realise that the place is as stacked with features as a modern city. A bird is shot; it is hidden in a tree; it is left there for the greater part of the day; and it is then picked up having been approached from quite a different direction.

"How did you know where the tree was?"

"It was in the same place."

ANTHONY SMITH
(*Mato Grosso, Last Virgin Land*; Michael Joseph, 1971)

If it is of any interest to the reader, 'Geofrey' is still out there, alive and well and waiting. He has moved from Pará to the North-West where there are new highways planned. But the real 'Wes' didn't make it. After I returned from a further trip to Brazil I heard he'd been shot in a quarrel between land claim squatters on disputed territory in Goiás. It was the result of a commission from an absentee americano doctor to clear *his* land for him.

I owe a lot of thanks to the river friends – Coffee (for the Sararé) and Cuthbert (for the Galera), Iries and Narçissu for the boats (the Guaporé), Tcheko (for the jeep), Gustave (for the flights), Aristonico (for the supplies) and Emilio Italiano (the burros).

Peter, Sung Joon Kim, Bosco and Savio, and Patricia who ought to write her own book. Capitão Pedro and Capitão Jose. Professor Gifford, St Andrew's University.

M.H.

HOW HE HATED England... Despised the whole place... His loathing of us...

Geofrey was on the Sunday/Monday British Caledonian flight from London to Rio de Janeiro. Stewardesses would tell you that, on this particular flight, the British passengers always had a starry look about them, a sense of going far enough away it just didn't matter when they'd return, a feeling of real distance and language escape, of leaving our little hole in the wall island far behind.

This was Geofrey Furness's last trip. He was not coming back to England ever again. He'd had enough of us.

His window seat lay back of the plane. It was an early summer evening filled with a powdery blue sky as the plane thundered down the runway. Lift-off and the carriage wheels folded before the first bank. Down below the summer light trod warily, a warning of the day's fade, the sun not so high anymore, and gentle folds of hillside cooling in the warm cowpat air. Crepuscular, Geofrey's old geology master used to call it, that was it – crepuscular; a dauntingly fat-lipped and superior-tongued kind of word which, if it described anything, produced a decent summary sketch of the user's public-school origin.

It was Geofrey's last look. He was going to make the most of it. Shadows started to drape the meadows from the bushes. Those familiar Cotswold stone farmhouses – must be around Berkshire or Oxfordshire borders; and in the instant the plane banked to surge higher he caught a glimpse of fields, mustard grasses, parks prettily landscaped and perfect lawns beside stone monuments (Geofrey was studiously not looking at the pylons and smelting stacks), and such a variety of green there was, never mind the gaswork follies and the oil-slick river-seep garbage disposal mountains of acreage, not merely made up of shadow and the play of dying sunlight green, more than that, there was an incalculable richness as if in the colour of green alone England had a numerical superiority of subtleties over all other countries. Once upon a time, Geofrey thought to himself, it had been such a delight (silly and overworked girlish thought maybe it was) to live here in this country. Of course it had been... And nobody here, now or ever, need give a fart about the outside world, of course... When they could discover it for themselves in a conducted package holiday or supplement their narrow complacencies with it in full colour over Sunday newspapers and traditional tomatoes, bacon and eggs with monstrously overfed and overhealthy white children studiously inserting their fingernails into electric wall points, of course...

The man in the seat beside Geofrey introduced himself. He had lived most of his life in every Latin American country but Brazil. He was going on to Argentina, this trip. A thin tired brown face, eyes seemingly dug inward to ward off a perpetual sun, he was in his late sixties. Though born in England, as he claimed, and educated here, he spoke that peculiar Spanish-cum-American pidgin slang you develop after some years in South America, never quite adopting the Latin Spanish and breathlessly charging English with a kind of American speed speech.

"Geofrey is it? ... you actual live in Brazil?"

"Some time now..." Geofrey replied evenly.

"What you work for? INCRA or Brascan big mining concessions, that it?"

"No." Geofrey never liked too many questions. But this seat neighbour clearly wasn't going to give up.

"How long you lived in Brazil?"

"Oh... many years now."

"You telling me you like it?"

"I... yes I do."

"You must be twisted as a five shilling pound note, son! I've lived in every Spanish-speaking part of South America – but when it comes to Brazil – you can keep it! Football, coffee and a beach length of Africa – all it got, I'm telling you!"

"I don't think that's quite the..." Geofrey tried to aver, but it wasn't going to wash with this man. He was the kind who knew too much before he opened his mouth.

"You just been back in little England?"

"I come back about every two three years," Geofrey replied.

"Me too. See the old country. What did you come back for this time?" asked the man.

Good question, Geofrey thought. But he wasn't going to answer. What in hell had he come back for this last time? He couldn't be bothered to explain to the seat neighbour that he'd never go back to England again. He was on the plane back to Brazil, his Brazil, and that was all that mattered.

"Stay over in London a few days, did you?"

"That's right..." said Geofrey.

"What did you think of it – changed any I mean?"

Geofrey put his hand out and thumbed the seat button. The whole chair levered itself backwards. Perhaps this might be just hint enough for the neighbour.

He remembered what it was he had come back to England for. And it had been only a matter of a couple of weeks. The shortest trip back he had ever made. Why had he made this quick flight over? To begin with, it was out of a sense of duty. The London lawyer had written to him in Araçatuba, state of São Paulo, to tell him of his mother's death. The letter had taken four months to reach him. The lawyer didn't know that Geofrey had already moved up north more than a year back. Geofrey had been living in the tiny community of Chimboa up towards Santarém on the Amazon, and regular mail was rare indeed.

When he opened the letter, four months too late, he realised there was little he could do. She had been buried, by then. And all the lawyer could complain about was the number of cables he had sent out earlier to Araçatuba. Well, sometimes, in certain areas of Brazil, cables fare worse than letters do.

But Geofrey did make the trip home, nevertheless. He wanted to clear everything up finally. Although, to the best of his knowledge, there were no other relatives, he wanted to wipe the slate clean, perhaps give that lawyer a rocket for not knowing the new Amazon address at Chimboa, pay the man his fees, and find out what mother had left in her deposit account for him.

Geofrey lay back in his tilted seat and remembered the details of those past couple of weeks in England. He remembered the way he felt when the incoming plane dipped its wing through the low grey sky and he saw Gatwick Airport spread beneath him, with body tilt and sole and heel cavity bumps as the wheels rolled out for the landing. He remembered his thoughts. He hadn't seen the old country for three years, and this England to him was a cottage industry of mortgage keepers and property pigs at swill in the overdraft vat; an island community of greed merchants chasing pennies; for Geofrey was one of those people who had rejected us, he wanted those wide open spaces abroad where such corners as our tiny island of mixed economy capital thinly disguised in the form of democratic socialism couldn't affect him, you see – he could no longer live in a society within which he had no control. Too complex an organism. Too rarefied an existence. And Geofrey had decided on, of all places, Brazil.

Geofrey leaned back in the plane seat. He remembered what he had come back for, this last time. He had come back for a few days to cut himself adrift from us, for ever. It had been a final last couple of weeks among us. Geofrey thought back, he remembered every detail . . .

*　　*　　*

At the Customs line-up it was a slightly peculiar feeling to discover he could no more go through the glass door to a booth marked 'UK passports only'; Geofrey had to stand with his Brazilian passport in a very much longer queue. He had acquired Brazilian citizenship in the last twelve months. The process was almost complete. He was now a foreigner, in a strange land, and although he could speak our language, he no longer wanted to understand us, our snobbish and peculiar ways, our class-dominated stratas, our complacencies, our rituals and our indomitable (from time to time) resiliences. Geofrey hurried with his suitcase to the airport exit.

He asked the taxi-driver to take him to Curzon Street.

"The Flying Wheel," he said.

"The what, mate?"

"One hundred and seven Curzon Street."

"You mean one of them red houses at the top end?"

"That's right."

"It's a block of offices now."

"Don't be so silly!"

"It is I swear! Pulled them down late last year."

"Block of offices!"

"Sure – that's progress isn't it, mate?"

"I won't believe it until I see it."

The taxi-driver grinned at Geofrey, and switched his meter—

"It's your money, chum!"

He always stayed at The Flying Wheel when he came home. It was a seedy hostel for RAF and RFC Veterans; Geofrey had a permanent in to the place because his father, during the war, was a partner in the club. Geofrey's father died in a raid over Arnhem. The partnership didn't mean much, except a free hotel room whenever he came up to London, whether it was as a schoolboy or as a university student. In the past ten years he always made his base at the club when he flew over from Rio on the Sunday/Monday British Caledonian Special.

The taxi eased up outside a tall white office colossus in Curzon Street, the taxi-driver leant back and slid open his partition—

"What I say?"

"You should have taken me to Ladbrokes on that!" said Geofrey.

"Where do you want to go now?" the taxi-driver searched in his mind, "– Vauxhall Gardens!"

"Good cheap hotel."

"Sussex Square? OK?"

"Fine," said Geofrey.

Geofrey had lived in Brazil for fifteen years. He first went out there in 1958 at the age of twenty-four. There was a quality about him which was prematurely old. Whenever he thought of England he did so with idiosyncratic mannerisms; he still referred to Wimpy Houses as *Lyons Corner Houses*, policemen were still public-schoolish *rozzers*, socialists were Daily Telegraphese *lefties*, and he liked to call the radio *the wireless*. People get like that when they stay away from us for so long, it becomes a kind of defence mechanism, a way of looking at England in a cosy perspective, cynosure for the cynic for one who can't or won't see the change in us.

Geofrey was the sort of expatriate who thought of 'beating it up' in Berkeley Square, or thereabouts (that is, if no developer had pulled the place down for more office blocks), and use the facilities of a club for which his membership card was long since out of date. He'd meet a friend in the bar of the Sloane Square Hotel who'd smile when Geofrey brought out his old phrases, who was sure to say—

"Well you have been away a long time haven't you?"

Or there was always an absentminded chum up in the glass-encased restaurant at the White City (he never missed the dogs on Thursday evenings) who might say to him—

"Have you improved your *Spanish* in Brazil, Geofrey?" But that hurt. That really struck home to the expatriate. It was like being pummelled against the ropes in the Fourth's light middle finals at school, the rest of the house shouting and gunning for you, but when the referee wasn't looking, I'll never forget that blind squirt thought Geofrey, his opponent odious Marchy Clutterbuck caught him one well below his waist-band, and Geofrey for the remainder of that term at Haileybury lived with the social insecurity of his left ball suspended in that bony socket just behind his pubics. Laughter in the showers, swimming-pool changing-room derision . . .

Hitler only had one ball – lada dadada da dumdum!

Geofrey made a couple of calls on old friends. He visited the lawyer who had some papers for him to sign. He had to sign further documents at his mother's bank to take possession of her small estate, there was a current account with an overdraft (lawyers' fees, funeral costs etc), and a deposit account of £4,000. Most other matters had been dealt with in his absence. The house his mother lived in was rented from the Church Commission. The furniture was placed in a warehouse to wait on Geofrey's word. Her personal papers, clothes and mementoes were in the keeping of his mother's neighbour in Windsor.

Geofrey sat in his little room on the second floor of the terrace hotel in Sussex Square. It was cold here in London, and there was so little for him to come back for. He didn't miss his mother much. What had she ever done for him? After his father died, she palmed him off to grandparents, and after the war he lived with her for less than three years. He was at an expensive boarding school, his grandparents paid for that, and he knew he had inherited from his mother a selfishness which he had always despised to find in her.

He hired a car and drove out to Windsor. It was always a pleasant sensation for memory to see the castle rise up in the trees from the slip road off the motorway. But in the last twenty-four months many other things had changed. Geofrey turned left down the High Street, it was a four-mile drive past the hospital and the kindergarten school he remembered, and then the road branched into a triangle.

The tall grey house his mother used to live in was surrounded by a batch of brightly red-tiled estate bungalows. Geofrey parked the car and watched a file of children hesitate at the pavement. The air was filled with a busy clattering concrete sound. The corner shop where, as a child, he raced to buy sweet milk tablets, was no longer there. Why should I expect it to be, he asked himself? That old lady Mrs Whateverhernamewas must be long dead.

He looked across the road from the house. That was where his mother kept up a pretence of good old English class. She used to encourage him to stop by at the pretty white-wood cottage, down a drive, what seemed to him a smuggler's cove of sinister green trees and huge bushes, a cloistered arboreal wilderness, to invite himself to tea with Lady Bourne May. Ah dear old Lady Bourne May, with her summer jams and yellow sun umbrella out on the Russian dacha-like porch tapping her white high-heeled tennis boots, counting her ration coupons through a pair of spectacles which only had one lens, the right eye'd lens, he recollected. Come here, Geofrey ... it's perfectly all right, you can tell your mother you can build the wigwam underneath the monkey tree and if you and your friends want to roast chestnuts just be sure you blow the fire out afterwards, I don't want the tree up in flames.

That's all right, Lady Bourne May, he replied, squeaky piping boy's voice, I have no friends, I just want to roast my own chestnuts.

Such a peculiar boy you are, you should have lots of boy-friends at your age, Geofrey.

I like to be alone, because it's nicer that way.

The tired wood supports of the wide gate which opened on to the Lady Bourne May's drive were still there. Nothing else was. That green wilderness thick with birds and berries and fir floors deep in evergreen spikes was vanished. Geofrey leant against the remains of the gate, a concrete broadwalk led to rows of nasty white garages, and behind them stood a caravan site. About a dozen fibreglass caravans in a ring fence of barbed wire, and not a single tree was there left.

He remembered Lady Bourne May's dog – Scotty; he helped her bury him under the monkey tree. That beautiful Victorian planted folly tree, perhaps it came from Japan, so thick and strong it once was he built his own tree-house on a Piccadilly Circus of boughs more than twenty feet from the ground.

Geofrey thought of that little white dog, Scotty, stumpy legs leaping in the snow, barking bright-eyed yappy animal a bus ran over on a Friday afternoon. Yes, that was the place, Scotty's grave must be right underneath that blue and gold caravan with it's pylon high TV aerial. No sign of the tree, though.

The road was called High Standing Hill when he was a boy. He and his mother and Lady Bourne May sat out in deckchairs to watch the King and Queen ride open carriage to Ascot up High Standing Hill. And Lady Bourne May could recognise practically every last person in the first four carriages.

Although this was war-time, everything at the bottom of High Standing Hill seemed to have a gentle endearing quality about it. To a boy, on occasional visits to his mother, with a garden like Lady Bourne May's to run in, people did seem kinder, there was a mildness, a gentleness, a soft flowing very middle-class assurance that no matter what Mr Hitler got up to, very little would change. And the sweet-shop would always sell milk tablets, Scotty the dog would always be burrowing for rabbits he couldn't possibly catch under the monkey tree, and Lady Bourne May would never empty her gauze-covered larder cabinet of her delicious jams, home-made almond and date cake and sugar-topped raisin buns flavoured with cinnamon.

Now, High Standing Hill had another name, it was called Hospital Road. As for Lady Bourne May's wilderness garden, that was Evergreen Caravans Ltd. And the white-wood cottage with the Russian verandah was no more.

Geofrey could have stayed longer. He might have had the courtesy to take a bunch of flowers to his mother's grave at the Windsor Park cemetery. But he didn't. A coldness gripped him. He had no tears. It was all finished. There had been a certain passing of years, and that was that; there had been 1943 and bad old Mr Hitler, there had been 1956 when he joined the army in National Service, and there came 1958 when he left England for good.

Always on his own, too much of a selfish one, and what sentiment he could have felt for the past was now a loathing; there was no place for him in this country.

He was standing in Leicester Square, with his Brazilian passport safely tucked in his inside pocket, listening to the jumble of foreign accents all around him, literally three out of every four people were foreigners, London was awash with Swedes, Germans, Americans and Japanese, and he felt peculiarly British listening to them. I must be going mad, he thought. It wasn't this bad three years ago when I came back.

Tonight he'd have a quiet meal on his own in Jimmy's in Soho (nobody had taken that away yet), and perhaps a few doubles in Jules' Bar in Jermyn Street before British closing hours.

The rush hour was descending fast. At the back of Simpsons in Jermyn Street a tall woman with a weight of baskets and packages collided into Geofrey. He helped the woman pile her goods back into their precarious position against her chest. Then she looked at him and, before she could speak he too recognised her.

"Geofrey! ... Isn't it?"

It was Alison, all right. They hadn't met since 1963. By then she had children and a new home somewhere in London, and very far removed from him.

"Christ! What a coincidence!" he blurted out; but on second thoughts, he didn't think he meant to sound so encouraging.

"Like a Noël Coward comedy, what?" she said.

He looked very blank at her.

"I mean," she added hastily, "meeting like this, after all this time!"

He nodded. Alison always did have cultural pretensions.

She took his arm and laid half her packets against him, and they made their way towards Jules' Bar, it was a bit of a battle, because most of London was trying to get through them to reach the tube station in Piccadilly.

"I'm taking you to the very place for a quick drink." She smiled up at him.

"Where's that?"

"You know perfectly well where!" she had to shout above the traffic.

Jules' Bar was always the same. The dark fat seats were lined with old Cavendish Hotel days, and there was a carefully fostered gloom, cavernous with echoes of shrouded forgotten gossip from the early fifties. Alison didn't look too good. That Leslie Caron baby-face he remembered so well was turning to fat, fatty round and cunning little tired tyre marks at the corners of her eyes. She looked at his hair—

"I can see you're not going bald!"

"Thanks a bunch!"

"No. I mean it. Everyone else I know – all my husband's friends, their hair is falling out like spring snow."

"How's Charlie?"

"He's going bald too."

"That's nice. Anyone else going bald I used to know?"

"Are you still in Brazil?" she asked, there was a hesitancy in her voice, as if she could hardly bring herself to ask such a question, it all seemed so absurd, so far-fetched, for a man like Geofrey to settle in a place like that.

"Not at this moment in time no – but in general, I'm a Brazilian," he said confidently.

"I'll never understand you, Geofrey ..." and with afterthought, "none of us will, I suppose."

"That's right," he said.

"I mean – how do you live? Where do you live?"

"I live in a kind of wood chalet hut right out slap in the middle of nowhere."

"How extraordinary."

"And I like it," he said firmly.

"But Geofrey – it's none of my business, but – what is the

point of living there? What are you doing – day by day? Is it fun?"

"No. It's not fun at all. It's extremely unpleasant."

"I see," she clearly didn't.

"I sit in my hut and I've got a bit of land – not much by Brazilian standards – and I'm waiting."

"For what?"

"I'm waiting for the Army to build a bloody great road right through my land, and then I'm waiting for the Japs and Germans to come along with their electronic probes, and find I've got nickel and bauxite and oil underneath my hut – and I'll be rich."

She looked at him as if he was belted in a strait-jacket and eight male warders were trying to bundle him into an ambulance.

"How long have you been waiting?"

"In Brazil, everything takes time."

"How long?"

"Where I am now – in Chimboa – about three years."

She stood up abruptly. A quick undisguised glance at her watch. Her long skirt trailing, she wore tight-fitting expensive-looking leather boots stitched in a patchwork pattern of various colours. Teeth just a touch stained yellow from nicotine. Fussy bustling manner of good taste and confidence, a wife with a well salaried husband, two cars, a daily, and a free box in the Albert Hall they can borrow off a friend to hear Neil Diamond or some nostalgic R&R revival group, rustle of ten pound notes in a coy Boer War tobacco tin, simply distraught she won't be able to get a taxi this time of night—

"Geofrey I'm sorry I do apologise" – if it was one thing girls like this are good at it is the meaningless apology – without one whit of an attempt at disguising lack of sincerity, "I must go now. I have to put the children to bed. Nanny's night out. Charlie's in Birmingham – business – and I'm on my own and . . ."

He stood up. A perfunctory kiss for her. Her mouth opened wide with an idea—

"Look. I'm sorry rushing away like this. So interested in you and Brazil. Come to supper tonight? Won't you? Oh please?"

"Are you sure Charlie is in Birmingham?"

"Of course he is," with impatience.

Yes, he said, all right, he said; and she was gone with a whirl of packages and stumping leather heels in the glass doorway.

He sat in the gloom on the fat bench seat, and the barman found him a bottle of Southern Comfort. There was a time when he knew her well. That first year in the army in Malaya, in 1956. She had been a nurse out there. Charlie was his best friend, and though Geofrey found her first, first fell in love with her, and was first with a bungling love grope in a jeep beneath a bamboo awning in the fuel store compound, Charlie was the one who won out in the end.

He didn't want to remember too much about it. Perhaps he and Alison had tried to make love a couple of times, in that sweat heat, and Geofrey had failed miserably; he became frantic about it, fear, impotence, self-recrimination ate into him, and out of desperation he asked her marry him. He shouldn't have asked her that particular night. But how was he to know? Alison and Charlie spent that day together, and Charlie had seduced her with every inch of confidence Geofrey so badly lacked.

It hurt for a while. He and Charlie were once such inseparables. He confesses all his impotencies to Charlie, then his best friend after listening to the sob story for weeks on end, ups and screws the girl himself. So much for best friends. There were to be no more of them in Geofrey's future.

Silly youthful blind years, all right so they were, but Geofrey still ached for that girl; this lonely boy who chopped off caterpillars' heads in Lady Bourne May's garden grew up into an uncomfortable loner, with no confidence in his sex, a sullen personality quick to resent, long to forgive his best friend, even after Charlie and Alison's wedding. Charlie lacked tact then, too. He wrote to Geofrey asking him if he'd like to be best man, do the honours old thing make up yes? To please us, he wrote, and Geofrey never spoke to him again.

He bought a bottle of wine at an off-licence duly noting the curious VAT tax everybody must pay now, in addition to the retail price, he picked up an evening paper at a corner stall and queued for the bus Alison explained he must take to come within walking distance of the house.

It was a curious sensation looking at the news. He was told there are 20,000 homeless families in London, that millionaires trebled their fortunes by keeping office blocks empty, the cost of living according to the Retail Price Index was going up at the rate of 18 per cent a year as against wages which rose at (net) 14 per cent, and when a girl typist received £45 a week with vouchers a Scots miner collected a £26 basic ex over-time, for every new hotel room built the government provided a £1,000 subsidy, meanwhile a pensioner was forced to spend two thirds his pittance on rent for a gas-fired single room.

Alison lived in a tall terrace house in a square in Islington. The paint outside was very new and there was a swish of Morris patterned curtains across balcony windows on the first floor. She came to the door with a corkscrew in her hand, and when she saw the bottle he carried—

"I must have been clairvoyant!" she smiled out loud.

Supper was laid out in a Formica and polished wood recess behind the kitchen and Alison turned knobs and rotated timing mechanisms on a wall of cookers which looked as complex as an ICBM chart operator's table.

"Charlie's doing well ..." he murmured.

"Well, of course you haven't seen him for years – I don't suppose you want to anyway – but you remember how keen he was on printing? He has this small press of his own – and Conservative Central Office gave him a contract for bumpf posters and circulars – and it all grew from there. He's got a German partner, and they print most of their stuff in Holland."

"Ah yes."

"Printing is much cheaper in Holland – don't have the same awful union troubles."

"Course not."

"But you mustn't go back to Brazil thinking we are the new rich – I mean, for example, we bought this house eight years ago for £6,000, and what's more we had two sitting tenants – awfully difficult it was to get them out, do you know Charlie had to arrange an overdraft from the bank to give them lump sums so as they would agree to go? We didn't have time to find them alternative accommodation. Now they say – insurance valuers say the house is worth £50,000, isn't that amazing?"

"Oh yes."

"But we don't go out much – watch telly most evenings – had a bit of luck last year – just before the mortgage people stopped handing out loans for second homes. We found this dear black and white cottage in Suffolk. Friend who also lives near said a builder was trying to buy it to knock it down, so we rushed in and just managed to pip the man to the post. Awful luck really when you think of it – he wanted to knock it down and put up back-to-back chalets. Charlie found out how old the cottage was – got a Grade Three preservation order stamped on it and the council gave us a grant for the roof, and then we ripped out the tiling in the bedroom and found a Jacobean iron grate and . . ."

A certain numbness spread over him. What was she talking about now? Oh, she'd bought a Renault car, and you know how reliable these are supposed to be, well, the first week I had it, it—

"I'm afraid that's the end of the wine you brought, Geofrey."

And she was telling him to be very quiet, and if he followed her like that, she'd give him a peep at the children, and there they were in wash yellow painted rooms at the top of the house. They're always asleep by eleven. Two healthy-looking boys, walls of prints, football socks dangling out of drawers and long modish hair. Perhaps ten or eleven years old

He and Alison sat in the upstairs sitting room. He persuaded her not to compulsively switch on the television. She glanced at him with a kind of sulky distress, as if to say, there really isn't any more I can tell you about myself and Charlie, and the kids and the house.

Her chatter slowed up. Geofrey lay slumped in the armchair. He hardly dared to speak. A violence welled up inside him. So this was what he'd missed. These two sleeping lads upstairs could have been his. He liked to imagine, a shade wistfully, this woman could have been his wife. There was a defined and carefully perimetered map to Alison's existence; this was how it would be through the seventies, through the eighties, this bland complacency fattening in a consumer's market, a genteel decay vacuum-packed with suitable phrases for inevitable events, clothes and actions custom-tailored for a lifestyle, aspic preserved human jars, containers of i.q. intelligences, men and women undeniably overburdened with charm and response and alertness, push-button contributors of millions to doubtlessly deserving starvation causes. Geofrey helped her place the smokeless fuel in the grate, the flames leapt with the aid of packaged firelighters. A cold anger crept through him. He was a murderer of these selfsame complacencies in himself.

"Alison?"

She knelt by the fire, her fingers mimed sudden cold, there was a certain look in her eyes, a distant remembering of him, but long in the past, long and far away—

"Do you think, perhaps, you and I might have stayed together like this ... instead of Charlie," he said.

"I'd almost forgotten," she white-lied.

"No you hadn't."

"I don't think it would have ... Geofrey," she said.

"I thought I loved you so much I was going crazy inside," he said.

"What would you have done? Taken me to Brazil?" the slight sarcasm in her smile.

"On the contrary I might have worked hard here – done what Charlie has done – made this made that ..." he tailed away unconvincingly.

"You're not like that, Geofrey."

"No?"

"You like to do everything your own way. Tell nobody what you're up to. You don't want people – you don't want to mix like Charlie can or – why don't you admit it?"

"In other words you and I never had a chance?"

"That's right ... I'm sorry," softly.

"... You don't have to try to be kind to me," he murmured, after a pause.

"I don't understand."

"You found a better lover he happened to be my best friend and you both took off. Right?"

"Wrong."

"You want to conserve this you want to slap a Grade Three preservation order on that as if this whole country is a sort of museum piece and you want to sit in this centrally heated pinewood polished mortgaged coffin till the day you die. Right?"

"It's not that I mind you being so bloody rude, Geofrey," she sat back on her heels, a tiredness in her words, mouth curled in bored irritation. "You couldn't live here. You despise people like Charlie – who I happen to love – but you tell yourself you despise him for some adolescent wrong he did you. You lie to yourself. It's all nonsense. You hate us and despise everything we stand for, but you're too bloody scared to come out with it. You're too scared because you have nothing inside you to replace people like Charlie and me with! That's the truth! You look at me – sneer at me and think it looks so cosy and middle-brow, way of life or whatever it is that's the bee in your bonnet – I'll tell you it's difficult it hurts sometimes I ache in myself to live like this! Charlie and all! Don't sit there telling yourself I've sold off all my instincts and all my sensitivities, don't think I don't wake at night screaming and crying because I know no more how to justify my little way of life than you do!"

She thought, perhaps, Charlie had kept some very good brandy in the cupboard under the stairs. She was right. She came back with a remarkably good-looking vintage. She stood by the cane and glass trolley where the glasses were, she was saying how silly it was to shout like this, let's make up, there is so much to talk about besides—

"... Now I want to hear about Brazil. And—"

He stood by the door. His voice was calm and flat but quite emphatic.

"Alison, you don't fucking want to know any such thing, you can watch it on telly on a Sunday afternoon documentary until your eyes turn square! Let's get that straight!"

She followed him out of the door. A flushing red bloomed on her cheeks. But she wasn't going to reply. Geofrey, just as she remembered him years ago, had a cold withdrawn manner once he became angry, as if every word he uttered he really wanted to swallow back and forget about.

At the front door he turned to her. She wanted to say I suppose this means we'll never ever meet again. Well, I'm sorry, I didn't want it to turn out like this.

She didn't, though. Just as well. For Geofrey already knew it.

Friends drove him to a house near Oxford for a Sunday lunch.

"You'll love them, dogs and kids and croquet and they've got at least three hundred acres."

Geofrey smiled to himself. He didn't bother to explain. They'd only think he was doing the smug sneer arrogant expatriate thing.

But 120 hectares or thereabouts where Geofrey came from was equivalent in his mind to the amount of space the GLC car park behind Trafalgar Square took up.

Lunch was on the lawn. (Of course it was.) Geofrey ate on his knee with the assistance of a black terrier. It hadn't begun to rain. It would. In due English time.

A tall girl with a very loud voice spoke about 'the third world', and Geofrey winced to himself, he supposed this was one of the new phrases they used back here to refer to anything further away across the sea than the Scilly Islands.

She was intelligent he'd been warned, that's right Geofrey just the sort of girl you ought to take back with you to Brazil the kind of girl who would love a challenge.

She wore flapping clothes in a pointedly gypsy fashion with bangles and rings and clattering Moroccan droopy things which rivalled her voice for distraction; she has a 'first' the voice murmured, connected by marriage to Welsh border politics.

"Tell me," she asked, "did you improve your *Spanish* in Brazil?"

He quite visibly slowed. The prime piece of roast beef on the end of his fork which he'd kept so prizedly till last was snapped sniffed and gobbled down the terrier's pink tongue.

He looked across the lawn, over the trees, birch, ash and laburnum and Victorian policy evergreen, to the soft folds of the hills in the distance, and there was the start of a valley where pylons strode across the first fields of the valley basin, and then and there he made up his mind this was the last time he'd come back to England.

The very last. That bloody membership card to a club now long out of date was going down the toilet. As for friends – you mean these cosy sods borrowing money from the banks against their mortgages and their life insurances to buy yet another German car, you mean these dwarfs who take out yet more loans against doubled and tripled paper values of their houses to pay up a sixty per cent bite from the Inland Revenue, mean all these charming wives with children and nannies who are for ever apologising to him that they just simply somehow never have the time to write, and anyway Geofrey, there never is much to write about from here is there—?

Geofrey contacted the British Caledonian office in Regent Street. They had a seat for him on the next Sunday evening flight to Rio. From Rio he'd fly north to Belém on the Amazon, the rest was easy.

There is a certain comfort in not having any goodbyes to make.

You are left alone shuttered inside yourself. The climacteric atmosphere of arrivals and departures in an airport increases that drama of isolation. Geofrey very much appreciated the feeling. It was perfect fare for loners. For those guys who wanted to remain untouched by others. Those singular types who, out of thick-skinned blandness or sheer bloodymindedness or small paranoias inbuilt with spite and fear, call it what you will in someone like Geofrey, need only to speak to themselves and to hear their own answers. Something along the lines of that homily – only islands produce single children, and continents produce brothers. Geofrey was a single ...

*　　　*　　　*

That Latin American bore beside Geofrey lowered his seat back on a par with our hero who was aboard the plane bound for Rio never to return to us.

"Geofrey, is it ... ?"

"That's right ..." in at least a civil tone.

The chundering roar of the plane reverberated in Geofrey's ear. He kept his head close to the slide curtain by the window. But the Latin American expert wouldn't go away.

"I just about lived almost every damn country South America – except Brazil. What you do in Brazil, son?"

"I used to buy cattle ..." said Geofrey, "but I don't do that any more, really."

"You don't look you retired either?"

"No I ... I used to buy cattle down in the south. Then I moved up to the Amazon. Bought a piece of land. That's about it."

"What you do with the land?"

"Not exactly anything. I just sit there."

"Where is it?"

"Right out nowhere north Amazonas. You wouldn't have heard of it. Nothing there at all – coupla shacks."

"You got to live. What do you do? I mean – with this land?"

"I don't do anything. I just sit there and wait. That's all I do." There was a defensive edge to Geoffrey's voice. He wasn't going to explain what you do with a piece of land middle of nowhere in central Brazil to a know-nothing like this bore beside him. How could he understand the joy of it? The way you just sit and wait with all those other brasileiros out there, dreaming and scheming, that one day, big brasil nut boom bust day, the miracle might happen to you and your land. The saudade of it, the hopeless singing the optimistic tears. Nobody but a Brazil nut would understand it.

"Let's get this straight," the bore bit hard, "you sitting in the middle of the jungle doing nothing – just waiting – sitting on all this land you got doing nothing with it?"

"In a little while I might buy some stock. I don't have any money now to buy beef."

"What kind of land is it – is it fertile?"

"Not particularly."

"Will it grow anything?"

"Not too well."

"They say most of that mato stuff inside load of crap first rains come all get washed away with the topsoil."

"So they say ..." Geofrey murmured.

"Then you got nothing – lot of red rock and black tree stubble."

"They say so ..." murmured Geofrey again.

"Is it true?"

"Perhaps."

"Well what—"

"And perhaps not." Geofrey wasn't prepared to let him complete his obvious next question, "Perhaps there is so much land that, in the end, it don't matter if a little bit gets leeched." Geofrey was quickly sinking into the pidgin Latin American patter you can so easily pick up. The adverbs and the pronouns were fading from his tongue.

"Well ..." the tired deeply lined face with the know-all voice scratched his head, "it makes no sense sitting on a heap of earth slap middle of the forest, no sense at all."

"I'm waiting for the new highway to come through. They driving a big road up from the Cuiaba/Porto Velho route. Big six-lane fist of a road right through the central plateau of all

Amazonas south of the Amazon. That's what I'm waiting for."

"You must have a hell of a lot of patience, son, because, mark my word – when people like you do find one of these roads come close enough in to your land, and you start thinking the road will be your fortune – I'm telling you, you got it wrong. You think you can sell off your land make vast profit to land-prospecting big industrial concerns make you fat offer for mineral rights. You think oil down there right under your chicken strip massaranduba tree – rich Japs want to pay you zillions for it! I just don't believe all that Brazil miracle nonsense. You want to know how much it costs to keep Brazil miracling? It cost say twelve billion dollars they borrowed from shit knows where! What happens when they got to pay it back? What happens when they can't borrow no more? What happens when the roads creep over with mato all over again because it is too expensive to maintain them? All I say – you must have a hell of a lot of patience, son."

"I have ..." almost inaudible. A stone between Geofrey's teeth. He bit hard.

"I hate to put you down, son, all those land dreams and the like, but ..."

"Think nothing of it ..."

"And how long you lived out there on this piece of land you bought?"

"Not long ..."

"And you speak Portuguese?"

"I believe so ..."

"You speak it well?"

"Told I do ..."

"Son, when I hear Portuguese," the know-all said expansively, "it's like listening to a disease of the throat!"

He went on to describe the purity and joy in speaking Latin Spanish. The uplift and the dignity of the language compared to Portuguese.

Geofrey wasn't the rising kind. Nothing the man said could make him blow his stack. He'd worked too hard out there at becoming a Brazilian. All those years he'd practically gutted his larynx like a fork raked over a herring spine to pronounce those slushy imprecise tones, and now he had such a command of the tongue he could fall into any *giria* from Amapá to Rio Grande do Sul. He loved his disease of the throat.

He wanted his Brazil. He was going back to that humid bath for good, never to return to us, and in his going lay a realisation that there was no place left for him any more in the old country. Insular colony of the righteous, island outpost of Europe, post-war exporter of the mini car, the folding bicycle and the jump-jet, driver on the wrong side of the road the left, inventor of the environmental unsaleable the Concorde plane ... no more for Geofrey this old world of ours.

At any rate, it was the last time a black terrier on an Oxfordshire lawn gobbled Geofrey's big forkful of roast beef potato gravy and Yorkshire pudding with horseradish sauce.

* * *

Geofrey has been in Brazil fifteen years. He went out to Araçatuba shortly after he'd finished his National Service in Malaya, and that was where he first heard about the dream of Brazil. Malayans talked about Brazil with a certain sneer. Tender sardonic delight in a nineteenth-century Brazil which was raped. It was in Malaya those hijacked Brazilian rubber roots were first planted in the last century, that English colonel who shot his way out of the Amazon in a gunboat loaded with seeds. And that was the start of the rubber bust on the Amazon.

In ten years the price of rubber fell by seventy per cent. Jack-booted millionaires in Pará and Santarém and Manaus left deserted their French Empire marble palaces. Gold plated faucets and diamond bracelets and Titian paintings were auctioned off in Havana. Steamboats furnished in Witley Court Edwardiana tilted in the mud, rust rather than brocade decorated the saloons, and liana strangled the crimson velvet upholstery. Brazil became a word for laughter to the new planters in Malaya, the British Empire in the guise of zoological specimen hunter had pirated the greatest commodity Brazil had to export. Geofrey was fired by these stories. He had to go to Brazil.

He lived among the British colony in Araçatuba. And for years, while he possessed no real capital of his own, he worked to become a cattle buyer for the English fazendeiros. He saved his money. But he knew he could never afford the kind of rich pasture Araçatuba had.

Then the rumours of the trans-Amazonian highways started. After the fiasco of Brasilia, there was yet another dream of Brazil. Open up the interior. For months the papers wrote of nothing else. And Geofrey first heard of this place called Chimboa.

There was talk of a trans-America highway from Mexico to the tip of Tierra del Fuego. Talk of a Brazilian road the BR 406 which would traverse the whole continent south of the Amazon from Rio Grande do Norte to the eastern wall of the Peruvian Andes at Cruzeiro do Sol.

It was three years ago when Geofrey knew at least one road was under way. (Courtesy of the World Bank.) It was a 2,000-kilometre strip of red dust straight as a pencil for hundreds of kilometres from Cuiaba in the centre of Mato Grosso to a place called, but not found on any map, Chimboa.

Geofrey was cautious. Photographs in papers were unreliable. Only last month the *Globo Araçatuba* had described a picture of the Eiffel Tower as the new Embratel/NASA satellite radio link. A gigantic road in a state like Mato Grosso, only one of the twenty odd states which make up modern Brazil and yet this State of Mato Grosso alone is two and a half times the land size of all France, had to be seen to be believed. Geofrey flew to Cuiaba. He borrowed a Wyllis *Rural* and he drove six hundred kilometres west of Diamantina to find this BR 165, as it was called.

Under a mile-high cloud of red dust the army had started to cut a highway wide as a ten-lane motorway into the forest. It was worked on a twenty-four-hour shift, there was a mobile hospital, an attendant helicopter, there was a church in a stripped-down railway carriage floated on the back of a lorry, and there was even a whore house for Saturday nights. The road builders were ploughing through an area of thin forest which opened on to dustbowl seca land at the rate of twenty kilometres a week. But this was the dry season, when the rains came progress would be much slower and when they met the first of the big rivers which fed the Amazon from the south the mato and the liquid rot of vegetation would bring them almost to a standstill.

The gypsies from Cuiaba came out to the site on Saturdays.

The army let them through reluctantly. Geofrey met Eleanor, fat gypsy Jewess, colourful long-skirted cigano, she pulled at his trouser pockets, tapped his wallet with her palms—

"Tell fortune?"

"No."

"What you do here? You're not a Brazilian, americano spy?"

"No."

"How much money you got to give Eleanor?"

"None."

"What you want here, gerente, Englishman like you?"

"Have you heard of Chimboa?"

"Sure. Everyone heard."

"What is Chimboa?"

"It's a nothing – nothing place – nothing there."

"Is this road going all the way?"

"Give me your hand quick – I read it – I know what you want buy land up in Chimboa – road come through and you rich, right? I know you."

"How do you know all this?"

"Everyone say same thing – all talk the same, get to Chimboa and buy the land, find minerals and oil and gold they all say the same."

"Is it true?"

"Give me palm – cross my hand with fifty cruzeiros and I tell you."

"No thanks."

Geofrey smelt the insanity of the dream, there was an intoxication in the air, a blood rush to the mind, perhaps it was true, after all the failures in the past, this maybe was the dream which would return the promises of Brazil; and all around him he could see it in the Brazilians' eyes, the return of that secretive gleam, the mystery and treasure of hope had come back. Geofrey hurried.

*   *   *

Brazil never was a banana republic. Too big for that. No one group of mad dog fascists ever milked the country of its greatest resources and then fled to a Liberian residency with the goods safely tucked away in a Swiss vault. But there has always been a familiar pattern of control.

In our century a hero of the Left like Carlos Prestes was on the verge of rallying the northern states when the army crushed him. At one time, Getúlio Vargas, who was if anything a precarious ally of the Left, could rely on a proletarian vote to fend off the armed forces. And João Goulart, though suffrage still restricted to the literate, appealed to the masses with proposed rent controls, agrarian reform and nationalisation of oil. Then the military moved again. And whenever they struck, it was always a return to the ironically named estado novo.

Brazil has had its booms – the gold, the rubber, the diamond, the oil, it was João Goulart who put his finger on the biggest boom of them all, the land.

Goulart wanted to shift the shanty-dwellers from the city surrounds on the east coast to the interior. He wanted to give each family ten hectares, on the condition they would move there, stay there and work the land. Once again the army seized power and Goulart fled. But he touched a nerve. The future of Brazil was not in concrete nightmares like Brasilia a few hundred kilometres inland, absurd lonely buildings on a dehumanised planalto extravaganza of marble and glass and nowhere for people to walk built for tourists who needn't leave their hotels; the future was in the millions of square hectares in Acre, in Mato Grosso, in Rondonia, Pará and the Amazonas.

After Goulart came another estado novo. Congress was suspended. Basic legal rights were no longer guaranteed. Military high command announced presidents called Costa e Silva, or Castelo Branco or Medici. But nobody was hurriedly quitting the country with vast hidden profits. There is such a sense of nationalism and insularity no Brazilian really wants to leave his country. Why leave here, when here was everything?

And a lawyer, Roberto Campos, came up with the answer. This urbane man with his rich friends from Washington took a kind of twisted advice from Goulart's agrarian ideology. Yes, why not open up the whole of Brazil, somewhere in this green desert there ought to be twice the bounty of the Libyan oil fields and the minerals of Siberia under the mato.

The dream was as contagious to the two per cent rich as it was to the eighty-nine per cent poor. Forget about Goulart's appeal to the little man, his promise of work to the shanty-dweller, somehow smear Goulart with the *wickednesses* of Chinese communism, and make the great start of selling Brazil in the world's market. Ask the World Bank and IMF for a twelve million dollar loan. Sell half if not two thirds of the entire state of Bahia (an area of land the size of West Germany) to American corporations, hand over to the USA controlling interest in five out of the largest nine manufacturing companies in Brazil. Bring the Japanese, the americanos, the Germans and the Lebanese here, whisper to the supposed free world that by the turn of this century half its resources will come out of Brazil. Forget about Goulart. Slice the cake. Sell it off. Make another cake. Auction that. Above all, build the roads. Build such highways, inland, straight red scars that dwarf anything the Inca or the Roman imagined, build 30,000 kilometres of road to open up the dark green heart. If Goulart's vision was of a smallholder's utopia, Campos had a dream of capital's last outpost in the west.

Estado novo?

* * *

Geofrey hurried. He flew to Santarém on the Amazon, and a diesel launch took him south, up river, to the collection of tin huts and telegraph poles the army had put up in Chimboa. At that time no civilian thought of flying in there, and the army gave no flight facilities in their cargo planes. Geofrey arrived at Chimboa, took one look at the huts and the little casa de planta shanty street, and he made up his mind on the spot. He took samples of the land at varying heights, he slept out in his rêde strung between trees, and after three days, he took a canoe back up north. From Santarém he ferried to Manaus. From Manaus he flew to São Paulo.

It wouldn't be a bad comparison to say Geofrey bought a

parcel of land north-west of Chimboa the size of Manhattan Island. The Ministry of the Interior sold him, with options on other land he hadn't got the available cash to pay for, a stretch of sertão and planalto and oddly rising bumps of serra at terms which worked out at about two English shillings an acre.

Much of the land was worthless, he knew this at a glance, it needed fifty acres to support one cow, but in certain places where streams fed the soil and where in the dry season there was still moisture on the lower plains, and no matter how thin the subsoil, the land here would last ten years or more, and that was far enough into the future for Geofrey.

He had sufficient funds to *form* the best of the land, perhaps after a second year a bank would lend him money against the increased value of his land and he could buy cattle. And Geofrey knew cattle. He was no great expert on land, it didn't matter, he had so much of it, and the BR 165 was coming closer each month; if this was going to be the great Brazilian boom he was in there in front of everybody else.

Nobody could elevate Chimboa to the status of a village once he'd seen it. Before the promise of this great trans-Amazonica highway it was a collection of planta roofed shacks which, from the air was simple enough to be mistaken for an Indian aldeia. Then the army came. They chose an area of sertão far enough away from the river for a landing strip for their FAB cargo planes. They built a water filter plant and they erected telegraph poles which travelled fifty kilometres into nowhere on either side of Chimboa. Each pole was capped with a basin sized arc lamp. And from a distance, say ... coming in to land in one of the army's Korean war vintage planes you'd have the impression things were really moving out here. At night the broad strip of dusty street could be floodlit and that shining new water plant could mean nobody any more has to boil their own water.

But you had to get closer to understand the Brazilian way.

For reasons never explained the generator for the impressive row of poles never arrived. For other reasons, just as complex no doubt, the engine to drive the filter plant never came up river on its raft.

Nobody who lived in Chimboa before the army got here was surprised at this. They kept their kerosene lamps burning just the same. And in the hut on a stilt platform which served as the pensão the gas-driven refrigerator remained the one gadget of any size which actually did function. The army put down boardwalks against the mud, and where a couple of frame stores stood they hastily put up a verandah-fronted post office, it was very reminiscent of a wild west Hollywood stoep. John Wayne would not look at all out of place here. There was the rail where the vaqueiros hitched their horses. There were, indeed, what might pass as cowboys in boots and stetsons lounging in front of the pensão, and the wind nudged the dust into scuddies of red cloud which drifted in the humid air. The difference being ... the horses were just too decrepit to ever appear in a Hollywood bangy-bangy (all Brazilians call their westerns that), somehow those boots never quite achieved the glamorous swagger of true Texan footwear, nor were their hats ten gallon, more of a five-pint size with a black plastic ribbon.

The Chimboans wore guns. Packed against the cowskin saddle mat there was invariably an antiquated over-and-under rifle. There is a kind of a law against carrying arms in Brazil. But people in the interior seldom took any notice. Tied to a man's belt you'd often see a holster which never quite fitted the German or Japanese revolver. And in places like Chimboa, there was another law, albeit unwritten, any Brazilian who hid his pistol was considered dangerous. If he showed his friends the gun on his hip there was a certain honesty about his intentions. If he concealed it well ... look out, steer clear. And who can tell? The traveller is left to wonder if this is just another John Wayne fantasy built out of seeing too many bangy-bangys.

A Tupi group of Aripuana indians drifted up to Chimboa from their reserve in the south-west. They appeared harmless and when Geofrey discovered them on his land he invited them to build him a wood bungalow with a porch. He paid them with goods from the store, took out to them cheap cotton trousers and shirts, and they had a liking for pinga, as well. Pinga was a fermented sugar cane brew, it worked out at about three English pennies a bottle.

Much has been made of the threat to the indian by the building of these great highways but, for some like the Capitão Pedro and his Aripuana group the closer they got to the road the better. They were the kind of indian long past first contact with branco. A taste for alcohol, they liked those flat rubber slip-on sandals with one tongue for the toe. And Capitão Pedro spoke good Portuguese. Eventually they would become the shanty-dwellers of Chimboa, long after the road had turned the place into a Kansas City.

Geofrey sat beside a group of vaqueiros on the porch in front of the pensão. A man passed around a cup of chá de mato. They each sucked at the green liquid through a straw. Geofrey watched a cloud of red dust rise up on the horizon of the dirt track to Santarém.

It was the first vehicle that had come down from the Amazon this week. The Brazilians guessed it was an army truck. The patrão of the pensão said he'd made no new orders. Geofrey watched the dust bowl with even more curiosity. He knew the army preferred to use the river or the air-strip for their supplies. It was too much of a risk to bring a lorry down that track. It had holes the size twenty-pound bombs blew out. And if your back axle went there wasn't a chance in ten days anybody would come by.

The travelling dust bowl bobbed and weaved down the long lonely track. Mato and undergrowth, brush and shifting red sand on either side of the track. Now it was a brown cloud, now grey, now it was yellow the sun catching the dust particles until their shadow re-aligned the vehicle. The air so thick, pregnant and paused like a glycerine drip, and the vaqueiros couldn't hear the engine yet, it was so far off on the planalto.

Wes and Linda had filled the back of their pickup with petrol canisters. There'd be no gas in a place like Chimboa, leastways not for sale. And they needed enough to make the round trip back up to Santarém. That was two thousand kilometres of petrol. Wes believed in planning ahead. He knew what these Brazilians were like. *Brazil nuts* he called them. He had them all worked out before he set foot on their soil.

Dwight Weslie was the kind of forty-five-year-old you could talk yourself into believing anything between thirty-eight and sixty. He stood about half an inch above five feet, but his tall Texan boots with their inward sloping heels gave him a much needed extra four inches. He was fair to ginger skin, much given to freckles, and if he ever took his stetson off you'd find a clear clean ginger bald round pate shiny and dappled. But he never ever did take his hat off, and he let long wisps of red hair dangle over his ears from the side. He had pugnacious shiny face, wide open green eyes, and somehow the pug bully look in his face was accentuated by a stubble no razor could ever quite trim away.

Linda was mouse. She had a nice easy American face, the shadows were quick around her eyes, and when she smiled there was an effortless plastic manner about it. She had never been born with the whiteness of her capped teeth. A good width of your hand taller than Wes, she had an upright way of standing, never to swell in folds beneath the cloth her buttocks inside her Levi's were pads of sparse flesh, which explained the stiltedness of her hips and the boyish strides she took.

When Wes stopped the pickup outside the pensão and the rattle of the engine died the air was filled with a remarkable silence, a silence of looking and waiting, and the red dust the pickup lifted behind it was so slow to sink in the soft air.

If you don't know the Brazilian stare it's worth considering. And long before you meet up with it.

Nowhere else in the world is there anything like it. Those vaqueiros can fold their hands together in their laps, and there falls over their deep caboclo colouring an appearance of total passivity, they shut their mouths over front molars which have long since departed, and the eyes open wide like a jacaré presented suddenly with a leg of prime boi two metres from its nose, and the eyes of the Brazilians settle back with an imaginary knife and fork to receive, store up, imbibe, it's a consuming process, more of a grand digestion of new information on the retina, this novel presence in front of them must be etched into the lining of their minds, and the sight of Wes and Linda that sponge liquid heat day in Chimboa was their meal of the month.

Not since Geofrey got here, and he with his perfect Portuguese near faultless in any *giria*, who they could always refer to as the americano behind his back because out there everybody with a mother tongue of English is an americano, had the vaqueiros of Chimboa got their eye-teeth into such an estrangeiros' arrival.

Wes strutted like a turkey-cock to unwind his legs. He put down his pocket Berlitz school phrasebook and opened his mouth, the vaqueiros caught gold glint of teeth.

"Descoolpey yuh all you mother fuckers," Wes reached behind with both his hands to pull the wet transparency of the cotton shirt from his skin, "and se pode falla inglês because that about all this fuckin' disease of the throat Portuguese I know? Yah get!"

Not a vaqueiro moved.

The brooding meal-making eyes barely lifted from Linda's breasts, beneath the damp tartan vest there was the swell of her body and hers were the first americano nipples those vaqueiros had seen since the Medici government banned the Italian (and only) edition of *Playboy* magazine Brazil ever allowed on the bookstalls.

Geofrey hesitated, too.

He'd learnt the custom of never trying to be noticed, out here. What was it in the americano's voice? A mid west or a north of the southern states accent, where did that annie-get-your-gun with a tin-plate tooth-support rattle in the adenoids voice come from?

"Now I don't expect any of you guys to read me the American Constitution," Wes tried again, "but I'd appreciate you saying something ..." and again – "huh?"

Linda licked her lips nervously, a moustache of moisture edged beneath her nose, it was so uncannily quiet with all these John Wayne figures on the stoep out front, she closed her eyes for a moment to shield from the heat, and for no good reason she believed she saw an image of that white rabbit Louisa with pink eyes which her Aunt Mim gave her for her thirteenth birthday. That rabbit was an unlucky gift that was. She looked up, the plumpish guy with piggy eyes was saying—

"Can I help you? Are you stopping ..." Geofrey emphasised the "here?". Les beamed ninety dollars of gold teeth.

"Linda?" Wes said.

She had only glanced at herself in the driving seat mirror, his voice boomed again—

"Hey Linda! Leave your face where it is!"

"Rude bastard," she whispered to herself.

"Howling eggs honey, it's a limey!" Wes shouted out impatiently.

Geofrey felt the blush rouge his cheeks. Something had made him speak up with a Haileybury school clip to his words. That odd mixture of a plum and a lisp, his tongue too far forward on his teeth, with a public schoolboy hint of disguised superiority.

"I'm Wes . . . and this is Linda. Don't pay no mind to her she's as stupid as she looks. She's with me."

"What are you doing coming down here? You can't go no further south until the road comes through. This is a cul-de-sac," said Geofrey.

"Cul—?"

"Dead end," Geofrey helped a little more.

"That's right, right on the nail you are skipper, Linda and me, me I mean me, I'm looking for land, out here in this very place—" but Geofrey was too busy watching the vaqueiros slide off their haunches to circle around the pickup to look for the damage the Santarém Road must have inflicted. Meanwhile, Wes could barely hang it all out quick enough, – "an' this new road comin' through an' all these rumours about them givin' the land away, nothing happened to Brazil like this since Henry Ford old goffer Ford tried to manufacture tyres up on the big one!"

"Big one what?"

"The *big one*, the Amazon yuh limey fucker the big *R*!"

There wasn't too much light at the end of Geofrey's tunnel. Never mind being called a fucker, he could hardly keep pace with the speed and noise of Wes's speech; somehow being called a fucker, and a friendly fucker at that, was at least a fair introduction to Dwight Weslie which he could interpret.

"You intend to stop here – in Chimboa!"

"We brought our own *readies*, do they cook for us out here?"

Geofrey sighed softly. You call hammocks *rêdes*. You pronounce them *hedgies*. Only Wes found a new pronunciation. Yes, indeed, Wes was coming through.

"It's the usual," said the limey, "supper at six, the patrão turns the lamps off at nine."

"Jeeesus God my pa used to tell me you grow old quicker in the dark. What does it cost?"

All that day Linda spoke little. But Geofrey liked her silence. It didn't matter at all if she really was as dumb as Wes said. Geofrey studied her face, it was even more silent, more remote when Wes was screaming at the top of his bull voice. She didn't actually flinch at the noise, but he could see a kind of angry recoil behind her pale eyelashes.

Wes's behaviour was so outrageous Geofrey had to hand it to him, it did the trick. When the army passed by and demanded they strip the entire pickup for drugs, the stubby little man, the wide-lipped americano, shouted so loud and so long at them those khaki figures eventually melted away in confusion. Wes had an overpowering nature, the Brazilians were the type to believe if a man shouted so hard he must have some semblance of authority to back it up with. And when the prefeito asked Wes for his gun licence, after catching sight of the rifle stock in the back of the pickup, though Wes had less than a dozen Portuguese words, he knew his man all right. He shoved a fifty cruzeiro note into the Brazilian's hand, tickled the prefeito's face with a gentle humorous slap, and shoved him off the stilt porch of the pensão with the ease of a man cracking lice between his fingernails and flicking it into the street.

"How can you possibly make yourself understood in this country if you won't learn the language?" Geofrey asked.

They were sitting outside the pensão. The fat patrão lingered behind them.

"Answer – you bawl loud enough for something you want in life they understand you from Hong Kong to Peoria!" Wes turned to the patrão, he opened his mouth wide and the patrão observed the americano's fine gold teeth with considerable awe, and Wes ushered into the air the sound weight behind a four hundred pound boi – "... ONE ICE COLD BRAHMA BEER YUH PIG AND BRING IT ME IN A GLASS!"

The patrão was behind his bar, in and out of his gas-powered freezer and across the room to the porch with beer and glass before the echo subsided. Wes grinned mischievously. Geofrey calculated the patrão had never put a beer in a glass in his Chimboa life before. It was a bravura performance and Geofrey acknowledged it. Wes was a survivor, out here.

"You're a soft enough looking guy, what are you, a kind of lawyer or something?"

"I live here."

"You kiddin' me!"

"It's a fact ..."

"But what can you do?"

"I'm a farmer."

"On your own?"

"Quite ..."

"Jeeesus – only a limey could be sitting out here in the middle of this. Now you ain't told me half the truth have you?"

"Haven't I?"

"You doin' something else – come on now—?"

"I'm waiting ... that's all."

"Waiting?"

"I'm waiting for the road ..."

"I knew it!"

"Oh?"

"You waiting for this road because one day yuh think it'll make you King Ranch rich? Right?"

"If you say so ..."

"Course I fucking well say so!" Wes's gold teeth mined a clacking laughter.

Linda's hammock was stretched across an open door, if there was any breeze that night she'd have the advantage of it, it was a kind of air-conditioned Chimboa privilege for her. There was caution in how Wes chose to sleep. He rigged up his rêde from the back of the pickup to the verandah roof beam. He was just in sight of Linda and if anybody touched the pickup he'd feel it the instant. There was no lavatory of any kind for Linda, but the patrão put a bucket by her rêde; the only other women in Chimboa were cafusos, itinerant mother whores for the porceiros by the shantyshacks, casual cooking labour in the pensão, and they didn't bother with buckets.

Wes and Linda certainly travelled light. Geofrey mentally checked the canvas sacks in the back of the pickup, there was little else – about half a dozen stacked G800 size retreads, and petrol canisters tied back with chicken wire for the return journey to Santarém.

At night the army kept to itself behind the air-strip. But indigenous Chimboa ate at the pensão. There was always the undignified scramble for chairs the moment a cafuso produced the bowls of beefy and rice and hot sauce and paste paper tasting manioc pulp. Before Wes grabbed his chair Geofrey noticed what appeared to be a revolver as thick as a pocket Bible against the stubby americano's hip. The vaqueiros were quick to follow his gaze.

"Well Jeff! ... just what is a limey like you doin' out here?"

"I—"

"And I want yuh to give me your life story inch by inch like it was the Bible you were telling."

"I—"

"But first, mostly, I'm gonna tell you mine!"

And it was worth hearing if you liked a Kurt Vonnegut read. But it certainly was far from the truth. One way or another, Wes had fought (at the top of his voice, naturally) a confusing series of battles on behalf of his grateful country from Guadalcanal to Formosa Straits and from the beaches of Tobruk to the final assault on Crete. The account didn't hold water the same volume he put back pinga with suck of lemon and ice scrapings from the patrão's freezer. Wes had been married a couple of times, in each case it was the woman who had done him wrong, and Linda's pale lashes quivered when he pounded the table with his fist.

"Women are whores ... !"

"Now he don't really mean what he say," Linda pipes.

"All women are whores – you included!"

But he was grinning and stroking her hair, and she tossed the long fringe out of her face and kept her mouth tightly closed.

Wes even believed he had twins somewhere in Japan. But the authorities—

"Just pulled me out of there so fast, I had no time to count them! And being the war you know ..."

He had worked merchant ships, one time he logged up in Canada on the State border of Washington. His home town was in Oklahoma, and that was where he met up with Linda. He had driven to a small town, nothing more than a street of stores, pool hall and gasoline station, to bury a brother-in-law. Linda lived a short way out of the place. She worked in the fields with her mother, and they were dirt poor.

Geofrey managed to squeeze an inquiry about Wes's accent beneath the flood of narrative, but it was Linda who spoke up—

"You thinking it sounds like a Texan speaking don't it?"

"Well ..."

"You don't need pay much attention to Wes's Texan voice. Wes believes he's a spiritual Texan don't yuh Wes honh?"

He grunted.

"You know what Texans call us in Oklahoma?" she looked up at Geofrey, her small fingers gently touched Wes's fist which lay on the table, "they call us oakies! They think they better'n us."

There were reasons, Wes hinted darkly, why he could not go back to the States, he had been forced, rather – obliged to leave the country hurriedly and about all the IRS allowed him to take out was a ten thousand dollar saving he had kept in his brother-in-law's deposit box.

"But why Brazil?"

"It's here, son, it's all here, come 1980, 1990, don't matter what you own long as you got land, this country's goin' save the West."

"Is that your political testament?"

"My what? Son, my politics is – what yuh can find at the end of a loaded rifle yuh can keep! Right?"

"What do you say, Linda?"

"Oh I guess I go right along with what he say?"

"That's right," said Wes happily, "an' even if I'm wrong Linda so stupid she still go along with it."

"Now I want you to know," added Linda stoutly, "I still got a mind of my own. Never did say I could talk about politics did I? So don't you put me down, like that!"

"Lindypants I don't want you getting roused up like that," Wes pinched her skinny buttocks inside the stained Levi's, he glanced across at the limey, "... Linda's one of them people who really do care about things. Linda cares very hard. She thinks all the time about hurting little animals and causing pain to pets and dogs and cats and birds, tell him it's true, Linda?"

She nodded dumbly, but she wasn't going to say any more. Afterwards, she thought, if he bothered to ask her she might tell this English guy she once dreamed of becoming a veterinary surgeon when she was at first grade, that's what she dreamed of, and she could have done it but her mother didn't want her to stay on at school after she was fifteen. And then ... perhaps not, Linda reconsidered, because it was blood that made her feel so weak, and when her white rabbit Louisa her Aunt Mim gave her died on her, spilling all that blood like it did, Linda vomited up two meals and an hour of strawberry malteds at Howard Johnson's, somehow the sight of blood made her knees jelly up, and that was why that particular ambition would never have come to anything. But Wes wouldn't understand even if she told him. He so rough.

"What do you know about farming, Wes?"

"I know as much as these Brazil nuts know."

"Yes?"

"You seen how they treat their land? Do you know how stupid the average Brazilian is? He more stupid than Linda is stupid – and that's pushing it some!"

Geofrey blinked.

"We goin' work our asses off we goin' to farm – here right here somewhere – and this road BR whateveritis comin' through comin' right past our front stoep won't it Linda?"

"Would you believe it – Wes has been studying the subject such a long time now—?" said Linda.

Somewhere he had found an old estado novo map with all the great highways on it the army promised to build. One of those Brasilia printed maps of such optimism they make topographical New York look like a National Park – sometimes there are more roads drawn across the forest interior of Brazil on these sort of maps than you can find in the whole of suburban São Paulo. And right slap in the centre of three great highways in the cartographer's imagination stood Chimboa.

"This place here, Jeff, is in the middle of all the Amazonas, give it a decade or fifteen years, and what have you got?"

The land boom light shone like a beacon in the oakie's eyes. One of these days, he added, centre of the Amazon basin south of the big river Chimboa will become the new Kansas City.

"You see Jeff ... I got a vision. Me and Lindy cannot fail, there'll come a time when all these Brazil nuts they just fade away they don't see it at all they the most unbelievably stupid pig ignorant sons of whores – and all women are whores son don't you forget that – may not look like it now but couple of years time this shovel of dirt pensão'll be a – we're sitting in the main bar of the Hilton Amazon hotel and it's right under our nose – Howard Hughes walk in this door he'd turn that air-strip into the biggest jumbo-jet skating rink South America ever saw – do you know what the experts say is under these rocks the bauxite the zinc the copper the industrial diamonds the – this is the vision I got, Jeff, and it ain't possible it can't come true!"

Geofrey raised his eyebrows in quizzical arcs, he looked at

Linda, she pushed her hair away from her eyes and leant like a child against Wes as if she needed his support, and the mosqus careened and zinged in a cloud above her head—

"What do you think Linda!"

"Oh I go along and agree with ever' word he says sometimes I think Wes talks a lot of wisdom don't you?" her eyelashes had a sheen of perspiration from the heat of the kerosene lamp which swung from the beam support in the ceiling.

The patrão took the plates away, and he commenced dowsing the lamps, although he left one alight; and three of the more courageous vaqueiros stood behind Wes in a semi-circle. They could not take their eyes away from the square-shaped bulge in his hip pocket. Wes hunched his shoulders uneasily.

"Tell those guys will you," he spoke softly, "they don't stop staring at Linda's tits so help me I might crack open their heads!"

"They are not looking at her tits ..." Geofrey lowered his voice. He tried to motion with his eyes to Wes's hip pocket. Wes touched his hip. The vaqueiros watched with that long meal-eating look.

"Just tell them not to crowd behind me will yuh, Jeff?"

"They want you to show them what you've got in that pocket."

Linda looked very confused, even a trifle taken aback; if what the limey says is true that these Brazil nuts prefer to look at Dwight's back pocket instead of her sweet nipples, what kind of guys are they?

"I'm afraid you don't understand," said Geofrey, "nobody can carry a gun and not show it. And that thing in your pocket looks like a revolver."

Wes was about ready to stand up and start screaming, his mouth flew open, the gold teeth sentinelled his larynx, and his fat dangerous fists were shoving the table away from him when Geofrey spoke with a quiet reasoned urgency—

"I'd be grateful for my sake, if not for Linda's, you'd take it out and place it on the table. That's all. They don't want a fight."

"Honh—?" Linda gently touched his closed red knuckle fist. He relaxed his grip on the table. He felt in his pocket and drew out a tobacco tin. He laid it in front of Geofrey.

"It ain't no gun yuh limey fucker yuh kook – look it!"

Wes, with worldly contempt, pulled open the tin and held it

out. Inside were two neat rolls of US hundred dollar bills bound with elastic.

"That's Linda and me's ten thousand dollars, that's all! Now you fuckin' well tell them guys," his voice rising rapidly, "don't ever think of looking in my back pocket again!"

The vaqueiros slipped across the room, and where they stepped out on to the verandah the darkness and the liquid mosquito-riding night consumed them. Geofrey apologised. He said the tin really did give the impression of a small flat German-make revolver.

"The hell it did!" snapped Wes.

And out here, this is how you must behave, this is how your Brazil nuts react to certain situations, but they won't bother you again, Wes.

"Damn right, they won't! I'll cut all their teeth out and set fire to their eyeballs!"

Wes did a bit of steaming and humping his high-heeled boots on the board floor, but for all his noise and his righteous capering, and the knotted muscles of his broad shoulders, and the way he projected his chin it seemed as far out as the brim of his hat, there was an element of caution behind the clowny gestures and the preposterous mien. This little runt oakie was a fighter. It could just be – he'd survive out here. This runt oakie with a mouth wide as a toucan's had a kind of built-in all-purpose early warning system. And in a place like Brazil, where they say they like you and they only want to please you but behind your back they are cutting you up in sections they are hating you so much, no Brazil nut was going to waste time bothering even liking Dwight, behind his back or to his face, and that's where he was safe.

Dwight Weslie stomping and bawling five foot of nothing all raggedy ass Peoria punk American ape-tree-top-true-grit of corn valley, in *his* terminology, sawn off stetson high roller, *his* view of things, last grand funk pioneer of the Brazil nut bust, *his* dream, boom boom go the land strike, *his* words – he all right, he make it, he safe.

* * *

Geofrey waited for a few more days. He wanted to see how long the americano's enthusiasm for Chimboa would last. It wasn't easy for either Wes or Linda to hang out in a place like this. Every moment of the waking day those black saudade eyes were pinning them against the horizon. They felt like microbes beneath a miroscope. They had no language, and every time the oakie opened his toucan mouth to speak a crowd began to form around him.

Nothing was going to deter Wes. He had made up his mind about Chimboa. This was to be the new Kansas City of the Amazon basin. So contagious was his enthusiasm, sometimes Geofrey could himself see, rocking at night in the straw-weave rêde Capitão Pedro's Aripuana family made him, waiting for the last frugal lamp in the patrão's shack to snuff out, the avenidas and praças of a Chimboa splendid and affluent beneath columns of concrete apartment houses; there would be bars that never closed, tiled bathrooms with showers with real faucets which didn't siphon brown river water at you, the sky at night barraged with the winking incandescence of blue and gold neon, and even the returned light from the moon on these incongruous towers would bleed the stars for whiteness.

Wes believed it pioneer's gold he had run into the limey. Geofrey showed him over his land, they spent nights up in the limey's wood house, their hammocks slung across the verandah. While Linda cooked beefburgers with a relish sauce (and that was just about all Linda could cook), Wes insisted on buying a portion of Geofrey's land.

"You got more land here than yuh can ride across in a day. Now you don't want all this I mean all of it?"

"When I bought it I had little choice, the parcel came in one lump—"

"But yuh don't want all of it?"

"No . . ." slowly.

"You can't look after all of it yourself, right?"

"When I can afford to buy cattle I'll have to hive some of it off."

"No no yuh don't understand – sell it to me now sell me and Lindy a fair block of it – and we be your neighbours. How does that strike yuh, buddy!"

"Well . . ."

"You want me and Lindy as your neighbour folks now don't yuh? Now tell us – ain't that true?"

"I . . . suppose that would be fine."

"You bet your sweet life!" the voice rising in the planta roof beams of the hut, "ain't it so, Lindy!"

"Fine by me . . ."

"Now, whadya say to that, limey?"

As far as the rains were concerned it was a good time to sell anything which might pass for grazing. The rains this year lasted well into June, and miles of red earth which had long since lost its topsoil yet retained that quick grass the retreat of the wet season always harvested. A strange grass, a cheat amongst grasses, like the mão de cabecho the colonial Brazil ghost with hands made of hair which melted in the daylight this grass melted in the first few weeks of the dry season. And the sun burning at its pitch would shrink these red miles into a rust ash, what water the foliage had willed would waste away into a soil made skeletal.

There was a stretch of land on a slight gradient looking south, it had a temporary fertile look about it, on its lower slope stood a pink flowering oiticicia tree, all around there was buriti and macaiba palm, and at first glance liana and tree strangler gave this green a dense mysterious quality. You'd find sudden clearings with pools, and Geofrey took the americano to the one place which, in Wes's mind, clinched the deal. It was a natural spring pool, encased in slabs of grey marble like stone, deep enough to bathe in.

They climbed to the high point above the palms and the green illusion of spring's short-lived liana, and Geofrey pointed to a fuzzy cloud shape on the horizon of trees, more than a hundred kilometres to the south.

"See that . . . ?"

"Yearh . . . some kind of sand storm blowing up," said Wes knowledgeably.

"Oh no."

"No? . . . some kind of waterfall spray is it?"

"That's the road, Wes. That's the road coming through. You can make your house up here and watch them build the road closer every day," said Geofrey.

Wes squinted his eyes. The rising curling blot of dust must be five hundred feet in the air. Below it, where those D.C.9 yellow cat excavators clawed beneath the red rock down to the mud, there were more than two hundred builders, each man covered from head to foot in fine rusty silt. So thick was it, at times, they couldn't see more than their arm's length in front of them.

"Limey?"

There was a soft, sleek, almost worshipful sound in Wes's voice, a supplication—

"You know how much money I got. I ain't kidded yuh."

"Of course."

"Now there's no bullshit between you and me. We want to be friends, right? We need each other out of here, right? Now I know you goin' give me a fair offer a fair deal for this parcel of land, I know it because you got that bullshit plum in your mouth of old England – tell me that's so?"

Geofrey hesitated. Linda wanted to say to him, it ain't everyday Dwight drops his shouting and his bull roaring because most of the time he so afraid he can't stop himself, but this time he means it, it's no pretence, mister, and you don't have to be very clever or even very British with your suckeggs accent, to see Wes is about as stupid and vulnerable as I am. He don't expect anything from you like favours, he wants you to treat him honest, that is all, so when you hear Wes whine like this it means he put his heart in your hand. Don't crush him, mister.

"Can you stick it out here, Wes?"

"Of course I can!"

"Can Linda?"

"I –" Linda began.

"She's with me ain't she?"

Linda sat on her knees in the red earth, she saw the dustbowl cloud above the horizon where the men worked the BR 165 highway through the forest, she could hear the excitement in Wes's voice, she could read it in his face; this was the prettiest parcel of land he'd ever seen outside of Oklahoma Wes was saying to Geofrey.

"I got to buy off you, those Brazil nuts would cheat me till I bled."

"A good point," Geofrey replied.

"It makes sense don't it?"

Linda's grey eyes under those pale lashes looked up at Geofrey as if to say you let us stop here, I'm tired too you know, I can't keep following this old runt oakie going nowhere with his ten thousand dollars, be honest with him if you can, he's got to stop running some place and all this looks awful green, be kind to Wes because he's just a little man, a little guy, nothing has ever gone right for him and he needs help, he won't ever tell you so but he needs it all the same. Wes is full of crap as they say, but he all I got, and he the only guy I ever met who asked me to go to South America with him.

"I can't give you a price, Wes. I don't even know how much land there is here. I must work it out. Let's say – by the end of the week," said Geofrey.

Wes scuffed his toes in the earth, he pushed his stetson back of his head, and said he and Linda would stay up there for a while just sitting up there, and they'd watch that dust cloud above the horizon, you go on ahead, we'll catch you up.

Capitão Pedro and his Aripuana family were thirty strong. They were fourth and fifth cousins removed, half brothers whose parents lay in mists of sororal wedding ceremonies, nieces wed to uncles and plain ordinary young bloods who gave to Pedro the lip-service of sons, and like him had no time for the indian reserve north of Porto Velho.

The women cropped manioc and maize. Before they met up with Geofrey they never expected to stay long in one place. At the close of each dry season they'd leave the land stripped bare to build another maloca a moon's walk away in the forest. When they moved east towards Chimboa from the banks of the Rio Teles Pires they had plenty of arcos da fleché and straw rêdes, to sell to the motoristas on the new road. And they were prepared to get as close to branco as they could. They weren't ashamed. They had no premium on pride.

To get clothing for the winter they'd march up to a shack, quite naked on purpose, and hold out their arms with a look of entreaty. The shocked branco wife would rush back inside and throw at them through a window any old pile of shirts and trousers she could find. The Aripuana family would run back into the palm and pillar cactus sertão where cascades of liana like giant spider webs made a green smothering creeper, and they'd put their clothes back on. They'd giggle and race home with their booty, real vagabundos . . .

Geofrey knew where to find them. Both seasons they maintained a fire in a planta conicle thatch on the side of their clearing. On a dry day in the windless haze, when the air stroked you like the touch of warmly moistened wool, a thread of burning sap and vegetation twisted high as the urubu could fly.

Before he met the Aripuana Geofrey knew nothing about indians, or amerindians as the anthropologist insists on calling them, and he thought no more of them than did the average Brazilian. They were lazy. There were few of them. They hunted for the least they needed, they spent their lives devising methods to do what was most meagrely required of them to keep the group together and no more. When Geofrey discovered them on his land, the Capitão (all indian groups like to call their elder this) admitted they were safer on his land and if he wished they'd work for him. They knew if they camped on branco territory, or too close to the military, they'd be hunted down. FUNAI, the new indian protection service, would be called in. Then, men with rifles and clubs would come in trucks to herd them back to the reserve in the south.

At the first streak of lemon in the morning sky Geofrey rode out to them. There was still too much water for the Wyllis jeep that far to the west of Chimboa. He hacked his horse through sertão where the forest was sparse, and the early hour gave his skin a cool shivery sensation; for he knew that if noon was like liquid tar, such a morning of first light in Brazil was champagne.

This year the Aripuana had built a circular maloca without a thatched roof of planta. They had acquired tarpaulins and stretched them across a skeletal frame of sugar cane joists. Their fire spiralled in gathering mushrooms of black through the pyramid shaped palhoca hut at the edge of the clearing. Inside the palhoca strips of wild pig and gutted bacalhau fish hung-on animal gut wires for smoking, crinkled salt rub leather twists of elephantine churrascaria.

Geofrey's Portuguese was infinitely better than the old Capitão's. But only Pedro amongst this particular group knew the branco's language. He had taught himself out of fear. He was the eldest, and every group of indians in the contacted-to-integrated stage for their own protection needed one spokesman at least. These groups had learned the hard way. If they were going to be cheated and robbed anymore by the branco, at least they could understand the words with which they were being cheated and robbed.

The limey sat in the warmth of the ashes outside the palhoca hut, strange as it was he realised he was sweating much less perched so close to the dry heat, and he waited there for the Capitão to put on a pair of cotton drill trousers. Pedro always did this when Geofrey arrived. It wasn't anything so crawly as deference, it was more a gesture from the Capitão, he could look like branco just as much as any of those vaqueiros in Chimboa. He could impersonate them.

Geofrey gave the old man a bottle of white rum cachaça, a half kilo of rapadura, a kind of brown sugar candy, crisp with a treacly flavour; they both sat cross-legged by the embers of the fire, rat-tailed dogs of skin and bursting rib cages scratched and rolled in the warm ashes, and belly pop babies waddled picking up shit lumps, a mother shouted out when they tried to eat them.

Geofrey told the Capitão how grateful he was to the group in the past, they had formed land and built his wooden house. But in the future there were to be some changes. He had the prospect of new money, and he wanted all available grazing land for the beef stock he intended to buy. He asked Pedro to take his group towards the sloping sertão west of where the pink flowering oiticicia tree stood. They could crop there if they wished, and they would find another americano for whom, if they wanted, they might work.

"But that land is red dirt," said the Capitão.

"You will have to work harder to crop."

"After the moisture has dried off cropping will be impossible."

"Do you want to go cropping elsewhere – on a Brazilian's fazenda?" asked Geofrey.

"No."

"Why not?"

"You know why gerente . . . they will kill us hunt us down and destroy us."

"Do you want me to tell the FUNAI people you are here on my land?"

"No."

"Why not?"

"They will come here with trucks and take us back to Porto Velho. And they'll send me to prison for leading my family here."

"I need all this good land here – it will *form* easily – in due course I can ringfence it –"

"We could stay – help you work for you –"

"Do you want to stay when I ask the vaqueiros to help me drive the beef?"

"No, gerente."

"You know what they will do."

"They will lay animal traps for us and take us into Chimboa with our feet in wire."

The Capitão spoke with a sad dutiful voice, all his meanings were tinged with if not a whining – a kind of sad mellifluence, pedantic and slow, an abnegation of his spirit. He could hide nothing. He was Geofrey's serf. In choosing this americano for a master he knew he fared better for his group than he could with any other bugre branco.

"If you do what I say I will have you back on the good land as soon as it is formed. You can work it the season after the next season. I'll share some of the crop with you."

"How can I tell the others this?"

"You will have to find a way."

"They will say I have let them down."

"That is your affair."

"They will ask me to step down from Capitão."

"I'll be sorry."

"They'll say I have made a secret bargain with you and that I will profit from it for myself."

"You are a strong man you tell them they are lies."

"What will I tell them when they find there is not enough cropping on the other side – and there is not food enough for the wet season?"

Geofrey could not answer. The narrow black eyes fringed with few lashes commenced to draw tears. Geofrey looked away.

"Why have you done this?" asked the Capitão.

"I have my reasons."

"Yes..." the old indian stood up with surprising agility.

His feet were grey from the ashes all around. The visit was at an end. And the Capitão, for his own face, must demonstrate in front of the young blood indians his leadership. No, he will not shake Geofrey's hand, the Aripuana never touch branco if they can help it, even though it is an estrangeiro branco, even an americano branco.

"You are the chefe," said the Capitão with finality. The other indians crowded so close, just to touch Geofrey's horse, press their palms along its flank, and the Capitão betrayed no humiliation in his glance, he stood his ground with a passive calm, he couldn't afford to show his family the sadness and the resignation he felt, otherwise they would turn on him, they would turn on him as quickly as they would cut a dog's throat if there was no wild pig by the close of the dry season, the Capitão stood passive and calm at the edge of the clearing and Geofrey mistook even that for what he believed to be an expression of the idle and the cowed.

* * *

Geofrey worked hard at the Brazilian spirit of jeito. Jeito is a wrinkle. Jeito is seeing around a corner before you get to it. Jeito is the chicken who asked himself why he did it before he actually crossed the road. When a Brazilian says no and he means yes but you'll have to be nice to him for it – that is jeito. If a cigano makes you cross her palm with a ten cruzeiro note saying "don't worry it safe as in the Bank of America" and she squeeze your genitals with a magic word you so surprised you don't have even the time to blush and then she closes her fist and opens it again – the ten cruzeiros vanish... that is jeito, too.

Jeito is a tricky wrinkle. It is a peculiar mixture of sadness and the desire to please and a cunning born for making small triumphs. Such that, when a brasileiro claps his arms around you and begs you to stay in his home with him he means go swing your rêde in the pensão round the corner and he'll come and take supper off you. And no soon as he tells you how he loves you he must turn back to a friend and casually denounce you because there is no sucking up to estrangeiros. And no matter how often he comes up to you – someone you've never clapped eyes on before – comes up and takes a cigarette out of your pack in your shirt pocket, smile please and offer him a light to go with it, because hard as you search you will never find where he keeps his own cigarettes.

Geofrey liked to look upon the bull americano Wes, with the dust of dreams in his nostrils, with jeito. Like the Brazilians he wanted to please the oakie and like the porceiros on the pensão stoep he wanted to see Wes take a fall.

"Why don't you like this americano, gerente?"

"He doesn't understand it here."

"But you all come from the same country?"

"No."

"What you think of him then?"

"Nothing but bugre estrangeiro . . . come here to steal as much as he can."

When they asked Geofrey why he sold such a piece of red dust to the americano, they'd smile behind their black eyes at his reply, they could appreciate the trick in the deal, the americano would take a great tumble, and they'd lie in their hammocks on the pensão verandah and they'd wait for it with their meal-making eyes.

"You will sell the land to him, gerente?"

"Why not? . . ."

The strip of southward-facing land inclined to a higher plain, its stone pool and delicately flowering oiticicia tree all of which looked so temporarily green – amounted to near four hundred hectares. Before the sale could be made out, the vendor had to inform the army authorities by the air-strip, just in case they envisaged any use for this parcel of land, and he had to give advance notice of this sale to the prefeito in Chimboa. The prefeito was a black-skinned German Brazilian called Haroldo, he was mestico, from a black mother and a Bremen born tapper who died in the great gold bust days during the thirties east of Chimboa in Minas Gerais. Surly man, slow to reason, easy to panic, with a long black aquiline nose. He had built his planta shack close by the air-strip, he liked to be near the army, it was a demonstration of his mayoral authority. The army welcomed him into their canteen, and he kept their filtered water in plastic buckets behind his door.

"How much you get from this americano for the land?"

"US $7,500 for it."

"You know what we call that?"

"You tell me."

"Jeito."

"Ah yes."

Haroldo held Geofrey's arm in a warm grip. Behind the fat fat black German lips there lay a wryness—

"How long he stay here this man?"

"How long do you want him to stay?"

Haroldo smiled. But very quickly, then it was gone, and the dark eyes shuttered out the humour with a glinting bile, not a flicker of sadness was there.

"I must look at your passport, gerente . . . then everything will be in order."

Geofrey watched the man open the identity folder. The neatly folded cruzeiro notes were conjured away. Haroldo licked his counting fingers.

The limey and the oakie set out for the land claim office of the Ministry of the Interior in Santarém. Geofrey's Wyllis *Rural* was piled with petrol canisters and spare tyres. Wes hugged a bottle of Katina pinga between his knees and talked all the way. He had so many plans.

He and Linda for the first year must work the land together. He'd put down maize and sugar cane, barley, guava and fig, and manioc, thus he'd crop a twentieth of the land. And after *forming*, the rest would become rough grazing.

"It ain't that easy though – I need those Brazil nuts in Chimboa come up and slash and burn off the top vegetation, and I'll need cash for that, too."

The oakie stood in the jeep to wipe the film of red dust from the windshield. Geofrey pummelled the four-wheel drive over the axle busting ruts in the dirt track, and the transplant Texan in Wes's voice—

"Take me all these next two seasons take two more dry seasons and I got ten head of cattle per *hecatare*, and that ain't birdshit!"

On the greenest sertão, fed by wet season streams, a hectare couldn't support three head.

"Don't see why not ... three year away have me six hundred cows and forty bois. You tell me what you get per head for steers? You don't get less'n a hundred dollars from them canning corporations."

A hundred and fifty head and three bois out of that sertão and even the vaqueiros will start tipping their hats at you.

"So that's sixty thousand dollars by the fourth year and I'm buying into more of your land, son!"

If you had a drought season in any one year out of four you wouldn't have enough spinach on that land to put into Popeye's pipe. But Geofrey kept his mouth shut, and he concentrated on the ruts in the track before him.

"Now I trust you Jeff ... we got enough between us to show those Brazils how to grow lampshades. You honest with me. I know Britishers, that suckeggs in your mouth polite crap, ain't it a God-gave miracle I found yuh!"

Linda lay alone in Geofrey's home while they were gone. She said she'd make herself useful, tidy the place up. Wes didn't argue. But Geofrey noticed the curiosity in her expression. Before they left he showed her where he kept his two Japanese rifles. But she'd be safe, nobody would come out that far.

There was a front room the length of the verandah. Wicker chairs, a folding card table, a lamp with a cleric green shade and a wall of shelves summed up the furnishings. The shelves stored Geofrey's possessions – cartridge boxes, medicines, tools and wax and chicken wire, beer cans and tar mix, ropes, leathers and a buckram-backed photograph album.

A partition wall framed two more rooms behind. A mattress thrown over a tarpaulin cloth. In an iron-bound Booth's shipping line style tea-chest jackets and trousers were rolled into tight bundles, shirts and socks in a lower compartment. A spare pair of tall yellow leather boots stood in a fruit box. The last room served for washing, a mirror and shaving brush on a ledge beneath the window and in one corner a stone jar water filter.

Just inside the front door there was a grey aluminium fogão for cooking. An oil black pan stood on the oven plate. Linda was intrigued by this soft spoken Britisher. A loneliness about him, an unlikely physical presence, not at all the pioneer of

Poker Flats. The album of snapshots confused her. Moon-faced lad standing on an English pebble beach studying a dark and cold sea. Beside homely grandparents in front of an Edwardian house solid and nasty, fringed with a bed of azaleas. A seventeen-year-old Geofrey, hair plastered back, mouth agape somehow managing not to come last out of six in a sports day hurdle race. Only one girl there. A leggy creature in a nursing uniform trying to hide her face in mock exasperation. Gummed to the fly leaf a faded brown to yellow formal shot of an RAF officer father, two studs to his epaulet and the same soft rounded features.

Certain things were missing from the album. Things she could not possibly guess at. Those images of an isolated boyhood. A lone child buried in his fantasies. There were no shots of adoring parents clambering down beach-heads to net shrimps with an only son, no army pals on furlough riding bikes through Devon villages khaki vested roaring with laughter as one of them topples over a low stone wall from a narrow bridge. An elusive quality about him, this britisher. A loner too selfish to share emotions. His suckeggs accent.

It was difficult for her to understand the photographs she saw. She had never even left Oklahoma until Wes dragged her into Texas on that one trip they made. Geofrey's appearance gave so little away. Plump, medium height, pale brown lifelessness in his hair, his genial hesitant smile which forecast little laughter. But the limey had different eyes. They bulged with that over-taste for pinga and lemon sucks, they bored with an implacable strength. As if to say I'll be delighted to help but most of all I want to find a way you can be of use to me.

In the evenings Linda lit the oil lamp and waited with a childish delight for the mosqus to swarm in a cloud above the light. She occupied quite considerable stretches of time catching them and crushing them in the centre pages of a pocket Bible she found. She held the thick book open until they practically settled for a lesson from Paul to the Corinthians, and she would slam the book shut with that absurd sense of triumph you get even if just one mosqu is crushed. For Linda's light skin was deep into that sensitised area where at the least whisper of an insect the hairs would crawl on her arms.

Sometimes, before she pulled back the wood blinds and

light from the lamp threw her head and shoulders in long shadow across the clearing in the night, she had a shivery sensation, as if out there in the tree fringe of mato and tall grasses, instinct presage of being watched, she was not alone; and she often touched the barrel of one of Geofrey's rifles, it gave her that extra measure of confidence, before she lay in the soft dark to sleep, lying stiff and straight waiting for the perspiration to seep cold into the mattress, and night to dissolve her.

Geofrey's lawyer had the deed of sale ready within a day. He was clearly somewhat miffed nobody had invited him to waste everybody's time by going out to this place Chimboa, which barely existed, to make a land search. That extra source of income would have done him nicely. He warned Dwight Weslie of the risk in buying land without a search. But—

"Hell, I know it's this limey's land I'm buying. I'm sitting right beside him ain't I?"

"I have a perfect legal right to sell you the land," said Geofrey quietly.

"That's right," said Wes, "it ain't as if I'm buying Brooklyn Bridge from you, is it now?"

At the municipal building they stamped the oakie's fourteen signatures and were about to tell Geofrey it would take them at least a month before they could make a decision on the land tax and how much Wes must pay annually (it was only a matter of pennies anyway) when Geofrey showed them a letter from Haroldo, the prefeito, and then everything seemed in good order. They had to make one final trip to the umpteenth office down the end of a corridor. A clerk shoved a separate slip of paper under the oakie's nose. It was a closely printed formal declaration.

"Read it me, son."

"It's a new clause all land sales have here. It asks you if there are to your knowledge any indigenous on your land?" explained Geofrey.

"Hell, you tell me what indigenous means – then I'll sign!"

"Indians."

"Brazilian indians?"

"Amerindians."

"Up in Chimboa?"

"It's possible."

"I ain't seen no such thing, have you?"

"No," said Geofrey.

They stayed an extra night in a corrugated roof pensão on stilts some five kilometres up from the town. At this point the Amazon is so wide – near fifty kilometres across – at the lips of the Tapajós' meeting with the Amazon; where the black and green thrust from the Tapajós smears the south bank an olive white colour. It is called the running of the waters here, the olive and the yellow flow side by side, and the southern shore line is quite mosquito-free.

When the sun lowered below the palm and fig fringe where the river twists, it bled its bright orange into awesome streamers beside the yellow and the olive and the ochre slicks in the water; it became a slow sea of giant-coloured snail trails. In the dying light, fall of mist on a liquid leather surface, so wide and unhurried seemed its progress east, a sea beggaring the eye for a far shore-line opposite, the Amazon appeared motionless.

The men slung their rêdes between the poles on the upper floor of the pensão. Wes lowered his voice, all round them sleeping figures swayed in their cotton cradles, and there were few lights at this time of night along the favela shore-line, tied below to the stilts outboard motor canoes lightly strained at ropes—

"What reason you got for staying out here, limey?"

"Do I have to have one?"

"I mean – England being such a comfortable little place and all that. You got to have a reason?"

"I like it here."

"Don't give me that, son. Nobody likes it here, nobody really likes it!"

"Yes, I do."

"You running from something – somebody?"

"No."

"What about folks back home?"

"I don't think I have any left now, a cousin or two perhaps. All that's so far in the past I don't think about it."

"But you go back?"

"I used to."

"But you will, huh—?"

"I don't know..." said Geofrey slowly, "it's the kind of

place you go back to when you are old and about to die, the kind of place you return to in the end with all the money you've made, I like to think of it as being a sort of geriatric ward you return to for a long sleep."

"Come again?"

"Like a country hotel at the end of a driveway of elms, there's a fire in the grate and they put you into the bed they've prepared for you and—"

"Psst!" a harsh spit from one of the hammocks swinging in the dark, "...dormi! Psst!"

"But limey – suppose all this comes to nothing out here? All these plans – like the road – the land – minerals..."

"It can't..."

"You right..."

"This is the place..."

"Damn better be..."

"Psst! ..."

Before they drove back, Wes filled the Wyllis with what he'd bought, axe heads, tools, a buzz saw, plenty of rope and black tar mix and concrete mix, tin cutlery and bowls and boiling pans, kerosene canisters, sacks of rice and maize, dried salt beefy and cans of powdered milk, and a stone water filter jar.

Linda was standing on the verandah watching the swirl of red dust behind the Wyllis in the distance. They were a mile off through the stump and palm and tall grass sertão, but she could make out the shape of Wes standing on the running board shouting out something impossible to hear and waving his arm, and she reminded herself to give them no impression, not on any account, that she had felt afraid or lonely in the house while they were away. A rising warmth, a sense of wellbeing filled her, Wes's waving arm meant the land was theirs, and they were staying.

She was running forward, calling out that she had finally beaten that grey fogão by the door, that crazy stove thing there, the limey has, and you'd better like it because it took the whole morning to make it.

Geofrey walked over to one of the sheds in the clearing. He kept a case of pinga buried in the earth there. Makeshift cooling process it might be, but not to be sniffed at in the boondocks place like this. Yes, it was still there. The Aripuana hadn't come looking for it. The earth was undisturbed. Wes was dancing about and shouting and banging his funny little pointed Texan-style toes. Linda wore a splash of bright lipstick, and she showed Geofrey all the rubbish she'd thrown out of the house. Wes was talking about cutting trees, stripping and building and measuring, there were shovels to fit handles to, and there were horses they had to buy from those guys in the pensão at Chimboa. The alcohol made Linda burst into a fit of giggles. Geofrey mixed pinga and black guarana resin with cachaça white rum and splits of lemon. And the mosqus plunged.

* * *

Wes and the limey couldn't wake of their own accord the next morning. The sun frazzled their eyelids until they had to hide from it. Both of them swung in their rêdes on the porch, it was almost noon. Linda was inside. Though she tried to sit up on the mattress, when she kicked out at the mosquiteiro her sides ached with a sharp pain just back of her ribs, there was a swollen feeling, and she breathed in with a gasp.

Geofrey said he knew how to make the perfect hangover antidote. He stumbled towards the fogão and reached for a pan. He heard Linda's gasp for breath behind the thin screen wall.

"Don't let it worry you," he called out, "that's only your liver giving you hell. Soon fix that."

"My God..." she murmured softly. He heard that, too.

The limey crushed green bananas into a batatadoce mash in the frying pan. He filled a smaller pan with farofa, manioc flour, and deluged the paste with oil. He lit the stove and waited patiently for the portions to sizzle.

He went outside to the shed which protected his earth-hole. He pulled another pinga bottle out and tripped clumsily in his bare feet back to the house. He had left his boots under the hammock on the porch boards.

Linda took one look at the meal he had prepared and threw up her arms. Geofrey laid a plateful of banana batata topped with farofa beside the mattress in the back room. She shuddered.

"The perfect pick-me-up," he said grimly.

"The hell it is!" she growled.

Linda closed her eyes and curled up tightly in a ball back beneath the mosquiteiro. She waved at him go away.

"I could be sick just looking at that muck."

Wes and Geofrey gulped the stodge antidote on the porch together. They swung back and forth sharing the pinga bottle between them.

"Painful stuff..." murmured Wes.

"Nothing like it for the cure..."

"Do I have to drink more of this white gasoline to make me feel better too?"

"When you're ill from pinga – best thing for it – take another half bottle. See you straight."

"I don't rightly know..." said the oakie, shaking his head from side to side, "if I can even stand up."

"You don't?"

"Limey, can you feel your toes?"

"Eh..." Geofrey concentrated on his digit extremities for a moment, "no I don't think I can."

"Me neither!"

They cut lime-shaped lemons and sucked at the halves. From time to time they shaded their eyes from the sun at midday. The light broiled on the porch, and the planta leaves in the roofing crackled nervously above their heads.

There is a roughly carved track which drives through the seca forest trees at the edge of Geofrey's slash-and-burn. From the verandah you can see anyone along the track for a mile before he reaches the clearing.

It was the oakie who first noticed it. He casually sat up and shaded his eyes with his hands. There was a handful of dust moving on the horizon along the track between the trees. Although the little dustbowl was less than a mile away the sun danced curious tricks on the oakie's sight. The red finger of dust shimmered as if somebody had placed an oily filter lense over Wes's gaze.

"Wake up you bastard...!"

"Huh?"

"Somebody coming."

"Vaqueiro wanting work – I don't want to see him."

"Licketysplit he comin' whoever he be."

Geofrey looked up. The figure causing the dustbowl was out the trees now and pummelling his animal over the slash-and-burn at no end of a dangerous pace.

"He ride like that over those stumps he'll cripple the horse," said the limey.

Geofrey could see the rider. It was the patrão from Chimboa. Fat Narcissu. He'd never seen Narcissu on a horse all the months he'd been in Chimboa. Narcissu pumped the grey speckled mule towards the house. There was a nasty wedge of a bit in the animal's mouth. Much too large for it. Narcissu wasn't one for taking risks on a horse, clearly. The mule tried unavailingly to roll it's gums away from the bit, it slathered painfully.

Narcissu wheeled the mule alongside the porch rail. As he slipped his heavy body to the ground the sackcloth saddle clung to his arse. The patrão peeled it away from his wet legs with a certain sheepishness.

"You ride around much more like that Narcissu you'll kill yourself no end of damage," said Geofrey.

The oakie chucked the bottle at the patrão. Narcissu smiled and nodded, his breath wheezed in his throat, the pinga upturned into his mouth with a deep draught.

"...Me, I don't often ride," Narcissu began, "too much weight to carry. Can't trust a mule."

"I can see that."

"Gerente, excuse me – for interrupting you—"

"You welcome anytime – my house is yours."

"I thought I come and tell you myself. The prefeito sent me on up he said I should tell you—"

"...What?"

"He said you come down right away and see who arrived in Chimboa."

"Well, who?"

"Nobody ever arrives in Chimboa, right?"

"Who has?"

Nobody except americanos buying land like yourself – got all the time in the world to wait for the road—"

"Narcissu..." Geofrey spoke calmly, he motioned the patrão to sit on the edge of the boards by the step, "I know nobody ever comes to Chimboa. So who's arrived?"

"You won't believe it," said the patrão, trickling the pinga down his throat with a tantalising pause, then— "... Haroldo tell me you won't believe it."

"I won't until you tell me."

"The prefeito said you interested in buying and *forming* the land developing this land for beef, you think some day, perhaps, these guys from the east will come with machines to drill, find minerals and oil up here, right? Make you incredible rich, gerente, right?"

"Whad he saying?" piped in the oakie.

"The prefeito say you come down right away and see this guy who just come in. Come in from the south on a motorcycle brand new smart polished cycle he got and he drove right past the army and the road builders, so he must have some pretty powerful authority permission they let him through – he made the rest of the journey through that wet forest to get to Chimboa. Fantastic, no—?"

"What's his name?"

"Won't say. Secretive type."

"Brasileiro?"

"I guess so."

"Guess?"

"He's yellow. He's chinês or japonês."

"What he speak?"

"Speak better than I do."

"No accent?"

"Just like you or me..." the compliment registered. Geofrey smiled appreciatively.

"Give me a clue, limey, will ya?" Wes muttered, but Geofrey had no time to explain. The patrão's words went off like a fuse bomb in his skull—

"Chefe, the prefeito said I ought to tell you, come and tell, this nissei guy got a large steel box on the back of his motorcycle and he's riding all around the edge of the village right out over this side of the air-strip taking samples of the earth and testing it with steel prods from this box he got."

Geofrey sucked in his breath. The pinga haze cleared from his eyes. Suddenly, he was reaching for his boots and shouting to Wes to do the same. Narcissu dribbled on—

"...The prefeito said to me to tell you it likely this guy some big official from SUDAM or americano nickel company from Belém and he got all this steel box equipment because he think maybe perhaps Chimboa's sitting on a bucket of oil the size of the pacific ocean. That's what Haroldo told me."

Geofrey repeated the story to Wes as they climbed into the Wyllis. Narcissu sat on the porch and fanned his face with his shirt, he said he'd be along in a short while, maybe after he finishes this bottle, anyway you guys go on ahead and there's Brahma Chopp beer in the kerosene freezer back of the pensão. Help yourself, gerentes.

"What are you waiting for, son?" Wes yelled encouragement, stiffening his stetson down over his eyes, "put your heel down on that gas pedal, a miracle has happened!"

It sounded the kind of outlandish incident out here which could cause a forest fire of rumours. In the first place the stranger was yellow – curious, he won't give his name – more curious, he won't say what this steel box of tricks is for what he doing in Chimboa and why he should risk his neck dragging a motorcycle through that swamp lowland forest north by the road works which the builders themselves haven't yet tackled – curious enough to panic anyone, let alone two pinga plunged americano pioneers.

The pensão was empty. They raided the freezer behind the fogão screen and lounged back against Narcissu's wicker bench, Wes draped his heels over the handrail and bit off the beer-tin tab with his teeth. It was unusually quiet. Nobody stirred on the wide street below them. A grey woolly saguim monkey with a pygmy black leather face cracked cashew nuts on the beam above them. The little macaco was tethered by an arm's length of chain. The patrão's pet. A water bowl and a food basket balanced on the beam, it was Narcissu's little act to throw cashews for the macaco to catch.

There was no sign of the chinês. Or japonês. Or whatever he was.

"You think he's hiding from us?"

"Certainly not."

"All we gotta do – sit here and wait, right?"

"Narcissu will be along soon. He said the chinês was staying for supper," said Geofrey.

It was an hour later when Linda finally got herself together. She dressed and drank three tin cups from the stone jar water filter in the corner of the front room. There was nobody about. The guys might have told me, she thought. I got pins and knives and swords and things sticking into my head it hurts so bad.

She steadied herself on her feet. She stepped from the verandah and walked gingerly around the outside of the house. Might clear my head, she believed.

And she saw him. She had to blink to be sure she was seeing right.

The boy was kneeling on the ground at the edge of the slash-and-burn testing the earth with steel prods. The prods were attached to a small battery of coloured dials which came out of a steel box. Linda didn't know what to think. It seemed so incongruous. A few yards away from the boy, well, to be honest, he was more of a man, a slim boyish guy in sky blue Levi's and wearing one of those half-ass white Brazil nut stetsons you can buy in any rodoviaria store – a few yards from him lay a shiny new orange motorcycle.

Linda stopped short. In that moment he must have seen her. He left off whatever it was he was doing with his bleeping electric probe machine and hurried across the clearing. Now she could see his face. He was yellow-skinned, a good-looking young guy with a disarming grin. Where in hell he'd come from, Linda wondered.

"Hi," she said simply.

"You American?" he asked as he stopped in front of her.

"Sure I am."

"My name's Antioch. Antioch Tibushi. I didn't want to come any nearer just in case your husband got suspicious and threw me off. You got a husband I take it—?"

"I ain't married," said Linda, pert and quick.

"Is this your house?"

"Nope. Belongs to a friend. He's a Britisher." Linda suddenly felt quite different. She realised she hadn't spoken to anyone new in months. And this guy seemed so neat and clean. There was something very tidy and positive about him. As if he just didn't belong out here.

"I'm Linda..." she said slowly, "come on in out the

sun . . . I'll make you some of that green jungle tea stuff they all seem to drink out here."

"Anything will do . . ." Antioch replied, as he followed her back up to the verandah, "you got some plain ordinary Nescafé?"

Linda grinned and wiggled her hips as she climbed the steps. There must be a tin somewhere, she murmured.

It was a long cold cream bath of an afternoon. Geofrey counted six mangy dogs walk past his Wyllis he'd never seen in the village before. All three of them – Wes and Narcissu and the limey – sat out front of the pensão with their feet up on the handrail surrounded by a mess of empty Brahma beer cans. It was unusual for Geofrey, but even he felt a spasm of impatience. As for the oakie – he was fit to bursting with mad dog land profit dreams. He couldn't help himself—

"You just suppose," he repeated for the fourth time, "this guy got some special contract from one of them big USA syndicates – like Hanna Mining Company send him out here buy up land claims for iron ore—"

"They wouldn't send anyone until the road came through," Geofrey mildly rebuked Wes.

"It takes time sure – that's what they in business for multiple conglomerates like Kaiser Minerals like General Electric Company like Bethlehem Steel – Bethlehem Steel practically own the whole of Minas Gerais damn it – you heard of Bethlehem Steel Corporation ain't you?"

"Of course . . ."

"If it ain't it must be the other . . ."

"What must?" with a sigh.

"Stands to reason don't it – this guy gotta represent somebody to come all the fucking boondocks way out here tell me that so, it's so ain't it?"

"Perhaps . . ."

"No use playing that ass-hole stiff limey upper lip now son – if he this guy say to you, I'm from Hanna Incorporated Brazil nut etcetera here boy you can have twenty million dollars for that bauxite aluminium electrolyte nickel zinc iron ore and copper you keep beneath that thatch house whadyacallit you hang your hammock in call home – he say that to you, you'd get him to a land attorney in Santarém to sign the deeds if you had to swing ape top of the trees like Tarzan bullshit all the way there! Am I right?"

"He hasn't offered us anything. We don't even know why he's here."

"Son . . . in this world you need optimism. I may have nothing else, but I got that. Sure as owls hoot. Right—?"

"The man hasn't even come back. Maybe he's gone north by now, Wes . . ."

Wes lifted his heels from the handrail. He stood up and whistled a low thin sound between his teeth.

"Oh yes the man has . . . yes sir he has," said Wes softly.

Geofrey didn't need to follow the oakie's gaze. He could hear it too. The putter-pop-putter of a motorcycle.

Wes leaned over the porch to see better. The bright orange machine sparked a red wake of flying feather dust behind it. The rider scooped the front wheel to halt the machine outside the pensão. Narcissu hurriedly carried himself behind the fogão screen. It might be safer to watch from there.

Geofrey pulled his feet down so he could see the bike more clearly. It was one of those brand new São Paulo built Honda CB 175s. Five gears and a rearside mount double-plated second petrol tank.

On the pillion rack stood the shining tin box of tricks.

Antioch Tibushi climbed the steps, pulling at his fancy blue mist goggles, there was an unexpected trimness about him, something clean and young and unruffled. Yes, that was it, thought Geofrey, he looks like he couldn't perspire if you kept him a night in a Malayan Turkish bath.

". . . Ola!" Antioch beamed at the two seemingly struck dumb and rather mesmerised figures on the patrão's front porch. The smaller of the two, the one with the tank shoulders and tomato-shaped freckle red face who had heels on his boots the height your mother once used to wear hers, took a step towards him.

". . . Ola to hell with it, mister, do you speak English?" asked Wes.

"Sure," Antioch replied smartly, "why not?"

The accent was that of an easterner. A little high-pitched maybe, thought Wes, but as much like a New York sophisticate as he'd ever heard.

"You American, son?"

"I'm Brazilian."

Wes studied the youthful and undeniable Japanese features, he sucked in his breath and wrinkled his eyebrows into quizzical curlicues.

"You puttin' me on...?"

"I can assure you..." said Antioch with a disarmingly pleasant grin.

"Where'd you learn to speak English like that then?" Wes pouted.

"I did four years at Princeton University."

The oakie felt his neck and lower cheeks redden with pin-prick nerves. He jutted his chin forward—

"Huh?"

"Princeton Agricultural Course for eighteen months."

An awful blankness spread across the oakie's face. His palms opened and closed involuntarily, spastic like responses you get from pulling that gut inside a chicken leg back and forth; though he stood his ground, Antioch could not help recognise the mistrust and incomprehension in the florid little fellow.

"If you want to say what in hell is a yellow-skinned Brazilian with an easterner's accent doing out here – well, go ahead," Antioch replied swiftly, "it's no skin off my back."

"Aw...bullshit to that son," suddenly Wes was all smiles and tippetytoeing the boards as if he was in dancing pumps, "here sit down with us...you wanna beer?"

"I don't drink."

"You wanna smoke?"

"I don't do that, either."

"What kind of business you in then, son?"

"I'd rather not say."

"I mean some people," Wes continued regardless, "said rumour has it you been walking over this land here and abouts poking it with gadgets. What you got in that tin box of tricks of yours?"

"I'm afraid...that's also my business."

"You ain't telling us—"

"Let's say...let's call it my little secret."

"Let's...!" Wes murmured little sir echo of disbelief.

"You know how it is in a place like this," Antioch grinned without the slightest trace of malice, "after all if you had a great million dollar plan you wouldn't go round shouting it from the trees would you—?"

"You mean . . . you mean," Wes stuttered, mouth agape, his ninety-dollar gold fillings leading with his chin, "you mean you ain't what you supposed to be?"

"I only came back this way, after I'd finished what I came to do, to tell the patrão I wasn't staying for supper, after all," said Antioch.

Huh . . ." Wes mouthed. He turned back to look at the limey a silent appeal writ large on his face.

"So, if you don't mind," Antioch spun round and climbed down the steps towards his gleaming orange Honda, ". . . perhaps you'd be good enough to say I won't be stopping over night."

Antioch had slipped his fancy goggles back on and mounted the machine before Geofrey could pull himself together. He ran down the steps, but that fraction too late, because Antioch had already kicked the bike into action.

"Now . . . wait a minute!" Geofrey blurted out at the young rider, "there's no need to rush away like this. You mustn't pay any attention to my friend's bad manners. He – he can't help that. He's a good soul at heart and all that sort of thing. Now you're not really leaving this minute are you—?"

"I'm afraid I am. I've finished what I came for," Antioch replied evenly, "and I've plenty more work to do before I reach the Amazon."

"There is nothing between here and Santarém."

"I know that," cool as silk, Antioch.

"Now wait a minute, please . . ." Geofrey followed Antioch like a lamb as the machine completed a full circle to face north, "I appreciate you are in a hurry but this is ridiculous."

Antioch closed the throttle, stubbing his heel for a moment in the ground to arrest the machine, he glanced up at the puffy-faced young-man-grown-old beside him with pinga eyes—

"You out here to make your fortune that's what you doing out here, sir – you and your friend—?" Geofrey gaped.

"I'm no different from you, mister. Just the same goes for me," Antioch called out behind him above the hornet hive exhaust, "good luck to you . . . !"

Geofrey stood in the middle of the street. He watched the

orange Honda bounce away along the Santarém track to where the string of telegraph poles stopped. The putter-pop-put became a thin nasal whine. A layer of red dust like the probe of a fat mosqu settled on the limey's eyelashes.

Wes took a beer can and kicked it in a high arc over the street. Mad dog money dream land eldorado frustration streamed out of him—

"Howling eggs whad I say I did wrong that son of a whore what happened!"

Linda took some trouble to mince a strip of salt beefy. She heated it slowly with dendê oil, sweet-tasting yellow palm extract, and the leather-textured beefburgers were ready by the time Geofrey and Wes returned in the early evening.

They were morose at first. Until she started to chatter about this strange yellow guy with a motorcycle called Antioch (what kind of name anyway is that, huh?), who'd appeared out from nowhere at the edge of the clearing. No, he wasn't Chinese, he said he was Brazil born of Japanese parents and he'd been educated real well in the States. Would you believe that, honh? she asked.

"We met him," said Wes dourly.

"I'm so glad – I told him all about you both and he said he'd drop by if you were still there when he'd finished his work and all."

"You told him what?" Wes suddenly hollered.

"Sure honey..." she said, wide-eyed and innocent, "told him about the limey here, and the land and the plans we got. Why?"

Wes looked the colour of one of those grey marbled stone slabs by the pool up on that land he had bought.

"Linda..." Geofrey asked, "did he tell you what he was doing what he was looking for?"

"Didn't he tell you?"

"No."

"Oh, he's a real nice guy, Japanese Brazil nut you know ...he's following all along where this road is coming by you know..."

"And?" pressed Geofrey.

"He's got this plan see, he's going to find a real pleasant piece of land not much you understand nothin' like as big as we got here – an' he's going to grow lettuces. He says nobody has thought of growing lettuces before this far north. Says come three or four years he'll have the lettuce monopoly south of the whole Amazon basin. Bright, huh?"

Wes turned on the limey –

"Ya son offa bitch mother whore! That Jap boy got nunca mais sweet nothing at all! He ain't come buying our dreams, man!"

* * *

Those following weeks Geofrey made himself scarce. He was lucky to hitch a ride east on a Protestant Mission flight which stopped over at the air-strip. With the new dollars in his pocket he could look for beef. He knew the best place to buy. North of the Ilha do Bananal, by a network of small rivers, some of which feed west towards Chimboa, there is a well-known million hectares ranch. To get there Geofrey persuaded the flight to drop him at Araguaçema. He might borrow a jeep by the air field. At the worst he'd find a vaqueiro to ride up with him to the ranch.

The road-builders had cut a swath of broken tree trunks and burnt shrub fifty kilometres closer to Chimboa. Soon the big yellow cats would start to claw at the sandstone beneath. For once again the ground altered. From the seemingly impenetrable thickness of the mata seca, that drying out green forest foliage, where the road emerged now, there was cerrado; a kind of scattered wilderness of fern and shrub and razor leafed bush. It was no less arduous to cut a super-highway here, but the builders made better progress. There was still more deep forest to cut through in the river flood areas up front, before they reached the strange open sertão basin which surrounded Chimboa. And there was much doubt they'd reach the perimeters of the sertão before the wet season started again. Brazil has several kinds of forest, from the massaranduba-tree bearing mata seca, the palmito dense rain green world, to the hevea bordered river tracery, but there are so many more – stony ground serra cactus plumaged, pantanel of waist deep marsh still as a painted ballroom floor, and the disconcertingly untruthful sertão of Chimboa. Sertão which promises a richness of matter and liana as if there is water to outpour all the sun of the dry season. Yet this very sertão, luxuriant and matted, is the frailest of the forest, the quickest to fade, it conceals a soil less than a season of slash-and-burn can leech to red rock aridity. And it is a fair warning to those who would strip all the forests for minerals or oil or cattle, with no regard for the future, land like sertão required three wet seasons to revive from its first cover crop of kudzu.

Wes built his hut. He laid a board foundation raised a few feet above the flat earth where he chose his site. The adze spliced him uprights and he raised the joists and cross-beams into position. He and Linda balanced themselves precariously on the roof supports and tamped spliced green cana into strips for waterproofing. Over this they laid palm and buriti leaf in a thick thatching. At the front entrance they draped palmyra leaves over a criss-crossed lean-to, it added shade to this side of the house, and soft wood poles held the structure up. This was the porch, if the supports were strong enough to tie rêdes beneath it.

He batoned planks to small trees and created a corral. Now they possessed two horses the vaqueiros had stolen from somebody else, and how was Wes to know that? Now Linda kept four chickens and a cock in a wire coop, and Wes took up baking—

He jammed flat slab stones into a rough square over an iron grating, and he baked quite serviceable bricks under the sun. He baled buckets of yellow mud from the rims of sinking streams. He made a mix out of tar and horse dung and pine resin. They dried without crumbling. Narrow cane shoots slotted into the bricks, when they dried Wes drew the canes out of the mix and the hollow tubers kept their shape. He concreted the pegs beneath the boards and in-filled the foundation with mud. Wood hatches were made to fit the window squares, and every evening they both washed themselves down in the stone pool below.

He built a fogão for cooking with the bricks. Wes buttressed the wall which faced most of the day's heat with them. He dug a trench out of a natural formed cranny which fed to a stream and made a lavatory out of the bricks. Cane poles covered with palmyra leaves in the shape of a wig-wam gave the convenience a measure of privacy. He asked Linda to come and see it—

"What do you think that is?" he asked proudly.

"How do I know what it is!" she replied.

"For Christ's sake, it's a shit-house!"

"It is? You could have fooled me!"

"I built it specially for you."

"Well that's nice of you Wes... but I been quite happy out in the bushes," she said.

"You don't understand what I'm saying. This is the first shit-house anybody ever built in Chimboa. First time sanitation ever come to this place. How about that?"

"My me ...!" said Linda.

"It takes an American to build a shit-house. That's my philosophy. Now you go on in there and try it."

"But Wes—"

"Go on."

Linda stooped beneath the broad-lipped palmyra leaves and sat glumly on the mud brick convenience.

"You the strangest man I ever met," she said out loud, "I thought you come to Brazil here to avoid civilisation and shit-houses and all that sort of thing."

"Are you using it?..."

"Give me a chance!..."

"Are you using it?"

"All right!"

"Using it now?"

"All right for Christ's sake! Jeeesus! I'm using it!"

A seraphic smile spread across the oakie's face. He walked back to the house. Dumb broad got nothing but peanuts between her ears. First shit-house Chimboa ever seen in a thousand years.

They always woke with the lemon light of morning before five. Often, Linda swam by herself in the stone pool, soaping herself down watching the early dragonfly skate the surface with a strummed buzz of its wings. The house always smelt of resin when she woke. And where the pool lay, some distance from the house, a morning mist rose out of the vegetation rot all around. It was followed by the shrill clack clacking of first birds.

Most common was the little cinnamon-coloured curutia which plunged through the leaves and lianas like a paper dart. Those were the best hours of the day. By nine the sertão was at its noisiest, the sun being high enough to make pools of sweat in the cups above your earlobes, and Wes could hardly grip the adze firm enough for the moisture which slicked like slime in his fists.

Porceiros say the armoured leguan, fat forest lizard, gives the command to cease clacking, when the morning heat becomes intolerable. It is often by a stone pool heavily scuttling, and it lifts its long tail when it cries—

tui tui tui . . .

And the curutia stops darting, still is the rubbed nut in the cheesegrater action of the grilo, and what water there is begins to steam, like vapour from the mouth of an exhausted runner, in the boiling light.

Linda was slow to notice the change in Wes. And what she did notice, she shrugged away. He got so engrossed in the work, that was why he never spoke to her for a whole day at a time. And he got so exhausted he couldn't sleep, he silently ate the meals she prepared and lay back in his rêde staring at the warm blue night. He couldn't stop working. He lived off his nerves. A determination breathed fire in his eyes. When he did talk his voice became harsh, there was ever a resentment behind it, as if he didn't care one way or the other if she wanted to share the life. She didn't exactly feel unwanted, that never occurred to her, but his manner suggested he expected her to leave at any moment, and even if she did it was no skin off his back. Linda shrugged the thought away.

Linda barely remembered her own father. He was a share cropper. When she was eight he left home and never came back. She and her mother worked a patch of land together a few miles outside a small town. They were poor white. When she was older she heard boys in the pool hall call her white trash. She never got invited to those spin-the-bottle parties the girls in town gave, they all had cars and they didn't speak to her much.

She had gone to the store twice that month, the second trip was to explain why her mother couldn't pay up the grocery bill. That was when she met Wes. She stood at the counter and the storekeeper froze when they heard his voice. They heard it across a street and thirty yards down a turning. Wes was bawling somebody out the length of the town street. Linda was curious. She'd had walk-outs with boys, before. Clumsy hot demands, her legs twisted impossibly in back seat convertibles, sprawled in the grass back of a dance floor Thanksgiving Day ball callow fumbling hungry hot adolescent fingers juke box electronics in the jugular of the night *you mine now, Lindy* familiar as a cola caramel sundae or divinity fudge.

She always liked the idea of an older man. Wes stopped bawling and grinned at her. He let her drive his pickup home. She mowed down somebody's white-wood painted mail box and steered three times into a ditch. He laughed and said she was so stupid he'd never met anyone so stupid in all his life. But he liked her. He told her he was twice her age and he let her stroke his bald freckled dome, and he'd never ever allowed any of his wives to do that. There was something pathetic and disarming about the guy, all he stood was five feet nothing with these barn wide shoulders and a mouth which was perpetually open. Don't you ever stop shouting? I was born shouting. I came out of the womb shouting! She liked his loneliness. She liked what he said. How he'd wasted years. All those jobs which came to nothing. And the travelling, he'd worked the way he described it in just about every State of the Union there was, and now he could talk of nothing but this place Brazil. She didn't know which side of the map it was on. He showed her the ten thousand dollars he kept in a tobacco tin. He said to her this was his last chance to make out. You come with me. Like that. Right out of nowhere. You come with me. You just a dirty old man looking for young girls. I ain't going there with you. And he started to shout again. She had to shake out her ears. Fruit picking white trash what you got to stay here for? He asked. He said we ought to fuck first, and then we'll see your mother, then I'll drive you to Texas. Ever been there? No I ain't. And they did. She never once stopped to ask herself how much she really liked him. But she stuck to him. And if he shouted too much she learnt to plug her ears with cottonwool.

Wes bought some sheets of tarpaulin from the army at the air-strip. He tacked the sheets to crossbeams and made a ceiling out of them. He didn't trust the planta roof. He knew what the rains would be like. Every noon, too tired to work any more, he rode out with stripped sugar cane stakes. He had tied lengths of cotton to each stake. He rode out across the sertão to mark the perimeters of his land.

A cafuso in Chimboa taught Linda how to drain the poison sap from bitter manioc through gauze. She had prepared enough to fry the white potato like pulp on the stove when the door behind her casually opened.

A slim brown indian, quite naked, funny little sticks in his ears and nostrils, and smoothly distended belly, stood inside the house. He didn't speak. He stood still and grinned a silly toothless smile. She swung round. He held out his hand to her. He was offering her something. Her skin prickled. She sucked in her breath and let out a scream. Her arm lifted the pan up high. The manioc flew like streaming custard across the room.

She was transfixed. That sheepish curl on his lips. The strange hairlessness of his body, the oiled slippery appearance of his skin. A length of gut held up his penis vertical to his stomach, and a black crown of rope thick hair fringed over his ears.

Wes was near enough to the hut to hear her. He plunged the horse through the bush, whacking it from side to side with a swishing cane.

The Aripuana was one of the Capitão's many nephews. Although they had observed these new americanos at a careful distance, nobody had plucked up enough courage to approach them. This young blood was filled with curiosity. He could go back to the Capitão and show them the gifts of clothing he was sure Linda would throw at him. He brought with him a pair of dead birds. And he had carefully decorated himself with the wood splits in his ears and nose. He liked to take these brancos by surprise.

Linda pushed past the young blood and raced out on to the porch when she heard Wes's horse. She raced ashen faced. Our oakie pioneer leapt off the horse with his cane stick raised. But he too stopped short when he saw what Linda was pointing at. He seemed paralysed for a moment by the indian's presence. Somehow the young blood didn't look human. The peculiar stillness in the way he stood; that smile . . . unchanging.

Wes approached him. He smelt a pungent sickly odour from

the indian, of animal grease and rot vegetation. Those dead birds held out in his hand. An offering.

"Will you take a look at that..." breathed Wes.

"Do something will you honey, he hasn't got any clothes on," said Linda.

"One of them pig indians right on our land Linda..."

"Shall I give him a pair of your pants?"

"What for?"

"He walked in the door and I was cooking just like that." Linda could not take her eyes off the sleek brown man in dark shadow of the doorway.

"You stay like that see," murmured our pioneer to the indian, "I want to show you that's not the way you step into my house no clothes and nothing scaring the girl out of her picky mind!"

Wes circled around him. The indian pointed to the oakie's pants, he mimed the putting on of the pants. Wes slashed him with the cane stick. Slashed him again across the face. The young blood dropped the birds and knelt against the wall. There was no attempt to fight back. He didn't try to avoid the stinging blows. Wes swung at him, again and again, but the sheepish smile never left the fat brown lips.

Linda ran inside and pulled at a pile of clothes in a fruit box on the floor. She came out holding a pair of cotton Levi's.

"Don't hit him like that!" she shouted. The young blood was like a dog tied to a post, and Wes wouldn't stop. Linda grabbed at his arm.

"Don't hit him any more, please!"

Wes stood away, breathing hard. His eyes were wide and staring, fixed with curiosity on the young blood, why didn't he get up and run what was the matter with him lying down like that as if he wanted more whipping—? The indian moved slowly to the far end of the wall. He sat back with a sadness in his face, a peculiar look of regret, but he wasn't frightened, it was more a resigned expression, now he knew what these branco were like, he could go back to the group and show them the slash marks.

"You wouldn't believe he'd be so pig stupid!" Wes said.

"Give him these." Linda shoved the Levi's at Wes. Wes pushed them away.

"Don't be so stupid."

"Please Wes – that's all he wants – he ain't got no other clothes. Please—"

Wes kicked the dead birds across the ground. Linda dropped the pants she was holding. She picked the birds up by the string they were attached to.

"Give one of them a pair of pants you'll have them back like a football squad!" said Wes.

The young blood was on his feet. All in one motion. A quick fluid action. Before Wes could move he was striding quickly and quietly away, yet unhurried seemingly, without any appearance of running hard, loping steps towards the bush and liana thickness of the sertão, never once looking back. The trees swallowed him.

"You didn't have to do that!"

"How was I to know what you screamed for?"

"Hitting him like an animal—"

"That's what he is – animal – a matter of coincidence he looks human."

"No sense in hitting him like that."

"Course there is!"

"What did he do!"

"Walked in your door – my door – like that, skinnydip naked ain't that enough insult?"

"I was scared that's all."

"That's right. How do you know what these animals do out there?"

"He meant no harm – you could have given those pants."

"Dumb broad you are - that's what he came for. He most probably got a two-piece suit and a pair of boots hidden out there in the trees."

"He hasn't..."

"Did you smell him, Linda?"

"I guess so, but—"

"Smells high as dead pig in a heat wave."

"You don't go hitting him!" she shouted with feeling. Her face felt flushed and hot. She was so angry.

"By God I'm goin' find the rest of them wherever they are," Wes's tone was exultant, "you know what it mean him coming by like that?"

She was gone. She ran into the house and slammed the door behind her. Wes was oblivious.

"Indians work for free," he called after her, "they're on our land, they belong to us. We got indians, Linda! ... Linda—?"

Linda scraped the manioc pulp off the wall, she felt numb and shaky, outside Wes was shouting to himself. And tears began to cascade down her cheeks. She never liked to see anybody hurt, least of all that animal indian human thing. All right, so perhaps he was an animal, that don't mean Wes can cut up mad dog going ape hitting him like that. Maybe an indian thing like that had no soul, neither had her white rabbit Louisa her Aunt Mim gave her, but all he wanted was clothes. For Christ's sake!

She had read somewhere, one of those dentist waiting room *Reader's Digest* magazines maybe, that these kind of confrontations only happen to Americans when they go abroad. You have to expect this sort of thing, that's what she'd read. Culture shocks, they called it. All Americans receive culture shocks, and that's what that indian thing on the porch with wood spindles in his nose was.

He went out looking for them every morning. He packed bottles of pinga and white sugar sacks strapped against the rug cloth saddle, he packed a carton of Minister filtro cigarros and a bag of rice; when he found his indians he was going to trade with them. And if he'd already seen one there must be dozens more of them out there, somewhere. It took our stub tall oakie pioneer a week to notice the thread of wood smoke above the trees over to the west of his land. He had never quite thought of looking for them in the sky. Then it clicked. The smoke rose too far west for him to reach it that day. The following morning he woke with the curutia darting paper bird, rot mist vegetation blurred his direction, by the time the sun tripped its heat hammer Wes was drenched with sweat, but he could see that same spire of smoke. In the palm swamp monstera and caladium leaves slowed the horse completely. Wes had to chop with the machete and his tall heels wallowed in the green matter. If the indians had made a path it was unlikely he'd know even if he walked right across it. The leaves gave way to the slashing blade with a leather-like reluctance.

The clearing appeared abruptly. The dense buriti fell away and Wes halted with the horse close behind him. There was the maloca. Newly built. Half a roof of planta and palm leaves over a frame of gut-bonded cana. Wes wiped the moisture from his eyes. By God there were indians all right. His indians on his land. Shrivelled brown women their bean bag breasts slapping against ribs, pot-bellied babies rolling in the warm dust of the fire. Those skinny dogs all bone haunch and tail hadn't barked yet. He was pleased he had crept up on them so sneakily. I must be stealthy as a polecat.

The Capitão coughed delicately just behind the pioneer's ear. All eighteen young bloods, brothers, cousins and nephews stood in a semi-circle less than five yards away behind Wes. Slanting light which fell through the creeper green ceiling wasp ringed their brown bodies. They had been watching him for days. Riding round and round the westerly side of his land. Coming closer all the time, but never quite finding them. They were almost worried they might have had to send a cousin out to show Wes the way.

Capitão Pedro didn't want to let this branco down. When he was certain Wes could find his way to the maloca he instructed the men in his group accordingly. They each rubbed red and white stripes down their chests, they added a few extra touches like the splints of wood in their ears, and they tied painted palm leaves scissored into fringes around their ankles. The Capitão wanted to see this branco's expression when he arrived. After all, if he was going to meet his first group of indians he might as well see them at their peacock best.

Wes stood his ground and beamed broadly at them. None of them would shake his hand. So he put the machete carefully back on to the saddle hook and introduced himself—

"My name Wes . . . and I've come to tell you I'm your friend . . . and eh . . . and I thought you ought to know you're squatting right slap centre of my land . . ." and they weren't paying any attention to what he said. Two of them ducked low beneath his chin to study the gold teeth in his uppers and lowers with considerable fascination. One young blood poked his finger into the oakie's mouth and scratched the gold tooth. Wes grinned at him.

"And . . . these is . . ." Wes faltered, touching the bags of sugar and pinga bottles, "... this is what I brought you. Like a gift see ... right?"

The Capitão immediately understood. He took the horse away from Wes, and led our pioneer into the clearing. The brown faces all round him watched with furrowed frowning interest. The other young bloods stoned the dogs away, the animals ran whimpering across the ground. Just before the other young bloods got their hands on the gifts, the Capitão snarled at them that these were brought specifically for him, and he was the one member of the group who knew how to talk to branco like this strange creature with a wide-brimmed stetson and high heels.

It could quite truthfully be said that Wes walked tall into the clearing. He had good reason to. There wasn't one indian who stood an inch above him. And the first thing he recognised was what a quiet group they were, little people greased and slippery skinned, how all their motions were slow, as if a perpetual tiredness enveloped them, and their long almond eyes glittered black curiosity at him.

When they spoke their mouths filled with ta-pa-pi-kwu-oho-tapa sounds. They had a matter-of-fact nature, their tired seeming movements were not out of slothfulness but out of a healthy regard for doing what was least required of each in this forest. After the Capitão placed Wes opposite him on the ground in the shade side of the maloca, the largest hut, women brought across all the gifts and laid them at the Capitão's feet. They touched the pinga bottles with a kind of thanklessness, there was no show of gratitude, anything so mundane as that, and they tapped the fat sugar sacks as if to say he could have brought us more if he'd loaded up two horses.

The Capitão decided against putting on a pair of trousers, in deference to Wes, now that they were sitting down. It was so enjoyable to watch this branco's face. The bug-eyed uneasiness in Wes. With a touch of mime and his dozen or so Portuguese words the oakie and the Capitão got along quite nicely. And every time he spoke Wes tried to lower his voice to a reasonable pitch.

"You see ... all this land here – far as from here to right over there – and to over there – and across to my home – home hut house like this mine – I own it all. And I want to try to explain this to you. OK? ... Am I making sense am I getting through?" Wes drew a picture of the land between the maloca and his house on the ground, and he pointed to the maloca and he touched his own chest to make a point, and the young bloods crowded and jostled around him, "... now I'm not saying I don't want you on my land. I do, you stay just as long as you like but in exchange I want you to do – you and you and all of you – do something for me. Right."

The Capitão only replied in Portuguese, the young bloods could understand neither of them, but to Wes's surprise, the Capitão seemed to understand almost everything he said. The old indian nodded and scratched at the map drawn out in the earth, and so far as Wes could follow it all, he was in perfect harmony with the Capitão. Of course, it was very important for the Capitão to give his own group the impression he could communicate with this branco. In the long run, it didn't take much guesswork on the Capitão's part to understand Wes.

The children were emboldened. A little girl wrapped her legs around the oakie's left boot and tried to pull it off him. Wes laughed and let her wrestle with it. A woman hung a necklace of capyvara wild boar teeth around the pioneer's neck. He was reluctant to take his stetson off to aid her. But the Capitão made it known to him he'd like to wear the stetson. Wes hesitated, for an instant the Capitão looked crestfallen, he was trying to say only he would wear the stetson, and none of the other Aripuana would. Wes relented. The Capitão stood up. He pulled the stetson to a similar angle. But none of the group was paying him any attention. They were fascinated by the oakie's bald pate. Wes controlled his embarrassment, he let them stroke the shiny dome, ginger dappled with freckles. They asked him how he made it. Wes tried to explain it grew naturally that way. Why is that, they were asking—? Wes mimed it was on account he had a big brain box and there wasn't enough hair to cover it up.

The Capitão didn't swallow that one.

Wes stayed talking with the Capitão for two hours and more. The Capitão treated it all very seriously. The other men in the group wandered away. The Capitão agreed with almost everything Wes put to him. Yes he'd do this, yes he'd see to that. Wes was astonished. These people expected him to come there making demands on them. They wanted him to announce his authority over them. Even the Capitão. There was no resentment. No quarrel at all. But there were minor wrinkles. No he couldn't give the Capitão his wristwatch. No, the machete was the only one he possessed. If they wanted more pinga, they'd have to come to his home for it, because it might look suspicious to those guys in Chimboa if he kept riding away with bottles of the stuff swinging from his saddle. As for the stetson – or these boots – well, that was out of the question.

They made Wes feel like a king.

A very pretty brown sister, wide black eyes and fat breasts painted with ochre, agoutis or paca teeth circlets interspersed with parrot feathers at her wrists and neck, brought the king an oval of sweet cassava bread. It weighed more than four kilos. He must take it home with him, she explained. It is our gift to you. And she placed the bread in his hands and smiled at him. If Wes noticed anything at all in her smile, so busy was he taking in the delicate mould of her body her perfectly shaped limbs rounded without any hint of fatness, he could have registered a look of bland regard, as it was in all the other women of the Aripuana, without those prerequisites the civilizado wants among his own kind – sympathy or warmth, self-conciousness or desire to connect in some way, this bland regard in the pretty young sister was saying to him – stay or go, help us or leave us alone, we expect nothing from you because we have so little we can give to you, you are branco civilizado you have everything, anyway.

A young blood brought him his horse. The Capitão would not shake hands. But he was the last of the group to stand at the edge of the clearing, to watch Wes ride away. Some of the dogs raced beneath the hooves yapping until the indians stoned them off. The children ran to the trees after him. But they ran silently, they did not wave or shout. Wes glanced behind him. The Capitão stood firm.

All the way back, the bread swinging in a sack at the stirrup, Wes tried to figure it out. He felt so proprietorial. These were virtually his subjects. These soft brown bodies covered in a high stinking grease were in the kingdom of Dwight Weslie. Yet they were not afraid. They were prepared to place themselves in the very palm of his hand. But they didn't expect anything from him, perhaps the pinga and the occasional sack of rice that was nothing, and they took for granted that his word was law. Jesus it can't be that easy! Where'd all these stories come from about tribes killing east coast Brazil shanty trash settlers? All these indian things want to do – shoot birds out of trees and harvest manioc for the wet season. They don't even possess a rifle between them. The king clipped his horse at a pace, and he tried to follow the barely visible path the Capitão had shown him....

"Those indigewhadyamacallem, Jeff," the oakie said to Geofrey when his pal the limey returned that week, "now... you telling me you never knew they were on my land?"

"Cross my heart and hope to die I didn't."

"I seenem."

Beady bright red possession burning in Wes's face, some kind of new animal he discovered must send out east ask the zoos what price they'd give for it.

"When I sat down with that old Capitão thing he said they're goin' settle there. You didn't know that either?"

No, Geofrey didn't.

"So I said – no I told them – this is my backyard all mine what you goin' to do about it? And I gave them gifts. And they said they really wanted rifles had I got any. I wasn't going to give them rifles now was I? More damn sense than that. Would I give them pinga for bows and arrows? Who wants bows and arrows time like this! I said I'll get you pinga on condition."

"What condition?"

The Aripuana group began work for Wes that week. The day Geofrey got back, they were already shovelling the earth, slashing and burning the land around the hut, cutting a path out towards the table sertão which looked green enough for pasture one day. There was such a triumph in Wes's face, sense of conquest without pain, possession without having had to give up a dime of his, he said you know it's like a hundred years back slaves and black ass Africans imported into the south, all you need show them is a bottle of pinga or cachaça white rum and hold up a cane stick swish it over their heads and they just knuckle under.

"Jeff I got a whole household squad staff right on my back porch working each morning for me."

"Has Linda taken to them?"

"She bawls me out everytime I hit one of them but you got to understand they work so slow they don't know how to work together systematically they animals man, but if I hold them to it. Shout a bit and—"

"Is Linda afraid of them?"

"No no – she goes along – I say to her don't ever let them in the house honey they got fingers like electric magnets, but she watches them out the window. And I had to tell her to give them some of my pants because I don't like for her to see their nuts dangle when they bend down."

"You're a lucky man."

"That's what I keep telling myself! I don't need those guys round the pensão they got dollar-shaped eyes."

"As long as the indians are on your land you can do what you like with them."

"I believe it now . . . when you told me before I thought ridiculous but now I don't I speak to the old fellah and he nods his head everytime I ask him for anything."

Oh, and the oakie said they were like a pack of animals, except for the fact they walk and talk, they walking and talking animals but they different from you and me, this pig shit sour cream smell they got well you get used to that, and the way they can never be anywhere in one place together in one concerted effort when I tell them, well that's what they are – kind of pathetic half humans creeping about inside the forest. They better off working for me.

"Now tell me you envious of me, Jeff, tell me I done the right thing, huh?"

"Did you see any women in the group?"

"Yearh yearh I saw."

"Young girls I mean—?"

"Plenty of them sure."

"You like them?"

"I don't need to like them, I own them. They mine. Now ain't that true?"

"I mean—"

"I know what you mean all right . . . they certainly kind of different looking. It's the skin they got it's like it was oiled specially or—"

"Did the Capitão offer you one as a gift?"

Now Wes wasn't the kind of man to leave that part of the story undecorated. Hell, that Capitão thing said I could have the choice of three girls I saw. He made them stand there and I looked them over, right in front of all the men indians. But there was one. Like a kid, but a bit older, small very neat and small, and she come up to me with a loaf of bread size of a kerosene can, got beads banging around her neck and wrists, little moon brown face all smiles, and she practically dropped her tits right in the palm of my hand.

"She's for me. That one."

"I'm sure she is."

"And who'd ever tell Linda?"

"I won't."

"That's right. You my buddy, pal."

The buddy knew a lot more than he told that night. For no matter how cowed Pedro's Aripuana ever became or how abject contact with branco ever made them, that they gave girls away, that even the Capitão might offer his own wife who had a body like parched cow-hide, that they'd even dream of such a thing – these were fistfuls of civilizado romance, they were the pathetic wish creations branco has arrogated to himself so often before; and the oakie was talking like those mateiros and eastern porceiros in the shanty huts beside the road where the yellow claw steel cats were coming through the forest. Satanic child instincts, softly mouthed obscenities hideous favela trash libido leers in the moist night when the moths made immolation dives at the kerosene lamp to burn out their eyes.

Just like a moth, murmured Geofrey. The oakie couldn't hear. He was too busy playing king.

* * *

Geofrey rammed the Wyllis *Rural* around bush and ditch. The earth was drying out enough to take it. He drove up past the pink-flowering oiticicia tree. It was an easy time for him.

He had bought the cattle from the ranch at Araguaçema, but there'd be a long wait before the fazendeiro could rope the beef to the rafts he must send down river to Chimboa. He had to wait out the coming weeks.

He cut the engine and walked towards the stone pool. Palm and bush straggled around him. He could hear the water splashing, and he stopped by the shade of a palmyra to observe. He could have turned back, but he didn't. The palmyra was a good vantage point, and he believed he was hidden enough. He watched Linda bobble her head in the pool. She splashed her face, soap rinsed out of her hair, she flapped on to her back to float.

Her body had a white larvae pulp texture, apart from the deepening colour of her arms her nakedness was clearly a stranger to the sun. She kicked her long stick legs and the water addled the swallow's nest of brown pubic of her crutch.

She could see him all right. She'd heard the Wyllis bump and grind up towards her. I can see you, creepy crawly guy, think you gotten enough cover under that palm tree, you want something to really look at – here – hey here – look at this, limey! She had to jump up out of the water to grasp the edge of the stones. She flicked an ankle up and over the side slipped on to the stones. She rubbed the towel through her hair quickly, and laid herself out flat on the stones. The towel made a pillow. Geofrey didn't move. She bided her time, then—

"... You seen all you want to see, Geofrey?"

His skin prickled. He tried to grin. It was an embarrassed expression.

"... You can come a little closer, I don't mind. Come on, Geofrey."

She didn't move her head. She shaded her eyes with her hands and studied the puff cotton threads of cloud high in the hazy blue.

"You can come out now, Geofrey, come on."

He ducked his head beneath the low stooping palm leaves and walked towards her. Weedy explanations drifted through his mind's ear and out the other.

"I don't mind ... honest I don't," she said, still not moving her head, "so long as Wes don't find out. And how'd he ever find out?"

"I ... didn't mean to ..."

"Yes you did, why lie?"

"Well ..." diffidently.

"Did you never go swimming with girls? Never go swimming with nothing on?"

"Eh no—"

"About time you started to – last fall I spent best part of two weeks camping and swimming with nothing on at all in Red River – why don't you take your clothes off and jump in?"

"No thanks I'd rather not – I really meant to tell you – that's why I stopped – it's quite a distance from here to the house and you don't want those vaqueiros riding by do you?"

"Geofrey," she said with precision, "you were spying on me, you don't have to invent explanations. Why don't you admit it?"

"All right – I'm sorry."

"No need to be. I'm not ashamed."

"I wish you'd put your clothes on now. Linda – just in case."

"Wes ain't around. It don't bother me none."

"Where is he?"

"He's chasing some of those indian things they wouldn't come and work for him, for I don't know why they wouldn't so he got it into his head to go out and rustle them out like a wild west sheriff. He's made himself a whip eight feet long and he takes it to them. So I fetch myself here and keep a healthy distance."

"It's not easy to make indians understand what you want – especially if you are Wes."

"He never stop shouting and beating them, I guess I can't bear to listen. He goes ape on them and that's the funny thing they don't fight back they just smile those silly smiles they got and they come back for more. It's crazy!"

"You don't like that?"

"I don't like see any animal get hurt."

"Wes has changed."

"Changed? He ain't the same guy I first came here with. He so different. He don't talk to me like he used to. He don't sleep. Sometimes right in the middle of the night he goes across the clearing up by the high point there and he sits and watches the lights down over the road where the builders are – way across the valley – and he stays there till light."

She stood to her feet. She was quite close to him. Quirky mischievous smile on her lips. He could touch her by just lifting his hand. Her breasts were very white gentle mounds kissed with bright nipples.

"You can swim can't you, Geofrey?"

"Yes, why?"

She was a step closer. That larky grin on her face. It was so unexpected, he hadn't thought of it. He was too near the edge of the stone pool rim. Something told him that perhaps she was going to put her clothes on after all. When she pushed him with both her flat hands and—

"Because I'd hate to see you drown!"

—he trod air backwards, Geofrey executed a near perfect somersault into the water. He surfaced and coughed up a lung-sized gargle and was surprised at the depth of the water in the centre. He stroked to the side and pulled at the stone rim. The water weighted his clothes, air sockets gurgled up from the bottom of his boots.

She'd skipped to the far side to fetch her Levi's and sweat shirt and sneakers. She laughed gaily as she reached her arms into the shirt and jerked it down over her damp straight hair. Geofrey shook out his ears.

"I told you you ought to swim more often! That's for snooping. Are you mad at me now?"

"First time anybody's dunked me since I left school," he said. And – no, he wasn't mad. He asked for it. You win, Linda.

"That's what I said to myself when I met you – you know there's something about a limey like this – he looks like he's never really played, you know, fooled around or done anything in his life that give him a mite of pleasure."

Geofrey sat down on a patch of grass away from the reflected heat of the stones around the pool. She tucked her toes into the sneakers and threw him her towel. He wiped his eyes.

"Ain't it true?" she asked him.

He was saying he lived most of his childhood on his own, preferred no company to any, and if it seemed peculiar, well you have to understand that only someone as self-sufficient as this can stick it out in a place like Chimboa godawful bush mato outpost slap centre of the Amazonas.

"You a funny guy, Geofrey – really are – what do you do for girls?"

"I don't."

"Well I know you like girls. I seen you staring bug-eyed through that palm tree."

"What do you want me to tell you? That I'm in love with my mother? That I'm waiting for a truckdriver to come by I picked up in Santarém?"

"You lived all this time in Brazil – you could find a nice Brazilian friend—?"

"You think a carioca would follow me out here to live? In this?"

"No, I mean ... you just don't seem to care about anybody – anybody else that is."

She took her towel back and screwed it into a turban shape around her head. She pushed the straggles of hair up underneath.

"There once was a girl ..." he said slowly.

"I know ..." she smiled coyly at him, "I seen her. That girl in the picture album thing, you got family photos in. That the one?"

"Yes."

"You asked her to marry you?"

"Yes I did."

"And she gave you the thumbs down?"

"She married my best friend."

"But Geofrey ..." her eyes opened wide, "that ain't exactly the end of the world is it?"

"After that – I came to Brazil. It may sound odd to you but perhaps I'm an old-fashioned kind of guy. Girls don't grow on trees for me. And I've never met a person who thinks about Brazil same as I do – and I don't expect to."

"Oh I don't reckon that's so. I don't believe you I really don't. Like the way you watched me hidden and all thinking she don't notice me here – you afraid of something aren't you? What you got to be afraid of – is it sex? Somebody do something wrong to you when you was a kid? That it?"

"There's no room for anybody else with me in my life. No room out here. I'm alone."

"Well ..." she breathed out a hot humid air yawn, faint

drowsiness grilo monotony scraping sleep, "there's enough space out here for you to be so alone you could forget what people actually look like."

"Linda? ... What is there for you here, with Wes?"

"I've never thought about it."

"Yes you have."

"I mean about Wes and me. I never think about what this kind of living means that what you mean if I thought about that I'd pack my toothbrush and be gone by the morning. Well it's what the books calls culture shock. And I've had more culture shocks right now than I ever thought possible."

"Wes is twice your age."

"You look at him. Fit as a bull he is."

"You'll leave him. One of these days. You'll walk out go straight back to your mother in that little town you come from."

"Perhaps I will. Just perhaps. But you ought to know something about me – I'm not afraid of work – or being dirt poor or that – I'm straight with everyone I speak to I'm honest and I won't do nothing to Wes until he do it to me first. Wes ain't going to ask me to marry him. I know that. But there's nobody quite like that guy. Besides, he's the first man ever did ask me to go to Brazil with him. And I owe him that."

She said she hoped his wristwatch was waterproof, and if he'd bring up the Wyllis and give her a ride to the house she'd boil some of that dreadful smelling green tea you Brazilians like so much and you can suck it through a straw long as you want on the porch and Wes would be back soon, there's pinga I keep cool in the earth just like you showed us to, and plenty of lime lemons to suck, you can talk about the road and the minerals and indian things, swinging in the hammocks to keep the hive of mosqus off of you, because that's just about all you guys ever do seem to want to do, right?

* * *

The new work-force up at the clearing around the hut was

no assembly line machine skilled efficiency; you ask an Aripuana to leave a tree where it is he cut it down, tell him slash it he burn it, persuade him meet you today he arrive tomorrow, give him an axe head he lose it – the indians could never quite do what Wes wanted of them. They were children, seemingly wayward and silly, never hurried, and they so quickly became bored with a task. And the pioneer bawled them out until his lungs ached.

Wes started to kick. He used his cane stick. He 'rationed' them their pinga and bags of sugar and rice. An indian broke an axe haft a few moments after the oakie had made it, Wes could fashion hafts out of iron wood he was so adept at it, and Wes cracked. He swung the indian clean in the air by his pudding bowl hair until the eyes streamed. But the indian fell back, that same sheepish passive smile, and he'd carry on. Whatever he did to them they never retaliated, they even playfully devised tricks for avoiding the blows, and the more his blows rained on them the more natural the more the norm of branco it appeared to be to them, and they came back for the punishment and the pinga. Black almond eyes silent and acquiescent to a degree, twittering ta-pe-puta-tumu-oke-i giggles, they unwittingly goaded rage like a vomit in the oakie's throat.

Linda saw the change in him. In everything he said there was a coarsening. Fits of anger spilt over the tiniest matter. He had come back to the hut that morning. She hadn't stirred. He was fucking her and she wanted none of it, she was another object for the release he wanted, by the open screen door the shutters were pulled back and two Aripuana were watching them, she yelled out but Wes refused to stop, he bent her arms back and smiled grimly down at her. He wanted those indians to watch. Every bit of strength he showed them was a newly won possession for him. Linda spat at him, twisted her body and rolled from beneath, she drew the shutter across the space. The punching and kicking became his one sure reality.

The Aripuana *formed* a piece of land around the home the size of a football ground. Certain trees – fig and palm Wes painted with a slash of white – were left standing. Parts of the earth were burnt black, stumped massaranduba and furnace heat cracked seams littered the compound area, stones too heavy to lift shrapnelled the ground. Beyond the clearing where the young bloods had hacked away the liana the tall grass held an illusion of richness. There, the red earth and the revealed clay beneath would hold its moisture. But only for a while. As long as the king was happy about it, that was all that mattered.

On some days a tiredness took hold of him, it was a drained sensation. However much he kicked those whadyamacallems it left him an emptiness. He wished to sweet Jeeesus they'd stand up to him, for once hold their ground and answer him back. That's what he was looking for – a good reason, an excuse justified by the spiralling norm of his brutality to kill off one of them. They were becoming a hydra-headed punchbag. It wasn't enough for the king. He began to believe he would never truly own them until he killed. Until he took life – pyramidic logic consuming him – until he could see their expressions after it, their cowedness and their brown smiles over toothless chasms, a death to give him an ultimate sense of well-being, only this could assuage the emptiness.

A coldness grew between them. She wouldn't have him touch her. Something inside closed against him. Little things – her skin shivering beneath his fingers, little looks – of self-disgust when he had finished. She started to hide in the house, the closed shutters gave her darkness, she withdrew and he sensed the shame she felt. At night she stayed out under the palm porch swinging alone in her rêde. She even let the mosqus gather in a cloud over her head, they'd perch on her fingertips where the blood was closest to the skin gossamer pins slake slanting into her, but she wouldn't step inside to sleep with him, she wouldn't ask for the mosquiteiro, no matter how often he shouted, in the liquid eye of the night she'd defend herself with silence.

"Where you put that cane stick of mine, Linda?"

"How do I know . . ."

"You hid it."

"I don't touch it . . ."

"Yes, you hid it."

"I don't even see it, Wes!"

"Where!"

"Hurting me . . . !"

"You don't like see me hitting them, you close up the shutters and sit in the dark middle of the day and try to pretend it ain't happening! Give me it?"

"Let go of me – pulling like that!"

"Tell me—?"

"Ye-e-es I hid it! ... Now stop doing that!"

"... All right."

"They may be animals – you treat them worse than animals – I hid it I hid it. Leave me alone will you!"

"... All right, Linda. Fine fine—"

"Fuck off out of here now will you please."

"... All right ... won't serve no purpose even if you think it will. I can find another cane stick like that. They all over the ground outside."

"You do that then."

"I can even tell an indian thing go and bring me one and cut like I want it—"

"You do!"

"Won't stop me hitting."

"I closed my ears."

"Won't stop me hitting them and that's what they expect that's what they like them and me – it's our relationship and I don't ask you to understand. But I do!"

"Not listening ..."

"You put your hands over your ears much as you like you hide behind the shutters sit in the hot dark until there ain't nothin' left of you but a pool of sweat – shit! – don't you understand I'm winning!"

Silence. Her tears. Don't even know if they are tears. Could be perspiration rolling like pearls down the bridge of her nose. He was out the door shouting for somebody to get into line. Her neck where he'd gripped her still felt his nails. Hair feels like he pulled a fistful of roots out with him. She'd draw the shutters back. In the gloom find a corner beside the wood wait until the shirt is saturated wring it out in the stone pool later lie out afloat on the water watch urubu climb and stiffen in the haze height they swoop down kick the water at them no corpse this.

* * *

Wes had arranged for nine of the young bloods to meet to form a new parcel of land. He told them they must be there at exactly half the sun's dial above certain trees. As usual they arrived in dribs and drabs. Three of them got there more than two hours later than the appointed time, which was approximately five thirty in the morning.

He turned on the three. He told them he don't need them. They can't do this to him. Got to be there just as he says. Their sheepish grins, wondering expressions, why hasn't he got his usual cane stick with him? He picked up large stones and threw them. He chucked stone after stone until they understood the 'game' – that they had to run – and they ducked and twisted in the sertão. He caught one indian a cracker of a blow on his head. Blood gushed. The indian climbed back to his feet and wobbled. His stomach felt sick. He doubled-back to get out of range.

Linda was hardly out of the rêde when she heard him run up. She slept in shorts and a sleeveless cotton vest. The indian leant against the porch upright and held his head in his hands. Red all over his fingers. She wanted to run inside and pull back shutters. But the young blood slipped to his knees. Dizziness gripped him. He was smiling up at her. She hesitated. He was mouthing at her soft ta-pu-te-tei-pui-pui-na. Tapping his head lolling it from side to side.

She found the oakie's fruit box. She took the indian a pair of Wes's pants. But he wouldn't take them. His head – pointing for her – his head. And she took his hand very gingerly, leading him inside the hut, taking a deep breath, not bearing to look at the free flow of blood—

"Sit there... over there... that's right."

She was shaking all over. The strange oiliness of his skin. It's soft touch. The young blood sat on the fruit box and she wiped at the wound with a cloth. She poured a cupful of water from the filter jar and made him hold steady while she cleared away the matted hair.

"You keep still... like that... OK, now this might hurt... got to be done, you see..."

She drenched another rag with cachaça alcohol, and held his head, the indian stiffened abruptly at the burning sensation. She tied straps of shirt over the rag and wound them round his head.

He kept wanting to feel with his hands what she was doing. She slapped his hands down and knotted the ends of the cloth.

All his limbs were shivering. And his body felt so cold beneath her touch. Red clots married the cotton binding to his head. She brought him a shirt and pushed it into his hands.

"Now that just plain stupid – you put it – go on put it on – catch death of pneumonia start shaking like that, hear me—?"

He took the pants from her, too. He slipped his legs into them. She boiled a pan of green chá de mato and made him suck at the thick mixture through a straw. He still smiled at her, that gentle witless fat creasing grin, passive lips now asking for something more – he mimed to her—

"You want what?"

Mimed again.

"Want see yourself in a mirror? A mirror is that it?"

She took out her vanity box, and lifted the little plastic mirror top of her powder base. He inspected the dressing around his head with considerable curiosity. He wanted to keep the powder case, but—

"Oh no. Only one I got see. You come back tomorrow show you again. You come back and I'll look at the wound again."

It was clear she wanted him to leave. He understood. He turned to look at her from the ground below the raised level of the porch. That silly smile again.

"Go along you go ... off you go now," and she waved her arms at him. He was running now with one hand jammed to the bandaging in case it came away. He had to find the others. He had to show them what he'd got. Linda fell across the rêde on the porch, she tipped the cachaça bottle into her mouth, God she'd never thought of doing that before, touching the thing like that, mending the wound, cold and shaky now, I'd never have believed it if you told me a month ago I'd be doing that for an indian, and his smell, that smell he has – rancid buttermilk and summer skunk dead on the highway.

That evening before Wes got back, the indian returned with four others. They all had cut marks on their bodies, like somebody had found a new cane stick sharp as a knife and slashed at them all day. The indian with the bandaging wanted her to wipe their cuts as well. He mimed and pointed and they smiled their gummy pink grins at her. For pity's sake I'm not a missionary, I'm not an MD on vacation, get out of here—

"Go on! All of you. Leave me alone! Please!"

She ran inside and bolted back the door. Before they could run up to the porch she had closed the shutters and curled herself in a corner in the darkness. Their feet pattered on the boards outside. Funny ta-pei-i-ye whispers. Then they skipped off the porch, their sibilant chatter much fainter now, and they were across the cleared compound, slipping into the palm and liana selvedge of the sertão.

* * *

In the day, Wes squatted on the high ground and watched the plume of red dust rise up among the trees where the road builders were carving the super-highway. Soon they'd get so close he'd hear the roar from the yellow D.C.9 cats and he'd even be able to make out the sun's sheen on their mustard helmets. There ... he could just see the shape of it, a red rut of a snake wriggling through the green, then at times it became a straight line for a hundred kilometres or more, but as it closed towards Chimboa through the changing land stratas it twisted more. When it finally arrived here, he told himself, and the technicians geiger counted the value of the minerals underneath and when the banks rolled in with their caravan trailer counters, you'd hear the laughter of new millionaires rise as high as where the flowering pink oiticicia tree stood on his land. Those Brazil nuts would switch on the lamps atop the telegraph poles, somebody would fetch an electric ice-box from Santarém and plug it in, there'd be no more kerosenes to wank about with, and this pile of shanty spittoons will be a concrete Kansas quicker'n any macaco can gibber up in an iron-wood.

As for Linda – little Lindypants will leave. Won't even be a note. All there'd be – her Levi's and her face paint box missing. Army nut take her to the air-strip. Stand there and look dumb enough – that she can do – she'd hitch a cargo flight up north to Boa Vista. I could have been that stupid I might have married her.

He rode way west of the indian's maloca that day. There the land was high enough to find with the naked eye the dipping basin of mato several hundred kilometres away where the Rio Teles Pires made its flooding descent to the Amazon. It was a fat river this time of year, brown weighted water slowly draining its mother mato until it must cascade mud brown and bitter yellow into the arterial sea of the Amazon. High above the trees urubru wait, black vulture colon shapes, heavy eyes filled with prey, breathless hang of talons in the creamy air. Must turn back now. Horse ain't got eight legs.

He wasn't looking for them (and when you do you don't find them), but there were two brown bodies running up ahead of him. His horse heaved beneath his heel. He'd catch them. But there was no path on this rocky incline. Tumbled trees festered with green climber. His horse refused to climb across.

Wes was wrong. Only one indian he'd seen. Now the trees and liana grew more thickly here. And she had turned back for no apparent reason, she was coming back towards him with a prim and delicate stride, an offer to help on her face, it was this same pretty young sister who gave him that oval sweet cassava bread his first call at the maloca. She wore beads and a bone triangle over her pubics and there was a faint powdering of ochre dust on her stomach. She took his bridle and pulled the animal over the dead trunks.

Wes ambled the horse forward and she walked beside. She didn't know any of his twelve words of Portuguese and he was quite relieved for that. He watched how she moved her feet. With a sure and certain gait she placed the heels forward, he never saw her toes touch the ground there was such a springing swiftness in the arch of her feet. Her toes stubbed like tiny fists, they were resilient and supple as a sloth's palm.

He jumped down to walk with her. She stood a hand shorter than him. Beyond the broken trees there was fern, flattened by the rains now cracked and dry in brown and rust patterns, and above them hung a cobweb of strangler.

He touched her shoulder. And she paused. As gentle as he could be he brushed at the urucum of ochre on her belly with curiosity. She saw it cling to his fingers and she smiled and pushed them towards his face and they planted whorls of red dust against his forehead. She liked that. Her tongue spread her lips with a wide grin, only a girl young as herself can keep all her teeth as she has done, and her splayed nostrils crinkled humorous circles around her nose.

Afterwards he'd congratulate himself on how easy it had been. After he'd sat with her and palmed her breasts with that dust on them; after he'd smiled a lot, and she plucked at his gold fillings with her finger nails, and her quiet acquiescence as if she didn't mind at all what he did, even when he pulled the triangular shell tanga from her pubics. She didn't appear to breathe she lay so still, and his fingers slipped beneath the fold of skin. She studied him with a calmness. There was an unmistakable oiliness about her body, greased firmness like the inner wall of a snail's shell.

Gentle as he'd ever be, he spread her beneath him, all the while feeling so amazed at her passiveness, he pulled at his clothes and there was a sense of matter-of-factness and a waiting in her, but tempered with no apprehension of a body being abused, nothing like that at all, only when he entered her did her eyes change. They became black pools filled with a void-like distance. He could have been a million kilometres from here.

But she responded. Her body involuntarily eased upwards to meet the pumping head of his cock, still her eyes remained obsidian. They had an unflinching unreflective bolt. In her mind she closed something away from him it was a certain secret tiny grain of mystery much more important to her than the crude sperm spasm hunt of his senses. Though he had this possession of her – pumped avarice – branco arrogated spoil – this making a death of her rising senses – he knew there was no coming in that closed and forbidden area of this little sister so expressed in the pools of her eyes. That secret, for a while, was hers.

Then he heard the noise. A foot on bark. Dried crack. Wes was very quick. He didn't need to look. He knew the indian was behind him. Flashed across his mind what he had first observed – the two of them running together in front of his horse. How quickly he had forgotten.

The little sister was rolling away. Crying out and jumping to her feet, ducking into the trees. Wes twisted to the side with embarrassed panic. His hands fastened his pants. The Aripuana held a knife. Slim and wasted like an old cutlery blade. Haft of soft wood bark. He held it out at arm's length, the sharp edge glinted at the oakie's throat. Wes scrambled as best he could. He had seconds. No knife fight lasted longer. His horse hadn't strayed more than a few yards. The young blood wouldn't hurry. There was caution in his brown face, the same curled passive smile, and broken black square in the rind of gum. Wes remembered which side of the skin saddle his axe was holstered. He'd have to duck and run, if he could do it quick enough, not allowing the indian more than an instant to strike into his shoulders, there was a chance.

* * *

Linda had seen some of the Aripuana women do it before. They laid out wet clothes by the stone pool and rubbed them with stones large as their fists to press out the dirt.

She placed dunked garments, pants and shirts of hers and the oakie, on the slab stone edge of the pool and slapped soap on to a stone one of the Aripuana had left behind. Then she dunked them again and wrung them out. She spread the clothes as smoothly as she could against the hot stone. Heat broiled the day now, and the least movement wilted her. She didn't believe she could produce any more perspiration. It still poured off her. She lay back, the fingers of her hand trickled in the pool beside her, she kicked her sneakers off and closed her eyes.

Perhaps it was no time at all, though she believed she must have dozed away for a while, when she felt someone tugging at her arm.

Two women from the Aripuana group were standing above her. She did not have to shield her eyes from the sun when she looked up, they blocked the cruel heat from her. The younger woman, not more than thirty, fragile features already puckered with lines far beyond her years, thin breasts drooping with unselfconscious usedness nipples bled for milk out of angry hunger – she was pointing to the sun and then touching Linda's face, and pretending to sharply pull her hand back in haste as if Linda was on fire.

She wanted to move away from them. They were too close to her. Strange oiled leather like touch in the woman's fingers. She was still grinning and stroking the air to gain Linda's attention—

"You mean..." Linda spoke out, "if I sit here in the sun I'll get ill sun do something to my head?" she banged her forehead with her fist, "...Make me go crazy? Right?" and the Aripuana women nodded their heads vehemently, yes they understood, that's exactly what they meant. Linda smiled and thanked them. But she wished they'd go away.

They both crouched beside her. They hung their hands in front of their round bellies. The white between their toes looked like daubs of cream paint they had forgotten to wash off. The women studied Linda carefully. Particularly, the younger one. She was fascinated by Linda's clothing, or if not her clothing her sex within her clothing, because she wore her normal jeans.

She couldn't take her eyes off Linda's Levi's. She pointed to Linda's crutch and murmured in a streaming soft hiccupping glottis to the other indian. She reached forward, but slowly, child taking a toy it does not own, as if to say don't be angry with me please, and she pinched Linda's breast. She rubbed her hand over the nipple with the experimental curiosity of a visitor from outer space. Linda grinned weakly at her. After all, it's not every day of the month you lie down in the sun for a breather and an indian thing woman comes up to you to tweak your right nipple is it?

"That's right..." she said quietly, "I'm a girl just like you are. How about that?"

The indian took Linda's expression for approval, she knelt forward on her knees and clumsily scratched at the fly in the front of the jeans, eventually she managed to work down the zipper. Apart from the fact that she wished they'd just go away, Linda fluctuated between two vague emotions – faint blushing awkwardness and gawky timidity. She had no time to laugh out loud with mock-confidence, or push the woman away, she did not know how to react in such a curious situation. The older woman from the Aripuana leaned closer too, she was as eager to find out about this americano as her friend was. The prying brown fingers slid beneath Linda's knickers and brushed her pubic hair. They explored an inch or two more and then retreated. Linda rearranged her clothes as deftly as she could.

The women were now giggling together. It seemed to Linda they were saying yes she is a woman all right, and now we know, we don't have to argue about it anymore. We can go back and tell the others what we did, and they might be jealous of us.

"All right? ..." Linda asked, "shape up all right did I?" And whatever it was they thought she asked, the Aripuana women nodded in furious agreement. And they chattered gaily to Linda, as if in all confidence Linda could understand every word, lisp of tongue in the roof of the mouth, black gaps in the gumshoe front of their jaws, glottal throats emitting a soft descent of vowels.

Perspiration hovered on her eyelashes, the palms of her hands slithered against the stone, and Linda quickly stripped to jump into the water. The Aripuana women hesitated, as if Linda had taken possession of the pool and it no longer belonged to them. But Linda waved, laughed, kicked the water in the air at them, and they turned to look at each other for confirmation. Both women held hands and jumped together. They fell into the pool with a shriek. Linda casually lay on her back and showed them how to float. When they could not quite do it first try, she held their backs for them and they gulped air for fear drowning. Linda's foot slipped and she dunked her face down accidentally. She rose blowing bubbles. They laughed out loud. Hands splashing foam out of the water. Above them the hot sky was a sapphire haze, heat danced.

* * *

As time went by Geofrey was none too sure of his new cattle. How long would they take to get here? What sort of shape would they be in when they did? Lorries, he knew, were to take them from Araguaçema where the vaqueiros would herd them. At the river they would have to strap them down to the rafts and pole the live freight west towards Chimboa. It wasn't an easy water route. The rivers twisted and reluctantly fed their way west, to Chimboa, because all the while the fat pull of the Amazon to the north was their true magnet.

Parcels of his land were drying up, strips of sertão he'd rather graze the new beef on than let the sun destroy. But they were only the cheapest parcels. He had much better land than that; unlike the oakie. But the rains were now a long way off, and no such thing as spring existed out here, soon the cracks in the earth would grow shrill with insects seeking shade, and even tree strangler would shrivel up too much for the emerald snake and the cobra cipo to mimic it any longer.

That evening, swinging in the rêde on the porch, mosqus gathering, he heard Wes ride up. No moon to see by but he could hear the horse's nostrils. He lit the kerosene and when he hung the lamp up against the planta thatch he was surprised at the sullen exhaustion in Wes's face. The oakie's forearms were covered in dry clay, dust and grained dirt gave his features a red-nosed comical expression.

"You look like you've been swallowed by a cobra and come out the tail end! . . ."

Wes slumped on to the floor in a heap. His back against the wall. He was silent for a while. Geofrey pushed a basket of lemons towards him. The pinga stood on the table by the door. Wes crushed the splits against his teeth and sucked noisily at the bottle until the burning sensation ate into his throat. He began slowly to explain. He'd been out all day up there out to the west, that high point where you can see the Teles Pires basin, and his horse baulked at some tree stumps. A whadyamacallit jumped him with a knife. Right out of nowhere. Just with no reason in the world come at him. So he took his axe out of the saddle sack and swung it at the indian thing you know like to frighten him a little perhaps but the guy kept coming with this ridiculous smiling look on him and—

"I didn't mean to do it like that! I swung it round and he ran at me. Right into me. I took out his stomach. Broke him apart."

"He was alone?"

"Yearh yearh."

"There was nobody else?"

"That's what I say."

"But why? For what reason did he—"

"Am I expected to ask him sit down and ask him and he's coming at me running ape savage knicker naked what else could I do?"

"What happened?"

"I waited, man. He crawled for a little. Lay all balled up – blood everywhere – kept lookin' at me until his eyes went soft. Losing all that blood and gut – he died."

Wes broke the ground with his axe and scooped out the clay beneath. He buried the indian there. It was dark when he finished, gut and blood and mucus shovelled away, that quick damp darkness of toad croak and tree slither. He rode straight to Geofrey.

"You gotta tell me what do I do?"

"What can you? It was an indian and he's gone now."

"But I can report it – tell them it was an accident—"

"If you did that – the army would have to telegraph the police at Santarém – they'd keep you under lock and key up at the air-strip. The police would arrest you – most probably me and, well, because I know you, I speak your language, they'd arrest Linda – and we'd all be sitting in a Brazil jail for the next six months. Do you want that?"

"No ..."

"Want them to confiscate your land off you? Take my new beef away from me? If there is one thing a Brazilian loves – it's to find a foreigner in trouble, it's like Christmas every day of the year for him. Want that?"

"No ..."

"The Capitão won't go looking for the indian. Indians go away, come back sometimes months on end – he'll expect to see him some time in the future."

"I can't leave it like that ..."

"What are you feeling, Wes – remorse?"

"Sure I feel as guilty as hell—"

"About one indian?"

"Well, I—"

"What I hear from what Linda tells me you don't exactly give them an easy time when they're working for you."

"Sure I muscle them along a bit – they so stupid – they need it—"

"A Brazil nut kill an indian he forget about it the next minute."

"Anybody go looking for him won't even find I covered the earth back like it was."

"Nobody's going to look for an indian."

Wes felt the heat of the alcohol ease into his body. His taut nerves relaxed a little. Why was he talking like this to the limey? He'd wanted all along knock off a whadyamacallem. But he'd wished it had been right out in front of them, not like this hidden and dark, with nothing but guilt and fear rising in his throat. Shit! The limey was right, it was one indian thing, that's all. Geofrey believed no more than a quarter of the oakie's tale. There was more to it. The little runt seemed paralysed. The sap run out of him. They sat together silently, the pinga drained to the bottom of the bottle. Geofrey, out of after-thought—

"You've got that new buzz-saw ... ?"

"The adze, why?"

"Wait a few days. Until their curiosity has died down. If you feel that bad about it – make a gift of the adze to the Capitão.

"If you do that," Geofrey added, "the Capitão will forget. He'll forget about that indian in seconds."

"Sure ..." Wes nodded. There was an insatiable look about him, a hunger where his conscience craved, but the truth was buried deep within him there was no way it could come out, like a shrike grain of sand it lodged in his nerve ends.

"If you do that," Geofrey added, "the Capitão will think you're a king."

He rode back that night with Wes. The tough little man was devastated. His teeth chattered and he babbled as they rode in the dark. Geofrey said he must explain it to Linda. Explain it all. For her sake. There was much worse to face out here than one dead indian.

Linda was awake on the porch when they arrived. Geofrey recognised the nervousness in her, her sudden flood of hospitality, you gotta come in, gotta stay for an hour Geofrey you have, as if she was terrified of being left on her own with Wes.

He didn't stay. He wheeled the horse and caught a glimpse of Wes's silent expression. He wouldn't be doing much shouting this night. He imagined Linda sitting cross-legged on the floor listening to Wes. The oakie would paint the picture a bit. This indian thing running out of nowhere ape crazy with this knife in his hand. Wes remembering he might have been too harsh on him once. Roughed him up a little, one time. It was just a grudge, Linda, he'd been drinking that cachaça rum, you should have seen the way he looked at me. He'd have killed almost anyone he bumped into. It so happened it was me.

The lights from the hut faded behind Geofrey. Yellow squares in the distance, no brighter than the fire-fly whizzing across his nose. Harsh noise of the forest at night, all around him, sometimes he lit the ground in front of his horse with a flashlight, sharp crack and bark the throat of the night dry like tinder, then a crashing and slithering snort exclamation from a wild roedor somewhere in the sertão to the side, roedor hunting cotia, cotia searching for marsupial, marsupial in blind haste for fear of toad adder. Curutia beak dipped in downy breast wait for light. Jacaré snout in the drying gulleys wait for calf's clumsy step in pantanel marsh. Top of the tallest iron-wood, black hood of prey, the urubu just wait ...

And why didn't Wes take out his revolver? He need not have killed then. No Aripuana would attack senselessly like that. If the Capitão and his group wanted they could find a five centavo piece in a square hectare of mato. He'd find it all out in due course. Wes would bring him that adze. The Capitão would come by.

* * *

Linda didn't believe a word of it. No matter what Wes said. That didn't alter the fact – she was terrified. She wouldn't bathe any more in the stone pool. She wouldn't step out of the house, except for a trip to the 'convenience' across the clearing, and even then she made Wes wait for her. She wouldn't look out of the open shutters to see the Aripuana. She slung the hammock behind the door.

But the indians came, in their normal casual numbers, to work on the land every day. Wes didn't shout so much, he didn't swing his cane stick with his usual swagger, he was very subdued. Slowly he got his bearings.

One morning was very different.

Wes rose with the lemon light. He went out to saddle up. The bridle and the stirrups were kept in a small shed to the back of the house. He draped them over his back and reached for the axe he kept beneath a strip of tarpaulin. It was still there. But it wasn't as he left it, the night before. It was chopped into little pieces. Careful little sliced chunks. The whole haft. It looked like an outsize box of matches.

The Capitão eventually called on Geofrey. So silent was he the limey didn't see him until he stood a couple of yards away from him. The old fellow crouched on the boards and his sad voice droned in the thick afternoon air. Geofrey said little. He gave away nothing. When the Capitão asked him for his advice, Geofrey shrugged. You must decide for yourself, Capitão. When the indian left, as he watched him lope across the clearing to the trees, Geofrey remembered the adze the oakie gave him. The gift for the old man. It still lay in Geofrey's shed behind him. He wasn't going to call the Capitão back. It was too late for that, now.

Wes employed all the caution he could muster. He put aside his stick cane to beat the indians with. He allowed them to come and go in their casual manner, and no matter how much he steamed up inside, he said nothing. Naturally enough his workforce slowed up. But he watched them carefully. He studied them like fleas under his microscope. The young bloods gave him no sign. They slashed and burnt the land, they were no less in awe of him, and for a while Wes was lulled into believing that perhaps it was true – one dead Aripuana meant nothing, even though the indian had been their sib blood.

Then came the first wrinkle. On that occasion he hardly noticed some of the young bloods were missing. So lulled was he, he shrugged it off, maybe they had had a pinga-filled night in their maloca, and they were too ill to come up to the clearing. The next day it was different, half as many came to work for him. And the following day was the same pattern. He was down to six Aripuanas. He waited in the first light of the new morning, and a strange thing occurred, because two indians stepped into the clearing some distance away from him as if they were ready to begin *forming* the land; Wes waved at them, they paused, turned to each other, and ran off into the sertão. They never came back.

Wes grew silent and morose. Each morning he rode out to the edge of the clearing where the steep incline of the land gave him a vantage point looking south, but no indian came. Around the hut the chickens laid their eggs for Linda, and she watered a home garden patch she had planted for vegetables, their two horses shaded themselves beneath a palmyra in the corral the oakie built for them, but there was a difference. The air seemed to be filled with quiet menace, as if eyes brown and black almond long eyes watched and waited at the edge of the clearing. And at night, though the skirt of forest and drying liana was noisy enough, an eeriness, a prickling fibre tingling sense of isolation surrounded the place.

And Linda cracked. Wes had ridden way west in the dawn. She stood on the porch and looked across the stubby grass strip, root and foliage blackened and slashed, the silence of it, the empty heat, and a greater sense of being unwanted here than she had ever before felt overwhelmed her. The perspiration through her clothes was cold. How could Wes understand? Why should he listen? He was planets removed from her, deep in nightmares of pride and embattled dreams of possession. Runt oakie on a planalto outpost shotgun paranoid stomping his Brazilian Alamo. He didn't need her. Least of all to hear her complaints. Peanut pioneer made tall by his own brutality how could he understand I want to cry salt rivers and my heart wants to lie curled in the palm of his hand like a kitten and I might be safe, even in all this mess, how could he respond to that? And ... forget I even said it. That's not the way out of here. He ain't got no palm, all he got a fist. Crush you like a chinaberry seed.

There was a lot of movement in Chimboa down by the landing stage to the river. The vaqueiros shouted and whistled, kicking their horses into the shallows. Geofrey waited for his raft of calves. Caboclo boys moleque-coloured poled the raft to the shore. Linda tried to attract his attention. She couldn't wade through the mud in case she fell. He was knee-deep in it reaching for the raft as it aimed into the landing stage.

She knew he was ignoring her on purpose. She waited until the men had unstrapped the calves and kicked the animals to their feet. Geofrey and another mateiro punched the ears with soft metal clips. The vaqueiros roped each calf and hauled them through the water desperate bulge-eyed skinny animals. As for Linda, well Geofrey wasn't going to talk to her in the middle of all that, he wasn't going to appear that friendly in front of the Brazilians. That was his way. When the last calf was herded from the bank up along a dirt track, she pulled the Englishman aside—

"I must speak with you!"

"Can't you see I'm—"

"Geofrey will you listen!"

"All right. Don't shout. Don't draw attention."

"If you don't help us, those indian things goin' kill us – me and Wes!" she blurted out.

"Don't be silly."

"They won't come back no more and Wes is going crazy waiting for them."

"You don't know what you're talking about – indians don't kill anyone. You've no idea what the Aripuanas are like either of you – why do you talk like that?"

"One day they'll come back sure as eggs they'll – they've found out what Wes done!"

"What are you shaking like that for? Those indians are harmless. Tribes like that have been gunned down and cheated and robbed so long – they're not going to kill anyone! Listen to me will you?" How soft and chubby his face was, how could this guy possibly be so confident, when she could feel the danger all around her?

"I want you to help us."

"Want?"

"Do – do something!"

"Go to the Capitão and tell him it was an accident. That's for Wes. Tell him I'm sorry it won't happen again. That's for Wes, not me. He's the king, isn't he? Besides, you don't have any idea they know about it. You don't know."

"Tell me why they stopped coming up to the farm?"

"They could all be sick – pick up a virus in the river."

"Or why Wes's axe was all broken up like that?"

He hesitated. For, sometimes an indian will leave a broken weapon beside a body in order the guilt may be transposed to the arrow or the knife. If they find an axe which has been used to kill a man with they can break the haft into tiny pieces to release the spirit of murder from it. But what would it do to tell Linda that?

"Wes must fend for himself."

"You his buddy ain't you?"

"He knows out here – you cannot rely on anybody else it just brings trouble on them also."

"I came to tell you, because someone's got to listen to what I have to say. It's me talking. Don't you understand? I'm included in all this."

"I realise it's difficult for you, but—"

"He became an animal. That's what Wes come to. I'm also talking about myself, see. Wes don't want to know nothing but guns and killing and winning – I need help – it ain't the same guy I first come out here with."

"But you came, nevertheless."

She wanted to hit him so hard, to take away that suckeggs in his voice, that confidence, if he'd only look hard enough he'd see the pain she was in.

"Any decency ..." she began slowly, "I thought he had, it's – oh it's all gone now. I can't take no more, Geofrey."

"What did you expect?"

"I thought leastways there'd be – you make me so foolish saying it – some kind of tenderness. Ain't that meant to be love? Something I'd find in his heart he'd give to me and it would be special. Ain't that love? I never once stopped and thought he meant all that women-are-whores kind of thing ... never did ..."

She waited for the Englishman to pull off his boots. He scraped the soft mud and shook out the brown water. He scuffed his bare feet in the dry grass. If he'd only say one kind word to her. Just give her a blink of sympathy, one little look or a smile, and stop play-acting this pioneer crap, give her a dime of kindness. She ached for that small mercy.

"Is that how it is?" he asked.

"The truth."

"Then I'm sorry."

"Come again?"

"You're a lot braver, Linda, than I'd ever have thought." His piggy eyes unwaveringly stared at her, and if it was kindness she wanted so desperately to believe she saw in them, she could be forgiven the illusion.

"Well . . ." she shrugged. Her quick plastic smile, all too easy a trick of the lips to disguise the tears that were surely coming. A toss of her head. Skinny hips no Levi's will ever quite stitch a hold on. Pale girl, cricket thin bones who the boys in the pool hall called white trash because she never had enough money to take the bus into town with. Aunt Mim's white rabbit gift. Jugular night hot clumsy fingers *you mine now, Lindy*. She wanted to reach out and take his arm as if that little touch of warmth was all she needed to spend another night out there in the hut with the oakie king— ". . . That's about the nicest thing I ever did hear from anyone in the whole of Brazil!"

Her tears smiled.

* * *

And those indigewhadyamacallems never came back to work for Wes. And the days dried the land out more. At noon an uncanny stillness, boiled and lanced by the sun, surrounded the hut. And things kept on disappearing. A bag of crushed maize, tin of tar, a double-edged saw, and axe hafts which Wes had carefully fashioned out of sapling iron-wood. No matter what the oakie did to protect his possessions, somehow each new morning yet another tool had gone astray. He felt he was encircled by black forest eyes; and occasionally, even with our planalto pioneer, his smouldering anger gave way to fear. Now he had less control of events, there was nobody he could run to for help, for the limey had explained all that to him months back – out here you must rely on yourself, period. You are alone up here in the south-facing hut above Chimboa waiting for this big road to come through, this is your dream, and nobody else not even Linda (least of all Linda) can share in it. The stillness of the noonday, like the fear, was nothing but a waking moment from a nightmare, he told himself, the dream was still there.

That morning Wes walked out to the shed to collect his saddle-skin and, glancing out of the corner of his eye he saw his horse was no longer tethered under the palm tree in the corral and even the rope had gone too, and turning back towards the house his mouth gaped involuntarily, helpless with rage he shouted at the top of his voice bull raw anger. Linda ran and hid, only she and the strange stillness heard him.

Most times she said nothing, she only spoke when he asked her to. She never gave him a chance to bawl her out, she worked so hard. In the oakie's terms she near worked her ass off. She cleaned and cooked, scrubbed the insects out of the floorboards, helped him burn off the ticks with lighter fuel, she cleared and stripped bush from the sertão with him through the height of the afternoon scorch. She was so scared she did anything he asked of her slavishly. But she kept away from his bed. That was the unspoken rule.

"Wanna come skinnydipping in the stone pool, Linda?"

"You go ahead ..."

"You don't ever do that any more, do you?"

"I—"

"What you so afraid of?"

"Wes, I'm not—"

"You afraid all the time somebody's goin' sneak up behind you stick you with one of their fish head arrows? That it?"

"No."

"Well what do you think then, huh?"

"I don't, Wes ..." softly.

"You so fucking afraid all the time you'll drop down dead from fear you will – you don't need wait for them indian things come and get you."

"Anything you say ..."

"Well there's nothing ain't goin' to happen because I'm king here on this land our land – and that's the truth."

"*Your* land Wes ..."

Fucking right. Don't think because you want to crawl around with your tail between your legs like this it makes any difference to me. I'm staying here. This is the place. No matter what happens.

They had freak days up there, too. A sticky grey sky fended off the sun. The air crackled with a thunder promise. Everywhere a dry tinder noise, but of course – no rain. At times it was quite windless, and a static pulse like the friction from the scrape of dried bones stung the air. Linda made a supper of beefy, fried manioc and feijão for him. She couldn't eat any. She flopped into her rêde under the planta porch, she pushed the door half open for a draught of air. As she lay back her fingers brushed a warm slimed object. Wes was still trying to get the beefy out of his teeth with a stick when she screamed. She leapt out of the hammock and stumbled against the boards. She shouted at him go look. He swung the oil lamp above his head, and bathed the porch yellow. In the hammock lay a black and yellow banded caninanha snake. It was quite dead. Its head was sliced away from its body. Its inert head, flicker tongue pressed against the roof of the mouth lips agape, looked like a morning tulip.

Linda shrunk against the boards in a corner, she crossed her legs beneath her and clutched her toes with her hands. She rocked to and fro. Wes took out a bottle, but she shook her head.

"That's about it, Wes ..."

"Huh?"

"I don't need no more convincing ..."

"Don't get so upset—"

"I'm just not taking it any more."

"That's exactly what they want you to do. You show them you're terrified they'll come back do it again on you."

"I can't take any more. I've had it right up to the neck, I've had it!"

"They trying you on, and—"

"First the tools, bags of corn, the cans, then the horse then this – that what you call tryin' anything any more! Can't you see sense?"

"That all you got to say?"

"Yes ..."

"That all it means to you – this place?"

"When I first came out here I never expected anything – but I never expected this, neither."

"*That all—?* I'm saying."

"Yes ..." she felt the prickly heat rise up behind her eyes and she didn't want him to see, anyhow it would be a waste of tears on him, she buried her face in her elbows and long strands of mouse-coloured hair curtained her forehead, Linda had to swallow hard to conceal the choke in her throat, "... yes, *that all*, Wes," she murmured, vacant and toneless, her heart emptied.

In the morning he rode out on Linda's pony. He mentioned something, quite off-hand, about measuring up a parcel of land for a ring fence. She noticed he packed both rifles and his pistol. He'd be back late, he said. She fed the chickens and watered the vegetable patch, and she observed how every new day the earth became more of a rust red colour, drying up and parching her few plants. Then the stillness in the air got at her. She couldn't stay there alone.

She took two hours to walk to the store in Chimboa. She bought a few things and tried to waste the hours sitting by the river. She watched boys repairing a wood canoe and idly hoped the Britisher would come by. Before she walked back she drowned some cachaça shots at the patrão's table. There was one vaqueiro she liked. A slim youth who smiled a lot and kept an ebony toothpick between his teeth all the day. He rode her back with her basket to a point just below the stone pool, from where it was but a short climb to the house.

She didn't expect Wes to be back. She knew he was punishing her, he'd be gone well into the dark evening, knowing how she hated it so much now, this creeping stillness all around her, fruits of black eyes staring at her through the palms. She shivered as she made the last of the climb, and faced the hut across the slash-and-burn clearing.

As she reached for the door a strange smell curled in her nostrils. Sweet and sick. Her fingers came away from the steel ratchet on the door with a soapy cloy to them. When she looked down her fingers were covered with blood. She looked again, blood was smeared over both sides of the door jamb. Inside the house there was more. Smears across a wall where Wes had plastered white coating over the wood, blood wiped across the table, over the fruit box on the floor, and at her feet a heavily dripped glob of it wide as a jacaré's egg. She ran outside again. She stood stick still, everything looked quite regular, except that – all her chickens in the wire coop were gone. Not a sign of them.

She bundled shirts and canvas sneakers and her only button cardigan into a bag, along with her passport and vanity case and an extra pair of Levi's. She ran straight out of the door, not once looking back. She had made up her mind, and – *that all* there was to it.

She was tired and it would be a long walk there. But there was a rough path through the bush and palm Geofrey's Wyllis had crushed down. She had to make towards the east, where the sertão sloped gently in the direction of the Chimboa/Santarém dirt track. And she was careful, she detoured in such a way, no matter how soon Wes rode back, he wouldn't be able to follow her. She was more afraid of that, of him catching up with her and taking out his cane stick and bawling her out, hitting her and dragging her back up to the hut, than meeting any of those indian things on the way. The long haul took her the rest of the day. The sheen from the heat striking up at her from the ground caused a strange drumming in her head. Her vest dripped with moisture. She covered her hair with a satin choker she found in the bag. She'd have to slow up. But she didn't until she could see Geofrey's house, she pushed herself forward until, from a rise between twin palmyra palms she could make out the yellowing planta thatch roof in the distance. Her breath was coming fast in short gulps, the noise in her ears was not just from the curutia shriek or chip-chip of grilo in the undergrowth, it was a zinging buzz she could not shake off, it clumsied her steps and made her eyes dizzily blink. She chose a spot and lay down in the sandy red earth. She could imagine the coolness of the stone pool she had left behind, and how the flowers of the tall oiticicia tree seemed like voluptuous armfuls of pink passion orchids, but it was all in her daydream, for she'd never go back to them again. More than an hour must have passed, when she woke the sun had burnt into her eyelids, and when she sat up for a while everything she looked at was bleached white. The heat was gentler now. The tinny rattling sertão sound had faded, the butterflies no longer swarmed around the nectar flowers on the bushes – Brazilians call any of these papagaios - but she was looking at clumps of flame red inflorescences which burst petal stars on the euphorbia bushes tired robbed pollen beauties which trespassed to the edge of the clearing around Geofrey's house, they too were now folding in dismay as their bushes dressed longer shadows across the earth.

She paused on the perimeter of the blackly stumped slash-and-burn clearing, from there she could see Geofrey on the front step shaking hands with the old indian, the Capitão; the wrinkled brown creature hastily took his hand away from the Britisher as if he'd held a hot coal, it was clear he didn't like the familiarity of the handshake, and it was the insensitive Britisher who caught him by surprise. The Capitão wore cream faded pants and single thong slippers. On each forearm he had bracelets of old Coca-Cola cans. Linda waited. She had no intion of going anywhere near that wrinkled indian thing. Eventually, she could make out the smile on the Britisher's face as he said goodbye to the Capitão. The indian kicked dirt grains out of his slippers and loped away in the opposite direction.

Geofrey was pouring fresh water in a bucket he held beneath the earthen-ware filter jar, when she stepped inside the room. She untied the satin wrap around her hair and dropped her bag at her feet with an emphatic gesture.

"Hallo mister limey ..."

"How did you get here?" he looked up, "I didn't hear your horse."

"Walked."

"All the way!"

"I rested up on the slope, I must have dozed off—"

"You walked! You could die in that heat."

"I mighty near did – and what would you care?"

He pushed a wicker chair towards her, he didn't have to look very deeply into her face to see, "... has something happened?"

"I'm staying here – with you, Geofrey. Just until you can get me on a plane or a car out of this place. I'm leaving, and don't you tell me I can't. And I'm staying here until I do leave, and don't you tell me I can't do that, either."

He looked rather blank. Kind of dopey abashed expression. What in God's name ever did surprise this strange pallid guy?

"Have you told Wes?"

"Never you mind about him – you've got to get me outa here. OK?"

"No it isn't. Have you told him?"

"He can find out for hisself."

"You haven't?"

"No ..."

"Linda you're putting me in a spot – it just isn't that easy."

"Ain't that the one thing you hate most of all – getting yourself in a corner?"

"All I'm saying is—"

"I'll sleep out almost any place – now you help me because it's the only thing I've asked you to do, and I need help now."

"I'm afraid I have only the bed."

"I'll take the hammock out there on the porch, right?"

"Well . . ."

"I'm staying with you, Geofrey – I'm staying."

"We'll have to make some arrangement – you can't sleep out there on the porch—"

"Any terms you like. OK?"

"I suppose so . . ."

"And you'll get me away—"

"I'll try . . . but—"

"And you'll keep Wes off me?"

"If you want that."

"You tell him yourself, I won't see him I won't have him coming here near here and there's no more talking about it! That's my decision."

Geofrey said he'd speak to the oakie.

"How long before I can leave?"

He said he'd try to put her on the next raft of calves that came through. She could take a flight out north from Araguaçema.

Is there no other way, she asked?

"Look . . . I can't drive you up to Santarém. I've got to live here with Wes after you've gone. I can only—"

"You mean you don't want to be seen helping the americano's girl? That it? Don't want those vaqueiros looking at you asking dirty questions, right?"

"I'd rather it looked orderly, that's all. They know I have no reason to take you up north. I don't want them to think we've got secrets."

"Sure sure – you want to be just like them – you want to be a Brazilian like them and it's too much bother looking after crazy foreigners, ain't I right?"

"Linda, I am a Brazilian now!"

"You kidding yourself!"

Geofrey did his best to explain, yes he'd try to do the decent thing, she could stay with him, and he hoped neither the patrão or the prefeito came by – why should they? she asked – and he'd keep to the rêde on the porch etcetera she could have the bed etcetera and the house she must consider her home etcetera.

"You ain't scared of me are you?"

"I don't think so."

"Because you don't have to pull all that stiff upper tooth stuff with me."

"What are you getting at?"

It was such a little thing she wanted. She confirmed in her mind what she knew. For example, how he'd been undressing her with his eyes all these months. That reserve of his which could only hint at the sensual from the discreet distance of shadow beneath a palm some yards away from the stone pool where she bathed. And yet, it wasn't as crude as that, she acknowledged. This little thing she wanted – the relief she could find in the recognition of it – shared between them – him to just once say how much he liked her, say it in a gentle manner, in that suckeggs voice of his, above all say it in a way it could never be shouted; anything . . . but that familiar oakie's bull roar, her skin cold beneath his touch, and eyes shrunken back with loathing.

"Nothing ever struck you . . . about me?"

"Like what?" he asked.

"Nothing ever made you hide under a tree and watch me swim skinnydip out there – in the stone?"

"Well, I apologised for that."

"You so fucking indifferent limey – what's the matter with you? You sick?" she blurted out.

"Don't shout – I'm not Wes."

"You never ever once said to me you pretty Linda! . . . I meant."

"I'm sorry . . ." Geofrey paused, "Yes – as a matter of fact you are. Very."

"And you ain't never told me you like me before – I know you do – but you never did, ain't it true?"

"I do. Fair enough?"

"So . . ." she stared down at the rough boards in the floor, "Geofrey . . . ?" behind the boiled banter and the runt hardness she had copied from Wes there was a different warmth, an eggshell sliver of tenderness, something no hundred Dwight Weslies could ever take away from her, and she stood closer to him, hazed grey eyes, pale lashes, that trick of a quick plastic smile. "... You want me don't you?" tinsel thin twang in her throat, girlish hesitancy, echo of guitar whines, reluctant sex pulse in the warm dance hall night, dusty streets and boys with greedy fingers, *how can you get back home if you ain't got the money for the bus Linda? I can drive you but it'll cost you some, you mine now Lindy.*

Geofrey swallowed abruptly. Funny little blotches in the puffy skin. A dodging shift in the gear of his eyes. Pinga distended loneliness in his pupils.

He gaped at her.

"Well, do you or don't you want me? . . . after all, I'm asking?" smiled up at him. Plastic turkey-pie wishbone ease.

"If you put it quite that bluntly—"

"I do."

"Eh yes ... thank you very much."

She put her head back and laughed out loud. Little pink ribbed throat arched with chuckles. He was like a Sunday preacher over the tea table, newly washed and pressed cotton table cloth, toasted wheat cakes and chocolate whip sauce, English tea-bags in bitty cups, molasses and rye bread, her in her off-white dimity dress, 'elbows off the table honey', and apple jelly and candy bananas later. Thank you very much he said to her. His suckeggs voice and all. She couldn't stop smiling.

Geofrey tied a kerosene lamp to his saddle. He didn't need to light it, it was easy enough to see in the dark that night. The horse hung its head in the gloom closer to the ground as if to smell it, beneath its hooves with a scurrying grunt a marsupial fled into the trees, rat-like almost the size of a young pig, a mucura most likely, and the horse shivered.

When Geofrey reached the oakie's clearing he could not make out the shape of the hut in the distance. There were no lights on. But he was there, Geofrey could sense it, Wes was sure to be there.

* * *

Earlier, when the quick dark struck the sun down, Wes had come back. And he knew she'd gone the minute he stepped inside. The face paint box of hers was missing. Sure sign that was. Her extra pair of jeans gone. Just what she was like – had about three possessions in the whole world including her passport and a box of paper panties the humidity had destroyed. The finality of her goodbye breathed in the air. He could hear her voice. Filibusters of self-justification.

I'm sorry, Wes. You keep your indian things. You love them so much you hate them so much they've gotten hold of you like a disease. Ain't a finger I can lift make any difference. You and the limey will get on fine, sit out there on your porches sucking lemon splits and soaking pinga until what did you say—? Those Brazil nuts learn to grow lampshades out of the earth. When I get home they ask me whatever happened to that dwidget runt with the big adenoids you went out there with, that boondocks place? Oh, you mean Dwight, Dwight got this mosqu fever and if he weren't mad dog bug-eyed most moments he made up the rest of his time by riding up and down this red desert place shooting indians. Not indians not indians like you know indians soap opera indians but little fat creatures live out in the trees in the densest part smell like skunks in a heat wave by Red River.

You don't say, Lindy? I don't say a word of untruth!

Wes hid his bottles in the earth under a flat stone just as the limey showed him to. He fetched his pinga out, cut up the lime-shaped lemons, and sat in front of an up-turned crate which served as a table and stripped clean both his rifles and his revolver. What I bring her out here for? Kid like that. That stupid. Bird nest brained drugstore pickup bushy tailed about Brazil. If you love me mister just as much as you say and you expect me to go all that way there with you, you'd better show me on the map just where Brazil is because my geography never did teach me that far afield. Holy cow, Dwight! Is that it? How did it get that big without me ever knowing about it?

* * *

Geofrey unstrapped his lamp and lit it before he crossed the compound to the porch. The door was open, and the oakie sat in the darkness with his back against the wall, a liquid look in his eyes, the sudden yellow glare from the kerosene garishly lit up Wes's face. He hardly blinked. He moved his knees and a rifle slid to the floor with a clatter.

"You can't sit in the dark like this."

"I can."

"Bloody morbid . . ."

"Suckeggs you bastard!"

"Thought I'd come out – pay a visit."

"Like fuck you did. Now don't give me that!"

Geofrey didn't know how to handle it, he'd never been in this position before, in fact this was the very sort of thing he'd spent most of his life trying to avoid; look here, Dwight it's none of my business – and – I'm awfully sorry – and – she's made up her mind you see – and – there is nothing I can do about it.

"Piss on that, limey."

"Well, I—"

"You don't even have to start."

Wes poured a shot from the bottle into a tin cup. He cut a lemon and rolled it across the table towards Geofrey.

"Help yourself . . . my home is yours ain't that what they say?"

"Wes, she's scared out of her wits."

"That so."

"If you leave it to me, I can get her out."

"Out?"

"She's going home."

"Where'd she get the money from?"

"Says she's got it – enough to fly to Miami."

"Did she say she stole it from me?"

"No, and I don't think she did."

"Well . . . you do just what you like."

"Is that all you have to say?"

"You want me to burst into tears?"

"I thought – perhaps – if you loved her—"

"You an expert on that, too?"

"I don't even begin."

"All I want right now is to be left alone," said Wes, "I want it like this, I want those whadyamacallems back on my land here working for me and I'll get them – don't doubt that son—"

"Suppose they don't?"

"But you see they will. They have to. They mine they my animals and they know it."

"Two weeks ago you were terrified of them."

"Not any more. That's exactly what they'd like me to be. Now I understand that. Now I'm seeing things the way they do."

"I see."

"And there's something else I'm beginning to get too."

"Oh—?"

"Between them and me there's a bond. They need me because they're on my land and they're better off here than any place else. Don't matter what happens I can wait they've got to see it my way because I'm the king."

"Can you survive on your own?"

"Don't be so silly! That's all Linda talk, I'm communicating with them. I know they're there. Each day I go out I know they watch me. They're thinking of nothing but me and I know it."

"Have you tried to see them? In the maloca?"

"I wouldn't dignify them with a visit. I'm waiting until they come to me – and they'll come, friend, they will."

"You know I'll help you."

"That's right, you my buddy, pal. Come a time – this road make us so rich we'll import Lindas in and out of here like rabbit freight."

"All right," said Geofrey. "Then I'll get her out. And you won't have to see her."

"The hell with her!"

Moths making shadows large as your head dived at the kerosene lamp, scratch and lense shutter quick fold of burnt wings, sweet acrid powder smell, their antennae begging scorch deaths.

"You know, when you and she first came out here I thought – not that it was any of my business – thought there was some love between you two."

"Sure there was."

"There was?"

"Now it all gone. That all."

"I thought perhaps you were going to marry her?"

"I'm more than twenty years her age. I got sense you know. She don't want to marry an old man like me, mister."

"She did at some time."

"All right perhaps she did ..."

"Did you?"

"I never asked her and she never asked me, neither."

In the silence they watched the suicide insect shadows zoom around the walls. The pinga had softened Wes considerably. He wanted to talk about other things. The road, the minerals, those old war exploits of his, anything but Linda. He liked the war tales, they made him feel twenty years younger. And he was so good at telling them now, told them so well now he believed every word himself, as if they were legend turned into fact. But Geofrey wasn't staying. He sucked lemon through his teeth and drowned back the last shot in the tin cup.

Wes followed him out to the horse. Geofrey snuffed the lamp and strapped it against the saddle. The night was like a sweaty palm, its oily texture creamed against their faces. Geofrey sat in the saddle and untied the halter from the corral post.

"Limey ...?"

"Yes?"

"I ... I don't mean half those foul-mouthed things I said."

"Sure ..."

"No no I mean it. I don't want no harm to come to Linda. All it is – she can't take it out here, and I knew it first day I met you she couldn't."

"You'll find somebody else."

"And that ain't the point, either. I don't want anybody else. I'm just like you. That's what happens out here people like you and me that's what happens. Right?"

"I believe it's so."

"Linda meet up some soda jerk smart-ass kid with a Ford Thunderbird take her swimming in Red River live their lives out of a deep-freeze and send kids to a university grow up with an education. Right?"

"No doubt of it."

"That's how I see it."

"Goodnight, Wes."

"I don't have nowhere else. Nothing goin' come my way

any more in this life – but this here – what I got. And I consider myself more than lucky I got this – it's like living in a dream out here – but the dream more than that the dream coming true it's real. OK?"

"I hope so."

"Course it is. And something else I want to tell you limey – I never told a soul not Linda not nobody."

"What?"

"I'm an old man. That's what they call you in America, look at my age say – you old now son, nothin's new for you any more. Credit you got left ain't worth spit, that's what they say."

Geofrey swung the horse around. The lamp bounced against his knee. Clack and clatter chorus – macaco and macaw and leaf-nosed bats swaying on liana – from the perimeter of trees at the edge of the oakie's slash-and-burn.

"But out here I ain't old. I'm forty-eight goin' on twenty-two. I'm new. Baby born new. Because – and I want to tell you this ..."

"I'm listening."

"My last chance this is – understand that?"

"Yes."

"It's the last chance I got. Ain't no more cards left in the pack. OK? You follow?"

"Goodnight, Wes," and Geofrey nodded, he understood.

Below them, in the southerly distance, where the sertão sloped away from the natural plain of the compound, the only lights they could see were the pinpricks from the road-builders' huts. Wes watched them as Geofrey eased his horse along. He could imagine those great yellow steel cats still and dormant at crazy angles in the red earth, surrounded by rows of felled iron-woods, and the huts mounted on wheels ready to be pulled forward a few more yards by tomorrow night.

"All I do at night ..." murmured the oakie, "is watch those damn lights down there on the road. And I tell myself they just moved half a kilometre they have moved that bit more nearer to here today. That's my kick ..."

Geofrey was too far away to hear. He dug his heels in and the horse trotted forward. Wes stood in the dark until the hooves melted into the cries of the trees. Fire-flies ricocheted like matches you struck aflame and flicked into the sky. Wes reached into the hole under the flat stone for another bottle. He flopped into the hammock on the porch by the open door, it had always been Linda's hammock, her rêde, far enough away from his bed, and he spilt the first mouthful over his stomach when he tried to swig and swing in one movement. He looked up. He kicked his boots off and swung his legs up.

The mosqus gathered delicate tingle wings, and he pressed his stetson low over his eyebrows. But behind such unimportant things as mosqus stood the stars. Bright bright stabs in the night. And if he looked hard enough with that blur in his gaze, behind even the stars there'd appear a grainy shooting series of colours, no matter how often he shook his head or closed his eyes from them, and those silver shooting light grains wouldn't fade.

* * *

Geofrey took his time. He wiped the horse down and led her into a fenced field. In the dark he slapped back the shutters at the front of the house, and after filling the stone jar water filter from a barrel for the morning, he bolted the door with a log barricade. There was a Brahma Chopp tin of warm beer on the shelf, he kicked his boots across the boards and juggled with a half empty packet of Minister cigarros. The can spat at him when he levered the finger clasp and winged insects whirred up in the coolness of the night at the unexpected flare from a match.

Linda had put herself to sleep in his bed. But Geofrey could not convince himself of her presence. There was a disappearing quality about her personality; a lacklustre – the kind of girl no matter how many group photographs you made of her posed beside other summer swimmers on Red River Bend during a hot afternoon Linda would always be the one who never stood out. The slim blonde, no not quite a blonde a brunette, not quite that either – a mouse blonde nothing colour, would hesitate behind healthy laughing Oklahomans, faint and watery in the picture, she'd stand there with a self-induced wheyness, literally begging to be over-exposed on the negative. You couldn't quite touch her in her presence, or see her in her absence in the mind's eye, and if you had heard her speak you'd have heard a million echoes of that drawl; and Geofrey considered that, suppose someone came to him sometime in the future and said oh you remember Linda, did you know she died in an automobile accident in Tucson God knows what she was doing there why she even went there believe they said redneck croppers put her in the back of a pickup and she had a fight with one of them he said something rude to her and the driver lost control of the wheel; if she died like that and the certain someone came and told Geofrey – he'd just shrug, pale trick of a girl fleeting in his memory, he'd shrug and say to himself 'that fits, that about sums up Linda', and he'd remember how he had never kept a photograph of her, even.

He placed a candle in the corner and stood at the bottom of the bed. She'd found the mosquiteiro he had long ceased to use, it was wrapped like a grubby wedding veil around her head and shoulders. The candle flame crackled as it burnt moth wings. Geofrey undressed and lay beside her on the bare mattress. There was no point in keeping sheets, they saturated in an hour or so, and at least the mattress was thick enough to absorb the moisture. With a mechanical motion, as if he believed, in his clumsiness, it was expected of him, Geofrey put out his arm and pulled her round until Linda lay on her back. She was already awake. She loosened the wound mosquiteiro from her neck and pushed it back of her head. Geofrey thought of the oakie, the little bull he couldn't impersonate, and he felt afraid. Linda rolled her legs out from their curled position. Her voice, transparently clear in the night air—

"Turn out the light will you . . ."

His fingers found the flame, and warm wax adhered to them. She was waiting for him in the dark, he told himself, more in truth – he reassured himself; and he peeled back the gauze mosquiteiro he touched the arch of her ribs, taut sinuous bone cavern, and his wrist brushed the scarcely perceptible mounds of her breasts; button stiff nipples beneath his fingers sparked a shivery feather-light tingle in his stomach. The soft sound was the casual slide of her legs, and he believed it to be a stir of sensual anticipation; her flower vulva opened against his palm, and his pressure there sweet finger dip in flesh nectar made gentle strokes. She lay still. Not the least murmur. Where was her supposed celebratory skin shudder, her sensual retort to his awkward probing? Geofrey was unaware of his clumsiness as he kneeled to press his legs between hers. Now accustomed to the dark he was all the while aware of her eyes. Quite expressionless open stare up at him. He realised in that moment she had made no gesture. Her fingers hadn't moved. Her arms akimbo against the mattress. And a new panic invaded him, there was no urgency from her no silent gift of receiving not a hint of her own emotions, and he wilted, the confidence drained from him like shallow pools in the sand salt waves hauled back at ebb-tide, and, hard as he tried, no amount of pulling on his flaccid cock could lift its head. Coffee cup rattle of canteen laughter amongst the National Service boys on the Malayan British army camp, 'Geofrey? Trouble with Geofrey he's a professional virgin', 'You mean Geofrey? Too bloody mean to pay for it – if he had it he wouldn't know it, anyway.'

Hitler he only had one ball la da la da de da la la.

He rolled over to the side again. There was enough of the mosquiteiro between them for him to cover his legs. Perspiration seeped from his shoulders into the mattress. At least, he commiserated with himself, he did have this unreasonable ache in his genitals, a robbed itching. The want of her was there all right, but something else – bite of failure, lack of unselfconsciousness, shrivelled his body. He lay awake, the least sound clear as a cracker bang in his ear, unable to think, and sleep not wanting to disturb him propped his eyelids open.

"Did you see Wes ...?" her voice was remote, disembodied.

"He's all right."

"He's drunk—"

"And that—"

"That what you mean by all right?"

"He'll cope."

"What did he say?"

"Talked about the land and—"

"About me I mean?"

"He said..." slowly.

"I ain't afraid. You tell me what he—"

"He said you can go. That's all."

"Jeeesus! Like he's doin' me a favour. I'm going, period."

"I even think he's relieved."

"Like he's glad?"

"Yes."

"Didn't say he missed me?"

"Do you expect him to?"

"Or – who goin' cook for me now – did he say?"

"No."

"Did he show you lights down in the valley the hut lights by the building of the road? Did he tell you his war experience stories?"

"He wanted to."

"Must be true, I guess..." she said with a sigh, "what you said, that old freckle face he all right."

She was quiet. Nothing would make him turn towards her. He huddled at the edge of the bed. Linda sat up, the mosquiteiro fell between them. She kicked it down. It came away from his legs. She leaned across him and placed her lips against his shoulder. She puffed her cheeks, a hot surge of warmth-girlish trick from schooldays – melted into his skin. She wiped the perspiration from his face, her thin fingers felt the shutter quick butterfly flicker of his eyelashes.

"You an odd guy you are..."

"Please..." he pulled away.

"No I mean it – you think you go at me like some red-eyed Brazil nut think Linda just a bit of tail for the night, trying to pretend you some stud with a belly full of beer – that ain't you, Geofrey..." she said softly, "now is it?"

"I'm sorry whatever I did I'm sorry."

"Why should you be?"

"I've said I am."

"Why? I didn't help you much did I?"

"Well..." he murmured, "they do say it's more difficult in the heat in this kind of climate."

She chuckled sweetly. Chimes of smiles behind her teeth. No barely hidden derisiveness. She curled closer. His back was cold with moisture.

"They *do* say that do they?" with gentle irony.

"I'm not Wes..."

"Who asked you to be him?"

"Well—"

"You be just as you are, nice and gentle Geofrey the limey ... huh?"

Her hair fluttered in prickly drops over his face. She reached for his head. She held him in her hands. Her mouth close against his. No hurry about it at all. An evenness of motion. And his tongue inched along the curved inside of her lip.

"Better ... ?"

"Linda, I—"

Her breath in his nostrils, not pulling away from him, smiling lips now, the words mouthed between their lips, a trespassing pulse wakened his blood, and he felt the words smother in between their lips.

"Ain't no hurry about it, Geofrey ..."

He nodded in the dark.

"I'll make you happy ..."

Yes.

"Plenty of time yet ... promise you."

Sense of ease. His tautness fading.

"Not now ... later ..." she stroked his face, her fingers played delicately around his nose and his lips, whispered touch against his eyelids, "... there'll be another night. I'll make you happy ..." she curled away from him, her spine moulded knobs of bone, skeletal seeming seriatim of vertebrae, beneath the painfully thin skin.

Long after he was certain she slept, he got up and wiped his body down with a towel. He dipped his face and his hands in a bucket of water to lose the clamminess. He did not know how long it was he dozed. When he woke later, he could feel her body beside him, she was trembling, as if from cold. It couldn't have been that, he knew. And though she slept, the trembling had a coughing motion about it, a rising and falling of her shoulders, skinny elbows pressed against her ribs moving like tiny bellows to the threshing pump of her lungs, barely audible sobs – what he could only guess to be tears and an inconsolable dream. He did not touch her.

In the morning she was a lark. Crashing pans in a wood washtub by the door, pumping up the fogão cinders, making a wood crate with a hole in it above the shit drop that she might sit with decorum and piddle without a splash.

"What do you call a bed pan in England, Geofrey?"

"A goes-under."

"Goes under the what?"

"Goes under the bed!"

They ate sour manioc loaf and goiabada jam for breakfast. The way the limey liked his coffee was black soup finger thick boiled with sugar, not what we'd call sugar, but cane pap whittled out of tubers. In her breezy vernacular she talked about screwing, and he said he could only describe it as having a bash or beating it up, in that purposeful quaintness of his, as if he'd removed it far enough away from his own reality, and she peeled with laughter.

"My old grannie called it spooning."

As she asked him in such a point blank way, Geofrey described a couple of adolescent love matches in a tennis court changing room he once experienced, after most of the players had gone home for high tea, when sporting fingers hesitated at the corners of white frilled knickers, fetish touch caught in a limbo of child/nursery clothing, and hands which pulled clumsily at the fly front buttons of a pair of shorts, boy-scout erections frozen in the mind, prematurely stumped growth to adulthood. And Geofrey's coy manner of describing dusky yellow girls his mates in Malaya queued up for on a Saturday night in a red-light district; off limits to military personnel. And of course, he was the exception. But there once was a horsy girl who borrowed her parents' bungalow in Sherbourne—

"Otherwise aside from that my sex life has been pretty non-existent."

"What happened to the girl in the – the bungalow—?"

"That was quite a thrash if you like. In fact she said – just before her family arrived that night on a surprise visit – said I was a bit of a lion on the sheepskin rug in front of the blazing fire!"

"Geofrey, what I want to know is, you all alone out here got all this Brazil nut way of life you got, there must be something real nasty about you somewhere or you wouldn't stay here—?"

"Oh, there is!"

"I can understand that. I can't see you properly if there ain't. You must have a streak – right?"

"I have to stay here. Brazil is a waiting place. Everybody waits. That is what I learn. Pray that someday when the road is through they'll find a Siberia of minerals under me here – and nothing can stop me."

"Is that all?"

"And it's impossible to describe the feeling – it's sadness it's saudade it's yearning for a future – you catch it like a virulent grippe."

"You never strung up your great-aunt and left her in a closet and ran off with her knitting needles? You never assassinated the President of England? You didn't try take the crown jewels from the Tower of London that's where they are ain't they—?"

"Not quite ..." only his eyes worried her, little features in a bland almost podgy face, there was no light in them not a spark of the spirit's levity, "but to keep it like it is – stay here like I am – I'd kill for it."

The change was unmistakable. His voice was that of a very young man grown suddenly old. Of a schoolboy who has had a machine gun shoved into his arms and told to go out and shoot some people he's never met or laid eyes on in his life before, in the name of Queen and Country. An adolescent believing himself made man by sticking it out here in this sertão and red rock and palm and liana river slither, a loner too selfish to make contact with others, onanism made paranoid by the size of the land and its promise.

"It may not be quite what some of my friends in England see me as – kind of malaria infested goon sitting it out year after year – and you learn in Brazil if you wait long enough, sit with a vaqueiro on his porch and share his dream long enough – it will happen."

"You think Wes has a chance?"

"He'll find out for himself. Kind of person comes here shouts like that kicks and punches his way like that – he feeds off people like me. He needs me out here so he can fantasise his dreams. He won't ever truly understand. Like the Brazilian does. As I do. It won't happen single runt oakie makes a million overnight just not on – a pipedream – how can he learn what I have? That you must wait, must face out everything that come along, and wait again and wait some more."

"He's a fighter."

"It isn't guts. It's sleep you need when you come here, the kind of sleep which puts aside all the outside – Europe, America – each day is like a recurring sleepwalk, you can't afford to wake from it."

"What friends you got, Geofrey, in England?"

"I had friends . . ."

"There's nobody, right?"

"No room for them, any more . . ."

You can consider me your friend. I'd like that Mister Limey, I would. Perhaps you can't imagine what I felt, oh I know you wanted to redneck screw me last night, fuck me with that kind of gut thing you imagine I respond to, well you wrong mister, so wrong. And after I did nothing I watched you turn away from me, could see the humiliation you thinking you're no substitute for stud runt freckle nose, and then it was me who changed. Of a sudden. I wanted to lie with you, quite quiet with you like a little animal, not screwing or any, and reach out and hold you, say to you there is no panic, nobody need go mad dog ape Warren Beatty over Linda, and all the time I was growing warmer, deep inside me, you were so defenceless, right? And I could have cried I felt so good, I was there to nurse you, well nobody ever told me I was a nurse before. Feeling pity and all that bullshit, like I did the day Aunt Mim's rabbit Louisa she gave me died. Pity like hot tears ache burn in my eyes, pity I'd never before thought of longer than I can think.

As is happened that was the morning Linda ran clean out of her one-a-day malaria tablets. She was in despair about it – just the kind of thing can happen to me, I could drop down dead the day before I leave without them pills, and nobody give a damn. Geofrey couldn't reassure her. No matter how much he reiterated he'd caught malaria as often as four times in one year when he bought cattle in Araçatuba for the English fazendeiros – you lie still in a rêde for ten days, booze enough, and you sweat it out.

There was a favela hut near pensão in Chimboa, and it boasted a broadly painted dentista sign. The man had no more qualifications than a horse thief to be a dentist, a doctor, a vet or a mortician (all of which sundry services he was prepared to offer), and the wise in Chimboa, i.e. the living, steered clear of the place.

Not surprising at that, either, when you saw what he kept in the hut: there was a giant stripped down steel chair, painted black, shot through with incised holes, it was rescued from a pre-world-war Bolivian cargo plane crash-land; but any easily tortured mind could mistake it for a sale item from an Alcatraz death chamber. And he had an antique – circa 1920 Manaus gold teeth boom – oil driven rotor drill the length of your forearm.

The dentista's prime source of income in Chimboa was burying the dead and extracting their gold fillings. The fillings paid for the funeral, and then they were recycled among the army mouths on the air-strip.

Geofrey knew the man kept a store of various they-fell-off-the-back-of-a-lorry drugs in a fruit box beneath the famous electric chair and he bought a bottle of Korean War vintage quinine solution. A mouthful of this taken once a day with a shot of pinga will kill you soon enough, he explained to Linda when he returned, but at least you can't say after you died from malaria.

He who might become a Brazilian is surrounded by mimicry in the forest glades of the sertão: a caterpillar silkspins a coat of twigs, certain butterfly wings copy the shape of a bee, a luminous beetle – a fire-fly, a burnet moth – the wasp, a harmless adder stripes itself venomous coral snake blue, red and yellow: and of the hundred and fifty known species of treefrogs, seventy-five are peculiar to Brazil, in particular the nose frog which swallows the eggs she has developed in the throat of her male until they hatch by leaping out of her stomach – she paints herself black giant red horror eyes the size of a puma's.

Geofrey asked Linda if she'd like to go hunting with him that evening. In the dark? Certainly – best time catch wild pig. How? I'll take you. He'd built a platform halfway up a massaranduba tree. Plantain, twined and stretched, helped to disguise it. To hunt with any success, he said, you must imitate the dark.

She watched him load his rifle. He bound an ordinary flashlight to the barrel with black masking tape. The tin thumb-switch had a neatly bored hole through its centre. He knotted a fine thread of gut in the hole and stretched it taut to loop over the rifle trigger. He gingerly carried the weapon across the compound. Linda followed him to the forest edge.

In the chattery howler monkey dark they perched up on the massaranduba platform. Half an hour, then an hour passed. Linda gently tugged the pinga bottle from his lips and took a swallow. It was confidence, not warmth, she wanted from the alcohol. Little insects dropped on her, they crawled around her neck. Her legs ached, trapped beneath her in a crouch.

It seemed to her all the moist night air was filled with sounds. Crackle and slither of invisible paws. Below them, there came another noise, this time heavier, even clumsy. Geofrey swung the rifle towards the noise. His elbow jerked into Linda's ribs. He drew a deep breath, quite audibly, and the noise appeared to stand still.

As he pulled the trigger the flashlight threw a bright ring of light between two trees, and after this explosion her hearing became suddenly fuzzy and distant. A small pig with what appeared to be an outside head ringed with white – musk pig or bearded peccary – stood frozen in the sharp beam of light between the trees.

She glimpsed its pink glint eyes in the moment it twisted to lunge off into the undergrowth when Geofrey fired again. The pig tumbled sidelong to the ground and kicked with its legs as if it was in full flight. Linda held the rifle for him. Geofrey dropped and raced towards the animal. His machete sliced through the panic grunt in the pig's throat. The fat haunches quivered, as if bowels were the last to be informed of death.

Geofrey gutted the pig and hung its carcass on the porch over a tin bowl to bleed. However much he complained she persuaded him to take off his saturated clothes. She splashed him down with a bucket of water and wiped his face and his body. Linda with microscopic patience squeezed out the ticks from his neck and forearms with lighter fuel. In turn, he did the same for her.

They were light-headed from the pinga, exultant at the evening's kill, and she giggled when she asked him if it was true Britishers only took a bath once a week. After he stripped the gun, Geofrey bolted the door and snuffed out the kerosene wick. He was still afraid.

"... want me to hold you, then—?"

There is a little blue flower which, with some hunting, you can find in the sertão. Of a peculiar shyness—

"... to do that, like this—?"

so much so it seldom opens until long after the noonday broil has receded.

"... no ... you don't do nothing."

Distant pollen kin to the hyacinth it lifts its head in a garden of termite mounds and those reedy candelabra uprights in the red earth,—

"... it hurt you—?"

tall uva grasses, preferring the leathery shade of macaiba palm and pillar cactus.

"... you don't panic? ... right—?"

Strangely only the larger insects like the hawk-moth can reach a proboscis beyond the bluebell pubic stamens to the stigma ovum, so unwilling to surrender and withdrawn is this flower.

"... now you can ... honh—?"

Geofrey had shown Linda how to creep up to the flower, point her finger at it commandingly, 'dormi' he told her, and saying 'dormi' she instructed the flower and almost at once the obedient bluebell lids closed as if in sleep.

"... want me saying? ... real dirt things—?"

Gaily, she hunted about the palms nannying each blue flower she found.

"... out loud ... oh, honh!"

And in a matter of moments she had a whole dormitory of comatose liliaceaes at her feet.

"... want me tell you sick awful crude words—?"

"No ..." he lied.

"... want me say out loud obscene ass-hole mouth things—?"

No.

"... now you fucking me ... cunt screw fuck shit suck doin' it! ... you fucker honh come now ... you come ... hon! ... oh, honh!"

He was curled away from her in a way that it was uncomfortable for her to reach over an arm to hold him. She wiped the perspiration from his back with a vest. His face buried itself in his hands and he made no movement. Linda tried to drag the mosquiteiro from the bottom of the bed, it had slipped too far, and she was tired enough not to bother.

"Geofrey . . . ?"

He was already asleep.

"Jeeesus Geofrey . . . making love to you kind of cross between TV parlour quiz and drum majorette cheer leader some dumb university ball game!"

She felt the sudden cooling of his skin, now that the perspiration had stopped. She stretched the vest over his shoulder. In her reflection on the day, it seemed to her it had been the most crowded and yet the easiest twenty-four hours she had known since she first arrived, in Chimboa. She remembered a word—

". . . what you said – dormi wasn't it—?"

She could sense the dead weight helplessness sleep clothed his body with, and she slid down cricket thin comma shape beside him, stale sweet moist skin heat in her nostrils, the mattress bulged on either side.

". . . dormi, mister. Honh—?" she murmured in the milk warm night.

* * *

Wes sat up at nights on the porch floor with his rifles between his knees waiting for them. There was no way he could see them, but they were there, he knew, they were there in the trees at the edge of the clearing, behind his back when he turned away, crouching and listening, glottal accents mute in their throats, able to detect the crunch of his tall boots as if they were wearing them themselves, and Wes believed he could smell them they were so close to him at times.

But what else could they do, he asked himself—? They might set fire to the hut he had built, but he'd get more than one of them if they got that close with his rifles. They could steal the pickup, if they could do it without him hearing, if they could start the engine without the key, and if they could actually sit in the front seat and drive it.

They were children, he was confident about that, just kids, they'd soon tire of the game, they'd bicker amongst one another, when the rainy season approached they'd discover they had nothing shored up for the winter and they'd be on their knees begging for maize and manioc. Pig ignorant kids, that was all.

He must have dozed off, without seeing the first flicker of lemon light across the sky. The rising sun poured orange glare under his eyelids. He woke with a start, he rubbed his eyes, and ran across the clearing to be sure his other horse had not been taken.

There was no horse in the makeshift corral. The wire gate lay wide open. Perspiration waltzed into his palms. A tingling rage held him rooted to the ground. Now he had no horse left. That one had been Linda's. All forty dollars of it. It never had been more than a long-legged ten-year-old mule, but that's about all you can expect one of those vaqueiros to sell you out here.

He sawed off planks and battened back all the shutters with them. He nailed down every door to the cluster of huts at the side of the house and wedged beams in a diagonal fashion across the entrance door to the house. Maybe they were watching him, telling themselves what princes they were catching him asleep and off his guard going away with his last horse – he wasn't through by any means; as long as they saw the rifle he slung over his back and the pistol and the machete he swung at his hip he believed they reckoned him still to be the king.

"And that ain't all you goin' see of me today *indigi*," he suddenly said out loud, standing slap centre of his slash-and-burn clearing, "... because I am king, this is my land, and no bunch of bullshit indian things piss on me!"

If the forest heard him there was little indication. Black-draped urubu funereal poise atop buritis solemnly pumped their wings. Curutias paper-darted in the liana. Shrilled hysterically, tree to tree free-finger-falling ... the macaco laugh.

It took him four hours to reach the maloca clearing where he last found Capitão Pedro and his Aripuana. Wes had slipped a bottle of pinga into his holster, the revolver was pirate-style under his belt. With a bit of natural ingenuity he exchanged the rifle sling for a belt of rounds, the new sling lay heavily against his back, and his long walk there was in the noon heat. Though he wore no socks, those Texan tall boots were absurd footwear for the sertão, the welts chafed him raw and the heels slewed unsteadily in the muddy earth.

He prided himself he'd catch them all dozing in their hammocks. He'd find all that equipment they'd stolen off him hidden in the palhoca hut, he'd come upon them unawares trying to ride either of the two horses they'd taken, he'd...

He had already walked a third of the way, his stetson rim was dark with perspiration, and he admitted to himself all that kind of bravura was pure folly. He'd catch them at nothing. Because they were everywhere, their eyes made his skin prickle beneath the shirt, for each new step he took he felt a pair of narrow eyes beneath ridges of black hair crawl into his pores, he believed they were so close now. Sometimes he stopped dead in his tracks, perhaps listen to a footfall hear brown fingers scratch hold of tree bark, but there was not a movement, the only sound there new to him was the noise of the heat. The sun's sheen scolded anything that moved; and this sertão, just as with the forest, which changed terrain so quickly – from catinga stunt vegetation to sudden tracks of mata ciliar gallery forest cathedrals unexpectedly tall in a swamp basin – made the loneliness so much more acute.

Then the spire of smoke from the group's permanent fire twisted high in front of him. He unshouldered the rifle and remembered the denseness of the vegetation which surrounded the clearing up ahead. He ducked low and ran as hard as he could, swishing cashew trailers and bordoleta vines tracered by him like a ticker tape parade. Nothing was going to make him afraid of them. He was going to give them hell if...

He stepped into the clearing, turning from side to side, twisting and turning with the rifle butt on his hip Guadalcanal-style TV spin-off gotta protect those last LCIs left in the harbour. But...

It was very empty in the Aripuana clearing. Nobody was there at all, all the women and children gone, not even a hangtail dog. Just the pile of spreading embers, the parakeets they tie – bald and scrawny creatures kept for their feathers, and a pair of baby macacos twirling their tails around a chain attached to a tree.

He was sure they were there still. He could feel them. They were inches away. He ducked his head to see into the liana-capped huts. Not an *indigi* soul. He thumbed back the safety clip, and in rapid succession fired four shots over his head.

The staccato noises levelled off against the trees into hollow crump sounds. Grey discharge fumed in the air above him. Black powder puffs hesitated in the thick atmosphere. The monkeys hauled themselves upright by their tails and crouched closely against each other. Their fingers chattered in their mouths. A parakeet's wing, somewhat low on feathers, batted the air, bald patches of white in the red and green, like boiled chicken tissue.

After the blasts the forest showered out new noises. A crackling chorus gained confidence, half laughs half a maze of clucked choral scratchings encircled the oakie pioneer, freckle-nosed stetson-bearing desbravador (he who tames) of the forest. And he waited. Did he expect them to bring him his horses out of the trees loaded with Goodyear-tyre-sized cassava loaves? They had heard him all right, and they were staying out there in the shrivelling bush, he could play pistoleiro until the urubu turn white.

He had made his point, he liked to tell himself; then Wes looked up to note the declining arc of the sun. Though he feared none of them, king as he knew he was, he had to get back now. The long walk would bring him close to the warm fall of dusk, that cooling period before the mosqus ascend, filled with the shy blue eyes of the dormi flower and 'Queen of night' cactus exhaling essences of vanilla, and instinct caution warned him.

He was to hurry.

* * *

Geofrey knew it wouldn't be long before they found out that the americano girl had moved in with him. One of the vaqueiros would ride past and see her. He'd ride back to the pensão in Chimboa, he and Narcissu the fat patrão make a meal out of it, those listening figures on the porch watching the dust settle like vapour clouds, and somebody else was sure to meet up with the prefeito. Then it would only be a matter of hours before the prefeito, Haroldo, drove up to the house on a seemingly innocent pretext. That was how it would be. And every day after that, trying hard as he knew how to avoid it, there'd be that barrier between him and the Brazilians. He'd become a stranger to them again. Those years wasted. All his efforts to dissolve the shadow of the outcast come to nothing.

During those first few days he rode down to the village each morning. He was careful never to put an outright question to avoid curiosity. He listened and waited for the word, and that was the Brazilian way. Word told him there was no new supply truck from Santarém, which might take Linda back up north. The landing stage by the river was empty, and though he considered the road south to Porto Arthur – filled with those 986 h.p. frontloader yellow cats and the army of road-workers – no jeep was strong enough to plough the swamp lowland to reach the portion of the road already completed. When he approached the coronel at the air-strip, the tall bony man shook his head with condescension, he unbuttoned his jacket hypnotically swinging a brass crucifix at Geofrey—

"We are under government orders not to give civilians flight facilities, gerente."

"I wasn't really thinking of myself!" Geofrey murmured, "...suppose somebody has an accident out here, there is an emergency, or—"

"Still nothing I can do. I am acting under orders."

"Of course..."

"My job here is to keep this military station occupied until the road gets through from Porto Arthur. My job is to protect the road-workers."

"Protect?"

"Protect them from indians—"

"Ah, yes..."

"Protect them from Communist-inspired guerillas who might hide in the serra."

"I did not know there were any."

"Neither did I gerente, but there might be. You see, there are rumours of these Communist bandits to the west of the Rio Teles Pires, I must protect the road from them."

"Protect Chimboa from the rumours."

"Of course ..." said the coronel, without a trace of irony in his voice.

Geofrey conjured up a picture of half a dozen idealistic students, Paulista youths from middle-class homes hiding out in the forest, on the run from the authorities in fear of the city police legendary enquiry 'techniques'; perhaps they tried to distribute radical pamphlets in the library of the São Paulo University, they might have subscribed to a banned political group, Marighela inspired and now they were hiding out in the serra with a stolen machine gun and a couple of World War Two Mannlicher Carcano carbines. It didn't require an air-borne Division to protect Chimboa from them.

"What you want to leave here for, anyway, gerente?" smiled the coronel.

"Oh, but I don't."

"You have to stay here, no? Wait for the road come through – make your fortune, no?"

"I wouldn't think of leaving here. I love Brazil," Geofrey was quick to reply.

"So that is why I cannot allow free rides in my planes," the coronel smiled thinly, tucking his crucifix beneath his vest. He emphasised the word 'free' Geofrey noticed. Ah, so that was it. It was a matter of jeito, was it? Perhaps, the coronel meant, perhaps if you pay me enough I could arrange it gerente, but on the other hand you know the penalties for trying to bribe an officer, no?

Geofrey certainly wasn't going to take that risk. He could not guess what the coronel's price would be, even if he had one, but he knew any bribe he offered would place him under the officer's thumb, he'd be a pawn again, an estrangeiro outcast. That – he didn't want.

Linda locked herself inside the limey's house each morning he rode away. She surrounded herself with shutters. Shutter in her mind to keep out Wes. Shutter off the all too familiar slash-and-burn clearings. This wasn't her country, the forest and the thick heat shrivelled her soul, and when this happened out here nothing could be worse, each long pulsing hour became an unbearable trap. Monotony dripped like a water torture. All she could think of was—

"...Did you ask, Geofrey, did you really try?" she said when the limey returned in the afternoon.

"No supply truck has come in."

"What about the air-strip then?"

"They won't take you."

"There must be a way!"

"You must wait. There might be a launch on the river, soon."

She could think of nothing else. Though she tried. She made love to this withdrawn and soft spoken man, she coaxed him into it, it gave her a certain sense of control, but even this sex became a mechanical gesture. Geofrey, the real Geofrey protected himself with layers of reserve. The centre of the man was a dream area, filled with this strange mix of emotions, simultaneously a waiting and a yearning, and yet again it was tinged with an abstract sadness, a loneliness, something untranslateably called saudade, peculiar only to a Brazilian. She could not reach that.

After they had made love, Geofrey made a bombilla of maté – thick green leaves boiled into a tea beverage which you sucked at through a straw – and he left her inside the house. He swung in the hammock on the porch, letting the mosqus cloud over his head, and for an hour or more his piggy eyes stared out across the darkening shadows of forest and clearing, it was a consuming process, as if his eyes wanted to digest the whole landscape, a meal-making cascade of senses on his retina.

In this he was very much like Wes, at least to her way of thinking. She dared not ask him what it was he looked at through the sweating dark palm of the evening. There was such an air of fatality in the way he swung there, just like those vaqueiros in Chimboa, a waiting and a wanting spirit about him, quiet and passive, of a containment, unique perhaps to all Brazil nuts that one day the land promised would indeed deliver, red dirt made mineral wealth, dry sertão made untold oil strikes, the road ever the road made industry comparable in size to anything the old world has to offer.

She was asleep when the empty pinga bottle rolled across the boards out on the porch. In the morning she brought him slices of cassava bread pasted with goiabada jelly. His eyes were pink and watery as if he had lain awake the whole night, watching the dark and waiting for the lemon light of the day, and that is exactly what he had done.

"OK?"

"Fine, thank you."

"Like to sit out here all night just staring out?"

"It may sound strange, but—"

"Tell me, Jeff . . ." she hesitated a fraction, "what is it makes you stay here?"

"I thought you knew—"

"I know all about the road and waitin' for it, I mean that ain't the real answer I was looking for."

"That's right – the road."

"Suppose it don't bring all it promise—? Something go wrong—? World discover oil and minerals some other place—"

"It can't."

"Suppose nobody wants to buy Brazilian beef from you? Maybe they find something wrong with it – it got a special Brazil disease nobody ever thought about before—?"

Geofrey grinned at her. He lowered his eyes as if to say you don't know what you're talking about, and he watched a crowd of eager ants race around a piece of jelly he had dropped on the floor.

"I know you think Linda just pig ignorant about these sort of things – have you ever thought what would happen to you – it all come to nothing out here? What would you do then, honh huh?"

"I'd have no choice."

"Course you would – you could go back to little big Britain, and all those crown jewels and things you got there."

No thanks, he said softly, I'm not going back anywhere, because, well . . . there is no going back. Ever.

It wasn't just the loneliness or the landscape's monotony which hurt her so. There were times when she dared not listen outside, even open her eyes. If Geofrey was gone during the the day, riding with his young beef herd, though she always bolted the door behind him Linda felt wretchedly afraid. Her paranoia crushed her. Suppose Wes descended here? Beat her till she bled, then in tears begged her to go back with him? That nosy prefeito might come waving some ass-hole redtape document to be signed—? Or the patrão from the pensão, a cable for Geofrey perhaps, his next raft-load of stock was on its way—? Suppose the vaqueiros discovered her in the limey's house? Now they'd consider her a whore. Now she belonged to anybody. That was their way. And they'd prove it.

You know when you are being watched. You have learnt to recognise all the symptoms after these months up at the oakie's slash-and-burn clearing. The roots of the hair have a tingle sensation. You make clumsy mistakes with your hands you wouldn't do ordinarily. You are undressing behind transparent walls and your ears prick at the least sound.

Linda knew when the old wrinkled indian thing, Capitão Pedro, was coming before he stepped out of the trees, she was so smart now with her instincts. Quite regular, it seemed – he came to talk with the limey. On each occasion Linda made herself scarce. She climbed out of the back window and ran across to Geofrey's horse. She liked to ride bareback around the clearing on the fringe of the trees. Though she was always careful, he was a tall one this horse, too strong for her, she knew.

It made the limey laugh to see her hide like that from the old Aripuana. She said to him – I don't understand how you can stand the smell of him. Well, reasoned Geofrey, if he smells like that to us can you imagine what we smell like to him! She wouldn't listen.

At first she didn't think it strange. The two men always sat so calm and relaxed out on the porch, sucking green tea through straws, jawing heaven knows what. Then she began to notice how frequent these meetings were. So much so, she was climbing out of the back window practically every other afternoon, leastways it seemed like that to Linda.

One day a certain oddness struck her. She was watching them from her safe distance. The way they stood together, kind of rapt silence between them, something they shared she couldn't grasp, like contemplative stone statues staring out over the sertão, not saying a word to each other – Linda felt a shivering sensation and the sweat down her spine was suddenly cool.

* * *

The Capitão and Geofrey had finished talking about the more important matters. Usually, at this stage, the old indian would slip away across the clearing. But, on this occasion he lingered. As if he wanted to say something else, talk on a separate matter, now that there was nothing more to be discussed about the little americano.

Geofrey yawned and leaned back against the post on the verandah. The Capitão was describing the Aripuana Reserve his group had retreated from two seasons ago. He was almost whispering the account. They hated being so near the road on one side, and the big farmers behind them. They had felt trapped. Besides, there were too many other groups around. Particularly groups like the newly contacted Cintas Largas. They were dangerous, the Capitão told Geofrey. No good to us.

Geofrey listened politely. It seemed the Capitão was explaining that, after all this time he was known as an Aripuana, that wasn't the true name of this group. Aripuana was a kind of umbrella trade name to cover the area between the Roosevelt River and Porto Velho, flowing from the Aripuana headwaters.

Geofrey, in truth, didn't care one way or the other what the Capitão wanted to call himself. Any name was fine by him. But the Capitão was persistent—

"Now you ask me question . . . why did I make us leave down there?"

"I don't know, Capitão . . ."

"And why is it – our real name is Surui – our aldeia was Surui – ask me why that is?"

"All right . . ." Geofrey crouched by the wall, a tired heat series of prickles invaded his eyelids, "why was it you left? Why is your name Surui, Capitão?"

The old indio was pleased at that. Now he could tell the branco all he intended to. He had never told any other branco, and he wanted to get it off his chest.

"You see . . . we always were a small group. The Surui. There are many more of us – but our group never got any larger, my family group. And I want you to ask me why we left the Reserve down there – when we were good friends of Francisco Meirelles who looked after us—? Please, gerente?"

"All right, I'm asking . . ."

"When we first met the missionarios they kept bringing us

gifts, and we thought that that was all there was to the branco world. They come in they give us more gifts, until we felt we only had to look like poor indios and branco would shower down more gifts on us. Until... you do want to know what happened to us?"

"Yes..."

"We started to work for a big fazendeiro near Posto Sete de Setembro. But he gave us money instead of gifts. And then the missionarios became angry with us and stopped bringing us gifts like food and clothes. And they stayed away for long periods as if they didn't want to speak to us. Later, we found the only place we could spend our money was by buying from the shop the fazendeiro built for us on the land. Now ... gerente, you going ask me what come next? And how clever I was?"

"How clever were you, Capitão?"

"I discover – because by then I could speak good Portuguese that the fazendeiro was charging us ridiculous prices for things like – he charging us twenty cruzeiros for a packet of Hollywood filtro cigarros. So I find out all the money we work for go back to him and I decide we must leave."

"What happened then?"

"The fazendeiro say he threaten to kill us if we leave – tell the missionarios and Francisco what bugre thieves we were – and we ran off."

"To where?"

"We stay by the road at Riozinho – beg from the motoristas because the missionarios would still have nothing to do with us and the fazendeiro come to them telling lies."

"Is that all, Capitão?"

"No – it get much worse, now. You listen?"

"All right ...

"What was the real trouble that descended on you Surui?" Geofrey obediently obliged.

"Some days – half the moon something like that the missionarios go back to Sete de Setembro because the fazendeiro was complaining he could find no indians to work for him. That we had told other groups not to go near the bugre. And there was an accident. Some of the missionarios were killed on the land near the hut which was once our shop.* And we got all the blame for this. Nobody would speak to us now."

"What did you do?"

"I was going to ask you to ask me that," the Capitão was quick to get down to business, his lisping putty tone rapid and low, "we did nothing. Or for the while . . . then, the other brancos arrived."

"Who were they, Capitão?"

"They were the ones who said they had bought all the land we were on at Riozinho – and they said to us we must go immediately. They wanted to build glebas for other branco the pobre branco and it wasn't good news to have us sitting on the gleba pavement where they might shop – so they told us. We didn't know what to do. Until the day – these missionarios came back to us and said 'you wretched indios are in real bad trouble now. You caused deaths. You sitting on land this company called Itaporanga has bought from the Ministry of the Interior. What are we going to do with miserable troublemakers like you Surui?' . . . And I made up my mind. We'd go I said. And we did."

"I see . . ."

"And I swore I'd tell nobody but you – that we were Surui – because everybody say we have given Surui a bad name. We just nothing now – just bugre Aripuana – no name nothing indios."

The Capitão, with a certain theatrical flourish wiped his eyes, but Geofrey could see no tears there.

"Well, I'm sorry about all that," Geofrey breathed with obvious relief, "it is a sad tale, indeed, Capitão. And I fully realise it."

"And this is where we came to – we took moon after moon to get here – because here is far enough away from those places down there which I'll never go back to."

"Quite . . ."

"They can say what they like – say we got no dignity given Surui a bad name bugre trash indios they can say. We not going back."

* In November 1971, four FUNAI workers and a Brazilian journalist were killed by unknown indians in a hut bordering a large farm close by the Roosevelt River. It was generally supposed to be the result of constant friction between the Cintas Largas groups and seringueiros.

"No ..."

"And ..." the Capitão looked positively chagrined, "that is the end of our story, gerente."

Linda kept her distance on the edge of the clearing. She could see the men poised strangely still on the verandah. They were both staring out across the forest roof. She looked to follow their gaze and she could see nothing. Just the same monotony of trees and sky and stubble clearing. She wondered what in hell a guy like the limey has to say to that animal thing. She shrugged. Weren't no business of hers. She was on her way home, please God, and that was all she need think about.

After the Capitão had gone, Geofrey felt a little curious about the old indio. Why had he bothered to tell him that flat-footed meandering account of the group? Geofrey didn't care if the group was called Aripuana, Surui or sweet fanny anything, they just little men in the forest who do what he say.

Linda hated to sound too curious about those strange meetings Geofrey had with the animal thing, but she did ask him—

"You telling them things when you speak to that man – telling them to go back and work for Wes?"

"In their own time they will," Geofrey said.

"What makes you so sure of that?"

"I'm surprised you even care about Wes's wellbeing—?"

"Well ... I don't, see," she murmured with a sulky voice.

"They have to stay here. On Wes's land at least they're safe from the army and those vaqueiros – the army would leap at the chance of a man hunt. They'd give anything for a bit of firing practice. That's why you never meet any missionaries or anthropologists out here. Army don't want them nosing about Chimboa."

"... honh?"

"Yes?"

"You wouldn't mind telling me ... just what is an anthropologist, Jeff?"

* * *

There was nobody now he could listen to, not that he even wanted to. Wes liked it alone. He was going to tough it out. No matter how much they hid from him. But by knowing they were there, almost beside him as he walked over the *formed* land, so close to him perhaps their shadow duplicated his own, and at night guessing the trick silent stealth of their bodies as they circled around him, him feeling no anger at all, there was a certain comfort in what he liked to call this bond between him and his whadyamacallem. One of these days time come they must shore up for the rain season they'll come begging on their knees they'll come. And whatever it is they think I've done them wrong by, or what gives them the right to think they can steal the last empty Brahma beer can I got to toss out the door, they have to come back eat shit to me. Look it – there's this bond between us – they want me to hurt them. Maybe they pig stupid but they understand that, it gets through, nothing else do.

He wandered a long way off from the hut, he was intentionally giving them an invitation. He took no gun, and he sung and shout top of his voice while he split buriti boughs with his axe. Wanted to show them his muscle. His squat square body lathered in sweat, the axe rising and falling, sun glint like Inca gold on his blade, he wanted to draw all the attention he could, show them no fear, take only three or four of them sneak up behind and finish him off, or poison tip those useless arrows of theirs the newspapers like to write so much about, creep up on him on all sides (those arrows so useless they can't hit a fifty-seater omnibus unless they get within five yards of it) ... watch me now, *indigi*. Don't I make a target?

There was one instance which did drain his confidence. It made him feel a little bit of his luck slip away. His judgment a fraction askew. He walked below the rocky pool to where the flowering oiticicia tree stood. Now it was peculiar, he admonished himself, how he'd been so busy thinking of nothing but his brown indian things, that he hadn't looked at his favourite tree for a long time.

As he approached he couldn't see it yet above the bush on the sertão. He expected its wild pink blooms to startle the green and red of the terrain it witnessed, as it had always done. The tangled bushes fell away from him, and he drew in his breath, faint whistle of air in his teeth. His oiticicia looked very different. The tree, such an early flower out here and at its best a giant's fist of carnation colour, had changed out of all recognition.

This, his favourite tree, was a legendary creation. Perhaps the oakie's delight in his oiticicia reflected something of this. In the old days of the indians, that is to say more than seventy years ago, what the anthropologist likes to call the birth of contact between branco and the indigenous, there was a great Tupi tribe to the east of the Rio Teles Pires called the Kawahib. They were never quite made extinct, in later years they made many subgroups, but the Kawahib were among the first of the great tribes in isolation the branco decimated. Booms of rubber and gold hunted them down. The Kawahib always grouped together, sometimes as many as five thousand in one maloca, and because of this they were feared all the more; man hunts were organised, death-dealing branco out of terror and land greed possession destroyed this tribe. And it is a peculiar fact that – like the jé group, the Bororo, further south of here, the more the Kawahib closed its ranks into one community and the more vast a piece of land they claimed title to – such tribes become lethargic. Their green river world so huge it knows no perimeters, their numerical strength grouped under one maloca seemingly invulnerable, such as the Kawahib, became easy targets. And branco always knew where to find them, they did not know how to disperse into subgroups because they were a family of thousands, they could not splinter into a network of cells for their own protection, moietic unity grown goliath was the seed of their destruction.

The oakie's favourite tree was once a Kawahib legend.

The oiticicia was the first pink bride of the Brazilian spring. At full flower it married the moon, and at night the white disc ran a gauntlet of clouds to fasten itself to the oiticicia, its pinkness groomed with white and silver radiants of pearl. And like a bride, so eager to dress for the ceremony of quick spring, in such a hurry for her moon love, she must be the first to give up all her pollen. She must be vanquished, suffer for her early heart, left deserted by her hunting moon god chauvinist in the heavens.

The oakie's tree was now a witch. The flowers were black sagged rinds. They dropped down, petal and petalfold stained with an oily substance. There was no pink any more in the branches, you could have been forgiven for thinking somebody had tossed a barrel of tar mix over the whole tree.

Wes felt a sliver of fear. The blackened tree made his sertão appear even bleaker. For the first time he tasted dry mouth salt defeat about the land. The shrub and liana and wet creeper were shrivelling fast. The broad bladed water-grass, so bold in the first flush of the flood rains in retreat, could not disguise the baldness of the red earth, it was rutting beneath the top-soil. Wes had led himself to rely on his oiticicia tree. It was his beacon of fertility. Now it had become a widowed tree. The moon rode hyena husband high in the blue heaven, transparent hunter, no lover any longer of the sap-fled oiticicia.

Wes listened to the forest with the ears of an animal. He began to detect the derision in the macaco's laugh. The trees were filled with a crowd of raucous despisers. They hated him, with their ironic jeers, he believed to himself. He was the clown, now. They were the big top audience, howling monkeys who vaulted the green pavilion tiers, roedor, cotia and wild pig who scuffled in the grunt dark, mourning urubu attendants who wait to carry off the stricken performer.

But Wes kept his bravura. He liked to show himself. Present himself to the watching eyes as a perfect target. Those indian things would make their first big mistake. They'd give a show of confidence. That was what he wanted.

In the lemon cool drip of the morning he went down to the rocky pool. Vapour wet stone like a clear grey marble slabbed its sides. Where the level of the water had shrunk no lichen grew. It had a clean look. Scrubbed by the sun. He placed his rifle and revolver on a flat of rock. He took off his clothes and slid into the pool. Before he plunged towards the centre where it was deepest he tightened the black chin cord of his stetson. He splashed forward until the water rose to his eyebrows and he had to kick with his feet to keep himself afloat. Wes was no swimmer. He managed to balance himself by flailing the surface with his muscular red arms. As best he could he pulled his feet up to float back on the water. He rubbed soap across his chest and he lathered his neck and face. He could not look up at the violent rim of the sun which pecked the top of the trees – there was so much soap in his eyes. He trod water and sneezed out loud to clear his sinuses.

The black lace beneath his chin slipped again, it tightened across his lips and he had to spit it away. When he removed his hands from the sting in his eyes, cupping his palms with water to splash back over his face ... he saw them.

There were about a dozen Aripuana indians, evenly spaced apart, standing around the pool's edge.

He rubbed his eyes to be sure he was seeing straight. Yes, indeed, he was. A pulse throbbed in a vein on the side of his forehead.

But he did not hesitate. He stroked his fat arms across the water towards the guns.

The rifle and the revolver were not there any more. Not where he thought he had placed them. He spun around, reaching for a handhold against the slabbed stone, water whirlpooling at his waist. Perhaps he'd put the guns on the far side ...? He looked. But he hadn't done so. And where were his clothes? They too were gone.

The young bloods looked very different now. They seemed to be new men. They wore slashes of red and yellow urucum on their faces. Bracelets of parakeet feathers and Coca-Cola cans on their arms and legs. Broad daubs of brown paste down their chests.

They were no longer those callow bodies who worked so indolently around the hut. No longer the cowed and giggling things he had kicked into submission. Some wore shorts, others wore only the string piece attached to their genitals. Brown noses punched flat and bowls of oiled black hair cut into sharp steps above their ears.

It was unlikely the oakie had seen such ceremonial dress. But the young bloods were decorated just exactly as they could be seen in any one of those interminable *holy cow mother do modern indians really look like this?* German and English TV documentary films the present Brazilian government has sponsored. Those Aripuana looked like the kind of thing two grips, two soundmen, a director in a khaki bush hat waving a waterproof light meter and eight sweating technicians not excluding the patient cameraman counting the ticks in his elbows, could spend an idyllic month filming down in the south in the eastern Mato Grosso with, albeit, government approval.

Casual as he could contrive to be, Wes swam back into the

centre. He splashed water at them with his ankles. He tried a hoarse shout of confidence—

"What you want, boys!"

They didn't move.

"You want work?"

They stood.

"Want to come back to me?"

Not a tremble of expression in their faces.

"Huh? ..."

Brown statues. Studies in silence. Gravamen of black eyes, liquid eyelashes, elongated hazel-nut lids. Then one or two of them flickered with interest. They had noticed the alloy glint from the oakie's wristwatch.

His freckled red and white body an object of curiosity, strange repellent skin the colour of vulnerableness, muscular but blotched, out of all context in this sertão of forest and brush, this americano's (no, not even that, to them he was just branco, pure and simple, for the Aripuana there were no continents there were no nations) fat shoulders looked like the floundering belly of a river porpoise, lung-fish or playful canoe bumping manateé.

"Now get the hell out of here! Fetch me the Capitão! You wanna discuss work? Hear me!" His bull roar.

"—"

"You want work!" His voice to a scream.

"—"

" ... Scare me none red yellow brown all painted up mother cunt son suckers I drive into town tell those army grunts on the strip you out here what you think they fuckin' do to you, lynch posse man, come out here fuckin' cut your nuts off stuff your mouths with, *just stand easy there*, when I tell them from me how you ain't in no place like where you should be they peel you skin you alive change you into lampshades quicker you can spit boy, yah got that?"

"—"

"Piss blood heathen animal sodomite ass-hole peepers too fuckin' indolente make enough contos buy old Coca-Cola can, *back off that pool will yah*, I'm a fuckin' Christian ex-Korean marine war vet got more medals, *whad you doing with those rocks?* second class than you indige swamp waps can count stars, yah hear?"

"—"

"Damn right you guys got nothing but Jesus fuckin' Christ ape shit peasant peanut butter liquid between your ears, *put down that stone, man* when I done with you bring down on your hole-in-the-wall heads guaran-damn-t-yah won't have one mother fuckin' dime bit, *step away you listen,* chance in shit kingdom come save your necks, *whad you doing with that, don't* for I got rights like I got fuckin' branco King dominion over your dog souls, *don't* I'm a true fuckin' baptised by Holy Roller loyal citizen of the United States of America and swore allegiance to the learned by heart whole nut cracking 23 Articles of the Constitution, you guys, Old Glory in my Southern Bones, you animal things, *so move your asses off that* and yah, *don't*—"

The first rock glanced across his shoulder blade. He couldn't tread water. He waited for his own buoyancy to bring him back up to the surface. His stetson floated away from him. The lace torn.

The moment he surfaced another rock whumped into the water beside him. He went under. Before he could cough out breath, water swilled into his larynx. Yet, strangely, the strike of the rocks didn't seem to hurt. The water softened their impact, the pain had a delayed mechanism. His feet threshed for balance. When he touched the floor of the pool he lunged back up to try grip hold of the stone slabs.

A rock nailed itself against his forehead. Sick scuffling feeling, sense of surprise. Then, backwards, his knees uppermost, hands flailing to hold, too far away now, and a wall of blood clotted over his eyes.

When he surfaced there came to him an instant of recognition. Red to see. Sky bathed in it. Sun dripping on him, blood sun. Only the outlines of the whadyamacallem. Shooting freezing pain in his legs, a crack inside his head, something else thudding down at him, gulf of black growing, under now, this time can't come up on my own.

An infinitesimal point in Wes's brain registered that last hit, a discharge of creeping warmth, all nerve ends robbed, air and blood gargle in the throat. A balloon inside his mouth, his lips forced to open wide to release the torrent.

The young bloods waited.

The blotched red and white shape no longer resembled a river porpoise. It seemed shrunken, more the size of a fat bacu fish, red streamers from its forehead, blood wrinkles on the surface of the pool, drifting there beneath them.

They broke the rifle in half and buried it with the oakie's pistol. The clothes they took with them. As they walked away, one young blood paused at the lip of the stone pool. He watched the still pudgy wrists rise towards the surface. And there was a glint of gold in the branco's mouth.

The Aripuana speeded to a trot. They said nothing between them. They skipped along through the palm and bush towards where the trees lay thickest. Their eyes were downcast, almost soulful, like children barely able to kindle guilt, of a mollified righteousness, they might have worried a little for the spirits of the forest for they had to be appeased over this matter, perhaps within a very short space of time a wild pig or a timbu must be slaughtered and they will burn it with some of the branco's clothes in order that the sacrifice take up the burden of guilt. That was how it should be. The pig did the killing. The spirits will be appeased. The pig or the timbu did it, it must be that way, the blame transferred.

The black stetson floated on the surface of the pool. It lay inches away from the dead man's head. The head was a ginger freckled dome, quite bald and of a shininess. All around it columns of red spiralled up. So close lay the stetson, you could almost believe the oakie would reach out for it, reach out for it and cover his naked pate, for so hot was it now and the brilliant dragonflies were keeping low in the shadow side of the stone rim, Wes you'd think would grasp that favourite hat of his to pull it down tight over his eyes, just like he always did.

* * *

It was only river word. An old mateiro who brought cana in his canoe to sell in Chimboa said there was a raft load of calves twisting its way up water. Then some of the vaqueiros, coming in from a ten-day beef drive on the Iriri River, said they'd seen it, too. Geofrey took heart. It must be his cattle. He knew it was a matter of days before someone discovered Linda up at his house. Perhaps now the pressure was off. He lounged on the porch of the pensão with his boots up against the rail. He watched the vaqueiros roll 'general' dice across the floor, and the patrão brought him a plastic beaker of green tea to suck. Fat Narcissu loosened the pyjama string belt around his waist. He trod warily over the rattling dice 'general' game. Geofrey drew on the straws and passed the beaker back to the patrão.

"The coronel says he got a supply plane coming from Manicoré – you know where that is, gerente?"

"On the Madeira," said Geofrey with gentle exactness. Narcissu hoped to catch him with questions like that. But the Englishman with his Brazilian passport knew every air-strip between Manaus and Goiânia. The patrão sucked at the straws and studied Geofrey through his bulge eyes.

"Big delivery he says. They got machines and plenty of stores. Maybe they got mail, too."

"Oh ..."

"Sure. Big sorting office send it to Manicoré from Manaus. Now I got nephews working there on the Belém steamers. I get a letter once a year from them."

Geofrey glanced across at the string mail pouch Narcissu hung against a post. It was always empty, nobody wrote letters from Chimboa. You would no more expect mail to arrive than see a vaqueiro ride an emer bird, tall grey and brown ostrich creature, along the main street in Chimboa.

"You don't seem too interested in the supply plane, gerente—?"

"If you told me it was bringing a dozen Germans with their mineralogy search equipment or some rich americano looking for bauxite I'd lay down on the ground and let him use me for a carpet," said Geofrey.

"You'd like a letter, no—?"

"No."

"Why nobody ever write you, huh?"

"There is nobody."

"You got a mother or a father?"

"No."

"A cousin, maybe—?"

"Maybe ..."

"Well, I got two hundred cousins, cousins and nephews, they write to me."

"They do!" Geofrey raised his eyebrows in a doubtful expression.

"Well, I see it this way – I got two hundred of them, at least three of them write me once a year," said Narcissu.

Invariably, when a big supply plane came in, there'd be a few newspapers to read – *O Liberal* or *A Manaus*. They'd always be about a month out of date. And they never told you much. Three quarters of it football, perhaps Alfa Romeo promise to build a factory in the Amazonas, some long-distance motorista rapes an indian girl (but it wouldn't read like that – 'indian tribe of women molest lone truck driver' – that's how it would read), possibly there might be a little item from England, 'Elizabeth, Queen of England, has an abortion: Government forced to resign?' stolen from gutter-press French magazine. You don't get news in a place like Chimboa, just the slow sweat drip of one day following another.

In the afternoon Linda cooked a meal of beefy, feijoada and manioc grated flour. Geofrey brought back a couple of beers from the pensão. Before he ate he dried his horse with strips of blanket. Yes, he told her, it sounded like his raft which was coming up river. If the cafusos have got lamps they'll sail it through the night. Maybe in the morning we both go down to the landing stage ...

Her heart didn't exactly leap. You wait, that's all. She'd learned that from the limey. You wait, they say it'll arrive tomorrow, it arrives three days later. There's a delay. Like three of the calves fell off the raft. Their ropes too loose. And it takes the cafusos two days to find some river thief they can sell the carcasses to. What always happens, said the limey, you say to them when they arrive they are three head short, the cafusos grin pink gums, lower their eyes, you know how it is gerente – nasty rapids a day behind us, these calves they just panicked. You shrug. And the cafusos drink the money away in the pensão. Narcissu delighted. Vaqueiros whisper and laugh. This americano Geofrey estrangeiro gerente big idiot now, they know something he don't. Secret pinga talk, night laughter.

She only heard the boardwalk outside creak. There was someone on the verandah. A hand thumped against the door. Geofrey strode across the room and opened it. The Capitão quickly stepped back, beckoning Geofrey. Unusual for Linda not to have six-sensed the old indian. She believed she could smell him before he ever reached the porch. She ran into the back room and pulled the screen door behind her.

The men stood outside talking in an urgent tone. Capitão Pedro's glottal throat rose to a pitch. She could only guess at the sounds. It wasn't anger she heard in the indian's voice, more a kind of alarm, a spitting mellifluent fear. And it seemed he wanted the limey to help him.

Geofrey shouted out at her before he closed the door. It wasn't clear to her what he said. She huddled against the back wall. Then she knew they were running across the clearing towards the horses. Both men mounted and she heard the hooves thud impatiently whilst Geofrey placed a halter over the indian's horse. Geofrey guided the second horse behind him, and he kicked his mount forward. Red dust scattered behind them in slow clouds.

It must be something important, she knew, because she'd never seen that old indian thing get up on a horse all the months she'd been here in Chimboa. Those Aripuana made no pretence at riding horses.

Geofrey was gone all the afternoon. Linda boiled a tureen of black beans and she softened a strip of salted beefy with a hammer for the evening meal. The head of the hammer developed a wobble as she beat the meat. There was a split more than an inch deep in the handle, and she went outside to the sheds to find another one. She had to duck beneath the planta thatch, the shed roof was so low, and she waited for her eyes to grow accustomed to the sudden gloom inside. A wide triangle of corrugated asbestos lay across a pile of equipment and empty kerosene containers. She pulled the asbestos away until it revealed the remains of a car axle and the cracked shell of a long disused sump. That wasn't all she revealed.

There was the adze. The adze Wes gave to Geofrey as a peace offering for the Aripuana. The adze the limey promised he'd give to the indians. It was just lying there. Nobody had given it to any indian thing. Beside it lay any number of axe hafts,

hafts that only Wes could have fashioned she so easily recognised them, those same hafts which used to disappear daily from the oakie's clearing. Linda dragged the asbestos up against the wall. All those other things she could see now. All kinds of tools and black tar mix cans, coils of rope, axe heads and twin-bladed saws, practically every single item which those indian animals had stolen from Wes over the weeks gone by.

She'd like to have dodged it. What business of hers was it, any more? In the morning, with luck, with Brazilian luck, she'd be gone. She thought of her oakie pioneer sweating it out alone in his slash-and-burn clearing. Toughing it out on his own with his indefatigable dream. All the while believing the limey to be his true partner, the one neighbour on this rubbish terrain he could rely on. Slowly, certain things dawned on Linda. There'd be some explaining to do. For she cared for that runt oakie, no matter how she was never likely to see him again, ever, she cared, and she had to know the truth.

Linda took all the tools up to the house. She laid them out on the table. Every one of them. She wanted to see the limey's expression when he walked into the room. She wanted to see his eyes, piggy secretive eyes, she wanted to see the first crack in that bland expression of his.

The dark falls so quickly when the mosqus ride the air. She ignited the wick and throttled the glass container back over the lamp. She carefully placed it on the table beside all the stolen equipment.

The Capitão thing was not with him when Geofrey rode the horses back. She heard him moving about in the dark outside, he took his time with the horses, and when he had finished he stopped to fetch a pinga bottle from his earth container before he came in.

He stood in the doorway. He was talking about a large boa skeleton he'd seen on the planalto. She felt she was sleepwalking, cold and dreamy, as if she was hearing his voice a mile away from where she sat.

Geofrey approached the table. With an automatic gesture he lifted up one of the axe hafts. He carefully put it back, quite delicately returning it to the rest of the stolen equipment, like a man studying a collection of rare and brittle porcelain. He breathed in deeply.

"Where did you find these ... ?"

"You know, limey ..."

"I'm asking you, Linda—"

"Just don't try telling me you know nothing about them, that's all! Don't think I been sitting here counting the ways you can lie to me about them, Geofrey! Don't bother your thieving skull about that – I want you to tell me truth, right!"

"There is nothing to tell you—"

"Don't tell me you and them indian things ain't hand in glove! You never gave them that adze because you never once intended to, that adze Wes asked you to give them! How come you got all this stuff they stole from Wes and me's porch? And you seeing that old indian guy all the time. He came here – day after day – and I never once thought until now – you were telling them all the time, give that tacky little oakie hell will ya because I want him off my land! You can thieve what you like – you don't need work for him don't be scared of that little runt – pay no mind to him some bum americano knows ass-hole nothing about what he doin' ... am I right?"

She could only shout. It was the only release she had. Perhaps that's why the oakie bawled out so much, only if he shouted loud enough would his spirit fly. Linda contemptuously shoved the adze into Geofrey's face. The shouting made her feel better. Tears had nothing to do with it.

"Geofrey—?"

He said nothing.

"All the time you been planning it, since that first day we arrive, so easy now for you – this trash whore she can go out first minute that raft come up river, Dwight Weslie – he got about a few weeks left alone out there, and he'll be begging you buy that land back off him so hard he'll near enough give it you back. You like to kid yourself you become so much a Brazil nut – suckeggs voice know-all you bullshitter you don't have to even try no more. You done it. You so fucking indistinguishable from those John Wayne guys down in the pensão you become as much shanty trash as they have there ain't no difference!"

The piggy eyes glinted with a seraphic look. He could even be smiling at her, a glimmer there, a kind of ponderous gratification, as if she had just paid him a compliment.

"Why ... ?" she asked in a whisper, "you tell me why ... ?"

"If you expect me to burst into tears, say I'm sorry, go running back up the hill take these things to Wes you got—"

"Go to hell!"

"If somebody like Wes wants to come out here – make a fool of himself that's his cup of tea – if he hadn't come across me do you think he would have survived more than a week out here?"

"You cheated him."

"I was willing to help in so much—"

"You took his money quick enough."

"Anybody would take Wes's money. Man like that he's born to be taken every day of the living month, Linda."

"This was his dream – he trusted you, man. He told you what he wanted, and he said you was his buddy and that crap, and he believed in you. He such an idiot he still does. He think you on his side. He trusted you."

"Linda, it's too late now ..." she barely noticed the change in his tone. Nor had she paid any attention, she was so busy shouting, to the way he referred to the oakie. As if it was all in the past.

"First you wanted his dollars, right?"

"He had his land."

"Even I can see what it's worth – it's a red dust shit-house and palm tree thing, there ain't nothin' can grow—"

"He could have made it work – he knew there was a chance. They bring the road through, God only knows what minerals and the rest they'll find under his land."

"Is that all you can say—"

"If you think you can make me sit down and write a confession—"

"Don't you feel anything? You feel a little guilty or something because I found you out cheating—?"

"Nobody has cheated him. The indians came to me because they were terrified of him. He was his own enemy. It had to happen. Everything about Wes was always disaster. You know that, Linda."

"Did you say *was*?"

"Yes."

"What the hell do you mean by that?"

He cut a lemon and sucked at it. Geofrey tipped a tin mug of pinga down his throat. He pushed the bottle across the table towards her. The axe hafts clattered on to the floor.

"Here ..." he said slowly.

"You bastard you tell me something I don't know!" A grain itch of suspicion triggered in her mind. Unreasonable panic, out of all proportion to anything she had heard from the limey, flooded her thoughts.

"Wes is dead," Geofrey murmured, he stared at the floor where an axe haft rolled to a standstill, "he drowned in that stone pool where you used to swim. I went up there with the Capitão and I saw him. The Aripuana found him. Been dead two days I should guess. We fished him out and buried him." Geofrey paused, he took a lemon suck between his teeth, and he reached into his pocket. He drew out a steel-banded wristwatch. He held it up for her. Her eyes were staring wide.

"His watch, isn't it?" he said.

She felt numb. Her breath shivered under her tongue. Her knees felt like soft hollows, filled with a downy pillow substance. Geofrey was telling her how Wes had died. That is what he was telling her, she reminded herself. That is what she had just been told. Jeeesus Christ Linda, leave your face where it is and come and watch me teach Brazil nuts grow lampshades will ya. And Geofrey was telling her again. Now you tell me – how'm I goin' say 'Aunt Mim you know that white rabbit Louisa just died on me'? how'm I going to tell her that when she gave it me in the first place?

"Linda?" Geofrey said sharply.

She was years away. She was a child being told off for a broken vase which could never be replaced. An empty corner in her heart was closed away for good, like that vase her Ma kept because it was the only gift that husband of hers ever gave her, once that was broken, there was nothing to replace it with. *You mine now, Lindy.*

She ran out the door.

*   *   *

She didn't know how long she sat out there in the dark, in the slash-and-burn clearing. The lamp in the limey's house glowed dully some fifty yards or so away from her. She crouched, hugging her knees, staring into the noisy warm night. At first she felt cold and she trembled. Instinct fear for unseen creatures in the trees ahead of her made her curl herself up tightly like a safety pin. Geofrey hadn't gone after her. For a while she had to be alone like that, and she became accustomed to the gloom, sparking fire-flies alighted on her fingers, she even gained a scintilla of confidence. Perhaps because it was because no tears came. Or because her eyes began to delight in the company of those darting fire-flies, they had such curious rhythms, at times she believed that hundreds of them where she sat switched on and off with such uniformity it seemed like an electric switch-board magician controlled them by pulling a lever. And no tears came.

Who would cry over Dwight Weslie, she asked herself, when he never said or did one thing all his life to invite you? That runt oakie with his planalto big farming mineral discovery dream what he give – nothing; what he expect – nothing again. At least so long as she knowed him. That was the way he'd always been. You could never quite picture him as a kid. Born that way. Come out of his mother like that. Day he was born he most probably come right out of the womb strutting all of his five foot nothing in a pair of texan stud yellow leather boots with that same bald patch looking like a kitchen table you just that minute scrubbed down, putting on all that lone star drawl bullshit, and shouting so loud all the time his voice must have broke when he was in the cradle. Little guy like that has to shout, he so small you'd never see him if he didn't, otherwise no one would pay him no mind at all.

That fall when she and Wes drove across to Texas talking about nothing but this place Brazil, she first heard somebody describe him. What he say—? Who that runt little oakie? the person said. Nobody ever called Wes anything else. If there be a Lord, Dwight Weslie be up in those stars now, screwing down his stetson, bull roaring them angels, demanding a new pair of lone star boots because even up there he's still shorter than just about everybody else.

Oakie up in the stars. Scattering ten thousand dollar dreams.

Indian animal things turned into spirits hounding him with their heavenly silence. Angels of Grace and Aunt Mim's white rabbit Louisa telling him lower his voice in God's rafters. What you done Dwight Weslie? say Peter at the Gate. I ain't done anything yet, but I was sitting on a fortune of minerals waiting for this damn road to come through, it pig stupid bring me up here when I own half the suburb of tomorrow's Kansas City. I'm the kind of pioneer you need down there.

Geofrey snuffed the kerosene wick. She could see the candle he held, as he walked across the porch to his hammock, it flickered and trailed faint sparks in the dark. Linda waited, she'd give the limey time to finish the last of the bottle she knew he always drank himself to sleep with, and in due course the little candle on the porch rail faded to nothing. A howler monkey bayed razor teeth in the trees, there was a scattering sound in the palm and iron-wood fringe of the forest, cobra had found shrew-mouse, rat-tailed armadillo savaged plucky cotia, tapir trampled upon opossum, a certain larger creature had made a kill of a smaller one.

She walked back. When she brushed her arms with her hands she could feel the nubby indentations of the ticks which had lodged in her skin. But she didn't care about them now, she was used to them, those first revulsions had fled from her. And tomorrow she'd be gone. She could hear the ropes from Geofrey's rêde creak. He was still swinging. So perhaps he hadn't finished that bottle of pinga. She didn't bother to bolt the door behind her. There was nothing out there, nothing at all, except maybe Wes stomping his planalto in the stars and those seemingly tireless fire-flies, which, no doubt, were like the comets of the heavens to the ceaseless driver ant.

"Are you all right ...?" His voice was thick and slow. The empty bottle hadn't rolled across the boards yet.

"Fine ..." she murmured. She wasn't going to shout any more. A slime warm tiredness dulled her senses. There was no anger left.

She lay on the mattress, disregarding the mosquiteiro. In front of her the door lay open, across the room the window space looked out over the porch. She put her hands behind her head for a pillow and waited for the mosqus. It was strange, she admitted to herself, how she had no tears.

"You say that raft come in tomorrow . . . ?" she said softly, but it carried clear enough to where he lay out on the porch.

"Perhaps the day after . . ."

"Fine . . ."

"There's some left . . ." he hesitated. "Want a drink? Perhaps it may—"

"Stick to it, limey. You need it more than I do. Your conscience need it . . ."

There came a silence. The ropes of his hammock pulled against the porch poles. Then—

"You'll be gone in the morning, Linda . . ."

"All I think about . . ."

"I have to stay out here, that's what people like you won't understand. There is no going away for me – anything outside just incidental, anything threaten me incidental too. I found this place, don't you forget that, whatever you think of me, years of finding it took, and it got all I want."

"What would you call that, limey—?"

"It promises . . ."

"Excuse me—?"

"I listen to the sound of that road coming through – there'll be a time I can stand on the pensão porch actually hear those big yellow cats on the road – nothing ever in my life before promised me so much."

"Do anything for that limey – wouldn't you?"

"As you say . . ."

"Give up all your friends, all your old ties?"

"They never were . . ."

"All you have to do – you have to hate enough . . . huh?"

"If you want to put it that way."

"Forget enough . . . right?"

"In the morning . . ." his voice was slurred and heavy, "you'll be gone."

She heard the pinga bottle roll across the boards. She imagined it slipping between his pudgy fingers. Their lifeless grip. Delicately and as unsuspected as the mosqu dancing on his lips stupor sleep descended.

"Even kill . . . Geofrey? . . ." she whispered, ". . . right?"

Promise? What he mean by promise? He was like a child, untouched, not wanting to be touched, he not done one hundredth the things Wes seen and done, like a mean kid waiting for a new toy his Ma promised, and it such a good toy she promised him he'd have he won't dare tell on it to the other kids. Brazil promise what? Brazil promises suckeggs nothing.

Linda sat up to loosen her Levi's. Not knowing how tired she was. She dragged her sneakers along the boards to ease off the heels. Her head against the window sill – she did not realise she had closed her eyes until an hour later when she woke uneasily. The rim of the woodwork had left a deep crease across her forehead, it was like a welt you got from a hard slash with a cane stick.

Come the dawn and chirrup of early curutia paper-darting in the liana, Linda didn't waste much time. First light of lemon she was sitting in the passenger seat of the limey's Wyllis before Geofrey had time to make a pot of coffee. She never spoke a word. Sat there and waited. Hair silkily flailing over her eyes. The pale lashes flicked down.

She had her passport, those few dollars she had always kept back, half a loaf of manioc bread, her vanity box and a brown plastic leather suitcase. She was ready.

He wasn't going to speak. A few more hours and he'd be alone again. That raft had to be at the landing stage this morning. He shivered a little. Alcohol always made him feel cold when he woke. Before he pulled the porch door back after him he glanced across at the table in the front room. The oakie's steel-banded wrist-watch lay there. Linda had forgotten it, he supposed. Geofrey shrugged to himself. It was of no importance. He wasn't going to remind her, too much had passed between them for little things like that to make any difference, it was all too late for such sentiments and common kindnesses. There was no chapter in his book for our old world mores out here.

He choked the engine and reversed the wheels in the dusty earth, the rain wipers shaved the powdered windscreen in a fan shape. Linda said nothing.

The path from the river makes a junction between two favela huts as you enter Chimboa. As the Wyllis drove up Haroldo, the prefeito, called out to the limey. He ran after the jeep until Geofrey braked hard and clouds of dust rose up behind the vehicle.

"Your raft! It come in!" Haroldo panted alongside the jeep.

"I guessed," said Geofrey.

"I told the vaqueiros go straight down there before you come."

"Thanks."

Haroldo cautiously studied Linda's face. He could see the suitcase on the metal floor behind her. So that little americano's whore was going some place was she? Haroldo put his foot firmly on the running board, quickly aware of his rank as prefeito of Chimboa which the State's civil authority had invested him with, he assumed his responsibility. It is the prefeito's duty in any military occupied area to check out all arrivals and departures. In particular these know-all yankee land speculators. Up on the Amazon he knew there were half a million Brazilian families living in desperate poverty still waiting for land claim grants for a few hectares after years of patience and promises. What was so welcome about these americanos with their dollar dreams in the light of that?

"Where she going?" Haroldo asked.

"Taking the raft up to Araguaçema – they fly her out to Belém. Going home," said Geofrey.

"Tell her – give me her passport."

Geofrey smiled wearily at the prefeito. Yes, he supposed, Haroldo must have his little say in the proceedings, flex his prefeito muscle, and the patrão in the pensão will give him a free shot of cachaça when he repeats his story in the evening.

"Give him your passport, Linda," said Geofrey.

She looked up nervously. What in hell for? I'm an American citizen, her expression said.

"He's the prefeito, and I've told him you're leaving. This is a military occupied area so long as the road is being built this way – he has to check you out."

She opened her bag and pushed her passport towards Haroldo. The prefeito laboriously peeled back the pages until he found the visa stamp he required. Linda stared at the man blankly. She could feel her heart hammering in her throat. Haroldo ignored her, it was as if she didn't exist, and he spoke rapidly to the limey. Geofrey seemed to hesitate.

"... So tell me—?" asked Linda.

"He says your visa has almost run out and it is his duty to report you for this if you don't immediately get a renewal."

"He don't have to worry on that score. Because I'm taking the first flight for Miami I can find."

"He says you won't be welcome back here if you don't get a renewal because he can make it very difficult for you."

"He can stuff his visa renewal up his Brazilian ass-hole if he thinks I'm ever coming back to this hole in the wall!"

Linda snatched the passport from between Haroldo's fingers and snapped her bag clasp shut over it. Panic and white hate rage surged inside her. Nobody was going to stop her leaving now.

"Who the hell do you think you are – telling me when I can or cannot come back – you won't see me you bum ever again – won't see me no more come back to this shit-house pile of shacks! You tell him that!"

"What she say?" Haroldo asked.

Geofrey tried a benign smile. It came out a little pasty.

"Keep it calm," said Geofrey to her, "he doesn't like foreigners and he's naturally suspicious, that's his job in life."

Any thread of caution she had ever learnt from the oakie out here was snapped. That deadened ache she had felt in her body since last night was fading fast. She'd had enough, had so much she was up to her neck in it, now it was breaking.

"Whatever you got to say mister prefeito it ain't worth a nickel of dust, there's nothing you can do to me ain't nothing you can say or do make any difference I'm leaving, period, you think I'm coming back here you must be cuckoo clock crazy!" she snapped at Haroldo.

"What she say?"

"You don't like strangers? Have you ever considered strangers might not like you either? What you got to offer the world anyway that so fucking holy? I seen your eyes staring day since I first got here – like the rest of you guys on that pensão porch – thinking all the time here's some fluffy whore's tail yankee trash you gonna wank your nights away dreaming 'bout!" and now she could feel the tears coming, and she was glad of it, now those tears were breaking.

"What she say?"

"You don't like strangers, huh? What about this guy here beside me? What about him? And his fucking perfect Portuguese lick your boots language! Want me to tell you what kind of a stranger he is? He's a murderer, he's a killing lying thief murderer, what you got to say 'bout that! Oh, it's so subtle how he done it – I can tell you – you don't like strangers like me, what about this limey!"

As she started to scream out her eyes flooded. She pushed back her hair and spat at the prefeito—

"You ask this guy Geofrey what happened to my oakie! You ask him about them indian things! What they robbed and stole! You go up there and find my oakie's grave and you won't think this guy such a fucking ass-hole Brazilian! He's a murderer!"

Haroldo stepped away from the running board. The force of her high-pitched scream seemed to blow him backwards. His eyes opened wide.

Linda's head rocked to and fro. Soft saliva sobs jerked the breath back into her body. She crouched in her seat and her shoulders shook. Tears streamed over her mouth.

Geofrey spun the wheel hard to the left and accelerated down the path to the landing stage. Haroldo stood in the middle of the road scratching his head. For the life of him he couldn't think what that little house of dreams fire-fly americano whore in trousers was getting so excited about. When she screamed like that, pink adder tongue spitting, it sounded like last year's razor blade scraped against graphite.

Geofrey left her inside the Wyllis. He waited at the water's edge until the vaqueiros hauled the last of the young beef stock from the raft. A mateiro was beside him. The man had two donkeys to send up river. Geofrey signed a receipt for the mestico in charge of the raft. He helped him load on board a number of empty kerosene canisters to be returned to Araguaçema. The men tied the donkeys flat against the boards, and the mestico held out his hand for a note. He didn't get it. He got a fifty centavo piece.

The limey opened the back of the jeep. He took out the plastic suitcase and the vanity box. Linda wiped her eyes and followed him across the landing stage. She kept her eyes lowered as if she was studying the hand wide borboleta wings, red and brown, speckled grey and green, which fluttered above the mud shallows. She stepped on to the raft. The limey gave the mestico a nod, he spoke softly to the man, and the mestico lifted Linda's cases.

"Now you know what to do ..." Geofrey said, with a kind of

school master plum in the throat manner, "there is only one flight from Araguaçema – to Belém. From there you can fly up to Georgetown. There'll be a Miami flight for sure."

"Don't think about my good, mister."

"I'm not only doing it for your sake."

She stepped away from him. She clutched the vanity bag and pushed the suitcase along with her heel. She could have been mistaken for a college student taking a field study course during vacation. Perhaps not, for – if you looked closely – those eyes though red with tears were tired craters, faded irises, drained of their true colour, like transplants from a woman three times her age.

"You got what you wanted, mister limey."

He was silent.

"You got the land you got Wes's money you got the cattle stock you wanted – just about everything, right—?"

"If you like – if that's how you feel – you can come down with me to the military on the air-strip. We can tell them everything that has happened. About the indian being killed, about Wes dying, about those other indians. Tell them everything. Make a clean breast of it all. Then they'll lock you and me up and lock those Aripuana indians up until the moon drops out of the sky. Until we settle it in court. You want that?"

"I want out. Far away from you as is possible."

"As for Wes – there was nothing I could do once—"

"You killed him."

"I had to bury him like that. You bury a body within twenty-four hours out here, it's the law."

"You killed him."

"He could never have survived out here."

"It was you limey – you killed him."

Nothing showed on his face. He stood stiffly at attention in the red mud on the bank. His lace boots squelched in the ooze. Beside him naked boys caught the butterflies in their fingers. They stripped the wings with casual cruelty and hooked the remains of the insects to sticks for fish bait. Their wide eyes, little Brazil nuts, coffee dark, mestico and cafuso mix, their toes wriggled in the gummy mud.

"You tell me it, Geofrey—?"

He looked up at her.

"Tell me once – why? Why you did it?"

She believed a faint colouring spread across his cheeks. The bland look dissolved.

"Tell me now. Nobody will hear. Nobody will send the Consul down from Belém to get you. Tell me—?"

"You'd have to . . ." and he paused, as if he was searching in the pocket of his mind for the right coin, "you'd have to live a long time out here, Linda, to understand that," and though he might as well have not replied at all, she noticed the change in his tone. He spoke so quietly the words barely breathed in the hot morning air.

It was like standing on an outsize boxing ring, she thought to herself. Only difference being it was floating, and now it was slowly moving away from the landing stage. Beneath her the brown water rolled in oily droves, thin waves moiled against the river bank.

"I ain't saying I'll forget you and what I think you are, not ever," Linda looked at the limey as the raft moved away.

". . . Goodbye," he said.

She sat cross-legged beside the canisters and the uncomfortable shapes of the strapped-down donkeys. The mestico poled the raft until it faced the river at the right angle. It lurched into mid-stream, the brown swaying waters carried it evenly as it commenced its northward swing towards the Amazon. But before it reached the great river it would turn east along a network of tributaries for Araguaçema.

Behind her, the limey became an upright toy soldier in sweaty denims. She could not make out his piggy eyes any more. The mestico manipulated the raft round a bend in the river as tight as thirty degress. It looked like forest all the way.

Though the vaqueiros were out working his calves up towards his land there was still quite a crowd on the porch in the pensão. As he approached, Geofrey could see Haroldo and fat Narcissu comparing envelopes. After all these months, the big supply FAB plane had at last brought a delivery of mail. Before he could climb the porch steps Narcissu was shouting gaily at him and waving a small and unmistakable blue airmail envelope with Her Majesty's stamp on it. Geofrey took it and he immediately recognised the handwriting. Though he hadn't received a letter from this particular person for certain untold years, he knew the writing all right. How could he ever forget that hand?

Narcissu was bubbling away about his cousins. Those that had written and those that had not. Open it open it read it out to us, Narcissu was shouting, is it a sweetheart? It looks like a woman's writing! Geofrey smiled and shook his head. Later, he said.

He'd left the Wyllis on the river path junction by the favela huts. He'd hardly crossed the road before Haroldo caught up with him.

"Gerente!" said the prefeito, as if he meant why aren't you staying with us, the patrão's handing out free cachaça to celebrate.

"I have to see my cattle – pay off those vaqueiros."

Haroldo lingered beside the running board as Geofrey started the motor.

"Yes, Haroldo—?"

"I ask you this, Gerente—"

"Go ahead."

"What did that prostituta say to me – shouting at me like that?"

"Just now?"

"Sure, just now."

"Oh, she said ..." Geofrey looked at him straight between the eyes, he smiled broadly and lifted the gear stick, "she said how much she loved Brazil, how much she loved us all, and how soon she wanted to come back."

Haroldo spat into the earth, as he watched the Wyllis drive off, bumping and weaving the ruts in the dusty street. That house of dreams fire-fly americano whore must be crazy, he thought.

It was long after midday when the limey and the vaqueiros had finished branding the calves. After he paid them off, Geofrey walked for an hour in the sertão. It was the hottest part of the day. He liked to do that. He could take the sun as well as any of those riders. He could see his planta thatch bungalow way up ahead of him. Its low porch held up by the hammock poles. There was the adze which once belonged to the oakie to clean, and that letter from England to open.

Geofrey was usually so observant, he liked to believe he remembered every tree on the perimeter of his clearing, but on this occasion memory played him a strange trick, perhaps it was merely a lapse, maybe his momentary euphoria overlooked everything else; because – when he stepped inside the house he did not notice, it didn't even cross his mind, how Dwight Weslie's steel-band wristwatch no longer lay on the table in the front room.

* * *

On an early evening, the Capitão of the Aripuana came to see Geofrey. He wore a pair of faded jeans and was without his usual flapping nylon shirt. His feet were bare, and Geofrey could not help but recognise the black stetson on the old man's head. The indian was shadow silent. You couldn't hear him until he stood a foot away from Geofrey on the porch in the fading light.

"Capitão ..."

"Gerente ..."

"Todo bom ... ?"

"Bem ..."

"You come to ask me what I'm going to do about the dead americano?"

"I already know," replied the Capitão.

"How?"

"You going to do nothing because you are afraid of the soldiers."

"So are you Pedro. If I went to them tell them at the air-strip they'd come out here hunt you all down."

"If you did that ..." the old indian hesitated, he was careful to avoid any sense of real threat in his voice, "I'd say to them you hid the americano's body and you told us to steal from him."

"They don't believe indians, Capitão."

"They won't believe estrangeiros, either."

Geofrey offered up the bottle of cachaça he held in his hand. The indian slugged back a deep mouthful. Then he corked the bottle with a fold of bark and he slipped it beneath his belt. He didn't ask the Englishman if he could keep it. He knew Geofrey would not comment, he'd let him keep it, but in the past he'd always been careful to ask. He felt different now. He was celebrating a new certainty. It might be short lived but he could feel it grow in him. A welling up. Those shadows of countless disappointments and hopeless encounters with the branco in the past were fading a little. And the Capitão had been through it all, all those sixty odd years the anthropologist likes to play domino counters with – spot one the uncontacted, spot two the intermittent-contact, spot three the permanent-contact, not forgetting the blank domino for the extinct group, and the double six 'triumph' of the integrated-contact – like the Bororo, Pedro's Aripuana had run the gamut of branco hospitality. It was a better life to hide like this, working this americano's land and hoping against hope that the military never find out.

"All right ..." said Geofrey, "what else do you want?"

"Well, I cannot let the group stay where they are, gerente. If the rains come and we haven't enough manioc the younger ones will replace me."

"You can move the maloca back on to my land," said Geofrey.

The Capitão perched on the edge of the verandah. His thickly veined hands gripped the rail. A dwarf body, a trunk too long for his legs, tired skin folds around his ribs, defeated by age.

"When I was a boy ... the Aripuana hunted all this territory, and more ten times more, only boundary we had was the horizon. Until branco come," said the indian.

"It is all changed now."

"Now there's the road."

"In time, they'll forget about the americano, if that's what you're worried about. They'll be too busy in Chimboa watching the road come through."

"What you think? Americano like you—? What you think of that dead little americano the shouter – one we killed—?"

"You didn't kill him. Remember?" said Geofrey sharply.

"Ah yes," replied the Capitão, "the stones killed him. The spirit in the stones. They killed him. Now I forget that sometimes."

"He was no friend of mine."

"All americanos are friends they all work together."

"Not me, Capitão."

The indian shook his head with an admonishing frown. Oh

no, he gestured. In the dark the Englishman couldn't quite see him do that.

"You too, gerente."

"I'm different. Land I'm from I can't go back to. I can't work with them."

"No?"

"They are white worms and they live underground and I will never go back and work with them."

"You hate them so much you want to stay out here?" It was hard for the indian to hide the incredulity which crept into his voice.

"Right ..."

"It's a strange thing, you know ..." the Capitão stepped closer as if he wanted to study the contours of the Englishman's face, "if I did not know you I could mistake you for one of those vaqueiros in the village – you could be one of them."

"That's the finest compliment anyone has ever paid me," Geofrey replied.

The Capitão looked puzzled. He wiped the wet away from his eyes. The evening air was dense with moisture. Humid hands of night carried a faint vanilla smell, sweet and sticky tinged with an aroma of decay, as if somewhere close by the verandah a voluptuous bloom ... maracuja passion or yucca palm-lily was being shredded by termites.

"Is that what you've come all this way for" murmured the Capitão, "become a branco like those in the village—?"

The old man shuffled his lips in the pursed half light, it was almost inaudible. He stepped down into the darkness below the level of the boards. The Englishman had not as yet lit any of the lamps. A single candle burned behind him. Later, when the mosqus died off, he'd burn the kerosene.

"Capitão ... ?" Geofrey spoke out loud, and the indian stood still submerged in the gloom out front of the house, the night air hung limp and breathless around him, "Capitão, you must trust me. And I must learn to trust you. Capitão, are you listening? We have a bond you and I ..."

There came no reply. The Capitão had vanished. Geofrey lay deeper in the hammock, his toes balanced on the verandah rail. He kicked out at the porch post, the hammock began to swing.

The Capitão was trotting across the slash-and-burn clearing.

The Englishman's *formed* land. He remembered those bonds his tribe kept with the old style branco. Those seringueiros who used repeater rifles, those garimpeiros vagrant prospectors who dumped blankets filled with viruses beside the maloca, pinga bloated bug-eyed mateiros rivers of nickel trash dreamers who stole wives and daughters from the old style Aripuana caciques.

Now the branco came again with those roads and talked of nothing but land, land for favela shanty claims, for latifundio farms the size of a Holland, for beef fazendas, for cotton and maize and Japanese tomato fields, and mining camps. Now the young bloods of the Aripuana were the new pariahs, without papers or common rights, nothing more than talking animals, as rare as the sloth and as vulnerable, begging sandals from shacks to walk to town in, exchanging bows and arrows at a favela armazém on the outskirts for a coffee and a packet of Hollywood ('Ollywoodji) filtro, those same outskirts of towns you were banned to be in after dark, the special indigenous curfew.

And how the branco the bugre branco hated them, they were terrified of people like his young bloods, the branco did not want to believe in them, did not like to be reminded of his own caboclo origin, the indians were a life the branco had to unconsciously stamp out because they were irrelevant to his wants, that was what branco stood for all of branco stood for, and so did those who wished to join Brazilian movimento, like blind men crushing beetles underfoot, only with new techniques, new guns of deceit, new paper documents bombs of legal cunning.

And the Englishman had talked of *bonds* to the Capitão.

Bonds?

* * *

Brown-faced moon children clapping their hands and shrieking, all around him gurgling with laughter, glottal sibilants ... that afternoon Geofrey showed the Aripuana how to drive the pickup which belonged to the dead americano. The Capitão and his nephew young bloods stood to the side, a few of the women watched with them. The children clambered all over the vehicle, they kicked at each other to gain the driver's seat.

When the engine turned over, the Englishman slipped the handbrake and three of the little kids clung fearfully to the steering wheel as he guided them to the edge of the stone pool. The pickup bumped and heaved to a standstill. Geofrey pulled down the gear stick and on a sharp order from him all the children leapt clear and the vehicle steered itself into the pool. Its back up-ended and flopped over with a sail splash. Oil bubbles black as coal lumps floated to the surface. An inch above the water the exhaust pipe steamed in the hot afternoon haze. Like rainbow tanagers prancing in bromelia clumps the children screeched with laughter.

It was naturally important for the Capitão to demonstrate his authority to his nephews. He liked to confirm to them such abilities as he had. In a loud voice he stood behind the Englishman and warned the children not to come near this pool again. The children stared at him blankly. They couldn't understand a word. He spoke in Portuguese. Only Geofrey knew what he was saying. As for the nephews – it was clear enough that their Pedro could communicate with this pinga-eyed americano, this bugre branco they must learn to be humble towards. The young bloods shuffled uneasily. The women and children scattered. Capitão Pedro had made his point. You could see that by the flush on his old onion face.

"Everything will soon be just as it was," said Geofrey.

"I hope so, gerente."

"Now you have destroyed the pickup, too" said Geofrey.

"I have?" asked the Capitão.

"Yes. You."

"You mean the spirits have – don't you?"

"If you like."

The old indian didn't like to hear he had directly killed or destroyed anything. The Englishman ought to have remembered that. After all, he was the one who believed he knew their ways. The Aripuana children didn't destroy the dead branco's pickup, the water destroyed it, the water you see in the stone pool.

"You won't have much else to do," said Geofrey.

"There's the hut," the indian replied.

"Yes. Only the hut."

In Chimboa very few questions were asked. Nobody appeared to notice Dwight Weslie's absence. It was obvious he was no longer around. Nor was his pickup. He must have driven back up to the Amazon, to Santarém, he wasn't the type of estrangeiro to stand around and count his losses on the patrão's porch. But a couple of the vaqueiros asked about the little americano. Geofrey shrugged. He said his guess was as good as theirs. Perhaps he'd been eaten by a jacaré down by the Teles Pires River. They liked that. They could picture it in their minds, make a whole meal of a picture out of it. They liked that all right. They said to each other – rattling their aluminium star spurs flicking their toy-sized John Wayne issue stetsons to the back of their heads lifting their boots up against the pensão stoep which wobbled precariously under the weight – they said there are a whole lot more americanos in Brazil they hear about who ought to go the same way down the Rio Teles Pires!

As for Dwight Weslie's hut? It was carefully dismantled beam by beam. Not a shred of tarpaulin, not a pot or a sheet of asbestos was left behind. There was not a nail there a young blood might have overlooked. The slash-and-burn clearing would stay like that during the dry season. As soon as the rains return bush and liana, creeper and green fungus matter would change all that.

Geofrey planned on making a ring fence almost two miles long. Even that wouldn't secure a fifth of his boundaries. But he had to cost it. One day in the near future he'd ride south to that branco trash following behind the road-builders, those porceiros who erected their favela shanty huts beside the completed portion of the road. They'd come and work for him, and they'd work for less than the thirty dollars a month he'd have to pay a vaqueiro. In any case, he didn't want those vaqueiro bangy-bangy style hoodlums on his land every day. They might get inquisitive, ride too far west, they'd be sure to notice the smoke from the Aripuana clearing. That was the last thing the Englishman wanted to happen.

In the evening when the humidity allowed the burn of the day to cool quickly, he swung in his rêde and waited for the mosqus to gather in a cloud of violin whines above his head. He was so used to them now, their blood hunger couldn't disturb him. It was one of those evenings when you expected to hear thunder. Across the trees catch a crescent of grey wash lightning the whole sky was so heavy, and in the sun's wake metallic strips of green mingled with blood orange cut away the flesh of the cloud formations on the horizon. The green seeped into a lemon light meringue paste, the blood orange drained into sentimental pastel pinks. Movement you could only follow if you had the time and the pinga to lie out on the Englishman's verandah above Chimboa, and if you had Geofrey's patience, his ability to wait, that sense of saudade.

Recently, Capitão Pedro and his Aripuana had made themselves scarce. There was a reason for it, Geofrey ruminated to himself, perhaps the indians had got wind of something. Geofrey had noticed the sudden increase of troop movement around the air-strip. One of those doido jeep-driving soldiers might have strayed on to a track leading west. He could have seen the smoke from the maloca. Or some chicken-brained Paulista youth soldier with one of the cafuso girls from Chimboa demoraring out in the sertão with a horse blanket and a contraceptive. Perhaps they had frightened off the Aripuana group.

Word was in Chimboa a bunch of indians had gone south of the road-builders to the favela shacks. They had sold a couple of horses 'they must have stolen from somewhere' to the chefe at the porceiros' armazém.

Some of the vaqueiros on the patrão's porch wanted to ride down to the shacks and steal the horses back. They were sure the animals belonged up here in the Chimboa area.

If the Aripuana are moving so much, Geofrey considered, like going so far south to the road to sell those horses, then this was bad news for the Capitão. It meant that, perhaps, he had already lost control of his family group.

Geofrey split a lime-shaped lemon and sucked the half dry in his mouth. He took a hefty pull at the pinga bottle, the liquid stung his mouth deliciously. He remembered his letter. That day it arrived he glanced at it once and put it away. Now he wanted to look at it again. It was a common enough habit for anyone. You keep a letter in your breast pocket for a couple of days, take it out and look at it again, with the hope that you might have missed something, or that there is a hidden meaning between the sentences you had not noticed before.

Alison's letter was concealed inside an empty packet of

Minister filtro to keep it dry, in Geofrey's shirt pocket. He lit the kerosene lamp and hung it against the porch rail. When he opened the letter ... no, he had not been mistaken. The words were the same. There was no hidden secret between the lines.

Dear Geofrey,

I thought on an impulse – I'd write and tell you how sad I was when we met last. The way you stormed out. It's been months now, but it worried me dreadfully. You see, whatever you may think of us and how we live out our cosy lives here in London – I don't think you should go away like this saying how you'll never come back and that kind of thing, how you despise people like Charlie and me – taking with you all these false assumptions, thinking you can keep them for granted.

You see, when we bumped into each other those months back and you came home with me, it wasn't anything like it appeared to be. Nothing like the truth at all.

Charlie and I have been separated for more than a year. I think I lied to you about how much I was in love with my husband, but that wasn't the worst lie. Charlie has a girlfriend somewhere in Baker Street. He never makes contact, the boys ask after him, just as you did, I have to say oh darling your daddy has to stay out of town to work on an important contract. And I had to lie to you, too; saying something to the effect how successful Charlie's career is. Well, don't kid yourself, it isn't. He has a small firm, living off bank overdraft, and now that interest rates have gone through the ceiling the firm will have to shut down.

I had to get all this off my conscience, I saw your expression, your loathing, and I just had to put up a front.

You were always the loner weren't you? The unlikeable one, the selfish type who could never see the point in games. Always taking your own advice, only listening to your own voice. Maybe you are the kind who succeeds in the world. You make yourself so unpleasant, fighting and grinding away with your little chip of disgust for the rest of us. I find it so sad.

You swallowed all my lies hook line and sinker didn't you? My brave little front. I don't suppose you will get this letter, I only know your Araçatuba address. Even if you should, it hardly matters does it? I can't see you least of all shedding a tear over me and Charlie. Goodbye.

Love. Alison.

Love? There wasn't too much of that either between the lines, Geofrey thought. He couldn't quite understand what she meant by shedding tears. Was there meant to be something poignant or artistically dramatic about that last meeting they had in the Islington house—? If that was so, it eluded Geofrey. Am I supposed to drop a tear because Charlie's beating it up somewhat in Baker Street with a secretary girl? Drop a tear for Alison's sake? She must be crazy. Their fat little tea-cosy lives don't deserve to be pissed on if they were on fire.

He lay back in the hammock and waited for the fire-flies to plunge through the planta roof. He carefully folded the letter back into the Minister filtro box. That was the trouble with people like Alison – always hoping they might break your blandness, slip beneath your skin with their horrible little problems. Always there were those who couldn't survive without help, like Alison, like Dwight Weslie, like the Capitão Pedro, and in the end they come back to me because I appear confident. There are no cracks to show. If they only knew how long it took to get this way, how many years it took perfecting that strange Brazilian game of patience. It is saudade. It is a land which always promises. It is a yearning and a waiting, a waiting as simple as that for fire-flies to come tumbling through the roof, and as complex as being able to walk down the street in Chimboa and not one vaqueiro will bother you with his meal-making eyes.

How could Wes have understood that? Those rich quick nellie nervous dreams of his. What the fuck does he know about Brazil? This oakie who wanted to rape the country. You have to stay here, wait here, make love to Brazil, eat its red dry earth until you no longer vomit it up, breathe this cold cream air until your lungs feel like water melons. Pig runt oakie and his drivel was a natural for a fall. He could have had a worse fate down in Diamantina or Barra do Bugre. They would have murdered him, but slowly, they'd have hung him out to spin slowly in the wind until he was a raisin. Those *Fourth Reich* Germans in Barra would have eaten him.

Etchawwk! Etchawwk! Etchawwk! ... Howler monkey in the trees on the perimeter of his slash-and-burn clearing. As the night cooled the mosqus tired of their blood hunt. Moths and sandflies danced self-immolation waltzes around the kerosene lamp.

Geofrey had begun to learn just which parts of his land were good. He had seen the oakie's errors. Those parts where the sertão broke into richer grasses, parcels of hectares which could be sown at the close of the next rain season – they would grow well; and none of this was on the side of the incline which overlooked the road above the stone pool.

He told himself he could lie out there on his porch for ever, like that. In his mind he could see that BR 165 coming through, it worked for him like an instant polaroid on his retina, those road-building guys in their steel helmets crashing great yellow forklift cats into the red earth, jerking giant's teeth of rock to the side, flooded by arc-lamps all through the night, dysentery and malaria and leishmaniasis in exchange for triple rates before the rains come they'd reach the first telegraph poles on the outskirts of Chimboa; and the military would open the air-strip there'd arrive the Pará governador and a brass band from Santarém, locusts of six seaters would zoom in, and the surveyors the builders the speculators land-agents and geologists would pour in; there'd be mineralogists from Minnesota, engineers from Japan, drilling experts from Yucataw, blue silk-suited Germans with bleeping electronic gadgets feeling the red brown ochre earth like it was the voluptuous body of a new whore, priceless and incalculable her fee whose bauxite and zinc and casserite and molybdenum copper-lined vagina must yield to their technical probes; and Lebanese shoe salesmen (proliferating like termites in the Amazonas for some reason) and Cypriot cloth merchants and smart Paulista lawyers making land claim searches all bitterly complaining about the humidity like a plunge into ether and warm milk and carioca accountants asking the patrão at the pensão for batidas (he don't even know how to make one himself, Narcissu) and receiving a low class caipirinha instead. They'd come. They'd pour in. World Bank funds and IMF inside their Brazil nut credit card minds. What was it they all promised? São Paulo to be the Chicago of the South Americans, Cuiaba to be the Detroit, Goiânia the Los

Angeles and Chimboa the new Kansas City . . . in less than twenty years.

He could see straight out towards the east from this part of the verandah, lying as he had learnt to lie best in the rêde, flattening it out from one far corner to the other so that there would be no dip, to his east more than four thousand miles away was England, truncated to an empire of bank high interest loans and mortgage payments, hypocritical to a war in Ireland it won't even admit to being a war, unacceptedly impoverished by an entry into a European Economic Community it cannot conceivably benefit from. Islandic community heretofore glutted with Commonwealth tariffs, perfectly seeming reasonable people fed on social services from the cot to the grave, suckeggs voice usurer auctioneer of off-shore oil rig rights it can barely claim any legal title to, celebrator of royal weddings in the middle of economic crises, convener of nobles in ermine and dubber of soccer footballers titular, the whole place a kind of curiosity shoppe which buys junk and sells antiques; yet a community of peoples which at the last resort remains the one true international arbiter of commonsense the outside world still pays lipservice to. Originator of class warfare, one time pirate of the uncharted New World, England – raised choral voice of tea-cosy-sized sentiments at its annual venue for paranoia the London Proms, island of tiny white cliffs made plastic mole hill with fibreglass caravans, mother of rain and cloud, employer of millions offering a wage average lower than any other country inside the Common Market, it would be to Geofrey should he ever return to us, cottage industry receptacle of all his earthly loathing – a death his live body would never cease dying from.

Somewhere in the back of his mind he recalled the words of an English explorer who once declared you must first let the veil of civilisation descend behind you before Brazil will truly let you enter, even so you remain the estrangeiro until you discover you can wait for this promise of Brazil until you can wait for as long as the Brazil nut himself can wait, a waiting you can only explain by palm top black urubu poise, or the monotony of the grilo, or by the unblinking patience of jacaré in the river shallows. It is a waiting until all size and humidity becomes nothing, and like Geofrey you accept the loneliness of a sky which can find no horizon, all cruelties and all lies insufferable black eyes of saudade staring at you saying what you come steal from us now, gerente? mean nothing to you, because if you are a Geofrey it is here where the last gunfight in the west can be waged where the peacock strutting John Wayne cannibal capitalist can yet wake on a morning and find himself rich; where ten per cent of the poorest take two per cent of the wage cake and ten per cent of the richest take forty-eight per cent of the cake, in this decentralised market economy a beefburger stall or a second-hand truck can turn into a million dollar network overnight, nightmare land of one armed bandit promise out of whose ten major industries the USA has a controlling interest in six. Here, if you are a Geofrey, is a piece of land both INCRA and SUDAM and the banks will pay you to develop once the road is through, land both Embratel and Petrobras will offer you deals to make you rich – as the blonde starlet once described the sexual proclivities of a movie mogul – beyond human belief.

And the Brazil nut has waited through a hundred years of boom/bust exploitation to bring him a new dream, he has taken out a twelve billion dollar overdraft against mineral/land/possibly oil collateral which he can hardly begin to estimate, and it is this land (or what little of it he has kept for himself against Germans, Japanese and Americans) which promises to deliver him the minerals of Siberia and oil fields of Libya tamped on to an Alaska of mining the size of Europe.

His estado novo bust.

* * *

There is a moment in the forest at the edge of a fazenda's slash-and-burn clearing when the noises at night start to tremble, there is a stutter of uncertainty, the macaw closes its beaked cavern the grilos give a hiccup to their scratching and bufo toad stands on its hindlegs as if it would like to learn to walk that way. Silly fellow.

Geofrey's rêde swung rhythmically from side to side, and he let go his hold on the pinga bottle. It rolled across the boards and plumped into the red earth darkness below. For an instant the forest, should you have listened carefully to this tremble, has told you of a new presence.

Geofrey's eyes closed. The sour from the lime-shaped lemons rinsed out the back of his throat. His palms cupped as much moisture as the cold cream touch of the night placed in a buriti leaf. The mosqus had died away.

Deep in his mind a voice was telling him to wake up. You must listen gerente, to that sound, that tremble hiccup in the blue night. Why must I? There is nothing to fear. No one can touch me. I haven't made one mistake. There is nothing here to be afraid of. Outside of here, yes, outside where hate forbids one to ever return to those friends and places I was once a part of. They are white worms aren't they? Living subterranean lives. As forgettable as a fire-fly's leap before the scintillant cascade of stars in the eastern sky.

A wrinkled hand attached to a thin bony wrist held up the neck of a decapitated chicken, it rubbed the red froth nerve-end spout of the neck against the door of Geofrey's house until the blood trickled into the valleys of the wood around the door handle. The warm blood smelt faintly sweet sick, oiled glisten, humid limned in the dark... it dribbled black rivers.

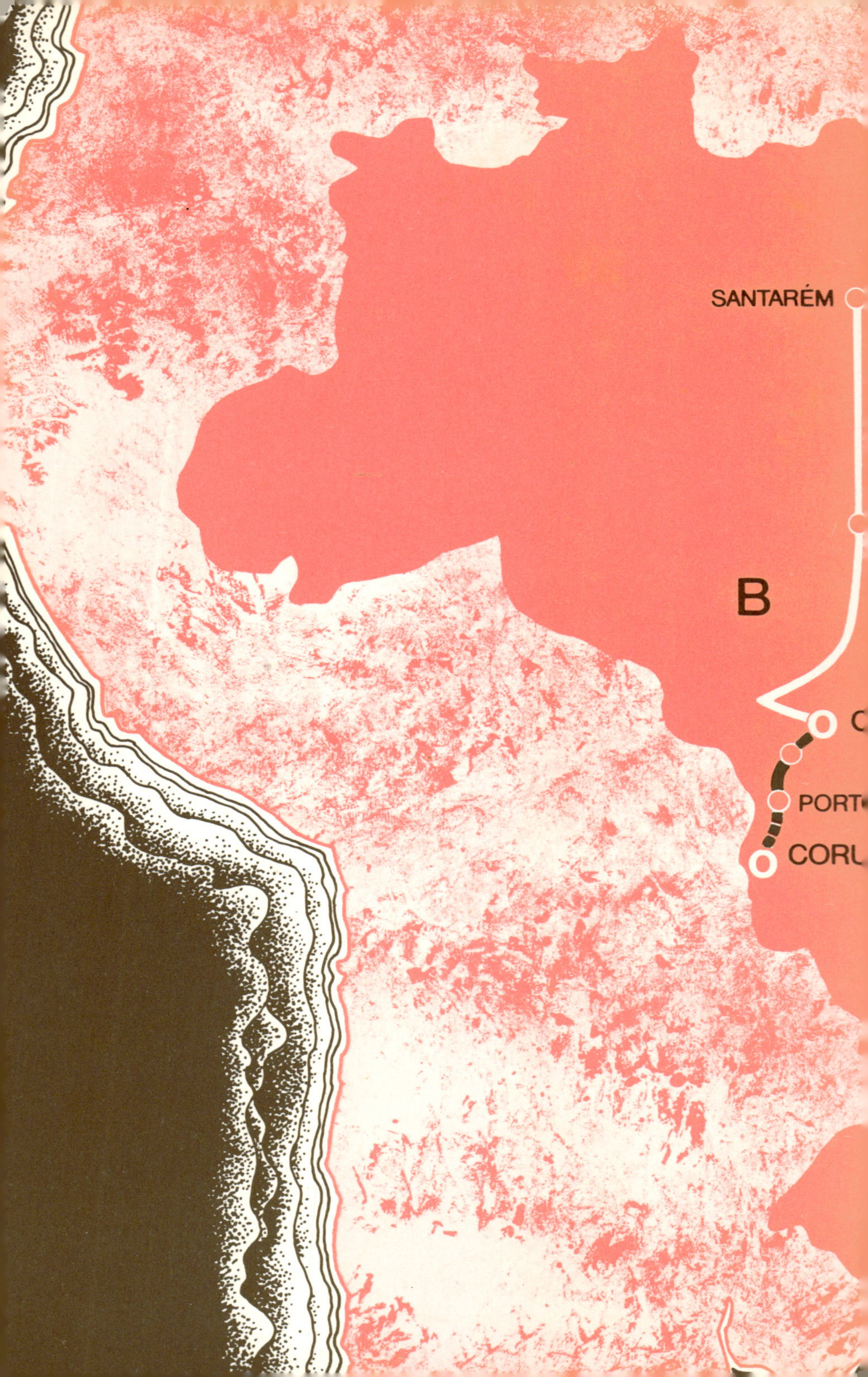
SANTARÉM
B